By Timothy Zahn

STAR WARS: The Hand of Thrawn
Specter of the Past
Vision of the Future

STAR WARS: The Thrawn Trilogy
Heir to the Empire
Dark Force Rising
The Last Command

The Blackcollar
Cobra
Blackcollar: The Backlash Mission
Deadman Switch
Cascade Point
Cobra Bargain
Cobra Strike
A Coming of Age
Spinneret
Time Bomb & Zahndry Others
Triplet
Warhorse
Distant Friends

Conquerors' Trilogy:
Conquerors' Pride
Conquerors' Heritage
Conquerors' Legacy

VISION OF THE FUTURE

TIMOTHY ZAHN

BANTAM BOOKS

NEW YORK • TORONTO • LONDON • SYDNEY • AUCKLAND

STAR WARS: VISION OF THE FUTURE
A Bantam Spectra Book / September 1998

SPECTRA and the portrayal of a boxed "s" are trademarks of Bantam Books,
a division of Bantam Doubleday Dell Publishing Group, Inc.

Library of Congress Cataloging-in-Publication Data
Zahn, Timothy.
 Vision of the future / by Timothy Zahn.
  p. cm. — (Star Wars)
  ISBN 0-553-10035-1
  1. Science fiction. gsafd. I. Title. II. Series: Star Wars
(Bantam Books (Firm) : Unnumbered)
PS3576.A33V57   1998
813'.54—DC21   98-23098
                                              CIP

Published simultaneously in the United States and Canada

Bantam Books are published by Bantam Books, a division of Bantam Doubleday Dell Publishing
Group, Inc. Its trademark, consisting of the words "Bantam Books" and the portrayal of a
rooster, is Registered in U.S. Patent and Trademark Office and in other countries. Marca Regis-
trada. Bantam Books, 1540 Broadway, New York, New York 10036.

PRINTED IN THE UNITED STATES OF AMERICA

BVG   10 9 8 7 6 5 4 3 2 1

TO THE STAR LADIES, THE WILD KARRDES,
THE CLUB JADERS, AND MY BOTHAN SPIES

AND ESPECIALLY TO

TISH PAHL
MINISTER OF FORMATION:
BOTH IN- AND DISIN-

CHAPTER

1

The Imperial Star Destroyer *Chimaera* slid through the black of space, its only companion the silent gas giant world of Pesitiin far below.

Admiral Pellaeon was standing at the forward viewport, gazing out at the dead planet, when Captain Ardiff arrived on the bridge. "Report from Major Harch, Admiral," he said briskly. "All damage from that pirate attack has been repaired. Your ship is back to full fighting readiness."

"Thank you, Captain," Pellaeon said, carefully hiding a smile. In the thirty hours since the failed attack on the *Chimaera*, Ardiff had gone from believing it to be a raid by New Republic General Garm Bel Iblis, to suspicions that it had been engineered by dissident Imperial elements, to similar suspicions involving similarly dissident Rebels, and was now apparently convinced that a pirate gang was responsible.

Of course, in all fairness, Ardiff *had* had the past thirty hours to cogitate on his theories. The techs' preliminary report on the debris from that destroyed *Kaloth* battlecruiser had certainly influenced his thinking, too. "Anything new from the patrols?" Pellaeon asked.

"Just more negatives, sir," Ardiff said. "Still no indications of activity anywhere in the system. Oh, and the sensor-stealthed assault shuttle you sent on the attackers' escape vector also just checked in. Still no trace."

Pellaeon nodded. As expected, really—anyone who could afford to buy and fly a battlecruiser usually knew a few tricks about hiding it. "It was worth a try," he told Ardiff. "Have them try one more system; we can transmit that far without relays. If they haven't picked up the trail by then, order them back."

"Yes, sir," Ardiff murmured.

Even without looking, Pellaeon could sense Ardiff's hesitation. "A question, Captain?" he prompted.

"It's this communications blackout, sir," Ardiff said. "I don't like being so completely out of contact this way. It's like being blind and deaf; and frankly, it makes me nervous."

"I don't much like it myself," Pellaeon conceded. "But the only ways to make contact with the outside universe are to either transmit to an Imperial relay station or punch our way onto the HoloNet; and the minute we do either, everyone from Coruscant to Bastion will know we're here. If that happens, we'll have more than the occasional pirate gang lining up to take potshots at us."

And, he added silently, it would be the end of any chance for a quiet meeting between him and Bel Iblis. Assuming the general was indeed willing to talk.

"I understand all that, Admiral," Ardiff said. "But has it occurred to you that yesterday's attack might not have been an isolated incident against an isolated Imperial ship?"

Pellaeon cocked an eyebrow. "Are you suggesting it might have been part of a coordinated attack against the Empire?"

"Why not?" Ardiff said. "I'm willing to concede at this point that it probably wasn't the New Republic who hired them. But why couldn't the pirates have set it up on their own? The Empire has always come down hard on pirate gangs. Maybe a group of them got together and decided the time was right for revenge."

Pellaeon stroked his lip thoughtfully. On the surface, it was a ridiculous suggestion—even on its deathbed the Empire was far stronger than any possible aggregate of pirate gangs could hope to defeat. But that didn't mean they wouldn't be foolish enough to try. "That still leaves the question of how they knew we were here," he pointed out.

"We still don't know what happened to Colonel Vermel," Ardiff reminded him. "Maybe it was this pirate coalition who snatched him. He could have told them about Pesitiin."

"Not willingly," Pellaeon said darkly. "If they did what it would take to make him talk, I'll decorate Bastion's moon with their hides."

"Yes, sir," Ardiff said. "But that brings us back to the question of how long we're going to stay here."

Pellaeon looked out the viewport at the stars. Yes, that was indeed the question. How long should they wait here in the middle of nowhere in the hope that this slow attrition of the Empire could be stopped? That they could end this war with the New Republic with a shred of territory and dignity still intact?

That they could finally have peace?

"Two weeks," he said. "We'll give Bel Iblis another two weeks to respond to our offer."

"Even though the message may not have reached him?"

"The message reached him," Pellaeon said firmly. "Vermel is a highly resourceful, highly competent officer. Whatever happened to him, I have no doubt he completed his mission first."

"Yes, sir," Ardiff said, his tone making it clear that he didn't share

Pellaeon's confidence. "And if Bel Iblis doesn't come within that time frame?"

Pellaeon pursed his lips. "We'll decide then."

Ardiff hesitated, then took half a step closer to his superior. "You really believe this is our best hope, sir, don't you," he said quietly.

Pellaeon shook his head. "No, Captain," he murmured. "I believe it's our *only* hope."

The wedge of approaching Sienar IPV/4 patrol ships broke in perfect formation to both sides, and the Imperial Star Destroyer *Relentless* glided smoothly between the re-forming clusters toward its designated orbital position. "Very impressive," Moff Disra growled to the slim man beside him, hearing his heart pounding in his ears as he gazed across the bridge at the green-blue world framed in the forward viewport. "I trust you didn't haul me all the way out here just to watch the Kroctarian home defense force's maneuvers."

"Patience, Your Excellency," Major Grodin Tierce said quietly at his side. "I told you we had a surprise for you."

Disra felt his lip twist. Yes, that's what Tierce had said. And that was *all* Tierce had said. And as for Flim—

Disra shifted his gaze to the Admiral's chair, feeling his lip twist a little more. Their tame con man was sitting there, bold as bricbrass in his blue-skin makeup and glowing red eye surface inserts and his white Grand Admiral's uniform. The absolute laser-trimmed image of Grand Admiral Thrawn, a masquerade solidly believed by every Imperial aboard the *Relentless* from Captain Dorja on down.

Trouble was, there weren't any Imperials on the planet below them. Far from it. Kroctar, merchant center and capital of Shataum sector, was deep in New Republic territory, with every bit as much military firepower as one would expect such a world to have. There was no guarantee that any of *them* would be impressed by Flim's eyes and uniform and acting ability.

And if they weren't, this cozy little triumvirate Disra had formed was about to blow up in their faces. Flim might look like Thrawn, but he had all the tactical genius of a garbage-pit parasite. Tierce, a former stormtrooper and Royal Guardsman under Emperor Palpatine, was the military brains of their little group; and if Captain Dorja saw an allegedly lowly major rush over to the allegedly brilliant Grand Admiral to give him advice, this whole illusion would explode into soap scum. Whatever bluff Tierce was running here, it had better work.

"Transmission from the surface, Admiral," the comm officer called from the portside crew pit. "It's Lord Superior Bosmihi, chief of the Unified Factions."

"On speaker, Lieutenant," Thrawn said. "Lord Superior Bosmihi, this is Grand Admiral Thrawn. I received your message. What may I do for you?"

Disra frowned at Tierce. "*They* called *us*?" he muttered.

Tierce nodded, a small but satisfied smile playing around his lips. "Shh," he said. "Listen."

"We offer you greeting, Grand Admiral Thrawn," a nasally alien voice boomed over the comm, "and we congratulate you most heartily on your triumphal return."

"Thank you," Thrawn said smoothly. "As I recall, you were somewhat less enthusiastic at our last meeting."

Disra threw Tierce a sharp look. "During his sweep through this sector ten years ago," Tierce murmured. "Don't worry, he knows all about it."

The alien gave a blubbering laugh. "Ah, yes—you remember most clearly," he admitted cheerfully. "At that time the fear of Imperial power and the lure of promised freedoms still held sway over us."

"Such lies held sway over many," Thrawn agreed. "Does your choice of words imply the Kroctari have come to a new understanding?"

There was a disgusting, wheezy-sounding noise from the comm. "We have seen the crumbling of the promise," the Lord Superior said regretfully. "There is no longer any order emanating from Coruscant; no focused goals, no clear structures, no discipline. A thousand different alien species tug the galaxy in a thousand different directions."

"Inevitably," Thrawn said. "That was why Emperor Palpatine first inaugurated the New Order. It was an attempt to reverse the collapse you now see coming."

"Yet we were also warned not to trust Imperial promises," Bosmihi hedged. "The history of the Empire is one of brutal subjugation of nonhuman species."

"You speak of the rule of Palpatine," Thrawn said. "The Empire has freed itself from his self-destructive anti-alien bias."

"Your presence in a place of command is some evidence of that," Bosmihi said cautiously. "Still, others still say the bias exists."

"Others still lie about the Empire in many ways," Thrawn countered. "But there's no need for you to take my word for it. Speak to any of the fifteen alien species currently living under Imperial rule, beings who cherish the protection and stability we offer."

"Yes—protection." The Lord Superior seemed to pounce on the word. "The Empire is said to be weak; yet I perceive that you still have great strength. What guarantee of safety do you offer your member systems?"

"The best guarantee in the galaxy," Thrawn said; and even Disra felt a shiver run through him at the veiled power and menace that was suddenly in the con man's voice. "My personal promise of vengeance should anyone dare attack you."

There was a noise that sounded midway between a swallow and a burp. "I see," Bosmihi said soberly. "I understand that this is rather sudden, and for this I apologize; but on behalf of the Unified Factions of the Kroctari people, I would like to petition you for readmission into the Empire."

Disra looked at Tierce, feeling his jaw drop a few millimeters. "Readmission?" he hissed.

Tierce smiled back. "Surprise, Your Excellency."

"On behalf of the Empire, I accept your petition," Thrawn said. "You no doubt have a delegation standing ready to discuss the details?"

"You understand my people well, Grand Admiral Thrawn," the Lord Superior said wryly. "Yes, my delegation does indeed await your pleasure."

"Then you may signal them to approach," Thrawn told him. "As it happens, Imperial Moff Disra is currently aboard the *Relentless.* As he is a specialist in political matters, he will handle the negotiations."

"We will be honored to meet with him," Bosmihi said. "Though I doubt his presence there is in any way the coincidence you imply. Thank you, Grand Admiral Thrawn; and until the meeting."

"Until the meeting, Lord Superior Bosmihi," Thrawn said.

He gestured to the crew pit. "Transmission ended, Admiral," the comm officer confirmed.

"Thank you," Thrawn said, rising almost leisurely from his command chair. "Signal TIE interceptors to stand ready for escort duty. They're to meet the Lord Superior's shuttle as soon as it clears atmosphere, flying in full honor formation. Captain Dorja, I'd like you to meet the shuttle personally and escort the delegation to Conference Room 68. Moff Disra will await you there."

"Understood, Admiral," Dorja said. He strode from the bridge, throwing Disra a tightly satisfied smile as he passed, and stepped into a waiting turbolift in the aft bridge. "You might have said something," Disra muttered to Tierce as the turbolift door closed behind the captain.

The Guardsman shrugged, a microscopic movement of the shoulders. "I wasn't absolutely sure this was what they wanted when they called," he said, gesturing Disra through the aft doors toward another turbolift. "But it seemed like a good guess. Kroctar has several potentially dangerous neighbors, and Intelligence reports the Unified Factions have become extremely disillusioned by Coruscant's inability to decide how tight a restraining bolt they want to keep on intersystem fighting."

They reached the turbolift and stepped into a waiting car. "Kroctar's the first," Tierce continued as the doors closed and they began to move. "But it won't be the last. We already have transmissions from twenty other systems whose governments would like Grand Admiral Thrawn to drop in for a chat."

Disra snorted. "All they're trying to do is shake up their enemies."

"Probably," Tierce agreed. "But what do we care why they want to rejoin? The point is that they do, and it's going to send shock waves from here to Coruscant."

"Until Coruscant decides to take action."

"What action can they take?" Tierce countered. "Their own charter specifically allows member systems to withdraw anytime they choose."

There was a beep from the turbolift comlink. "Moff Disra?"

"Yes?"

"There's a transmission coming in for you, Your Excellency, under a private encryption designated Usk-51."

Disra felt his stomach try to cramp. Of all the stupid, brainless— "Thank you," he said as calmly as he could manage. "Have it transferred to Conference Room 68, and make sure it's not monitored."

"Yes, Your Excellency."

Tierce was frowning at him. "That's not—?"

"It certainly is," Disra bit out. The turbolift doors opened—"Come on. And stay out of sight."

Two minutes later they were in the conference room with the door privacy-sealed behind them. Activating the comm display set into the center of the table, Disra pulled the proper encryption datacard from his collection and slid it into the slot. He keyed for reception—

"It's about time," Captain Zothip spat, his eyes flashing, his bushy blond beard bristling with anger. "Don't you think I've got better things to do than—?"

"*What!*" Disra barked. Zothip's head jerked back, his own tirade breaking off midway in sudden confusion. "Do . . . you . . . think . . . you're . . . doing?" Disra continued into the silence, biting out each word like the crack of a rotten snapstick. "How *dare* you take such an insane risk?"

"Never mind your precious image," Zothip growled, some of his insolence starting to come back. "If consorting with pirates is suddenly an embarrassment for you—"

"Embarrassment is not the issue here," Disra said icily. "I'm thinking about our two necks, and whether we get to keep them. Or hadn't you noticed how many relays there are in this transmission?"

"No kidding," Zothip said with a sniff. "And here I thought it was just your wonderful Imperial comm equipment kicking ions again. So where are you, out at your vacation home counting your money?"

"Hardly," Disra said. "I'm aboard an Imperial Star Destroyer."

Zothip's face seemed to darken. "If that's supposed to impress me, you'd better try again. I've about had my fill of your precious Star Destroyers."

"Really." Disra smiled coldly. "Let me guess. You got overconfident, went in blazing, and Admiral Pellaeon clipped your tail feathers for you."

"Don't mock me, Disra," Zothip warned. "Don't ever mock me. I lost a *Kaloth* battlecruiser and eight hundred good men to that Vader-ripped *katchni.* And the payment's going to come out of somebody's hide. Pellaeon's, or yours."

"Don't be absurd," Disra said scornfully. "And don't try to blame it on me. I warned you not to actually engage the *Chimaera.* All you were supposed to do was make him think Bel Iblis was attacking."

"And how did you expect I was supposed to do that?" Zothip shot back. "Insult his family? Transmit lists of ancient Corellian curses?"

"You pushed an Imperial too hard and he pushed back," Disra said. "Consider it a useful lesson painfully learned. And hope you don't need to learn it again."

Zothip glared. "Is that a threat?" he demanded.

"It's a warning," Disra snapped. "Our partnership's been extremely profitable for both of us. I've had the chance to play havoc with New Republic shipping; you've had the chance to collect the merchandise from those ships."

"And have taken all the risks," Zothip put in.

Disra shrugged. "Regardless, I'd hate to see such a valuable relationship dissolve over something this trivial."

"Trust me, Disra," Zothip said softly. "When our relationship dissolves you'll find a lot more than that for you to hate."

"I'll start making a list," Disra said. "Now go lace your wounds; and next time you want to talk to me go through proper channels. This encrypt's one of the best ever created, but nothing's totally slice-proof."

"The encrypt's that good, huh?" Zothip said sardonically. "I'll have to remember that. Should bring a good price on the open market if I ever need quick money. I'll be in touch."

He waved a hand offscreen, and the display blanked. "Idiot," Disra snarled toward the empty display. "Moronic, brain-rotted idiot."

Across the table, Tierce stirred. "I trust you're planning to be a little more politic than that with the Kroctari," he said.

Disra shifted his glare from the display to the Guardsman. "What, you think I should have let him cry on my shoulder? Or said 'There, there,' and promised to buy him a new battlecruiser?"

"The Cavrilhu Pirates would be a dangerous enemy," Tierce warned. "Not militarily, of course, but because of what they know about you."

"Zothip's the only one who really knows anything," Disra muttered.

Tierce was right—he probably should have played it a little more calmly. But Zothip still shouldn't have contacted him directly like that, especially not when he was away from the security of his office.

Regardless, he wasn't going to admit an error in judgment in Tierce's presence. "Don't worry—he's making too much out of this arrangement to toss it all over a single battlecruiser."

"I wonder," Tierce said thoughtfully. "You should never underestimate what people will do out of pride."

"No," Disra said significantly. "Or out of arrogance, either."

Tierce's eyes narrowed fractionally. "What's that supposed to mean?"

"It means you've pushed things too far," Disra said flatly. "Dangerously far. In case you've forgotten, Flim's job was to inspire the Empire's military and bring them solidly into line behind us. It was never part of the plan to openly provoke the New Republic this way."

"I've already explained Coruscant has no legal basis for action—"

"And you think that will stop them?" Disra shot back. "You really think fine points of the law will make any difference to terrified aliens who think Grand Admiral Thrawn is breathing down their necks? Bad enough that you talked me into letting Flim show himself to the Diamalan Senator. But now *this*?" He waved a hand in the direction of the planet.

"The Diamalan incident accomplished exactly what it was intended to," Tierce said coolly. "It created doubt and consternation, stirred up old animosities a bit more, and silenced some of the last calming voices the Rebellion still has."

"Wonderful—except that now *this* little trick has completely negated that one," Disra countered. "How can anyone wonder if the Diamala are lying when a whole planet has seen Thrawn?"

Tierce smiled. "Ah, but that's the point: the whole planet *hasn't* seen him. Only the Lord Superior's handpicked delegation will have seen him; the rest have only their word that Thrawn has returned. And since part of his message to the neighboring systems will be that Kroctar is under Thrawn's protection, his sighting will be as suspect as the Diamal's."

"You always make it sound so reasonable," Disra bit out. "But there's more here than you're letting on. I want to know what."

Tierce lifted his eyebrows. "That sounded like a threat."

"It was half a threat," Disra corrected him coldly. "Here's the other half." Reaching into his tunic, he drew the tiny blaster concealed there.

He never even got a chance to aim it. Before the weapon was even clear, Tierce had thrown himself onto the conference table, the momentum of his leap carrying him sliding headfirst on elbow and hip toward Disra across the polished laminate. Reflexively, Disra leaped to his right, trying to move out of reach of the approaching hands; but even as he lifted the blaster, Tierce rolled partway over and grabbed the center comm display, using it as a pivot point to both change direction and also roll him onto his back, swiveling his feet around in front of him, and then pushing off of it to increase his speed.

The maneuver caught Disra flat-footed. Before he could move again to correct his aim, one of Tierce's feet caught the blaster squarely across the side of the barrel, sending it spinning across the room.

Disra took a staggering step back, the bitter taste of defeat choking his throat, hands lifted in a futile gesture of defense as Tierce hopped off the table. He'd had one chance to wrest control of this grand scheme back from the Guardsman, and he'd muffed it.

And now Tierce would kill him.

But once again, Tierce surprised him. "That was extremely foolish, Your Excellency," the other said calmly, crossing the room and retrieving the blaster. "The sound of a shot would have had a squad of stormtroopers down on you in nothing flat."

Disra took a careful breath, lowering his hands. "That works both ways," he managed, knowing even as he said it that the Guardsman wouldn't need to bother with anything so crude and noisy as a blaster if he wanted to kill him.

But Tierce merely shook his head. "You insist on misunderstanding," he said.

"And you insist on working behind my back," Disra countered. "Gaining a system or two isn't worth the risk of scaring Coruscant into action. What's going on that you aren't telling me?"

Tierce seemed to measure him with his eyes. "All right," he said. "Have you ever heard the phrase 'the Hand of Thrawn'?"

Disra shook his head. "No."

"You answered that rather quickly."

"I was working on this plan long before you came on the scene," Disra reminded him tartly. "I found and read everything in the Imperial records that pertained even remotely to Thrawn."

"Including everything in the Emperor's secret files?"

"Once I was able to find a way into them, yes." Disra frowned as a sudden thought struck him. "Is this what your little trip to Yaga Minor last month was really all about?"

Tierce shrugged. "The primary purpose was exactly as we discussed: to alter their copy of the Caamas Document to match the changes you'd already made in the Bastion copy. But as long as I'd broken into the system anyway, I did spend some time looking for references."

"Of course," Disra said. Nothing so crude as a direct lie, simply a conveniently neglected bit of the truth. "And?"

Tierce shook his head. "Nothing. As far as any existing Imperial record is concerned, the term might not even exist."

"What makes you think it ever did?"

Tierce looked him straight in the eye. "Because I heard Thrawn mention it once aboard the *Chimaera.* In the context of the Empire's ultimate and total victory."

Suddenly the room felt very cold. "You mean like a superweapon?" Disra asked carefully. "Another Death Star or Sun Crusher?"

"I don't know," Tierce said. "I don't think so. Superweapons were more the Emperor's or Admiral Daala's style, not Thrawn's."

"And he did just fine without them," Disra conceded. "Come to think of it, he did always seem more interested in conquest than wholesale slaughter. Besides, if there were another superweapon lying around, the Rebels would almost certainly have found it by now."

"Most likely," Tierce said. "Unfortunately, we can't make it *quite* that final. Did your extensive research into Thrawn's history happen to turn up the names Parck and Niriz?"

"Parck was the Imperial captain who found Thrawn on a deserted planet at the edge of Unknown Space and brought him back to the Emperor," Disra said. "Niriz was the captain of the Imperial Star Destroyer *Admonitor,* which Thrawn took back into the Unknown Regions on his supposed mapping expedition a few years later."

" 'Supposed'?"

Disra sniffed. "It doesn't take much reading between the lines to see that Thrawn tried his hand at Imperial Court politics and got his fingers burned. No matter what they called it, his assignment to the Unknown Regions was a form of exile. Pure and simple."

"Yes, that was the general consensus among the Royal Guard at the time, too," Tierce said thoughtfully. "I wonder now if there could have been more to it than that. Regardless, the point is that neither Parck nor Niriz—nor the *Admonitor,* for that matter—ever returned to official duty with the Empire. Not even when Thrawn himself came back."

Disra shrugged. "Killed in action?"

"Or else they did come back, but are in hiding somewhere," Tierce said. "Perhaps standing guard over this Hand of Thrawn."

"Which is what?" Disra demanded. "You say it's not a superweapon. So what is it?"

"I *didn't* say it wasn't a superweapon," Tierce countered. "I just said superweapons weren't Thrawn's style. Personally, I see only two likely possibilities. Did you ever hear of a woman named Mara Jade?"

Disra searched his memory. "I don't think so."

"She currently works with the smuggling chief Talon Karrde," Tierce said. "But at the height of the Empire, she was one of Palpatine's best undercover agents, with a title of Emperor's Hand."

Emperor's Hand. The Hand of Thrawn. "Interesting possibility," Disra said thoughtfully. "But if the Hand is a person, where has he or she been all these years?"

"Gone to ground, too, perhaps," Tierce said. "The second possibility's even more intriguing. Remember that above all else Thrawn was a master strategist. What could be more his style than to leave behind a master plan for victory?"

Disra snorted. "Which after ten years of Imperial reverses would be totally useless."

"I wouldn't dismiss it quite so quickly," Tierce warned. "A strategist like Thrawn didn't see battle plans solely in terms of numbers of warships and locations of picket lines. He also considered geopolitical balances, cultural and psychological blind spots, historical animosities and rivalries—any number of factors. Factors which could very likely still be exploited."

Absently, Disra rubbed his hand where Tierce's kick had jammed the blaster painfully against the skin. On the face of it, it was absurd.

And yet, he'd read the history of Thrawn's accomplishments. Had seen the record of the man's genius. Could he really have created a battle plan that could still be used ten years and a thousand defeats later? "What about that five-year campaign I found in his files?" he asked. "Was there something in there I missed?"

"No." Tierce shook his head. "I've already been through it. All that is is a rough outline of what he was planning to do after the Bilbringi confrontation. If the Hand of Thrawn is a master strategy, he hid it away somewhere else."

"With Captain Niriz and the *Admonitor,* you think?" Disra suggested.

"Perhaps," Tierce said. "Or else the ultimate victory lies with a person called the Hand. Either way, there's someone out there who has something we want."

Disra smiled tightly. Suddenly, it was clear as polished transparisteel. "And so in order to lure that someone into the open, you've decided to parade our decoy around a little."

Tierce inclined his head slightly. "Under the circumstances, I think the risks are worth taking."

"Perhaps," Disra murmured. "It assumes, of course, that it wasn't all just a load of tall talk."

The corner of Tierce's lip twitched. "I was aboard the *Chimaera* with the Grand Admiral for several months, Disra. Before that, I watched him from the Emperor's side for nearly two years. Never in all that time did I hear him make a promise he wasn't able to carry out. If he said the Hand of Thrawn was the key to ultimate victory, then it was. You can count on it."

"Let's just hope whoever's holding the key comes out of hiding before Coruscant gets nervous enough to take action," Disra said. "What do we do first?"

"What *you* do first is get ready to welcome the Kroctari back into the

Empire," Tierce said. Placing Disra's blaster on the table, he pulled a datacard from his tunic and set it down beside the weapon. "Here's a brief rundown on the species in general and Lord Superior Bosmihi in particular," he continued, starting toward the door. "It's all the data we had on board, I'm afraid."

"It'll do," Disra said, stepping to the table and picking up the card. "Where are you going?"

"I thought I'd join Captain Dorja in escorting the delegation from the hangar bay," Tierce said. "I'm rather looking forward to seeing your negotiation skills in action."

Without waiting for a reply, he stepped through the door and was gone. "And to seeing whether or not the Royal Guardsman and con man still need the Moff?" Disra muttered aloud after him.

Probably. But that was all right. Let him watch—let Flim watch, too, if he liked. He'd show them. By the time the Kroctarian delegation went home, both of them would be absolutely convinced that Disra wasn't just some tired old politician whose brilliant scheme had somehow gotten away from him. He was a vital part of this triumvirate, a part that was not going to simply fade into the background. Especially not with a guarantee of ultimate victory almost within their grasp.

He had started this; and by the Emperor's blood, he would be with it to the very end.

Sliding the datacard into his datapad, he tucked his blaster away into its hidden holster and began to read.

There were no planets visible from the bridge of the Imperial Star Destroyer *Tyrannic*. No planets, no asteroids, no ships, no stars. Nothing but complete, uniform blackness.

Except for one spot. Off to starboard, barely visible within Captain Nalgol's view, was a small disk of dirty white. A tiny sliver of the comet head the *Tyrannic* was riding beside, peeking through the ship's cloaking shield.

They'd been flying like this for a month now, completely blind and deaf to the rest of the universe outside their insular existence.

For Nalgol, it wasn't really a problem. He'd pulled duty on one of the Empire's most distant listening posts when he was a cadet, and the mere fact that there was nothing outside to look at didn't bother him. But not all of the crew were as tough as he was. The vids and combat practice rooms were getting triple duty these days, and he'd heard rumors that some of the probe ship pilots were being offered huge bribes to take a passenger or two on their trips outside the darkness.

At the height of the Empire's power, Star Destroyer crews had been the elite of the galaxy. But that glory was far behind them; and if something didn't break soon, Nalgol was going to have a serious personnel problem on his hands.

Outside, there was a brilliant flash from the upper portside quadrant. Relatively brilliant, at least: the glowing drive from one of their probe ships, carefully made up to look like a battered old mining tug. Nalgol watched as it circled around to vanish beneath the arrowhead-shaped hull toward the hangar bay.

No, the unremitting blackness didn't bother him. Still, he had to admit it had felt good to stretch his eyes there for a moment.

There was a step on the command walkway beside him. "Preliminary report from Probe Two, sir," Intelligence Chief Oissan said in that tone of voice that always sounded to Nalgol like someone smacking his lips. "The warship count around Bothawui has gone up to fifty-six."

"Fifty-six?" Nalgol echoed, taking the other's datapad and skimming the numbers. If he remembered the list from yesterday's probe run— "Four new Diamalan ships?"

"Three Diamalan, one Mon Calamari," Oissan said. "Probably there to counter the six Opquis ships that arrived two days ago."

Nalgol shook his head in wordless amazement. From the beginning he'd had quiet but serious doubts about this mission—the idea that the Bothan homeworld would become a focal point for *any* military activity, let alone a confrontation of this magnitude, had been ludicrous on the face of it. But Grand Admiral Thrawn himself had apparently come up with this scheme; and plagued if old red-eyes hadn't been right.

"Very good," he told Oissan. "I want Probe Two's complete report filled within the next two hours."

"Understood, Captain." Oissan seemed to hesitate. "I don't mean to pry into top-level affairs, sir, but at some point I'm going to need to know what's going on out there if I'm to do my job properly."

"I wish I could help you, Colonel," Nalgol said candidly. "But I really don't know a lot myself."

"But you *did* receive a special briefing from Grand Admiral Thrawn at Moff Disra's palace, didn't you?" the other persisted.

"It hardly qualified as a briefing," Nalgol said. "He basically just gave us our assignments and told us to trust him." He nodded in the direction of the comet and the other two Star Destroyers riding cloaked alongside it. "Our part is simple: we wait until all those ships out there have battered themselves and the planet into as much rubble as they're going to, then we come out of cloak and finish them off."

"Finishing off Bothawui will be a good trick," Oissan commented dryly. "I doubt the Bothans have scrimped on their planetary shield system. Thrawn give any idea how he's going to handle that?"

"Not to me," Nalgol said. "Under the circumstances, though, I'm inclined to assume he knows what he's doing."

"I suppose," Oissan muttered. "I wonder how he got all those ships to face off like that?"

"Best guess is that rumor you picked up from your fringe contacts just before we cloaked," Nalgol said. "That thing about a group of Bothans having been involved in the destruction of Caamas."

"Hardly seems something worth getting worked up over," Oissan sniffed. "Especially not after all this time."

"Aliens get worked up over the strangest things," Nalgol reminded him, feeling his lip twist with contempt. "And from the evidence out there, I'd say Thrawn found exactly the right hot spot to hit them with."

"So it would seem," Oissan conceded. "How are we supposed to know when to come out of cloak and attack?"

"I think a full-scale battle out there will be fairly obvious," Nalgol said dryly. "Anyway, Thrawn's last message before we went under the cloak said there would be an Imperial strike team on Bothawui soon, and that they'd be feeding us periodic data via spark transmission."

"That'll be useful," Oissan said thoughtfully. "Of course, knowing Thrawn, he'll probably have the battle timed for the comet's closest approach to Bothawui, to give us the maximum benefit of surprise. That's about a month away."

"That makes sense," Nalgol agreed. "Though how he's going to get them to follow that tight a timetable I haven't a clue."

"Neither do I." Oissan smiled tightly. "That's probably why he's a Grand Admiral and we're not."

Nalgol smiled back. "Indeed," he said; and with that admission, one more layer of his private doubts seemed to melt away. Yes, Thrawn had proved himself in the past. Many, many times. However this magic of his worked, it was apparently still working.

And under the spell of Thrawn's genius, the Empire was about to get some of its own back. And that was really all Nalgol cared about.

"Thank you, Colonel," he said, handing back the other's datapad. "You may return to your duties. Before you do, though, I want you to check with Probe Control about whether we can increase our probe flights to twice a day without drawing unwanted attention."

"Yes, sir," Oissan said with another tight smile. "After all, we wouldn't want to miss out on our grand entrance."

Nalgol turned to gaze out at the blackness again. "We won't miss it," he promised softly. "Not a chance."

CHAPTER

2

From somewhere in the deep recesses of his mind came an insistent warbling; and with a jolt, Luke Skywalker snapped out of his Jedi hibernation trance. "Okay, Artoo," he told the droid as he rolled out of his bunk, and took a moment to reorient himself. Right; he was aboard Mara Jade's ship, the *Jade's Fire,* heading toward the Nirauan system. The system where Mara herself had disappeared nearly two weeks ago. "Okay, I'm awake," he added, flexing his fingers and toes and working moisture back into his mouth. "We almost there?"

The droid twittered an affirmative as Luke snagged his boots, a twitter that was echoed from the direction of the cockpit. The echo was Mara's Veeone pilot droid, who had been flying the *Fire* ever since Luke and Artoo had come aboard at the Duroon rendezvous point, and who up till now had refused to let either of them anywhere near the ship's controls.

An overprotectiveness that was about to come to an end. "Artoo, go back to the docking port and make sure the X-wing's ready to fly," he instructed the little droid as he headed toward the cockpit. "I'm going to take us in."

A minute later he was seated in the *Fire*'s pilot's seat, reviewing the layout of the controls and displays one last time. The Veeone droid, perhaps recognizing Luke's expression as one he'd seen often enough on Mara's face, had decided not to argue the point. "Get ready," Luke told the droid, resting his hands on the controls. The counter ran to zero, and Luke pushed the hyperdrive lever forward. The starlines flared and shrank back down into stars, and they were there.

The Veeone whistled softly. "That's the place," Luke confirmed, gazing out at the distant sun, its tiny red disk looking cold and aloof. The planet Nirauan itself was nowhere to be seen. "We're looking for the second planet," he told the droid. "Can you get me a reading on it?"

The Veeone twittered an affirmative, and the nav displays came to life.

"I see it." Luke nodded, checking the reading. It was a pretty fair distance away.

Which was by deliberate design, of course. The *Fire* had impressive shields and armament, but charging to the rescue with quad lasers blazing would be unlikely to do Mara any good, no matter what the situation she was in. Stealth and secrecy were the plan, and that meant leaving the *Fire* hidden out here while he and Artoo sneaked in in their X-wing.

He keyed the comm unit to the docking bay. "Artoo? Is everything ready?"

There was a confirming warble. "Good," Luke said, looking back at the nav display. They were, he estimated, a good seven hours away from the planet by the X-wing's sublight drive. A long time to sit in a cramped cockpit worrying about Mara, besides giving whoever was down there a straight vector back to the *Fire*.

Fortunately, there was another way. "Start calculating our two jumps," he instructed Artoo, keying on the *Fire*'s automatic weapons systems. "No more than five minutes each way—we don't want to take any more time with this than we have to."

Artoo twittered an acknowledgment, and got to work. "Now, you're clear on what you're supposed to do?" Luke asked the Veeone as he keyed the drive to low power and started the *Fire* moving. There was a convenient clump of small asteroids drifting through in the darkness just ahead that would make a perfect hiding place. "I'm going to put the ship in with those rocks; and then you're going to sit there and pretend to be one of them. Okay?"

The droid gurgled reluctant agreement. "All right," Luke said, easing the ship up into the asteroids. One of them, about shockball size, bounced lightly against the hull, and he winced in reaction. The *Fire* was Mara's most prized possession, and she was more protective of it than even the Veeone was. If he dented the hull, or even just scratched the paint, he would never hear the end of it from her.

He finished his maneuvering with exaggerated care, and managed to get it into position without any further collisions. "Okay, that's it," he said, unstrapping and keying control back to the Veeone. "You've got the code I gave you—we'll transmit that on our way back so you'll know it's us. Anyone else . . . well, don't let the ship shoot at them unless you're fired on first. Not until we have some idea what's going on down there."

Two minutes later, keeping a wary eye out for the floating rock pile outside, he eased the X-wing out of the *Fire*'s docking bay and headed into deep space. Artoo had the course already plotted in, and with a burst of starlines they were off.

Luke had told him to keep it under five minutes, and the droid had taken him at his word. Two minutes after heading out, following Artoo's instructions, he dropped the X-wing back out of hyperspace, turned it around, and headed back in. Two minutes after that, they were there.

Artoo whistled softly. "That's the place, all right," Luke confirmed, gazing out at the dark planet hanging in space in front of them. "Just like the pictures the *Starry Ice* brought back."

And Mara was down there somewhere. Stranded, maybe injured, maybe a prisoner.

Or maybe dead.

Pushing that thought firmly away from his mind, Luke stretched out to the Force. *Mara? Mara, can you hear me?*

But there was nothing.

Artoo gave a questioning warble. "I can't sense her," Luke admitted. "But that doesn't necessarily mean anything. We're still pretty far out, and she may not be strong enough to reach this far. She could be asleep, too— that would limit her range."

The droid didn't respond. But it wasn't hard to guess that his thoughts were paralleling Luke's.

And there was also the vision Luke had had three and a half weeks ago at the Tierfon medical facility. That image of Mara floating lifelessly in a pool of water . . .

"Anyway, there's no point in worrying about it," Luke said, pushing that vision into the back of his mind as best he could. "Do a quiet sensor scan—nothing that'll set off their detectors. Or at least, nothing that'll set them off if they work the way ours do."

There was an acknowledgment, and another question scrolled across the X-wing's computer display. "We'll take the same route in that she did," Luke answered. "Down the canyon to the cave where she disappeared. Once we get there, we'll take the X-wing inside and see what happens."

Artoo twittered an uneasy-sounding acknowledgment. Glancing at the course record Talon Karrde had given him, Luke eased the X-wing toward the planet, wishing for a moment that Leia were here with him. If those creatures that Mara had run into were intelligent, it might take not only Jedi skill but also diplomatic finesse to deal with them. Finesse that Leia had, and that he didn't.

He grimaced. On the other hand, they probably weren't very happy back home that he'd taken off this way without notice, let alone if he'd tried to bring Leia along with him. No, Leia's diplomatic skills were needed most back in the New Republic.

What skills would be needed here he'd find out soon enough.

They were still well outside the planet's atmosphere when the X-wing's sensors picked up the two alien spacecraft rising from the surface toward them. "So much for stealth and secrecy," Luke murmured, studying the sensor profiles. They definitely looked like the ship he and Artoo had spotted on their way out of the Cavrilhu Pirates' nest in the Kauron asteroid field.

That ship, though, had cut and run before he could get a close look at it. Now, as this pair rose rapidly toward him, he could see that his first impression of the craft had indeed been correct. Roughly three times the X-wing's size, they were an odd but strangely artistic combination of alien manufacture melded with that of the all-too-familiar TIE fighter design. At the bow of each ship was a slightly darkened canopy, through which he could just barely make out a pair of Imperial-style flight helmets.

Artoo whistled pensively. "Steady, Artoo," Luke warned. "It doesn't necessarily mean they're allied with the Empire. They might have found a TIE fighter somewhere and borrowed from it."

Artoo's grunt showed his opinion of that one. "All right, fine, probably not," Luke said, eyeing the incoming ships. A minute later they were on him, rising slightly above the X-wing and altering course as they curved into flanking positions on both sides. "You getting weapons readings?"

The droid whistled, and a rough schematic appeared on the computer display. The ships were quite heavily armed. "Great," Luke muttered, stretching out with the Force to try to get a feel for the situation. But all he could detect were the basic emotional backgrounds of the three beings aboard each ship. Alien minds thinking alien thoughts, with no point of reference for him to latch on to.

On the other hand, their flanking positions were more suited to escort than attack. More importantly, Luke's Jedi senses weren't indicating any immediate danger. For the moment, at least, they were probably relatively safe.

And it was time to start acting friendly. "Let's see if we can talk to them," he suggested, reaching for the comm switch.

The aliens beat him to it. *"Ka sha'ma'ti orf k'ralan,"* a surprisingly melodious voice said in Luke's ear. *"Kra'miral sumt tara'kliso mor Mitth'raw'nuruodo sur pra'cin'zisk mor'kor'lae."*

Luke felt his stomach tighten. "Artoo?" he asked.

The droid warbled a worried-sounding confirmation: it was indeed the same transmission Karrde and Mara had picked up from the alien ship that had buzzed Booster Terrik's *Errant Venture*. The transmission, according to Mara, that had included Thrawn's little-known complete name.

Grimacing, Luke keyed his comm. "This is New Republic X-wing AA-589," he said. If the aliens didn't speak Basic, of course, this wasn't going to do any good. Still, it wouldn't do to just sit here and ignore them. "I'm looking for a friend who may have crashed on your world."

There was a short pause. Watching out the canopy, Luke had the distinct impression that the two alien ships had pulled in just a hair closer to him. "New Republic X-wing," the voice came again, this time in quite passable Basic. "You will follow us to the surface. You will not deviate from our guidance. If you do, you will be destroyed."

"I understand," Luke said. There was a click from the comm; and suddenly the two alien ships dropped toward the surface. Luke was ready, following and sliding quickly back into his place in the formation. "Show-offs," he muttered under his breath.

He had spoken too soon. A second later the two ships again twisted away, this time curving slightly up and then hard to starboard. Artoo screeched as the portside ship shot uncomfortably close over his head, the tone of his displeasure rising sharply as Luke cut the X-wing hard over to again match the maneuver. He had barely settled back into his place in the center when they did it again, veering to portside this time.

Artoo grunted. "I don't know," Luke told him as he caught up with his escort again. "Maybe there's some kind of defense system they've got set up that requires a specific approach if you don't want to get blasted. Like the pirates had at their asteroid base, remember?"

The obvious point scrolled down the computer display: according to the *Starry Ice*'s record, Mara hadn't followed any such complicated approach. "Maybe they set it up in response to her sneaking in," Luke suggested. "Or we could be coming in over a different part of the planet than she did—we haven't been able to pick up a geographic match yet."

Artoo grunted. "Or they could be trying to create an excuse to open fire," Luke agreed grimly. "Though why they'd think they'd need one I don't know."

The alien ships performed three more sets of maneuvers on the way down, none of which Luke had any particular trouble matching. But as they reached the upper atmosphere they seemed to tire of the game, settling into a hard, straight drive toward the western horizon. Luke stayed in formation, splitting his attention between the ships and the ground far below, and stretching out to the Force for any signs of trouble.

They were twenty minutes into their drive, and Artoo had finally made a match between the topography below and the *Starry Ice*'s records, when the familiar tingling began. "We've got trouble, Artoo," Luke told the droid. "I'm not sure what kind yet, but it's definitely trouble. Give me a quick status rundown."

He ran an eye over the display as the status report appeared. There were no other air- or spacecraft registering on the X-wing's sensors, nothing in their escort's power usage or weapons systems that indicated attack preparation, and the X-wing's own systems were reading fully operative. "How far to the fortress Mara found?" he asked.

Artoo beeped: less than fifteen minutes at their current speed. "Sometime in the next ten minutes, I'd guess," Luke told him. "Be ready." Taking a deep breath, settling his hands on the controls, he consciously relaxed his muscles and immersed himself in the Force.

They were registering six minutes to the fortress, and the canyon Mara had flown down had just appeared paralleling them on the distant horizon, when it finally happened. In perfect unison the two escort ships threw a quick spurt of power to their forward thrusters, dropping from flanking into following positions behind the X-wing as their velocities blipped down.

And from nozzles nestled half-hidden beneath their cockpits spat a deadly salvo of blue fire.

But their target was no longer there. An instant before the aliens' thrusters had fired, Luke had caught the subtle disturbance in the Force; and by the time their weapons flashed he had thrown the X-wing into a sharp climb, curving up and around in a tight loop that would take him back around into attack position behind his attackers.

Or at least, that was the normal endpoint of the maneuver. This time, though, Luke had other plans. Instead of pulling out of his loop behind the aliens, he held the X-wing's nose pointed toward the ground for an extra pair of heartbeats. Then, at what seemed like the last second, he twisted the starfighter into a stomach-wrenching, twin-rotational turn. An instant later they were running bare meters above the ground on a vector perpendicular to their original course.

"What are they doing?" Luke called, not daring to take his eyes away from the landscape long enough to look for himself.

The droid's warning screech and a sudden tingling in the Force were his answer. From behind came another volley of blue fire, most of it going wide but a few shots splattering off his rear deflector shield. "Any new friends joined them?" he called.

Artoo warbled a negative. That was something, anyway. Still, those ships were good and the crews clearly knew what they were doing. At two-to-one odds, Luke was going to have his hands full. Especially since—

Artoo twittered an urgent question. "No, leave the S-foils as they are," Luke told him. "We're not going to shoot back."

The droid's question was a disbelieving whistle. "Because we don't know who they are or why they're here," Luke told him, eyes measuring the ground ahead. Just beyond Mara's canyon the terrain abruptly became something shattered-looking, broken into granite-walled cliffs and deep, sharp-edged crevices. "I don't want to kill any of them until I know who and what they are."

Artoo's rejoinder became another screech as the latest enemy salvo blew a thin layer of metal from the top of the starboard S-foil. "Don't worry, we're almost there," Luke soothed him, risking a quick glance at his status displays. No serious damage yet, but that wouldn't last long once the attackers got a little closer.

Which meant that his best hope was to keep that from happening.

Behind him, Artoo whistled suspiciously. "That's exactly where we're going," Luke confirmed. They were nearly to the shattered landscape now; and off to portside he spotted a likely looking gorge. "Oh, relax— it's no worse than some of the other things we've pulled off," he added, twisting the X-wing's nose toward the gorge. "Anyway, we haven't got a choice. Hang on—here we go."

Beggar's Canyon on Tatooine had been a tricky but familiar obstacle run of twists and corners and switchbacks. The Death Star trench had been far straighter, but with the addition of turbolaser fire and attacking TIE fighters to keep it interesting. Now, the Nirauan cliffs took the challenge a step farther by adding unpredictable curves and breakpoints, with varying widths and depths, jutting rocks, and clinging tree vines.

The newly signed Rebel recruit at Yavin would have recognized the risks involved. Even the cocky adolescent on Tatooine would have hesitated at the stupidity of tackling such an unknown labyrinth at such high speeds. The seasoned Jedi Luke had become, though, knew he wouldn't have a problem with it.

He was mostly right. The ship sliced through the first series of twists with ease, Luke's piloting skill and prescience in the Force combining with the X-wing's innate maneuverability to leave the alien ships far behind. He shot through an open valley, changed direction toward a new canyon—

And nearly lost control as a burst of blue fire raked across the portside fuselage.

"It's all right," he called back to Artoo, feeling a flash of annoyance with himself as the X-wing plunged again into the relative safety of his chosen ravine. This had happened before: focusing his attention—and the Force—too narrowly in one direction had a tendency to blind him to anything happening outside that cone. Clearly, at least one of the alien pilots had been smart enough to abandon the chase and fly up over the maze to wait for the target to show himself.

But the gambit had failed; and if the terrain cooperated, he wouldn't get another chance at it. The X-wing emerged into a second valley, this one smaller than the first, and veered off into another ravine. Letting the Force guide his hands, Luke watched the cliffs around him, looking for just the right place . . .

And then, suddenly, there it was. On both sides of the X-wing steep cliffs rose upward, one of them angling sharply toward the other until only a tiny ribbon of daylight showed at the top between them. Lines and clusters of drab and scraggly bushes clung to various parts of the craggy rock, with a thick matting of brown bushes and squat trees covering the canyon floor below. Ahead and behind, the canyon curved sharply to either side, leaving this center part as an isolated bubble surrounded by rock.

It was the perfect place to go to ground.

Artoo didn't squeal or screech as Luke swung the starfighter around in a hundred-eighty-degree skid in a classic smuggler's reverse. Probably, Luke decided as he fed power to the thrusters, because the little droid was too busy holding on for dear life. For a handful of seconds the X-wing bucked beneath him, and he fought hard for stability as it tried to flip out of control. Outside, the canyon walls shooting past began to slow, and as they did so he eased off on the drive and keyed in the repulsorlifts. The deceleration pressure crushing him against the seat cushions faded; spinning the X-wing around to face forward again, he threw a quick look around. Directly ahead, a pair of squat but bushy trees rose up from the canyon floor, straddling what appeared to be a dry creek bed, their trunks just the right distance apart. Killing the last of the X-wing's forward velocity, he dropped its nose down to slide neatly between the tree trunks.

"There," he said, running the last steps of the landing cycle and shutting down the repulsorlifts. "That wasn't so hard, now, was it?"

There was a weak and slightly shaky whistle from behind him. Apparently, Artoo hadn't found his voice yet.

Smiling tightly, Luke popped the canopy, wincing at the high-pitched scratching sounds as dozens of thorn-edged leaves scraped across the transparisteel, and slid off his helmet and gloves.

The air flooding in from outside was cool and smelled vaguely mossy. For a long minute he listened, stretching out with Force-enhanced senses for sounds of pursuit. But there was nothing except the normal sounds of wind rustling through the leaves and the distant chirps of avians or insects. "I think we've lost them," he told Artoo. "At least for now. You figured out where we are?"

Artoo beeped, still sounding a little dazed, and a map appeared on the computer display.

Luke studied it. Not too bad, but not too good either. They were no more than ten kilometers from Mara's cave, but most of the territory between here and there consisted of the same kind of narrow gorges and rocky cliffs they'd just been flying through. At least a full day's travel, probably two, possibly three.

On the other hand, the very roughness of the ground would give them better cover than they could reasonably have asked for. All in all, a pretty fair trade.

But it wouldn't be much of a trade if the aliens found them before they even got started. "Come on," he said, easing out of the cockpit and rolling out to the ground. The attempt to avoid the leaf thorns was only partially successful, but only a couple of them actually drew blood. "Let's get the pack sorted out and get out of here."

It was the work of a few minutes to break out the camo-net Karrde had sent along and to pull it snugly over the X-wing. Then, as an extra precaution, he cut up some of the smaller bushes and tree limbs with his lightsaber and scattered them on top of the net. It wasn't perfect, especially at close range, but it was the best he could do in the available time.

Karrde's people had also put his survival pack together, assembling the supplies and loading them aboard the X-wing while Luke hurried through the datawork necessary for getting off Cejansij. And as Luke had come to expect from the smuggler's organization over the years, they'd done a first-rate job of it. Split into two separate carrypacks, the supplies included ration bars, water filter/bottles, medpacs, glow rods, a good supply of syntherope, a spare blaster, a survival tent with bedroll, and even a small selection of low-yield grenades.

"I'm surprised they didn't try to cram a landspeeder in," Luke grunted as he hoisted one of the packs experimentally onto his shoulders. It was heavy enough, but the weight had been well distributed and would be reasonably easy to carry. "I guess we'll have to leave the other pack here. You ready to do a little climbing?"

Artoo warbled questioningly, his dome swiveling to peer first one direction down the canyon and then the other. "No, that's where they'll expect us to come out," Luke told him. He pointed upward toward one of the cliffs towering over them. "That's our route, up there."

The droid swiveled his dome again, whistling skittishly as he leaned way back to look up. "Relax—we won't have to go all the way to the top," Luke calmed him. "See that gap about two-thirds of the way up? If I read the aerial pictures right, that should lead into a cut that'll take us the rest of the way to the top."

Artoo warbled forlornly, looking back and forth along the canyon again. "No, Artoo, we can't go that way," Luke told him firmly. "And we don't have time to argue the point. Even if those ships can't get in there, they may have smaller ones back at the fortress. And they can always come in on foot, too. You want to be sitting around when they get here?"

The droid beeped emphatically. Swiveling himself around, he started bumping determinedly along the dry creek bed toward the base of the cliff below the gap Luke had pointed out.

Smiling, Luke gave his pack one final settling shrug. Then, stretching out with the Force, he lifted Artoo high enough off the ground to clear the undergrowth and headed toward the cliff.

As it turned out, the climb had looked more daunting than it really was. Though certainly steep enough, the wall wasn't nearly the impossibly vertical slope that it had seemed from the canyon floor. Hand- and footholds were plentiful; the whole cliff face seemed to be dotted with narrow ledges and small caves, and the bushes and vines provided sturdy hand-holds as well.

The only problematic part was Artoo, but even that quickly settled into a more or less comfortable routine. Finding a secure place to stand, Luke would use the Force to lift the droid up past him to a narrow ledge or conveniently spaced pair of caves, hold him in place while using the syntherope to lash him to the nearest bushes, then climb past him to the next convenient resting point and repeat.

Artoo didn't care for any part of the procedure, of course. Midway up the cliff, though, he at least stopped complaining about it.

They were almost to the gap, and Luke was once again catching up to the point where he'd anchored Artoo, when he heard the faint voice.

He stopped, one hand gripping a lumpy vine, and listened. But there was nothing but the distant insect chirping he'd been hearing since they landed. Running through his Jedi sensory-enhancement techniques, he stretched out his hearing; but though the chirps became louder and more varied, the voice he thought he'd heard wasn't there.

There was a loud squeal from above him: Artoo, whistling softly in his enhanced hearing. "I thought I heard something," he murmured back, the words booming in his head. Hastily, he eased his hearing back to normal. "It was like a voice—"

He broke off at Artoo's startled twitter. "What is it?" he asked, looking up. The droid was facing down and along the cliff; turning his head, Luke tracked along his gaze—

And froze. Perched on a thorn-leafed bush not three meters away was a small, slack-winged brown-gray creature.

Watching him.

"Take it easy," Luke soothed Artoo, taking a moment to study the creature. About thirty centimeters long from head to talons, it was covered with smooth-looking skin. Its folded wings were more of the same, though it was hard to guess their size, and arched slightly over in a way that reminded Luke of hunched shoulders. The head was proportionally small and streamlined, with a pair of dark eyes nestled beneath fleshy folds and two horizontal slashes beneath them. The upper slash was undulating with the steady rhythm of respiration, while the lower was pressed into a tight slit. A pair of segmented, wide-taloned feet gripped the bush it was perched on, apparently not bothered in the least by the sharp thorns. The overall effect was like something halfway between a mynock and a preying makthier, and he wondered if it was related to either of those species.

Artoo gave another warble, this one wary. "I don't think it means us any harm," Luke assured him, still watching the creature. "I don't sense any danger from it. And we're a little big for a snack for something that size."

Unless, of course, they hunted in packs. Still watching the creature, he stretched out with the Force, searching for others of the species. There were definitely more of them in the canyon, but most seemed to be fairly distant—

The lower slit on the creature's face opened, revealing twin rows of tiny sharp teeth, and emitted a loud chirp.

Who are you?

Luke blinked in surprise. There was the voice he thought he'd heard, except that this time it was clear enough to understand. But had it come from—? "What?" he asked.

The creature chirped again. *Who are you?*

He was right: it was the creature who'd spoken.

Only it hadn't spoken. Not really. But then how had Luke understood—?

And then, abruptly, he understood. "I'm Luke Skywalker," he said, stretching toward the creature with the Force. "Jedi Knight of the New Republic. Who are you?"

The creature emitted a short series of chirps. *What do you do here, Jedi Knight Sky Walker?*

"I'm looking for a friend," Luke said. His guess had been right: while he couldn't understand the creature's actual chirping language, he was pulling the essence of the communication from its mind via the Force. An extremely rare event, in his experience, and it probably implied the creatures were at least marginally Force-sensitive. "She landed near here nearly two weeks ago and then disappeared. Do you know where she is?"

The creature seemed to shy back a bit. It fluffed its wings partially open, resettled them across its back. It chirped again—*Who is this friend?*

"Her name is Mara Jade," Luke said.

Is she another Jedi Knight?

"Sort of," Luke hedged. Mara had dropped by his Jedi academy occasionally over the past eight years, but she'd never stayed long enough to complete her training. Actually, there were times Luke wondered if she'd ever truly begun it. "Do you know where she is?"

The wings fluffed again as the creature chirped. *I know nothing.*

"Really," Luke said, letting his tone cool just a bit. He didn't even need the Force for this one; he'd watched Jacen, Jaina, and Anakin pull this trick enough times to recognize guilty knowledge when he saw it. "What if I told you a Jedi can always tell when someone's lying?"

From behind him came a loud and authoritative chirp. *Leave the young one alone.*

Luke turned his head. Perched on the bushes and craggy rocks on the other side of the cliff face were three more of the creatures. They were each twice as big as the first one; but even without the size differential the subtle differences between adult and young were instantly apparent. "Your pardon," he said to them. "I wasn't trying to intimidate him. Perhaps you can help me in my search for my friend."

One of the creatures spread his wings and gave a short hop to a bush closer to Luke, twisting his head one way and then the other as if studying the intruder out of each eye individually. *You are not one of the others. Who are you?*

"I think you know," Luke said, a quiet sense prompting him to play a hunch. "Why don't you tell me instead who you are?"

The creature seemed to consider. *I am Hunter Of Winds. I bargain for this nesting of the Qom Qae.*

"In the name of the New Republic I greet you, Hunter Of Winds," Luke said gravely. "I presume you know of the New Republic?"

The elder Qom Qae fluffed his wings exactly the same way the young one had. *I have heard. What is the New Republic to us?*

"I suppose that depends on what you want it to be," Luke said. "But that's a matter for diplomats and bargainers to discuss. I'm here to help a friend."

Hunter Of Winds chirped decisively. *We have no knowledge of any strangers.*

But we do, the younger Qom Qae chirped from behind Luke. *The Qom Jha spoke of—*

Hunter Of Winds cut him off with a squawk. *Is your name Seeker After Stupidity?* he demanded pointedly. *Be silent.*

"Perhaps you've merely forgotten," Luke suggested diplomatically. "A nesting bargainer must have many other matters to think about, after all."

Hunter Of Winds fluffed his wings. *What happens outside this nesting does not properly concern us. Go to another nesting of the Qom Qae, or to the Qom Jha if you dare. Perhaps they will help you.*

"All right," Luke said. "Will you guide me to them?"

They are outside this nesting, Hunter Of Winds chirped. *They are not our concern.*

"I see," Luke said. "Tell me, Hunter Of Winds, have you ever had a friend in danger?"

The Qom Qae spread his wings, his two companions following suit. *This conversation is ended. Young one: come.*

He leaped out from his bush, gliding away toward the canyon floor below on outstretched wings, his two companions following. Turning back, Luke saw the young Qom Qae follow them.

Artoo grunted contemptuously. "Don't blame them too much," Luke told him with a sigh. "There may be cultural or political entanglements here we don't know about."

He resumed his climb. "Or they may just be wary of getting involved in someone else's fight," he added. "We've certainly seen enough of that over the years."

Five minutes later they'd reached the gap. Luke had been right: the cut continued upward toward the top of the cliff at a much more leisurely angle while still keeping them under tree cover the whole way. "Perfect," Luke said, peering up along it. "Let's get up to the top and see where we go from here." Collecting the syntherope, he started to coil it—

And suddenly Artoo emitted a startled squawk.

"What is it?" Luke demanded, grabbing reflexively for his lightsaber as he spun around. There was no danger around them that he could see or sense. "Artoo, what is it?" he asked again, turning his attention to the droid.

Artoo was gazing back down into the valley along the way they'd come, moaning mournfully. Frowning, Luke followed along the droid's line of sight—

And felt his breath catch in his throat. Down on the valley floor, their X-wing had vanished.

"No," Luke breathed, gazing hard at the browns and grays down there. His first, hopeful thought was that his camouflage job had simply been better than he realized and that the starfighter was still right where they'd left it. But a moment of careful searching with Jedi-enhanced senses put that hope quietly to rest.

The X-wing was indeed gone.

Artoo warbled anxiously. "It's all right," Luke soothed. "It's all right."

And to his own mild surprise, he found he actually meant it. The X-wing's disappearing act was frustrating and annoying; but oddly enough, there was no sense of danger or fear accompanying it. Not even any serious concern, despite the fact that the loss of their ship meant no chance for a quick escape should the situation warrant it.

A prodding from the Force? A sense, perhaps, that the X-wing was merely misplaced and not actually lost?

Unfortunately, he realized soberly, it could just as easily be a prodding in the opposite direction. That the loss of the ship didn't matter because he would not be leaving this world alive anyway.

Unbidden, an image of Yoda rose from his memory: the old Jedi Master sighing with weariness as he settled onto his bed for the last time. Luke could remember his gut-churning fear at Yoda's frailness; could recall the exact tone of his own voice as he protested to Yoda that he must not die. *Strong am I with the Force,* Yoda had gently reproved his student. *But not that strong. Twilight is upon me and soon night will fall. That is the way of things . . . the way of the Force.*

Luke took a deep breath. Obi-Wan had died, Yoda had died, and someday it would be his turn to face that same journey. And if this was the place where that journey would begin, so be it. He was a Jedi, and would face it as one.

In the meantime, the reason he had come here had not changed. "Nothing we can do about it now," he told Artoo, turning away from the valley and returning to the task of coiling the syntherope. "Let's get to the top and see where we go from there."

From directly above came a soft chirp. *There are better ways to pass.*

Luke looked up. The young Qom Qae was back, hovering on some updraft he'd found and gazing down at them. "Are you offering to help us?" he asked.

The Qom Qae bent one of his wings slightly, the change in air pressure sending him sidling over to the cliff face beside Luke. He caught one of the bushes in his talons as he reached it, folding his wings behind him. *I will help you,* he chirped. *The Qom Jha have said another has arrived and is with them. I will take you there.*

"Thank you," Luke said, wondering if he should ask about his missing X-wing. But after the young Qom Qae's skittishness earlier it probably would be better to leave any interrogations for later. "May I ask why you're willing to take the risk?"

I am known to some of the younger Qom Jha, he chirped. *I do not fear them.*

"I'm not necessarily talking about the Qom Jha," Luke said, wanting to make sure the young alien genuinely understood the risks. "The others Hunter Of Winds spoke of may also try to stop us."

I understand that. The alien fluffed his wings. *But you asked Hunter Of Winds if he had ever had a friend in danger. I have.*

Luke smiled. "I understand," he said. "And I'm honored to have your assistance. I'm Luke Skywalker, as I said, and this is my droid, Artoo. What's your name?"

The Qom Qae spread his wings and made a short hop to a bush in front of them. *I am too young yet to have a name. I am called merely Child Of Winds.*

"Child Of Winds," Luke repeated, eyeing him thoughtfully. "You wouldn't by any chance be related to Hunter Of Winds, would you?"

He is my sire, Child Of Winds chirped. *It is indeed true about the wisdom of the Jedi Knights.*

Luke suppressed a smile. "Sometimes," he said. "But we should get moving now. Along the way, perhaps you can tell me more about your people."

I would be honored, Child Of Winds said, spreading his wings eagerly. *Come, I will show you the path.*

CHAPTER

3

The communications blister on the New Republic Dreadnaught *Peregrine* was something of an anachronism among modern warships, a throwback to the pre–Clone Wars design philosophy that had prevailed at the time the *Peregrine* and its *Katana*-fleet sister ships had been built. Not only was the ship's entire primary antenna array located in the blister, but so were the complex and delicate encryption/decryption computers.

The handful of other *Katana*-fleet Dreadnaughts still in New Republic service had had their comm blisters extensively renovated, with the encrypt/decrypt equipment moved inside into a more sheltered area between the bridge and Intelligence ops. But somehow, no matter how often the renovation procedure was talked about, the *Peregrine* always seemed to slip through the cracks in the work schedule.

Wedge Antilles had wondered about that on occasion. There was, he knew, still some bad blood between General Garm Bel Iblis and a few of the New Republic's upper echelon, dating back to Bel Iblis's years of running his own private war against the Empire after his falling-out with Mon Mothma. Wedge had always suspected the lack of renovation on this, the general's flagship, was tied to that animosity.

It wasn't until Wedge and Rogue Squadron had been permanently assigned to Bel Iblis that he'd learned the truth. Intelligence sections, Bel Iblis had explained to him, were crowded and public places, and having a decrypted signal piped to bridge or command room gave abundant opportunity for anyone with a modicum of skill and a surplus of curiosity to tap into the conversation. A comm blister, in contrast, was about as isolated a place as one could find aboard a warship; and having the encrypt/decrypt computer close at hand meant that the message began and ended right there. Whenever any really private transmissions were due, that was where Bel Iblis was to be found.

He and Wedge were there now. At Admiral Ackbar's personal request.

"I understand your concerns, General Bel Iblis," Ackbar said, his face filling the comm display, his huge eyes swiveling around to take in Wedge as well. "And I do not disagree with your assessment. But I must nevertheless turn down your request."

"I strongly urge you to reconsider, Admiral," Bel Iblis said stiffly. "I appreciate the political situation on Coruscant, but that can't be allowed to blind us to the purely military considerations here."

The Mon Cal's lip tendrils seemed to stiffen. "Unfortunately, there are no longer any pure military considerations involving the Caamas issue," he rumbled. "Political and ethical questions have pervaded everything."

"Unusual combination," Wedge murmured under his breath.

One of Ackbar's eyes swiveled briefly toward him before turning back to Bel Iblis. "The final line of the situation is that any serious New Republic presence over Bothawui at this point would be construed as support of the Bothans against their critics."

"It would be nothing of the sort," Bel Iblis objected. "It would be a voice of calm and reason in the middle of a very dangerous flash point. There are sixty-eight warships here already, all of them engaged in a twelve-way glaring contest with each other, all of them ready to jump if any of the others so much as sneeze. There has *got* to be someone here who can mediate any problems before they collapse into all-out war."

Ackbar sighed, a darkly rasping sound. "I agree with you wholeheartedly, General. But the High Council and Senate are in ultimate authority here, and they have come to a different conclusion."

Bel Iblis threw a baleful glance at Wedge. "I trust you'll continue trying to change their minds."

"Yes indeed," Ackbar said. "But whether I am successful or not, you will not be the one chosen for the dubious honor of mediator. President Gavrisom has already selected another task for you."

"More important than keeping the peace over Bothawui?"

"Far more important," Ackbar assured him. "If Bothawui is the flash point, then it is the Caamas Document which is the spark."

Wedge felt a sudden premonition hit him. Could Gavrisom actually be considering—?

He was. "President Gavrisom has therefore concluded that the New Republic's best chance of defusing the controversy is to obtain an intact copy of the document," Ackbar continued. "To that end, you are to proceed immediately to Ord Trasi, where you will begin assembling a force for an information raid on the Imperial Ubiqtorate base at Yaga Minor."

Wedge stole a furtive glance at Bel Iblis. The general's expression hadn't changed, but there was just enough of a tightness in his jaw to show he was thinking along the same lines Wedge was. "With all due respect, Admiral," Bel Iblis said, "President Gavrisom must be joking.

Yaga Minor is possibly the most heavily defended system in Imperial *or* New Republic space. And that's just considering a straight-line attack, where it doesn't matter which enemy positions come under fire. Having to keep the enemy data system intact adds five extra layers of difficulty to the whole operation."

"The President is well aware of the challenges involved," Ackbar said, his voice even more gravelly than usual. "I'll be honest: I don't like this any more than you do. But it has to be tried. If war breaks out over this issue, we don't have enough ships or troops to either force or maintain a peace. The entire New Republic could conceivably collapse into total civil war."

Bel Iblis looked at Wedge again, turned back to the display. "Yes, sir," he said. "Unfortunately, I'm forced to agree with your assessment."

"I may also say," Ackbar added, "that if there's any way this can be done, you are the one who can do it."

Bel Iblis smiled wryly. "Thank you for your confidence, Admiral. I'll do my best."

"Good," Ackbar said. "You and your task force are to leave Bothawui immediately for Ord Trasi. I'll be quietly sending you the rest of your ships over the next two weeks, at which time I expect you to have a battle plan formulated and ready to go."

"Understood," Bel Iblis said. "What about special equipment or units?"

"Anything the New Republic can supply is yours," Ackbar assured him. "Tell me what you need, and I'll have it sent to you."

Bel Iblis nodded. "We will of course need total secrecy on this," he warned. "If even a hint leaks to the Empire, what little chance we have will be gone."

"The secrecy will be complete," Ackbar promised. "I've already set a cover story in motion which should convince any Imperial spies that the ships are secretly being assembled in the outer regions of the Kothlis system for the defense of Bothawui, should that become necessary."

"That should work," Bel Iblis said. "Provided they don't head to Kothlis and take a look for themselves."

"Two Rendili Space Docks have already been moved to the Kothlis system," Ackbar said. "They'll be equipped with dummy ships carrying the proper IDs and markings for the benefit of any Imperials who happen by."

"Interesting." Bel Iblis cocked an eyebrow. "So this isn't just some slice-of-the-moment idea Gavrisom came up with last night. This has been in the works for some time now."

The Mon Cal nodded his massive head. "The preparations were begun the day after the riot at the Combined Clans Building on Bothawui," he said. "With General Solo's implication in that incident, the President knew it would no longer be possible for the New Republic government to make any overt political moves without our motives coming under fire."

"I understand the reasoning involved," Bel Iblis said heavily. "Ord Trasi it is, then."

"A liaison team from my office will be waiting there when you arrive," Ackbar said. "Good luck, General."

"Thank you, Admiral. Bel Iblis out."

The general touched a key, and the transmission ended. "Which doesn't mean I entirely agree with it," he commented under his breath to the blank display as he turned to Wedge. "Well, General. Comments?"

Wedge shook his head. "I was on an information raid once, back when we were trying to get data on Grand Admiral Makati out of the Boudolayz library," he said. "I think the bit-pushers estimated afterward that we were about eighty percent successful. And that was Boudolayz, not Yaga Minor."

"Yes, I've read the reports on that raid," Bel Iblis said, stroking his mustache thoughtfully. "This is definitely not going to be easy."

Wedge grimaced. "Meanwhile, Bothawui keeps collecting warships like a floodlight collects night insects. Eventually, sir, someone's going to try to take advantage of that."

"I agree," Bel Iblis said. "Which is why I asked you to come up here with me this afternoon."

"Oh?" Wedge said, regarding him closely. "Then you knew this was coming?"

"Not the Yaga Minor raid specifically," Bel Iblis said. "But I had a feeling Coruscant would turn down my request to stay here and keep order. It also occurred to me that if my task force was ordered away—as we now indeed have been—that Rogue Squadron isn't technically part of that task force."

Wedge frowned. "You've lost me, General. I thought we'd been permanently attached to you."

"To me, yes," Bel Iblis agreed. "But not to my task force. It's a fine but very important technical distinction."

"I'll take your word for it," Wedge said, trying without success to sift confirmation of that point from his own memory of the New Republic's military regs. "So what does that mean?"

Bel Iblis swiveled the encrypt station chair around and sat down. "It means I agree with you that someone is likely to take advantage of this mess," he said, folding his hands in his lap. "Possibly this shadowy Vengeance organization that keeps throwing riots and demanding the Bothans pay through the snout for their part in the destruction of Caamas."

"Yes," Wedge said slowly as a sudden thought hit him. "And since the Bothan contribution to that attack was to sabotage the Caamas planetary shields . . . ?"

Bel Iblis nodded. "Very good. Yes, my guess is someone's going to try to take out Bothawui's shields."

Wedge whistled softly. "Do you think that's even possible? The Bothans are supposed to have one of the best shield systems in the galaxy."

"They did once, back at the height of the Empire," Bel Iblis said. "Whether they've kept it up I don't know. But of course an enemy wouldn't have to take down the entire grid to do serious damage. Dropping the shield just over Drev'starn would open up a hole you could pour a lot of turbolaser damage through."

"Yes," Wedge murmured. "Trouble is, it wouldn't be just the Bothans who'd get hammered."

"That is indeed the problem," Bel Iblis agreed soberly. "At last count, there were over three hundred megacorporations with their headquarters on Bothawui, plus thousands of smaller companies and at least fifty pledge and commodity exchanges."

Wedge nodded. It wouldn't exactly mean universal economic chaos if they were hit, but it would add a considerable degree of extra anger and resentment to the stew already heating up out there.

And with all those warships trying to stare each other down overhead, it might do considerably more than just heat the stew. "What do you want me to do?"

Bel Iblis seemed to be studying his face. "I want you to go down to the surface and make sure that doesn't happen."

Wedge had had a sneaking suspicion that was the direction this conversation was going. It came as something of a shock just the same. "All by myself?" he asked. "Or do you think I might need the rest of Rogue Squadron, too?"

Bel Iblis smiled. "Relax, Wedge, it's not as bad as it sounds," he said. "I'm not expecting you to stand in front of the Drev'starn generator dome, a blaster in each hand, and hold off the Third Imperial Heavy Armor. So far Vengeance has shown more trickery and subterfuge than brute force; and trickery and subterfuge are things a couple of clever X-wing pilots ought to have a good chance of spotting."

So the proposed scout party was up to two now, Wedge noted, thereby doubling their chances of rooting out this theoretical splinter in a sand hill. "Did you have anyone in particular in mind as the second clever X-wing pilot?"

"Of course," Bel Iblis said. "Commander Horn."

"I see," Wedge said between suddenly stiff lips. A search for a hidden saboteur . . . and Bel Iblis had immediately come up with Corran Horn. Could he somehow have deduced Corran's carefully hidden Jedi skills? "Why him?"

Bel Iblis's eyebrows lifted slightly. "Because his father-in-law is a smuggler," he said. "He's bound to have a network of contacts Horn will be able to access."

"Ah," Wedge said, relaxing a bit. "I hadn't thought about that."

"That's why I'm a senior general," Bel Iblis said dryly. "You'd better get below and give Horn the good news. You heard Ackbar—I only have a couple of weeks to pull all this together, and I'll want you back with the squadron when we hit Yaga Minor."

"We'll do what we can," Wedge promised. "You want us to take one of the *Peregrine*'s unmarked shuttles?"

Bel Iblis nodded. "X-wings would be a little conspicuous. Leave your uniforms, too, but take your military IDs in case you have to pull rank on some bureaucrat. I'll let you know when I want you at Ord Trasi."

"Understood," Wedge said.

"Good," Bel Iblis said. "I'm going to stay up here for a few minutes— I can transmit to the other commanders from here as well as I can from the bridge or my office. Ackbar said *immediately*, though, so as soon as the other ships are ready, we go. You'll need to be off the *Peregrine* before that."

"We will, sir," Wedge said, moving toward the door. "Good luck with your battle plan, General."

Bel Iblis smiled faintly. "Good luck with yours."

They were just hitting Bothawui's atmosphere when Corran, who'd been leaning against the side viewport looking back toward the shuttle's stern, turned around and settled himself back into his seat. "They're gone," he announced.

Wedge glanced at his displays. The ships of the *Peregrine* task force were indeed no longer registering. "That they are," he agreed. "We're on our own now."

Corran shook his head. "This is crazy, Wedge. And you say he specifically told you to take me?"

"Yes, but it didn't have anything to do with your hidden talents," Wedge assured him. "He thinks you'll be able to access Booster's smuggling network."

Corran snorted. "That might work, if Booster was speaking to me these days."

Wedge glanced sideways at him. "What, he's not still mad about that trick we pulled with the *Hoopster's Prank* off Sif'kric, is he? I thought we decided they weren't carrying any contraband and let them go."

"No, they weren't; and yes, he is," Corran said. "Clean or not, the Sif'kries decided they didn't want smugglers carrying cargoes for them and banned the *Hoopster's Prank* forthwith from future pommwomm shipments."

Wedge winced. "Ouch."

"Doesn't mean they won't get in anyway," Corran continued with a shrug. "It just means they'll have to come up with different ships or new ID camouflage or something. But it's a nuisance, and Booster hates nuisances. Especially official nuisances."

"Mm," Wedge said. "Sorry about that. Maybe Mirax will be able to calm him down."

"Oh, I'm sure she will," Corran said. "Come to think of it, though, I'm not sure Booster even has any interests on Bothawui. The planet's got so many other smuggling groups crawling all over it that he may have decided to leave it alone."

"Oh, that's handy," Wedge grumbled.

"Hey, *you're* the one who wanted to get back to the exciting life of an X-wing pilot, remember," Corran reminded him. "You could have been safely flying a computer somewhere on Coruscant if you'd wanted."

Wedge made a face. "No, thanks. Tried it, didn't like it. So you're not expecting us to find any help down there at all?"

There was a brief silence. "That's an interesting question," Corran murmured at last, his voice sounding odd. "Actually . . . I think I am."

Wedge threw him a frown. "You are what? Expecting to find help?"

"I think so, yes," Corran said, that same strange tone in his voice. "Don't ask how or where. I just . . . I think so."

"Let me guess," Wedge said. "Jedi hunch?"

Corran nodded. "Jedi hunch."

Wedge smiled. "Good," he said, already feeling better about this whole mission. "In that case, we don't have anything to worry about."

"Well, no," Corran said slowly. "I don't think I'd go so far as to say *that*."

CHAPTER

[Beware to the starboard,] the Togorian female at the *Wild Karrde*'s sensor station called, her normally fluid mewling speech now clipped and harsh. [At the two-five by fourteen angle.]

"I'm on it," another tight voice came over the bridge comm unit. The edges of a hundred asteroids rolling sedately past the viewport flickered with reflected light as one of the *Wild Karrde*'s turbolasers flashed, then blazed even more brightly as the target asteroid shattered into dust and fire.

Seated in the back of the bridge out of the way, Shada D'ukal mentally shook her head. Negotiating an asteroid field was never an easy task, but it seemed to her the Togorian and at least one of the turbolaser gunners were getting themselves far too worked up over the whole operation. Either they were naturally excitable, or else young and inexperienced. Neither possibility exactly filled her with confidence; both made her wonder about their captain's wisdom in bringing the two of them along in the first place.

Perhaps the captain was feeling the same way. "Calm down, H'sishi," Talon Karrde cautioned the Togorian from his seat behind the helm and copilot stations. "You, too, Chal. Just because this asteroid field is larger than others you've encountered doesn't mean it has to be treated any differently. A light touch, blast only the rocks that are of immediate danger to us, and let Dankin maneuver the ship around the others."

The Togorian's ears twitched. [I obey, Chieftain,] she said.

"Yes, sir," the gunner's voice added.

Not that the admonition made any appreciable difference, at least not that Shada could see. H'sishi still continued to snap out her targeting locks, and Chal still fired full-power turbolaser blasts whether the target warranted that much of a kick or not.

But then, maybe it wasn't just them. Maybe they were merely sensing and reacting to the nervousness Karrde himself was feeling.

Shada shifted her gaze to focus on his profile. He was hiding it well, actually, with only cheek and jaw muscles betraying the tension there. But Mistryl training included the reading of faces and body language, and to her eyes Karrde's steadily growing apprehension was as obvious as a navigational beacon.

And the upcoming stopover at Pembric 2 was only the first leg of their trip. What would he be like, she wondered uneasily, by the time they actually reached Exocron?

There was a particularly bright flash outside as a particularly large asteroid was blown to dust. "Oh, my," a gloomy, metallic voice murmured from Shada's right.

She turned to look at the C-3PO protocol droid strapped into the seat next to her. He was staring at the viewport, wincing with every turbolaser blast. "Trouble?" she asked.

"I'm sorry, Mistress Shada," he said, managing to sound prim and miserable at the same time. "I've never entirely enjoyed space travel. And this in particular reminds me of a rather unpleasant incident in the past."

"It should be over soon," she soothed him. "Just try to relax." The Mistryl shadow guard had never used droids all that much, but one of Shada's uncles had had one when she was growing up and she'd always had something of a soft spot for them.

And in Threepio's case, she felt a particularly personal sympathy for his position. Leia Organa Solo's personal translator droid, he had been suddenly and summarily offered to Karrde for this voyage—no notice, no questions, no apologies. In many ways, it echoed Shada's own long and unquestioning service to the Mistryl.

A service that had come to a sudden and permanent end a month ago on the windswept roof of the Resinem Entertainment Complex, where Shada had dared to put her personal honor above direct orders from the Eleven, the rulers of her shattered world of Emberlene.

Would the rest of the Mistryl be hunting her now? Her old friend Karoly D'ulin had hinted that that would be the case. But with the New Republic simmering toward self-destruction in a flurry of petty wars and revived grudges, surely the Mistryl had more important things to do than hunt down even a perceived traitor.

On the other hand, if Karoly had reported Shada's reasons for her defiance—had repeated the words of scorn for leaders who had now forgotten the proud and honorable tradition the Mistryl had once held to—then the Eleven might indeed consider her worth the effort to track down. Of all motivations to action, she had long since learned that injured pride was one of the most powerful.

And one of the most destructive, as well. To both the victim and the hunter.

A motion caught her eye: Karrde half turning in his seat to look at her. "Enjoying the ride?" he asked.

"Oh, it's great fun," she told him. "Nothing I like better than doing tight maneuvers with a cold crew."

The Togorian's fur expanded, just a little. But she didn't comment, and she kept her eyes on her displays. "New experiences are what give zest to life," Karrde said mildly.

"In my line of work, new experiences usually mean trouble," Shada countered. "I hope you weren't planning on sneaking in, by the way. The way your people are lighting up the field, all of Pembric 2 knows we're coming by now."

As if to underline her words, the asteroids outside flickered with a multiple sputter of turbolaser fire. "Actually, according to Mara, most ships have to do some blasting on the way in," Karrde said. His fingers, Shada noted, were tapping gently but restlessly on his armrest. "Even the locals who supposedly know the routes in and out."

[We have cleared the asteroid field, Chieftain Karrde,] the Togorian mewled.

Shada looked back at the viewport. There were still some asteroids floating past, but for the most part the sky was indeed clear.

[The planetary landing beacons are in sight,] H'sishi added, turning her head and fixing her yellow eyes on Shada. [Your junior crew drone may now cease her nervousness.]

Shada held that gaze for another two heartbeats. Then, deliberately, she turned away. Most of the *Wild Karrde*'s crew had been verbally poking at her, in one way or another, ever since their departure from Coruscant. Mazzic's people had done the same back when she first joined his smuggling group—the usual reaction, she had long ago realized, of a tight-knit crew who have just had a stranger thrust into their midst.

One of Mazzic's techs had unwisely crossed the line from verbal to physical jabs, and as a result had spent a month in a neural reconstruction facility. Out here, at the edge of civilization, she hoped the *Wild Karrde*'s crew wouldn't have to learn the lesson the same way.

The pilot half turned around. "What now, Chief?"

"Take us into orbit," Karrde told him. "There's only one place on the planet that can handle a ship this size, the Erwithat Spaceport. They should be calling with landing instructions anytime now."

Right on cue, the comm crackled. *"Bss'dum'shun,"* a sharp voice snapped. *"Sg'hur hur Erwithat roz'bd bun's'unk. Rs'zud huc'dms'hus u burfu."*

Shada frowned. "I thought you said they spoke Basic here," she said.

"They do," Karrde said. "They must be trying to throw us." He cocked an eyebrow at the droid beside Shada. "Threepio? Do you recognize it?"

"Oh, yes, Captain Karrde," the droid said with the first sign of enthusiasm Shada had seen in him since the trip started. "I am fluent in over six million forms of communication. This is the dominant Jarellian dialect, a language whose antecedents date back to—"

"What did he say?" Shada interrupted gently. Protocol droids, in her limited experience, would go running on side trails all day if you let them, and Karrde didn't look like he was in the mood for a linguistics lesson.

Threepio turned around to face her. "He has identified himself as Erwithat Space Control, Mistress Shada, and asks our identity and cargo."

"Tell him we're the freighter *Hab Camber*," Karrde said. "We're here to buy some supplies and power."

Threepio turned back to him, his posture indicating uncertainty. "But, sir, this ship is named the *Wild Karrde*," he objected. "Its engine transponder code—"

"Has been carefully altered," the pilot interrupted sharply. "Come on, they're waiting."

"Patience, Dankin," Karrde said. "We're in no particular hurry, and I doubt Erwithat Control has anything better to do right now. Just deliver the message as stated, Threepio. No, wait," he interrupted himself, a sly smile twitching at the corners of his mouth. "You said this was the dominant Jarellian dialect. Are there any others?"

"Several, sir," Threepio said. "Unfortunately, I am versed in only two."

"Good enough," Karrde said. "Deliver our answer in one of them." He settled himself back in his chair. "Let's see how far they're prepared to go with this game."

Threepio delivered the message, and for a long moment the comm was silent. "Attention, unidentified freighter," a voice growled reluctantly in Basic. "This is Erwithat Space Control. State your identity and cargo."

Karrde smiled. "Apparently, not very far," he commented, keying his transmit key. "Erwithat Control, this is the freighter *Hab Camber*," he said. "No cargo; we're just passing through and hoped we could buy some supplies and power."

"Yeah?" the controller said. "What sort of supplies?"

"Do you handle merchandising duties as well as space control?" Karrde countered.

"No, I just do the traffic," the other growled, sounding more annoyed than ever. "Let's hear your bid for landing rights."

Shada blinked. "Landing rights?" she muttered.

The controller had sharp ears. "Yes, landing rights," he snapped. "And that little crack is going to cost you an extra three hundred."

Shada felt her mouth drop open. Crack? What crack? She filled her lungs for a nasty retort of her own—

"We'll bid a thousand," Karrde said, warning her with a glance.

The controller snorted audibly. "For a freighter that size? You're either joking or a fool."

H'sishi hissed something under her breath. "Or perhaps merely a poor independent trader," Karrde suggested. "What if I make it eleven hundred?"

"What if you make it fifteen?" the controller countered. "That's New Republic currency, too."

"Of course," Karrde said. "Fifteen hundred; agreed."

"Landing Pad 28," the controller said, his grudging annoyance replaced now by open gloating. Briefly, Shada wondered how much of that fifteen hundred would be going directly into his pocket. "Beacon'll guide you in. The money's due on arrival."

"Thank you," Karrde said. "*Hab Camber* out." He keyed off the comm. "Chin?"

"Beacon come on, Cap't," the older man at the comm station reported, squinting at his displays. "They guiding us in."

"Key the vector over to the helm," Karrde instructed. "Dankin, take us in. Watch out for fighters—Mara said they sometimes send escorts for unfamiliar ships."

"Right," the pilot acknowledged.

Karrde looked at Shada. "You game for a little walk around once we're down?"

Shada shrugged. "We junior crew drones are only here to serve. Where are we going?"

"A tapcafe called the ThrusterBurn," Karrde told her. "Assuming my map is correct, it's only a couple of blocks from the landing pad we've been assigned. The man I'm hoping to meet should be there."

"I didn't think we needed any supplies this soon," Shada said. "Who are we meeting, and why?"

"A vicious yet cultured Corellian crime lord named Crev Bombaasa," Karrde said. "He runs most of the illegal operations in this part of Kathol sector."

"And we need his help?"

"Not particularly," Karrde said. "But getting his permission to travel through the area would make things easier."

"Ah," Shada said, frowning at his profile. This didn't sound like the casually fearless Talon Karrde she'd heard so many stories about from Mazzic and other smugglers. "We're worried about things being easy, are we?"

He smiled. "Always," he said. His tone was light, but Shada could hear an odd hollowness behind it.

"Ah—Captain Karrde?" Threepio spoke up hesitantly. "Will you be needing my services on this visit?"

Karrde smiled. "No, Threepio, thank you," he assured the droid. "As I said, Basic is the official language down there. You can stay on the ship with the others."

The droid seemed to wilt with relief. "Thank you, sir."

Karrde shifted his attention back to Shada. "We'll go lightly armed—sidearm blasters only."

"Understood," Shada said. "But I'll let you carry the blaster."

"Worried about things getting violent?" Dankin put in.

"Not at all," Shada said coolly, getting up from her seat and heading for the bridge door. "I just prefer that my opponents not know what direction the violence is going to come from. I'll be in my cabin, Karrde—let me know when you're ready."

Twenty minutes later, they were down. Fifteen minutes after that, upon payment of their landing fee and a brief negotiation regarding additional "protection" costs with a trio of white-uniformed Pembric Security Legionnaires, Karrde and Shada were walking down the streets of the Erwithat Spaceport.

It was not, to Karrde's mind, what one would exactly call an inspiring place. Even at midday a haze seemed to shroud the whole city, diffusing the sunlight and adding a dankness to the occasional breezes that stirred the hot air without any perceptible cooling effect. The ground was composed of wet sand, molecular-compressed where walkways were needed, a far cry from the permacrete that was the modern construction standard. The buildings lining the walkways were made from some kind of plain but solid-looking white stone, its onetime cleanliness now marred by the brown and green mottlings of dirt and mold. A sprinkling of pedestrians roamed the streets, most showing the same general deterioration as the spaceport itself, and here and there a hurrying swoop or landspeeder could be glimpsed between the buildings.

It was, in short, very much the way Mara's report from seven years ago had painted it. Except probably a little shabbier.

"Terrific place," Shada commented from beside him. "I get the feeling I'm a little overdressed."

Karrde smiled. Dressed in a form-fitting dress glittering with subdued blue lights, she did indeed stand out dramatically against the general drabness. "Don't worry about it," he assured her. "As I said earlier, Bombaasa is a cultured sort of crimelord. You can never be too overdressed for that type."

He glanced at her. "Though personally, I have to say I prefer the silver and dark red outfit you wore when we first met at the Whistler's Whirlpool on Trogan."

"I remember that outfit," she said, her voice oddly distant. "It was the first one Mazzic bought me after I became his bodyguard."

"Mazzic always did have good taste," Karrde agreed. "You know, you still haven't told me why you left his service so suddenly."

"You haven't told *me* anything about this Jorj Car'das character we're looking for," Shada countered.

"Keep your voice down," Karrde said sharply, glancing around them. There didn't seem to be anyone within earshot, but that didn't necessarily mean anything. "That's not a name you want to casually toss around here."

Even staring straight ahead, he could feel Shada's eyes on him. "He's really got you spooked, hasn't he?" she said quietly. "You weren't exactly thrilled about all this when Calrissian talked you into hunting him down; but he's *really* got you spooked."

"You'll understand someday," Karrde told her. "After I'm able to tell you the whole story."

She shrugged, her shoulder brushing briefly up against his arm with the motion. "Let's compromise," she suggested. "Once we're off Pembric, you can tell me half the story."

"Interesting proposal," Karrde said. "Agreed; but only if you in turn tell me half the reason why you left Mazzic."

"Well . . ." She hesitated. "Sure."

They turned a corner, and Karrde felt his mouth twitch. A long block away, fronting onto an open square, was the entrance to the ThrusterBurn tapcafe. Parked in front of it were perhaps twenty stripped-down speeder bikes. "On the other hand," he said quietly, "getting off Pembric may not be quite as easy as we hoped."

"Looks like a swoop gang's having a meeting in there," Shada commented. "There are the sentries—to the left, under the overhang."

"I see them," Karrde said. There were four of them: large, tough-looking young men in reddish-brown jackets sitting astride their swoops. They were pretending to talk together, but it was clear that their full attention was aimed in the newcomers' direction.

"It's not too late to scrub this," Shada murmured. "We can go back to the ship, get out of here, and take our chances with whatever Bombaasa decides to throw at us."

Karrde shook his head minutely. "We've been objects of official curiosity ever since we landed. If we try to leave now, Bombaasa's people will intercept us."

"In that case, our best bet is to walk right up to the place like we own it," Shada said briskly. "Keep your hand near your blaster—that'll keep their attention on you. Not close enough that they try to draw first, though. If it comes to a fight, let me throw the first punch; and if it looks like I'm losing badly and you get an opening, make a run for it."

"Understood," Karrde said, finding himself amused despite the seriousness of the situation. Shada had mostly kept to herself aboard the *Wild Karrde,* not joining into the normal shipboard camaraderie or showing any real interest in getting to know the crew. But yet here she was, slipping back into the role of bodyguard, preparing to defend Karrde's life even at the cost of her own.

What struck him the most was the sense that, down deep, she genuinely meant it.

The four sentries let them get to within a few meters of the rows of parked swoops before saying anything. "Tapcafe's closed," one of them called.

"That's all right," Karrde said, not breaking stride as he glanced incuriously over at them. "We're not thirsty."

The swoopers had looked like they were lounging casually on their vehicles. They weren't. Before Karrde and Shada had taken two more steps they'd zoomed across the square and skidded to a halt between the newcomers and the parked swoops. "I said the place is closed," the one who'd spoken repeated darkly, the long maneuvering vanes of his swoop pointed with unsubtle threat directly at Karrde's chest. "Go away."

Karrde shook his head. "Sorry. We have business with Crev Bombaasa that can't wait."

One of the others snorted. "Listen to him," he said derisively. "He thinks he can just walk in on Bombaasa anytime he wants. Pretty funny, huh, Langre?"

"Hilarious," the spokesman agreed, his face not showing any evidence of humor. "Last chance, murk. Leave in one piece or in a bunch of 'em."

"Lord Bombaasa is going to be very displeased if you don't let us in," Karrde warned.

"Yeah?" Langre sneered, nudging his swoop forward. "Like I'm really scared."

"You should be," Karrde said, taking a step backward as the maneuvering vanes poked perilously close to his chest. Shada, he noted peripherally, hadn't moved backward with him but was still standing where he'd left her, shrinking wide-eyed back from the swoop snorting and vibrating its way alongside her as if terrified by its presence. "Lord Bombaasa doesn't like to be kept waiting."

"Then I guess we ought to hurry up and put you in a box for him," Langre said, sneering a little harder. He nudged the swoop forward another meter, forcing Karrde to take another rapid step backward. Not quite rapid enough; the tips of the maneuvering vanes jabbed sharply against his chest before he could get out of the way.

One of the other swoopers chortled. Grinning maliciously, Langre gave the swoop another burst of the throttle, clearly intent on knocking Karrde down this time. The movement brought him directly alongside Shada—

And in that instant, she struck.

It was doubtful Langre even saw it coming. One moment Shada was standing there, transfixed like a frightened animal in a hunter's sights; the next moment she had swung her left leg back, rotated her upper body toward the swoop, and slammed her right fist into the side of his neck.

There may have been a distinctive "pop" accompanying the flat crack of the blow; Karrde wasn't sure. What he *was* sure of, as Langre did a sideways cartwheel off his swoop onto the ground, was that this one was definitely out of the fight.

The other three had excellent reflexes. Before Langre even hit the sand they had twisted their handlebars around and roared off in different directions across the square, forestalling any attempt Shada might have made to similarly take them down. Cutting close to the surrounding buildings, they curved around and stopped short, turning their swoops around to point toward Shada.

"Get out of the way!" Shada snapped to Karrde, moving to the center of the square and dropping into a low combat stance. Turning her head back and forth, she looked at each of the swoopers in turn as if daring them to take her on.

For a few seconds they seemed to ignore her challenge as they discussed the situation in a hand-signal code Karrde didn't recognize. Taking advantage of the lull, he backed up until he reached the edge of the square. So far the swoopers hadn't shown any inclination to draw the weapons they were undoubtedly carrying, but that could change at any time. Watching them closely, he dropped his hand to his blaster—

"I don't think so," a gruff voice said in his ear.

Carefully, Karrde turned his head, the caution dictated by the hard muzzle suddenly pressed against the small of his back. Three hard-faced men in Security Legion uniforms were standing there, the last of them in the process of closing the concealed doorway that had opened up in the building behind him. "You're just in time, Legionnaire," Karrde said to the leader. This was probably futile, but he had to try. "My friend's in danger out there."

"Yeah?" the other said, pulling Karrde's blaster from its holster. "Looked to me like she was the one who started it. Anyway, trying to bluster your way in to see Bombaasa is a crime all by itself around here."

"Even if Bombaasa decides he's glad we dropped in to visit?" Karrde countered. "You'd be in serious trouble."

"Nah," the Legionnaire said, sticking the appropriated blaster into his belt and coming around to Karrde's side. "That's why we got these," he added, hefting his weapon as he stepped a prudent meter away from his prisoner. It was, Karrde saw now, not a blaster but an old Merr-Sonn tangle gun. "If Bombaasa decides he wants to see you, hey, we just cut you loose. If he doesn't"—he grinned evilly—"then you're already wrapped for burial. Real convenient."

He gestured with the tangle gun. "Now shut up. I want to watch this."

Throat tight with frustration, Karrde turned back to the square. The *Wild Karrde*'s crew wouldn't be able to get here fast enough to help, even if he could get to his comlink to alert them. He could only hope that Shada was as good as she claimed.

And at that moment, their private consultation finished, the swoopers attacked.

They didn't all charge at once, as Karrde had rather expected them to. Suspecting perhaps that Shada would try to maneuver them into head-on collisions if they did that, two of them instead began tracing out a loose encircling ring around her while the third drove hard and straight directly in.

Shada stood her ground, but just before the maneuvering vanes reached her chest she dropped back flat onto her back. The thug whooped with glee as his swoop shot past over her, a triumphal shout that turned into a squawk of surprise as Shada tucked her legs to her chest and kicked hard straight up, catching the swoop just forward of the directional thrust nozzles and bucking the swooper right out of the saddle.

It only took a second for him to get himself reseated and regain control. But in the enclosed area of the square that was a half second too long, and with a horrendous crash both swoop and thug slammed full-bore into one of the buildings.

The Legionnaire beside Karrde whistled softly. "That's two," he commented. "She's good."

Karrde didn't reply. Shada was back on her feet now, and the two remaining swoops had pulled their circle a little farther back as if afraid to let her get too close. If they decided that she wasn't worth the risk of another wreck and pulled their blasters . . .

And then he noticed one of the swoopers glaring at the trio of Legionnaires; and with that single look he realized that the use of blasters was now completely out of the question. With this many witnesses watching, pride alone dictated that they deal with her without weapons.

The two swoops were still circling. "Come on, Barksy," the head Legionnaire called. "Not afraid, are you?"

"Scrub it, murk," one of the swoopers snapped back.

"That's *Lieutenant* Murk to you, scum," the Legionnaire murmured under his breath.

Abruptly, Barksy swung his swoop out of the circle and charged inward. The same basic technique his predecessor had tried, and Karrde found himself holding his breath as Shada again fell back onto the sand ahead of its advance. Surely the swooper couldn't be so stupid as to try the same trick again.

He wasn't. Even as Shada hit the ground he pulled back hard on his handlebar controls, the swoop's nose rearing up as the vehicle slid a couple of meters farther before pulling to a hard stop. With a triumphal shout, he swiveled a hundred eighty degrees and brought the swoop's nose down hard on the spot where Shada had landed.

But Shada was no longer there. Instead of simply hitting the sand and staying there as she had the last time, she had instead thrown her body into a convulsive, wavelike movement as she hit the ground, her arching back and legs bouncing her off the sand and up into an impossible-looking hand-and-foot grip on the underside of the swoop. Somehow she managed to hold on through the spin and nose-slam; and as the swooper leaned over, openmouthed, for a closer look at the empty ground where his victim should have been, she unhooked one of her feet from its perch and landed a solid kick against the side of his head.

Beside Karrde, the lieutenant clucked his tongue. "I don't believe it," he muttered, clearly as stunned as Barksy had been before Shada's kick cleaned all confusion from his mind. "Who is this bahshi, anyway?"

"One of the best in the business," Karrde assured him, pitching his voice in the sort of low, confidential tone that just naturally seemed to go along with the half step he took toward the man. Another step the same size, he estimated, and he would be close enough. "Actually, that was nothing," he added, lowering his voice still more and simultaneously taking that extra half step. "Wait till you see what she does to this one."

He threw a careful glance to his side. The lieutenant was hooked, all right, staring in glassy-eyed fascination at the drama in the square, waiting to see what magic the mysterious woman would pull next from her sleeve.

The last swooper seemed to make up his mind. Pulling out of his circle at the far end of the square, he leaned low over his handlebar controllers and charged. Shada feinted left and then dodged right, the end of the jutting thrust nozzles missing her hip by bare centimeters. The swooper spun the vehicle hard around, clearly hoping to catch her from the side with the long nose of the swoop. But he had misjudged his speed, and the swinging maneuvering vanes scythed past her with plenty of room to spare. It took him a few more meters to kill his spin and momentum, bringing himself to a halt no more than three meters from Karrde and the Legionnaires. He swiveled around again to face Shada, shoulders hunched with anticipation—

And with a smoothly casual movement, Karrde plucked the tangle gun from the Legionnaire's hand and fired.

The swooper screeched an air-blistering curse as the semi-plastic webbing slammed into his back, whipping around him and pinioning his arms solidly to his sides. "As you were, gentlemen," Karrde said mildly, taking a long step away from the Legionnaires and shifting his aim to cover them.

"Cute," the lieutenant said. Oddly enough, he didn't seem particularly upset. "Real cute."

"I thought you'd like it," Karrde said, nodding to the other two Legionnaires. "Your weapons on the ground, please."

"That won't be necessary," a suave voice said from somewhere above him.

Karrde risked a quick glance, but he could see no one. "No, I'm not there," the voice assured him, a touch of amusement in his tone. "I've been watching your performance from inside my casino, and I must admit to being impressed by your work. Tell me, what is it you want here?"

"To see you, of course, Lord Bombaasa," Karrde said to the hidden speaker. "I had hoped to collect on an old debt."

The lieutenant made an uncomfortable-sounding noise in his throat. But Bombaasa merely laughed. "I'm aware of no debt I owe you, my friend. But by all means let us talk about it. Lieutenant Maxiti?"

"Sir?" the lieutenant said, straightening automatically to attention.

"Give the gentleman back his blaster and escort him and the lady to the casino. And have your men clean the garbage out of the square."

The interior of the ThrusterBurn was a sharp contrast to the climate outside—a sharp contrast, for that matter, with nearly every low-rent cantina and tapcafe Shada had ever been in. The air was cool and comfortably dry, and while the booths lining the walls were dark enough to ensure privacy, the rest of the tapcafe was bright and almost cheerful.

Not that the current clientele was the sort that would appreciate such homey touches. There were about twenty of them, stamped-templet copies of the four she'd disposed of outside, all glaring balefully at the newcomers from their group of tables in one of the corners by the curved bar. Briefly, Shada wondered if Bombaasa had told them their sentries were being unceremoniously carted out of the square outside, but quickly dismissed the thought. A man who owned this kind of tapcafe would be unlikely to risk it by deliberately inviting a fight inside.

Nevertheless, she kept an eye on the swoopers as Lieutenant Maxiti led them across the main area to an unobtrusive door at the back of the dance floor.

The door opened as they approached, giving them a glimpse of a small back room, and a large, dark-eyed human stepped out. He threw a measuring glance at Karrde, an even longer look at Shada, and then nodded to the Legionnaire. "Thanks," he said to the latter, dismissing him with that single word, then looked back at Karrde. "Come on in," he invited, stepping aside to let them pass.

The back room had been fitted out as a compact casino, with four tables around which a dozen or so beings of various species were busily engaged in a variety of card and dice games. With their minds and hopes pinned to their money, it was doubtful any of them even realized anyone new had come in.

All except one. A short, pudgy human with thin, sticklike arms, he sat alone at the largest table, his slightly bulging eyes focused unblinkingly on Karrde and Shada as they stepped into the room. Two large men with the same bodyguard look as the one now closing the door behind them stood at attention beside the pudgy man's chair, also eyeing the newcomers.

Shada grimaced, not liking this at all. But Karrde didn't hesitate. "Good day, Lord Bombaasa," he said, stepping right up to the edge of the table. "Thank you for seeing us on such short notice."

The two bodyguards seemed to tense, but Bombaasa merely smiled thinly. "Like the legendary Rastus Khal, I am always available to those who intrigue me," he said smoothly. "And you do indeed intrigue me."

His insectlike eyes shifted to Shada. "Though for a moment there I thought you had run out of tricks," he added. "If your companion hadn't snatched the lieutenant's tangle gun, you would have been in trouble."

"Hardly," Shada told him coolly. "I caught a reflection of him moving toward the Legionnaires and guessed he was about to try something. If it didn't work, he was going to need my help right away, and the swooper would keep."

Bombaasa shook his head admiringly. "An amazing display, my dear, truly amazing. Though I'm afraid that in the process you've ruined your gown. Perhaps I can arrange to have it cleaned before your departure."

"That's most generous of you, my lord," Karrde said before she could answer. "But I'm afraid we won't be able to stay on Pembric that long."

Bombaasa smiled again, but this time there was a distinct glint of menace to the expression. "That remains to be seen, my friend," he warned darkly. "And if you're another New Republic or Kathol sector emissary seeking to annex my territory, you may find your departure considerably delayed."

"I have no ties to any governmental group," Karrde assured him. "I'm merely a private citizen here to ask a favor."

"Indeed," Bombaasa said, toying idly with the subtly glittering throat pendant around his neck. "I have the distinct impression you don't realize what my favors cost."

"I believe you'll find this one has already been paid for," Karrde countered. "And it *is* only a small favor, after all. We have an errand to run inside your cartel's territory, and we'd like safe passage through your various pirate and hijacking gangs until we've completed it."

Bombaasa's eyes widened politely. "Is that all," he said. "Come, come, my dear sir. A large, tempting target like your freighter, and you want safe passage?" He shook his head sadly. "No, you don't understand my fee scale at all."

Shada felt her muscles tensing, consciously relaxed them. All three bodyguards were armed and competent-looking; but if nudge came to punch, she doubted any of them had ever faced a Mistryl before. Unfortunately, unlike the case with the swoopers, she wouldn't have the luxury of leaving them damaged but alive. She would have to take out the one behind them first . . .

"My mistake," Karrde said, his tone almost offhanded. "I assumed that when someone had saved your life you would be more grateful."

Bombaasa had been in the process of lifting a finger toward the body-guards standing beside him. Now, at Karrde's words, he froze, the finger poised in midair. "What are you talking about?" he demanded cautiously.

"I'm talking about a situation that occurred here a little over six years ago," Karrde said. "One in which a rather dapper gentleman and a young lady with red-gold hair foiled an assassination plot against you."

For a pair of heartbeats Bombaasa continued to stare at Karrde. Shada threw a surreptitious glance at the two bodyguards, mentally plotting out her attack plan—

And with a suddenness that startled her, Bombaasa burst out laughing.

The other gamblers in the casino paused in their activities, turning to gape momentarily at what was apparently an uncommon sound in their quietly desperate little world. Bombaasa, still laughing, gave a hand signal, and the bodyguards visibly relaxed. "Ah, my friend," he said, still chuckling. "My friend, indeed. So you're the mysterious chieftain the young lady spoke of when she refused to accept any payment."

"I'm the one," Karrde said, nodding. "I believe she also suggested that a man of your obvious breeding wouldn't mind carrying the debt until it could be properly repaid."

"She did indeed." Bombaasa waved a thin hand at Shada. "And now you bring this one. I would never have expected there to even exist two such beautiful yet deadly ladies, let alone loyal to the same man."

He cocked an eye toward Shada. "Or *are* you committed to this man, my dear?" he added. "If you would be interested in discussing a change of career, I could make it well worth your while."

"I'm not committed to anyone," Shada said, the words hurting her throat as she said them. "But for the moment, I'm traveling with him."

"Ah." Bombaasa peered closely at her, as if trying to gauge her sincerity, then shrugged. "If you should change your mind, you have merely to come see me," he said. "My door will always be open to you."

He returned his attention to Karrde. "You are right: I do indeed owe you," he said. "Before you leave, I'll provide you with a special ID over-lay for your ship that will identify you as being under my protection."

His lips compressed. "However, though it will certainly protect you from members of my cartel, it may at the same time create extra danger for you. Over the past year a vicious new pirate gang has relocated to this area, one which we have so far been unable to either eliminate or bring under our control. I suspect they would consider a freighter under my protection to be a particularly intriguing challenge."

Karrde shrugged. "As you pointed out earlier, we would be a tempting target regardless of that. We are, of course, not nearly as vulnerable as we appear."

"I have no doubt of that," Bombaasa said. "However, the enemy is quite well equipped, with a sizable fleet of SoroSuub *Corsair*-class assault starfighters as well as a number of larger ships. If you can spare the time, perhaps you would allow my people to do some quick upgrades of your weaponry or shields."

"I appreciate your offer," Karrde said, "and if circumstances were otherwise I would be all too happy to accept. But I'm afraid our errand is a pressing one, and we simply can't afford to take the time."

"Ah," Bombaasa said. "Very well, then. Leave when you must—the ID overlay will be ready when you are." He smiled slyly. "And of course, for you there will be no exit visa required."

"You are most generous, my lord," Karrde said, bowing slightly at the waist. "Thank you; and the debt is now paid." Taking Shada's arm, he turned to go—

"One other thing, my friend," Bombaasa called them back. "Neither of your associates gave me their names when they were here, nor would they tell me yours. I would appreciate it if you would satisfy my curiosity."

Beside her, Shada sensed Karrde brace himself. "Of course, Lord Bombaasa. My name is Talon Karrde."

The pudgy figure seemed to sit up a little straighter. "Talon Karrde," he breathed. "Indeed. Some of my, ah, business associates have spoken of you. Often at great length."

"I'm sure they have," Karrde said. "Particularly those Hutt agencies with whom your cartel has ties."

For a moment Bombaasa's eyes narrowed. Then his expression cleared and he smiled again. "The Hutts are right: you indeed know far more than is healthy for you. Still, as long as you don't seek to extend your organization into my territory, what have I to fear?"

"Nothing at all, my lord," Karrde agreed. "Thank you for your hospitality. Perhaps we shall meet again someday."

"Yes," Bombaasa said softly. "There is always that chance."

The Legionnaire lieutenant, Maxiti, offered to get them a ride back to their landing pad. But Karrde declined. It was only a short walk, after all, and after a taste of the Pembric climate the somewhat austere conditions aboard the *Wild Karrde* would seem that much more pleasant.

Besides, after the tone of that last exchange with Bombaasa, it wouldn't do to look as if they were hurrying to get away from him.

"Who's Rastus Khal?" Shada asked.

With an effort, Karrde brought his mind back from dark visions of vengeful crimelords having second thoughts. "Who?"

"Rastus Khal," Shada repeated. "Bombaasa dropped the name right after we were shown in."

"He was a fictional character from some masterpiece of Corellian literature," Karrde said. "I forget which one. Bombaasa is quite literate, or so I've heard. Apparently, he likes to consider himself a cultured sort of cutthroat."

Shada snorted. "Cultured. But he deals with Hutts."

Karrde shrugged. "I agree. One reason the Hutts and I don't get along, I suppose."

For a minute they walked in silence. "You knew he was connected with the Hutt syndicates," Shada said. "Yet you told him who you were. Why?"

"I'm not expecting Bombaasa to renege on his deal with us, if that's what you're worried about," Karrde said. "Cultured beings always repay their debts, and Mara and Lando did indeed save his life."

"The question wasn't so much about Bombaasa as it was about you," Shada countered. "He didn't need to know who you were, and I've seen your expertise at dodging questions you don't want to answer. So why did you tell him?"

"Because I'm guessing word of this encounter will get back to Jorj Car'das," Karrde said quietly. "This way, he'll know it's me who's coming to see him."

He sensed Shada frown. "Excuse me? I thought the idea was for us to sneak up quietly on him."

"The idea is to see if he has a copy of the Caamas Document," Karrde corrected her. "If we appear suddenly, without any warning, he's liable to simply kill all of us before we have a chance to talk to him."

"And if he *does* know we're coming?" Shada retorted. "Sounds to me like all it does is give him more preparation time."

"Exactly," Karrde said soberly. "And if he feels ready for us, he may be more inclined to listen before he shoots."

"You seem convinced he'll shoot."

Karrde hesitated. Should he tell her, he wondered, exactly why he'd allowed her to come on this trip?

No, he decided. Not yet. At best she would probably feel insulted or offended. At worst, she might refuse to go along with it at all. "I think there's a good chance he will, yes," he said instead.

"Knowing that it's you."

Karrde nodded. "Knowing that it's me."

"Uh-huh," Shada said. "What did you do to this guy, anyway?"

Karrde felt a muscle twitch in his jaw. "I stole something from him," he told her. "Something he valued more than anything else in the universe. Probably more than he valued his own life."

They walked in silence for another few steps. "Go on," Shada prompted.

Karrde forced a smile. "I only promised you half the story today," he reminded her, trying to put some lightness into his tone. "That was it. Your turn."

"What, why I left Mazzic?" Shada shrugged. "There's not much to tell. I left because a bodyguard who becomes a target herself can't do much good for anyone else."

So Shada had become a target. That was very interesting indeed. "May I ask who's suicidal enough to be gunning for you?"

"Sure, go ahead and ask," Shada said. "You're not going to get an answer, though. Not until I get the rest of the Car'das story."

"Somehow, I was expecting you to say that," Karrde murmured.

"So when do I get it?"

Karrde looked up through the haze at the dim glow of Pembric's sun. "Soon," he promised. "Very soon."

CHAPTER

"The sixth sumptuous hour of the fifteenth glorious day of the yearly Kanchen Sector Conference now begins," the herald intoned, his deep voice echoing across the bowl-shaped field where the various delegates sat, squatted, lay, or crouched, according to their species' particular physiological design. "Let us all hail and magnify the Grandiose Elector of Pakrik Major, and bid him express his sublime and all-encompassing wisdom in his leading of this gathering."

The assembled beings called or growled their agreement with the herald's sentiment. All but Han; and lounging beside him on the feathery matgrass, Leia had to smile in private amusement. Coming out here had been Han's idea, after all: a temporary respite from the bitter dissension and the gnawing suspicions that had been churning through the New Republic government ever since that partially destroyed copy of the Caamas Document had come to light.

And it had been a good idea, too. In the half day since their arrival Leia had already begun to feel the tension draining out of her. Getting away from Coruscant was exactly what she'd needed, and she'd taken great pains to mention that to her husband at least twice now and to thank him for his thoughtfulness.

At the moment, unfortunately, all her reassurances were falling on deaf ears. Once again, Han had failed to take into account what Leia privately referred to as the Solo Embarrassment Factor.

"And let us similarly hail and magnify our glorious visitors from the New Republic," the herald continued, waving his hand in an expansive gesture toward where Han and Leia were stretched out. "May their sublime wisdom, awesome courage, and magnificent honor enlighten the sky above our gathering."

"You forgot our uplifted eyebrows," Han muttered under his breath as the assembly roared out their greetings.

"It's better than Coruscant," Leia chided him gently as she half rose and waved. "Come on, Han, be nice."

"I'm waving, I'm waving," Han grumbled, leaning up on one arm and waving reluctantly with the other. "I don't know why they have to do this every hour."

"Would you rather have people accusing us of helping cover up attempted genocide?" Leia countered.

"I'd rather they just left us alone," Han said, giving one last wave and then dropping his hand back down. Leia lowered hers as well, and the approving roar of the delegates died away.

"Patience, dear," Leia said as the herald bowed deeply and yielded the podium to the elaborately dressed Grandiose Elector. "It's only for the rest of the day—you can put up with it that long. Tomorrow we'll head over to Pakrik Minor and get all that peace and quiet you promised me."

"It just better be *real* peaceful and quiet," Han warned, looking around at the crowd of delegates.

"It will be," Leia assured him, reaching over to squeeze his hand. "They may be all pomp and pageantry here on Pakrik Major, but over there among the tallgrain farms we probably won't find anyone who even recognizes us."

Han snorted, but even as he did Leia could sense a lightening of his mood. "Yeah," he said. "We'll see."

"Carib?"

With a wince of tired knees Carib Devist got up from where he'd been crouching, careful not to bump into either of the two rows of tallgrain pressing close around him. "I'm over here, Sabmin," he called, waving his coring tool as high over the stalks as he could reach.

"I see you," Sabmin called back. There was the crackle of brittle leaves being brushed against; and then Sabmin emerged through a gap in the row. "I had to come right—" He broke off, frowning at the tool in Carib's hand. "Uh-oh."

"Save the uh-ohs for polite company," Carib said sourly. "Just say *shavit* and mean it."

Sabmin hissed softly between his teeth. "How many colonies?" he asked.

"So far, just the one," Carib said, waving the corer toward the tallgrain stalk he'd been digging into. "And I *did* find an empress, so it's possible I got the whole infestation. But I wouldn't bet money on it."

"I'll alert the others," Sabmin said. "Probably should get word to the tri-valley coordinator, too, in case this isn't the only valley the bugs are moving into."

"Yeah." Carib eyed his brother. "And what wonderful news have *you* brought me?"

Sabmin's lips compressed. "We just got confirmation from Bastion," he said quietly. "New Republic High Councilor Leia Organa Solo is definitely over on Pakrik Major. And the attack on her is definitely on."

Reflexively, Carib glanced up at the half-lit planet hanging in the sky overhead. "They must be crazy," he said. "Attack a New Republic High Councilor, just like that?"

"I don't think they really cared who they got to attack, so long as it was a New Republic official," Sabmin said. "Apparently, the Grandiose Elector sent out a blanket invitation to Coruscant asking for a representative. My guess is that the request was prodded by some Imperial plant, with an eye to the fact that we were already in place here and could act as backup. It was just luck that Gavrisom decided to send Organa Solo."

"Yeah," Carib said darkly. "Luck. Did this come over Grand Admiral Thrawn's personal authorization?"

"I don't know," Sabmin said. "The notice didn't say. But it *has* to have come from him, doesn't it? I mean, if he's in command, then he's in command."

"I suppose so," Carib conceded reluctantly. So there it was. The war was about to be brought suddenly and violently to the Pakrik system. Right to their doorstep . . . and the long wait was over. The quiet existence of Imperial Sleeper Cell Jenth-44 was about to come to an end. "You say we're the backup. Who's the primary?"

"I don't know," Sabmin said. "Some tag team in from Bastion for the occasion, I'd guess."

"And when is it supposed to happen?"

"Tomorrow," Sabmin said. "Organa Solo and her husband are supposed to be coming over here to Minor once the conference breaks up."

"And there's no indication whether the attack is real or just supposed to look real?"

Sabmin gave him a startled look, an expression that quickly turned knowing and thoughtful. "Interesting point," he said. "With Thrawn involved you can't take anything for granted, can you? No, all I know is that there's an attack coming and that we're supposed to stand ready in case Solo's better or luckier than expected."

Carib grimaced. "I suppose even Solo's luck has to run out sooner or later."

"Yeah." Sabmin eyed him suspiciously. "What are you thinking?"

Carib looked up at the sky again. "I'm thinking we have to play this by ear," he said quietly. "One thing's for sure, though: if the battle comes anywhere near our valley, no matter who's winning, we're definitely not going to just sit by and watch. We've invested too much here to let it go without a fight."

Sabmin nodded. "Understood," he said soberly. "I'll pass the word to the others. Whatever happens tomorrow, we'll be ready."

Ahead, through the alien greenery, a stand of gnarled trees brushed past the screen to Pellaeon's left, and the AT-AT simulator bucked to the right in response. "Watch those trees, Admiral," Major Raines's voice warned in his helmet headphone. "You probably won't knock yourself over that way, but I've seen walkers get hung up so bad you had to send a couple of troopers down to blow the tree off at the roots. Takes time, and you're a sitting flink until you get free."

"Acknowledged," Pellaeon said, easing over away from the trees. Simulated AT-AT combat, frustrating though it could be sometimes, was far enough outside his normal command duties that it was actually a form of relaxation for him.

Though of course nothing that included combat was ever truly outside a Supreme Commander's duties. The better Pellaeon understood how mechanized equipment handled on difficult terrain, the better he would know how to deploy them in future operations.

Assuming, of course, the Empire ever again had occasion to launch ground assaults.

Firmly, he shook the thought away. One of the reasons for coming down here, after all, had been to distract himself from the continued and frustrating lack of response to his peace offer on the New Republic's part.

He was past the stand of trees now. Easing back on his speed, he keyed for a side view to see how Raines was handling the jungle.

Very straightforwardly, actually. Keeping an eye farther ahead than Pellaeon was doing, he was using his forward laser cannon to cut down potential obstacles well before they became a problem.

A fairly noisy technique, of course, and one that gave any enemies that much more advance warning. On the other hand, AT-ATs were hardly the weapon of choice where stealth was required, and Raines's method was definitely moving him through the jungle faster than Pellaeon. Lifting his gaze, trying to stifle the reflexive impulse to watch where his AT-AT was about to step, he squeezed off a few tentative shots.

"That's the way, Admiral," Raines said approvingly. "Just try to anticipate where the trouble's going to be before you're too close to aim the guns where they can do any good."

Pellaeon grunted. "Better yet, avoid using AT-ATs entirely in this situation."

"Whenever we can," Raines said. "Unfortunately, troublemakers like to hide themselves in places like this and then put up energy shields over their heads. Besides, there's nothing like an AT-AT clumping through the trees to scare the sneer off someone's face."

There was a click from the headset. "Admiral, this is Ardiff," the *Chimaera*'s captain's voice came. "Lieutenant Mavron is on his way in." There was just the briefest pause. "He reports, sir, that he has a vector."

Pellaeon felt his eyes narrow. Mavron's mission had been a long shot, one last attempt to find out something about the force that had hit them six days ago. If he said he'd found a vector . . . "Have him report to Ready Room 14 as soon as he docks," he instructed Ardiff, shutting off the simulator. "I'll meet you there."

Ardiff was waiting alone in the ready room when Pellaeon arrived. "I assumed this was to be a private meeting, so I cleared the other pilots out," he explained. "Is this about that HoloNet search?"

"I hope so," Pellaeon said, waving him to one of the chairs around the central monitor table and sitting down himself. "Ah—Lieutenant," he added as the door slid open and Mavron stepped inside. "Welcome home. A vector, you said?"

"Yes, sir," Mavron said, setting a datapad down on the monitor table and easing himself into a chair with the peculiar stiffness of a man who has been sitting in a starfighter cockpit for too long. "The HoloNet relay at Horska did indeed still have their records for transmissions from this area just after that raid against us."

"You were able to pull them all, I presume?" Pellaeon asked, picking up the datapad.

"Yes, sir," Mavron said. "Unfortunately, I couldn't get any names, but I did get endpoints for the transmissions." He nodded toward the datapad. "I took the liberty of sifting through them on the way back. The one I marked struck me as the most interesting."

Pellaeon felt his jaw tighten as he found the lieutenant's mark. "Bastion."

Ardiff rumbled deep in his throat. "So it *was* an Imperial behind that attack."

"There's more," Mavron said. "The original endpoint was Bastion; but then it got relayed a few more times and wound up somewhere in the Kroctar system."

"Kroctar system?" Ardiff said, frowning. "That's deep in New Republic territory. What would someone from Bastion be doing there?"

"I wondered that, too," Mavron said, his voice suddenly grim. "So I stopped off at Caursito on the way back here and pulled a copy of the TriNebulon for that day. If the timings are correct, a few hours after that transmission the Unified Factions of Kroctar announced that a treaty had been negotiated between themselves and the Empire. The mediator of record—well, according to Lord Superior Bosmihi, it was Grand Admiral Thrawn."

An icy chill ran up Pellaeon's back. "That's impossible," he said, his voice sounding strange in his ears. "Thrawn is dead. I watched him die."

"Yes, sir," Mavron said, nodding. "But according to the report—"

"*I watched him die!*" Pellaeon thundered.

The sudden outburst surprised even him. It certainly startled Ardiff and Mavron. "Yes, sir, we know," Ardiff said. "Obviously, it's some kind of trick. Lieutenant, I imagine the rest can wait until you file your complete report. Why don't you go get yourself cleaned up."

"Thank you, sir," Mavron said, clearly glad to be given the opportunity to escape. "I'll have my report filed within an hour."

"Very good." Ardiff nodded. "Dismissed."

He waited until Mavron had gone and the door was once again closed before speaking. "It *is* a trick, Admiral," he said to Pellaeon. "It has to be."

With an effort, Pellaeon pulled his thoughts back from the memories of that awful day at Bilbringi. The day the Empire had finally and irrevocably died. "Yes," he murmured. "But what if it's not? What if Thrawn really *is* still alive?"

"Why, in that case . . ." Ardiff trailed off, his forehead wrinkled in sudden uncertainty.

"Exactly," Pellaeon said, nodding. "The time when Thrawn's tactical genius could have done us any good was—when? Five years ago? Seven? Ten? What could he possibly do now except bring the New Republic down on us in panic?"

"I don't know, sir." Ardiff paused. "But that's not what's really bothering you."

Pellaeon looked down at his hands. Old hands, gnarled with age and darkened by the sunlight of a thousand worlds. "I was with Thrawn for just over a year," he told Ardiff. "I was his senior fleet officer, his student"—he hesitated—"perhaps even his confidant. I'm not sure. The point is that he chose the *Chimaera* and me when he returned from the Unknown Regions. He didn't just pick us at random; he *chose* us."

"No, there wasn't much Thrawn did at random," Ardiff agreed. "From which it follows that if he's back . . . ?"

"That he's chosen someone else," Pellaeon finished the other's sentence, the words a sharp ache in his heart. "And there can be only a very few reasons why he would do that."

"It can't be position," Ardiff said firmly. "You *are* Supreme Commander, after all. And it certainly can't be competence. What's left?"

"Vision, perhaps," Pellaeon suggested, tapping the datapad gently with a fingertip. "This peace proposal was my idea, you know. I came up with it, I argued for it, and I crammed it down the Moffs' throats. Moff Disra was one of those who loudly and strongly opposed it. Moff Disra of Bastion. Coincidence?"

For a moment Ardiff was silent. "All right," he said. "Even if we grant all that—which I don't, by the way—why send a pirate or mercenary group out here to attack us? Why not simply come here and tell you directly that the treaty idea is off?"

"I don't know," Pellaeon said. "Perhaps it isn't off. Perhaps this is exactly where Thrawn wants me to be. Either preparing to talk to Bel Iblis, for whatever reason, or else—"

He pursed his lips. "Or else simply out of his way. Where I can't interfere with whatever he's planning."

The silence this time stretched out painfully. "I don't believe he would do that to you, sir," Ardiff said at last. But the words carried no genuine conviction that Pellaeon could hear. "Not after all you went through together."

"You don't believe that any more than I do," Pellaeon said quietly. "Thrawn wasn't human, you know, no matter how human he might have looked. He was an alien, with alien thoughts and purposes and agendas. Perhaps I was never more to him than just one more tool he could use in reaching his goal. Whatever that goal was."

Almost hesitantly, Ardiff reached over and touched Pellaeon's arm. "It's been a long road, sir," he said. "Long and hard and discouraging. For all of us, but mostly for you. If there's anything I can do . . ."

Pellaeon forced a smile. "Thank you, Captain. Don't worry; I'm not going to give up. Not until I've seen this through."

"We're staying here, then?" Ardiff asked.

"For a few more days," Pellaeon said. "I want to give Bel Iblis every possible chance."

"And if he doesn't show?"

"Whether he does or not, we'll be going to Bastion next," Pellaeon said, hearing a touch of grimness in his voice. "For this and other matters, Moff Disra has some explaining to do."

"Yes, sir," Ardiff said, standing up. "We'll hope that this whole Thrawn appearance is just some trick of his."

"We most certainly will not," Pellaeon reproved him mildly. "Thrawn's return would revitalize our people and bring nothing but good to the Empire. I would never want it said that I valued my own pride above that."

Ardiff colored slightly. "No, sir, of course not. My apologies, Admiral."

"No apologies necessary, Captain," Pellaeon assured him, getting to his feet. "As you said, it's been a long, hard road. But it's nearly over. One way or another, it's nearly over."

The entry procedures at the Drev'starn Spaceport were considerably tighter today than they'd been the last time Drend Navett had landed here on the Bothan homeworld. Hardly surprising, considering the events of the past five days. With the surprise Leresen attack against their orbital manufacturing plant and the subsequent multispecies military buildup in the sky overhead, tensions were growing at a rapid and eminently satisfying pace.

And the Bothans' normally business-friendly procedures had suffered as a result. Once little more than a formality, exit from the spaceport quarantine area now required a complete ID check and cargo scan.

Not that that mattered to Navett. This time through, there was nothing in his cargo that would raise even a paranoid Bothan's fur. And his ID was as perfect as only Imperial Intelligence could make them.

"Your identification and personal effects appear to be in order," the Bothan customs official said after the fifteen-minute procedure that seemed to be the norm today. "However, the Importation Department will have to run further tests on your animals before they can be allowed into the city proper."

"Sure, no problem," Navett said, waving his hand in one of the expansive gestures typical of the Betreasley district on Fedje where his ID claimed he'd been born. He had no idea whether the Bothan would notice subtleties of that sort, but the first law of infiltration was to wear a role the way a stormtrooper wore his armor. "Hey, I done this on dozens of planets," he added. "I know how this quarantine thing works."

The Bothan's fur rippled, just noticeably. "On many worlds, you say?" he asked. "Is there some problem you have with maintaining ownership of your shops?"

Navett frowned, as if trying to decipher his way through a complicated sentence, then let his face clear. "Naw, you got it all wrong," he said. "I'm not tryin' to set up a place I can settle down in. 'Sides, unless you got a bunch of guys to run the racks for you, you can't make a go of the exotic pet business unless you keep movin'. Lot of potential stock you'll never even hear about unless you go where they come from."

"Perhaps," the Bothan murmured. "But I suspect you will not find much of a market on Bothawui in these troubled times."

"You kiddin'?" Navett said, letting some oily smugness show through. "Hey, this place is perfect. A planet under siege—lots of tension—that's exactly where folks are going to need a pet to get their minds off their troubles. Trust me—I seen it happen dozens of times."

"If you say so," the Bothan said with a ripple of his shoulder fur, obviously not caring whether this slightly uncouth alien made a profit here or not. "Leave me your comlink frequency and code and you'll be notified when the quarantine is ended."

"Thanks," Navett said, collecting his documents together. "Make it fast, okay?"

"It will be as quick as regulations require," the Bothan said. "A day of peace and profit to you."

"Yeah. Same to you."

Five minutes later Navett was walking down the street, jostling his way through the mass of travelers hurrying in and out of the spaceport. Passing up the rows of for-hire landspeeders, he put his back to the setting sun and headed off on foot toward a row of cheap hotels bordering the spaceport area.

With his back to the sun, he spotted the shadow coming up behind him a few seconds before Klif dropped into step at his side. "Any problems?" the other asked quietly.

"No, it went real smooth," Navett said. "You?"

Klif shook his head. "Not a one. He took the bribe, by the way, but he wouldn't promise we'd get the animals out any sooner."

"Not with a bribe that small," Navett agreed, smiling to himself. An insultingly small gratuity from the pet dealer's assistant, and none at all from the dealer himself, ought to nicely reinforce their carefully constructed image as small-timers trying to turn a fast profit without the slightest idea how the game was played.

And with the Bothans, an image like that practically guaranteed them to be the focus of private amusement, back-room contempt, and complete official disinterest.

Which meant that when the time was right for the Drev'starn section of the Bothawui planetary shield to come down, it would.

"You see Horvic or Pensin in there?" Klif asked. "I didn't spot either of them."

"No, but I'm sure they got in all right," Navett said. "We can tap the rendezvous point tomorrow if we can find a shop fast enough."

"I picked up a rental listing," Klif said. "Most of them come with apartments above them."

"That'll be handy," Navett said. "We'll look through it tonight and see if there's anything in the right area. If not, we can always check with a rental agent in the morning."

Klif chuckled. "Don't worry—we've got plenty of bribe money left."

"Yes," Navett murmured, looking around. Fifteen years ago, according to rumor, it had been information from Bothan spies that had led the Rebel Alliance to Endor and resulted in the death of Emperor Palpatine and the destruction of the second Death Star. In the years since then, Bothans had been involved with the Black Sun organization, the destruction of Mount Tantiss, and any number of other blows against the Empire.

He didn't know the full scope of the plan that was under way here; but of all the worlds Grand Admiral Thrawn might have chosen for destruction, few would have given him more personal satisfaction than this one.

They had reached their chosen hotel now, and as they started up the steps an ancient droid standing warden beside the door stirred himself. "Good even, good sirs," he wheezed. "May I call for a baggage carrier?"

"Naw, we can handle 'em," Navett said. "No sense wasting good money on a droid."

"But, sir, the service is free," the droid said, sounding confused.

But by then Navett and Klif were past him, pushing through the doors and strolling into the lobby. They were, he noted, the only hotel guests carrying their own bags.

But that was all right. Let the Bothans and their more sophisticated guests snicker at them behind their backs, if they chose. When the fire began to rain from the sky, the laughter would turn to screams of terror.

And Navett would be enjoying every minute of it.

CHAPTER

It was on her fifteenth day in the darkness of the Nirauan cave when Mara Jade awoke to discover a rescuer had finally arrived.

It was not, however, any of the potential rescuers she would have expected.

Mara?

She sat up suddenly in her bedroll, blinking her eyes reflexively open despite the fact that in the pitch-darkness there was absolutely nothing to see. The sense of someone calling to her had been wordless, but as clear as if her name had been spoken aloud. She stretched out with the Force . . .

And as she did so, the sense of his presence came drifting in to her. His presence, and his identity.

It was Luke.

The tone of his emotions changed, the hard edge of anxiety permeating it turning abruptly to relief as he sensed her response and knew that she was unhurt. A new touch of anticipation flowed into his mind, and as she focused she could sense a physical darkness around him. Best guess was that he was in the cave, she decided, probably working his way her direction.

Which unfortunately meant that his anticipation was a bit premature. Finding the cave was one thing; finding each other within its multiple twistings was going to be something else entirely.

But Luke already had that covered. To her wordless question came a renewed sense of assurance from him; and even as she frowned, she caught a sense of others around him, beings who he seemed to be following. Apparently, some of the mynocklike creatures who had hauled her in here in the first place were acting as guides.

She looked up at the ceiling and walls around her. More of the creatures were up there, silently watching her. "Skywalker's coming," she called up into the darkness. "You happy?"

They were. Even with her frustrating inability to hear their words directly, there was no mistaking the surge of excitement that rippled through them. "I'm so pleased," she said. Standing up, she felt her way toward the subterranean creek gurgling its way through the rock a few meters away. She'd picked this spot early on in her captivity as a place where she would have water available, and in the days since then had learned to navigate the trip without using her glow rod.

She reached the creek, located the conveniently placed flat rock where she kept the small bottle of personal cleaning solution from her survival kit, and stripped off her jumpsuit. The outfit itself was one of the top-of-the-line brands that was standard issue aboard Karrde's ships and shrugged off dirt and oils with ease. Mara herself, unfortunately, did not; and if she had company coming it seemed only reasonable to make herself presentable.

The water was shallow, swift-moving, and icy cold. Mara splashed it all over herself, trying not to sputter too much with the thermal shock. A few drops of cleaning solution rubbed vigorously into skin and hair, another agonizing dip into the liquid ice of the creek to rinse off, and she was through. An only marginally warmer breeze flowed along the same path as the water, and she stood in the draft for a few minutes, brushing off excess water and fluffing her hair until she was mostly dry. Getting back into her jumpsuit, she collected her things and headed back to her encampment.

Just in time. She was still sorting her equipment back into their proper niches in her pack when she caught the first flickers of reflected light against the rocky walls and high ceiling. Rolling up her bedroll and tucking it into her pack, she sat down on her "chair"—another mostly flat rock—and waited.

It seemed to take an inordinate amount of time before the bouncing light finally resolved itself into a Jedi Master carrying a glow rod; but when it did she finally understood the reason for the slow trip. Luke himself was burdened down with what looked like the sort of everything-but-a-set-of-alluvial-dampers survival kit Karrde's people liked to put together; and trundling awkwardly but gamely along beside him on the uneven ground was his R2 astromech droid.

"Mara?" Luke called, his voice echoing through the cave.

"Right here," Mara called back, standing up and waving her glow rod. "You sure took your time."

"Sorry," he said dryly, making his way to her. "We couldn't find the local airspeeder-hire stand and had to walk. You look good."

"You look terrible," she countered, running a critical eye over him. His jacket and the jumpsuit beneath it were stained with dirt and sweat and dotted here and there with small rips and punctures. "How far did you walk, anyway? Halfway around the planet?"

"No, only about ten kilometers," he said, shrugging the pack off his shoulders onto the ground and running a hand through his hair. "But it was cliffs and wilderness all the way."

"And thornbushes, apparently," Mara added, gesturing toward the tears in his jumpsuit. "You want to get cleaned up? There's a stream right over there that doesn't have too much ice floating in it."

The droid gurgled. "Maybe later," Luke said. "How have they been treating you?"

Mara shrugged. "Ambiguously," she said. "At first I thought I was being held prisoner. But they didn't seem to mind if I moved around the immediate area, so I thought I might have been mistaken. On the other hand, they also wouldn't let me go too far in any direction, and they've still got my lightsaber and the blaster they took from me."

"Your blaster?"

"Yes, my blaster," Mara said, putting a drop-it tone into her voice. The aliens had taken both of her main weapons; but they'd missed the tiny backup blaster snugged in its holster against her left forearm. Up till now she hadn't had occasion to use it, but she didn't want Luke announcing its existence, either. "And my lightsaber," she repeated. "So now I'm not sure what's going on."

"Yes, my Qom Jha guides told me you have trouble understanding them," Luke said. Apparently, he'd gotten the message about the blaster. "It sounds to me like the reason they brought you in here was to keep you safe."

"I was afraid of that," Mara said, feeling her cheeks warming and hoping the chagrin didn't show. Bad enough that someone had had to come all the way out here to the edge of Unknown Space to rescue her after she walked the side of her head into that rock. Even worse that it had to be Luke Skywalker, Jedi Master, who probably had a million better things to do with his time. But for the "rescue" to be from what was essentially an impromptu alien baby-sitting service was embarrassing beyond words.

"Don't worry about it," Luke said quietly.

She blushed harder. "Blast it, Skywalker, stay out of my mind."

She felt his own flush of embarrassment at the unintended intrusion. "Sorry," he apologized. "But I didn't mean it that way. They say they needed to protect you because you were being hunted by the Threateners from the High Tower."

Mara frowned, her embarrassment abruptly forgotten. "The Threateners?"

"That's the Qom Jha name for them," Luke said. "Beings similar to us, they say, and allied with the Empire."

"Terrific," Mara murmured. With her attention these past few days focused on survival and the exploration of her surroundings, the reason why she'd come to Nirauan in the first place had rather been lost in the back of her mind.

But now it was suddenly back in a rush: the mysterious spaceship she and Luke had spotted skulking around the Cavrilhu Pirate base, and the one that later had buzzed Booster Terrik's private Star Destroyer. Alien beings and alien technology, but with a distinctly Imperial flavor mixed into the design. "So we were right," she said. "They *were* hunting for Imperials at the Cavrilhu base."

"It's starting to sound that way," Luke said. "Though don't forget we only have the Qom Jha word for that. We'll need to check it out for ourselves."

"Um." Mara eyed him. "So they can talk to you, huh?"

"Through the Force, yes." Luke paused, eyes slightly unfocused as if he were listening to a faint sound. Mara stretched out to the Force herself, but aside from the creatures' normal chirping she could still catch only the familiar almost-voices making almost-words. "You can't hear that?" he asked.

"Not understandably," Mara admitted. The thought annoyed her almost as much as having to be rescued. "What are they saying?"

"At the moment, not much," Luke said. "They're waiting for their Bargainer to arrive. I gather from an earlier conversation I had with a group called the Qom Qae that that's the local term for leader or spokesman."

"Ah." Mara frowned as a ripple of displeasure ran through the almost-voices. "I get the distinct feeling they don't like the Qom Qae very much."

"Yes, I know," Luke agreed, his tone a little uneasy. "Actually, it may be partially my fault. I think they're displeased that I brought a Qom Qae in here with me."

"Not necessarily the most politic thing you could have done."

"He spent the last couple of days guiding me here," Luke said, sounding a little defensive. "He wanted to come inside and see you, and I decided he'd earned that much. Besides, whatever's going on probably concerns both groups."

"Could be." Mara glanced around them. "Where is this guide of yours?"

"Up there somewhere," Luke said, playing the beam from his glow rod around the ceiling. Each of the mynocklike Qom Jha twitched as the spot of light passed, shying away from the glare.

All except one, a somewhat smaller creature whose leathery hide seemed to be a slightly different color than that of the beings clustered closely around him. Also unlike the others, who hung casually from cracks or bumps in the ceiling, he was perched awkwardly upright on a rock jutting out from the wall. "That him?" Mara asked.

"Yes," Luke said, holding the light there a moment and then turning it back toward the ground. "He's called Child Of Winds."

Mara nodded, thinking back to her flight in through the deep canyon and all the small caves she'd noticed pockmarking the rock walls along the way. "I take it the Qom Qae are cliff-dwellers?"

"His nesting is, anyway," Luke said. "His father is also their Bargainer."

"Friends in high places," Mara said. "That could be handy."

"I'm not sure 'friends' is exactly the word I would have used," Luke said dryly. "They seem to have made off with my X-wing when I wasn't looking, and Child Of Winds either can't or won't tell me where they took it. It must have taken a whole lot of them to even move it."

"It did," Mara said with a grimace. "I know because I watched the Qom Jha do the same thing with my Defender, hauling it into the cave to who knows where. Looks like they've got more in common with the Qom Qae than they might like."

"Actually, your Defender isn't very far away," Luke said. "Artoo and I spotted it on our way in. He gave it a quick scan—it didn't seem to be damaged."

"That's a relief," Mara said, a small amount of the weight lifting from her back. The Defender might be useless for getting her home, but without it she couldn't even get off the ground. "After everything Karrde went through to get his hands on it, he'd kill me if I lost it. When's he getting here with backup?"

Luke winced. "Well, to be honest . . . I told him not to send anyone else."

Mara felt her mouth go a little dry. "Did you, now," she said, striving to keep her voice calm. If Luke was starting to slip back into his old omnipotent-Jedi habits . . . "You don't think the two of us tackling a whole fortress full of unknown enemies is giving us too much of an advantage, do you?"

An odd look flicked across his face. "That's not it at all," he protested. "I just didn't think it would be a good idea for a full battle force to come storming into the system. Especially since we didn't know whether or not you were a prisoner."

"I suppose that makes sense," Mara conceded, the knots untying a little. "I guess that means you don't have a Star Cruiser skulking in the outer system, either?"

"I doubt the New Republic could spare even an armed transport right now," Luke said, his expression turning grim. "Things are getting very nasty out there."

"Let me guess. Caamas and the Bothans?"

"Caamas, the Bothans, and a thousand worlds using Caamas as an excuse to pick up on old grudges against their neighbors," he told her. "And frankly, I'm starting to wonder if there's any way at all of stopping it."

"That's a cheery thought," Mara growled. "Let's deal with one problem at a time, all right? Starting with confirming these Threateners are the same ones we're looking for. We think we spotted one of those alien ships on its way in when we came out of lightspeed, but it was too far away for a positive identification."

"Oh, they're the right ones," Luke assured her. "I had two of them escort me in, then try to shoot me down."

Mara grimaced. "I guess that says whose side they're on."

"Not necessarily," Luke cautioned. "Or at least, not permanently. We might be able to persuade them—wait a second. The Bargainer's here."

Mara nodded; she'd already sensed the anticipation flowing ahead of the new arrival. "You're going to have to translate for me," she told him. "I wish I could hear them myself."

"It would sure make things easier," Luke agreed, forehead wrinkling with thought. "I wonder if—here, give me your hand."

"My hand?" Mara echoed, frowning, as she extended her left hand toward him.

"I can sense them," he explained, taking her hand with his right and gripping it firmly, "and we can sense each other. If we can make that link strong enough . . ."

"Worth a try," Mara agreed, stretching out to the Force. The aliens' communications were indeed clearer now, like whispered words beneath the chirping just a little too soft to hear. She stretched out harder, frowning with concentration.

"Let's try this," Luke said, stepping close to her side and turning to face the same direction she was. Shifting her hand from his right to his left, he slipped his right arm around her waist and leaned over to touch the side of his head against hers.

And in that moment, like a faulty display whose self-tuning had just come on-line, the vague sounds and sensations she'd been picking up for the past two weeks abruptly coalesced into words.

—*the Bargainer for this nesting of the Qom Jha*, the words flowed through her mind. *I am known as Eater Of Fire Creepers. The Qom Jha rejoice that you have come to us at last.*

"We're glad to be here," Luke said gravely. "I'm Luke Skywalker, as you seem to already know. This is my friend and ally, Mara Jade."

A wave of emotion swept the chamber. *Why do you bring her here to us, Master Walker Of Sky?* Eater Of Fire Creepers demanded, an odd sort of caution in his tone.

Luke frowned. "I didn't bring her; she came of her own volition. Is there a problem?"

Did you not heed our message regarding this Jaded Of Mara? Eater Of Fire Creepers asked. *You surely must have received it by now.*

"I've received no messages from you," Luke said. "When and where was it sent?"

I do not understand, Eater Of Fire Creepers said, sounding wary now. *What do you mean by no messages?*

"I mean no messages," Luke said. "I'd never heard of you or this world until I was told by Mara's friends about her capture."

But the messages have been delivered, Eater Of Fire Creepers insisted. *It was so promised by the Bargainer of the Qom Qae—*

He broke off, his wings fluttering ominously. *You—Qom Qae,* he bit out. *Stand forward and speak in your nesting's defense.*

There was a sudden commotion by the section of wall where Child Of Winds had been perched. Mara flicked her glow rod that direction, just in time to see the small Qom Qae drop toward the floor to avoid three Qom Jha attempting to pounce on him. They altered direction toward him; changing direction himself, Child Of Winds curved up and over toward a wide crack in the opposite wall near the ceiling. "Leave him alone!" Luke called sharply. "He's just a child."

He is a Qom Qae, the Bargainer spat as Child Of Winds dived head-first into the crack. *He bears the responsibility for his nesting's treacheries.*

Luke let go of Mara's hand and took a long step away from her. "You will not harm or harass him," he said in a tone of command, his words punctuated by the *snap-hiss* and brilliant green blade of his lightsaber. "Leave him alone, and I will question him."

A Jedi with ignited lightsaber, in Mara's experience, was a sight that normally caused sentient beings to pause for a moment or two of sober reflection. The Qom Jha either didn't understand, didn't care, or else assumed that five meters of vertical space would be adequate protection from the glowing weapon beneath them. In the green light Mara could see Child Of Winds trying to wedge himself more tightly into the limited protection of the crack, his claws slashing ineffectually toward the three Qom Jha fluttering around him. A half-felt command from the Bargainer, no longer understandable now that Luke had moved away from her, and another group of Qom Jha detached themselves from the ceiling and moved in toward the confrontation.

And it was time, she decided, to remind the aliens exactly who it was they were dealing with here. Tossing her glow rod over to her left hand, she snatched her backup blaster from its forearm holster with her right and fired three precisely placed shots into the wall around Child Of Winds's hiding place.

With a startled screech the attacking Qom Jha shied back from the blasts and flying rock chips, fluttering for a moment before settling into new positions on the ceiling away from the besieged Qom Qae. Another half-sensed command from the Bargainer, and a taut silence descended on the cavern. "A minute ago you called him Master," Mara called toward the aliens. "Is he a Jedi Master to be respected and obeyed, or isn't he?"

There was a rush of almost-words. "Translation?" Mara murmured.

"He said, 'You have no place to speak thus to the Bargainer of the Qom Jha,' " Luke told her, shifting his lightsaber to his left hand and stepping back to her side. Keeping a wary gaze on the ceiling, he again put his arm around her and touched his head to hers—

—*indeed, even now you hang clutched to crumbling rock,* Eater Of Fire Creepers's voice came into her mind again. *Do you deny you are the same Jaded Of Mara who once flew with the nesting of the Empire?*

Luke's arm seemed to tense across Mara's back. "What do you mean?" he asked cautiously.

Those in the High Tower have made great rustlings and bargainings about this being, Eater Of Fire Creepers said, his tone dark. *Perhaps it is our trust in you which hangs from crumbling rock, Master Walker Of Sky.*

"Or maybe the crumbling rock is in your own heads," Mara countered before Luke could reply. "If any allies of the Empire are talking about me, it's because I'm near the top of their list of enemies. Or didn't you bother to listen to the entire conversation?"

The Bargainer fluttered his wings again, but this time there was a touch of uncertainty to the gesture. *Their language is not easily understandable,* he conceded. *Yet we have been betrayed once already by the Qom Qae, and do not wish to add one betrayal to another. Master Walker Of Sky, you said you would force the Qom Qae to speak in his nesting's defense?*

"I said I would question him," Luke corrected mildly, closing down his lightsaber. "Child Of Winds, come down here."

There was a moment of hesitation; and then the Qom Qae worked his way out of the crack and dropped down to land on a stone beside Luke. *I am here, Jedi Sky Walker,* he said, keeping a wary eye on the ceiling.

"Did your nesting of the Qom Qae receive messages for me or for the New Republic from this nesting of the Qom Jha?" Luke asked. "And did your Bargainer promise Eater Of Fire Creepers your nesting would deliver those messages?"

Child Of Winds seemed to hunch his wings over his head, a heavy sense of nervous guilt rippling from him. *It is not my place to bargain for my nesting,* he said. *Hunter Of Winds—*

Hunter Of Winds is not here, Eater Of Fire Creepers cut him off brusquely. *You will answer the question.*

Child Of Winds sank lower into his wings. *It is as you say,* he conceded reluctantly.

"Well, that's handy," Mara muttered. "We could have known about this place years ago."

"Sounds that way," Luke said. "Why weren't the messages delivered, Child Of Winds?"

Hunter Of Winds concluded it would not be safe, the young Qom Qae said. *A Qom Qae would need to attach himself to one of the Threateners' flying machines and endure a long journey through the cold and dark before he could reach you.*

That is no reason for betrayal of your bargainings, Eater Of Fire Creepers said contemptuously. *The Qom Qae have flown thus through the darkness many times, or so they claim. Admit that it was cowardice and fear that caused your betrayal.*

You of the Qom Jha are safe in your caves, Child Of Winds shot back. *We of the Qom Qae live in the open air.*

Do the Threateners not threaten us all? Eater Of Fire Creepers demanded, fluttering his wings.

Do the Threateners come into your caves to seek vengeance from the Qom Jha? the young Qom Qae countered. *Their vengeance would rest solely on the Qom Qae.*

Did the Qom Jha not first risk their lives seeking to learn the Threateners' plans? Do the Qom Jha not continue to take such risks?

Do the Qom Jha learn anything of value? Did you not mistake this friend and ally of Jedi Sky Walker as one flying in the Threateners' nesting?

"Enough," Luke called into the argument. "Whatever has happened is over and done with, and trying to share out the blame won't gain us anything. Fine, so the messages weren't delivered. But we're here now, and we're ready to help you."

"The question," Mara added, "is whether you're worthy of our help."

Luke half turned to frown at her. "What are you—?"

"Quiet," she muttered. "Trust me. Well, Eater Of Fire Creepers?"

There was another awkward silence. *We fear the Threateners,* the Bargainer conceded almost grudgingly. *The Qom Jha and Qom Qae alike fly in the shadow of their talons. We would seek to have this threat removed, if you are willing.*

"Yes, we understand your wishes," Mara said. "But that's not the question. The question is whether you deserve our assistance. And if so, how you intend to prove it."

What proof do you seek?

"For starters, we'll need assistance getting into the High Tower," Mara said. "I assume your people have been getting in from somewhere in this cave system; we'll need guides to that entrance. After that, we may need some of you to run interference or scout out the territory."

The Bargainer fluttered his wings. *Your request will put this nesting in danger.*

"Your request puts *us* in danger," Mara countered. "Would you rather we just call off the whole thing and leave right now?"

There was a brief undercurrent of conversation, either too fast or too alien for Mara to pick up. "I hope you know what you're doing," Luke murmured.

"No matter how you slice it, we're going to need guides," Mara said. "Anyway, I've dealt with this sort of culture before. Anyone who calls their leader 'Bargainer' expects to be bargained with. Offering to do something for them free of charge and hoping they'll reciprocate usually doesn't work. Makes them suspicious, for one thing."

Beside Luke, Child Of Winds stirred. *What will you do with me now, Jedi Sky Walker?* he asked.

"Don't worry," Luke said. "I'll make sure you're given safe passage out of here and back to your nesting."

The Qom Qae hunched his wings. *I cannot go back.*

Luke frowned. "Why not?"

They will not take me back, he said. *I have disobeyed the Bargainer of the Qom Qae, and will not be allowed to rejoin the nesting.*

Luke cocked his head to the side. "Won't be allowed to rejoin?" he asked pointedly. "Or won't be allowed to rejoin without punishment?"

The young alien's emotions twitched. *I would prefer to go with you to the High Tower,* he said. *If I may see directly the dangers posed by these Threateners, I will understand them better. Perhaps I will be able to persuade others of the Qom Qae to assist you.*

"As I said: bargainers," Mara said wryly.

"Yes, I'm beginning to understand," Luke said in the same tone. "I appreciate the offer, Child Of Winds. But this is likely to be very dangerous."

Will your machine travel with you?

Mara glanced over at the astromech droid, standing off to the side warbling quietly to himself. "That's a good question," she agreed. "He'll definitely slow us down."

"True, but if we want any chance of accessing the High Tower's computer systems we'll need him along," Luke pointed out.

"Assuming he can even interface with those networks," Mara warned. "They *are* aliens, you know."

"We know they use Imperial technology in their spaceships," Luke reminded her. "Chances are good they'll have at least a couple of our computers up there, too."

If your machine travels with you, why may not I? Child Of Winds spoke up again. *Once in the bright lights and open air of the High Tower, I would be a better scout than these cave-dwellers.*

"Except that you don't know anything about the High Tower," Luke said. "Besides, considering the rivalry between your two nestings, I don't think Eater Of Fire Creepers will want you poking around his territory any longer than you have to."

Child Of Winds fluffed his wings. *Then perhaps it is time that rivalry is ended,* he said loftily. *Perhaps it is time for one brave and honorable Qom Qae to stand forth and heal the crumbled rock beneath our talons.*

Luke and Mara exchanged looks. "You?" Luke hazarded.

Do you doubt my sincerity? Child Of Winds retorted. *I, who defied the Bargainer of my own nesting to bring you here?*

"It's not your sincerity we're questioning," Luke assured him. "It's—well—"

It is my age, then, the young Qom Qae said, his tone distinctly huffy now. *You do not believe that a child still called by his father's name can accomplish great deeds.*

Abruptly, Mara noticed that the discussion on the ceiling had ceased. Eater Of Fire Creepers and the other Qom Jha were listening closely to the conversation going on below them.

And it occurred to her that with a member of a rival nesting along on the trip, whoever Eater Of Fire Creepers sent with them would bend over double to show how much more helpful the Qom Jha could be. "No, we're not worried about your age," she told Child Of Winds. "After all, I was still almost a child when I went on my first mission for the Emperor. Luke wasn't that much older when he began to fly with the warriors of the Rebellion."

She could feel Luke's frown. But he'd obviously picked up on her tone, because he nodded agreement. "She's right," he told the Qom Qae. "Sometimes the desire to succeed and the willingness to learn are more important than age or experience."

"The 'willingness to learn' part meaning you obey orders," Mara added sternly. "If one of us tells you to stop, move, duck, or get out of the way, you do it and ask questions afterward. Understand?"

I will obey without question, Child Of Winds said, and there was no mistaking the youthful exuberance in his tone. *You will not regret your decision.*

Luke looked up at the Qom Jha. "The Qom Qae have given us the services of their Bargainer's child," he said. "What do the Qom Jha offer as proof of their own worthiness?"

It will be hard indeed for the Qom Jha to match such a valuable gift, Eater Of Fire Creepers said, a distinct note of sarcasm to his tone. *Still, we can but try.*

He fluttered his wings in silent command, and three of the Qom Jha dropped from the ceiling to land on rock perches in front of Luke and Mara. *Splitter Of Stones, Keeper Of Promises, and Builder With Vines have all defied the dangers of the caverns to enter the High Tower. They will guide you there and protect you as best they can from the dangers of the caverns.*

"Thank you," Luke said, inclining his head. "It appears that the Qom Jha are indeed worthy of our assistance."

The Qom Jha are pleased to be so considered, Eater Of Fire Creepers said. *The way is long, though, and for beings without flight the journey to the entrance will require several suncycles. When you reach the place and are prepared to enter, send word back and other hunters of the Qom Jha will join you to serve as protectors.*

"That will be most helpful," Luke said. "Again, I thank you."

"And I'll want my blaster and lightsaber back, too," Mara added.

They will be returned at once, Eater Of Fire Creepers promised. *We will speak again, Master Walker Of Sky. Until then, farewell.*

He dropped from the ceiling and flapped away into the darkness beyond the reach of the glow rods, followed by the rest of the Qom Jha. A minute later, only Child Of Winds and their three Qom Jha guides remained.

"That seemed to work out all right," Mara commented.

"It did indeed," Luke agreed. "I take it all back."

"Take all what back?"

"Whatever doubts I might have had," he said. "You were brilliant. How soon can you be ready to go?"

"I'm ready now," Mara said, running a critical eye over him. "But then, I've just been sitting around for the last two weeks with nothing to do but count rocks. The question is whether *you're* up for a hike or if you'd rather take a few hours to rest up first."

The droid warbled feelingly. "I think Artoo's voting for a rest," Luke said with a smile. The smile faded. "But, no, I think we ought to get moving as soon as we can. You heard the Bargainer—we've still got a long way ahead of us."

"And you've got a million better things to do back home," Mara said, feeling a fresh surge of guilt.

"I didn't say that," Luke said mildly.

"Doesn't mean it's not true," she growled. "Look, if you want to leave, I'm sure the Qom Jha and I—"

"No," he said quickly.

Quickly; and just a little too sharply. "Someone step on your foot there?" she asked, eyeing him curiously.

But if there had been any clues in his expression, they were buried now. "I need to be here," he said quietly. "Don't ask me why."

For a few heartbeats they gazed at each other. Mara stretched out with the Force, but Luke's emotions weren't giving away anything more than his face was. "All right," she said at last. "Let me get my pack. I don't suppose Karrde thought to send a spare glow rod along with you."

"As a matter of fact, he sent three," Luke said, crouching down beside his pack and pulling one of them from an outside pocket. "Oh, and I should refill these water bottles before we leave. You said there was a stream nearby?"

"It's right over there," Mara said, waving that direction as she stepped over to her pack and squatted down beside it. "Hang on a second and I'll show you."

No, she wouldn't ask, she decided as she secured the seals. Not now. But she would find a way to bring up the subject again later.

Because whatever it was, it was something that had Luke worried. And anything that worried a Jedi Knight was something that deserved very careful attention indeed.

"Okay," she said, getting to her feet and slinging the pack over one shoulder. "Follow me. And watch your step."

CHAPTER

7

"That's it," Han said, nodding out the *Falcon*'s viewport. "Pakrik Minor. Not much to look at, is it?"

"It's beautiful," Leia assured him, gazing out at the speckled blue-green world looming in front of them. A vacation. A real vacation. No Coruscant; no politics; no Caamas issue; no ancient vengeances and smoldering wars. Not even any children, droids, or watchful Noghri underfoot. Just her and Han and silence. "Farms and forests, you said?"

"That's all there is," he promised. "And we're going to get a little of both. Sakhisakh called while you were at the closing ceremonies and said they'd found a nice little inn run by a farm family right at the edge of one of the forests."

"Sounds wonderful," Leia said dreamily. "Did he give you any more grief about him and Barkhimkh having to wait for us at the spaceport?"

"Oh, they're still not happy about leaving us alone like this," Han said with a shrug. "Especially not after that riot on Bothawui. But they know how to obey orders." He smiled slyly. "And I think he felt better when I told him we'd be running under a fake ID."

Leia blinked. "A what?"

"Yeah—didn't I tell you?" Han asked, radiating innocence. "I brought along an old smuggler ID to book the room with."

She sent him one of her repertoire of patient looks. "Han, you know we can't do that."

"Sure we can," he said, as usual ignoring the look. "Anyway, you're supposed to be leaving everything to me, remember?"

"I don't remember lawbreaking being on the program," Leia said. But the tensions were already starting to fade away, and she discovered with mild surprise that the issue of false IDs wasn't even sending a ripple of guilt through her conscience. Considering some of the things she'd done in her life—including open and active rebellion against a legally established government—this was hardly something to get worked up over. "You wouldn't get away with it if Threepio was here."

"Not without having to listen to a lecture, anyway," Han said, making a face.

Leia smiled. "Oh, come on, Han. Admit it—you miss him, too."

"I do not," Han protested. "I just—never mind."

"Never mind what?"

Han grimaced. "Thinking about Threepio makes me think about Karrde; and I still don't like the idea of him heading off to the Outer Rim with that Shada D'ukal woman. I know you didn't pick up any treachery when we talked to her, but I still think she's trouble."

Leia sighed. Shada D'ukal, former bodyguard to the smuggler chief Mazzic, who had casually slipped through the Noghri screen around their Manarai Mountain apartment and invited herself into their private strategy session with Karrde and Lando. A potentially powerful ally? Or an equally deadly enemy? "I don't particularly like it, either," she told Han. "But Karrde's a big boy, and it was his idea to take her along. Did you ever get in touch with Mazzic to ask about her, by the way?"

Han shook his head. "The word's still floating around the fringe that I want to talk to him, but nothing came through before we left Pakrik Major. 'Course, now it'll have to wait till we get back."

Leia raised her eyebrows. "You mean you didn't even tell your smuggler contacts we were going to Pakrik Minor? You *are* serious about this being a vacation."

"Nice," he growled.

Silence descended on the cockpit. Leia watched Pakrik Minor as it came steadily closer, trying to recover the mood she'd had before the topic of Karrde and Shada had come up. But for some reason the peace refused to come. She stretched out with the Force, trying to calm her thoughts and emotions . . .

On the control panel, the proximity warning began beeping. "Crazy hotshots," Han muttered, frowning at the displays. "What in space do they think they're doing?"

And with the shock of a slap to the face Leia suddenly understood. "Han, look out!" she blurted.

He reacted instantly, old smuggler's reflexes combining with unquestioning faith in his wife's Jedi abilities to send the *Falcon* into a sharp sideways drop—

Just as a pair of brilliant red laser bolts sliced through space above them.

"Deflectors!" Han snapped, straightening out of his drop and throwing the ship into another turn.

Leia had already hit the switch. "On," she confirmed, keying the weapons panel and taking a quick look at the aft display. There were three small ships back there, starfighter size, firing again as they scrambled to match the *Falcon*'s maneuvers. No IDs on any of them. "Is this part of the entertainment?"

"Not on my ticket," Han gritted. "Thanks for the warning."

"You almost didn't get one," Leia confessed, squeezing off a salvo of shots from the *Falcon*'s upper quad laser battery. All four shots missed. "I thought the sense nagging at me was just me worrying about Karrde and Shada."

"Well, you can start worrying about us if you'd rather," Han said, throwing the ship into a spiraling loop. "Whoever these guys are, they're good."

"I didn't want to hear that," Leia said, keying the comm. Time to call for help from Pakrik Defense.

But their attackers were way ahead of her. "They're jamming our transmissions," she told Han grimly. "Even the private New Republic frequencies."

"Like I said, they're good," Han grunted, leaning the *Falcon* into another evasive turn. "You notice they waited until we were too close in to the planet to jump to lightspeed, too."

More laser bolts flashed past, closer this time. Leia fired another burst in response, again missing. "They're too maneuverable for the targeting linkage down here to handle," she said.

"Yeah, I know," Han said. "I'm heading up to the upper quad. Get ready to take over."

Leia winced. Up there at the top of the ship, with nothing between him and the attackers' lasers except the *Falcon*'s shields and a few centimeters of transparisteel . . .

But he was right: one of them had to do it. And even with her Jedi skills to draw on, she wasn't nearly as good a gunner as he was. "I'm ready," she said, gripping the copilot's helm yoke. The only way to protect him now was to make sure none of those lasers connected. "Any suggestions on strategy?"

"Just try to keep us out of their sights," Han said, leaning some more on his yoke. Almost reluctantly, the *Falcon* pulled out of its loop— "Okay; go," he said, keying control over to Leia's side and in the same motion sliding out of his seat. "Got it?"

"Got it," Leia acknowledged. "Be careful."

"Yeah," Han said, and sprinted out of the cockpit.

Leia gave him five seconds to get to the ladder, then spun the ship into a dip-and-turn maneuver designed to confuse an attacker into overshooting his target. But their pursuers were too smart to be taken in quite so easily. A glance at the aft display showed they were still there, sticking to the *Falcon* like starving mynocks. Another salvo shot past, this time a few of the bolts spattering off the *Falcon*'s deflector shield.

"Okay, I'm here," Han's voice announced over the comm unit. "How you doing?"

"Not as well as I'd like," Leia told him. "I think they've found the range."

"Yeah, I noticed," he said dryly. "It's okay—she'll hold together. Just keep 'em off a few more seconds."

"I'll try," Leia said, throwing the ship into another wrenching evasive pattern and trying desperately to come up with something more concrete than just trying to stay out of their way. But there was just so little here to work with. There was Han and her and the *Falcon,* with the attackers crowding them from behind and the sky-filling disk of Pakrik Minor starting to crowd them from in front.

Pakrik Minor . . . "Han, I'm going to take us in toward the planet," she called into the comlink. "Even with them jamming us, if we can get in close enough *someone* ought to notice what's happening and call in an alert."

"Sounds good," he said. "But be careful. These guys aren't built for atmosphere maneuvers, but neither are we. Hah!"

"What?"

"Got one. Didn't slow him down, but I think I took out his shields. Get 'er moving."

The deadly game continued. Leia pushed the *Falcon*'s sublight drive for all it was worth, twisting their tortured way toward the growing bulk of Pakrik Minor. The hail of laser fire continued, most of it missing, but enough of the shots were connecting to become distinctly worrisome. Already the red indicators on the status boards outnumbered the green, with their number creeping up with every salvo. Unbidden, a memory flashed: her first ride in the *Falcon* as they tore madly away from the Death Star, blasting their way through the TIE fighter sentry line in their bid for escape.

But Luke had been with them then, and Chewie and Threepio and Artoo. And the *Falcon* had been younger, less temperamental. Besides which, Vader and Tarkin had in fact wanted them to escape . . .

Abruptly, the memory was shattered by a brilliant flash from above and behind her. "Han—!"

"Got him!" Han's voice crowed from the comlink. "One down, two to go. She holding together?"

Leia threw a quick look at the status boards. "Yes, but just barely. We've lost the ion flux stabilizers and we're down to less than half power on the sublight. Looks like another direct hit and we'll lose the rear deflector, too."

Han grunted. "Sounds like it's time to try something clever. You ever done a smuggler's reverse?"

"Once or twice," Leia said cautiously. "But I already tried a dip-and-turn, and that didn't do any good. They probably know all about smuggler's reverses."

"Yeah, but you're not going to do it like they expect," Han said. "You're going to swing the *Falcon* around like you're bringing her to a hard stop; but instead you're going to keep spinning the rest of the way around until you're pointing at the planet again and then gun her for all she's got. That ought to throw them off guard."

"And if it doesn't?"

"Hang on, I'm not done," Han said. "You give them a few seconds to hit their drives to try to catch up; and *then* you do a straight smuggler's reverse. With any luck, they'll shoot straight past us."

"Or ram straight into us," Leia said with a grimace. "You ready?"

"Ready. Do it."

"Here goes." Setting her teeth, Leia killed the drive and twisted the *Falcon* hard over. The stars spun dizzyingly around—she caught a glimpse of the two fighters braking hard to keep from overshooting their target— the sunlit bulk of Pakrik Minor swung back into view—

And she threw full power to the drive again, the acceleration pressing her back into her seat. "Han?"

"Perfect," he reported with grim satisfaction. "Can you give me any more speed?"

"Sorry, this is it," she told him, checking the displays.

"That's okay, it'll do," he assured her. "Get ready. Smuggler's reverse . . . *now*."

Bracing herself, Leia cut power and once again threw the *Falcon* into a spin. The attacking fighters swung back into view ahead of her, much closer this time and framed by the glow of their sublight drives flaring at full power. Killing the rotation, she threw power to the drive.

The attackers tried. They really did. But even with their smaller size they had a fair amount of inertia, and with that much power already committed there was no possible way for them to stop. With their minds radiating frustration and helpless anger, they shot past the *Falcon*.

Or rather, one of them did.

The shock of the impact threw Leia out of her seat, the awful crunching sound from somewhere aft ringing in her ears. "Leia!" Han's voice shouted as the echoing noise was joined by a dozen warbling alarms. "Leia!"

"I'm all right," Leia called back over the din. "Han, we've been hit."

"Are we leaking air?"

"I don't—I don't know," Leia stammered, blinking at the proper status board as something tried to obscure her vision. She swiped a hand across her eyes; it seemed to help. "No—hull's still intact. But the drive and repulsorlifts—"

"I'll be down in a minute," Han cut her off. "Just hold her together."

A blaze of light and color caught the corner of Leia's eye. She looked up from the controls, startled to see Pakrik Minor rotating past in front of her again. The last remaining fighter was framed in the center of the planetary disk, waggling evasively as he tried to kill his speed.

But even as he swung back around, Han caught him dead center with a full salvo from the quad. With a brilliant multiple flash of fire, he was gone.

"Okay, that does it," Han called. "I'm on my way, sweetheart."

Leia nodded, swiping a hand across her eyes again and returning her attention to the status boards. The sublight drive was out, but the indicators weren't showing how much actual damage they'd taken. The repulsorlifts were in much the same shape; the doomed fighter must have hit the *Falcon*'s underside and scraped its way back to the stern.

Hit off-center, too—the ship was still doing a slow spin. She keyed the auxiliaries to try to straighten them out, noticing only then that the hand she'd swiped across her eyes had a bright streak of blood on it. Stretching out to the Force, she probed the injury and set the healing process in motion.

And then Han was there, dropping into the pilot's seat beside her. "Okay, let's see," he muttered, keying his own status board. He glanced at her, did a startled double take as he spotted the blood on her forehead. "Leia—!"

"I'm all right—it's just a cut," Leia assured him. "What are we going to do about the drive?"

"Fix it, that's what," Han grunted, climbing out of the seat again. "And we'd better do it fast."

He took off at a dead run. Leia finished adjusting the *Falcon*'s rotation and looked up again—

And caught her breath. Pakrik Minor, which had been uncomfortably large during the battle, now filled that whole section of the sky.

And was getting closer.

The *Falcon* had been with the two of them all their married life, and with Han even longer than that, and Leia knew it would hurt him terribly to let the ship go. But it was the height of foolishness to hold so closely to any possession that it killed you. Grimacing, she keyed for escape pod activation.

Nothing happened.

"Oh, no," she breathed, keying it again, and again. "No."

But the result didn't change. The escape pods were inoperative.

And she and Han were trapped in a ruined ship, plummeting toward the ground.

Swallowing hard, she keyed the comm. It would be close, but with the jamming now gone, maybe help could get to them in time.

But the comm indicator glowed red, one more casualty of the doomed fighter's impact. They were cut off, and all alone.

And they were about to die.

Leia took a deep breath, stretching out to the Force to silence the fear. Now was no time to panic. "Han, the escape pods aren't functional," she called, keeping her voice as steady as possible.

"I know," his taut voice came back. "I spotted that when I was up there. Try the restart booster."

She found the key, pressed it. "Anything?"

"Not yet," he said. "Let me try something else."

"You want me to come help you?"

"No, I need you up there at the controls," Han said. "And keep an eye out—if you spot another ship, try firing an emergency signal blast from the quads."

And hope that any such convenient ships weren't running backup for the last group. "Right."

The minutes dragged on. The red lights began to wink tentatively back to green as Han worked; but not enough of them, and not nearly fast enough. A whistling sound, soft at first but growing ever louder, began to fill the cockpit as the *Falcon* pushed its way through Pakrik Minor's upper atmosphere without the benefit of shields to dampen the sound and the friction. The deep black of space above her began to take on a slight haze as they drove ever deeper, and Leia could feel the temperature slowly edging up. Below her, the planetary features were beginning to take on form: here a lake, over there a mountain ridge, directly beneath and ahead a wide and fertile valley.

"Try the restart again," Han said into the silence of Leia's thoughts, his voice startling her.

"Right." She keyed the switch, and this time there was a tentative answering rumble from the drive.

"All right, easy," Han warned. "Don't try to stop us all at once—this jury-rig can't handle too much. Just ease in some power and see if you can start slowing us down. And if you've got any Jedi tricks up your sleeve, it's about time to give them a try."

"I'm already trying," Leia said, her heart aching within her. She *had* been trying, in fact, ever since realizing the full extent of the danger they were in. She'd tried to contact any Force-sensitives in the system, had quieted the distractions in Han's mind so that he could concentrate better on his work, had stretched out to the Force looking for guidance or inspiration. But none of it seemed to have helped; and with an almost overpowering sense of helplessness she knew there was nothing more she could do. She couldn't repair the sublight engines with a wave of her hand, or stop the *Falcon*'s inexorable fall planetward, or call for help where none existed.

We're doomed. Threepio's oft-repeated wail echoed through her mind. It was just as well he wasn't here, she decided. Or the children, safe on Kashyyyk under Chewbacca's care. Or even their Noghri guards. If it was their time to die, there was no need for anyone else to go with them. *Good-bye, Jacen, Jaina, Anakin,* she thought toward the stars, knowing that the message would almost certainly not reach them, wishing with a deep regret that she could see them one last time. On the status board, almost lost in the chaos there, the proximity warning began beeping—

And to Leia's shock, a small craft roared past overhead. "Han!" she shouted. "Another ship just—"

She broke off, the sudden surge of hope catching like a bone in her throat. The ship had slowed to match speeds with the *Falcon*, riding above and just ahead of it, and giving her her first clear look at it.

"A ship?" Han called excitedly. "Where?"

Leia took a ragged breath. A second ship had joined the first now, paralleling the *Falcon* above and to the right, a third had taken up position on the left, and the aft display showed one more flying directly above the sublight vents. "Never mind," she told Han quietly. "They're Imperial TIE interceptors."

CHAPTER

"They're *what*?" There was the staccato clank of a set of tools landing on the deck. "Hang on, I'm on my way."

Leia looked up at the ships pacing them. TIE interceptors, all right. In excellent condition, too, from what she could see of them, and she wondered where they could have come from. Surely the Imperials weren't launching an all-out attack on the Pakrik system; with the sector conference over and the delegates on their way back to their home systems there was nothing here they could possibly want.

Unless, of course, they were the backup for the first three fighters. In which case, they were here to make sure the job was finished.

With a screech of boots on hull plates Han skidded to a halt beside her. "What are they doing?" he panted, peering up at them.

Leia frowned. "Nothing," she said, realizing belatedly just how odd their lack of activity was. To just sit out there and watch them crash seemed overly sadistic, even for Imperials. At least for line soldiers; she'd known some Moffs and Grand Moffs who would have reveled in something like this.

"They're maneuvering," Han said suddenly, pointing. "That one on the left—see? He's drifting out a little."

"I see," Leia said. "But what's the maneuvering for?"

An instant later she got her answer. In perfect unison, a bright yellow disk connected by a yellow cable shot out from the underside of each of the four TIEs, slamming solidly onto positions on the *Falcon*'s upper hull. The cables went taut; and with a jerk that nearly knocked Han off his feet, the ship's descent abruptly slowed.

Leia looked up at Han, saw her own bewilderment mirrored in his face. "I'll be sat on by a Hutt," he murmured. "Grappling mags." He sank into the pilot's chair, looked over at her. "I give up. What's going on?"

Leia shook her head. "I don't know," she said slowly, stretching out with the Force. "But there's something about these pilots, Han."

"Like what?"

"I can't tell yet," Leia said again. "But something very strange."

"You're telling me." He nodded toward the viewport. "Well, whatever it is, we ought to find out about it pretty soon. Looks like we're already coming down."

He was right. They had passed over a line of low hills and the TIEs had now dropped to barely treetop height. Rolling along beneath them were vast fields of tallgrain, the neat rows rippling with the wind of their passage. They passed an access path, more fields, another path, still more fields. At the far side of this set were another collection of hills, taller than the group they'd passed a few kilometers back.

And at the base of the tallest of the hills, little more than a dark spot in the hazy afternoon sunlight, was a cave.

"Yeah, that's where we're going, all right," Han said. "Nice and private, unless whoever owns these fields happens to be out working them. Got a reception committee already waiting, too, I see."

Leia nodded, squinting against the sunlight at the figures standing outside the cave. "I count . . . looks like ten of them."

"Plus the four TIE pilots, plus whoever else is hanging around inside," Han agreed, reaching under his control board and retrieving his blaster and holster from the storage niche there.

"You have a plan?" Leia asked, eyeing the blaster.

"Not really," Han said as he buckled on the holster. "I'm not going to charge out shooting, if that's what you're worried about. If they wanted us dead, they would have just let us crash."

"Maybe they think the children are with us," Leia said, a shiver of unpleasant memories running through her. After all the times her children had been kidnapped or threatened . . .

"If they do, they're going to be real disappointed," Han said, his tone deadly. Deliberately, he checked his blaster and shoved it back in the holster. "And in a lot of trouble, too."

He nodded toward her waist. "Almost time for the party, hon. Shouldn't you be getting dressed, too?"

"Right," Leia said, pulling her lightsaber out of her board's storage compartment and hooking it to her belt. Calming her thoughts, she reached out to the Force for strength and wisdom. "I'm ready."

A minute later they reached the hills; and directly in front of the cave, as Han had predicted, the TIEs slipped into full repulsorlift mode and eased the *Falcon* smoothly to the ground. They released the grappling mags and reeled them back in, and with practiced ease lined up and began maneuvering one by one into the cave.

"At least that explains how they showed up from nowhere," Han commented as he shut down what was left of the *Falcon*'s systems. "Three'll get you the hand pot this is one of Grand Admiral Thrawn's sleeper cells."

"I always thought those were just a myth," Leia said, gazing into the darkness of the cave. "Disinformation the Empire came up with after Thrawn—well, after we thought he was dead."

"I'm still not convinced he isn't," Han growled, standing up and stepping back toward the door. "No point in putting this off. Let's go see what they want."

One of the reception committee was waiting at the bottom of the ramp as Han unsealed the hatchway. He was a tall man, roughly Han's height and strongly built, with dark eyes and a thick shock of long black hair. "Hello," he said, nodding as they started down the ramp. His voice was genial enough, but there was a definite tension in his face and stance. "Either of you hurt? Councilor, you're bleeding."

"Just a scratch," Leia assured him, rubbing at the dried blood. That odd sense she'd felt with the TIE pilots was back again, stronger than ever. "It's already mostly healed."

The man nodded, some of his black hair dropping across his eyes with the movement. "Yes, of course. Jedi healing techniques."

"Where's the rest of your group?" Han asked, glancing around as they reached the bottom of the ramp.

"Checking out your ship," the man replied, pointing behind them.

Leia turned. The others they'd seen waiting were walking around under the *Falcon*, looking and poking as they assessed the damage. "That second Korlier did a number on you, didn't it?" the first man continued. "You're lucky—if he'd rammed you a little higher up, he'd have taken out your power core and probably breached your hull along with it."

"So those were Korlier Flashships, huh?" Han said, his tone that of one professional exchanging shop talk with another. "I've heard of them, but never seen one before."

"They're not very common," the man agreed. "But since the Korlier Combine doesn't put serial numbers on any of their models, they're a favorite of people who don't want their identities traced."

"Sort of just the opposite of TIE interceptors," Han said pointedly, nodding back toward the cave opening.

The man gave him a bittersweet smile. "Something like that," he said. "My name's Sabmin Devist, by the way. Welcome to Imperial Sleeper Cell Jenth-44."

"Nice to be here," Han said with only a hint of sarcasm. "So what happens now?"

"We talk," a voice came from their right.

Leia turned. Coming around the side of the *Falcon* was a man dressed in a TIE pilot's flight suit. About Sabmin's height and build, she noticed, with a shorter version of his same black hair and a well-trimmed beard. "My name's Carib Devist, Councilor Organa Solo," he said as he crossed toward Sabmin. "I'm sort of the spokesman for this group."

"You're Sabmin's brother?" Leia asked. The family resemblance was obvious.

Carib smiled faintly. "That's what we tell people," he said. "Actually . . ."

He stepped to Sabmin's side. "Seeing as you're a Jedi, I don't suppose it'll take you long."

Leia frowned, wondering what he was getting at. The two of them just stood there, watching her, Sabmin's hair rustling in the breeze . . .

And then, abruptly, it hit her. Sabmin, Carib—

She twisted her head. Behind them, the men who'd been examining the *Falcon* had come out from under the ship and were standing silently in a row, also watching. Different clothing, different hairstyles, some with beards or mustaches, here and there a scar—

But otherwise identical. Completely identical. "Han . . . ?"

"Yeah," he said; and as she focused on his thoughts, she knew that he'd caught on, too. "Brothers, huh?"

Carib shrugged uncomfortably. "It sounds better," he said quietly, "than clones."

For a long minute the only sound was the soft hiss of the breeze rustling through the tallgrain stalks. "Ah," Han said at last, his voice studiously casual. "That's nice. So what's it like being a clone?"

Carib smiled bitterly—the exact same smile, Leia noted with a private shudder, that Sabmin had shown a minute earlier. "About as you'd expect," he said. "It's the sort of secret that gets heavier with time and age."

"Yeah," Han said. "I can imagine."

Carib's face hardened. "Excuse me, Solo, but you can't possibly imagine it. Every time one of us leaves this valley it's with the knowledge that every outside contact puts our lives and those of our families at risk. The knowledge that all it will take will be one person suddenly looking at us with new eyes, and the whole carefully created soap bubble of the ever-so-close Devist family will collapse into the fire of hatred and rage and murder."

"I think you're overstating your case a little," Leia suggested. "We're a long way past the devastation of the Clone Wars. The old prejudices aren't nearly so strong anymore."

"You think not, Councilor?" Carib countered. "You're a sophisticated woman, a politician and diplomat, fully accustomed to dealing with the whole spectrum of sentient beings. And you're good at it. Yet you, too, are feeling uncomfortable in our presence. Admit it."

Leia sighed. "Perhaps a little," she conceded. "But I don't know you as well as your friends and neighbors do."

Carib shook his head. "We have no friends," he said. "And if we're a long way past the Clone Wars, we're not nearly so far past Grand Admiral Thrawn's use of soldiers like us in his bid for power."

"Is that who you're working for now?" Leia asked, studying Carib's face. There was something disturbingly familiar about him . . .

"The orders have come in over Thrawn's name," Carib said cautiously. "But of course, you can put any name on any order."

Beside her, Leia felt Han's sense suddenly change. "I got it," he said with a soft snap of his fingers. "Baron Fel. Right?"

"Baron *Soontir* Fel?" Leia asked, her stomach tightening with the sudden realization. Yes, *that* was who Carib reminded her of: a young Soontir Fel. Once the Empire's top TIE pilot, Fel had married Wedge Antilles's sister and then been forced to strike a reluctant deal with Rogue Squadron to save his wife after Imperial Intelligence Director Ysanne Isard set out to kill her. The rescue had succeeded, but an impeccably laid trap had subsequently snared Fel himself back into Isard's hands. At that point he'd disappeared, presumably to a brief trial and a quick execution.

Except that all that had happened only a few months after Endor, years before Thrawn had returned from the Unknown Regions and begun his cloning operation. Which left the question—

Han got there first. "So how come Fel lived long enough for Thrawn to get the cloning tanks up and running?" he asked.

Carib shook his head, a brief flicker of pain crossing his face. "We don't know," he said in a low voice. "Our flash-learning didn't include any of Fel's personal history. We assume—" He hesitated. "We can only assume that whatever sympathies he might have had toward the New Republic were burned out of him by Isard."

"Or by Thrawn?" Han asked.

"Or by Thrawn," Carib agreed heavily. "Otherwise, I doubt Fel would have been thought reliable enough to have clones taken from him. No matter how good a pilot he was."

There was another moment of silence. Leia stretched out with the Force, but if Carib was disturbed by the discussion of wrecked minds, it was masked by the odd clone-sense surrounding all of them. "Yet you saved our lives just now," she reminded him.

"Don't give them too much credit on that one," Han growled. "If they'd left us alone, we'd have hit dead center in this valley of theirs. You think their secret could have stood up to all the investigators who'd have swarmed over the place?"

"Yet our secret is now out anyway," Carib reminded him calmly. "Depending on what you decide to do."

"Maybe," Han said, his hand dropping casually to hover beside his blaster. "Or maybe depending on what *you* plan to do."

Carib shook his head. "You misunderstand. We have no intention of harming you. Nor do we wish to fight for Grand Admiral Thrawn and the Empire."

Han's forehead wrinkled. "So, what, you're surrendering?"

"Not exactly." Carib seemed to brace himself. "What we want—all that we want—is your word that we'll be left alone here."

Han and Leia exchanged glances. "You want *what?*" Leia asked.

"What, is that too high a price to pay for saving your lives?" Sabmin demanded. "Considering what you owe us—"

"Wait a minute," Han said, holding up a hand. "Let me get this straight. You were created by Thrawn?"

A muscle in Carib's cheek twitched, but he nodded. "Correct."

"This is *Grand Admiral* Thrawn we're talking about, right?" Han persisted. "The guy who wants to bring the Empire back? The guy who picked the best and most loyal TIE pilots, AT-AT drivers, and whatever to run through his clone tanks?"

Carib shook his head again. "You still don't understand. Certainly Baron Fel was loyal to the Empire, or at least what the Empire was before insane butchers like Isard took over. In his era, the Empire stood for stability and order."

"Which you in the New Republic could use a little more of at the moment," Sabmin put in pointedly.

"Let's leave the politics out of this," Leia put in quickly before Han could come up with a good retort. "I'm still confused. If Baron Fel was loyal to the Empire, and if you see the need to reestablish that kind of order—"

"And if Thrawn's really back," Han muttered.

"*And* if Thrawn's really back," Leia agreed, "then why would you want to sit this one out?"

Carib smiled sadly. "Because for once, the great Grand Admiral Thrawn miscalculated," he said. "There was one thing Fel cherished more than personal glory or even galactic stability."

He waved a hand around him, the gesture taking in the fields surrounding them. "He loved the soil," he said quietly. "And so do we."

And finally Leia understood.

She looked at Han. "He's kidding, right?" her husband asked, his expression and thoughts clearly not believing any of it. "I mean—look, Luke couldn't wait to get off that farm on Tatooine."

"Luke was on a moisture farm in the middle of a desert," Leia reminded him, letting her gaze sweep slowly across the neat rows of tall-grain, her own memories of the rich vegetation of Alderaan tugging at her. "It was nothing like this."

"You feel it, too, don't you?" Carib said softly. "Then you understand."

He looked around the fields. "This is our life now, Councilor. Our land and our families are what matter to us. Politics, war, even flying—that's all in the past." He brought his gaze back. "Do you believe us?"

"I'd like to," Leia said. "How far are you willing to go to prove it?"

Carib braced himself. "As far as necessary."

Leia nodded and stepped up to him, sensing Han's flicker of uneasiness as she left his side, and locked eyes with the young clone. Calming her mind, she stretched out to his mind with the Force. He stood impassively, allowing the probe without flinching . . . and by the time she stepped back again, she had no more doubts. "He means it, Han," she confirmed. "They all do."

"So that's it, huh?" Han said. "We're just going to head off and leave them here?"

"We'll repair your ship first, of course," Carib said. "The MX droids that handle maintenance on our fighters can probably have it running in a day or two."

To Leia's surprise, Han shook his head. "Not good enough," he said firmly. "You're asking us to protect an Imperial sabotage group. That's a pretty big risk for us, you know."

The group off to the side stirred. "What are you trying—?" someone began.

Carib silenced him with a gesture, a slight smile tugging at the corners of his mouth. "You always were an operator, Solo," he said dryly. "What do you want?"

"You don't want to fight anymore," Han said. "That's fine; neither do we. But if we don't get this Caamas thing resolved fast, none of us are going to have any choice in the matter."

"Your point?" Carib asked.

"We need to find out which Bothans were involved in the hit on Caamas," Han said. "And there's only one place we know we can get those names from."

Carib's lips compressed briefly. "The Empire."

"Specifically, the central Imperial records library on Bastion," Leia said, seeing now where Han was going with this. "The problem is that we don't know where Bastion is."

"We don't either," Sabmin said. "Our orders come from the Ubiqtorate through a special channel. We've never been directly in touch with Bastion or the current Imperial leadership."

"Sure, but there must be some way you can get an emergency message to them," Han said. "Imperial ops procedures can't have slipped *that* badly."

Carib and Sabmin exchanged glances. "There is a place at the edge of Imperial space where we can go," Carib said doubtfully. "But it's not supposed to be used unless there's vital information that can't wait for proper channels."

"I think we can come up with something that qualifies," Han said. "If we can, will you take me out there?"

"Wait a minute," Leia cut in. "Don't you mean take *us* out there?"

"Sorry, hon," Han said, shaking his head. "But if there's one person everyone in the Empire knows by sight, it's you."

"Oh, really?" Leia countered. "You think you're any better?"

"I wasn't ever president of the New Republic," Han pointed out. "Besides, *one* of us has to go."

"Why?" Leia demanded, a dull ache around her heart. Han had done a lot of crazy things in his life; but walking into the heart of the Empire was beyond even his old smuggler's rashness. "The New Republic has other people they could send."

"Yeah, but which ones can we trust?" Han asked. "Besides, we don't have time to go back and hunt up a team. The whole New Republic's balanced on a blade edge right now."

"But you can't go alone," Leia insisted. "And don't forget I'm a Jedi. Any trouble you get into—"

"We've got company," one of the clones announced suddenly, pointing.

Leia looked. Just clearing the distant hills, a low-flying craft was burning through the air toward them. "Carib, you'd better get the others into the cave," she told him, running through her Jedi sensory-enhancement techniques and squinting at the approaching vehicle. "Better yet, you'd better all go. That looks like our Noghri guards' Khra shuttle."

"Too late," Carib said, his eyes on the approaching vehicle as he gestured the others to stay where they were. "If there are Noghri in there, they already have us under surveillance. Trying to slip out of sight now will just make things worse."

The shuttle was almost to them, skimming low over the tallgrain and showing no sign of stopping. Han made an unintelligible noise in the back of his throat, and even Leia felt a twinge of uncertainty. It *looked* like a Khra shuttle, but at the speed it was making, that was impossible to confirm. If it was instead a follow-up attack . . .

And then, at almost the last second, the craft braked hard, coming to a midair halt. A short gray figure dropped out the passenger-side door, and the shuttle shot off again, swinging high over the cave and hills before circling back toward the group gathered around the *Falcon*.

"Councilor," Barkhimkh said gravely, recovering his balance quickly after his three-meter drop and marching toward them. He had no visible weapons, but with a Noghri that didn't mean a lot. "The Pakrik Defense monitor said that a ship had come under attack, and surmised it was yours. We are pleased to find you uninjured."

"Thank you, Barkhimkh," Leia said, keeping her voice as gravely unemotional as his. What he really wanted to do, she knew, was to express his deep shame and self-loathing that he and Sakhisakh hadn't been there to help protect them from the attack. But he would never reveal even a hint of such feelings in front of strangers. "We appreciate your concern," she added. "As you see, we were able to land safely among friends."

"Yes," the Noghri said, his eyes measuring the group with a single well-trained glance. "I presume you will now be"—his voice faltered just slightly—"returning with us?"

An almost undetectable slip; but for Leia it was enough. "No, it's all right," she said quickly, taking a step toward Carib. "They're not going to hurt us."

"You do not understand," Barkhimkh snarled. There was contempt suddenly in his voice, and a blaster just as suddenly in his hand. "They are Imperial clones."

"They're clones, yes," Leia said. "But they're on our side now."

Barkhimkh spat. "They are Imperials."

"So were the Noghri, once," Carib said quietly.

Barkhimkh's blaster twitched toward him, his large black eyes flashing. Any mention of their long servitude to the Empire by outsiders was considered a deadly insult. "No," Leia said firmly, reaching out with the Force to turn the blaster muzzle aside. "They saved our lives, and they've asked for sanctuary."

"You may trust them as you choose, Councilor," Barkhimkh said darkly. "But I do not."

But nevertheless the blaster disappeared. "There was an urgent transmission from Coruscant for you shortly after you departed Pakrik Major," the Noghri said, waving a stand-down signal toward his partner in the circling shuttle. "Did you receive it?"

"No," Leia said, frowning. She hadn't realized the Noghri were able to tap into their private communications. "It probably came in while we were being jammed. Did you get a copy?"

"Sakhisakh will bring it," Barkhimkh said, nodding his head fractionally toward the shuttle now landing off to the side. "We of course did not attempt to decrypt it."

Which didn't necessarily mean they couldn't do so if they'd wanted to. "Have him bring it into the *Falcon*, please," she instructed. "I'll go get the decrypt ready. You wait here with Han and help Carib and the others get repairs organized."

Ten minutes later, seated at the *Falcon*'s game table as Sakhisakh stood watchful guard between her and the hatchway, she slid the datacard into her datapad.

The message was short, and very much to the point:

> *Leia, this is General Bel Iblis. I've just received some vital information and urgently need to talk to you. Please stay on Pakrik Minor; I'll be arriving there in three days and will meet you at the North Barris Spaceport. Please treat this communication with the utmost security.*

Leia frowned, the skin on the back of her neck tingling. What in the worlds could Bel Iblis have found that he would need to come all the way out here? And why *her*, of all people?

There was the clank of boots on metal, and she looked up to see Han stride in past Sakhisakh. "Looks pretty straightforward, I guess," he reported, sliding into the seat beside her. "The head droid thinks they can have her back together in a couple of days. So what's this big important message?"

Wordlessly, Leia handed over the datapad. Han read it, his forehead wrinkling as he did so. "This is interesting," he declared, setting down the datapad. "How did Bel Iblis know we were here?"

"Gavrisom must have told him," Leia said. "He's the only one who knew we were coming to Pakrik Minor after the conference was over."

"Yeah, well, those three Korliers knew it, too," Han said pointedly, swiveling the datapad around to look at the message again. "How sure are you that this is really from Bel Iblis?"

"About as sure as it's possible to be," Leia said. "It has his signature code, plus the bridgebreak confirmation."

"That's, what, that crypt-embedded code trick Ghent came up with a couple of months ago?"

"That's the one," Leia said. "I don't think the Imperials even know the codes are in there, let alone have a way to access or duplicate them."

"Unless Ghent was using the same trick back when he was still working for Karrde," Han mused, rubbing his chin. "Could be the Imperials picked up on it then."

"No, Bel Iblis asked him that when he first proposed the technique," Leia said. "Ghent said it was something he'd just developed."

"Mm." Han read the message again. "No idea what this is about?"

"None," Leia said. "I guess we'll find out in a couple of days."

"Well, *you'll* find out, anyway," Han said. "Carib and I will be long gone by then."

Leia took a deep breath, the ache returning abruptly to her chest. "Han—"

"No argument, hon," Han said quietly, reaching over to take her hand. "I don't like it, either. But if we don't get this stopped, everything's going to go up in smoke. You know that better than I do."

"We don't know that," Leia argued. "We've got the New Republic government and Luke's Jedi students to help hold things together. If it comes to civil war, we can force the Bothans to pay whatever reparations are necessary, even if it winds up wrecking their economy."

"You really think the Diamala will let Gavrisom force them into that kind of self-destruction?" Han countered. "Not to mention the Mon Cals, the Sif'kries, and whoever else has lined up on the Bothans' side since yesterday? Come on, we didn't win the war with wishful thinking."

"Well, then, what about Karrde?" Leia asked, trying one last time.

"What about him?" Han asked. "Just because he's gone out looking for a copy of the Caamas Document doesn't mean he's going to find it. Matter of fact, he didn't seem too confident about it himself. If he had, he would have asked for half the payment up front."

Leia glared at him. "I'm being serious."

"So am I," Han said, squeezing her hand. "You think I *want* to go walking into the middle of the Empire? Look, you can talk all you want about holding things together; but if the New Republic blows, you and Gavrisom and all the Jedi in Luke's school aren't going to be able to put it back together. And if that happens, what kind of life are Jacen and Jaina and Anakin going to have? Or Chewie's cubs, or Cracken's grandkids, or anyone else? I don't like it any better than you do, but it's got to be done."

Leia took a deep breath, stretching out to the Force. No, she didn't like it at all. But at the same time, paradoxically, it somehow felt right. Not pleasant, certainly not safe, but right. "You aren't going alone, are you?" she sighed. "I mean someone besides Carib?"

"Yeah, I've got someone in mind," Han said, his voice an odd mixture of relief and regret. Relief, she suspected, because his Jedi wife wasn't going to insist he not go; regret for exactly the same reason.

Leia managed a smile. "Lando?"

"How'd you guess?" Han said, managing an answering smile. "Yeah. Him and a couple others." He half turned to look at Sakhisakh. "Not you, in case you were going to ask."

"I would advise you reconsider," Sakhisakh said. "A Noghri guard disguised as your slaves could be unobtrusive even on an Imperial world." His eyes flicked to Leia. "We have already failed you twice, Lady Vader, first on Bothawui and now here. We could not endure the shame and disgrace of a third such failure."

"Disgrace isn't going to matter much if you get us picked up ten steps off the ramp," Han pointed out. "Sorry, but Lando and me can do this ourselves. You just keep an eye on Leia, all right?"

"Do not fear," Sakhisakh said, a dark menace in his voice. "We will."

Under the table, Leia caught Han's hand. "So much for our little vacation," she said, forcing a smile that probably looked as unconvincing as it felt.

The look that flickered across Han's face made her wish she hadn't said that. "I'm sorry, Leia," he said in a low voice. "We never seem to get a break from all this, do we?"

"Not very often," she agreed with a sigh. "If I'd realized at the beginning how much all of this was going to cost . . . I don't know."

"I do," Han said. "You'd have died on Alderaan, Palpatine would still be running the Empire, and I'd still be shipping spice for slimetails like Jabba. All that by itself makes it worth it."

"You're right," Leia said, feeling slightly ashamed of her moment of self-pity. "When were you and Carib planning to leave?"

"Well, let's see," Han said consideringly, an unexpected glint of roguishness touching the somber tone of his emotions. "I've got to get a transmission across to Lando, and Carib's got to roll their freighter out and run a check on it. And he's a family man, too, so he's going to need time to say good-bye to his wife and kids. So let's say . . . tomorrow morning?"

Translation: he'd told Carib they weren't leaving till morning, with whatever excuses he'd needed to make it stick. "Thank you," she said quietly, squeezing his hand and trying the smile again. It felt much better this time.

"It's not what I was looking for," Han said. "But I guess it's better than nothing."

"Much better," she assured him. "But do you think all these crises can wait an extra night?"

"I don't know," Han said, sliding out of his seat and offering her his arm in one of those old Royal Alderaanian gestures he too rarely used. "But I guess they'll have to."

CHAPTER

Outside the curved transparisteel canopy came one last burst of bubbles from the blue-veined rock formation rising from the ocean floor. As if that had been a signal, the blazelights illuminating the area began to dim. The quiet buzz of conversation in the observation gallery stopped in anticipation.

Standing against the back wall, Lando Calrissian smiled in some private anticipation of his own. When he and Tendra Risant had first proposed this undersea mining operation, her family had been less than enthusiastic; but they had been openly critical of his idea to add an observation gallery so that paying customers could watch. Ridiculous, they had said—no one pays good money to watch miners mining, even aquatic miners in the admittedly unusual locale of the Varn ocean floor. But Lando had insisted, and Tendra had backed him up, and the family's financiers had grudgingly forked over the extra money.

Which made it that much more of a pleasure to watch packed galleries like this one waiting eagerly for the show.

The blazelights finished their fade, leaving the rock formation just barely visible as a dark shape against the slightly lighter seawater around it. Someone in the gallery murmured to a friend . . .

And suddenly there was a single point of blue-green fire at one edge of the rock. The point grew rapidly, becoming a line and then a pair of branches, and finally an arachnid-web of light as the blue veins of fraca ignited and burned.

And then the sheets of yellow bubbles appeared as the heat of the burning fraca set off the tertian beneath it, and for perhaps the next thirty seconds the entire formation was surrounded by a twisting fury of fire and light. Like a living creature writhing in the silent agony of its death throes—

And with a shower of multicolored sparks and one final flurry of bubbles, the formation collapsed into a pile of rocks.

Someone gasped; and as the sparks and bubbles faded and the blaze-lights began to come up again there was a ripple of spontaneous applause. The gallery's own lights came back, and with a buzz of excited conversation the audience began their exit back to the casino areas. Lando waited by the door as they filed out, smiling, accepting compliments, answering a scattering of questions covering the usual range of intelligent to banal, and as the last two Duros filed out he reset the doorway for general admission. The miners were scheduled to collapse one more ore formation today, but until that time the gallery would be open, free of charge, to anyone who wanted to come in and watch.

He was just starting down the corridor toward the Tralus Room when his comlink beeped. Pulling it out, he thumbed it on. "Calrissian."

"Transmission coming in on the surface link," the voice of Chief Command Officer Donnerwin announced. "It's encrypted and marked private."

"I'll take it in my office," Lando told him, keying off the comlink and changing direction. Tendra, perhaps, calling to say she'd wrapped up her Corellian trip and was heading back to join him. Or maybe it was Senator Miatamia or another Diamalan official with news about the security arrangements he was hoping to make with them for his ore shipments.

Either one would be welcome. Reaching his office, he sealed the door, dropped into his desk chair, and with twice the anticipation those gamblers back in the gallery had shown he keyed the comm.

It wasn't Tendra. It wasn't even Miatamia. "Hi, Lando," Han said, an all-too-familiar half smile on his face. "How're things going?"

"A lot better two minutes ago than they are now," Lando told him, the anticipation popping like a bubble and settling into the pit of his stomach like a bad feeling. "I know that look. What do you want?"

"I need you to go on a little trip with me," Han said. "Can you get away for a few days?"

The feeling in Lando's stomach got a little colder. No who-mes, no what-makes-you-think-I-want-somethings, no banter of any sort. Whatever was going on, Han was deadly serious about it. "That depends," he hedged. "How dangerous is this little trip likely to be?"

Again, there should have been some banter. There wasn't. "Could be pretty risky," Han admitted. "Could be worse than that."

Lando grimaced. "Han—look, you have to understand—"

"I need you, Lando," Han cut him off. "We're on a tight schedule, and I need someone I can trust. You've got the expertise I need, you know the people I need, and there's no one else I can get."

"Han, I've got responsibilities here," Lando said. "I've got a business to run—"

"Karrde had a business to run, too," Han interrupted again. "He's not going to like it if you say no."

Lando shook his head in resignation. No, Karrde certainly wouldn't be happy if he passed on this. Not after Lando had single-handedly talked him into heading out to Kathol sector to try to get an intact copy of the Caamas Document from the mysterious Jorj Car'das.

Whose ties to Karrde Lando still didn't understand. But that wasn't the point. The point was that Karrde hadn't wanted to confront Car'das, but he'd gone anyway. Now Han was calling the pot hand, and Lando was about twenty points shy of a twenty-three. "All right," he said. "But only because of Karrde. Where and when?"

"Right now," Han said. "You have the *Lady Luck* there?"

"On the surface, yes," Lando told him. "I can take the next shuttle up and be there half an hour later. Who are these other people you said we need?"

"Your old admin pal Lobot, for one," Han said. "And that Verpine he was working with for a while—what was his name?"

"Moegid," Lando said, feeling his eyes narrowing. "Han, this isn't what I think it is, is it?"

"It's probably worse," Han conceded. "Lobot and Moegid still running that little slicer trick you once told me about?"

"I don't know if they still are," Lando said with a sigh. "But I'm sure they still can. You haven't by any chance located—?"

He hesitated. Even with the transmission encrypted he didn't want to say the name aloud.

Obviously, neither did Han. "You mean the place we talked about at the Orowood?" the other said obliquely. "I think so, yeah. Get Lobot and Moegid and meet me two systems Coreward from where you didn't have any choice."

Lando smiled tightly. *They arrived right before you did,* the words echoed accusingly through his memory as clearly as if it had happened yesterday. *I had no choice. I'm sorry.*

I'm sorry, too, Han had replied as he and Leia, a squad of storm-troopers behind them, had walked forward into that private dining room on Cloud City to face Darth Vader. "Two systems Coreward it is," he confirmed.

"I'll be waiting," Han said.

The transmission ended. Lando leaned back in his seat, gazing unseeingly at the blank display. *The place we talked about at the Orowood.* They'd talked about several different places at that clandestine meeting. But only one of them could have gotten Han this riled up.

Bastion. The latest site of the oft-moved Imperial capital, its location and name of its host planet hand-sealed secrets. Probably one of the best-defended worlds in the galaxy; certainly the central focus of Imperial power; most definitely a place where the names Han Solo and Lando Calrissian were rather less than admired.

And one of the last places in the galaxy where a complete set of Imperial records would be stored. Records that might have the names and clans of the Bothans who had helped destroy the world of Caamas half a century ago. Records that could end the increasingly violent argument about whether the entire Bothan species should pay the penalty for that handful of anonymous murderers.

If they could find that crucial record. And get out with it alive.

He keyed the comm. "Donnerwin, send a transmission to Lobot at Dive Central," he ordered. "Tell him to get himself and the *Lady Luck* prepped—we're going on a little trip." For a moment he debated ordering Lobot to contact Moegid, decided against it. The *Lady Luck* had better encryption than the under-to-over comm, and the less information out there for snoopers to listen to, the better. "And get me a seat on the next surface shuttle."

"Acknowledged," Donnerwin said, unfazed as always by this sudden change in his boss's plans. "The shuttle leaves in twenty minutes. Do you want me to hold it?"

"No, I can make it," Lando told him, running a quick mental list. Everything he was likely to need was already aboard the *Lady Luck,* and barring any major disasters the casino/mining operation should be able to run itself for a while. At least until Tendra got back.

A pang of guilt jabbed into him. After all he and Tendra had been through together, she had a right to know why he was dropping everything like this. Especially if there was any chance at all that he wouldn't be coming back.

He swallowed, his mouth unexpectedly dry. He would come back, all right. Of course he would. Hadn't he flown right into the heart of the second Death Star and lived to tell about it? Sure he had. And he'd survived the destruction of Mount Tantiss, and that Corellian unpleasantness, and everything in between.

But he was older now, and wiser, with a business he really enjoyed and a woman who for possibly the first time in his life he felt truly and honestly connected to. He didn't want to lose any of it. Certainly not by dying.

But, hey, there was nothing to worry about. He was going with Han, and Han was about the luckiest old scoundrel he'd ever known. They'd come back okay. Sure they would. Guaranteed.

"Boss?"

Lando blinked, snapping out of his private pep talk and focusing on Donnerwin again. "What?"

"Will there be anything else?" the other asked.

"No," Lando said, feeling slightly ridiculous. "Just keep things running smoothly until Tendra gets back."

Donnerwin smiled. "Sure thing, boss. Have a good trip."

"Thanks."

Lando keyed off the comm, and with a grimace pushed back his chair and stood up. No, there was nothing foolish about a little healthy caution. It was far worse than that.

It was age. Lando was starting to feel old; and he didn't like it. Not a bit.

So fine. He would go ahead and take this little jaunt into the heart of the Empire. It would do him good, and might just save the New Republic on top of it.

Sure. It would be just like old times.

In her earphone came the sound of Calrissian's door opening and closing; and with a sigh, Karoly D'ulin pulled the device out of her ear. "*Shassa*," she murmured into the empty air.

The word seemed to hang in front of her, there in the tiny utility closet. An old Mistryl battle curse, but spoken now not with anger or combat rage but a deep sadness.

Her gamble had paid off . . . and now she was going to have to kill an old friend.

With practiced fingers she began disassembling the audio tap she'd put into Calrissian's office when she'd arrived here forty hours ago, a flush of anger intruding on her dour mood. Anger at Talon Karrde for being so predictable; anger at herself for anticipating his moves so precisely; anger at Shada D'ukal for putting her in this position in the first place.

What in the ashes of Emberlene had possessed Shada to defy the Eleven that way? she wondered. Loyalty, Shada had said up on that windswept rooftop. But that was clearly ridiculous. Mazzic was a grubby little smuggler—nothing more—with no more claim on Shada's loyalty than any of the dozens of other employers she'd worked for over the years. True, this particular job had lasted longer than most; but no matter what Mazzic might have thought, Shada had still been a Mistryl shadow guard all that time, ultimately answerable only to the Eleven Elders of the People.

So Shada had defied her orders, and as a result a Mistryl deal with a Hutt crimelord had gone sour, and the Eleven were demanding Shada's head. All Mistryl had been alerted to watch for her, and several teams had been sent specifically to hunt her down.

And out of all that flurry of activity it had been Karoly who had found her.

Even now, eight days later, the irony of it was still a bitter taste in Karoly's mouth. She hadn't worked with Shada for twenty years, yet had still managed to anticipate that Shada's next move would be in the direction of the New Republic hierarchy, though whether to join up or sell out

Karoly still didn't know. She'd arrived on Coruscant just in time to see Shada leaving the Imperial City, and had tracked her to an apartment owned by High Councilor Leia Organa Solo and her husband near the Manarai Mountains.

She might have taken Shada there—certainly surprise would have been on her side. But the Solos were rumored to have a cadre of Noghri warriors around them at all times, and even given that Noghri combat skills were probably overrated, it would still be risky for a single Mistryl to go up against them alone.

So she had called for backup. But before they could arrive Shada had left the building in the company of Talon Karrde. There again might have been her chance; but before she could do more than infiltrate into the inner landing bay Organa Solo and her protocol droid had arrived with a pair of Noghri in tow. She and the droid had gone inside, the Noghri taking up positions at the outer hatchway; and when Organa Solo had left a few minutes later it was without the droid. She'd collected her guards and left the landing bay.

And then, to Karoly's chagrin, the *Wild Karrde* had immediately sealed up and taken off, leaving her too far from her own ship to have any hope of giving chase.

The Eleven had been furious. So had the Mistryl hunter team who had dropped everything to rush to Coruscant at her call. Nothing had been said; but then, nothing had to be. Their expressions had been enough, and the sideways glances and muttered comments to each other as they'd headed back to their ships. They'd heard the story about Karoly letting Shada escape back at the Resinem Entertainment Complex, and it wasn't hard to guess that many of them were thinking she'd done the same thing here.

Which had made it that much more important that she prove them wrong. And so she'd played a long-shot hunch, keying back on a vague connection between Karrde and Calrissian that Mazzic had gotten whiff of a few years back.

A hunch that had now paid off. Solo had been careful in that transmission, but that single oblique reference to Karrde had been all she'd needed. Shada was off with Karrde, and Calrissian was being asked to join in.

And wherever he went, Karoly would be there, too. Calrissian had once been a smuggler, and every smuggler—former or otherwise—had a hidey-hole or two hidden aboard his personal ship. If Karoly could reach the *Lady Luck* even a couple of minutes ahead of Calrissian, odds were she could be snugged away out of sight by the time he started up the entry ramp.

And if it turned out he was planning to use her hidey-hole for something else . . . well, she would mark that target when she came to it.

In the meantime, there was her carrypack to throw together and a place on the next surface shuttle to reserve. Preferably with a seat closer to the exit than Calrissian's.

Waiting until the corridor outside was silent, she slipped out of the utility closet and headed at a fast walk back toward her room.

"Admiral?" Captain Dorja's voice came from the comm speaker in the secondary command room's inner circle of repeater displays. "The Ruurian ambassador's shuttle has just cleared the ship and is heading back to the surface."

Handing his drink to Tierce, Flim flashed Disra a smug smile and stepped over to the repeater displays. "Thank you, Captain," he said in that calmly measured Thrawn voice he did so well. "Prepare a course for Bastion, and inform me when the ship is ready."

"Yes, sir."

The comm unit clicked off. "About time," Disra growled, throwing a glare at Tierce. "If you ask me, we've pushed our luck too hard here already."

"We're familiar with your opinions on the topic, thank you," Tierce said, not quite insubordinately, as he handed Flim's drink back to him. "I'd remind you that three brand-new treaties is a very good return for a week's work."

"Only if Coruscant doesn't come down on us like a wounded rancor," Disra countered sourly. "You push them hard enough and long enough and they will."

"This hardly qualifies as pushing, Your Excellency," Flim said. His voice, too, was a little too close to insubordination for Disra's taste. "We haven't opened or provoked any hostilities, and we've gone only where we've been invited. On what possible grounds could Coruscant attack us?"

"How about the grounds that a state of war still exists between us?" Disra snapped. "Either of you ever think of that?"

"Political suicide," Flim sniffed. "We've been *invited* by these systems, remember? If Coruscant tries to stick its collective nose in—"

He broke off as a shrill whistle sounded from the repeater displays. "What's that?" he demanded.

"Emergency battle alert," Tierce said tightly, nearly splashing the rest of Flim's drink onto his pristine white uniform as he shouldered past the con man and dropped into the command chair. "Admiral, get over here," he added, his hands darting over the controls.

The tactical display came up, turning the room into a giant holographic combat display; and as it did so, the comm unit twittered. "Admiral, I believe we're about to come under attack," Dorja's voice said calmly.

"Eight *Marauder*-class Corvettes have just jumped into the system, heading our direction."

Disra consciously unclenched his teeth as he looked around the room for the flashing symbols that would mark the incoming Marauders. Of course Dorja was calm—he thought he had the great Grand Admiral Thrawn aboard his ship, with matters undoubtedly under control.

But he didn't, and they weren't. And unless Disra did something fast, this whole tenuous soap bubble was going to blow up right in their faces.

Flim was at Tierce's side now, and the major was reaching for the comm switch. "Tell Dorja he's to take over," Disra hissed toward them. "Tell him this is too small or too trivial for you to bother with—"

"Shh!" Tierce hissed, cutting him off with a glare and a chopping motion of his hand. "Admiral?"

"Ready," Flim said, and Tierce tapped the key. "Thank you, Captain," the con man said smoothly; and once again, it was suddenly Grand Admiral Thrawn standing in the room. "Have you identified them?"

"No, sir, not yet," Dorja said. "They have random-noise generators blanketing their engine IDs. Highly illegal, of course."

"Of course," Thrawn agreed. "Launch a half squadron of Preybirds to intercept."

"Yes, sir."

Tierce flipped off the comm unit. "Are you crazy?" Disra snarled. "A half squadron of starfighters against—?"

"Calm down, Your Excellency," Flim said, throwing Disra a coolly calculating look. "This was one of Thrawn's standard techniques to sniff out an unknown opponent's identity."

"More to the immediate point, it buys us time," Tierce added, his fingers skating madly across the computer console. "Marauder Corvettes, Marauder Corvettes . . . here we go. Mostly used by the Corporate Sector these days, with a few in assorted Outer Rim system defense fleets."

"Interesting," Flim commented, leaning forward to read over his shoulder. "What would the Corporate Sector want with us?"

"I don't know," Tierce said. "Disra? Any ideas on that one?"

"No," Disra said, pulling out his datapad. No, he didn't know why anyone in the Corporate Sector might want to attack them this way . . . but on the other hand, the mention of Marauders had triggered a vague memory at the back of his mind.

"Do you have a list of the other systems who use them?" Flim asked.

"Running it now," Tierce said. "Nothing really jumping out at me . . . there go the Preybirds."

Disra glanced up to see the marks indicating the starfighters speeding outward toward the distant intruders, then lowered his eyes to his datapad again. It had had something to do with Captain Zothip and the Cavrilhu Pirates, he remembered. There, that was the section . . .

"I need some suggestions here," Flim said urgently.

"Thrawn's standard pattern would be to let the Preybirds begin to engage, then pull them back," Tierce said. "How the enemy responded to the probe was usually enough to let him figure out who they were."

"That's fine for Thrawn," Flim bit out apprehensively. "Unfortunately, we're a little short of his brand of genius at the moment."

"Unless Major Tierce took classes in the technique with the Royal Guard," Disra added, snapping the datapad closed with a grand sense of triumph.

"Helpful as always, Your Excellency," Tierce said absently, still sifting through the computer records.

"Glad you appreciate me," Disra said. "They're Diamala."

He had the satisfaction of watching both of them turn to look at him, a look of stunned surprise on Flim's face, the same surprise tinged with suspicion on Tierce's. "What?" Flim asked.

"They're Diamala," Disra repeated, enjoying the moment to the fullest. "About three months ago the Diamalan Commerce Ministry bought twelve Marauder Corvettes to use in transport escort. And possibly for some rather shadier operations."

"You sure?" Flim asked, peering at the display. "It doesn't show here."

"I'm sure it doesn't," Disra said. "Captain Zothip was trying to buy them and was outbidden. As I said, they may be reserving them for shady operations."

"And how do you get from there to the assumption these are those ships?" Flim demanded.

"No, he's right," Tierce put in before Disra could answer. "That Diamalan Senator we dragged aboard the *Relentless* with Calrissian—remember? I never did think he was wholly convinced you were Thrawn."

"And if our Intelligence reports are right, he was the one who helped drive the governmental split on Coruscant over the whole issue," Disra reminded them.

"Yes, he was," Tierce said, turning back to the computer keyboard. "It appears he's decided to give us another test."

"The question being what we do about it," Flim said, looking across the room. "And the Preybirds are almost there."

"I know," Tierce said, gazing at the computer display. "Call them back."

"Already?" Disra frowned at the tactical. "I thought you needed them to—"

"I don't need anything," Tierce cut him off. "Call them back, and have Dorja set up for a Tron Boral maneuver."

"A what?" Disra asked, frowning harder.

"A somewhat esoteric battle technique," Flim explained, leaning over

Tierce's shoulder and tapping the comm unit back on. "That will do nicely, Captain," he said smoothly. "Recall the Preybirds, and prepare the *Relentless* for a Tron Boral maneuver."

"Acknowledged, Admiral," Dorja said briskly. "Will you be joining me on the bridge?"

Tierce looked up at Flim and tapped a spot on the computer display. "You won't need my assistance," Thrawn assured the captain, nodding acknowledgment to Tierce and leaning closer to read the indicated section. "A Tron Boral maneuver, followed by a full-closure Marg Sabl sweep by the Preybirds, and I think our unknown assailants will reconsider their plans. Assuming they're still alive to do so, of course."

"Yes, sir," the captain said, and Disra could almost see the other rubbing his hands together in anticipation. "Tron Boral maneuver ready."

"Execute, Captain."

Flim keyed off the comm unit again. "And that should be that," he said, leaning casually on the back of the command chair and gazing with interest at the tactical display.

"You see, we already have a battle plan to use against Diamala," Tierce explained, looking over at Disra. "Thrawn tangled with them a few times during his sweep through the Rebellion ten years ago." He gestured toward the computer. "All I had to do was pull up the record of one of those battles—"

"There they go," Flim interrupted him. "Running like hopskips."

Disra followed his pointing finger. Flim was right; the Marauders were indeed turning tail and heading for hyperspace. "But we haven't done anything yet," he protested, feeling slightly bewildered.

"Sure we have," Tierce said, his voice grimly satisfied. "Don't forget, they've got records of Thrawn's victories, too. The *Relentless* moved into a Tron Boral maneuver . . . and that was all they needed to know."

"Yes," Flim murmured as, across the room, the Marauders' marks winked out as they jumped to hyperspace. "With ships that weren't even registered to them, we responded with exactly the right move."

He tapped the comm again. "Secure from battle configuration, Captain," he instructed Dorja. "And inform the Ruurian governments that the threatened attack on their world has been frightened away."

"At once, Admiral," Dorja's voice came. "I'm sure they'll be pleased. Shall we continue course preparation for Bastion?"

"Yes," the con man said. "You may leave the system when ready. I shall be meditating if you require me."

"Yes, sir. Have a good rest, Admiral."

Flim keyed off. "And that," he added to Disra and Tierce, "is indeed that. If the Diamala weren't convinced before, five gets the sabacc pot they are now."

"Good for them," Disra said sourly. "You realize, of course, that all this little exercise accomplished was to bring us one step closer to scaring Coruscant into coming down on us."

"Patience, Your Excellency," Tierce said, keying off the tactical and getting up from the command chair. "I'm sure it also helped convince the Ruurians they've chosen the winning side."

"Yes," Disra said. "And perhaps brought us one step closer to the Hand of Thrawn."

Flim frowned. "The Hand of Thrawn?" he asked cautiously. "What's a Hand of Thrawn?"

Tierce pursed his lips, clearly annoyed. "Your Excellency . . ."

"What's a Hand of Thrawn?" Flim repeated.

"No, no, go ahead," Disra said to Tierce, waving a languid hand and preparing to enjoy this moment, too, to its fullest. Tierce and Flim got along together far too well for his liking. It was about time they both got a taste of some of the misgivings and suspicions about this arrangement that Disra himself had been feeling since it started. "It's your story. You tell him."

"I'm listening," Flim said, his voice suddenly dark. "What is this you haven't bothered to tell me?"

Tierce cleared his throat. "Calm down, Admiral," he said. "It's like this . . ."

It was, Disra reflected later, a good thing that the secondary command room was totally soundproofed. As it was, with all the shouting, he completely missed the characteristic deck vibration that marked the Star Destroyer's return to hyperspace.

CHAPTER

10

The first hundred meters were reasonably easy, even with Artoo's usual problems with uneven terrain. Mara had explored some of this section of the cave, and had studied most of the rest with glow rod and macrobinoculars, and she was able to pick out the best route.

But at that point the floor dropped off abruptly for perhaps ten meters; and when they reached the chamber at the bottom of the passageway, they were in new territory.

"How's it look?" Luke called to Mara as he used the Force to ease Artoo over one last boulder at the foot of their descent path.

"About like you'd expect," Mara called back. She had her glow rod out in front of her, her body silhouetted as the light was scattered into a hazy nimbus by the dust in the air. "You know, just once it would be nice to go on one of these little jaunts where we didn't wind up having to drag that astromech droid through rocks and bushes and sand and all."

Artoo beeped indignantly. "Artoo's usually done a good job of earning his keep," Luke reminded her, brushing the grit off his hands as he stepped to her side. "Anyway, when did we have to pull him through sand?"

"I'm sure we'll hit some sooner or later." Mara gestured ahead. "What do you think?"

Luke peered out through the haze. The chamber was short, no more than fifteen meters from where they stood to the far end, but it was indeed a mess. A maze of rocks and boulders littered the area, with the jagged blades of stalactites and stalagmites jutting randomly from ceiling and floor blocking their way. At the far end, the chamber closed down again to a narrow crack that looked barely wide enough to squeeze through. "Doesn't look too bad," he told her. "We can handle the stalactites with our lightsabers. The big question's whether that crack's too narrow to get Artoo through."

There was a rustling in the air and Keeper Of Promises fluttered to an upside-down perch on one of the stalactites. *Are you troubled, Master Walker Of Sky?* the thought formed in Luke's mind. *Is the path ahead too difficult for you?*

No path is too difficult for Jedi Sky Walker, Child Of Winds jumped indignantly to Luke's defense, flapping his way to a rock beside Mara. *I have seen him do great deeds in the outside air.*

Perhaps they were great in the easily dazzled eyes of a Qom Qae, Splitter Of Stones put in dryly from another stalactite a few meters into the chamber. *Those who have earned their names are more difficult to impress.*

"They're talking again, aren't they?" Mara muttered.

"The Qom Jha are wondering if this chamber is going to be a problem for us," Luke told her. "Child Of Winds is defending us."

"Decent of him," Mara said, unhooking her lightsaber and hefting it in her hand. "Shall we give them a little demonstration?"

Luke frowned at her. "Are you sure you can—I mean—"

"You mean can I do it?" Mara cut him off. "Yes, I can do it. Just because I haven't graduated from your precious Jedi academy doesn't mean I can't use the Force as well as anyone else. You want high or low?"

"I'll take high," Luke said, a little taken aback by the heat of her retort. He got his own lightsaber in hand and gave a quick look around the chamber, fixing the position of each stalactite firmly in his mind. "You ready?"

In answer Mara ignited her lightsaber, the light from its blade adding a blue tinge to the neutral white of her glow rod. "Anytime you are."

"Right," Luke said, trying to hide his misgivings as he added the green of his lightsaber to the mix. "Go."

In unison they cocked their arms and threw, sending their lightsabers windmilling across the chamber, their blades snicking neatly and efficiently through the protruding rock spikes.

Or at least Luke's did. Mara's . . .

She tried. She really did. Luke could sense it in her stance, in her outstretched hand, in the mental strain he could feel like a static discharge all around her.

But as Master Yoda had once said, *Do, or do not. There is no try.* And in this case, as it had been then, there was indeed no try. Halfway across the chamber, Mara's lightsaber seemed to falter, its rhythm breaking and the blade tip dipping to carve shallow furrows in the rock floor. It would recover and fly true for another second or two, only to slow or dip again as she again nearly lost her Force grip on it.

Twice Luke was tempted to reach out and help her; on such an easy task he could handle both lightsabers without any problem. But both times he resisted the temptation. Mara Jade angry and frustrated was bad enough; Mara Jade angry, frustrated, and feeling like she was being patronized was not a combination he felt ready to face.

Besides, the job was getting done, if a bit erratically. And as far as the secondary purpose of the demonstration was concerned, the subtleties of the performance were completely lost on the audience. The cacophony of squawks and chirps from the Qom Jha filled Luke's ears and mind as the stalactites dropped from the ceiling around them to shatter on the rocks below.

But neither the crash of rock nor the startled exclamations from the Qom Jha were able to drown out Child Of Winds's delighted squeals. *I was right—you see, I was right,* he crowed. *He is a great Jedi warrior, as is Mara Jade beside him.*

Luke felt a twinge as he called his lightsaber back to him, timing it to arrive at the same time as Mara's slightly more sluggish weapon. "War doesn't make one great, Child Of Winds," he admonished the young Qom Qae gently as he closed down his lightsaber and returned it to his belt. "Battle is always to be the last resort of a Jedi."

I understand, Child Of Winds said, the tone of his thought making it clear that he did not in fact understand at all. *But when you destroy the Threateners—*

"We're not destroying anything," Luke insisted. "At least, not until we've tried talking to them first."

"I'd give it up if I were you," Mara called over her shoulder as she picked her way across the chamber toward the narrow opening. "He'll understand after he's seen a couple of his friends die in battle. Not before."

Luke felt his throat tighten. Obi-Wan, Biggs, Dack—the list went on and on. "In that case, I hope he never understands," he murmured.

"Oh, he will," Mara assured him darkly, her voice echoing strangely as she leaned her head into the gap and waved her glow rod around. "Sooner or later, everyone does."

She leaned back out and unhooked her lightsaber. "You can come on ahead—there's only a short neck of extra rock here. Just take me a minute to cut it away."

Six hours later, Luke finally called a halt.

"About time," Mara said, wincing as she eased herself down into the most comfortable position possible on the cold rock. "I was starting to think you were hoping to make it all the way to the High Tower by tonight."

"I wish we could," Luke said, brushing some stones out of a saddle of rock across from her and sitting down. He didn't look nearly as tired or sore as she felt, she noticed with some resentment. She could only hope he was merely hiding it better than she was. "I have a feeling that we're running on a tight deadline with this."

"You're always running tight deadlines," Mara said, closing her eyes. "Has it ever occurred to you that every once in a while you could let someone else do all the work?"

She felt the texture of his emotions change, and wondered whether his expression would be hurt, angry, or indignant when she opened her eyes.

To her mild surprise, it was none of them. It was, rather, merely a look of calm interest. "You think I try to do too much?"

"Yes," she said, eyeing him closely. "Why? You disagree?"

He shrugged. "A year or two ago I would have," he said. "Now . . . I don't know."

"Ah," Mara said. First his statement back at the Cavrilhu Pirates' asteroid base that he was trying to cut back on his use of the Force, and now at least a tentative admission that he might be trying to do too much. This was progress indeed. "Of course, if you don't do everything, who will?"

From his perch on a rock, Child Of Winds said something, and Luke smiled. "No, Child Of Winds," he said. "Not even a Jedi Master can do everything. In fact"—he threw an odd look at Mara—"sometimes it seems that it's not the job of a Jedi Master to *do* anything."

Builder With Vines made a comment of his own. "Yes," Luke said.

"What did he say?" Mara asked.

"He quoted me what appears to be a Qom Jha proverb," Luke said. "About how many vines woven together are stronger than the same number of vines used separately. I think there must be a variation of that one on practically every planet in the New Republic."

Mara threw a sour look at the Qom Jha. "You know, I used to be able to hear Palpatine's thoughts from anywhere in the Empire. I mean *any-where*—Core Worlds, Mid-Rim, even a jaunt I took once to the edge of the Outer Rim."

"And yet you can't hear the Qom Jha or Qom Qae from across the room," Luke said. "Must be annoying."

"'Annoying' isn't exactly the word I was hunting for," Mara said acidly. "How come you can hear them and I can't? If it's not some professional Jedi secret."

His emotions remained unruffled. "Actually, that's exactly what it is," he said. "Not a secret, really, but the fact that you're not a Jedi."

"What, because I haven't been through your academy?" Mara scoffed.

"Not at all," Luke said. "There are ways to become a Jedi without going through an academy." He hesitated, just noticeably. "But as long as we're on the subject, why *didn't* you come back?"

She studied his face, wondering if this was a subject she really wanted to get into right now. "I had better things to do," she said instead.

"I see," Luke said; and this time she *did* sense a twitch in his emotions. "Such as flying all over the New Republic with Lando, for instance?"

"Well, well," Mara said, arching her eyebrows slightly. "Do I detect a note of jealousy?"

Once again, he surprised her. The flicker of emotion, rather than flaming to life like an ember in a breeze, faded instead into a sort of gentle sadness. "Not jealousy," he said quietly. "Disappointment. I'd always hoped you would come back and complete your training."

"You didn't hope hard enough," Mara said, forcing down a flicker of old bitterness of her own. "I thought that after all we'd been through together on Myrkr and Wayland I deserved at least a little special consideration from you. But every time I showed up, you said hello and then basically ignored me. Kyp Durron or one of those other kids—they're the ones who got all your attention."

Luke winced. "You're right," he conceded. "I thought . . . I suppose I was thinking that you didn't need as much attention as they did. Kyp was younger, more inexperienced . . ." He trailed off.

"And see what it got you," Mara couldn't resist pointing out. "He nearly wrecked the whole academy, not to mention you and the New Republic and everything else that got in his way."

"It wasn't all his fault," Luke said. "The Sith Lord Exar Kun was driving him toward the dark side."

"Do tell," Mara said, aware that she was drifting straight back into territory she had already decided to avoid for the moment. "And whose idea was it to set up the academy at Yavin in the first place? *And* who decided to leave it there after that mess with Exar Kun was finally sorted out?"

"I did," Luke said, his eyes steady on her face. "What are you getting at?"

Mara grimaced. This was *not* the time or the place to get into this. "All I'm saying is that you're not infallible," she said, once again deflecting the matter. "That by itself ought to be enough reason for you not to try to do it all yourself."

"Hey, I'm not arguing," Luke protested with a faint smile. "I'm a reformed person—really. I let you handle your own lightsaber back at that chamber, didn't I?"

"Thanks for reminding me," Mara said, feeling her cheeks warming with embarrassment. "I really thought I had better control than that."

"It's the long, sustained control that's often the hardest to master," Luke said. "But I've found some special techniques for that. Here, lift up your lightsaber and I'll show you."

Shifting her hip to free the lightsaber—and to incidentally move her leg off a rock that was starting to become uncomfortably sharp—Mara lifted the weapon out in front of her. "You want it on?" she asked, getting a Force grip on it and dropping her hand away.

"No, that's not necessary," Luke said. "All right, now, hold the lightsaber steady in front of you. I want you to keep an eye on it but to also visualize it in your mind, just the way it's hovering there. Can you do that?"

Mara half closed her eyes, her mind flashing back to their trek through the Wayland forest ten years ago. There, too, Luke had slipped easily into the role of teacher, with her taking the role of student.

But a lot had changed since then. And this time, perhaps, she would be the one who would be presenting the most important lesson. "Okay, I've got it," she told him. "What next?"

Mara was a quick study, as Luke had noted in the past, and easily picked up the rudiments of the focusing technique. He kept her practicing with it for another half hour, and then it was time to move on.

"I hope your droid's not going to run out of power before we get there," Mara commented as Luke used the Force to lift Artoo over yet another section of claw-slash ground. "I'd hate to think we'd dragged him all this way just so he could become a floor decoration."

"He'll be all right," Luke said. "He's not using much power right now, and your droid fitted him with some extra power packs on the way in."

"Wait a second," Mara said, frowning. "*My* droid, Slips? I thought you said you came by X-wing."

"We came down to the planet by X-wing, yes," Luke said. "But we came into the system in the *Jade's Fire.* I guess I forgot to mention that."

"I guess you did," Mara said shortly, a flush of anger making Luke wince as it flowed through her emotions. "Who in blazes gave you permission—? Never mind. It was Karrde, wasn't it?"

"He pointed out that your Defender doesn't have a hyperdrive," Luke said, hearing the defensiveness in his voice. "Two people in an X-wing cockpit gets pretty cozy."

"No, you're right," Mara said reluctantly, and he could sense her forcing back her reflexive protectiveness toward the one thing in the universe she truly owned. "You'd just better have it well hidden out there. And I mean *really* well hidden."

"It is," Luke assured her. "I know how much that ship means to you."

"You'd better not have scratched the paint, either," she warned. "I don't suppose you thought to bring the beckon call?"

"Actually, I did," Luke said, frowning slightly as he dug into one of the pockets of his jumpsuit. For some unknown reason an old memory flashed back: the time he'd gone back to Dagobah and stumbled across an old beckon call from some pre–Clone Wars ship. He hadn't known what it was, but Artoo had remembered seeing Lando once with a similar device, and so they'd headed to Lando's mining operation on Nkllon to ask him about it. Arriving just in time, as it happened, to help Han and Leia fight off a raid by Grand Admiral Thrawn.

But why should that particular memory come rising back now? Because Mara was here, and he'd seen his first vision of her at that same time? Or was it something about that ancient beckon call—or the *Fire*'s beckon call, or beckon calls in general—that was triggering something deep in his mind?

Mara was looking oddly at him. "Trouble?" she asked.

"Stray thoughts," Luke said, pulling out the beckon call and handing it to her. "You're not going to be able to call the *Fire* from here, though. We're way out of range, and I seem to remember the beckon call being strictly line-of-sight."

"No, there's also a broadcast setting," Mara said. "But the range *is* pretty limited. Still, there may be transmitters in the High Tower I can run the call signal through."

She sent him one last glower on the subject. "Though you can bet I won't bring it out of hiding until and unless we can neutralize their nest of fighters. Speaking of which, you never told me what happened with the pair you ran into."

"There's not much to tell," Luke said, unhooking his lightsaber and igniting it. A quick swipe, and yet another stalactite blocking their path went crashing to the ground in front of him. "They told me to stay with them, then ran through a series of quick maneuvers. I thought at the time they might be looking for an excuse to open fire."

"More likely wanted to see what kind of craft and pilot they were dealing with," Mara suggested.

"That was the conclusion I ended up with, too," Luke agreed, stretching out with the Force to lift Artoo over the shattered stalactite. "Anyway, they waited until we were a few kilometers from the High Tower and then opened fire. I ducked into that series of canyons your record showed and managed to lose them."

Mara was silent a moment. "You said they told you to stay with them. They spoke Basic?"

"Eventually," Luke said. "But they started off with the same message you and Karrde picked up when that other ship buzzed by Booster Terrik's Star Destroyer."

"Karrde gave you that, I take it," Mara said, her emotions turning suddenly darker. "Did he give you the rest of it?"

"He gave me your landing data," Luke said. "Was there more?"

"Yes, and none of it good," Mara said. "Point one is that Thrawn's name is buried in that message. Point two is that your sister recovered a damaged datacard near Mount Tantiss that was labeled 'The Hand of Thrawn.'"

The Hand of Thrawn. "I don't like the sound of that," Luke said.

"No one else who's heard it does, either," Mara agreed grimly. "The question is, what does it mean?"

"You were called the Emperor's Hand," Luke reminded her. "Could Thrawn have had that kind of agent?"

"That's the first thing everyone else has asked, too," Mara said, and Luke sensed a brief flicker of annoyance from her. "That, or whether it could be a superweapon like another Death Star. But neither of those were really his style."

Luke snorted. "No, his style was to rancor-roll some brilliant strategy over everyone."

"Succinctly put," Mara said. "Still, the datacard came out of the Emperor's private storehouse, so it must mean *something*. Palpatine wouldn't have created disinformation just for his own private amusement."

"Well, whatever it means, it would seem our friends in the High Tower are somehow connected to Thrawn," Luke said. "I wonder if they could be a group of his people."

"Oh, *there's* a cheery thought," Mara growled. "Let's just hope the whole species doesn't have the same tactical genius he did."

"Yes," Luke murmured.

But even as he ignited his lightsaber to clear more of the rock from their path another sobering thought occurred to him. If the Hand of Thrawn hadn't been an assassin or special agent . . .

"You're thinking again," Mara cut into his musings. "Come on, let's have it."

"I was just thinking that maybe the Hand of Thrawn might have been a student," Luke said, turning to look at her. "Someone he might have been grooming to take his place if anything happened to him."

"So where is he?" Mara asked. "I mean, it's been ten years. Why hasn't he shown up before now?"

"Maybe the Hand didn't think he was ready yet," Luke suggested. "Maybe he thought he needed more time or training before he could take Thrawn's place."

"Or else," Mara said, and in the harshly shadowed light of the glow rods her face was suddenly tight, "he's been waiting for just the right moment to make his move."

Luke took a deep breath, the cool cavern air tasting suddenly a little colder. "Like the moment when the New Republic is poised to tear itself apart over the Caamas issue."

"It's exactly how Thrawn would take advantage of the situation," Mara said. "In fact, with Imperial resources whittled down to practically nothing, it's about the only thing he *could* do."

For a long moment they just looked at each other, neither speaking. "I think," Mara said at last, "we'd better get into that tower and see just what's going on up there."

"I think you're right," Luke said, turning his glow rod in the direction of their travel and boosting its power another notch. About five meters ahead, the passageway they were in seemed to open up into a large chamber, large enough at any rate to swallow up the glow rod's beam. He took a step forward—

And paused as a subtle sensation tickled at the back of his mind. Somewhere up ahead . . .

"I've got it, too," Mara muttered from behind him. "Doesn't feel like my usual danger warnings, though."

"Maybe it's not all that dangerous," Luke said. "At least, not to us."

Artoo warbled, a sound that managed to be suspicious and forlorn at the same time. "He wasn't talking about you," Mara assured the droid. "You see it, Luke?"

"Yes," Luke said, smiling tightly. Up ahead, their three Qom Jha guides, who up until now had ranged freely back and forth ahead of their slower ground-walking charges, had all taken up rock perches just this side of the cavern mouth. "I'd say there's something in there they're not anxious to run into."

"Which they seem to have forgotten to tell us about," Mara pointed out. "Another test?"

"Could be," Luke said. "No—Child Of Winds, stay back here."

I see no danger, the young Qom Qae protested. But he nevertheless obediently swooped to a landing on a stalagmite near the opening. *What is the danger?*

"We're about to find out," Luke told him, getting a grip on his lightsaber and easing toward the cavern. "Mara?"

"Right behind you," she said. "Want me to handle the lights?"

"Please," Luke said, handing his glow rod over his shoulder to her. Stretching out with all his senses, he stepped into the opening.

For a long minute he stood there motionlessly, studying the terrain as Mara swept the beams from the glow rods slowly around. The chamber was impressively large and high-ceilinged, with a handful of shallow channels conducting rippling streams of water across the otherwise more or less flat floor. There were none of the stalagmites and stalactites they'd had to put up with through the rest of the cave system, but the lower wall areas were pockmarked with dozens of half-meter-diameter holes that seemed to extend deeply back into the rock. The whole chamber—walls, ceiling, floor, even the creek beds—was covered with what looked to be a thick coating of a white mosslike substance. At the far side, the chamber again shrank down to a tunnel like the one they were standing in.

"There must be openings to the surface," Mara said quietly, her breath a momentary warmth on the back of his neck. "No light, but you can feel the air moving. And there's water, too."

"Yes," Luke murmured. Air, water, and a plant base—even a moss one—meant there could be a complete ecology down here.

An ecology that might well include predators . . .

"You want to offer it a ration bar?" Mara suggested.

"Let's try a rock first," Luke said, stooping down to pick up a fist-sized stone. He threw it out toward the center of the chamber; and as it arced toward the floor, he caught it in a Force grip and twisted it sharply to the side—

And abruptly something snapped out from one of the walls and back again.

And in that movement, the stone vanished.

"Whoa!" Luke said, looking over at that part of the wall as Mara swung the glow rods that direction. "Did you see where that came from?"

"Somewhere over there, I think," Mara said. "It went by too fast—there. See it?"

Luke nodded. From one of the deep holes in the wall, a brief cascade of gravel dribbled silently out down the white moss. There was some movement from the moss as the gravel passed, then it settled down again and the chamber was again silent and still.

"I guess it doesn't like rocks," Mara commented.

"We should have gone with the ration bar," Luke agreed, reaching out to the Force and replaying his short-term memory. It didn't help; the grab had been just too fast. "Could you see what it was?"

"Some kind of tongue or tentacle, I'd guess," Mara said. "The main part of the creature is probably inside that hole."

"And he's probably not alone," Luke said, eyeing the other holes around the chamber. "Any suggestions?"

"Well, for starters, we're going to need a closer look at one of them," Mara said. "You picking up any sentience in there?"

Luke stretched out into the chamber with the Force. "No," he told her. "Nothing."

"So they're simple predator animals, then," she said, squeezing into the opening beside him and handing him the glow rods. "That helps. Get out of the way, will you?"

"What are you going to do?" Luke asked, frowning, as she pulled out her lightsaber and ignited it.

"Like I said: get a closer look," she said. Holding the lightsaber out in front of her, she caught it with a Force grip and started it spinning slowly.

Still spinning, it floated off to their left, keeping close in to the wall. It approached one of the holes . . .

And with a flash of light and the multiple crunch of shattered rock, it vanished into the hole.

Mara Jade! Child Of Wings gasped. *Your weapon-claw—*

"It's all right," Luke calmed him. He kept his eyes on the hole, not daring to look at Mara. If she'd miscalculated . . .

And then, with a second loud crumbling of rock, a long sluglike creature sagged out of the hole, covered with pink blood still oozing from a half-dozen deep cuts across its body. Moving in an almost grotesque slow-motion, it slid down the mossy wall and came to a stop against a stone on the ground. A coiled tongue rolled loosely out of the slack mouth, followed by Mara's lightsaber.

There was a gasp from one of the Qom Jha. *So that is what they are like,* Keeper Of Promises said.

"You hadn't seen one before?" Luke asked.

No, the Qom Jha replied. *We did not encounter them until thirty seasons ago.*

Luke cocked an eyebrow. "Really. Weren't they here before that, or had you just not run into them?"

I cannot properly answer that question, Keeper Of Promises said. *Only rarely have the Qom Jha ever come into this part of the cavern.*

"Trouble?" Mara asked as she reached out with the Force to retrieve her lightsaber.

"There seems to be some question as to whether this room was like this up until thirty years ago," Luke told her.

"Interesting," Mara said, looking at her now bloodied lightsaber with distaste. Easing it around the corner into the chamber, she wiped it off on an edge of the white moss. "Could be someone moved into the High Tower about then and wanted to discourage casual tourism."

"That's one possibility," Luke agreed.

"Well, I did mine," Mara said, inspecting her lightsaber again. "You can do the next—what, about thirty of them?"

"About that," Luke confirmed, doing a quick estimate of the number of holes in the cavern's walls. "You think they might be smart enough to realize we're too big to eat?"

"I'd hate to count on it," Mara said. "There's more than enough speed and muscle behind those tongues to break bone."

"Agreed," Luke said. "I don't suppose there would be any path across that would be out of their range."

"Wouldn't want to count on that, either," Mara said. "Anyway, it seems straightforward enough. We hug one wall and slice up each of them from the side as we get to it."

Luke grimaced. Straightforward enough, certainly, but rather bloody. The creatures *were* nonsentient, of course, and it *was* vitally important that he and Mara get past them. But he still didn't relish the idea of so much wholesale slaughter.

But maybe there was another way. "Keeper Of Promises, you've obviously run into these things before," he said, looking back over his shoulder. "What do they eat?"

Keeper Of Promises fluttered his wings. *There are migrations of insects at the beginning and closing of each season.*

"Hmm?" Mara asked.

"Migrating insects," Luke translated.

"Ah," Mara said. "Except when they can get fresh Qom Jha, I suppose."

Splitter Of Stones ruffled his wings warningly. *Do not be insulting, Jaded Of Mara.*

"Of course, that doesn't explain what they're eating right now," Mara went on. "Not much in the way of insects down here at the moment."

"At least not any visible ones," Luke said. Closing down his lightsaber, he eased into the chamber, keeping close to the wall. Extending his lightsaber handle out as far as he could, he gave the moss a sharp whack.

There was a sudden rumbling buzz; and abruptly a dozen large insects burst from unseen cavities in the moss, flying off madly across the chamber in all directions.

They didn't get very far. As suddenly as the insects had appeared there was a flurry of snapping tongues, and a moment later the chamber again settled down into silence.

Behind Luke, Artoo gurgled nervously. "Interesting," Mara commented. "That moss layer must be thicker than it looks." She eyed Luke. "I hope you're not going to suggest we beat the walls and try to sneak across while the feeding frenzy is going on."

"You're half right," Luke said, igniting his lightsaber and again stepping into the chamber. Easing the glowing blade tip into the moss, he carefully cut a meter-wide square of the material out of the general expanse. He closed down the weapon and returned it to his belt, got a good grip on the edges, and pulled.

With an oddly discomfiting tearing sound, a fifteen-centimeter-thick patch came away. Luke caught it across his forearms, trying to hold it more or less together, wincing at the sight of a hundred suddenly disturbed grubs scurrying across the surface or burrowing back into the moss.

"Lovely," Mara said, coming to his side. "And now it's feeding time?"

"That's the plan," Luke said, easing over toward the next hole in line and lobbing the patch in front of it. The tongue snapped out, and in a flurry of moss dust the patch vanished.

"Let's see if it worked," Mara said, stepping past Luke and stretching her lightsaber blade in front of the hole.

Nothing happened. "Looks good," she decided. "Better get the droid past while he's still chewing."

"Right," Luke said, turning and getting a Force grip on Artoo. "Child Of Winds, Qom Jha—let's go."

A minute later they were all on the far side of the lair. "Well, *I'm* impressed," Mara declared, easing out of her guard stance to join them.

"And it didn't require us to kill," Luke pointed out, igniting his lightsaber and stepping over toward the next predator lair.

"Except a bunch of insects," Mara said. "You have a problem with insects, by the way?"

He thought he'd been hiding it better than that. "They remind me of those droch things, that's all. No problem."

"Ah," Mara said, closing down her lightsaber and stepping around behind Luke. "Tell you what: you cut, and I'll peel. Okay?"

Two hours later, they finally stopped for the night.

"At least, I *think* it's night," Luke said, frowning at his chrono. "I just realized I never got around to changing this thing to local time."

"It's night," Mara assured him, leaning thankfully back against her chosen rock and closing her eyes. Later, she knew, she would pay for this with numerous aches and pains from the dampness and sharp edges. But at the moment it felt immensely good. "Night is defined as time for all good little boys and girls to go to sleep. Therefore, it is definitely night."

"I suppose so," Luke said.

Mara opened her eyes and peered across at him. There had been a flicker of something in his emotions just then. "No?" she asked.

He shook his head. "No, you're right," he conceded, a bit reluctantly. "We need to sleep."

Instead of what? Mara stretched out with the Force, trying to read deeper into his mind. But the way was blocked, with nothing she could detect except a barrier of uncertainty tinged with—

She frowned. Embarrassment? Was that really what she was getting?

It was. And for the great Jedi Master Luke Skywalker to even have such an emotion was definitely evidence of progress.

And given that, the last thing she wanted to do was make it easy for him. When he was finally willing to crack his shell far enough to ask her about her relationship with Lando, she would tell him. Not before.

And maybe by that time he would be able to hear the other, more troubling things she had to say to him.

Maybe.

CHAPTER

"So that's it, huh?" Wedge asked, leaning nonchalantly against one of the old-style Bothan lampposts that lined the park and gazing across the open expanse at the gleaming white dome in the center.

"That's it," Corran confirmed, frowning at his datapad. "At least, according to this it is."

Wedge shifted his gaze to the periphery of the park, to the encircling street and the shops with their colorful trade flags that lined it. It was apparently market day, and hundreds of Bothan and alien pedestrians were milling through the area. "They must be nuts," he told Corran. "Putting a target like that—"

He broke off as a couple of Duros brushed past him and headed off at an angle across the park. "In a public area," he continued in a lower tone, "is just begging for trouble."

"On the other hand, having a pole of your planetary shield array inside your capital city pretty much guarantees the safety of that city," Corran pointed out. "That's going to be comforting to all the offworlders who do business here."

"The Bothans always *have* been big on image," Wedge conceded sourly.

Even so, he had to admit the place wasn't nearly as vulnerable as it looked. According to the data Bel Iblis had pulled for them, the dome was constructed of a special permasteel alloy, had no windows and only one door, and was filled with armed guards and automated defenses. The shield generator equipment itself was two floors underground, with a self-contained backup power supply, a room full of spare parts, and a cadre of on-duty techs who could allegedly take the entire system apart and put it back together again in two hours flat.

"True; but image apart, they've also never been slouches at guarding their own rear ends," Corran pointed out. "They'll have safeguards seven ways from—"

He stopped as a group of Bothans, chattering animatedly to each other, pushed their way between the two humans. A pair of stragglers following the main group were even more self-absorbed; one of them ran straight into Wedge, nearly knocking him over.

"My entire clan's apologies, sir," he gasped, his fur rippling with shame and embarrassment as he backed rapidly away directly toward Corran. Corran tried to sidestep, but the Bothan was already moving too fast and slammed into him, too.

"You clumsy fool," the second Bothan berated him, grabbing Corran's arm to help him regain his balance. "You will indebt our entire clan to the sun-death of Bothawui. Our greatest apologies, kind sirs. Are either of you injured?"

"No, we're fine," Wedge assured him. He glanced at Corran for confirmation, caught just the hint of a frown creasing the other's forehead. "On second thought—"

"Excellent, excellent," the Bothan continued, clearly not really interested in the answer to his question as he took his companion's arm and steered them both toward the shops. "A fine and friendsome day to you, then, fine sirs."

Wedge moved close to Corran's side, watching as the two Bothans nearly ran down an old human woman at the edge of the crowd and then vanished into the general pedestrian flow. "What's the matter?" he murmured. "Are you hurt?"

"No," Corran said slowly, his frown deepening. "There was just something that felt wrong about—"

Abruptly, he slapped at his tunic, his frown exploding into a look of utter consternation. "Droyk! He took my wallet!"

"*What?*" Wedge snapped, grabbing for his own pocket.

And finding it empty. "Oh, sh—"

"Come on," Corran bit out, diving into the crowd.

"I don't believe this," Wedge snarled, diving in after him. "How in space did they pull *that* off?"

"I don't know," Corran called over his shoulder, shoving one pedestrian after another aside. "I would have sworn I knew all the tricks. I don't suppose you happened to notice the clan sigil they were wearing?"

"I saw it, but I didn't recognize it," Wedge told him, feeling like a complete and blithering fool. Everything they had—money, credit chits, and both their civilian and military IDs—were in those wallets. "The general's going to kill us if we don't get them back."

"Yeah—one at a time and very slowly," Corran agreed darkly. He shouldered his way through one last clump of pedestrians into a temporarily open spot on the walkway and stopped. "Anything?" he asked, craning his neck to look over the crowds.

"Nothing," Wedge said, looking around and wondering what in the name of Ackbar's aunt they were going to do now. The Bothan government didn't know they were here, and would probably be furious if they found out. Ditto for any New Republic officials. "I don't suppose you might be able to, ah—?"

"If I couldn't pick up anything when they were right next to me, I'm not likely to be able to do it at this distance," Corran said, sounding thoroughly disgusted with himself. "I hope you've got a backup plan ready."

"I thought *you* brought it," Wedge countered glumly. Unfortunately, about all they could do now was get back on their shuttle and rejoin the *Peregrine* at Ord Trasi.

General Bel Iblis, it was rumored, had an awesome repertoire of Corellian invective that only came to the surface when he was absolutely furious. Wedge himself had never personally been able to confirm the rumor. It seemed likely he would soon have the chance to do so. "You're never going to live this one down with Mirax," he warned with a sigh.

"Right—like you're going to be able to live it down with Iella," Corran growled back.

"Hey, there, my fine young boys. Join me for a drink?"

Wedge turned, to find an old woman with bright eyes standing beside him. "What?"

"I asked you to join me for a drink," she repeated. "It's such a warm day, and all that bright sunlight is hard on old eyes like mine."

"Sorry, but we're a little busy right now," Corran said brusquely, standing on tiptoe to peer again over the crowd.

"You young people," the woman said reproachfully. "Always too busy to sit down and enjoy life. Too busy to listen to the wisdom of the aged."

Wedge grimaced, turning his attention back to the crowd and hoping the old fool would take the hint. What she was doing ore-digging on the streets of Drev'starn in the first place he couldn't imagine. "Look, ma'am, I'm sorry—"

"But too busy to share a drink with a lonely old lady?" she went on, her voice turning sorrowful. "That's just plain scandalous. Especially when the lonely old lady is buying."

Wedge looked back, searching for a firm yet polite way to get her off his back. "Look, ma'am—"

And paused. Her hand had come up now and was holding two items up for his inspection. Two small, black folders.

Their wallets.

Wedge felt his mouth drop open a few millimeters, focusing for the first time on her face. It was the same woman the two pickpockets had bumped into during their hasty getaway. "Ah, Corran?" he said, reaching out and taking the wallets from the woman's hand. "Never mind."

"Wha—?" Corran demanded, the word strangling off midway as Wedge held out his wallet to him. Warily, he took it, his eyes leaving the woman just long enough to confirm that everything was still there. "May I ask how you came into possession of these?"

The woman chuckled, shaking her head. "You CorSec people are a stitch. Do they program you for sound, or just feed you the manuals?"

Corran glanced at Wedge. "We like to be precise," he said, his voice cautiously offended. "And it's *former* CorSec."

"Whatever," she said with a shrug. "Either way, you boys ought to be more careful—those are nice family holos you've got in there, and I'd hate to see you lose them. Now, Wedge, how about that drink? We really do have a lot to talk about."

"Yes, why not?" Wedge agreed cautiously, a whole list of unpleasant possibilities running through his mind. If she fingered them to the local criminal groups—or worse, to the Vengeance organization—or even if she merely demanded a hefty reward—"You obviously already know our names. And you are . . . ?"

"Moranda Savich," she said. "Sort of a second-string employee of your old friend Talon Karrde.

"And on second thought, you two are buying."

The waiter droid delivered their drinks, spilling the obligatory few drops onto the carved stone table, accepted Wedge's coin, and departed. "*Chakta sai kae*," Moranda said, lifting her glass. "Did I get it right, Corran? I've never been sure of the proper Corellian pronunciation for that toast."

"Close enough," Corran growled, lifting his gaze with obvious reluctance from the datapad and looking at Wedge. "Well?"

Wedge shrugged. "It looked okay to me."

" 'Okay' isn't good enough," Corran said darkly. "I also notice that the only way to confirm that this letter of introduction is really from Karrde would be to run the ID codes through Coruscant."

"So get your tails over to the New Republic liaison office and have them do that," Moranda said, taking a long drink of the pale blue-green liqueur she'd ordered. "We aren't exactly fat on time here, you know."

"Yes," Wedge murmured, trying to read that so totally unconcerned face. "Unfortunately . . ."

"Unfortunately, you can't do that?" she suggested, peering at Wedge over her glass. "Yes, I thought so. Awkward."

"Why do you say that?" Corran demanded.

"Why do I say what?" Moranda countered. "That you're on your own, or that that's awkward?"

"The first," Corran said. "You sound like you almost expected that."

"Oh, come on," she said scornfully. "I *did* get a long look into your wallets, remember. What other conclusion is there when you've got your military IDs buried back behind the civilian ones?"

"Exactly," Corran said, fixing her with the kind of glare that Wedge decided was probably standard Corellian Security issue. "Which means you already knew we couldn't check up on this story before you spun it for us."

"And what, created that on the fly?" she asked, pointing toward the datacard still in his datapad.

"Or had it sitting in with your collection of a dozen other forgeries," Corran shot back. "How are we supposed to know?"

Lifting her glass, Moranda drained it. "Never mind," she said, getting to her feet. "I assumed we were on the same side here, and thought we might be able to help each other. Apparently we can't. Try to hold on to your wallets a little better next time."

Wedge looked at Corran, caught the other's fractional nod. "Please; sit down, Moranda," he said, half rising from his own chair and catching her arm. It felt painfully thin beneath her sleeve. "Please."

She paused, throwing a speculative look at each of them. Then, smiling tightly at Wedge, she resumed her seat. "A test, I presume. Did I pass?"

"Well enough for us to at least listen some more," Wedge told her. "Let's start with exactly why you're here."

"Presumably the same reason you are," she said. "Karrde sees an explosion coming, with the Bothans in the middle of it, and wants to see if there are outside forces planning to squeeze the detonators."

"And you're all he could spare?" Corran suggested.

"Hardly," Moranda said. "He's got people all over the New Republic tracking personnel and equipment movements. Other people are sifting through every report and hint and speculation that crops up. I just happen to be the one on the ground here."

"With what instructions?" Wedge asked.

Moranda nodded in the direction of the tapcafe door. "There's a lot of firepower in orbit up there," she said. "They could start shooting at each other anytime. But if anyone wants to take a poke at Bothawui itself, they'll have to get rid of the planetary shields first. Karrde asked me to keep an eye on them."

"Is that why you were hanging around the Drev'starn generator?" Wedge asked. "Trying to see how someone might get inside?"

"I'd already done that," she said. "Actually, I was out there today seeing if I could spot anyone else casing the place." She smiled maliciously. "Which is why I latched on to you two. No offense, but you stand out in a crowd like a Wookiee at a Noghri family reunion."

Wedge nodded as understanding struck. "Is that why you had our pockets picked? So you could find out who we were?"

Moranda's thin lips twitched. "As a matter of fact, no, I didn't. I just happened to be watching when those Bothans lifted your stuff and made sure I'd be in position to lift it back from them."

Wedge looked at Corran. "You thinking what I'm thinking?"

"That someone may have noticed us," Corran said, running a careful glance around the tapcafe. "Could be. I don't suppose you might have any idea where those two pickpockets might have gone to ground, do you?"

"Sorry," Moranda said, shaking her head. "I only got here a couple of days ago and haven't had a chance to link up with the local fringe."

"But you *could* link up with them if you wanted to?" Wedge asked, still trying to get a feel for this woman. Karrde he more or less trusted; but Karrde had a huge organization, and he couldn't possibly know everyone in it personally. Moranda Savich could easily be playing both ends against the middle, or bleeding Karrde's organization for her own purposes, or even just using him for free room and board whenever she was between more unsavory jobs. If someone from Vengeance, say, were to offer her a big enough pot of money to betray him and Corran, would she do it?

Moranda sighed. "Look, Wedge," she said quietly. "I used to do a fair amount of con work, and in con work you learn how to read people's faces. I can tell you don't trust me. And I really don't blame you—we *have* just met, after all. But I've got that letter from Karrde, and I *did* get your wallets back. Offhand, I don't know what else I can do to persuade you."

"But you *do* want to persuade us," Corran said.

She smiled, a tight, brittle thing. "I was given an assignment," she said simply.

Wedge suppressed a grimace. He still felt odd about this, but her arguments *did* seem to make sense. If anything turned up later, Corran's Jedi senses would hopefully pick it up. "All right," he said. "For the moment, at least, let's pool resources. Any suggestions?"

"Well, obviously, the first thing we need to do is find out if anyone suspicious has arrived since that orbiting research station was destroyed a week ago," Moranda said, her tone all business now. "That's what started this whole military buildup, after all. If Vengeance decided to take advantage of that, they may have needed to move more of their people here."

"Vengeance or anyone else," Corran murmured. "The Empire, for example."

"Seems reasonable," Wedge agreed. "There's only one problem. That information is locked up over in the Bothawui Customs computers, and we haven't got access to it."

"Oh, that's no problem," Moranda assured him with an airy wave of her hand. "Come on, finish up, and we'll go to your place and talk about it."

"Sure," Wedge said, taking a long sip from his as yet untouched drink and getting to his feet. Whatever happened here, he decided, this was going to be most interesting.

Not that that was necessarily a good thing.

"Really?" Navett said into his comlink, looking up as Klif came into the Exoticalia Pet Emporium and closed the door behind him. "Hey, that's great. When can I come by and pick 'em up?"

"Anytime you wish," the Bothan Customs official's voice came from the comlink. From the background came the faint sound of a sneeze. "Preferably soon," he added.

"You bet we will," Navett said cheerfully. "Got customers coming in already wantin' to see what we got, and we have to tell 'em we haven't got anything yet. We can come over now, right?"

"I believe I've already answered that question," the Bothan replied as another sneeze sounded in the background.

"Oh—right," Navett said as Klif came over. "Great. Thanks a lot."

"A day of peace and profit to you."

"Yeah, same to you."

He shut the comlink off. "We're in," he told Klif, putting the instrument away. "And from the sneezing, I'd say at least some of the Bothans are allergic to our little polpians."

"Should make them eager to get rid of them," Klif said.

"I think it already did," Navett agreed. "You see Horvic?"

Klif nodded. "He and Pensin are in as maintenance staff for that Ho'Din dive two blocks back from the shield generator. Post-closing shift."

"Perfect," Navett said. If their schematics were right, that tapcafe was directly over one of the underground conduits carrying power cables into the place.

"Yeah." Klif's face soured. "Now for the bad news. The two Bothan lifters we hired muffed the job."

Navett swore. He should have known better than to trust local talent. "They get caught?"

"According to them, the actual lift went smooth as lake ice." Klif grimaced. "It's just that when they got back to me, they didn't have the wallets anymore."

Navett felt his eyes narrow. "What do you mean, they didn't have them?"

"Just what I said: they lost them. Best guess is that someone in the crowd saw them lift the wallets and returned the favor."

"You're sure they didn't just pocket the cash themselves?"

Klif shrugged. "Not absolutely sure, no. But it's hard to believe a pair of New Rep agents would be carrying more cash than I was offering." He pursed his lips. "Unless, of course, they *aren't* New Rep agents."

Navett pulled over a chair and settled thoughtfully into it. Could he have been mistaken about them?

"No," he answered his own question. "No, they're New Rep, all right. Probably military, too, from the look of them. The question is, who is this new skifter who's joined the party?"

"You don't think it was just another lifter taking advantage of the situation?" Klif asked.

Navett cocked an eyebrow. "Do you?"

"No, not really," Klif said heavily. "Too much danger of getting caught with the goods when the marks woke up."

"My point exactly," Navett said. "No, they've picked up a fringe ally. A very *good* fringe ally, too, from the sound of it."

Klif hissed softly between his teeth. "We don't have anyone to spare for a proper surveillance," he reminded Navett. "Maybe we ought to get rid of them."

Navett scratched his cheek. It was a tempting suggestion. A tricky job on a tight timetable was bad enough without New Rep military agents snooping around. If they could be quietly eliminated . . .

"No," he said. "Not yet. They can't possibly be on to us. We'll keep an eye out, and if they seem to be taking too much interest in us we may have to do something about it. But for right now, we'll let them be."

Klif's lip twitched. "You're the boss," he said. "I hope you're not making a mistake."

"If I am, it's a mistake that's easily corrected," Navett said, standing up. "Come on. Let's put on our earnest-but-stupid faces and go get our animals."

CHAPTER

From somewhere in the far distance came the warbling call of Noghri combat code. "The ship is approaching," Barkhimkh translated. "Sakhisakh can see it."

"I'll take his word for it," Leia said. Hemmed in by the closely spaced trees that clustered on this small hill overlooking Pakrik Minor's North Barris Spaceport, she could see precious little but greenery around her, a minuscule patch of blue sky directly above her, and the landspeeder they'd borrowed from Sabmin beneath her.

A slightly awkward situation, in her opinion, and probably unnecessary, besides. Given that that transmission had carried Bel Iblis's personal signature code and bridgebreak confirmation, it could be no one but the general on that incoming ship. But her Noghri guards hadn't wanted her to show herself until the ship's occupant was positively identified, and for the sake of their concerns she had agreed to do this their way.

She could hear the approaching ship now. "Sounds pretty small," she said, running through her Jedi sensory enhancement exercises to boost the distant whine into something clearer.

"It does indeed," Barkhimkh's quiet agreement boomed uncomfortably loudly in her sensitized hearing. "I will observe."

There was the crash of a body moving through foliage, the thunderous noise fading to whispers as Leia reduced her hearing back to its normal level. In the distance she heard the whine blip up, then drop off sharply as the ship settled onto its pad and powered down.

The sound faded away completely, and for a long minute there was nothing but the rustling of leaves around her. Leia waited, wondering what was going on out there. The grandly named spaceport was actually little more than a large open field with a handful of permacrete landing pads scattered around; it shouldn't take this long for Sakhisakh to get over to the ship and check it out.

Unless there was some kind of trouble. She stretched out to the Force, seeking guidance . . .

And then, drifting in on the breeze, came a second Noghri battle call. "There is no danger, and we may come," Barkhimkh said from her side, his voice slightly puzzled. "But he warns that all is not as expected."

Leia frowned. Not as expected? "What does that mean? Isn't Garm there?"

"I do not know," Barkhimkh said, climbing into the landspeeder and keying its repulsorlifts. "I could see only that the ship was indeed small, as you had already ascertained, and that it bore no markings."

"No markings?" Leia asked carefully. "None?"

"None that I could see," Barkhimkh said again, easing the landspeeder through the trees. "Perhaps at a closer distance they will be visible."

Aside from a dilapidated grain freighter at the far end of the field, the newcomer was the only ship in sight. It was indeed a small vessel, probably a two-person craft, with the lines of a diplomatic shuttle but of a design Leia couldn't remember ever having seen before. At the bow, where a diplomatic ship would have carried governmental markings, there was nothing. Midway along the side, the hatchway stood open, with a short ramp leading down from it to the permacrete. "Has Sakhisakh gone inside?" she asked.

"Yes," Barkhimkh answered. "He is waiting with the pilot and passenger."

Pilot *and* passenger? Leia nodded mechanically, her eyes on the ship's bow. Now, as they neared the craft, she could see for the first time that there were indeed faint markings on the hull where some sort of insignia had once been.

And even with just the outlines visible, there was something vaguely familiar about the design. Something that was triggering an equally vague but nevertheless disturbing memory . . .

The landspeeder came to a stop at the ramp. "Councilor Organa Solo," Sakhisakh called down gravely from the open hatchway. "Your visitor humbly requests the honor of your presence."

"Of course," Leia said, matching the Noghri's formal tone. Sakhisakh knew Bel Iblis quite well; who could be in there that would make him go all formal this way? "Would my visitor like to present his request in person?"

"He would," Sakhisakh said, bowing slightly and stepping back out of the hatchway.

And as he did so, a new figure stepped into view. A tall humanoid, covered with soft golden down, with subtle purple markings around his eyes and shoulders. "Peace to you, High Councilor Leia Organa Solo," he said, his voice smooth and rich, yet with an undertone of deep and ancient sadness to it. "I am Elegos A'kla, Trustant for the Caamasi Remnant. Will you join me aboard my ship?"

Leia swallowed hard as the memories came flooding back. Her visit as a child to the secret Caamasi refugee camps on Alderaan, and the hundreds of colorful flags flying Caamasi family crests that she'd seen there.

Crests like the one that had been removed from the bow of Elegos's ship. "Yes, Trustant A'kla," she said. "I would be honored."

"Please forgive my intrusion upon your privacy," the Caamasi said, backing away as she started up the ramp. "I am told you and your bondmate came here for rest, and I would not normally have violated your aloneness. But I greatly wished to speak with you; and the one whom I brought with me said his errand was important to the point of terrible urgency."

"And that person is?" Leia asked as she stepped into the ship, stretching out with the Force. There was definitely someone else here. Someone familiar . . .

"I believe you are acquainted with him," Elegos said, stepping out of the way to the side.

And there in a chair in the back of the room, squirming nervously under Sakhisakh's watchful eye—

"Ghent!" Leia exclaimed. "What in the name of the Force are you doing here?"

"I needed to talk to you right away," Ghent said, his voice sounding even more nervous than he looked as he bounded out of the chair. "I wanted General Bel Iblis, but he's missing and I can't get hold of him. And you're President of the New Republic and all, so—"

"I'm not actually President at the moment, Ghent," Leia interrupted him gently. "I'm on a leave of absence. Ponc Gavrisom is in charge of the government."

Ghent blinked in surprise, and in spite of the seriousness in his manner Leia had to fight to keep from smiling. Ghent had once been Talon Karrde's top slicer, with such an awesome talent for breaking into and otherwise manipulating computer systems that Bel Iblis had made it his personal goal to lure the kid away from Karrde's organization. In the years since the general had succeeded in doing so, Ghent had proved himself over and over, rising steadily through the ranks until he now held the post of Crypt Chief.

But away from his beloved computers, the young man was about as naive and innocent and lost as it was humanly possible to be. The fact that, living in the heart of Coruscant, he'd still managed to miss Leia's leave of absence entirely was just about normal for him.

"Perhaps she can still be of assistance," Elegos suggested, stepping into Ghent's embarrassed consternation with typical Caamasi aplomb. "Why don't you tell her why you're here?"

"Yeah, sure," Ghent said, recovering his voice and digging a datapad out of an old and worn holder on his belt. "You see, General Bel Iblis gave me a datacard—"

"One moment," Sakhisakh's harsh voice cut him off. "Was it you who sent Councilor Organa Solo a message over Bel Iblis's name?"

"Well, uh . . . yeah," Ghent admitted, eyeing the Noghri warily. "I wanted the general, you see, but I couldn't get to him. And I found out Leia was here—"

"What do you mean you couldn't get to him?" Leia interrupted. "Where is he? Has something happened?"

"No, no, he's off in Kothlis system," Ghent assured her quickly, his eyes reluctantly shifting away from the Noghri to her. "Some kind of ship buildup—I don't know what for. But I couldn't get a message through to him, not even with top clearance codes. So when I found out you were here—"

"How did you find out she was here?" Sakhisakh demanded.

Ghent squirmed again. "Well . . . it was in Gavrisom's files. I mean, I wouldn't usually slice into High Council stuff, but it was *really* important. And then I met him—" He waved helplessly at Elegos.

"I was waiting at your office for you," the Caamasi spoke up, his voice sending a wave of welcome calmness through the room. "As my two colleagues made clear when you spoke with them, we are deeply concerned about the direction this matter has taken. Now, with overt threats toward the Bothan people, that concern has been greatly magnified."

He shrugged, the gesture rippling through his entire back up to his shoulders. "I had of course planned to wait until you returned to speak further with you. But Crypt Chief Ghent was so insistent that he see you immediately that I offered him transport, provided he was able to locate you."

"And provided he could use Garm's private signature code to make sure I'd come to the spaceport?" Leia asked, lifting her eyebrows at Ghent.

The young slicer winced. "I didn't think you'd come if it was just me," he muttered.

Leia suppressed a sigh. Yes, that was indeed classic Ghent. In actual fact, his name and expertise carried enormous weight among the upper levels of the New Republic government. Another fact he'd undoubtedly missed completely.

And as for bringing Elegos along, Ghent probably didn't have the faintest idea of how to fly a starship himself. Frustrating and annoying, but it all fit. "All right, relax," she said. "The interrogation is over, and all is at least temporarily forgiven. Now. What is this errand that was worth breaking half a dozen laws for?"

Wincing again, Ghent handed her the datapad in his hand. "It's really a message for Bel Iblis," he said. "But—look, just read it, okay?"

Leia took the datapad and keyed it on. On the other hand, she couldn't help wondering, if she'd known that it was only Ghent and not Bel Iblis who wanted to see her, would she have pushed harder for Han to take her along on his trip into the heart of the Empire? Even without Ghent's message the reasons had seemed right and proper at the time. But still . . .

And then the words popped onto the datapad display . . . and an icy chill ran through her. "Where did you get this?" she asked, her voice sounding unreal through the sudden pounding in her ears.

"General Bel Iblis brought it back from Morishim," Ghent said, his voice trembling now, too. "There was a Corellian Corvette that came into the system, only a Star Destroyer caught up with it and took it away."

"I remember reading Garm's private report on that," Leia said. "He wanted the incident kept quiet while he tried to find out what it was all about."

"Well, this was a transmission from the Corvette," Ghent said. "It was all mangled up, but I was able to sort through the jamming and untangle it." He took a noisy breath. "You see why I had to get it to someone right away?"

Leia nodded silently, staring down at the message.

> *—is Colonel Meizh Vermel, special envoy from Admiral Pellaeon, sent here to contact General Bel Iblis concerning the negotiation of a peace treaty between the Empire and New Republic. My ship is under attack by traitorous elements of the Empire, and I do not expect to survive. If the New Republic agrees to hold such discussions, Admiral Pellaeon will be at the abandoned gas mining center on Pesitiin in one month to meet with you. Repeating: This is Colonel Meizh Vermel . . .*

"Councilor?" Sakhisakh murmured quietly from across the room. "Is there trouble?"

Leia looked up at the Noghri, almost startled to find him there as thoughts swirled through her mind. A peace treaty. Not a temporary truce, but an actual, genuine peace. Something she'd been looking for and longing for since the days of Emperor Palpatine and her own youthful decision to oppose him and all he stood for.

And here it was, being offered to them by the Supreme Commander of the entire Imperial Fleet.

Or was it? Pellaeon was only offering to negotiate, after all. Were there preconditions that would be brought up at such a meeting, conditions that would turn the whole exercise into little more than a waste of time or, worse, a propaganda coup for the Empire?

Or was it worse even than that? Was it some sort of trap?

"Councilor?" Sakhisakh repeated, stepping to her side, his large black eyes gazing with concern up at her. "What disturbs you?"

Wordlessly, she handed the datapad to him. Because Pellaeon probably wasn't in charge of the Empire anymore. If Lando was to be believed—and if that wasn't some sort of trick itself—Grand Admiral Thrawn had returned.

And with Thrawn, nothing was ever what it seemed. Ever.

Sakhisakh spat something vicious-sounding in the Noghri language. "You cannot believe this," he growled, thrusting the datapad back at Ghent as if it were something unclean he was disgusted to even touch. "The Empire is the embodiment of lies and treachery. It will never be otherwise."

"It's often been that way, yes," Leia agreed soberly. "On the other hand—"

"There is no other hand!" Sakhisakh snarled. "They betrayed and murdered my people. They betrayed and murdered *your* people."

"I know," Leia murmured, the old ache rising again like acid in her throat.

"And if Thrawn has indeed cheated death," the Noghri went on, his voice turning to something deadly, "then there is even more reason to reject anything the Empire might say."

"Probably," Leia said. And yet . . .

"May I see it?" Elegos asked.

Leia hesitated. Technically, this was highly confidential New Republic business . . . "Yes, of course," she said, handing the datapad to him, her Force-sensitized instincts overruling the strict legalities of the situation. Before the destruction of their world, the Caamasi had been among the greatest mediators and negotiators the Old Republic had ever known, their skills in such matters rivaling even those of the Jedi. Elegos might well have some insight that would help her sort it all out.

For a long minute, the Caamasi studied the datapad in silence. Then, his blue-on-green eyes glittering with emotion, he lifted his gaze to her again. "I see no alternative," he said. "Yes, it may be a trap, but that is not certain. And if there is even a small chance that Admiral Pellaeon is sincere, that chance must be explored."

Sakhisakh regarded the other suspiciously. "I have long admired the Caamasi, Trustant A'kla," he said, his voice on the edge of challenging. "But in this, you speak the words of an unweaned child. Do you truly suggest Bel Iblis walk openly into the Empire's hands?"

"You misunderstand, my friend," Elegos said calmly. "I offer no such course for General Bel Iblis. Indeed, as you have already pointed out, it would be impossible even to suggest it to him."

"Why?" Leia asked.

"Because as Ghent has discovered, we have no means of communicating quickly with him," Elegos said. "And speed is vital, because this opportunity may even now be closing." He touched the datapad. "I do not know when the Morishim incident took place, but it is clear that forces opposing Admiral Pellaeon have already begun to gather against him. Even if all overt attacks have failed, he cannot wait forever for Coruscant's response."

Sakhisakh threw a wary glance at Leia. "Who then do you suggest be asked to walk into the Empire's hands?"

Elegos shook his head. "There is no need to ask anyone," he told the Noghri. "The choice is apparent and obvious. I will go."

Sakhisakh seemed taken aback. "You?"

"Of course," Elegos said. "Councilor Organa Solo, I have an obligation to return Ghent to Coruscant. If you will accept that obligation upon yourself, I can leave for Pesitiin immediately."

Leia sighed. Now, at last, she understood why it had seemed right for her to let Han go to Bastion alone while she waited here. "There's no need, Elegos," she said. "You can take him back yourself. I'll be the one going to Pesitiin."

Sakhisakh made a noise in his throat. "I cannot allow you to do that, Councilor Organa Solo," he rumbled. "To step into such danger—"

"I'm sorry, Sakhisakh," Leia said gently. "But as Elegos said, there's only one choice possible. I'm the only one here who has the authority to negotiate on behalf of the New Republic."

"Then bring someone else in from Coruscant," the Noghri demanded.

"As Elegos has also said, we don't have time," Leia said. "If Pellaeon is on schedule, he's been at Pesitiin for eleven days already. I have to go, and I have to go now." She took a deep breath. "If you can't handle dealing with Imperials, I'll certainly understand. I can take the *Falcon* and go alone."

"Please do not insult me," Sakhisakh said darkly. "Barkhimkh and I will of course accompany you. Even to death, if that is what awaits us."

"Thank you," Leia said. "Thank you, too, Ghent, for bringing this to me. You did the right thing, flagrant illegalities and all. Trustant A'kla, I thank you too for your assistance here."

"Wait a minute," Ghent said, his eyes looking confused again. "You're going out there? Alone?"

"Not alone," Sakhisakh growled. "We will be with her."

"Yeah, sure," Ghent said, looking back and forth between Leia and Elegos. "I meant . . . Elegos? Can't you—you know?"

"Travel alongside her?" the Caamasi said. "Certainly, I would be more than willing to do so. Though I have no official standing with the New Republic, my people have some small skills at negotiation." He regarded Ghent thoughtfully. "But as I have already explained, I have the prior obligation of returning you to Coruscant."

"Unless you're willing to take a shuttle over to Pakrik Major and find a liner to take you back," Leia suggested.

"But I didn't mean for you to—" Ghent's face twisted into something almost painful-looking. "I mean, I only brought you the message because—"

He sighed, a great exhaling of air that seemed to shrink him down like a collapsing balloon. "Okay," he said in resignation. "Yeah, okay. Sure, I'll go with you, too. Why not?"

Leia blinked. It was not the decision she'd been expecting from him. "I appreciate the offer, Ghent," she said. "But it's really not necessary."

"No, no—don't try to talk me out of it," Ghent said. "I got you into this—might as well stick through to the end. Everybody says I need to get out more, anyway."

Leia glanced at Elegos, caught the other's microscopic nod. Apparently, three days alone in a two-man ship with a Caamasi had done Ghent a world of good.

Or else the young slicer was finally beginning to grow up.

"All right," she said. "Thank you. Thank you all." She glanced around the room. "We'll have to take the *Falcon*, I'm afraid—this ship is too small for all of us. It's about a twenty-minute landspeeder ride away."

"Then let us go," Elegos said, gently prodding. "There is little time to spare."

Five minutes later they were racing across the Pakrik Minor landscape, the whistling of the wind the only sound as the five occupants sat wrapped in the silence of their own thoughts.

What the others were thinking during that trip Leia never learned. But for herself, a new and disturbing thought had suddenly occurred to her. A Jedi, she knew, could often see or sense into the future and, as she herself had often done, could similarly gain a sense of the rightness of the path being taken or the Jedi's own position along that path. She was seeing that rightness for herself now.

But could any Jedi, she wondered, see ahead to his or her own death? Or would the path leading to that moment always remain in darkness? Feeling right and proper, perhaps, all the way up to the point of passage?

She didn't know. Perhaps this would be the path where she would find out.

CHAPTER
13

From the far aft cabin, the warbling of the *Wild Karrde*'s bridge battle alert was a quiet, almost subtle thing. But Shada had been trained to notice subtle things, and she was awake and out of bed before the distant trilling had finished its down scale and shut off. Throwing on her robe, stuffing her blaster into a side pocket, she headed for the bridge.

The corridors were deserted. Shada picked up her pace, ears cocked for the noise of battle or the straining engines that would indicate escape or evasion. But the ship was eerily quiet, with the steady drone of the drive and her own softly slapping footsteps the only sounds she could hear. Ahead, the bridge door slid open at her approach; slipping her hand into her robe pocket and getting a grip on her blaster, she charged through the doorway.

And skidded to a slightly confused halt. The bridge crew were seated in their normal positions, some of them looking questioningly back at her abrupt entrance. Ahead, out the viewport, the mottled sky of hyperspace was rolling past.

"Hello, Shada," Karrde said, looking up from the engineering monitor where he and Pormfil had apparently been consulting on something. "I thought you were still sleeping. What brings you here at this hour?"

"Your battle alert—what did you think?" Shada countered, looking around again. "What's going on, a drill?"

"Not quite," Karrde said, stepping over to her. "My apologies; I didn't think you'd be able to hear the alert where you were."

"Listening for trouble is part of my job," she said tartly. "What is this 'not quite' drill of yours?"

"We're coming up on the Episol system and the world Dayark," Karrde explained. "There's a fair chance we'll run into some trouble when we come out of hyperspace."

Shada looked out the viewport. "That rogue pirate gang Bombaasa told us about?"

"Possibly," Karrde said. "Word of our voyage has undoubtedly preceded us."

"Not to mention word of your identity," Shada said.

Karrde's lip twitched. "Regardless, after that ship we spotted hanging around our Jangelle course change point, I thought it best if we hit the Episol system prepared."

"Sounds reasonable," Shada said. "Except for the part about you not thinking I needed to be informed."

"I didn't think there would be anything you could do," Karrde said mildly. "Unless they board us—which I guarantee they will *not* do—there won't be any hand-to-hand combat."

"Hand-to-hand is hardly my sole area of expertise," Shada said stiffly. "Or didn't I mention I'm fully qualified to handle those turbolasers of yours?"

The whole bridge had taken on an air of watchful silence. "You hadn't mentioned that, no," Karrde said. "But at this point it's largely irrelevant. The turbolaser bays are by necessity somewhat exposed, and if there's trouble I'd rather have you here where it's—well—"

"Where it's safe?" Shada finished for him. "Why, because it might not be pirates waiting for us out there?"

Dankin turned half around from the helm to look at Karrde. He opened his mouth as if to speak, thought better of it, and turned back around again.

"It's not Car'das," Karrde said, his voice carefully controlled. "Not here. If he was going to hit us at a distance, he'd have done so already. That means he's decided to wait until we reach Exocron."

"It's always nice to have something to look forward to," Shada growled. "In that case, let me take one of the turbolasers. I'm at least as good as Balig—probably better than Chal."

"We *could* put Chal at the spotting station," Dankin murmured.

Karrde's lip twitched, but he nodded. "All right, we'll see what you can do. Dankin, tell Chal to come back and take over spotting. H'sishi, how are we for timing?"

[We are four minutes one-half from arrival,] the Togorian at the sensor station said, her yellow eyes studying Shada with unblinking intensity.

"You'd best get up there," Karrde said to Shada, nodding toward the bridge door. "It's turbolaser two."

"I know," Shada said. "I'll check in when I'm ready."

Three minutes later she was strapped into the control console facing the big transparisteel bubble, running a prefire checklist and fighting back twenty years' worth of ghosts of other such battles, first with the Mistryl and then with Mazzic's smugglers. With most of those battles she'd been lucky enough to be on the winning side. With the others . . .

"Shada, this is Chal," the young man's voice came through her comm headset. "You ready?"

"Almost," Shada said, watching as the last of the self-check lights went green. "Yes, ready."

"Okay." If Chal was annoyed at having been summarily kicked out of his post, it didn't show in his voice. "Stay sharp; we're counting down now. Starting at ten . . . mark."

She listened with half an ear to the countdown, her hands resting on the controls, her eyes already starting the combat scan pattern her Mistryl instructors had taught her so long ago. The count reached zero, the mottled sky flared to starlines and shrank to stars—

And with a terrific jolt a laser bolt slammed hard into the *Wild Karrde*'s side.

[Seven targets waiting,] H'sishi snarled, the tone of her voice giving Shada the mental picture of all that gray-white fur standing on end. [Small attack vessels—*Corsair*-class.]

"Confirmed on number and class," Chal added. "Bearings—"

The targeting recitation was drowned out in the hissing roar of her turbolaser as Shada swung the weapon around and fired. One of the Corsairs, trying to sneak in under the freighter's docking bay, caught the burst squarely on its left flank and flashed into dust. His wingman, dodging most of the debris, scrambled wildly for distance but succeeded only in flying straight into a burst from Griv's turbolaser. What remained of the craft continued outward on an inertial trajectory, blazing like a flying funeral pyre.

"Two down!" Chal crowed. "Make that three."

"Everyone stay sharp," Karrde's calmer voice said. "We caught them by surprise this time. They know what to expect now."

Shada nodded silent agreement, taking a quick look at her tactical display. The four remaining Corsairs had pulled back, pacing the *Wild Karrde* but clearly not overly anxious to engage it again. Karrde, meanwhile, had the freighter burning hard through space toward the distant gas giant around which the Kathol Republic's capital world of Dayark revolved. "My guess is that they'll try their ion cannon next," she said. "Can we handle that?"

"Easily," Karrde assured her. "Certainly ion cannon that small. Here they come."

Breaking into pairs, the four Corsairs shot over and under the *Wild Karrde*, blasting away at full power with their ion cannon. Shada fired off a quick burst, catching one of them glancingly across the top quarter before both ships disappeared behind the *Wild Karrde*'s bulk. "Spotter?" she called.

"You took out his ion cannon," Chal confirmed. "Balig, you've knocked out his rear deflector—"

[They attack again,] H'sishi's snarl cut him off. Shada glanced at the tactical and swung her turbolaser around toward where the nearest Corsair should appear . . .

The attacker swung around the *Wild Karrde*'s hull, its lasers blazing uselessly away at the freighter's thick armor. Shada and Balig fired back, the twin turbolaser blasts catching him squarely across the bow and shattering him in a brilliant flash of light—

And with a deafening thunderclap something slammed straight through Shada's transparisteel bubble.

"I'm hit!" Shada gasped, fighting against the sudden tearing pain in her right chest and shoulder. All around her a cold wind whistled as the air rushed through the shattered bubble. Her right hand was useless; with her left hand she dug at her restraints, wondering distantly if she would be able to get loose and out of the bay before the vacuum took her. Perhaps now, at last, it was all finally over . . .

The wind was starting to diminish by the time she got the top restraint off. A bad sign. She shifted her hand to the lower strap, her vision starting to waver . . .

And with a second thud, more felt than really heard, the bubble and stars vanished into a plate of gray metal.

She blinked; but even as her oxygen-starved brain tried to figure it out, there was an ear-popping rush of air into the bay, and suddenly strange hands were snapping off the last of her restraints. "We've got her!" a voice shouted uncomfortably loud in her ear. "But she's been hit. Get Annowiskri down here, fast."

"Already here," a second voice came in from Shada's other side. There was a tingle of something in her arm . . .

She came to slowly, or at least slowly for a Mistryl. For a moment she remained lying quietly, her eyes closed, as she assessed the situation and her own physical condition. Her right chest and arm felt vaguely numb, and her scalp itched like it always did after a session in a bacta tank, but aside from that she felt reasonably fine. From the soft sound of breathing she could tell she wasn't alone; from the lack of background engine or machinery sounds it seemed the *Wild Karrde* had made it through to Dayark.

So it wasn't the end yet, and life remained before her. A pity. Taking a deep but quiet breath, she opened her eyes.

She was lying on one of the three beds in the *Wild Karrde*'s medical bay. Seated across the room, staring meditatively off into space, was Karrde. "I take it we won?" Shada asked.

Karrde jerked slightly, his gaze coming back to her. "Yes, we won quite handily," he said. "How are you feeling?"

"Not too bad," she said, moving her right arm experimentally. Aside from some stiffness and the numbness she'd already noted, it didn't seem too bad, at least as long as she didn't try to move it too far in any direction. "Arm needs a little more work."

"Yes, Annowiskri tells me you'll need at least one more session in the bacta tank," Karrde said. "I had you pulled out so that you could accompany me on a short walk outside the ship. If you're interested, that is."

"Of course I'm interested," Shada said. "Where on Dayark are we?"

"The main spaceport of the capital city Rytal Prime," Karrde said. "We put down about two hours ago."

Shada frowned. "And you're just going out now? I thought we were in a hurry."

"We are," Karrde said. "But we had to play host first to a small group of inspectors. They spent over an hour going through the ship with the proverbial flat-edge sifter. Ostensibly searching for contraband."

"I hope you watched them closely."

"Very closely," Karrde assured her. "At any rate, they've gone now, and Pormfil and Odonnl are making arrangements to get the ship repaired. In the meantime, the Kathol Republic military commander would like to have a word with us."

"About our attackers, no doubt."

"No doubt," Karrde agreed. "Perhaps focusing on how we managed to fight them off with so little damage."

Shada lifted her eyebrows. " 'So little damage' being a relative term, of course."

Karrde grimaced. "I'm sorry about what happened, Shada—"

"Forget it," Shada cut him off. Apologies always made her uncomfortable, even when they were sincere. Especially when they were sincere. "It was my idea, remember. So what's the plan?"

"I'm supposed to meet with a General Jutka at a tapcafe just outside the spaceport," Karrde told her. "They mostly speak Basic here, but there's a fair-sized contingent of Ithorian colonists, too, so I thought we'd take Threepio along in case we run into translation problems."

"Odd place for an official meeting," Shada commented. "Sounds like they don't know whether they want to be associated with us or not."

"I would say that reading is dead on target," Karrde agreed, eyeing her thoughtfully. "Your grasp of politics is quite good, especially for a simple bodyguard."

"I've never claimed to be simple," Shada countered, swinging her legs over the side of the medic bed. "Give me five minutes to get changed and we'll go see this general."

• • •

Ten minutes later the three of them were walking down the bustling street that bordered the spaceport, Karrde and Shada walking side by side with the gold-colored protocol droid shuffling along nervously behind them. "The natives seem curious," Shada commented in a quiet voice.

Karrde nodded. He'd already noticed the surreptitious glances of the Ithorian passersby and the out-and-out stares of some of the human ones. "Mara reported they were a wary but not particularly unfriendly people."

"Nice to know," Shada said. "Of course, that report is six years old now. Interesting outfits they're wearing—those shimmery coats with all the random tufts of fur still on them?"

"It's crosh-hide," Karrde identified it. "Native animal to one of the worlds in the Kathol Republic. Comfortable and durable, and those bits of fur can be left on either randomly or in any of a variety of patterns. Mara told me crosh-hide coats were just coming into style when she and Calrissian were here; I see it's bloomed into a full-blown fashion since then."

"Probably because it makes for instant identification of strangers," Shada said, catching hold of a pinch of her shipboard jumpsuit material. "Not much chance of us blending into any crowd with these on."

"Definitely a grain of truth in that," Karrde agreed. "This part of the galaxy has been largely left alone by outsiders, but they had some clashes with the Empire and there have been a few attempts by the New Republic to bring it into line with current political thought."

"A goal the natives aren't interested in?"

"Not really," Karrde said, looking around at the faded commercial signs flapping restlessly in the breeze. A few of them were in Basic, but most were laid out with Ithorian glyptographs or a flow-and-dot script he didn't recognize at all. "Threepio, we're looking for a place called the Ithor Loman," he said, motioning the droid to his side. "Do you see it anywhere?"

"Yes, Captain Karrde, it's right over there," Threepio said, lifting an arm to point at a blue sign labeled in Ithorian.

"Reminds me of Bombaasa's place on Pembric," Shada growled. "You know, Karrde, you might want to consider occasionally adding a few more people to these probe parties of yours."

"You wouldn't consider that a slight on your combat skills?"

"I think I've adequately proved my combat skills," Shada countered. "The point is that if you field enough people you can sometimes keep a fight from starting in the first place."

Karrde nodded, suppressing a smile. "I'll remember that. After you."

Considering the early morning hour, the tapcafe seemed unusually well populated, with both Ithorian and human locals in their crosh-hide jackets plus one or two obvious offworlders like themselves. "Any idea which one General Jutka is?" Shada murmured.

"I presume he'll be watching for us," Karrde said. "If not—"

He broke off as a short, slender man with short hair and a dapper crosh-hide jacket rose from a nearby table and stepped up to them. "Ah—visitors," he said cheerfully, his eyes sparkling with interest or bubbling good humor as he looked each of them up and down. "You must be the parties here to see General Jutka."

"Yes, we are," Karrde said. "And you?"

"Entoo Needaan E-elz, at your service," he said, giving a short bow. "Call me Entoo Nee."

"Interesting name," Karrde said, eyeing him. "That Entoo part sounds rather like a droid designation."

"Oddly enough, people do sometimes mistake me for a droid," Entoo Nee said, his eyes sparkling all the more. "I can't imagine why. If you'll follow me, I'll show you to the general's table."

He bounded off between the tables without waiting for an answer, his step as lively as his speech had been. "Curious little man," Threepio commented as they followed. "He does appear harmless, however."

"Never trust appearances," Shada warned him. "Personally, I don't think he fits in with this place at all."

"We'll keep an eye on him," Karrde told her. "That must be Jutka."

Entoo Nee had stopped beside a table in the back where a single, heavyset man was seated with his back to the wall, nursing a single drink. Wearing the by now familiar crosh-hide jacket, he nevertheless seemed to Karrde to be vaguely uncomfortable in it.

"That's a military man, all right," Shada said, echoing Karrde's own thought as Entoo Nee spoke briefly to the other. "You can tell he feels awkward being out of uniform."

Entoo Nee stepped aside as the others came up, gesturing brightly to the bulky man. "General Jutka, may I present our visitors," he said, suddenly looking a bit crestfallen. "I'm sorry—I didn't get your names."

"We didn't give them," Karrde said. "You can call me Captain. This is my friend Shada and my translation droid, See-Threepio."

The general muttered something in an unfamiliar language. "He says he wasn't expecting a full theatrical parade," Threepio translated helpfully. "In fact—"

"Enough!" Jutka spat. "Keep your droid shut up or I'll shut him up for you."

"Oh, my," Threepio gasped, taking a hasty step backward. "My apologies, General Jutka—"

"I said keep him shut up," Jutka cut him off. "I don't want to have to say that again. Now sit down."

"Certainly," Karrde said, sliding into a chair at the general's side and glancing back at Threepio. Entoo Nee had stepped to the droid's side and was talking soothingly to him in a low voice. "My mistake, General. I thought I was here for a conversation, not a series of threats."

"I apologize if you got that impression," Jutka said darkly, looking balefully up at Shada. She had ignored his invitation to sit down, moving instead around the other side of the table so that she was effectively standing over him, and for a moment Karrde thought he was going to issue a flat-out order for her to sit. He apparently thought better of it and turned his glare back to Karrde. "The fact is that you're a troublemaker," he said. "Troublemakers aren't welcome on my world."

"I see," Karrde said. "So in the Kathol Republic coming under pirate attack is the mark of a troublemaker?"

Jutka's eyes narrowed. "Don't push me," he warned. "I know who you're flying for—your ship's ID makes that perfectly clear. The last thing I want is to end up in the middle of some stupid war between Bombaasa and Rei'Kas."

"Rei'Kas?" Shada repeated, her tone that of someone who's just made a connection. "The Rodian?"

"Yes," Jutka said, frowning up at her. "You mean you didn't—?"

"No, we didn't know who our friends were out there," Karrde confirmed. "Many thanks. You know this Rei'Kas, Shada?"

"Only by reputation," Shada told him. "He used to be a strike team leader with the Karazak Slavers Cooperative. Quite a good one, apparently. He was also rough, violent, and vicious, and he irritated practically everyone he worked with."

Karrde nodded, feeling his mouth go a little dry. A vicious slaver, now in Car'das's territory. How many other criminals, he wondered, had also just happened to drift to this corner of the galaxy? "Interesting."

"Also interesting that the general knew his name when even Bombaasa didn't," Shada added. "You good friends with him, General?"

"My job is to protect the Kathol Republic," Jutka said, his tone vibrant with soft menace. "I have no such responsibility toward outsiders who come in unasked and meddle with matters that are none of their business."

Out of the corner of his eye, Karrde saw Shada's head turn fractionally as she gave the main part of the tapcafe a quick survey. "Are you threatening me, General?" he asked mildly.

"I'm delivering a warning," Jutka said bluntly. "You've hurt Rei'Kas, and he doesn't take kindly to that. He's got your ship marked, and as long as you're in his territory he's going to keep after you."

"We have every intention of leaving his territory," Karrde assured him. "After my errand is finished, of course."

"Do as you wish," Jutka said, grunting as he heaved his bulk out of his chair. "But I've given you fair warning. Don't forget that."

"I won't," Karrde said. "Thank you for your time."

Jutka scowled once and marched across the tapcafe. Pushing open the door, he strode out without a backward glance.

"And this is where Car'das picked to retire to, huh?" Shada said, sitting down in the chair Jutka had just vacated. "Lovely."

"Keep your voice down," Karrde admonished, looking around the tapcafe. No one seemed to be taking any particular interest in this corner of the room, but appearances meant nothing. "And I doubt retirement was ever in his plans."

Shada sent him a probing look. "You think Rei'Kas is working for him?"

Karrde nodded soberly. "I would say that's entirely possible."

He caught her eye movement and looked up as Entoo Nee pulled up a chair to their table and sat down. "Did you have a nice chat with the general?" he asked brightly. "That's good. That's very good."

He hunched himself closer to the table. "I've been talking with your droid," he said, dropping his voice conspiratorially. "He says you're looking for the fabled lost world of Exocron."

Karrde looked at Threepio. "Threepio?"

"I'm sorry, sir," the droid said, sounding miserable. "I didn't mean to give anything away. He asked if we were searching for Exocron, and I confirmed it without thinking."

"Please don't blame the droid," Entoo Nee said. "Your goal isn't a secret. At least, not to me. You're looking for Jorj Car'das, aren't you?"

Shada shot Karrde a look across the table. "Threepio, why don't you go over to the bar and get us a couple glasses of the local brew," she suggested. "On your way, listen and see if you hear anyone talking in Rodian."

"Yes, Mistress Shada," the droid said, sounding relieved at the chance to get away. "Right away."

He shuffled off. "Very clever," Entoo Nee said, grinning at Shada. "You think any spotters Rei'Kas may have planted in the crowd will talk Rodian to each other, eh? Very clever, indeed."

"Thank you," Shada said, fixing him with a look that was just short of a glare. "You were telling us about Jorj Car'das."

"Yes." Entoo Nee shuffled himself even closer to the table. "You're right to look for him on Exocron. That's where he is." He lifted a finger warningly. "But Exocron isn't easy to find. Most people in the Kathol Republic have never even heard of it. Most of those who have believe it to be a myth."

"So I've heard," Karrde said, fighting against a sudden sense of dread. How could Entoo Nee know why he was here? Unless, of course, he was working for Car'das? "Tell me why it's so hard to find."

Entoo Nee smiled even more broadly. "You don't need me to tell you that. Ah, but perhaps your friend doesn't know," he added, shifting his grin to Shada. "It's all the mini-nebulae and gas offshoots, you see, coming off the Kathol Rift. All of that reflected light and radiation scrambles sensors and communications—makes it terribly difficult to find anything at all. Searching the whole region could take you decades."

"And you can save us all that trouble, I suppose?" Shada asked.

"I can indeed," he said. "I can take you to Exocron. Right to Car'das himself, if you like."

He looked back at Karrde. "But only if Captain Karrde wishes."

With a strong effort, Karrde kept his expression steady. So the little man knew his name, too. "And what would this guidance cost us?"

"No cost," Entoo Nee said. "But no 'us,' either. It would just be you and me."

"Excuse me?" Shada said, lifting a finger. "Just you and him? What about the rest of us?"

"You'd have to wait for us here," Entoo Nee told her. "No other way, I'm afraid—my ship can only carry two people."

"How about if you ride with us and guide our ship in?" Karrde asked.

"Oh, no," Entoo Nee said, looking shocked. "I couldn't possibly do that."

"Why not?" Shada demanded. "Because Car'das doesn't want to see all of us?"

Entoo Nee blinked. "Did I ever say Car'das wanted to see any of you? I said no such thing."

Which wasn't the same as saying Car'das hadn't asked him to make the offer. "If I accept," Karrde said slowly, "when would we need to leave?"

"Wait a second," Shada put in before Entoo Nee could answer. "What do you mean, if you accept? You don't want to go off alone with him."

Karrde grimaced. No, he most certainly didn't. But at some point he was going to have to face Car'das. And if this was the best way to protect his people while he did that . . .

"Let me put it another way," Shada said, glaring at Entoo Nee. "I'm his bodyguard, and I'm not letting him go off alone. Not with you or anyone else. Clear?"

Entoo Nee held out his hands, palm upward. "But—"

He broke off as Threepio reappeared and set two heavy mugs of dark liquid onto the table. "Thank the Maker," he said breathlessly. "The clientele of this place are most unpleasant—"

"Never mind the local color," Shada cut him off. "Did you hear any Rodian?"

"As a matter of fact, I did," the droid said, half turning and pointing toward one of the tables across near the bar. "Three human males at that table—yes; the ones now standing up—"

"Uh-oh," Shada muttered, darting a glance at Entoo Nee. "Come on—time to get out of here."

"Don't bother," a softly vicious voice said from behind Karrde.

Slowly, he turned around. Two tables away, three men were sitting facing them.

And all three had their blasters drawn.

CHAPTER

14

"Oh, my," Threepio gasped, just audibly. "We're doomed."

Karrde looked back around. Behind Shada, the three thugs Threepio had just identified were striding between the tables toward them, blasters now in their hands as well. Across the rest of the tapcafe, the casual drinkers and loungers were either staring in surprise or morbid anticipation or else trying to beat a surreptitious retreat before the shooting started. "I suppose it would be a waste of breath to say you have the wrong people," he said, turning back to face the men behind him.

"No, go right ahead," the thugs' spokesman said sarcastically as the three of them got to their feet and fanned out slightly to cover their targets. "I always enjoy a good laugh in the morning. Hands on the table, please. So—did I catch the name right? Talon Karrde?"

"Yes, indeed," Entoo Nee spoke up brightly before Karrde could answer. "And this is Shada, and their protocol droid See-Threepio."

The spokesman impaled the little man with a glare. "You with them?"

Entoo Nee's eyes widened innocently. "Me? Not really, sir—"

"Then get out of here."

Entoo Nee blinked, threw a quick look around at Shada and Karrde, and scrambled up from his seat. "Do let me know, Captain Karrde, if you change your mind," he said.

He shot a quick smile at Karrde, another at the spokesman, then bounced his way toward the door. The spokesman watched him go, frowning; and as the little man pulled open the door, he turned back to face Karrde. "Change your mind about what?" he demanded as the thud of the closing door echoed across the tapcafe.

"He'd just made me an interesting offer," Karrde said, lifting his arms with conspicuous slowness and folding them across his chest. The thugs, their full attention on him and Shada, had completely missed the fact that someone had come into the tapcafe at the same moment Entoo Nee left. If he could manage to keep all of their attention on him for just a few more seconds . . .

And then someone across the room swore in astonishment. One of the thugs glanced around—"Shri—Xern!" he barked.

The spokesman spun around . . . and froze, his mouth dropping open with shock.

Silently, determinedly, H'sishi was striding toward them.

It took Xern another second to find his voice. "What in the name of the Rift is *that*?" he breathed.

"She's a Togorian," Karrde supplied, throwing a surreptitious glance at Shada. Her eyes were darting back and forth between the suddenly inattentive thugs, clearly measuring distances and assessing possibilities. That could be trouble. "Oh, and she's with me," he added.

H'sishi was still coming toward the semicircle of thugs, her mouth open far enough to show her fangs. "Tell it to stop," Xern snapped, his voice hitting a higher pitch as his blaster jerked around to point at the Togorian. "You hear me? Tell it to stop or we'll shoot."

"I wouldn't advise shooting a Togorian," Karrde admonished him mildly. "It only makes them angry."

Xern shot a look of disbelief toward him—

And in that instant Shada moved.

Her left hand, resting casually near her mug, snatched it up and with a quick flick of her forearm she hurled the contents across the table squarely into Xern's face. He bellowed, throwing up his forearm, too late, to try to block the wave of liquid. A convulsive jerk the other direction, and Shada had hurled the mug itself with crushing force into the throat of one of the other thugs. She started to leap up, yelping under her breath as Karrde grabbed her arm and held her firmly in her seat. There was the sputter of blaster fire and the sounds of bodies hitting the floor—

"Lower your weapon, Xern," Karrde said quietly. Even to his own ears his voice seemed a startling intrusion into the sudden taut silence filling the tapcafe. "Very slowly; very carefully."

Xern gave his eyes one last swipe with his sleeve and blinked them open . . . and for the second time in half a minute he appeared to be struck speechless as he stared at the scene around him in stunned disbelief. Disbelief at Karrde and Shada sitting unhurt at the table; disbelief at the crumpled bodies of his men lying around him on the floor, wisps of noxious smoke rising from the blaster wounds riddling their bodies.

And disbelief at the four crosh-hide-clad men at various tables scattered around the tapcafe pointing blasters at him.

"Your blaster, Xern," Karrde prompted again as the thug continued to gape, drops of Shada's drink dripping rhythmically off his chin. Shada stirred; but before she could move H'sishi had stepped to Xern's side and engulfed the barrel of his blaster in one massive hand. He started, almost as if seeing the Togorian for the first time, as she twisted the weapon to point harmlessly at the ceiling. She raised her other hand and dug a claw delicately into the back of his wrist, and this time he finally let go.

"Well done, everyone," Karrde said, getting to his feet as H'sishi stepped back, the blaster now reversed ready in her hand. "Dankin?"

"Here," the familiar voice came from a distinctly unfamiliar face as the other stood up at his table.

"Go give the bartender something to compensate for the mess," Karrde instructed him. "It's somewhat traditional in these cases," he added to Xern as Dankin crossed toward the bar, digging into his pocket. "Griv, stand by the door; Chal, Balig, go frontguard the way back to the ship."

"Right."

The other three headed for the door. "You're cute," Xern spat viciously. "Real cute. But if you think this is gonna get you out from under Rei'Kas's hammer, you're crazy."

"If I were you, I'd worry more about what Rei'Kas will do to you for losing your mob this way," Karrde countered. "I'd also worry about getting out of here before H'sishi decides you're too dangerous to leave alive."

"Oh, I'll leave," Xern said darkly. "But you'll see me again, Karrde. Just before you die." With one final glare, he turned and stomped out of the tapcafe.

"Well," Karrde said, turning back to Shada and holding out a hand to her.

She didn't move. "So you had backups in place all along," she said, looking up at him.

There was something distinctly discomfiting in her voice and face. "I thought you said you wouldn't take that as an insult," Karrde reminded her carefully.

"They're in disguise," she said.

Slowly, Karrde lowered his hand to his side. "They were all seen by the local inspectors who searched the ship earlier," he explained. "I had to assume some of the group were spies for the pirates, and would be able to recognize them."

"And the crosh-hide outfits?"

"Mara brought them back from her trip here," Karrde said, starting to feel sweat breaking out on his forehead.

Shada rose to her feet. "And you didn't think," she said quietly, "that I could be trusted with it."

For a second Karrde couldn't find his voice. The deep ache that had been in Shada's voice was so completely unexpected. "No, that's not it," he said. "I didn't—"

But it was too late. She had already turned her back on him, and was striding toward the door where Griv stood guard. "Are the repairs finished yet?" she asked.

Griv shot a quick look over her shoulder at Karrde. "Close enough," he said cautiously.

"Good," she said, stepping past him and pulling the door open. "Looks clear," she announced. "Let's get back to the ship."

Griv looked questioningly at Karrde again. "Yes," he murmured, heading toward the door.

The walk back to the *Wild Karrde* was very quiet.

Shada had stripped off her jumpsuit and had just gotten into her robe when the cabin door call chimed. "Who is it?" she called.

"It's Karrde," the other's voice came distantly through the panel. "May I come in?"

Shada sighed, wrapping her robe securely around her and knotting the waist sash. She had no particular desire to see him, especially right now. But she had committed herself to this trip, and she couldn't very well avoid the captain and still fulfill that commitment.

Besides, the pain of his casual betrayal of her trust had mostly subsided. Enough, anyway. "Come in," she called, tapping the release.

The door slid open, and Karrde stepped inside. "We've just made the jump to lightspeed," he told her, taking in her state of dress and dismissing it in a single glance. "Odonnl estimates seven days to Exocron."

"Good," Shada said briskly. "I should be back to full combat capability by then. Speaking of which, if you'll excuse me, I'm on my way to the bacta tank."

"The bacta can wait," Karrde said politely but firmly, gesturing her to a chair. "I'd like to talk to you."

She thought about refusing. But she *was* still committed to him and to this trip. "About what?" she said, sitting down, wondering if he was really insensitive enough to try concocting some feeble excuse about that tapcafe thing at this late date.

But he surprised her. "Jorj Car'das, of course," he said, pulling another chair over to face her and sitting down. "It's time you heard the whole story."

"Really," she said, keeping her voice neutral. He'd only promised to tell her this story on the way into the Exocron system; which, according to him, was still a week away. Was this his way of trying to make amends for his earlier thoughtlessness?

Not that it mattered. Too little, too late; but at least she'd get some useful information out of it. "Go on," she said.

His gaze drifted outward, as if to a time or place far away. "The story of Jorj Car'das goes back about sixty years," he said. "To the Clone Wars era and the chaos that it brought on the galaxy. There was a great need for smuggling during the conflict and afterward, of necessities as well as contraband, and a large number of organizations were hastily and rather haphazardly thrown together."

"That was when the Hutts really hit their stride, wasn't it?" Shada asked, interest stirring in spite of herself. There was very little she knew about that period, and she'd always wanted to know more.

"Many of them did, yes," Karrde said. "Car'das was one of those who jumped into the business, and whether through skill or simple blind luck wound up with one of the better organizations. Not one of the larger ones, but definitely one of the better ones.

"They'd been operating for about fifteen years when he was accidentally caught up in the middle of a big battle between some Bpfasshi Dark Jedi and—well, basically everyone else in that sector. According to Car'das's later story, one of the Dark Jedi commandeered his private ship and forced them to take off."

Shada shivered. That one she *did* know something about; a group of Mistryl had been involved on the defensive side of that conflict. Some of the stories she'd heard as a child from the survivors had given her nightmares. "I'm surprised he came back able to tell any stories at all," she said.

"So was everyone else," Karrde said. "The other four members of his crew never did return, in fact. But Car'das did. He suddenly reappeared two months later, settled back into control of his organization, and to all appearances life went back to normal."

"But the appearances were wrong?"

"Very wrong," Karrde agreed soberly. "It was quickly apparent to his inner circle that something serious had happened to him during those two months. He still had one of the best smuggling groups around, but suddenly he began pushing to make it one of the biggest, as well. He would move systematically into the territories of smaller groups and either buy them, absorb them, or destroy them, taking over their routes and clientele. Unlike the Hutts and other groups, he went for overall coverage rather than concentrated brute-force control, spreading himself thinly out all over rather than trying to dominate any specific systems or sectors. In a few years, he was already on his way to having something that could someday rival even Jabba's organization."

"Didn't anyone try to stop him?" Shada asked. "I can't see the Hutts sitting by and letting him outflank them that way."

"My dear Shada, *everyone* tried to stop him," Karrde said darkly. "But he was almost literally unstoppable. Somewhere, somehow, he had developed a knack for guessing precisely what his opponents were planning against him, and he was often able to counter their attacks almost literally before they were launched."

Shada thought back to the dozens of missions she'd gone on for the Mistryl, and the hours of painstaking research she'd had to put into learning her opponents' strengths and weaknesses, weapons and strategies, allies and opponents. "A handy talent," she murmured.

"Extremely handy," Karrde agreed. "But even as his organization grew, Car'das himself began to change. He became—I don't know. Moody, perhaps, inclined to flashes of screaming rage over little things that shouldn't have bothered him at all, or brooding alone for hours on end over charts of the Empire. More significantly, perhaps, after years of vigorous youth, he seemed to be aging rapidly. Much faster than one would have thought normal or likely.

"And then, one day, he got into his private ship, took off . . . and vanished."

Shada frowned. "Vanished. You mean . . . *vanished*?"

"I mean disappeared from the known galaxy," Karrde said. "He didn't go near any of his people; didn't contact any of his chief lieutenants; and if he was ever seen again by any of his enemies, they never announced the fact."

"When was this?" Shada asked.

"Twenty years ago," Karrde said. "At first there wasn't too much concern—he'd gone off on occasional secret trips before. But after three months had gone by and he still hadn't surfaced, his lieutenants began to talk about what they should do if he didn't come back."

"Let me guess," Shada said. "They wanted to hold a vote and see which of them would take over."

"I don't think voting was the procedure any of them had in mind," Karrde said ruefully. "In fact, the threat of violence was so thick that the suggestion was made that we simply split up the organization and each take a chunk."

"The trick being how you divide it to everyone's satisfaction," Shada said, noting the telltale word with interest. It was the first time in his recitation that Karrde had used the word "we." "So you wound up with a power struggle anyway."

Karrde's lips pressed briefly together. "Not exactly. I saw what would happen in that kind of struggle, and I wasn't totally convinced that Car'das wouldn't be coming back. So I . . . took over."

Shada lifted her eyebrows slightly. "Just like that?"

He shrugged uncomfortably. "More or less. It took planning and timing, of course, and a fair amount of luck, though I don't think I realized quite how much until I looked back on it from a distance of a few years. But yes, basically, just like that. I neutralized the other lieutenants and moved them out, and announced to the rest of the organization that it was henceforth to be business as usual."

"I bet that made you very popular," Shada said. "But I seem to be missing the problem here, at least as far as Car'das is concerned. He left and never came back, right?"

"The problem," Karrde said heavily, "is that I'm not sure he didn't."

Shada felt her eyes narrow. "Oh?"

"I took over the organization in a single night," Karrde said. "But that doesn't mean there weren't attempts by the ousted lieutenants and their cadres afterward to drive me out and take over themselves. There were eight different attempts, in fact, ranging from two immediate and abortive tries to an intricate scheme three years later that had probably taken the conspirators that entire time to plan."

"All of which failed, obviously."

Karrde nodded. "The point is that the leaders of four of those plots claimed during their interrogations that Car'das had been secretly behind them."

Shada snorted under her breath. "Smokecovers," she said scornfully, dismissing them with a wave of her hand. "Just trying to rattle you into cutting a deal."

"That was my conclusion at the time," Karrde said. "But of course there was no way for me to be sure. Still isn't, for that matter."

"I suppose not." Shada studied his face. "So what happened six years ago that made you send Jade and Calrissian out here to look for him?"

"It started further back than that," Karrde said. "Ten years ago, actually, just after Grand Admiral Thrawn died." His lip twitched. "Or perhaps merely faked his death. I was on Coruscant helping set up the Smugglers Alliance and Calrissian happened to show me something Luke Skywalker had found buried on a planet called Dagobah."

Shada searched her memory. "I don't think I've ever heard of the place."

"No reason why you should have," Karrde said. "There's absolutely nothing there—no cities, no technology, no colonies. What Skywalker wanted with the swamps I don't know, but it was obvious that stray electronic devices were out of place, which is probably why he brought it back. At any rate, from the markings I recognized it as the beckon call from Car'das's personal ship."

"Really," Shada said, frowning. A beckon call was the control for a fully slave-rigged ship, one that could operate on complete remote control whenever its owner signaled for it. The Mistryl never used full-rigged ships themselves, but she'd occasionally ridden on one with a client. Overall, they gave her the creeps. "Car'das had a full-rigged ship, did he?"

"Of pre–Clone Wars vintage, yes," Karrde said. "He bought it soon after he returned from that bout with the Dark Jedi. Said he wanted a decently sized ship that he could fly alone, without the need for a crew."

"And Skywalker just happened to find his beckon call lying in the mud on some deserted planet. How convenient."

"That was my thought, too," Karrde said. "But I checked with Skywalker, and the discovery seemed entirely fortuitous."

"Though whether that word can be applied to Jedi has always been arguable," Shada put in.

"True," Karrde conceded. "Still, it was the first clue we'd had in a decade; and even if it was some kind of plant, I thought it was worth the risk of seeing where it led."

"So you sent Jade to hunt him down," Shada said, remembering the conversation she'd overheard back in the Solos' Orowood Tower apartment. "And Calrissian insisted on tagging along."

"Basically," Karrde said. "They started at Dagobah and worked their way outward, searching through old spaceport records for where he might have stopped off for repairs or refueling. They also dug up hints about him here and there—some from the Coruscant library, some from various fringe characters, some from Corellian Security, of all places—and started putting the pieces together."

"Talk about your lifetime jobs," Shada murmured.

"It wasn't quite that bad, but it did definitely take some years," Karrde said. "Especially as they both kept getting dragged off on other business or pulled in to help fix whatever Coruscant's crisis of the month was. Still, the trail was already so cold that a month or two here or there didn't make much of a difference. They kept at it until they wound up in Kathol sector and Exocron.

"And there, as far as we can tell, the trail ends."

For a moment the room was silent as Shada digested it all. "I take it they never actually saw Car'das himself?"

With a visible effort, Karrde seemed to draw himself back from whatever ghosts of the past he was gazing at. "They had explicit instructions not to," he said. "They were to find out where he was—and with a world as well hidden as Exocron they also needed to find a route into the place—and then they were to come home. I would take it from there."

"And this was how long ago?"

Karrde shrugged uncomfortably. "A few years."

"So what happened?"

"To be honest, I lost my nerve," he admitted. "After what I'd done, I wasn't at all sure how I was going to face him. Had no idea what I was going to say, how I was going to even try to make amends. So I kept finding excuses to put it off."

He took a deep breath. "And now it looks like I'm too late."

Shada grimaced. "You think Rei'Kas is working for him."

"Rei'Kas, possibly Bombaasa, probably a dozen others we haven't heard about," Karrde said heavily. "But he's definitely on the move. Only this time he seems to be concentrating on piracy and slaving instead of smuggling and information brokering. The more violent edge of the fringe . . . and I can only see one reason why he would do that.

"To come after me. Personally."

For a moment the word seemed to hang in the air like a death mark. "I don't think that necessarily follows," Shada said into the silence, moved by some obscure desire to argue the point. "Why can't he just be building up a force to carve himself a little empire here in the backwater? Take over Exocron, maybe, or even this little so-called Kathol Republic?"

"He's been here for nearly two decades, Shada," Karrde reminded her. "If he was into empire-carving, don't you think he would have done it before now?"

"If he was into taking you out, don't you think he would have done *that* before now, too?" Shada countered.

"He may have already tried."

"And then, what, given up after the first three years?"

Karrde shook his head. "It doesn't make sense to me, either," he conceded. "But I knew Car'das; and he wasn't the sort of person who could just sit around doing nothing. He was a ruthless man, hard and calculating, who never forgave a wrong against him and never let anyone or anything stand in the way of what he wanted. And he lived for challenges—the bigger, the better.

"And he knows I'm here, and that I'm looking for him. That little man—Entoo Nee—is all the proof we need of that."

An involuntary shiver ran through Shada. The *Wild Karrde*, which had felt so safe and secure up till now, suddenly felt small and very vulnerable. "And so here we are. Walking straight into his hands."

"You, at least, should have nothing to fear from him," Karrde assured her. "You're not connected in any way with me or my organization." He hesitated. "As a matter of fact, that's why I agreed to let you come along."

Shada stared at him as understanding suddenly slapped her like an ice-soaked rag. "You're expecting him to kill you, aren't you?" she breathed. "And you think . . . ?"

"You're not associated with me, Shada," Karrde said quietly. "Everyone else aboard the ship is. I would have come alone, but I knew I couldn't survive the trip to Exocron in anything smaller or less well armed than the *Wild Karrde*. Car'das is a vengeful man; but like Bombaasa, he likes to consider himself cultured. I hope to talk him out of killing me, of course; I hope even more that he won't harm my crew. But if he's adamant on settling old scores . . . I hope at least I can persuade him to let you go back to the New Republic with a copy of the Caamas Document."

Shada shook her head. "Karrde, this is insane—"

"At any rate, that's the whole story," he cut her off easily, standing up and swinging his chair back to where it had been. "Oh, except for the fact that the huge data library Car'das had built up over the years vanished along with him, which is why we think he may have a copy of the Caamas Document. And now, you *do* need to get to that bacta tank. I'll see you later."

With a nod, he left. "Karrde, this is insane," Shada repeated again, quietly, to the empty room.

It was only later, floating in the bacta tank, that the other part of it occurred to her. Karrde was hoping, he had said, that Car'das would allow her to leave.

But he wasn't guaranteeing it.

CHAPTER

Splitter Of Stones said something in that irritating Qom Jha almost-voice and fluttered to his usual upside-down perch on a stunted stalactite. "Great," Luke announced. "We seem to be here."

Mara raised her glow rod beam from the ground in front of her and scanned the walls of the passageway, hardly daring to believe the grueling four-day trip was finally over. Cities or starships or even a quiet encampment under the open sky—those were her milieus of choice. This business of grubbing around dark, dusty tunnels with grime and dripping water and dank air all around was emphatically *not* her cup of elba.

But she'd survived it, and she hadn't wanted to kill any of the Qom Jha more than twice a day, and the astromech droid hadn't caused too many problems, and Skywalker had been unexpectedly congenial company. And now, they were finally here.

Of course, from now on they would be facing the High Tower, with all its unknown dangers. But that was all right. Danger was also one of her milieus of choice.

One of Luke's, too, come to think of it.

"There it is," Luke said, his own searching glow rod beam settling on a patch of rock along the wall a few meters ahead down the passageway. "Just this side of that archway."

"Archway?" Mara repeated, frowning as she turned her glow rod that direction. Surely someone hadn't actually built an archway down here in the middle of nowhere, had they?

No. It looked rather like an archway, certainly, with its more or less vertical side pillars creating a two-meter-wide bottleneck in the cavern passageway and its mostly circular upper arch butting up against the ceiling three meters above. But anything more than a cursory glance showed instantly that it was a natural formation, created by some trick of erosion or rock intrusion or long-gone water flow.

"It was a figure of speech," Luke said, shifting his light to the formation, too. "Sort of brings to mind that archway in Hyllyard City on Myrkr, doesn't it?"

"You mean the big mushroom-shaped thing you did your best to drop on us?" she countered. "The one we had to grind our way through three days' worth of forest to get to? The one where half the storm-troopers in the Empire were sitting around waiting for us to show up?"

"That's the place," he said, and she could sense his amusement at her recitation. "You left out where you wanted to kill me more than anything else in the galaxy."

"I was young then," Mara said briefly, shifting her light away. "So where's this opening?"

"Right there," Luke said, returning his glow rod beam to a crumpled-looking section of wall just below the ceiling. In the center of the light was a small open area that seemed to vanish into the darkness beyond.

"I see it," Mara said. There didn't seem to be any air coming from it; there must be some other blockage farther down the line. "Looks cozy."

"Not for long," Luke said, handing her his glow rod and igniting his lightsaber. "Everyone stay back—this'll probably throw rock chips around." He swung the blade into the wall, slicing into the stone—

And with a sputter of green light, the blade vanished.

Artoo screeched, and Mara caught the flash of astonishment from Luke as he stumbled briefly before catching his balance. "What happened?" she demanded.

"I don't know," he said, holding the weapon up close and looking obliquely into the end. "I thought I had it locked on . . . let me try it again."

He touched the switch, and with its usual *snap-hiss* the blade blazed into existence again. Luke watched it for a moment, then settled into a stable combat stance and again swung the tip of the blade into the rock wall.

And once again, the blade cut only a little ways into the rock before sputtering away.

One of the Qom Jha fluttered his wings and said something. "Yes," Luke said, and Mara could feel the sudden ugly suspicion in his mind as distant memories drifted up.

"Yes what?" she demanded.

"There must be cortosis ore in this rock," he told her. He held his glow rod up to the rock face, the light dancing off tiny sparkles.

Mara shook her head. "Never heard of it."

"It's apparently fairly rare," Luke said. "All I really know about it is that it shuts down lightsabers. Corran and I ran into some Force-users once who'd made sets of body armor out of woven cortosis fibers. It was quite a surprise."

"I'll bet," Mara said, a memory of her own drifting up. "So that's what the slab of rock was Palpatine had between the double walls of his private residence."

Luke lifted an eyebrow. "He had cortosis ore around his residence?"

"And around some of his other offices and throne rooms, too, I think," Mara said. "I never knew the proper name for the stuff. From what he told me, I gather that if your lightsaber has dimetris circuits anywhere in the activation loop, hitting the rock starts a feedback crash running through the system that takes only a fraction of a second to shut the whole thing down. A little something extra to slow down any stray Jedi who might come after him."

"The things you learn as Emperor's Hand," Luke murmured. "Do you know if there's any way to cut it?"

"Oh, sure—hundreds of them," Mara assured him, slipping her pack onto the ground. "Aside from the lightsaber thing, the stuff's basically useless. It's too weak and crumbly to build with—a good blaster carbine bolt will shatter it. Let me see—ah."

She pulled out one of the grenades Karrde had sent and shined her glow rod on the yield number. "Yes, this ought to work if you want to try it."

One of the Qom Jha put in another comment. "Keeper Of Promises thinks grenades would be a bad idea," Luke translated. "He says we're not that far from the High Tower itself, and that sound carries pretty far underground."

"He's probably right," Mara conceded, putting the grenade away and studying the rock where Luke had been cutting. "On the other hand, you're only getting a few centimeters at a time this way. Extra noise or extra delay. Your pick."

Luke ran a hand thoughtfully across the rock, and Mara could sense his concentration as he stretched out to the Force. "Let's try it with the lightsabers for a while," he suggested slowly. "At least a couple of hours. That should give us a better estimate of how long it's actually going to take."

"Fine," Mara said. "We can always switch to the grenades if we decide it's going too slow." She played her glow rod over the rock. "So along with caverns full of predators, we now have a wall that blocks lightsabers. How convenient for someone."

"It could be just coincidence," Luke said. But he didn't sound like he believed it. "Well, there's nothing for it but to get started." He frowned suddenly. "Unless you think this might damage the lightsabers."

Mara shrugged. "I can't see how it would, but I really don't know. Hopefully, we'll be able to pick up any trouble before it gets too bad."

"True," Luke agreed, looking down at his astromech droid. "Artoo: full sensors, and keep an eye on the lightsabers. Let us know if they seem to be overheating or anything."

The droid beeped acknowledgment and extended his little sensor unit. "We probably should start this as a triangle," Mara suggested, crossing the passageway and wedging her glow rod into a crevice where it would illuminate the area beneath the Qom Jha sneak hole. "Carving down at an angle on opposite sides. That should keep our blades out of each other's way, and angled cuts are usually better at weakening the underlying rock."

"Sounds good." Luke looked up at the three Qom Jha, grouped close together on the ceiling. "Splitter Of Stones, why don't you head back to Eater Of Fire Creepers. Tell him we're almost ready for the extra scouts he promised to send into the High Tower with us."

The Qom Jha said something. "No, but we will be soon," Luke said. "And you'd better take one of the others with you."

Sitting on a lump of stone beneath the archway, Child Of Winds flapped his wings and said something that sounded eager. "No, not you," Luke told the young Qom Qae firmly. "Keeper Of Promises, you go with him."

There was a brief comment from the Qom Jha that sounded vaguely condescending, and then Splitter Of Stones and Keeper Of Promises dropped off their perches and flapped off back into the darkness toward the cave entrance. Child Of Winds fired off a sarcastic-sounding shot as they left, then settled huffily back onto his rock. "I'll bet I'm missing some really witty repartee here," Mara said sourly, pulling her lightsaber from her belt and taking up position to the left of the cut Luke had started.

"Not really," Luke said, igniting his lightsaber and moving to the opposite side. "You ready?"

Mara ignited her lightsaber. "Let's do it."

They'd been at it for nearly an hour, and had completed the outline for their opening, when Artoo suddenly squealed.

"Hold it, Mara," Luke called, closing down his lightsaber and wondering briefly what was wrong. He'd been concentrating closely on the weapon and hadn't felt even a hint of any problem with it. He glanced over at Artoo—

And paused for a closer look. The droid's sensor unit was extended, but it wasn't aimed at the lightsabers. It was, instead, pointed down the passageway ahead.

"Mara?" he called, shifting the weapon to his left hand and pulling out his glow rod. He played it down the tunnel as, behind him, Mara shut down her lightsaber.

And in the sudden silence, he heard a noise. A rustling sound, like thousands of distant, throaty voices whispering wordlessly to each other.

A mindless rumbling that was echoed in his mind as he stretched out toward it with the Force.

And it was getting closer.

"I don't like the sound of that," Mara murmured, stepping to his side.

"Me, neither," Luke said, keying his glow rod to its brightest setting and sweeping it around again. Nothing was visible, but the way the tunnel twisted and bent in both directions that didn't mean much. He ran through his Jedi sense-enhancement techniques . . .

Fire creepers! Builder With Vines said excitedly from the ceiling behind him. *They are coming!*

"What?" Mara demanded.

"He said fire creepers are coming," Luke relayed.

"Uh-oh," Mara said. "Their Bargainer's name—'Eater Of Fire Creepers.' "

"Yes," Luke said, looking up at the Qom Jha. His wings were fluttering with some kind of anticipation. "I've been assuming a fire creeper was some sort of plant. Builder With Vines, what are these things?"

They are small but dangerous creatures, the Qom Jha said. *They will eat and destroy all things in their path, and can kill anything they find.*

"He says small but dangerous," Luke told Mara, sweeping the glow rod down the tunnel again.

"In which case, that much noise implies there must be one blazing lot of them on the way," Mara concluded grimly, looking around. "I get the very bad feeling we're about to meet a new species of roverines."

Luke shivered. He'd seen holovids of those infamous insect predators on their annual march across the Davirien jungles. Roverines traveled in swarms of hundreds of thousands, sometimes even millions, literally stripping the landscape of every bit of plant life as they passed over it.

Plant life, and any animals that were too slow or too sick to get out of their way, eating such stragglers down to polished bone. "Builder With Vines, how fast do they travel?" he called.

"Too fast," Mara snapped before the Qom Jha could answer. "Look—here they come."

Luke caught his breath. Ahead, just at the farthest spot the glow rod beam could reach, the front edge of a pulsating sheet of black had appeared, filling the entire floor and spilling perhaps a meter up the walls as well. Even as he watched, the edge flowed like some viscous liquid into a slight dip in the floor, reappearing as it flowed up again over the lip.

And Mara was right. They were coming far too fast.

"I'd say we've got maybe a minute before they get here," Mara said. "If you've got any clever tricks up your sleeve, this is the time to trot them out."

Luke bit at his lip, his mind racing. There was a way, he knew, to use the Force to create a low-level personal shield. But to maintain the shield long enough, especially against so many individual adversaries, would be practically impossible. Besides, it was doubtful he could also shield Mara that way, and she almost certainly didn't know the technique herself. Using the Force to move each individual fire creeper out of the way as they passed would be an equally impossible task, even with Mara working alongside of him.

And if these insects were anything like Davirien roverines, it would only take one of them getting through and sinking a poisoned stinger to shake their control and alert the rest of the swarm to the presence of food. No, their only hope was to stay out of the fire creepers' way entirely. Either somewhere farther down the tunnel, or else—

"The archway," Mara said suddenly. "We'll need footrests about two meters up—"

"Right," Luke said, igniting his lightsaber and stepping into the opening as he measured the distance with his eyes. Yes, it would just work. Assuming they had enough time to make the necessary preparations. "Artoo, close down all your openings," he called as he swung the tip of the brilliant green blade horizontally into the inner edge of the archway's side pillar half a meter above his head. If the cortosis ore extended this far out from the passageway wall . . .

Fortunately, it didn't. His lightsaber blade sliced cleanly inward a few centimeters into the rock, without a hint of trouble. "Child Of Winds, get to that opening up there," he called as he got a Force grip on the lightsaber and lifted it up to the rock over the cut he'd just made. "Find a place to hang on and stay there."

What about you, Jedi Sky Walker? the young Qom Qae asked anxiously, the fluttering of his wings nearly drowned out by the hum of the two lightsabers. *How will you protect yourselves?*

"You'll see," Luke assured him. He brought the lightsaber blade down at a not-quite-vertical angle, slicing out a rough wedge of stone and leaving behind a shallow horizontal ledge in the inner edge of the archway. The rustling of the approaching fire creepers was growing steadily louder. "Mara?"

"I'm finished," Mara called over the noise, the blue-white glow reflected from behind him vanishing as she shut down her lightsaber. "We've got maybe twenty seconds."

Luke looked down the tunnel as he pulled his lightsaber back to his hand. The leading edge of the swarm was barely five meters away, the entire passageway behind them absolutely black with the insects. "I'm ready," he told her, shutting down the weapon and returning it to his belt. "On three?"

"On three," Mara said.

Luke took half a step backward, and for a moment his back pressed against Mara's as they each gauged the distances and stretched out in their own ways to the Force. "On three," Luke repeated, trying to ignore the sound that seemed to fill the entire passageway. Across by one wall, Artoo moaned with fear. "One, two, *three.*"

He jumped upward toward his footrest, turning his body halfway around as he did so and hoping belatedly that the arc of his leap wouldn't be high enough to crack his head against the curved rock above him. As he came around to face the center of the archway he caught sight of Mara, also in midair with her back to the rock, starting to come down toward her own newly carved footrest. Her arms were stretched toward him, palms outward, as if she were reaching out to push him away. Luke got his own arms up, palms similarly outward, as their heels came thunking solidly down onto their footrests. Their palms met, their fingers intertwined—

Mara took a deep breath, exhaling it in a rush just audible above the noise of the fire creepers now swarming through the passageway beneath their feet. "I'll be Kesseled," she said. "It worked."

Luke nodded, taking a deep breath of his own. With their feet resting on the cutouts they'd made, their arms stretched rigidly out and their hands clasped to brace and support one another, they had in effect become a living archway within the stone one. And as long as they stayed that way, they would remain safe above the flow of insects.

But if either of them fell . . .

"Cozy, isn't it?" Mara commented, looking around. "Very symbolic, too. The great and powerful Jedi Master forced to rely on someone else for his survival."

"I wish you'd drop that," Luke growled. "I've already admitted I can't do everything."

"Which isn't quite the same as relying on other people," Mara said. "But okay; consider it dropped. Looks like we're just high enough."

Luke looked down. The river of fire creepers, as he'd already seen, sloshed a fair distance up the walls of the passageway as too many insects tried to travel through too small a space. Here at the archway, where the tunnel was still narrower, they roved even higher, with some of the insects passing barely centimeters beneath their footrests. "You think they can eat through our boots?" he asked.

"If enough of them climb aboard and start chewing, they can probably eat through anything," Mara said. "And all it'll take will be one of them noticing us to wave whatever chemical flags they use to whistle up the rest of the swarm."

Luke nodded grimly. "So in other words, if any of them look like they're getting close, grab them with the Force and get rid of them fast."

"Better still, throw them across the cave into a wall," Mara said. "What *I'd* like to know is what they're doing down here. There can't possibly be enough food in this entire cavern complex for a swarm this size."

"Maybe it's a shortcut from one part of the surface to another," Luke suggested. "There's that underground river we passed a ways back— maybe they come here for the water."

"Could be," Mara said, peering to the side. "I wish we'd had time to move our packs up off—what in *space*?"

Luke followed her gaze, just in time to see Builder With Vines swoop down in a shallow dive over the scurrying fire creepers and curve up again with what appeared to be some of the insects in his mouth. "He's eating them," he said, not quite believing it.

"Of course he is," Mara said. " 'Eater Of Fire Creepers,' remember?"

"But then—?" Luke floundered, thoroughly confused now. "Are they really not that dangerous?"

"Of course they're dangerous," Mara snorted. "You ever hear of the topshot in any clan who picked a name that made him sound calm and reasonable? This has to be the Qom Jha version of kick-the-rancor."

"Kick-the-rancor?"

"A slang term in Palpatine's court," Mara said. "Any stupid stunt where the risks were way out of proportion to the gain."

Luke worked moisture into a suddenly dry mouth as he watched Builder With Vines finish his snack and swoop down for another pass. Why in the name of the Force was he taking such a terrible risk?

And it *was* a terrible risk. Luke could feel the danger involved, his Jedi senses tingling almost as strongly as if the threat had been aimed directly at him. Surely Builder With Vines couldn't be that hungry. Could he?

"Offhand, I'd say he's showing off," Mara muttered, answering his silent question.

"For who? Us?"

"Hardly." Mara nodded toward the wall behind Luke. "For the kid."

Luke craned his neck to look. Balanced precariously on a stone near the Qom Jha opening, Child Of Winds was watching in utter fascination as Builder With Vines swooped over the mass of insects, his wings quivering with excitement or nervousness or envy. "Uh-oh," Luke said. "You don't think—?"

"I would hope he's not that stupid," Mara said. "But the Qom Jha have been riding him ever since we headed out on this little trip. He just might."

Luke grimaced. "Child Of Winds, you stay where you are," he ordered, putting Jedi firmness into his voice. "You're not to try to do what Builder With Vines is—"

And suddenly, a terrified shriek screamed through his mind. "What—?" he gasped, his body twitching violently with the shock of the sound.

"It's Builder With Vines," Mara bit out, her fingers tightening around Luke's to help maintain their balance. Luke looked down—

To a horrifying sight. Builder With Vines, his wings flapping frantically but uselessly, was struggling half-submerged in the living river flowing through the passageway. Dozens of fire creepers were already crawling across his head and wings, biting and stinging. Even as Child of Winds's terrified cry joined Builder With Vines's scream in Luke's mind a hundred more of the insects crawled onto the Qom Jha, their weight forcing him still deeper beneath the flow.

There was no time to waste. Stretching out with the Force, Luke hauled Builder With Vines up and out of the flow, holding him suspended in midair. He shifted his focus to the insects, grabbing them through the Force and throwing them off him.

"Don't bother," Mara said quietly. "There's nothing you can do."

Luke bit back the reflexive impulse to deny it. He was a Jedi—there had to be *something* he could do.

But no. She was right . . . and as Builder With Vines's mental scream died into the silence of death he let the body sink gently back into the mindless flow.

"Easy on the fingers," Mara said softly.

With an effort, Luke turned his gaze back to her, focusing on their joined hands. His fingers were all but white where he was squeezing hers tightly in frustration. "Sorry," he muttered, forcing himself to relax his grip.

"That's all right," she said. "You know, you've got a pretty good grip there. I thought you Jedi usually concentrated more on the mental aspects of the Force than you did in keeping in shape."

She was trying to deflect his attention, he knew, trying to turn his thoughts away from the horror he'd just witnessed. Sympathy from Mara was a new experience all by itself; but neither words nor sympathy had a puddle's chance of smoothing over the guilt and anger rising in his throat like a twisting sand-devil. "It's not all right," he snapped back at her. "I knew it was dangerous—I could have stopped him. I *should* have stopped him."

"How?" Mara countered. "I mean, sure, you could have used the Force to pin him to the ceiling. But what right would you have had to do something like that?"

"What do you mean, what right?" Luke bit out. "I was the one in charge here. Their safety was my responsibility."

"Oh, come *on*," Mara said, the sympathy still there but with a tinge of scorn around the edges now. "Builder With Vines was an intelligent, responsible adult being. He knew what he was doing. He made his choice, and he suffered the consequences. If you want to start feeling guilty about mistakes, start with ones that were actually your fault."

"Such as?" Luke growled.

For a long moment Mara gazed coolly at him, and Luke felt a sudden wave of misgiving ripple through his anger. "Such as?" Mara repeated. "Well, let's see. Such as not moving your Jedi academy off Yavin when you first found out a really nasty dark side power was infesting the place. Such as not slapping down a tipped turbolaser like Kyp Durron the minute he started showing dark side tendencies of his own. Such as not providing adequate protection for your sister's children against kidnapping, despite the fact it had already been tried a couple of times. Such as unilaterally declaring yourself a Jedi Master after less than ten years on the job. How long a list do you want?"

Luke tried to glare at her. But there was no strength behind the glare, and with a grimace of embarrassment he dropped his gaze from her face. "You're right," he sighed. "You're absolutely right. I don't know, Mara. It's been . . . I don't know."

"Let me guess," she said, the sarcasm gone from her voice again. "Life as a Jedi has been a lot foggier than you ever expected it to be. You've had trouble understanding what you're supposed to do, or how you're supposed to behave. You've been gaining tremendous power in the Force, but more often than not you've been paralyzed with fear that you're going to use it the wrong way. Am I getting warm?"

Luke stared at her. "Yes," he said, not quite believing it. How had she known? "That's it exactly."

"And yet," she continued, "sometime in the past couple of months, things have suddenly become clearer. Not that you've had any great lightning-bolt insights, but a lot of the hesitation has disappeared and you've found it easier to stay on what seems in hindsight to have been the right path."

"Right again," Luke said. "Though there have also been one or two pretty impressive revelations," he added, thinking back. "The vision on Tierfon that got me in touch with Karrde just in time to hear about you being trapped here, for one." He eyed her closely. "You know what's been going on?"

"Yes, it's been only slightly more visible than blindingly obvious," she said dryly. "Certainly to me. Probably to Leia and Corran and some of your other Jedi students, too. Possibly to everyone else in the New Republic."

"Oh, thank you," Luke said, trying to match her tone and not entirely succeeding. "That makes me feel so much better."

"Good. It was supposed to." Mara took a deep breath, and Luke could sense her reluctance. "Look, you're the one in the middle of this.

You're the one who has to make the final call on what's going on. But if you want my reading, it all started with that little jaunt you took out to Byss about nine years ago. Where you faced—whatever it was you faced out there."

Luke shivered. "The reborn Emperor."

"Or whatever," Mara said with an odd touch of impatience. "Personally, I'm not convinced it was really him. But that's beside the point. The point was that you decided—stupidly and rather arrogantly, in my opinion—that the best way to stop him would be for you to pretend to join up and let him teach you some of his dark side techniques."

"But I didn't really go over to the dark side," Luke protested, trying to remember those dark days. "I mean, I don't think I did."

Mara shook her head. "Debatable; but it almost doesn't matter. One way or the other, you still willingly dabbled in it. And from that point on, it colored everything you did."

One of Master Yoda's pronouncements floated up from his memory. *If once you start down the dark path,* his old teacher had warned, *forever will it dominate your destiny.* "It did, too, didn't it?" he murmured, half to himself, as all the errors and mistakes and, yes, the arrogance of the past nine years rose accusingly before his eyes. "What was I thinking?"

"You weren't thinking," Mara said, an odd mixture of impatience and compassion swirling together in her voice and emotions. "You were reacting, trying to save everyone and do everything. And in the process you came within a split blaster bolt of destroying yourself."

"So what changed?" he asked. "What happened?"

Mara's eyes narrowed fractionally. "You telling me you don't know?"

Luke grimaced, wondering that he hadn't seen it earlier. That critical moment off Iphigin, as he and Han had prepared for combat against the pirate gang Han had deduced was on its way. The moment when he'd seen the vision of Emperor Palpatine and Exar Kun laughing at him . . . "No, I know," he conceded. "I made a decision to stop using the power of the Force so much."

And suddenly, through that mixture of compassion and impatience came a wave of something completely unexpected. An overpowering flood of relief. "You got it," Mara said quietly. "Finally."

Luke shook his head. "But why?" he demanded. "The power's obviously there, available for a Jedi to use. Is it just because I touched the dark side that using it is so bad for me?"

"That's probably part of it," Mara said. "But even if you'd never done that you'd still have run into trouble. You ever been in a hullplate-shaping plant?"

"Ah—no," Luke said, blinking at the sudden change of topic.

"How about an ore-crushing facility?" she suggested. "Lando's had a couple of them at one time or another—you must have visited at least one of them."

"I've seen the one on Varn, yes," Luke said, the mention of Lando's name throwing a sudden damper on the cautiously growing feeling of excitement at these new revelations. Mara's relationship with Lando . . .

"Fine," Mara said, either missing the change in Luke's emotions or else ignoring it. "Sometimes small songbirds set up their nests in the upper supports of those buildings. Did you hear any of them singing when you were there?"

Luke smiled tightly. Again, it was so obvious. "Of course not," he said. "It was way too noisy in there to hear anything that quiet."

Mara smiled back. "Pretty obvious, isn't it, once you see it. The Force isn't just about power, like most non-Jedi think. It's also about guidance: everything from those impressive future visions to the more subtle real-time warnings I sometimes think of as a danger sense. Trouble is, the more you tap into it for raw power, the less you're able to hear its guidance over the noise of your own activity."

"Yes," Luke murmured, so many puzzles suddenly coming clear. He had often wondered how it was he could rebuild Darth Vader's personal fortress while Master Yoda had become winded doing something as relatively simple as lifting an X-wing from the Dagobah swamp. Clearly, Yoda had understood the choices far better than his upstart pupil.

And even in the short time since Luke had decided to try that same choice he'd already seen glimpses of why Yoda had chosen that path. Subtle bits of guidance, sometimes occurring as little more than vague and almost subconscious feelings, had been showing up more and more: protecting him from a quick capture back at the Cavrilhu Pirates' asteroid base, or quietly prompting him to accept Child Of Winds's assistance, which had led directly to this cavern and the pride-motivated aid of the Qom Jha. "I was on Iphigin a couple of months ago helping Han with some negotiations," he said. "The Diamala at the talks told Han that Jedi who used as much power as I did always ended up slipping over to the dark side."

"They may be right," Mara agreed. "Not all Dark Jedi come from botched training, you know. Some of them slip into it all by themselves."

"Not a very pleasant thought," Luke said soberly, thinking about his Yavin academy. Of his successes at Jedi instruction there, and his failures. "Especially given that I started teaching under dark side influence."

"Yes, I noticed that, too," Mara agreed. "Possibly one of the major reasons you didn't do very well with that first batch of students."

Luke made a face. "Is that why you didn't stay?"

"That, and the changes I saw in you," she said. "You didn't seem interested in listening to any warnings about what you were doing, and I decided that when it collapsed around you it wouldn't do either of us any good if I got caught in the rubble, too." She shrugged. "Anyway, Corran was there, and he seemed to have his head bolted on straight."

"He wasn't there very long, though," Luke murmured.

"Yes, I found that out afterward. Pity."

For a moment neither of them said anything. Luke craned his neck to peer to the side, wondering if the end of the fire creeper swarm was visible yet. This introspection was both embarrassing and painful; and besides, they had urgent work to do.

But the black carpet still stretched as far as the passageway's turns and irregularities permitted him to see. "What about you?" he asked, turning back to Mara again. "You were the Emperor's Hand. Why hasn't your life been dominated by the dark side?"

She shrugged uncomfortably. "Maybe it has. It certainly was from the time Palpatine took me from my home till I got rid of that last command he'd jammed into my mind."

Her gaze clouded over oddly, as if she were looking into some private place within herself. "Though it's funny, somehow. Palpatine never really tried to turn me to the dark side, at least not the way he turned Vader and tried to turn you. Actually, I don't think I was ever really in the dark side at all."

"But everything you were doing was the Emperor's work," Luke said. "If he was on the dark side, shouldn't you have been, too?"

Mara shook her head. "I don't know," she admitted. "But I wasn't." Her gaze came back, and Luke could sense the protective barrier going up again, as if she'd suddenly realized her private feelings had been a little too visible. "You're the Jedi Master. You figure it out."

"I'll work on it," Luke promised. Yes, the barriers were back up.

But not as high as they'd once been. Not nearly as high.

"In the meantime," she said, "do those sustained control techniques you taught me work on arm muscles as well as lightsabers?"

Luke focused on her arms, noticing for the first time that they were trembling slightly with muscle fatigue. "They do okay," he said. "But for muscles there's a better technique. Let me show you . . ."

It was another hour before the swarm of fire creepers finally finished its migration beneath them and disappeared down the cavern passageway. In their wake they left Artoo and everything metal or otherwise indigestible from their packs, though the packs themselves had vanished.

And, of course, Builder With Vines's remains.

Mara glanced once at the scattered bones, then firmly turned her eyes away. Yes, it was the Qom Jha's own fault that he'd gotten himself killed; and yes, on one level it was merely the balance of nature at work; and yes, she'd tried her best to keep Luke from taking any of the blame on himself. But none of that meant she had to like what had happened, or wanted to look at the results. "Good thing the food bars were in metal boxes," she commented, massaging her fingers as she prodded what was left of their equipment with the tip of her boot. "The water bottles didn't hold up nearly as well, though."

"There's plenty of water down here," Luke reminded her. He was standing near their cut, looking up at Child Of Winds. "We just won't be able to carry extra supplies with us. It's all safe now, Child Of Winds. You can come down."

The young Qom Qae didn't budge, that almost-voice going again. "I understand," Luke said gently. "But you have to come down. You're in the way up there, and we don't want to hit you with our lightsabers."

For a moment Mara thought Child Of Winds would decide he preferred to stay high up off the floor and take his chances with the lightsabers. Then, with clear reluctance, he spread his wings and fluttered down to a slightly awkward perch on top of the droid's dome.

"What now?" Mara asked, crossing to Luke's side. "Back to hack and slash?"

Luke shrugged. "The wall's not going to fall apart on its own," he said. "Unless you think we ought to risk using the grenades."

Mara peered down the passageway. Nothing was visible, but after that fire creeper swarm she was feeling a little spooked herself. "Let's stick with the lightsabers for now," she suggested. "If Splitter Of Stones gets back with the reinforcements before we're finished we'll consider it."

"Sounds good," Luke agreed, pulling his lightsaber from his belt and igniting it. "Artoo, keep an eye out for any more trouble."

The droid warbled a slightly nervous acknowledgment and extended his sensor unit again, nearly knocking Child Of Winds off his perch as he did so. "Okay," Luke said, taking his position to the side of their cut again. "Let's get started."

"Right," Mara said, igniting her own lightsaber. Luke's lightsaber slashed and died; Mara's followed similarly—

And that, she realized, was that. They'd had the conversation she'd known was coming, and had been dreading, since he first arrived here. And while he'd obviously not exactly been thrilled by the realization of how badly he'd wrecked the past few years, he'd taken the news better than she'd expected him to.

The question now was what he would do with this newfound knowledge. Whether he would take it solidly to heart and commit to what he now knew was right, or whether the lure of power and quick solutions would eventually drag him back to the easy path. The dark path.

She would just have to wait and see.

CHAPTER

16

From behind him came the sound of an opening door, and Han turned his head to see Lando step into the *Lady Luck*'s bridge. "Okay, it's done," the other announced, his tone tense and decidedly grumpy. "Everything's been shut down to standby. Engines, sensors, computer system—the works."

He crossed the bridge and dropped into the pilot's seat beside Han. "And I'd like to go on record right now as saying I hate this."

"I'm not exactly happy about it myself," Han had to admit. "But this is the way it has to be."

Lando snorted. "Says a self-admitted Imperial clone TIE pilot," he added accusingly. "You know, Han, I've done some crazy things in my time, but this one takes the prize."

Han grimaced, gazing out at the stars. It was crazy, all right. Somewhere out there, a hyperspace microjump away, was an Imperial Ubiqtorate contact station, with all the security and firepower and just plain nastiness that that implied.

And here they were, probably well within its defensive perimeter, sitting around like a belly-up gornt with their systems cranked way back to keep from being too visible to any auto-rovers the station might have out wandering the area. Waiting for an Imperial clone to come back and tell them where in the shrunken Empire the capital of Bastion was located. "Leia said he was all right," he told Lando.

"She said he was sincere and not planning to betray you," Lando corrected darkly. "She didn't say he was a competent enough liar to pull this whole thing off. Especially not in front of some congenitally suspicious Ubiqtorate agent."

Han eyed him. "You don't like clones, do you?"

Lando snorted again. "No, I don't," he said flatly. "Palpatine may have talked about alien species as being subhuman, but clones are *really* down there."

For a minute the bridge was silent. Han gazed out at the stars some more, rubbing his fingertips over his blaster grip and trying not to let Lando's nervousness get to him. Leia had agreed to let him come out here, after all, and Leia was a Jedi. Surely she'd have seen or felt or guessed if something bad was going to happen. Wouldn't she?

"Tell me about this Baron Fel," Lando said suddenly. "I mean the original one. What was he like?"

Han shrugged. "Typical Corellian, I suppose. Well, no, actually he wasn't. He was a farm boy, for one thing, who got bribed with an academy appointment to stop him testifying in a legal action against some big agro-combine official's son. We were at Carida together for a while, though I didn't hang around with him much. He was an honorable sort, I suppose—even a little stiff-necked about it sometimes—and a pretty fair pilot."

"As good as you?" Lando asked.

Han smiled tightly. "Better," he said, a little surprised he was actually admitting that out loud. "At least, with something the size of a TIE fighter."

"So how did he wind up getting cloned?" Lando asked. "As I remember the history, he quit the Empire, joined Rogue Squadron, then got recaptured. So the question is, why would anyone clone a guy who'd already turned once? I don't care *how* good a pilot he was."

"Leia and I asked Carib the same question on Pakrik Minor," Han said. "He told us he didn't know, that it wasn't part of the flash-learning they'd been given in the cloning tanks."

Lando grunted. "Look. They would have had to hold him for three or four years, minimum, before Thrawn got his cloning tanks up and running. Right?"

"They didn't need all of him," Han murmured. "C'baoth cloned Luke from the hand he lost at Bespin, remember?"

"Yes, but Luke's hand was one of Palpatine's trophies," Lando pointed out. "Why would anyone bother keeping parts of Fel in storage? No one even knew Palpatine had all those cloning tanks hidden away, let alone that Thrawn would show up and get them running again."

"Point," Han conceded. "So they probably kept him alive somewhere."

"Right," Lando said. "The question is where?"

"I don't know," Han said. "No one ever found records about him at any of the Imperial prisons or penal colonies we liberated. With his connections to Rogue Squadron, we would have heard if they had."

He hesitated. "The other thing you might not know is that a month or two after his recapture, his wife pulled the same sort of vanishing act."

Lando frowned. "I remember Wedge talking about that once. But you say 'vanishing'—I thought it was the Empire who snatched her."

"That's what everyone thought at the time," Han agreed. "But once they started sifting through the evidence, it was a lot less clear what had happened. Anyway, no one ever found a trace of her, either."

Lando shook his head. "If any of this is supposed to reassure me, it's not. The only way Isard could have gotten Fel back on the Empire's side would have been to braintwist him. You want to tell me what kind of clone is going to come from that?"

Han sighed. "I don't know. All I know is that Leia cleared him."

Lando nodded. "Yeah. Sure."

Again, silence descended on the bridge. This time, it was Han who broke it. "What are Lobot and Moegid doing back there?" he asked.

"They were practicing their slicing techniques before you had me shut the computer down," Lando said, still sounding grumpy. "They're probably checking over Moegid's equipment now."

"Did you tell them where we were going?"

Lando's lips compressed briefly. "I told them we were going into the Empire. I didn't tell them exactly where. Or why."

"Maybe you'd better go do that," Han suggested. "Moegid may need to brush up on Imperial computer systems or something."

"I don't think Verpine ever have to brush up on anything," Lando said. But he nevertheless levered himself out of his seat. "Sure, why not? We might as well all be worried together. It's better than sitting around waiting for the hammer to drop, anyway."

"Don't worry," Han called after him as he left the bridge. "It'll work out. Trust me."

There was no response but the metallic thud of the door as it slid shut behind him. Sighing again, Han turned his attention back to watching for Carib's freighter to return.

Trying hard not to worry.

The Ubiqtorate agent seated at his console gazed up at his visitor from under bushy eyebrows. "All right," he said in a voice that somehow reminded Carib of a thousand prasher worms scratching their wings against tallgrain leaves. "Your ID checks out."

"Glad to hear it," Carib said, trying to put some righteous indignation into his tone. To his ears, though, he sounded merely plaintive. "Does that mean you're finally ready to listen?"

The agent leaned back in his seat, regarding Carib coolly. "Sure," he said. "Provided *you're* ready to hear a list of charges against you if this big news of yours isn't as flacking urgent as you seem to think it is."

He slammed his stylus down on the desk in front of him. "Blast it, Devist, you know you're never supposed to come here yourself. All you people are supposed to know that. Everything you have to report goes through channels. *Everything.*"

Carib remained standing at attention, listening to the reprimand with half an ear and waiting with all the patience he could muster for the other to run out of words. The self-generated tirade, he knew, was one of the Ubiqtorate's classic tactics for rattling someone they wanted to be vulnerable.

But no. That wasn't something *he* knew. It was something Baron Soontir Fel had known. Something that had been artificially transferred along with his piloting skill to Carib and his brothers. Memories that were not his own, from a person who was not him.

And yet, on some level, *was* indeed him.

It was a mind-numbing thought, a painful and depressing blurring of identity that had cost Carib many a sleepless night back on Pakrik Minor before he'd finally made the conscious decision to bury it as far back at the edge of his mind as he could.

And he'd done a fair job of keeping it there . . . until the long-awaited, long-feared orders had come in from the remnants of the Empire—could it really have been only two weeks ago?—reactivating his TIE combat unit. Then, all the old uncertainties and questions and self-doubts had surged back to the front of his mind. He was a clone. A clone. A clone . . .

Stop it, he snarled at the word. *I am Carib Devist. Husband of Lacy, father of Daberin and Keena, tallgrain farmer of the Dorchess Valley of Pakrik Minor. Where I came from and how I came to be don't matter. I am who I am.*

He took a careful breath . . . and as he did so, the doubts once again returned to their uneasy sleep in the deep crevices of his mind. He was Carib Devist; and despite what anyone might say or believe, he was indeed a unique individual.

The Ubiqtorate agent was starting to wind down now, and with a flicker of private amusement Carib realized that for once the old intimidation tactic had backfired. Far from unnerving its intended victim, the tirade had instead given him the time he needed to collect his thoughts and his nerve and to prepare for verbal combat.

"So let's hear it," the agent snarled. "Let's hear this vitally important news of yours."

"Yes, sir," Carib said. "There was an Imperial attack on New Republic High Councilor Leia Organa Solo over Pakrik Minor five days ago. It failed."

"Yes, thank you, we know that," the agent said sarcastically. "Are you telling me you broke security—?"

"The reason it failed," Carib continued, "was because—"

"*I'm* talking here, Devist," the agent snapped. "You broke security for a story we could have pulled off Coruscant Hourly—?"

"—was because," Carib went on doggedly, "they were assisted—"

"Will you shut *up*? I'll have your skin pickled in—"

"—by an unknown alien ship," Carib finished.

"—a Hutt's slimy—" He broke off. "What do you mean, an unknown alien ship?" he demanded.

"I mean a ship with a completely unknown design," Carib said. "It had four outboard panels like the two on a TIE fighter, but the rest was definitely non-Imperial."

For a long moment the agent measured Carib with his eyes. "I don't suppose you happened to pull any records of the battle," he said at last, his tone challenging.

"Not of the battle itself," Carib said, pulling a datacard from his side pouch. "But we did get something of the ship afterward."

The agent held out his hand. Carib dropped the datacard into it, mentally crossing his fingers. Solo had cobbled this thing together during the trip here from a pair of records he and Organa Solo had had with them in their ship. Where they'd gotten the originals Carib didn't know.

And really didn't care, either. Combat, intrigue, galactic security—none of those were matters he and his brothers wanted anything to do with anymore. All they wanted was to be left alone to raise their families and tend their farms and live their lives.

And all he cared about at this immediate moment was that Solo's gimmicked record be good enough to fool this glowering bit-pusher into believing it. If it was . . .

The agent whistled under his breath, peering at his reader. "Tarkin's teeth," he muttered, shaking his head. "Are these energy readings correct?"

"That's what was there." Carib hesitated, but he couldn't resist. "So was it worth breaking security for?"

The agent looked up, but it was clear he wasn't really seeing Carib anymore. "I'd say so, yes," he said absently, keying his board furiously. "Sure. Just watch it when you head home, and keep with the zigzag. Dismissed."

And that was it. No thank-yous, no well-dones, no nothing. Just a petty little Ubiqtorate agent on dead-end duty at the edge of nowhere with visions of promotion dancing through his head.

But that was okay, Carib knew as he headed down the corridor. His part was done now, or almost done, and Solo would take it from here. He could go back to Lacy and his brothers and sink back into the quiet anonymity that was all any of them desired.

Unless . . .

He grimaced as a thought belatedly struck him. Yes, the Ubiqtorate agent back there had swallowed the bait in a single eager gulp. But that was no guarantee the military analysts on Bastion who would take the record apart would do the same.

And it was no guarantee at all that Grand Admiral Thrawn wouldn't see instantly through the scam. If he did, and if Solo was still in Imperial space at the time . . .

He shook his head once to clear it. No. He'd done what they wanted, and had risked his own neck to do it. What happened now was in their hands, not his. His part was done. Period.

Quickening his pace, he headed toward the docking tunnel where his freighter was berthed. The faster he got out of here and back to his farm, the better.

From off to the side, the speaker suddenly crackled. "Solo?"

Hastily, Han dropped his feet off the edge of the control board where they'd been propped and keyed the comm. "Yeah, I'm here, Carib," he said. "You got it?"

"Yes," Carib said. "He sent the droid probe off on vector forty-three by fifteen."

Behind Han, the bridge door opened. "Is that Devist?" Lando asked.

"Yeah," Han said as he punched up a chart. "You sure this is the vector to Bastion?"

"It's the direction the probe went," Carib said. "I'm sending you a copy of the recording."

"What I meant was are you sure he was sending it to Bastion," Han said as a beep from the board acknowledged receipt of the transmission.

"He didn't say anything one way or the other," Carib said. "But from the shining vision of promotion in his eyes, I can't see where else he would have sent it."

"How about to the main Ubiqtorate base at Yaga Minor?" Lando countered. "Isn't that his proper chain of command?"

"Usually, yes," Carib said. "But matters of immediate military importance go directly to the high command. Your unknown alien ship should come under that heading."

"We hope," Lando muttered.

"Besides which, there are military politics involved," Carib added. "Anyone stuck out on a contact station like this is here because the upper echelons have basically written him off. The only way to get out is to impress someone higher up in the military. Again, that means sending it straight to Bastion."

Han lifted his eyebrows at Lando. "Sounds reasonable to me."

"I suppose," Lando said suspiciously, peering with narrowed eyes at the freighter hanging in space outside the *Lady Luck*'s viewport. "So Baron Fel was pretty good with military politics, was he?"

Han winced. Whatever Lando's feelings about clones might be, there was no reason to go out of his way to antagonize Carib. Especially when the man was trying to help them.

Even more especially when they were sitting at the edge of Imperial space within spitting distance of a Ubiqtorate station. "Carib—"

"It's all right, Solo," Carib said, his voice studiously neutral. "Maybe you'll agree now I was right when I talked about this back on Pakrik Minor."

Han winced again. Carib's contention that there was still heavy prejudice against clones in the New Republic . . . "Yeah. Sorry."

"It's all right," Carib repeated. "My part's done; I'm heading home. Good luck to you."

The freighter curved away over the *Lady Luck* and flickered with pseudomotion as it made the jump to lightspeed. "He's sure in a hurry to get away," Lando growled.

"He's heading home," Han reminded him, turning his attention back to the chart. A course of forty-three by fifteen from the Ubiqtorate station would put it . . .

"Looks like the Sartinaynian system," Lando said, looking over his shoulder.

"Yeah, it does," Han agreed, nodding.

"Funny place to put an Imperial capital," Lando said, an edge of suspicion still coloring his tone.

"Oh, I don't know," Han said, skimming down the data the *Lady Luck*'s computer had on the place. "It was a sector capital once, so they're probably used to having a bureaucracy underfoot."

"Still a long way from the glittering towers of Coruscant, though," Lando said.

"Isn't everything?" Han countered. "Come on, we're wasting time."

Shaking his head, Lando dropped into the pilot's seat. "Sure. Let's just walk into the middle of the Imperial capital. Why not?"

"Lando, look—"

"No, it's all right, Han," Lando said with a tired sigh. "I said I'd do it, and I will. I just wish I didn't have to." He reached over and keyed the nav computer. "But wishes don't bring you the cards you want. Give Lobot and Moegid a call, will you, and tell them to strap in."

"Sure," Han said, reaching for his own restraints with one hand and going for the comm switch with the other. "Hey, don't worry. It's going to work out fine."

"Yeah," Lando said. "Sure."

. . .

"No!" Ishori Senator Ghic Dx'ono snarled, slamming a horny-tipped fist down on the table for emphasis. "It is completely out of the question. The Ishori will *not* accept anything less than full and complete justice for the Caamasi and the people of the New Republic."

"Justice is what we all seek," Diamalan Senator Porolo Miatamia countered, his voice the glacial calm of his species. "But—"

"You lie!" Dx'ono all but screamed, his ears flattened against his head. "The Diamala demand the impossible, and refuse to settle for anything else!"

"Senators, please," President Ponc Gavrisom cut in, his wings sweeping briefly between the other two as if trying to separate a pair of enraged shockball players. "I'm not asking for a resolution of the Caamas situation here and now. All I'm asking—"

"I know what you're asking," Dx'ono snarled. "But justice postponed is too often justice ignored." He jabbed a finger accusingly toward Miatamia. "And that is precisely the situation the Diamala are trying to engineer."

"The Diamala have every intention of seeing justice served," Miatamia said coldly. "But we understand that more urgent matters should take priority."

"Thrawn is dead!" Dx'ono snarled, leaping to his feet as if to physically attack the other. "He is *dead*! All Imperial records agree!"

Miatamia remained unmoved. "I saw him, Senator. I saw him, and heard him—"

"Lies!" Dx'ono cut him off. "All lies, created to distract us from the search for justice."

Seated in the small room behind the false wall, Booster Terrik shook his head. "Idiots," he muttered. "Both of them."

"Now, now, Father," his daughter Mirax Terrik Horn said, squeezing his arm. "Both of them are probably sincere, from their own different points of view."

"And we all know what road is lined with sincere people," Terrik said sourly, glancing back over his shoulder. "Where is that blasted Bel Iblis, anyway? I've got work to do."

"You've got nothing but overhaul and maintenance work on the *Errant Venture* scheduled for the next three weeks," Mirax admonished him firmly. "And you're not needed for a single bit of it."

Booster sent a glare at her, a glare that worked about as well as such looks had ever worked on her. Which was to say, not very. "I thought daughters were supposed to be a source of pride and comfort to their fathers in their old age," he grumbled.

She smiled. "When you get there, I'll see what I can do," she promised.

The smile faded as she turned back to the false wall. "This whole thing is starting to get out of hand. Have you heard that a hundred systems have already petitioned to rejoin the Empire?"

"My sources say it's only been twenty systems," Booster said. "Everything else is just rumors."

"Whatever the numbers, it's still something to worry about," Mirax said, a note of quiet dread in her voice. "If Thrawn is really still alive, and if all this turmoil persuades people they want or need his protection, then the Empire could regain its territory without firing a single shot."

"I doubt they're going to talk *that* many systems into coming back," Booster argued. But he didn't feel nearly as confident as he was trying to sound. "Anyway, there's not a lot we can do about it."

Behind him, the door slid open. "Ah—Captain Terrik," General Bel Iblis said, striding in and offering his hand. "Thank you for coming. I trust you've been well entertained?"

"If you mean the dance show, I've seen better," Booster said, jerking a thumb toward the loud drama in the next room as he reluctantly and briefly gripped Bel Iblis's hand. He and authority had never gotten along very well. "Speaking of dance shows, I've got a bone to pick with you over that nonsense in the Sif'kric system three weeks ago. The bureaucrats there still haven't released the *Hoopster's Prank* back to me."

"I didn't know that," Bel Iblis said, shutting off the speaker that was bringing the argument in from the next room and pulling over the room's remaining chair. "I'll give orders to have it sprung as soon as we finish here."

Booster eyed him warily. "The word 'finish' implies a start."

"Indeed it does," Bel Iblis agreed, positioning the chair to face the two of them and sitting down. "I didn't ask you here just for a private showing of Gavrisom's mediation skill. Incidentally, I presume I don't have to tell you that anything you heard here is to be considered confidential."

"Really." Booster frowned thoughtfully at his daughter. "Let's see. The Ishori scream when they debate and want a square meter of skin off every Bothan to give to what's left of the Caamasi. The Diamala want the same square meter, but only from the Bothans who helped destroy Caamas—exhuming them if necessary—as soon as anyone figures out who they were. Who do you think we should sell these big secrets to first, Mirax?"

She gave her father a patient look and shifted her attention to Bel Iblis. "We understand, General," she said. "What is it you want?"

"I let you see a bit of this private conversation because I thought it would help drive home the seriousness of the situation we're in," Bel Iblis said, nodding back toward the discussion still going on now inaudibly behind him. "The buildup of warships over Bothawui is being repeated all over the New Republic as worlds and species line up behind the Ishori and Diamala over this issue. The only way we're going to defuse the situation is to find out who exactly the Bothans were who sabotaged the Caamas planetary shields."

"As a dancer, General, you're no better than they are," Booster said. "Get to the point."

Bel Iblis locked eyes with him. "I want to borrow the *Errant Venture.*"

Booster stared at him, too stunned even to laugh in the general's face. "You must be joking," he got out at last. "Certainly not."

"What do you need it for?" Mirax asked.

Bel Iblis shifted his gaze to her. "We think there may be a complete copy of the Caamas Document in the Ubiqtorate base at Yaga Minor," he told her. "Gavrisom has decided to launch an information raid to try to get hold of it."

"A data raid on a Ubiqtorate base?" Booster echoed. "What poor sucker pulled *that* assignment?"

Bel Iblis regarded him coolly. "I did," he said.

For a moment the room was silent. Booster studied Bel Iblis's face, wishing the general had glazed over the false wall behind him when he'd turned off the sound. The argument back there, particularly the Ishori Senator's wide-armed flailing, was highly distracting.

As Bel Iblis probably intended it to be. "Okay," he said at last. "I get the picture—you need a Star Destroyer to sneak in through their outer defenses. Last I heard, the New Republic still has some captured ones. Why not use one of those?"

"Two reasons," Bel Iblis said. "First, they're all too well known. Disguising their markings and engine ID signatures would take too long."

"And probably not fool anyone for long," Mirax murmured.

Booster glared at her. Whose side was she on here, anyway?

"Right." Bel Iblis nodded. "Second, and more importantly, we can't pull any of them away from their assigned patrol duties without everyone in the sector instantly missing them. You know what an information raid is like: if the target gets even a whiff of your plans, you're sunk."

Booster crossed his arms across his chest. "Sorry, General. I sympathize with your problem and all, but no deal. I went through too much for that ship to risk it in some crazy scheme that's none of my business anyway."

Bel Iblis cocked his head slightly to the side. "You sure about it being none of your business?"

Booster uncrossed his arms far enough to tap at his upper chest. "You see a New Republic military insignia here?"

"You see the Diamalan Senator back there?" Bel Iblis countered. "They're allies with the Mon Cals on this Bothan situation; and you know how much the Mon Cals hate smugglers. If all-out war breaks out, one of the first things they're likely to do is move against all smuggling groups they can find, if for no other reason than to drain the potential pool of privateers the other side can use."

He lifted an eyebrow. "And with an Imperial Star Destroyer in your possession, where do you think you'll end up on their list of things to do?"

Booster grimaced. "Somewhere near the top?"

"That's where *I'd* put you," Bel Iblis agreed. "So helping me is very much in your own best interests."

He had a case, Booster had to admit. And he could feel the accusation behind Mirax's eyes as she gazed at him, reminding him of his glib comment not five minutes ago about how there was nothing they could do.

And it occurred to him—as it might not yet have to his daughter— that if Bel Iblis was going to Yaga Minor, Mirax's husband, Corran, and the rest of Rogue Squadron would probably be going in with him.

But to be asked to risk his beloved *Errant Venture* this way was just too much. Yes, it was falling apart, with half its systems questionable or totally dead, and with an operating cost that would make an Imperial baron blanch. But it was his. All his . . .

He paused. What in the worlds was he thinking of?

He uncrossed his arms and resettled himself in his seat, eyeing Bel Iblis speculatively. "Unfortunately, even if I said yes, you'd never get away with it," he pointed out. "You turn a halfway decent sensor array on the *Errant Venture* and a blind wampa could tell we're not up to Imperial standards anymore. We'd need turbolaser and tractor-emplacement upgrades, shield rebuilds, whole system replacements—you name it, we need it."

Bel Iblis's gaze had hardened noticeably during the recitation. "I see," he said dryly. "Airen Cracken warned me about you."

"Glad to hear he remembers me." Booster shrugged. "It's up to you, General. I'll lend you the ship; but in exchange, you have to upgrade the systems. And win or lose, those upgrades stay put when it's all over."

"The Mon Cals will love that."

"If war breaks out, the Mon Cals will be the least of my worries," Booster said bluntly. "Every two-bit pirate and smuggling group in the galaxy will be trying to get their hands on the *Venture*. That's my offer; take it or leave it."

"I'll take it," Bel Iblis said, standing up. "Where's the ship now?"

"Parked over in the outer Mrisst system," Booster told him, standing up as well and trying not to show his surprise. His admittedly spotty experience with New Republic officials was that they needed more cajoling and a lot more bargaining before they finally gave in. And New Republic military officials were even worse. "Where do you want it delivered?"

"I'll tell you once we're aboard," Bel Iblis said.

Booster frowned. "You're coming with us?"

"Along with two hundred of my crewers," the general said. "We'll assist you in flying the ship until we pick up a proper crew at the rendezvous point."

"I *have* a proper crew," Booster retorted. He should have known Bel Iblis wouldn't give in this easily.

"For running a mobile smugglers depot, perhaps," Bel Iblis said. "Not for impersonating an Imperial warship. I'll be bringing a full skeleton complement aboard before we leave the rendezvous point."

Booster drew himself up to his full height. "Let's get one thing straight right now, General," he said stiffly. "The *Errant Venture* is *my* ship. If I don't captain her, she doesn't go anywhere."

Once again, Bel Iblis surprised him. "Certainly," he said calmly. "I wouldn't have it any other way. I have a shuttle waiting; we'll leave at once."

"Whatever you say," Booster said, fighting against the bad feeling that, despite appearances, Bel Iblis had still not given in quite the way it sounded. "Mirax, you might as well take my shuttle and head back home."

Bel Iblis cleared his throat. "What?" Booster demanded suspiciously.

"I'm afraid Mirax will have to come with us," Bel Iblis said apologetically. "It's absolutely vital that we have complete security on this, and that means no one who knows about it can be allowed to wander around loose."

Booster drew himself up again. "If you think I'm going to let my daughter come on a raid against a Ubiqtorate base—"

"Oh, no, not at all," Bel Iblis hastened to assure him. "She and her son will stay behind at the rendezvous point with the prep crew."

Once again, Booster had the distinct feeling of having had the blocks knocked out from under him. "Fine," he muttered. "Well, let's get going. If you're determined to go marching into an Imperial base, we might as well get to it."

"Yes," Bel Iblis said. "And let me thank you once again for your help. Don't worry; it'll all work out fine."

"Yeah," Booster grumbled as he took Mirax's arm. "Sure."

CHAPTER
17

With one final truncated lightsaber sweep, the last of the chunks came away from the opening and crashed hollowly to the rocky floor. "There," Luke said, peering into the hole. "What do you think?"

Mara stepped close to his side and shined her glow rod into the opening. "Still going to be tight for the droid," she said. "But I think it'll do."

Luke glanced back over his shoulder, to the eight Qom Jha hanging from the passageway ceiling. Yes, it would do. More importantly, now that Splitter Of Stones and Keeper Of Promises had returned with the Qom Jha hunters Eater Of Fire Creepers had promised, they should get moving before they lost any prestige in their guides' eyes.

Or to put it another way, before they lost so much confidence in Master Walker Of Sky that they decided to back out of this trip entirely. They hadn't said much about Builder With Vines's violent death, but they were definitely avoiding the area where their friend had died.

And they weren't going out of their way to be nice to Child Of Winds, either. If he and Mara didn't get moving, there was likely to be more of the same trouble they'd already had too much of.

"I agree," he said, returning his lightsaber to his belt and stepping over to the shrunken collection of items that had been his pack before the fire creepers had gotten to it. Aside from the food bars in their metal case, the spare blaster power packs and glow rods, and some of the syntherope, there wasn't much left. The bedrolls, survival tent, medpacs, even the detonator casings on the grenades had all been ravaged into useless shreds. "I guess we just take whatever we can salvage of this stuff?"

"That's what I'm doing," Mara said. She had one of her ration boxes open and was sorting out the bars between the various pockets in her jumpsuit. "Soldiers' first rule: concentrate on the food."

"Understood," Luke said, starting to fill his own pockets. Artoo rolled unsteadily up to him on the uneven ground and with a beep of invitation slid open the hidden compartment in his dome. "I'm putting what's left of the syntherope in Artoo," Luke called to Mara, stuffing the coil into the compartment. "In case you need it."

"Fine," Mara said. "I'm ready."

"Me, too," Luke said, gazing into the darkness. "You want to stay with the same marching order?"

"You mean with you in front and me behind handling the luggage?" Mara asked, nodding toward Artoo.

Luke felt his face warming. "I meant—"

"I know what you meant," Mara said, giving him a wry smile. "But you're the Jedi; and if there's anything in there with big teeth, you've got the best chance of toasting it before it draws blood. So. After you."

Luke looked up at the waiting Qom Jha. "Sure," he said, shifting his glow rod to his left hand and drawing his lightsaber. "We're ready, Splitter Of Stones."

Follow me, the Qom Jha said, dropping off the ceiling and fluttering into the darkness.

It was quickly evident that their route wasn't so much a passageway as it was a narrow, V-shaped crack in the rock. Within the first three steps Luke was forced to return his lightsaber to his belt and wedge his glow rod into his tunic to free up his hands to help pull himself along. Behind him he could hear Artoo's continuous nervous twittering and the occasional muted thunk where Mara bumped him into one of the side walls.

Each time that happened, he had to fight back the impulse to offer his help. If Mara needed him, she would ask. Probably.

Fortunately, the crack was only no more than three meters long, with a yellowish wall blocking the far end. *This is the way inside,* Splitter Of Stones said from a perch at a small gap that broached the yellow wall near the top. *Beyond this wall is the High Tower.*

"I'd say we're here," Mara commented. "That wall's definitely artificial."

"Agreed," Luke said, wedging himself into a more or less steady position in front of the wall and drawing his lightsaber. "You and Artoo keep back."

The wall was quite thin and, more importantly, not made of cortosis ore. Three quick slices of the green blade, and they had their entrance.

Luke dropped through the opening, lightsaber and Jedi senses at the ready. Beyond the wall was a dark, high-ceilinged room, incredibly dusty, that extended out beyond the range of his glow rod beam. Spaced along the walls at two different heights were elaborately tooled wall sconces that looked like they had once held torches or torchlike lights. Above the sconces, at perhaps a dozen other points around the room, other gaps showed where sections of the yellow wall had crumbled away from the ceiling. Aside from the sconces, there were no other decorations or furnishings.

"Doesn't look like Hijarna," Mara muttered from behind him, waving her own glow rod around.

"What?" Luke asked.

"There's a ruined fortress on the planet Hijarna," she explained. "Karrde sometimes uses it as a meeting place."

"Yes, he said something about that when I saw him on Cejansij," Luke said. "He said if this fortress was like that one it could probably shrug off any attack he could throw at it."

"Him, or the New Republic in general," Mara said grimly. "The Hijarna fortress was made of some incredibly hard black stone that could eat massed turbolaser fire for breakfast."

She gestured with her glow rod. "My first look at the High Tower from outside the cave mouth reminded me of that one. But the wall material here isn't anything like it."

Artoo whistled, his sensor unit extended and rotating back and forth as if searching for something. "That doesn't necessarily mean anything," Luke pointed out, squatting down in front of the droid and peering at the datapad they'd rigged up to serve as translator for his more complicated comments. "They could have been built by two different groups of the same people."

"Maybe. What's he saying?"

"He says that from the fastenings he doesn't think the wall sconces were part of the original furnishings," Luke said. "For whatever that's worth."

He straightened up and pointed toward the unseen part of the room. "He also says there's a very strong power source operating somewhere over there."

"Really," Mara said with interest, taking a step in that direction and shining her glow rod into the darkness. "Let's go take a look."

No! Keeper Of Promises said sharply from above Luke.

"Hang on," Luke said to Mara, looking up. Keeper Of Promises was perched on one of the wall sconces, his wings quivering with agitation. "What's wrong?" he asked.

That way lies destruction, the Qom Jha said. *Others have searched that direction. None have ever returned.*

"He says there's danger that way," Luke translated for Mara. "Specifics unknown."

"Except that it eats Qom Jha, I presume," Mara said. "On the other hand, the only way out of here has to be that direction."

No, there is another way, Splitter Of Stones said from one of the other sconces. *Come.*

He flew across to the wall to their left and settled to a perch in one of the other gaps beneath the ceiling. *Here,* he said. *Here is the entrance to the hidden passage.*

"Really," Luke said, feeling his eyes narrow. The Qom Jha hadn't said anything about a hidden passage before. "And this hidden passage leads into the High Tower?"

Come, Splitter Of Stones said. *You will see.*

"Hidden passage, huh?" Mara commented as they crossed the room, Artoo rolling along behind them. "I don't recall that being mentioned before."

"Me, neither," Luke said. "It could have been just an oversight."

"Or an awkward but conveniently forgotten fact," Mara said darkly.

Artoo twittered questioningly. "Awkward because hidden passages usually also have hidden exits," Mara said to the droid over her shoulder. "And unless the Qom Jha have found a way through those exits, they won't know any more about the layout of the High Tower than we do."

"How about it, Splitter Of Stones?" Luke asked. "Have you and your people been inside, or haven't you?"

We have traveled all through the hidden passage was the somewhat sullen reply. *There are places where we can see the Threateners and hear what they are saying.*

"Let me guess," Mara said. "They've never actually been in the High Tower, but they're sure they'll be able to find their way around once we get them in."

"Basically," Luke said heavily. "Apparently, for all their talk, no one's actually been inside the place."

Some of the Qom Qae have been inside, Child Of Winds spoke up. *I know of some who have done so.*

Luke frowned at him. "They have? Who? When?"

Friends from other nestings have entered from above, Child Of Winds explained. *But they have always been quickly driven out, and have seen very little.*

"Still, that's apparently more than the Qom Jha have done," Luke said, looking at Splitter Of Stones again. The Qom Jha was maintaining a stiff silence, but Luke could tell he was not at all pleased with this revelation. "Have you yourself been inside, Child Of Winds?"

No, he said. *Only friends from the nesting nearest here.*

"What's the debate?" Mara asked.

"Child Of Winds says some of the younger Qom Qae of the region have poked around inside the upper areas of the High Tower," Luke said. "But how is it you're in contact with these others, Child Of Winds? I thought Hunter Of Winds said matters outside your nesting were of no concern to you."

They are of no concern to adult Qom Qae, Child Of Winds said. *But all children may fly freely wherever they wish.*

"Ah." So adult Qom Qae were territorial, but their children mixed together across nesting boundaries however they wanted.

And in the process played the role of informal ambassadors and information gatherers? Possibly. Something to remember if and when the New Republic decided to make official contact with them.

Beside him, Mara cleared her throat. "Is any of this no doubt fascinating conversation helping us get inside the High Tower?"

"Not really," Luke agreed, pushing the glimpse into Qom Qae social structure aside for now. Stepping to the yellow wall beneath where Splitter Of Stones was sitting, he ran an exploring hand across the surface. If there was a hidden door there, it was very well hidden. "You think we should look for a release, or open it the easy way?"

Mara's answer was the *snap-hiss* of her lightsaber. "Get out of the way," she said. "You, too, Qom Jha."

Splitter Of Stones fluttered hastily to one of the wall sconces. Three quick slashes, and Mara had a man-sized opening cut in the wall. Lightsaber held ready, she jumped into the gap and ducked to her right. Luke was right behind her, ducking to the left.

They were in a narrow passageway, no more than a meter and a half across, which like the room behind them extended to the right beyond the range of their glow rods. In the other direction, the passageway ended in a wall only a few meters away.

And leading up over their heads from that end was a set of stairs.

"Over here, Mara," Luke called quietly over his shoulder as he headed that direction. The stairs were narrow, and like the passageway itself extended past the range of his glow rod beam. Overhead to the left he could see just the hint of an angled and rising ceiling: another flight of steps, he decided, probably connecting with this set at some unseen landing ahead. Rising vertically along the inside edge of the stairway were a series of thick cylinders that ran from below the level of the passageway up into the darkness above.

"That's our way up, all right," Mara said from his side. "Uh-oh."

"What?" Luke asked, frowning as he stretched out with the Force. There was no danger he could detect.

"The stairs," Mara said, her glow rod shining downward on the lowest steps. "Now *that* looks like Hijarna building material."

Luke frowned down at it. "Any way to tell for sure?"

"A couple of blaster bolts ought to do it," she said. "But the noise would probably travel farther than we'd like. Anyway, at the moment it's irrelevant—we're not launching a full-scale assault on the place."

"Right—we're trying to sneak in," Luke agreed. "Looks like we'll have to go single file."

"I think we're all used to that by now," Mara said, playing her glow rod up and down the steps. "Reminds me of that secret passageway Palpatine had in the Imperial palace."

"Reminds *me* of the service shaft in Ilic on New Cov," Luke said, remembering that long walk he and Han had taken up those stairs to a landing area crawling with Imperials.

"You'd think just one of these secret-stair-builders would have the courtesy to install a turbolift," Mara said, shaking her head. "Or at least a droid carrier."

"It would be nice," Luke agreed. "Well, nothing for it but to start climbing. Let's go."

With the narrow but relatively open area ahead and above them, Luke decided to let Splitter Of Stones and his cadre of Qom Jha take the point, flying up and ahead of them. Luke went next, carrying the droid for a change, leaving Mara and Child Of Winds to bring up the rear.

Mara had groused a little about that, arguing that she wasn't tired and could handle the droid just fine. But Luke had declared the staircase safe enough for him to take droid duty, and had ignored her complaints.

Not that she'd complained too hard or too long. The droid had been getting heavier and heavier lately, and she was just as glad to be rid of the burden for a while.

"Any idea what these are?" she asked Luke, running her fingertips across the first of the thick vertical cylinders as she passed it. From this position on the stairs she could now see to the first landing, and a quick count showed there were twenty of the cylinders rising through the gap. "They don't look like ventilation shafts."

The droid warbled. "Artoo says they're power lines," Luke told her. "Probably bringing energy to the High Tower from that big power source he picked up."

"That's one blazing lot of capacity," Mara said, eyeing the cylinders uneasily. "Are all twenty of them pulling power?"

The droid twittered again. "Only three are active at the moment," Luke said. "But the others are still functional. Running to weapons or shield generators, maybe?"

"I was just wondering that myself." Mara felt her lip twitch. "From near the mouth of the cave you can see three towers rising from the fortress: three intact and one broken."

"Yes, I remember that from the record the *Starry Ice* brought back," Luke said, his voice and emotions tight. "You suggested that the shot that took out that tower might have also gouged out some of the ravine you flew in through. Is Hijarna stone that tough?"

"I don't know," Mara said grimly. "But Hijarna stone plus seventeen power lines' worth of shield generators might do the trick."

Luke whistled softly, shaking his head. "You know, this place is starting to look more and more impregnable by the minute. I don't think I like that."

"I'm *sure* I don't like it," Mara retorted grimly. "Especially in potentially unfriendly hands. It'd be worse than Mount Tantiss."

They reached the landing and the expected switchback and continued on up. For a while Mara tried to keep track of the stair count, but somewhere in the mid–two hundreds she gave up the exercise as useless.

They had passed the fourth landing when she began to detect the alien presence.

She kept at the sensation for the next few minutes until she was sure. Then, as they started to round the fifth landing, she leaned over and caught Luke's eye. "Luke?" she murmured. "Company."

"I know," he murmured back. "I've been picking them up for a while now. We must be getting close to the inhabited parts of the High Tower."

"The sensation seem at all familiar to you?"

"Very," he assured her. "They're the same species as the pilots who tried to shoot me down on my way in."

"I've never gotten that close to any of this particular group," Mara said, a sudden shiver running through her. "But I've definitely felt this sense before."

Luke seemed to brace himself. "Thrawn?"

She nodded. "Thrawn."

For a long moment they stood there in silence. "Well, you called it," Mara reminded him. "You said that might be a group of his people in there."

"It's starting to look that way," Luke said, looking up and waving toward him. "Splitter Of Stones?"

There was a rustling of wings, and the Qom Jha fluttered to a landing on one of the stairs ahead of Luke. "You said there were places where you could see or hear into the High Tower," Luke said. "How close are we to the nearest of those?"

Splitter Of Stones began to speak. Suddenly tired of this second-class status of hers, Mara reached over and took Luke's hand.

—*not too far away,* she heard the Qom Jha's voice echoed through Luke's mind. *Two and a portion more turns.*

"A portion?" Mara asked, frowning.

"The spot must be partway up one of the stairways," Luke said, glancing at the cylinders running alongside them. "At least these power lines should help mask our life-form readings if anyone's looking. That's convenient."

"It also means Artoo won't be able to pick up much of anything, either," Mara pointed out. "Not so convenient."

But that will surely not be a problem for you, Child Of Winds spoke up. *You have the Force.*

"True," Luke agreed.

"Some of us more than others, of course," Mara added, suppressing a grimace. As he had on that trek across Wayland ten years ago, Luke had been giving her more or less nonstop Jedi instruction during the trip through these caverns. But despite those efforts, she was apparently no closer to hearing this weird Force-driven communication of the Qom Jha and Qom Qae than she'd been when she first arrived on the planet.

And it was starting to bug her. It was starting to *really* bug her. What did she have to do to break through this invisible barrier to full Jedi powers, anyway?

She didn't have an answer. Luke might, but she didn't. And there was no way in the galaxy she was going to ask him. Not anytime soon, anyway.

Disgustedly, she let go of his hand. "Well, come on," she growled. "If we're going to do this, let's do it."

"Right," Luke said. If he'd picked up on her sudden sour mood, he didn't comment on it. "Okay, Splitter Of Stones, let's go. And warn your people to be especially quiet from this point on."

They resumed their climb. Mara followed along behind Luke, putting one foot in front of the other strictly on autopilot, her full attention turned outward as she stretched out to the alien presences growing steadily closer. None seemed to be very close, but from past experience she knew that with unfamiliar alien minds apparent distances could be misleading.

Two and a third flights of stairs later, as promised, they reached Splitter Of Stones's observation post.

"That's an exit, all right," Mara muttered, peering into the alcove that opened off to the side of the stairway. Roughly three meters wide and one deep, it ended in a door-shaped panel made of black stone equipped with a locking wheel and a pair of hand-grip releases. In the center of the panel was a tiny hole through which an equally tiny ray of reddish light shone through. "Looks like it swings outward."

"Yes," Luke murmured back, stepping into the alcove for a closer look. "Interesting, this locking wheel. Why lock it from this side?"

"Maybe it was for the exclusive use of certain high-ranking parties who wanted everyone else kept out," Mara said, stretching out with the Force. The alien presence was still pervasive, but still muted. "If you want to give it a try, this is probably as good a time as any."

"Right." For a moment Luke held his face against the door, peering through the peephole. Then, gripping the wheel, he turned it to the left.

Mara winced in anticipation, but the screech of rusted metal she'd expected didn't happen. In fact, the muted sound struck her as more like pieces of polished stone sliding smoothly against each other. Luke finished turning the wheel, then took hold of the two grip releases. "Here we go," he muttered, and squeezed.

Whoever had designed the self-lubrication for the locking wheel had apparently also designed the hinges. Again with only the faint rumble of stone against stone, the door swung open.

Mara was through the opening before the door had finished its swing, blaster in hand, her senses stretched fully alert.

They were at the end of a fairly wide corridor, she saw, that stretched for perhaps twenty meters before opening into an open, atriumlike area with a wide central pillar running vertically through it from which pale reddish light was streaming. Spaced along each side of the corridor were five recessed doors, each flanked by two of the wall sconces that they'd seen in the underground room below. Unlike those, though, the upper sections of these sconces were glowing with a muted white light, the illumination adding to the dimmer red coming from the pillar in the atrium. The corridor's floor and ceiling were covered in an intricate pattern of tiny interlocked tiles, while the walls were a contrasting plain silvery metal.

From the entryway behind her came a soft twitter. "Artoo says the red light is the same spectrum as the sun," Luke said from her side. "Either we're near the top or they're piping the light down here."

"I'd guess the latter," Mara said. "The decor's a surprise—the Hijarna fortress is nothing but plain black stone. Feel like a little reconnoiter?"

"Sure," Luke said. "Splitter Of Stones, if you or the others know anything about the High Tower you haven't told us, this is the time to do it."

There were more of the Qom Jha chirps and almost-speech; and abruptly all eight of them flapped past Mara and headed down the corridor. Reaching the end, they split up and vanished off in different directions. "He said they don't know anything more," Luke told Mara, "but that they're eager to learn."

"As long as they don't bring the locals down on us," Mara said, flicking off her glow rod and sliding it away into a pocket. "You'd probably better leave the droid here."

"I was planning to," Luke said. "Artoo, get back in the alcove out of sight and close the door. Child Of Winds—no, you stay here with Artoo."

There was an obvious complaint from the young Qom Qae. "Not now," Luke said firmly. "Later, maybe, but not now. Come on, Mara."

They headed out along the corridor, Child Of Winds still fussing behind them. "Looks like a residential area," Luke commented, nodding toward the doors they were passing.

"Yes," Mara said, frowning at the central pillar they were approaching. As they neared it she could see that it was shaped like a giant circular stairway, except with a smooth ramp instead of a staircase spiraling around it. And the edge—"Is that ramp moving?"

"It does look like it," Luke said, craning his neck. "Like a spiral slideway going up."

They reached the end of the corridor, and Mara eased an eye around the corner. More corridors like the one they were in were visible, spreading out like sunburst rays centered on the open area around the spiral slideway. "Definitely a barracks section," she said. "I wonder where the down ramp is."

"It's on the inside half of the up ramp," Luke said, pointing. "See—that inner section is going down?"

"I see it." Mara nodded. "Must be tricky getting across the up ramp when you want to get off."

"We'll probably get a chance to try it," Luke said, stepping close to Mara and putting his arm around her shoulder. She frowned at him, opened her mouth to ask what he was doing—

—*no one,* Keeper Of Promises's voice came as the Qom Jha fluttered into sight from one of the other corridors. *Some of the other passages end in walls, but most continue on into other such caverns.*

"Did you see anyone?" Mara asked.

We saw no one, Keeper Of Promises said in the slightly miffed tone of someone who's been asked a question he's already answered.

"Thank you." Luke tilted his head to look at Mara. "What do you want? Up or down?"

"Up," Mara said, easing away from him. It was always a little disconcerting to look at someone whose face was barely fifteen centimeters away. "All the command rooms and other interesting stuff at Hijarna were on the upper floors."

"Up it is," Luke said, releasing his grip on her and crossing to the spiral slideway. "Looks clear," he added, looking cautiously up into the opening as Mara joined him. "You picking up any danger?"

"No more than I have been for the past ten minutes," Mara said. "Sure, let's try it."

"Right." Luke waved at Keeper Of Promises. "Come on, Qom Jha—we're heading up."

They stepped onto the outer section of the slideway, both of them stumbling slightly as their bodies were forced to catch up with suddenly moving feet. "It definitely feels like we're getting closer to the aliens," Luke commented as the group of Qom Jha flapped past on their way to the next level. "I just wish I had a better benchmark for the species."

"Yes, it'd be nice to know how close they actually were," Mara agreed, watching above them as the Qom Jha split up again and headed off in all directions. One of the reinforcements—Flyer Through Spikes, Mara tentatively identified him—reappeared overhead as she and Luke reached the level, jabbering away. "He says they've found no one up here, either," Luke reported. "Splitter Of Stones has suggested—"

The flare of her danger sense was Mara's only warning. "Luke!"

"Down!" Luke snapped, igniting his lightsaber.

Mara was already dropping to one knee, spinning around as her eyes and blaster searched for a target. A movement just inside one of the corridors caught her eye—she tracked her blaster toward it—

And abruptly the world exploded into a flash of brilliant blue.

Instinctively, she ducked away from the bolt, her blaster spitting return fire. Another blue flash changed to green as Luke's lightsaber slashed across it, deflecting the bolt across the room. There was another blue flash, again caught by the lightsaber blade. Mara fired twice, had the satisfaction of seeing the half-hidden gunman duck back—

"Behind you!" Luke barked.

Mara dropped from her kneeling crouch to land flat on her stomach on the ramp, twisting around to face the other direction as she did so. Two burgundy-uniformed gunmen were visible back there, sprinting from the end of one of the corridors toward the protection of something that looked like a small service vehicle. She fired two shots—missed with both—

And abruptly one of the gunmen stopped dead in his tracks, raising his weapon toward her in a two-handed grip. Mara tracked her blaster toward him, a small part of her mind noting the blue skin of his face and hands and the glowing red eyes glaring out at her—

"Watch out!"

But the warning came too late. Even as Mara fired again and then twisted around to search out the new threat there was another flash of blue—

And a lance of agony jabbed into her right shoulder.

She might have gasped in pain; she wouldn't remember later whether she had or not. But suddenly Luke was crouching on the slideway beside her, his surge of fear dimly sensed through the waves of pain hammering at her. His hand briefly probed the area of the wound, and she could feel the pain ease somewhat as the Force flowed from him into her. "What do you think?" she managed through clenched teeth. "We seen enough for this pass?"

"Sounds good to me," he said, his lightsaber humming angrily as he swatted more of the blue blasts.

"Then—"

She blinked in surprise. Above her was the edge of one of the fortress floors; but it was pulling up and away from her. Even now, she could see, they were coming down to the level they'd started from. "How'd we get to the down part of the slideway?" she asked.

"You rolled onto it when you were hit," he told her, shifting his hand from her neck to a supporting grip cradling her shoulders. "Don't you remember?"

She shook her head. The movement sent a fresh surge of agony through her shoulder. "Combat reflex, I guess. Wait—my blaster!"

"It's all right—Keeper Of Promises picked it up," Luke assured her, shutting down his lightsaber. He half rose from his crouch, and she could feel herself also rising in the eerily intangible grip of the Force. "Here we go."

The level they'd come in on was starting to move past them now. Stretching out to the Force, carrying Mara with him, Luke leaped over the up section of the slideway to land on the solid floor beyond. Cradling her in both arms, he hurried down the corridor toward their hidden door.

"Look, I *can* walk on my own," Mara growled, glancing back over Luke's shoulder as he ran. Some of the Qom Jha were visible coming up behind them, but so far there was no sign of other pursuit. "You don't have to carry me—"

"Don't argue," Luke bit out, his mind frothing with concern and worry. "I just hope Artoo didn't lock the door—ah."

Ahead, the door was swinging ponderously open toward them, pushed by an obviously straining Child Of Winds. Trying to work past her pain, Mara stretched out to the door with the Force, giving him as much assistance as she could manage. The droid, rolling forward to help, squawked in surprise and hastily backed up just in time as Luke and Mara charged in, followed by four of the Qom Jha.

Seal the door, Mara heard Splitter Of Stones's order through Luke's mind as the Qom Jha flapped madly to a halt.

"What about the others?" Luke asked as two of the Qom Jha landed on the hand grips and began tugging.

They have gone into the other passages, Splitter Of Stones said. *They will try to lead the Threateners away from this area.*

"We can hope," Luke said as the door swung back into place. "Seal the door—I'm going to take Mara down to that last landing."

"No—go up," Mara said, digging out her glow rod with her left hand as Luke started down the stairs. "If they find the door, they'll probably assume we went down."

"Makes sense," Luke agreed, turning and heading up. "Artoo, you make sure they get it sealed and then stand guard."

A minute later they'd reached the landing. "I wish we still had our bedrolls," Luke said as he laid her carefully down on the cold stone and took the glow rod from her. "How does it feel?"

"Like someone's roasting an Ewok in there," Mara told him. "Not as bad as it was, though. Is that a pain-suppression trick you're using on me?"

"For what it's worth," Luke said, sticking the glow rod between his teeth and stripping off his jacket. "It's not nearly as effective on someone else as it is on yourself," he added, talking around the glow rod as he bunched the jacket and slid it under her head as a pillow.

"I knew there was something else I should have stuck around the academy long enough to learn," she said, hissing between her teeth as Luke set the glow rod down on her chest and began carefully pulling the burned edges of cloth away from the wound. "I don't suppose you offer a crash course."

"I usually like to ease into that lesson a little more gradually." Luke's lip twitched. "Ouch."

Mara looked down at her shoulder, and immediately wished she hadn't. " 'Ouch' doesn't even begin to cover it," she told him, feeling a little sick as she resolutely turned her eyes away. The burn was a lot nastier than she'd guessed. "I think I've just decided I'm going to miss the medpac more than I am the bedrolls."

"Don't give up just yet," Luke soothed. His fingers were stroking the skin of her shoulder and neck; and as they did so the pain again decreased. "I know a couple more tricks."

"That feels good," Mara said, closing her eyes.

"I'm putting you into a healing trance," Luke explained, his voice sounding oddly distant. "It can be a little slow, but sometimes it's as effective as a bacta tank."

"I hope this is one of those times," Mara murmured. Suddenly she was feeling very tired. "Yet another wonderful Jedi trick you'll have to teach me sometime. 'Night, Luke. Don't forget to wake me if the bad guys crash the party."

"Good night, Mara," Luke said softly. Softly, and uselessly—she was already sound asleep.

Is she going to die? an anxious voice asked from beside him.

Engrossed in Mara's injury and the setting up of the healing trance, he hadn't noticed Child Of Winds's arrival. Some Master Jedi. "No, she'll be all right," he said. "The wound isn't dangerous, and I have some healing abilities."

Child Of Winds sidled a little closer, peering with unblinking eyes at the woman stretched out at Luke's side. *Was it my fault, Jedi Sky Walker?* he asked at last. *Did I not open the door quickly enough?*

"No, not at all," Luke assured him. "It had absolutely nothing to do with you."

Then it was the Qom Jha who failed you.

Luke frowned at the young Qom Qae. Given the annoyingly persistent rivalry between the two groups, he would have expected a note of condemnation or at least lofty superiority in Child Of Winds's judgment. But there was nothing there but regret and sadness. "Perhaps," Luke said. "But it may not really be their fault, either. The Threateners may have detected our arrival and put together an ambush. And don't forget that cave-dwellers like the Qom Jha probably don't see as well in lighted rooms as you or I would."

Child Of Winds seemed to consider that. *If the Threateners laid a snare, they may enter this place to search for you.*

"They might," Luke agreed. "If they even know about it, of course. They might not—all the dust in here would indicate it hasn't been used for quite a while."

Still, they may know even if they do not use, Child Of Winds reminded him. *Your friend-machine and the Qom Jha watch and wait below. Should not someone also watch and wait above?*

"That's a good idea," Luke agreed. "Go tell Splitter Of Stones I want him to send two of his hunters to stand watch at the next stairway exit above us."

I will obey, the Qom Qae said, stretching out his wings. *But he will need send only one hunter. I will go myself to watch with him.*

Luke opened his mouth to object; closed it again. Child Of Winds had been chafing under the casual contempt of the Qom Jha ever since they'd reached the cave. This was something useful he could do that probably wouldn't be too dangerous. "All right, Child Of Winds. Thank you."

There are no thanks needed, Child Of Winds said. *It is only what is right for me to do for the Jedi Sky Walker.* He cocked his head for one final look at Mara. *And for his beloved companion.*

Spreading his wings, he flapped away into the darkness of the stairway, leaving that last comment echoing uncomfortably in Luke's mind. *Beloved companion. Companion. Beloved . . .*

He looked down at Mara, her familiar features thrown into starkly contrasting areas of light and shadow by the beam of the glow rod. *Beloved . . .*

"No," he murmured to himself. No. He liked Mara, certainly. Liked her very much. She was smart and resourceful, with a mental and emotional toughness he could rely on, plus a sharp humor and irreverence that made for a refreshing contrast with the automatic and unthinking awe too many people held him in these days. She'd been a trusted ally through some very hard and dangerous times, sticking with him and Han and Leia even when the rest of a hostile New Republic hierarchy had declared her untrustworthy.

And perhaps most important of all, she was strong and capable in the Force, with the ability to share his thoughts and emotions in a way that even a couple as close as Han and Leia couldn't experience.

But he wouldn't love her. He couldn't take that risk. Every time in the past that he had allowed himself the luxury of caring that deeply about a woman something terrible had happened to her. Gaeriel had been killed. Callista had lost her Jedi abilities and finally left him. The list of tragedies sometimes seemed endless.

Still, if Mara's theory was right, all of those disasters had happened while he was still under the lingering effects of his brush with the dark side. Would things be different now? Could they be different?

He shook his head firmly. No. He could try all the logic in the world—could come up with reason after reason why he could perhaps allow himself to have feelings like that again. But not now. Not with Mara.

Because hanging like a dark specter over all of this was the memory of that vision he'd had barely a month ago on Tierfon. The vision where he'd seen Han and Leia in danger from a mob; where he'd seen Wedge and Corran and Rogue Squadron in the heat of battle; where he'd seen himself on the Cejansij balcony from which he would later be taken to Talon Karrde and learn of Mara's disappearance.

And where he'd seen Mara surrounded by craggy rock and floating motionlessly in a pool of water. Her eyes closed; her arms and legs limp. As if in death.

He gazed down at her again, a quiet ache in his heart. Perhaps that was her destiny, an end to her life that he could do nothing to prevent. But until that was proved, he would tear his own life apart if necessary to prevent it from happening. And if part of that sacrifice was to keep her out of the shadow of destructive dark side influence he had had on so many others, then that was a sacrifice he would have to make.

But for now what she needed most was to be healed. And that would take no sacrifice, merely time and attention. "Good night," he said again, knowing she couldn't hear him. On impulse, he leaned over and kissed her gently on the lips. Then, stretching out on the cold stone next to her, he rested his head beside hers on a corner of his folded jacket and laid his arm across her chest where his fingertips could touch the area around her burned shoulder. Easing himself into a sort of half trance to aid in concentration, he stretched out to the Force and set to work.

CHAPTER

18

It took a few minutes' searching, but Wedge finally found the others at a small, open-air tapcafe half a block down from the space traffic registration office. "There you are," he said a little accusingly as he dropped into the third seat at the table.

"What's the problem?" Moranda asked, sipping at the pale blue-green liqueur that had been her constant tapcafe companion ever since they'd met her. "I told you we'd be down the street here."

"You're right—I should have guessed where exactly down the street you meant," Wedge countered, throwing a sour look at her drink. "Aren't you starting a little early in the day?"

"What, this?" Moranda asked, lifting the glass and turning it this way and that in the morning sunlight. "This is nothing. Anyway, you wouldn't be so heartless as to deny an old woman one of the last remaining pleasures of her declining years, would you?"

"That 'old woman' excuse is starting to wear a little thin." Wedge shifted his attention to Corran and the aromatic mug he was cradling. "And what's *your* excuse?"

Corran shrugged. "I'm just keeping her company. I take it the incoming-ship search went badly?"

"It didn't go at all," Wedge growled, glaring at Corran's mug. Now that he thought about it, a drink actually sounded pretty good. But after that rather self-righteous tirade he could hardly beckon a droid over and order something himself—

There was a movement at his side, and a mechanical hand set a mug down on the table in front of him, spilling a few drops first in the ancient annoying Bothan custom. "What's this?" he asked.

"We ordered it when we saw you coming down the street," Moranda said. "Figured that after dealing with Bothan bureaucracy you'd want something a little stronger than hot chocolate."

Wedge grimaced. So much for the grand mystique of command. "Thanks," he said, taking a sip.

"So what happened?" Moranda asked. "They wouldn't let you look at the records for incoming ships?"

"Not without fifteen forms of authorization," Wedge told her. "It's crazy. Doubly crazy given that everything on those lists is technically a matter of public record. If I wanted to sit at the spaceport and write down the names of every ship as it came in, I could do it."

"They're getting nervous," Corran murmured, swirling his mug. "Worried that Vengeance might start taking potshots at their best customers."

"Whatever, there's no point in kicking against a bureaucracy," Moranda said. "Let's think this through logically."

Wedge waved a hand in invitation. "We're listening."

"All right." Moranda took a sip of her drink. "I think we can all agree that if someone is after the Drev'starn shield generator, a frontal assault is out. Unless they brought a portable proton torpedo launcher with them, that building is far too well protected."

"Which means they'll have to rely on subterfuge," Corran agreed. "Fairly obvious so far."

"Don't rush me," Moranda admonished him. "Now, we can also assume they won't be able to suborn any of the techs or other people who work inside. But how about planting something on one of them?"

"You mean like a bomb?" Wedge asked doubtfully. "I doubt it. That's a big area down there. Any bomb strong enough to do any serious damage would be easily detected."

"Besides, if they have any brains at all, they have the workers change clothes before they go into the actual generator areas," Corran added. "That also protects against spy monitors being slipped onto anyone."

"So the workers are out," Moranda said. "What about the various underground conduits that bring in power and water?"

"There aren't any water conduits," Wedge said thoughtfully. "Water and food are supposedly brought in from outside and triple-scanned for contaminants." He looked at Corran. "Power, though, is another matter entirely."

"You might be onto something," Corran agreed, frowning as he drummed his fingers softly on the table. "Each shield generator is supposed to have its own self-contained power supply. But it's referred to as a *backup* supply, which implies the primary power source comes in from the outside."

"Where are you getting all this stuff from, by the way?" Moranda asked. "Not Bothan propaganda, I hope."

"No, we pulled it from New Republic military files," Wedge told her. "Unfortunately, what we had was a little skimpy on details."

"Typical Bothan paranoiac closemouthness," Moranda grunted. "I don't suppose you'd have any idea where exactly the conduits are located."

"Not even a guess," Wedge told her.

"Well, that's our second order of business, then," Moranda said. "Getting the complete schematics of that building."

Corran cocked an eyebrow. "I hope you're not expecting the Bothans to just give them to us."

Moranda snorted. "Of course not," she said. "That's why it's our *second* order of business. We can't very well go visit the construction records building during the day."

Wedge exchanged looks with Corran. "The building's only open during the day," he pointed out carefully.

"That's right," Moranda said, smiling encouragingly. "You catch on fast."

Wedge looked at Corran again. "Corran?"

The other made a face, but then he shrugged. "We do have our orders," he reminded Wedge. "And this isn't just to protect the Bothans, remember."

"I suppose," Wedge said reluctantly. So much for the mystique of command; so much for command at all. Still, Moranda was making sense. Unfortunately. "So if that's the second order of business, what's the first?"

"I thought we'd go pull the records for the last few days' worth of outgoing transmissions," Moranda said. "If Vengeance is plotting something, their group here probably has to report in every now and again."

Wedge felt his mouth drop open. "You want to go check *message traffic*? Do you have any idea how much of that there *is* from this planet?"

"That's exactly why they won't worry about it," Moranda said cheerfully. "They'll figure no one would be crazy enough to bother sifting through it all."

"Present company excepted, obviously."

"Well, of course." Moranda held up a hand. "Now, wait a minute, it's not as bad as it sounds. We can cut out all transmissions from major or established corporations—even if one of them was involved, they wouldn't send out anything under their own name. We can also cut out any nonencrypted messages, and we can cut out any message over, say, fifty words. That ought to give us something manageable."

Wedge frowned. "Why everything over fifty words?"

"The shorter the message, the harder it is to decrypt," Corran explained, sounding as dubious as Wedge felt. "One of the things I learned in CorSec. *My* question is, if we aren't going to be able to read it, why bother looking for it in the first place?"

"To find out where it's going, of course," Moranda said, draining the last of her liqueur. "The guys at this end can be as cagey as they want; but if they've got a sloppy contact down the line, we can still nail them. All we need is a likely system and I can call Karrde's people down on them from that end."

"It still sounds crazy," Wedge declared, looking at Corran. "What do you think?"

"It's no crazier than breaking into the construction records building after hours," Corran pointed out.

"Thanks for the reminder," Wedge sighed. "Sure, let's give it a try. I just hope the computer on our shuttle is up to a job like this."

"If not, the one on my ship can handle it," Moranda assured him, getting to her feet. "Come on, let's get moving."

"Captain?"

Nalgol turned away from the unremitting blackness hanging in front of the Imperial Star Destroyer *Tyrannic.* "Yes?"

"Relay spark from the strike team, sir," Intelligence Chief Oissan said, coming to a parade-ground halt and handing the captain a datapad. "I'm afraid you're not going to like it."

"Really," Nalgol said, giving Oissan a long, hard look as he took the datapad. Given the *Tyrannic's* blindness out here, it was unarguably nice to receive these brief reports from the Imperial Intelligence strike team on the Bothawui surface. But on the other hand, any secret transmission, even an innocuous one sent to an unobtrusive relay buoy, simply gave the enemy one more handle to latch on to.

And for that potentially dangerous transmission to contain bad news . . .

The message was, as always, brief. *Now ten days to completion of flash point. Will keep timetable updated.*

"Ten days?" Nalgol transferred his glare from the datapad to Oissan. "What is this ten days nonsense? The report two days ago said it would only be *six* days."

"I don't know, sir," Oissan said. "All messages to us have to be kept short—"

"Yes, I know," Nalgol cut him off, glowering at the datapad again. Ten more days in this clytarded blindness. Just exactly what the crew of this twitchy ship needed. "They just blazing well better be keeping Bastion better informed than they are us."

"I'm sure they are, Captain," Oissan said. "Paradoxically, perhaps, it's much safer to send out a long transmission on a commercial frequency via the HoloNet than it is to send a short-range spark to us out here."

"I'm fairly well versed in communications theory, thank you," Nalgol said icily. A prudent man, he reflected darkly, would have found a way to beat a hasty retreat after delivering news like this. Either Oissan wasn't as prudent as Nalgol had always assumed, or he was twitchy enough himself to be spoiling for a fight with his captain.

Or else this was part of a private evaluation of his captain's mental state.

And much as he would like to deny it, Nalgol had to admit this idleness and isolation were getting on his nerves, too. "I was simply concerned that the delay not upset Bastion's master plan," he told the other, forcing calmness into his voice. "I also wish I knew how in blazes they could lose six whole days out of a two-month timetable."

Oissan shrugged. "Without knowing what exactly their job is down there, I can't even hazard a guess," he said reasonably. "As it is, we'll just have to rely on their judgment." He lifted his eyebrows slightly. "And on Grand Admiral Thrawn's own genius, of course."

"Of course," Nalgol murmured. "The question is whether all those armed hotheads around Bothawui will be able to hold off another ten days before they start shooting. What's the warship count up to, anyway?"

"The latest probe ship report is in that file, sir," Oissan said, nodding toward the datapad. "But I believe the current number is one hundred twelve."

"A hundred and twelve?" Nalgol echoed, frowning as he pulled up the report. There it was: a hundred and twelve. "This can't be right," he insisted.

"It is, sir," Oissan assured him. "Thirty-one new warships have come in, apparently all in the past ten hours."

Nalgol scanned the list. A nicely matched set, too: fourteen pro-Bothan Diamalan and D'farian ships to seventeen anti-Bothan Ishori ships. "This is unbelievable," he said, shaking his head. "Don't these aliens have anything better to do?"

Oissan snorted under his breath. "From the news reports the probe ships have been bringing in, it's only because most of the New Republic *does* have better things to do that we haven't been buried by three times as many ships," he said. "But don't worry. I have faith in the New Republic's diplomatic corps. I'm sure they'll keep things calm until we're ready to move."

"I hope so," Nalgol said softly, turning to gaze out at the blackness again. Because after all this waiting, if he didn't get a clear shot at this alien-loving Rebel scum, he was going to be very angry.

Very angry, indeed.

The annoyingly cheery door chime of the Exoticalia Pet Emporium rang, and Navett stepped in through the back-room doorway to see Klif close the door behind him. "Business is booming, I see," he commented, glancing around the customer-free store as he walked between the rows of caged animals to the service counter.

"Just the way I like it," Navett said, leaning an elbow on the counter and gesturing the other to a chair. "You get those messages off?"

"Yeah." Klif circled behind him and dropped into one of the seats. "But I don't think any of them are going to like it."

Navett shrugged. "They can join the club. It's going to be awkward for us, too, you know—we're going to have to delay the delivery date for those three mawkrens. But there's not a lot any of us can do about it. It was the Bothans' idea to start keeping their techs locked in the shield building for six days at a time, not ours."

"Yeah," Klif said heavily. "I suppose we can't be expected to send our little time bombs in with the next shift any earlier than the next shift goes on duty."

"Don't worry about it," Navett soothed him. "Our cover is plenty secure, and it won't hurt Horvic and Pensin to wash dishes for the Ho'Din awhile longer. We can hover an extra six days without any trouble."

"Maybe not," Klif said darkly. "Guess who I spotted at the comm center while I was checking for messages."

Navett felt his eyes narrow. "Not our two New Rep military types?"

"In the skin and twice as pompous." Klif nodded. "And they had company: some old woman in a hooded cloak who seemed to know her way around better than they did. A fringe type, no doubt about it."

Navett scratched his cheek. "You think she's the one who got their wallets back from the Bothan lifters?"

"Well, they had their wallets with them," Klif said. "So I'd say, yeah, she's probably the one."

"Um." New Rep military types with a fringe lifter. Interesting. "Were they picking up or delivering?"

"Neither," Klif told him. "They were pulling a list of all outgoing transmissions for the past five days."

"Interesting," Navett said, drumming his fingers gently on the countertop. "Analysis?"

"They're on to us," Klif growled. "Or at least, they know someone's here." He lifted an eyebrow. "*And* they suspect it has to do with the Drev'starn shield generator, or they wouldn't have spent so much time hanging around there."

"Recommendation?"

"We vape them," Klif said bluntly. "Tonight."

Navett shifted his eyes past him to the display window across the store, gazing at the hundreds of pedestrians and dozens of vehicles hurrying past. Drev'starn was an immensely busy city, made all the more frantic by the presence of those warships overhead. Humans and aliens rushing around all over the place . . . "No," he said slowly. "No, they're not on to us. Not yet. They suspect something is in the works, but they don't know for sure. No, our best plan right now is to lay low and not let them draw us out."

Klif's lips puckered, but he nodded reluctantly. "I still don't like it, but you're the boss. Maybe all they're trying to do is get a handle on Vengeance; and they're not going to look for a group that big in a little pet store."

"Good point," Navett agreed. "We could even consider staging another riot for their benefit if they seem to be getting too close. If you're up to another performance, that is."

Klif shrugged. "Two riots on Bothawui might be pushing our luck," he said. "But I can get one going if we have to."

Across the room, one of the animals squawked twice and then fell silent again. Probably one of the pregnant mawkrens, Navett decided, muttering in her sleep. He'd better get those injections started if he didn't want a mess of tiny lizards running around underfoot six days before he needed them. "I just wish we knew who our opponents were," he commented.

"Maybe we can find out," Klif said, pulling out a datapad. "I followed them back to the spaceport and their ship. A surplused Sydon MRX-BR Pacifier, as it turns out."

Navett grimaced. The Pacifier had been the Empire's scout vehicle of choice, able to seek out new worlds and deliver a devastating pounding to them if it proved necessary. Considered by the New Republic to be too provocative for the delicate sensitivities of frightened primitives, their use had been summarily discontinued. Just one more reminder, if he'd needed it, of how badly things had been falling apart since Endor. "You get a name?"

"And a registration code," Klif said, handing him the datapad. "It's the woman's ship, unfortunately—she was the one who unlocked it—but we might still be able to backcheck them through it."

"Excellent," Navett said as he took the datapad. "The *Fingertip Express*, eh? Sounds like a lifter's ship, all right. A smart-mouth name for a smart-mouth lifter."

He handed the datapad back. "There should be a Bureau of Ships and Services office somewhere in Drev'starn. Find it and see what you can pull up."

"Aha," Moranda said from her ship's tiny computer alcove. "Well, well, well."

Sitting in the lounge just off the alcove, Wedge turned his eyes away from the expensive contour sculp on the wall in front of him, and his thoughts away from contemplation of how Moranda might have come into possession of such a prize. "You found something?" he asked.

"Could be," Corran said. Arms crossed and leaning against the wall, he'd been watching over Moranda's shoulder for the past two hours. "Three messages, all short and encrypted, have gone out in the past five days." He looked over at Wedge. "The last one just this morning."

"What time this morning?" Wedge asked, getting to his feet and crossing to the others.

"About ten minutes before we got there," Moranda said, peering at the display. "I guess we shouldn't have lingered over that drink. Too bad."

Wedge grimaced, a bad taste in his mouth. Too bad wasn't the half of it. With Corran and his Jedi skills along, they might actually have been able to identify and tag the sender if they'd been there in time.

If. "Where were the transmissions headed?"

"Toward Eislomi sector," Moranda said. "Specifically, in the direction of the Eislomi III HoloNet relay station."

Wedge suppressed a sigh. "In other words, a dead end."

"Looks like it."

"Still, if they've already sent three messages, they might send more," Corran pointed out. His voice was calm and controlled, without any trace of the frustration and disappointment Wedge knew he must also be feeling over this near-miss. "If worse comes to worst, we could always stake out the place."

"A waste of time," Moranda sniffed. "If they've got any brains at all, they'll spot a loiterer upwind from sixty paces away with their eyes closed."

"That depends on how the loitering is done," Corran countered stiffly. "And on who's doing it."

"What, you?" Moranda scoffed, looking him up and down. "Right. Like you wouldn't stand out like a stormtrooper at an Ewok roast."

"I thought it was like a Wookiee at a Noghri family reunion."

"No, no—you're versatile enough to do both."

"Oh, thank you," Corran growled. "Thank you very much."

"Both of you simmer down," Wedge interrupted sternly. "Corran's right, Moranda—he's exceptionally good at stakeouts. However, Moranda's right, too, Corran—we don't have the time or the troops to cover all outgoing transmissions, even if we were sure they'd use the same center again."

"At least we now know for sure that someone's operating here," Moranda offered. "That's something."

"Not much, though," Corran muttered.

"It occurs to me, though," Wedge said, raising his voice, "that there's still one route we haven't tried. Assuming Vengeance isn't homegrown—and considering its anti-Bothan sentiment, I think we can assume that—

they'll have to have found some place local to set up shop. Question: where?"

Moranda snapped her fingers. "A business. Has to be some kind of business."

"She's right," Corran agreed, his frustration and miffed professional pride suddenly forgotten. "An apartment wouldn't work—too risky to have lots of people coming and going at odd hours. With a business, you can always cover it as deliveries or cleanup crews."

"And working for someone else doesn't give you enough privacy when you need it," Moranda added. "*And* it'll have to be something fairly recently set up, *and* probably as close to the shield generator building as they can get."

"My thoughts exactly," Wedge said. "And since we can't hit the construction records building until later anyway . . . ?"

"What are we waiting for?" Corran demanded, detaching himself from the wall and heading for the hatchway. "Someone in Drev'starn must have a list of all new businesses. Let's go find him."

CHAPTER

19

"No," Captain Ardiff said, jabbing his fork for emphasis. "I don't believe it. Not for a minute."

"What about the news reports?" Colonel Bas countered. "Even stuck out here we've pulled in, what, five of them? If this thing's a hoax, it's a kriffing good one. If you'll pardon the language, sir," he added belatedly, looking with some embarrassment at Pellaeon.

"Language pardoned, Colonel," Pellaeon said, suppressing a smile. Bas had clawed his way up through the TIE pilot ranks to become the *Chimaera*'s fighter commander; and though he tried hard to fit in with the generally more cultured men who made up the officer corps, the saltier language of his youth did periodically intrude.

Personally, Pellaeon rather liked that. Not the expletives per se, but the fact that the man's language was an outward sign of honest and straightforward opinions or emotions. Unlike some Pellaeon had dealt with, Bas seldom if ever tried to hide his thoughts or feelings behind polite slip-talk.

"They're rumors, Colonel—that's all," Ardiff said, shaking his head. "Face the facts: Thrawn died. Admiral Pellaeon was there to see it. Now, if that was some trick—"

Pellaeon lowered his eyes to his plate and forked another bite of the braised bruallki, mentally tuning out the discussion. It was the same endless argument, with the same opinions and speculations, that had been playing its way around the ship in the week since Lieutenant Mavron had returned with the story of Thrawn's supposed appearance in the Kroctar system. Everyone from Ardiff on down had his own opinion on whether or not it was true, none of them could prove their opinion to anyone else, and the entire ship was about as tense as an overwound throwbow.

But the waiting, at least, was about to come to an end. He'd given General Bel Iblis a full month and a half to make his plans, and the

Chimaera itself had been here at Pesitiin for two weeks. Clearly, for whatever reason, Bel Iblis wasn't coming.

And it was time to go home. To return to the Empire, and to Bastion. And, on several levels, to find out what exactly Moff Disra was up to. He would give the order to prepare for departure as soon as he was finished with his meal. If Bel Iblis didn't arrive in the hour after that—

"Admiral Pellaeon, Captain Ardiff, this is the bridge," Major Tschel's voice came from the mess table speaker. "Report, please."

Ardiff got to the switch first. "Captain here," he said. "The Admiral's with me. What is it?"

"A ship's just entered the system, sir," Tschel said, his voice tight.

Ardiff flashed Pellaeon a sharp look. "A repeat performance by our pirates?"

"I don't think so, sir," Tschel said. "So far, at least, it's only a single ship: YT-1300 light freighter, minimally armed. They're transmitting a request to come aboard and speak with the Admiral."

Pellaeon took a deep breath. "Is there a name attached to the transmission?" he asked.

"Yes, sir," Tschel said. "She claims to be New Republic High Councilor Leia Organa Solo."

With the four TIE fighters riding escort positions on both flanks, the *Falcon* rose up out of sight of the distant sun, up into the shadow of the Star Destroyer's hangar bay. "We're committed now," Elegos said softly from the seat beside Leia.

"Yes," Leia agreed, her hands resting on the controls, watching as the *Chimaera*'s tractor beam reeled them steadily into itself. "We are indeed."

"Does that disturb you?" the Caamasi asked. "What are you thinking?"

Leia shrugged, a quick movement of tense shoulders. "On one level, of course it disturbs me," she told him. "Risks are always something a rational being prefers to avoid. But not all risks are bad. All in all, this is a good risk."

She half turned and tried a smile. "As to the other part of your question, I was just thinking that if Threepio were here, he'd probably be saying 'We're doomed' about now."

Elegos chuckled, a uniquely Caamasi sound. "Very good," he said. "I have not known much about you, Councilor, save what I have read and heard from others. This voyage, short though it has been, has been greatly instructive. Whatever happens next, I will always consider myself honored to have had these few days together with you."

Leia took a deep breath. The words themselves, taken alone, could be construed to have an ominous ring to them. But spoken with the Caamasi's quiet warmth, all potential threat or fear vanished. What came across instead was courage and hope and resolve; an inspiration and strength that came not so much from Elegos as it did from hidden reserves of her own. Reserves his words and presence were somehow able to draw out of her.

It was small wonder, she thought with distant ache, that the power-insatiable Senator Palpatine had wanted such a dangerous people destroyed.

There was a lone figure waiting at the foot of the *Falcon*'s ramp as Leia and the other three started down: a white-haired man of medium height, his face lined with age but with the parade-ground-straight back of a professional military officer. He wore the Imperial uniform well, Leia thought; he wore the chest insignia of a Fleet admiral even better. "Councilor Organa Solo," he said, nodding gravely as she approached. "I'm Admiral Pellaeon. Welcome aboard the *Chimaera*."

"Thank you, Admiral," Leia said, nodding back. "It's been a long time."

His forehead wrinkled. "I'm afraid you have me at a disadvantage," he said. "I wasn't aware we'd met."

"It wasn't a formal introduction," Leia told him. "But I remember my father pointing you out to me as one of the Fleet's most promising officers during the annual Grand Alderaanian Gathering at the Royal Pavilion when I was ten."

Pellaeon's lip twitched. "I remember those days well," he said quietly. "In some ways, I'd prefer not to."

His eyes shifted to Elegos, standing at Leia's left. "Perhaps you'll introduce me to the rest of your delegation?"

"Certainly," Leia said, passing over for the moment the distinctly unofficial status of the group. "This is Elegos A'kla, Trustant for the Caamasi Remnant."

Pellaeon smiled faintly as he nodded. "Trustant A'kla."

"Admiral Pellaeon," Elegos said, lowering his head in a Caamasi bow.

"On my right is Sakhisakh clan Tlakh'sar," Leia continued, gesturing to the Noghri beside her.

Pellaeon's smile remained, but Leia could sense a new brittleness behind it. "Of course," the Admiral said. "Alderaanian, Caamasi, and Noghri. Three beings with the most reason to hate the Empire."

Sakhisakh stirred— "We hold no anger toward you personally, Admiral," Elegos said calmly before the Noghri could speak. "Nor have we animosity toward the people of the Empire. Each of our worlds was destroyed by the hand of Emperor Palpatine, and he too is now dead. Continuing to nurture the fires of hatred would gain us nothing."

"Thank you, Trustant," Pellaeon said. "I appreciate your generosity and your wisdom." His eyes flicked briefly to Sakhisakh, then turned to Ghent, standing nervously at Elegos's other side. "And what particular grievance do you represent, sir?"

"Me?" Ghent asked, starting. "Oh, no, I'm not part of this group. I mean—I'm just the slicer who reconstructed Vermel's message for General Bel Iblis."

The last hint of a smile vanished from Pellaeon's face. "What do you mean, reconstructed?" he demanded. "Didn't the colonel present his message in person?"

"I'm afraid he didn't get that far," Leia said. "According to General Bel Iblis, his Corvette was intercepted by a Star Destroyer while on approach to Morishim."

Pellaeon's eyes had gone deadly. "Intercepted and destroyed?"

"No, or at least not at that time," Leia said. "The Star Destroyer brought his ship into its hangar bay and then escaped."

"I see." For a long moment Pellaeon stood there, his eyes gazing at nothing, his face hard and almost cruel, his emotions edged with simmering anger. Leia stretched out to the Force, trying to read past the emotion and wondering if she should break the silence or wait for him to do so.

Elegos took the decision out of her hands. "I take it Colonel Vermel was a close friend," he commented quietly.

Pellaeon's eyes and attention came back. "I will hope that he still is," he said. "If not, someone will pay heavily for his death."

He exhaled. "But you came to talk peace, not vengeance. If you'll follow me, I have a room prepared for us off the hangar bay."

"I'd prefer to hold our discussion aboard my ship, if you don't mind," Leia said. "I'm afraid my bodyguards insist on that."

For a fraction of a second there was a flicker of uncertainty, even fear, in Pellaeon's emotions. But then the fear faded, and he again smiled. "You have more Noghri aboard, of course," he said, glancing up at the *Falcon* looming over them. "No doubt watching even now with weapons at the ready."

"There will be no danger to you, Admiral," Elegos spoke up. "Not unless you yourself bring it aboard."

Pellaeon waved a hand at the ramp. "In that case, Councilor, I accept. Please; lead the way."

A minute later Leia, Pellaeon, and Elegos were seated around the *Falcon*'s game table—a distressingly informal place for such a momentous occasion, Leia thought with some embarrassment, but the only place on the ship where they could all sit comfortably together. Sakhisakh, without comment, had taken up a guard position where he could watch both their discussion and the entrance ramp. Ghent, also without comment, had gone over to the tech station and was busying himself with the *Falcon*'s computer.

"I'll get right to the point, Councilor," Pellaeon said, his eyes flicking briefly to Ghent and the Noghri. "The war that began twenty-odd years ago is effectively over . . . and the Empire has lost."

"I agree," Leia said. "Is this opinion shared by others in the Empire?"

A muscle in Pellaeon's cheek twitched. "I'm sure the average Imperial citizen has recognized that truth for quite some time," he said. "It's merely been the leadership who have clung to the hope that the inevitable could somehow be prevented."

"And does that leadership now agree with the two of us and the average Imperial citizen?"

"Yes," Pellaeon said. "Reluctantly, but yes. I've been authorized by the eight remaining Moffs to open peace negotiations with the New Republic."

Leia felt her throat tighten. She had heard Vermel's message; had come aboard and seen Pellaeon waiting alone for her . . . but only now did it suddenly seem truly real.

Peace. With the Empire.

"Yet as you have already said, the Empire has lost," Elegos spoke into the silence. "What then remains to be negotiated?"

Leia resettled her shoulders, sending a silent word of thanks in Elegos's direction for his subtle reminder of her duty here. She was representing the New Republic, and could not allow the emotional lure of peace to blind her to the hard intellectual realities of the situation. "Trustant A'kla makes a good point," she said. "What you would gain from a peace treaty is obvious. What would we gain?"

"Perhaps what we would gain is not as obvious as you think," Pellaeon said. "The New Republic is after all struggling with internal turmoil, with every indication that matters are getting worse."

He looked pointedly at Elegos. "Several of the Moffs, in fact, believe you're on the verge of collapsing into total civil war over this Caamasi issue. In the midst of such anarchy, the remnants of the Empire could easily be overlooked. Why then should we bother with the humiliation of a treaty at all?"

Leia's mouth felt dry. It was an all too reasonable question. "If you really believed we were about to destroy ourselves, you wouldn't be here," she pointed out.

"Perhaps," Pellaeon said. "Perhaps I merely don't believe the more virulent haters of the Empire would forget about us." He paused. "Or perhaps I may be able to keep that civil war from happening."

Leia frowned. "How?"

"Let me first state what the Empire would want included in any treaty between us," Pellaeon said. "We would want our current borders confirmed and accepted by Coruscant, with guarantees of free travel and trade between our worlds and those of the New Republic. No harassment; no border skirmishes; no propaganda pressure against us."

"What about the nonhumans living under Imperial rule?" Sakhisakh demanded. "Are we to merely accept their slavery?"

Pellaeon shook his head. "The Empire which once enslaved and exploited thinking beings is dead," he told the Noghri. "The human domination of Palpatine long ago became full cooperation between all the beings within our borders."

"Do all your subjects agree that they're now equals?" Leia asked.

"Probably not," Pellaeon conceded. "But once we had the security of a peace treaty, any Imperial system wishing to join the New Republic would be offered the chance to do so."

He lifted his eyebrows. "By the same token, we would expect systems within your borders who wish to rejoin the Empire to also be allowed to make that choice, with the same security and free trade guarantees extended to them."

Sakhisakh bit out a Noghri curse. "What people would be so foolish as to give you their freedom?" he demanded contemptuously.

"You might be surprised," Pellaeon said. "Freedom, after all, is a highly relative and subjective thing. And as I say, we're not the Empire you knew."

The Noghri rumbled under his breath again but remained silent. "Of course, all guarantees of safety would work the other direction as well," Pellaeon said, turning back to Leia. "No attacks by Imperial forces; no provocation; no hired privateers." His face twitched in an almost-smile. "And, of course, if we should happen to stumble across another superweapon Palpatine had hidden away, we would work with you to dismantle it."

Leia braced herself. "And what about the superweapon you're already using?"

Pellaeon frowned. "What superweapon?"

"The one that nearly defeated us once before," Leia said. "Grand Admiral Thrawn."

Pellaeon's lips compressed briefly, and Leia could sense the wave of uncertainty and quiet fear washing through him. "I don't know, Councilor. I have no idea at all what's going on there."

Leia threw a glance at Elegos. "What do you mean?"

"Exactly what I said," Pellaeon told her. "I've been here at Pesitiin waiting for General Bel Iblis for the past two weeks, and was running under a communications blackout for several days before that. I didn't even know Thrawn had been reported alive until a week ago."

Leia frowned, stretching out to Pellaeon with the Force. But there was no duplicity in his thoughts or emotions that she could detect.

"You say 'reported alive,' Admiral," Elegos said. "Does your choice of words imply you don't believe he has actually returned?"

"I don't know what to believe, Trustant," Pellaeon said. "Certainly I had every reason to think he was dead. I was there on the *Chimaera*'s bridge, standing at his side, when he appeared to die."

"Again, you say 'appeared' to die," Elegos persisted. "Did he or did he not truly die?"

"I truly do not know," Pellaeon said with a sigh. "Thrawn was an alien, with an alien physiology, and . . ." He shook his head. "Has he actually been seen by anyone from the New Republic? Someone whose word and judgment you trust?"

"My friend Lando Calrissian was intercepted and taken aboard the *Relentless*, along with the Diamalan Senator," Leia said. "Both of them claimed it was indeed Thrawn."

"The *Relentless*," Pellaeon murmured, frowning. "Dorja's ship; and he was one of those who did meet Thrawn personally. Hard to believe he would be easily taken in by a trick. Or, for that matter, that he would risk his ship without exceptionally good reason."

Leia hesitated; but there was no easy way to say this. "It occurs to me, Admiral, that these talks may be somewhat premature," she said. "If Thrawn is alive, then you are presumably no longer head of the Imperial military."

"If he's alive, he will most certainly relieve me of supreme command," Pellaeon said evenly. "However, at the moment that consideration is irrelevant. The military is subordinate to the Moffs; and the Moffs have authorized me to negotiate this treaty."

"Wouldn't that authority be rescinded, though, in the face of Thrawn's return?" Leia countered.

"It may," Pellaeon acknowledged. "But until I'm informed of such a decision, my authority stands."

"I see," Leia murmured, gazing at the old Admiral with a sudden new understanding. He had learned about Thrawn's return a full week ago; yet, instead of rushing back to learn more, he had deliberately remained here under communications blackout. Not just to wait for Bel Iblis, but to make sure he still had the authority to negotiate if and when Bel Iblis arrived. To start the ball rolling, perhaps beyond the ability of the Moffs or even Thrawn to easily stop it.

This was not a game, or at least not a game he was helping to run. Admiral Pellaeon, Supreme Commander of Imperial forces, genuinely wanted peace.

"Did Thrawn say anything to Calrissian and the Senator?" Pellaeon asked into Leia's musings. "I presume they were allowed to leave—very few people simply escape from an Imperial Star Destroyer."

"Actually, in some respects his message was similar to yours," Leia said. "He warned that the New Republic was headed for self-destruction and offered to help us avoid that."

"Are you considering his offer?"

"Unfortunately, his proposed method was deemed unacceptable by the Senate," Leia said. "He wanted to speak privately with the Bothan leaders, and from those conversations determine who had sabotaged the Caamasi shields."

"Interesting," Pellaeon said, rubbing his chin thoughtfully. "I wonder how merely talking with them would accomplish that. Unless the clan leaders do indeed know the truth."

"They claim they don't," Leia said. "And considering the growing threat to the entire Bothan species, I think they would give us that information if they had it."

"You suggested you might also have a way to prevent civil war," Elegos reminded the admiral. "Would you care to elaborate?"

Leia could sense Pellaeon pulling his attention back from his own thoughts. "I'm sure it's occurred to you that the crisis could be resolved by finding a complete version of the Caamas Document," he said. "In exchange for favorable peace terms, the Empire would be willing to offer you a copy of that record."

Leia shot a glance at Sakhisakh, saw the Noghri's own subtle reaction. If they were on schedule, Han and Lando should be right now conducting their own search for that record on Bastion. "Just like that?" she asked Pellaeon. "You'd simply turn it over to us?"

"Once we have it in hand, yes." He paused. "There is, however, one problem. If it does indeed exist, it would be located in the Special Files section of the archives, which is severely restricted and heavily encrypted. I don't have any way into those files; neither does anyone I know. If we're going to get to the document in time, the New Republic will need to loan us a top-rate decryption expert."

There was a sort of choked-off gurgle from the direction of the tech station. Ghent was still facing the control board, but his back had suddenly gone rigid. "Where would he need to go?" she asked Pellaeon, her eyes still on Ghent. "To Bastion?"

"No, to the Ubiqtorate base at Yaga Minor," Pellaeon said. "The commander there is a personal friend, and there's a somewhat isolated computer access station he could use. Bastion itself would be far too dangerous."

Leia looked back at him, her heart catching suddenly in her throat. "How do you mean, dangerous?"

"Bastion is the home base and stronghold of one of the most vehemently antipeace officials in the entire Empire," Pellaeon said grimly. "Moff Disra. He also appears to be up to his neck in a private little war using mercenary pirate gangs and illegally obtained funds."

"Yes, we've noticed all the pirate activity," Leia said, fighting to keep her voice steady. Han and Lando on Bastion . . . "You don't think Moff Disra would appreciate having a New Republic representative on his world?"

Pellaeon snorted. "Digging into private Imperial files? Hardly. Your expert wouldn't be there six hours before Disra would know about it. It wouldn't be six hours more before some convenient accident would happen to him. But he'd be safe enough on Yaga Minor."

"I'm glad to hear that," Leia said, looking again at Sakhisakh. The Noghri's face was rigid with the same ache and fear she herself was feeling. Han on Bastion, in the middle of a vengeful Moff's stronghold . . .

"Would it be possible for you to supply such an expert?" Pellaeon asked.

With a supreme effort, Leia pushed her fears away. "I don't know," she said. "I don't think so."

Pellaeon seemed taken aback. "You don't think so?"

"No," Leia said, glancing over at the tech station again. Ghent was still facing the control board, but his head was turned just enough to let him surreptitiously watch the conversation around the game table. "Perhaps later, after we have an official agreement. But not yet."

"By the time there's an agreement it might be too late," Pellaeon warned. "Our scout ships are picking up only occasional news reports, but even from what I know the situation in the New Republic is clearly getting worse. Even with an expert slicer at work, the project is going to take some time."

He grimaced. "And there's one other factor, as well. We suspect that one of Moff Disra's agents may already have found his way into those Special Files once. We don't know what he was looking for, but the Caamas Document is definitely one possible target. If we delay too long and he's able to get in again to erase the file, we may never learn the truth. Only if we act immediately—"

"All right," Ghent interrupted, swiveling abruptly around in his chair to face them. "All right. I'll go."

Leia blinked. Once again, he had taken her completely by surprise. "You don't mean that," she said. "This could be dangerous."

"The danger would be extremely small," Pellaeon insisted.

"Doesn't matter," Ghent said. His voice was trembling, but his jaw was set firmly. "On the way from Coruscant Elegos told me all about what happened to his world. It was terrible—everyone killed, all the animals, too. I hated the people who'd done it—I really hated them. And I hated the Bothans for making the whole thing happen in the first place."

He looked over at Elegos. "But he told me hatred was wrong, that it was one of those things that hurt the hater more than the people he hated. He told me there can be justice without hatred, and punishment without revenge. He said we were all responsible for what we do and what we don't do, and no one should have to pay for someone else's crimes."

He locked eyes with Leia. "I'm a slicer, Councilor Organa Solo. I'm a *good* slicer. And I'm responsible for what I do and what I don't do, just like you or Elegos. If I can help and I don't, I'm just as guilty as anyone else." He waved a hand helplessly. "I'm not too good at stuff like this. You understand what I'm trying to say?"

"I understand perfectly," Leia assured him. "And I very much appreciate your offer. The question is whether I can allow you to put yourself at risk this way."

"It would seem that should be a straightforward question for you to answer, Councilor," Elegos said. "As a Jedi, does Crypt Chief Ghent going to Yaga Minor seem the correct path?"

Leia hid a grimace. Once again, the Caamasi's perception had come through, reminding her of the true source of her insight and guidance.

Except that for once that source had failed her. Or perhaps more correctly, she had failed it. No matter how hard she stretched out to the Force, all she could see was the turmoil of her own fears for Han's safety. Fears that she'd managed to suppress until now; guilt that she'd allowed him—even encouraged him—to step onto a hostile world in the first place; resentment and anger that after all their years of sacrifice she and Han were still the ones who always seemed to be called on to risk everything for others.

Blinking back tears, she tried to push back the sudden surge of emotion. But it remained a restless churning pool washing across her mind and spirit.

And as the Jedi calm eluded her, so did any hope of reading Ghent's path.

"I don't know," she admitted at last. "I can't seem to get any kind of reading."

"Does that mean you can't guarantee his safety?" Pellaeon asked, frowning.

"No one's safety is ever guaranteed, Admiral," Elegos said. "Not even by a Jedi." He smiled faintly, an oddly melancholy expression. "Though, of course, most of us travel through our entire lives without any assurance at all that the path we are on is the correct one. No assurance except that of our own spirits within us."

"Elegos has been spouting that sort of stuff ever since we left Coruscant," Ghent said with a weak attempt at a grin. "I guess some of this nobleness stuff must have rubbed off on me."

Unsteadily, he got to his feet. "This is the right path. And I'm ready. When do we leave?"

"At once," Pellaeon said, sliding around the end of the table and standing up. "I'll put together a letter of introduction for General Hestiv and detail one of my most trusted pilots to fly you to Yaga Minor." His eyes flicked across Ghent's outfit. "I think we'll also put you in an Imperial uniform. Disra may have informers on Yaga Minor, and there's no point in drawing unnecessary attention by bringing an obvious civilian onto a military base."

"You won't be taking him there yourself in the *Chimaera*?" Leia asked.

Pellaeon shook his head. "Once you and I have finished our discussions, I'll be heading directly to Bastion. There are some rather pointed questions Moff Disra owes me answers for."

Leia swallowed. "I see."

"With your permission, then, I'll go arrange for Crypt Chief Ghent's transport." Pellaeon smiled faintly at Ghent. "I mean Imperial Lieutenant Ghent's transport. Come with me, Lieutenant."

Stepping past Sakhisakh, he headed for the *Falcon*'s exit. "Sure," Ghent said, starting after him. "So long, Elegos. You too, Councilor."

"Go in wisdom and courage," Elegos said gravely.

"May the Force be with you," Leia added. "And thank you."

Captain Ardiff was waiting in the aft bridge when Pellaeon emerged from the turbolift. "The *Millennium Falcon* has cleared the sentry perimeter and jumped to lightspeed," he reported.

"Good," Pellaeon said, looking past him to the viewport. In the distance, he could see the faint flickers of reflected sunlight from the solar panels of the TIE fighter escort as they headed back to the *Chimaera*. "And Lieutenant Mavron?"

"He and his passenger left half an hour ago." Ardiff lifted his eyebrows slightly. "May I ask . . . ?"

"How the talks went?" Pellaeon shrugged. "As well as preliminary talks ever go, I suppose. Organa Solo isn't about to commit the New Republic to a course of action based on my word alone, and I made it similarly clear that I can't accept her word as guaranteeing Coruscant's future actions. So there's a great deal of careful verbal dancing yet to be done."

"But she's willing to talk."

"She's very willing to talk." Pellaeon hesitated. "At least, about most things."

Ardiff frowned. "What do you mean?"

Pellaeon gazed out at the stars again. "There's something she wasn't telling me," he said. "Something important—that much I'm sure of. But what exactly it was . . ." He shook his head. "I don't know."

"Private information having to do with the Bothans, perhaps?" Ardiff suggested. "Or something more personal? She's been in political trouble on Coruscant before—could it be that she's about to lose her influence there entirely?"

"I hope not," Pellaeon said. "Political problems between her and Coruscant would make this process far more difficult than it already is. They might reject any proposal simply because she was involved with it."

"Or might support it *because* she was involved," Ardiff pointed out. "The polarization we're already seeing over the Caamas issue could easily bleed over into something like this."

"That's one of my biggest concerns," Pellaeon agreed grimly. "That peace will be rejected by some for no better reason than that their political enemies are for it."

He stepped past Ardiff onto the command walkway. "But all of us have only the cards the universe has dealt us," he said. "If Organa Solo refuses to show us some of her cards, we'll just have to play the game that way.

"And in the meantime," he added, "we have other matters to attend to. Set course for Bastion, Captain. It's time Moff Disra and I had a long, serious talk."

In front of the *Falcon,* the stars flared into starlines, and Leia slumped a little in her seat. "Do you think he really meant it?" she asked, turning to look at Elegos.

Elegos gave one of his full-body Caamasi shrugs. "I believe Admiral Pellaeon himself is sincere," he said. "As I presume you know with more certainty than I do. I suspect the question you really wish to ask is whether his sincerity can be trusted."

"I don't know," she said. "You're right, I don't sense any duplicity in Pellaeon himself. But with Thrawn back on the scene . . ." She shook her head. "Nothing was ever the way it seemed with him, Elegos. He could maneuver you into doing exactly what he wanted you to do, despite the fact that you *knew* he was trying to do it. Thrawn may be using this peace initiative of Pellaeon's for some other end entirely."

"Is that why you didn't tell him that Captain Solo was on Bastion?" Elegos asked.

Leia started. "How did you know about that?" she demanded. "I didn't tell you Han had gone there."

Elegos shrugged again. "You've dropped hints," he said. "As have the Noghri. It hasn't been difficult to put the pieces together." His blue-on-green eyes bored into her face. "Why didn't you tell Admiral Pellaeon that?"

Leia turned away from that gaze, pretending to study the *Falcon's* engine monitor. "We know that Imperials are encouraging at least some of the violence that's been occurring in the New Republic," she said, fighting through the sudden dryness in her throat. "That riot on Bothawui, for one—my Noghri guard found evidence that the shots that started it came from a rare Imperial sniper weapon."

"Interesting," Elegos murmured. "You didn't tell Pellaeon about that, either."

"The problem is we have no real proof of any of it," Leia said, shaking her head tiredly. "And even if we did . . . fighting Thrawn is like fighting a shadow, Elegos. He's never where you think he is, doing what you expect him to do. Everything he does is circles within circles within circles."

"Yet you cannot allow uncertainty to paralyze you," Elegos pointed out. "That path allows him to win by default. At some point, right or wrong, you must take action." His eyes seemed to bore into hers. "You must decide who you can trust."

Leia blinked back sudden tears. "I can't trust Pellaeon," she said bluntly. "Not yet. If Thrawn is orchestrating this whole operation, Han would be a terribly useful hostage or bargaining chip for him. I couldn't take the chance he'd find out from Pellaeon that Han was there."

"Yet you trusted him enough to allow him to take Ghent into a situation of potentially equal danger," Elegos pointed out.

"Ghent wanted to go," she said, knowing even as she spoke that such an argument was dangerously slippery ground. "Besides, he wouldn't be of any use to Thrawn."

"You know better than that, Councilor," Elegos said, the soft reproach in his voice a painful jab in Leia's heart. "Ghent is highly knowledgeable about New Republic encrypt and decrypt techniques. In a war situation, such knowledge would be of immense value to the Empire."

"We've already been over this," Leia reminded him, the first stirrings of anger coloring the guilt rumbling within her. Who was this Caamasi to tell her what was right or not right for her to do? "There's no way for us to avoid taking risks here."

"I agree," Elegos said. "And I don't suggest that your decisions were necessarily wrong."

Leia frowned, the growing anger turning to suspicious uncertainty. "What *are* you suggesting, then?" she demanded.

"That you're worried you used your power and authority to protect your husband more than you did a relative stranger," Elegos said. "That you're worried you've betrayed the trust that is yours as a High Councilor, a diplomat, and a Jedi."

"She does not need to answer to you, Trustant A'kla," a harsh Noghri voice came from behind them.

Leia turned her head to see Sakhisakh standing in the open cockpit door. "Trouble?" she asked him.

"No trouble," the Noghri assured her, stepping forward and taking up a position just behind her. "I came to report that no one is in pursuit, and that Barkhimkh is shutting down the weapons systems." He turned his dark eyes on Elegos. "If she chooses to protect her clan from danger, that is no concern of yours."

"I agree," Elegos said calmly. "As I've already said, I'm not here to pass judgment."

"Then why do you press her about it?" Sakhisakh demanded.

"Because as I also said, she herself is not convinced she did right," Elegos said, turning his gaze back to Leia. "It's important that she think this matter through and come to a conclusion, one way or another. Either to accept her decisions as right and continue on, or to acknowledge them as wrong and also continue on."

"Why must she do this?" Sakhisakh asked.

The Caamasi smiled sadly. "Because she *is* a High Councilor, and a diplomat, and a Jedi. Only when she is at peace with herself will she have the insight and wisdom we will all need to rely on in the days ahead."

For a long moment none of them spoke. Leia stared out at the mottled sky of hyperspace rushing past, the acrid bite of shame adding to the rest of the emotions swirling within her. Once again, Elegos was right. "You should have been a Jedi, Elegos," she said with a sigh as she unstrapped from her seat and stood up.

"I do not have a Jedi's ability to touch the Force," Elegos said, an odd note of regret in his voice. "And yet, you speak more truly than perhaps you know. It is a legend among my people that, at the very dawn of their age, the first of the Jedi Knights came to Caamas to learn from us the moral use of their power."

"I don't doubt the legend is true," Leia said, gesturing to the seat she'd just vacated. "Sakhisakh, if you'd take control here, I'll be in the cargo hold. I have some serious thinking and meditating to do."

CHAPTER
20

"Good day, citizen-scholars of the M'challa Order of the Empire," the ancient SE2 service droid behind the reception desk wheezed its usual greeting. "How may I and the Imperial Library serve you this morning?"

"Just assign us a computer station," Han said, putting a firm restraining bolt on his already grouchy mood. Already it was shaping up to be a hot, muggy day, and he felt both uncomfortable and stupid parading around the city streets in the traditional M'challa scholar's robe he and the others had been wearing ever since landing here on Bastion. The last thing he wanted to do was waste time trading banter with an SE2 droid. "We can handle our own data search, thanks."

"Certainly." The droid peered at him, then at Lando, then at Lobot. His gaze lingered on the latter, as if wondering why he was wearing his hood so close about his head on such a warm day. "You citizens have been in here before," he said. "Each of the past three days, if my memory has not degraded."

"We're doing a long-term study," Lando stepped in smoothly. "It takes a great deal of time."

"Would you like assistance?" the droid asked helpfully. "We have several research droids and interface counterparts available for hire at a purely nominal fee."

"We're doing fine," Han told him, striving mightily to keep from shouting in the droid's metal face. "Just assign us a station, all right?"

"Certainly, citizen-scholar," the droid said affably. "Station 47A. Go through the double doors to your left—"

"We know where it is," Han said, turning on his heel and stalking toward the indicated doors.

"And thank you," Lando added.

He and Lobot caught up with Han just inside the double doors. "You think you can draw a little more attention to us?" Lando growled as Han headed off through the maze of individual and group booths that filled the huge room, only a handful of which were currently occupied. "Maybe you should try kicking the droid back and forth across the desk a few times—that ought to do it."

"A lot of Imperials don't like droids," Han growled back. "Even scholars. Let's just get on with it, okay?"

Lando didn't answer, and Han felt a twinge of guilt for snapping at his friend that way. After all, Lando was doing him a big favor by even being here in the first place.

But his mood was already too sour for the guilt to make much headway against it. Three days of softfooting around the Imperial capital city having to put up with smarmy Imperials, overcharging tapcafe owners, and idiot SE2 droids was starting to get to him.

Especially considering how much progress they'd made so far in getting into the Special Files section. Namely, none.

They reached Station 47A and Han snagged a third chair from an unused booth to supplement the two already there. "All right," Lando said, activating the booth's privacy field as he sat Lobot down in front of the keyboard and then took the chair beside him. "You have a good contact with Moegid?"

Lobot's answer was to place his fingers on the keyboard. For a moment, nothing happened. Then, slowly, he began tapping the keys.

Hitching his chair up behind Lando, stifling a sarcastic remark that wouldn't have done anyone any good and was probably uncalled for anyway, Han sat down and tried to settle in. Maybe this time, they'd get lucky.

The ship had been quiet for nearly an hour before Karoly decided that, once again, she had guessed wrong.

It was aggravating. No, actually, it was infuriating. To have come all this way with Solo and Calrissian—to have spent days buried alive in this cramped smuggling compartment beneath the elegant living section of Calrissian's yacht—and then to not even find Karrde and Shada waiting at the end of the ride was maddening.

She took a deep breath in the darkness, ordering herself sternly to settle down. Maybe Karrde and Shada had simply been delayed, and were still on their way. She would just have to be patient and wait them out.

In the meantime, there was clearly nothing to be gained by hanging around in this hole feeling sorry for herself. Reaching above her, she worked the catch that popped the hidden access panel and eased it carefully to one side.

For a moment she remained motionless in a half crouch, listening for any indication that she might have been heard. Then she eased up and out into the corridor, breathing deeply as she flushed the stale air of the compartment out of her lungs.

No one was visible. Not that that was surprising, really. Solo, Calrissian, and that biocomp-wired cyborg they called Lobot had all gone off together that morning, leaving the Verpine presumably in his usual place in the aft control room. That had been the procedure every day since they'd landed here, and there'd been nothing in the snatches of conversation she'd overheard that might indicate the routine had been changed. Briefly, she considered sneaking aft to again try to figure out what the Verpine was doing, but decided against it. Her last two efforts in that direction had failed to discover anything useful, and she couldn't see wasting any more time on it.

Which left her with the question of what exactly she *should* be wasting her time doing.

There weren't all that many options, actually. For the past three days, she'd followed Solo and the others to what the SE2 on desk duty had identified as an Imperial Library. The first two days she'd sneaked in behind them to watch; yesterday, tired of staring through a privacy field watching them punch computer keys all day, she'd left them inside and scouted around the building and neighborhood.

Now, having sneaked back aboard the ship last night, she had tested the theory that Shada might actually be meeting with the Verpine while Solo and the others were out. But that one had fallen through, too . . . and as far as Karoly could see, she was out of options. For all the evidence to date, Shada might not be coming here at all.

And *that* was an *immensely* irritating thought. It would mean she had completely misinterpreted that conversation she'd eavesdropped between Solo and Calrissian, and had come out here on a total wild tresher hunt.

Wherever "here" actually was. It was Imperial space—that much had been obvious from the all-human populace even before she'd spotted her first Imperial Security uniform. But where in the Empire it actually was, she didn't know.

Not that it mattered all that much, except for the fact that if Solo and Calrissian managed to give her the slip it might mean trouble getting back home. Unlikely, though—from the way they'd been talking this morning, whatever their objective was they were still a long way from achieving it.

Still, Karrde *had* been mentioned in that conversation, so maybe he was just being cagey. Another quick scout around the library's neighborhood, she decided, then tag Solo again when they took their usual early-afternoon meal break.

And maybe this time they would actually say something worth listening to. Easing down the corridor, alert for any sounds, she headed for the hatchway.

. . .

"Another report from your new Empire, Your Excellency," Tierce said, laying a pair of datacards on Disra's desk. "The Ruurian governments have forwarded a copy of the fully executed treaty between their systems and the Empire."

"Systems?" Disra asked, picking up the datacard and frowning at it. "I thought our treaty was only with their home system."

"It was," Tierce said smugly. "Apparently, our little demonstration against those Diamalan Marauders convinced three of their independent colonies that they wanted to be on the winning side, too."

"Did it, now," Disra said, looking at the datacard with new interest. The Ruurian independent colonies were joint efforts with a half-dozen other species. "Did the other co-owners of those worlds agree?"

"Apparently so," Tierce said. "The treaties speak of the colony systems in their entireties, with no mention of specific regions or districts." He smiled. "Of course, the Ruurians *are* quite good at persuasion."

"They're not the only ones," Disra said, looking across the room to where Flim was hunched over in a chair, staring moodily out a window. "Congratulations, Admiral. You've picked up three more systems."

Flim didn't answer, and Disra felt his lip twist with contempt. Apparently, the con man was still sulking.

"Don't worry," Tierce said, following Disra's glare. "He'll get over it soon enough."

"Or else he'll soon find himself impaled on a sharp pole somewhere out in Unknown Space," Flim growled without turning around. "Right next to the two of you."

Disra looked up at Tierce. "What's his problem?"

"Nothing serious," Tierce said, dismissing the con man with a wave of his hand. "He's worried about that alien ship, that's all."

"Ah," Disra said, smiling tightly. Yes—the mysterious alien ship which that sleeper cell pilot had spotted and made a recording of off Pakrik Minor. "What's the status on that, anyway?"

"The analysts should be finished anytime," Tierce assured him. "I have a feeling this may be it, Your Excellency."

Disra felt a shiver ripple up his back. "You really think that was the Hand of Thrawn in that ship?"

"You saw the design," Tierce pointed out. "Part TIE fighter, part something else. Yes, I think that's the Hand, or else his agent, or else someone from Captain Parck. Whichever, I think we may finally have lured our target into the open."

Flim made a rumbling noise in the back of his throat. "Like you might lure out a Death Star," he muttered.

"You're overdoing the melodrama just a bit, Admiral," Tierce said, his patience starting to sound a little strained. "Whoever they are, there are a dozen ways we can keep them from getting close enough to figure out you're a fraud."

"And what if they want to say hello?" Flim countered. "What are you going to say then? That I've got laryngitis? That I just stepped out for a week?"

"Hold it, both of you," Disra cut them off as the comm light on his desk began to blink. "This may be it."

He keyed the comm. "Moff Disra," he said.

The man on the display was middle-aged, with the slightly nearsighted look of someone who has spent long years staring at a computer display. "Colonel Uday, Your Excellency: Imperial Intelligence Analysis. I have the final report on that record you sent me."

"Excellent," Disra said. "Send it immediately."

"Yes, sir," Uday said, glancing down and working keys off-camera. Another light on Disra's display winked on and then off again, marking the transfer. "I'm afraid there wasn't much we could get on the ship itself," Uday continued. "But what there was is in there."

"Thank you," Disra said, trying not to sound too impatient. The sooner he could cut off this garrulous fool, the sooner he and Tierce could start going over the report line by line. "You'll be receiving a commendation for your quick work."

"Two points, first, if I may, Your Excellency," Uday said, holding up two fingers.

"I'm sure it's all in your report," Disra said, reaching for the off switch. "Thank you—"

"According to the note that accompanied the file, the sighting was made by a TIE fighter off Pakrik Minor," Uday said. "That turns out not to be the case."

Disra froze, finger poised over the switch. "Explain."

"The file is actually a compilation of two separate sightings," Uday said. "One was made in the Kauron system, we think, the other either in the Nosken or Drompani systems. Neither was made by a TIE fighter, either."

Disra threw a hard look at Tierce. The Royal Guardsman's face had turned to stone. "How do you know?" he demanded.

"That they didn't come from TIE fighters?" Uday asked. "The sensor profiles are all wrong. I'd guess an X-wing or A-wing for the first one, some kind of well-equipped warship for the second. Not a New Republic ship—the verification signature is wrong for that." The colonel shrugged. "As to where they were made, that's easily pulled from the background star patterns."

Disra took a careful breath. "Thank you, Colonel," he said. "You've been most helpful. As I said, a commendation will be forthcoming."

"Thank you, Your Excellency," Uday said.

Disra stabbed the comm switch, and the colonel's face vanished. "Well," the Moff said, looking at Tierce again. "It seems we've been lied to."

"It does indeed," Tierce said, his voice soft, his expression gone suddenly deadly. "I think, Your Excellency, that we have been betrayed."

Disra swore viciously. "That kriffing clone. That *kriffing* clone. We should never have trusted them. Thrawn should never have started this kriffing project in the first place."

"Calm down," Tierce said, his tone suddenly sharp. "Thrawn knew what he was doing. And don't forget that a good many of those clones died fighting for the Empire."

"They're still an abomination," Disra snarled. He'd spoken with clones; had ordered them into battle; had even sold them to the Cavrilhu Pirates in exchange for Zothip's precious Preybird starfighters. They still made his skin crawl. "And you can't trust any of them."

"Can we get off Carib Devist and clone treachery for a minute?" Flim put in tautly. "Seems to me the question ought to be why he sent us a faked record in the first place. What did he have to gain?"

Tierce took a deep breath, clearly forcing calmness into himself. "That is indeed the question. Disra, how did the record come in?"

"Aboard a drone probe from the Ubiqtorate contact station at Parshoone," Disra told him. "Sent by the agent in charge—"

"Sent directly here?" Tierce cut him off. "No handoffs or course changes?"

"No," Disra said, one hand curling into a fist as it suddenly and belatedly struck him. "They wanted Bastion's location."

"And they got it," Tierce said darkly, his comlink already in his hand. "Major Tierce to Capital Security: full background alert. Possible spies in the city; locate and put under surveillance. Do not—repeat, do not—detain at present. Confirmation from Moff Disra will be forthcoming."

He got an acknowledgment and keyed off. "You need to send them a confirmation, Your Excellency," he said.

"I know," Disra said, frowning at him. "Excuse me if I seem unusually dense today; but you *don't* want them detained? Spies or saboteurs in my city, and you don't want them detained?"

"I don't think they're saboteurs," Tierce said. "After all, they've been here at least a couple of days and nothing has blown up."

"Oh, *that's* comforting," Disra said icily. "Why don't you want them detained?"

"As Thrawn often said, within every problem lies an opportunity." Tierce shifted his gaze to the side. "It occurs to me we have an extremely interesting opportunity here."

Frowning, Disra followed his gaze . . .

"You'd better not be thinking what I think you're thinking," Flim warned, his eyes flicking uneasily back and forth between Tierce and Disra.

"Of course we are," Tierce assured him. "A Rebel spy team, being confronted personally by Grand Admiral Thrawn? It would be the perfect cap to your performance."

"The perfect slab under my funeral pyre, you mean," Flim shot back. "Are you crazy, Tierce? They get one glimpse of me, and you're going to have a martyred Grand Admiral on your hands."

"Which might not be such a bad idea," Disra growled, keying confirmation of Tierce's security alert into his board. "Tierce is right—this is a perfect chance to demonstrate your omniscience."

"I can hardly wait," Flim said sourly, crossing his arms.

"Calm down, Admiral," Tierce said, nudging Disra aside and keying the display for a search grid overview. "We'll have them spotted in fifteen minutes, and the whole thing will be over in thirty."

There was a beep from the display. "Your Excellency?"

Muttering a curse, Disra keyed the comm switch. "Yes, what is it?"

A young, earnest-looking man appeared on the display. "Major Kerf, Your Excellency: spaceport control," he identified himself. "I thought you'd like to know that his shuttle has just landed."

Disra shot a look over the display at Tierce, got a shrug in response. "Whose shuttle has just landed?"

"I thought you knew, sir," Kerf said, looking a little bewildered. "He said he was on his way to the palace to see you, and I just assumed—"

"Never mind your assumptions, Major," Disra snapped. "Who is it?"

"Why, the admiral, sir," Kerf stammered. "You know—Admiral Pellaeon."

The waiter at the open-air tapcafe set the plate of mesh-cooked trimpian slices down on the table, accepted payment with a not-quite sneer, and strolled his way back toward the overhang where the bar was located. "He's a real gem, isn't he," Lando grumbled, glaring after him.

"Probably figures M'challa scholars wouldn't know good service if it fell over them, so why bother," Han said, picking up one of the slices and dipping it into the yellow-swirled miasra sauce, being careful not to let the sleeve of his robe drag into it. Despite the fact they again had no progress to show for their morning's work, he was actually feeling better than he had earlier.

Lando, on the other hand, seemed to have caught his bad mood. "So what, that means our money's no good?" he growled. "I tell you, Han, they're getting cocky again."

"Yeah, I know," Han said, taking a bite as he looked out at the people hurrying along the streets bordering the tapcafe. Hurrying about their business, with a light step and an optimism they probably hadn't had in years. And it didn't take a genius to figure out why.

Grand Admiral Thrawn had returned.

"They have to realize they're still completely overmatched," he pointed out around his mouthful. "They've got, what, a thousand systems left?"

"It's not a lot," Lando agreed, snagging a piece of the trimpian for himself and dabbing it delicately into the miasra sauce. Lobot, Han noted, without the distraction of conversation or moodiness to slow him down, was already on his second slice. "But you sure wouldn't know it by looking at them."

"Yeah," Han said, looking around some more. Happy people, cheerful people, confident that the universe was about to open up and rain wonders down on them again. It was enough to turn a bad mood really rotten . . .

He paused, the tangy bite of trimpian between his teeth suddenly forgotten. Beyond the pedestrians, the vehicular traffic had come to a momentary halt as a speeder truck halfway down the block maneuvered toward a loading ramp. And in one of the landspeeders a few meters back from the tapcafe—

"Lando—over there," he hissed, nodding toward the landspeeder. "That dark green open-top landspeeder. The guy with the thick blond beard?"

Lando pulled back the side of his hood for better visibility. "I'll be a scruffy nerfherder," he breathed. "That's not *Zothip*, is it?"

"Sure looks like him," Han agreed grimly, fighting the impulse to pull his own hood a little tighter around his face. Captain Zothip, head of the Cavrilhu Pirates, and one of the nastier forms of semi-intelligent rotscum he'd ever had the misfortune to cross paths with. Considering the bounty on Zothip's head, there shouldn't have been a civilized planet anywhere in the galaxy where he should have been able to show his ugly face.

And yet there he was, crammed into a landspeeder with five equally ugly bodyguards in the middle of the Imperial capital, shouting obscenities at the speeder truck as if he owned the whole town. "I'd say we've found the pirate-Empire link Luke and me have been looking for," he muttered. "Clones and all."

"I'd say you're right," Lando said, his robe twitching as he shivered. "I sure hope you're not going to suggest we follow him and confirm it."

Han shook his head. "Not a chance, pal. I tangled with him once a long time ago. I haven't the slightest interest in trying it again."

"Me, neither." Lando exhaled audibly. "You know something, Han? We're getting old."

"Yeah, tell me about it," Han said. "Come on, let's eat up and get back to the library."

He glanced up at the brilliant sunlight and blue, cloudless sky. "Suddenly this town seems a lot less friendly than it did five minutes ago."

The speeder truck finished its maneuvering, the traffic began to move again, and Solo and the others went back to their meal.

And setting a high-denomination coin down beside her own half-finished snack, Karoly left the tapcafe and slipped out into the stream of pedestrians. Suddenly, there was something more interesting than Solo and Calrissian and their library research to attract her attention.

Something far more interesting.

The dark green Kakkran landspeeder hadn't made it more than a street away when she found what she was looking for: an old, beat-up Ubrikkian 9000, untended, parked at the side of the street. Palming her Mistryl-issue inciter, she hopped into the driver's seat, taking the control stick with one hand and sliding the inciter beneath the readout panel with the other. The motor coughed reluctantly to life, and with a glance over her shoulder she pulled out into a gap in the vehicular stream. A casual observer would have seen nothing unusual; she could only hope that the owner wouldn't miss his vehicle until she was finished with it.

She wove in and out of traffic until she had trimmed enough off Zothip's lead to be able to catch frequent glimpses of the dark green Kakkran. The more official-looking buildings, including what was obviously the local governor's palace, were situated on the higher ground at the northern edge of the city off to their left. If the Imperial connection Solo had mentioned was real, the pirates should be turning off anytime now.

But to her growing surprise, they didn't. Instead, the Kakkran continued east, angling northward only after the palace was far behind them. They reached the outskirts of the city and headed out into the wooded hills that bordered the area to the north, and Karoly found herself dropping farther and farther back as the traffic thinned out.

The pirates changed roads twice more, curving farther and farther north, and Karoly began to regret she'd never gotten around to picking up a map of the area. The road they were on seemed to be taking them in a circle around the city, which made no sense to her at all unless they were trying to come up on the palace from behind.

She was still toying with that thought when the Kakkran suddenly pulled to the side of the road and disappeared into the trees.

She pulled off, too, slipping out of her Ubrikkian and heading into the woods on foot. She'd gone only a little ways when the sound of the repulsorlifts ahead of her cut off.

"You sure this is it?" a rough voice drifted back toward her through the trees. "Doesn't look like any escape route I've ever seen."

"Trust me, Captain," a more cultured voice assured him. "I scoped the place out thoroughly the last time we were here." Karoly got a glimpse of movement through the trees, headed for the cover of a squat bush—

"Here it is," the cultured man said; and as Karoly dropped into a crouching position behind the bush she saw one of the six pirates reach out an arm and swing away some hanging branches from a tree growing out of the rocky cliff face. "Your typical Imperial rat-run."

Zothip grunted, ducking down to peer inside. "Couple of land-speeders stashed away in there. The tunnel wide enough for 'em, Control?"

"I presume we'll find out," the cultured man said. "Grinner, get it started."

The pirates disappeared beneath the hanging branches, and a minute later there was the sound of a repulsorlift powering up. The sound revved, then faded away into the distance. Karoly gave them a count of ten, then eased to the tree and ducked under the branches.

She found herself in a small room, no more than twice as wide as the tile-walled tunnel that extended into the hills from its rear wall, with a small Slipter landspeeder parked along the side. In the distance, she could see the reflected glow from the other landspeeder's lights receding rapidly down the tunnel.

Using her inciter, she started up the Slipter, hoping the sound of the pirates' own vehicle would cover up the extra noise. Swinging it around, leaving the lights off, she headed off in pursuit.

"Report from Security Team Eight, sir," the young trooper at the comm monitor said, his voice academy crisp. "Three possibles have been spotted in a landspeeder outside the Timaris Building. Security Team Two reporting two possibles have just entered a jewelry store on the fourteenth block of Bleaker Street."

"I've got data feeds from both teams," the trooper at one of the computer displays added. "Running facial matches now."

"He'll be running them against the complete Fleet record system over at Ompersan, Your Excellency," the lieutenant standing beside Disra explained. "If they've ever crossed paths with the Empire, their faces will be in there."

"Very good, Lieutenant," Disra said, looking around the darkened palace situation room with a mixture of satisfaction and envy. Satisfaction, because the command team he'd installed here a year ago was working with the kind of speed and efficiency that had once been the proud hallmark of the Imperial military. Envy, because it wasn't him they were performing for. "Any suggestions, Admiral?"

Standing behind the main comm monitor station, Thrawn lifted his eyebrows politely. In the dim lighting his glowing red eyes looked even brighter than usual. "I suggest, Your Excellency," he said, the word "suggest" carrying just the barest emphasis, "that we first allow the analysis staff to do their work. There's nothing to be gained by showing our hand until we're sure who the spies are."

"Maybe they all are," Disra countered, suddenly tired of the polite condescension. In character or not—dangerous or not—it was high time he took the con man down a stroke or two. "Coruscant has been trying to learn Bastion's current location for a good two years now. I doubt they would waste that hard-fought knowledge just to drop one or two spies on us."

He could feel Tierce's eyes on him, and the heat of the Guardsman's disapproval of his verbal challenge. But Thrawn's blue-black eyebrows merely lifted politely. "What do you suggest, then, Your Excellency? That a saboteur team has been sent in to bring down our planetary shields in preparation for a major attack?"

Disra stared at him, the sudden jolt momentarily sidetracking his irritation. That was precisely the scheme they themselves were working against the Bothan homeworld of Bothawui. What in the Empire was Flim doing talking openly about such a thing here?

He was saved from his sudden confusion by the trooper at the computer console. "Report from Ompersan, Admiral," the other announced. "Suspected possibles have been cleared. All are listed as Imperial citizens."

"Very good," Thrawn acknowledged. "Continue the search. Your Excellency, I presume you have not forgotten your appointment."

Disra looked at his chrono, suppressing a scowl. Yes, Pellaeon would be arriving at the palace any minute now. And between that time crunch and the confusion his barbed remark about saboteurs had caused, the con man had managed to blunt the Moff's verbal attack without saying anything that could be construed as insubordination.

Just the sort of thing the real Thrawn might have done. Disra supposed he ought to be pleased. "Thank you for the reminder, Admiral," he said. "Carry on here. And let me know the minute—the *minute*—you find anything."

They had been back at work for half an hour when Lobot's fingers abruptly came to a halt. "What is it?" Han asked, the smell of the miasra sauce on his breath wafting by Lando's ear as Han leaned over his shoulder. "Are we in?"

"I don't know," Lando said, frowning at Lobot. The other's face had changed subtly, too, at about the same time his fingers had stopped typing. More importantly, the pattern of tiny lights on the frequency readout of his cyborg implant had changed. "Something's interrupted his contact with Moegid."

"Uh-oh," Han muttered under his breath. "You think they're on to us?"

"I don't know," Lando said again, studying Lobot's profile and wondering if he should try talking to him. Lobot's eyes seemed almost glazed over, as if he were in a trance or deep in thought. "I've never seen that comm pattern before."

"Um." Han reached out and experimentally touched Lobot's shoulder. There was no response. "Backup frequency, maybe?"

"Could be," Lando agreed. "I didn't know they'd set up a second biocomm frequency, but that would make sense. I just wish—"

Abruptly, the pattern of tiny lights changed again. "Beware," Lobot croaked out, his voice an eerie parody of a Verpine's insectine speech. "Security frequencies very active."

"Moegid's talking through him," Lando said, a tight sensation in the pit of his stomach. As far he could remember, Lobot and Moegid had never done *that* before, either. "Moegid, can you hear me?"

There was a long pause, as if some kind of awkward two-way translation was taking place. "I hear," Lobot said at last. "Beware. Security frequencies very active."

"They're on to us," Han said decisively, standing up. "Come on, let's get out of here."

"You think that's a good idea?" Lando asked, looking at the slightly blurred scene outside their privacy field. "At least here they'll have to come right up to us to get a good look at our faces."

"Only if they can't find a display unit to plug that droid out there into," Han said tartly. "Come on, give me a hand with Lobot—he might not be able to steer himself right now. Moegid, is there anyone snooping around the ship?"

They had made it halfway to the door, each of them gripping one of Lobot's upper arms, before Moegid's answer came back. "No one," Lobot assured them in the same Verpine croak. "Instructions."

"Stay put," Han told him. "We'll be there as soon as we can. Better cut off your transmissions to Lobot, too."

"And don't touch anything," Lando added. "You start up the engines and they'll have you targeted in half a minute."

"They might anyway," Han warned as they continued toward the exit. "Two will get you the hand pot they figured out the record Leia and I gave Carib wasn't taken at Pakrik Minor. All they have to do is run the records for any ships that arrived after that drone probe did."

"Unless Moegid got into the spaceport computer and changed our arrival date," Lando grunted.

"Was he going to do that?"

"He was going to try. I don't know if he managed it or not."

The lights on Lobot's implant changed again; and suddenly, like a sleepwalker suddenly coming awake, he straightened up in their grasp, his tread becoming steady and firm. "We'll just have to get back as fast as we can," Lando said, letting go of Lobot's arm and reaching beneath his cloak to loosen the small, undetectable slugthrower hidden there. Theoretically undetectable, anyway. "And hope we get there before they do."

Ahead, the lights from the pirates' landspeeder stopped bouncing. Karoly took the cue and brought her own vehicle to a quick halt, shutting down the repulsorlifts as soon as it was safe to do so.

Just in time. Even as the whine from her own repulsorlifts faded into silence she could hear the last echoes of sound as the vehicle ahead also powered down.

The lights were still pointed forward, away from her. Hopping out of her landspeeder, she headed that direction in a deceptively awkward-looking walk that struck a balance between speed and silence.

Not that the silent part was all that necessary. Zothip, in particular, didn't seem at all worried about noise. "Typical Imp rat-run, all right," his gruff voice boomed, unnaturally loud in the confines of the tunnel. "Where does this turbolift go?"

"Up into the palace, I presume," Control replied. He seemed to be at least making an effort to keep his volume down. "I've never actually—"

"Then where does this other part of the tunnel go?" someone else cut in.

"I don't know," Control said patiently. "As I started to say, I've never actually been in here."

Karoly was close enough to see them now, framed at the edge of the landspeeder's lights. "We'd better find out," Zothip grunted. "Grinner, call the turbolift and stay here with it when it gets here. The rest of you, let's go for a walk."

The five of them strode off through the illumination of the land-speeder's lights, Zothip in the middle with the four guards forming a protective box around him. The remaining pirate, Grinner, punched the turbolift call once, then turned back to watch his departing comrades.

Karoly had reached the rear of the landspeeder by the time the turbolift car arrived. She dropped down behind the rear quarter, freezing in place with blaster ready, as Grinner turned back around to where he'd be able to see her.

But with the lights blazing practically in his face, he didn't have a hope of spotting her back there in the shadows. He glanced once into the car, apparently confirming it was empty, and reached in to push the hold button. Then, satisfied that he'd carried out his orders, he turned back around to watch for Zothip's return.

There were, Karoly realized, not a lot of choices open to her at this point, and the ones she had weren't all that palatable. She could settle the Mistryl's score with Zothip right here and now, counting on surprise and her Mistryl training to make up for her numerical disadvantage. But from what she'd overheard, it seemed there was something very interesting going on between Zothip and someone in the palace above them. A planned assassination, perhaps? Or even a coup?

Not that she particularly cared what happened to Imperial governors. Or soldiers or Moffs, for that matter. The whole lot of them could crash and burn as far as the Mistryl were concerned. But pirates sneaking into a governor's palace on an Imperial world was just odd enough to have piqued her curiosity. Rising from her crouch, she eased silently up behind Grinner.

With his attention down the tunnel, and his mind who knew where, he never heard a thing. Sidling around behind him, watching to make sure she wasn't coming into his peripheral vision, she slipped into the turbolift car.

It was, as she'd guessed from the glimpse she'd gotten of its interior, a transplanted military turbolift car, probably scavenged from an old Dreadnaught. And as was the case with all such turbolifts, the door she'd just entered by was mirrored by another one on the opposite side of the car.

It hadn't been used recently; a single glance told her that much. But by the same token, it also looked like it hadn't been sealed.

There was only one way to find out for sure . . . and the time for that test was now. In the distance she could hear echoing footsteps, and as she looked back at the doorway she saw Grinner disappear in that direction as he took a few steps down the tunnel toward the returning pirates.

It was the work of five seconds to pull her climbing claws from her hip pouch, open them, fasten them securely to her hands, and ease their points into the crack between the closed doors. Setting her teeth, she began to pull them apart.

For a moment nothing happened. She pulled harder, putting Mistryl-honed muscle behind it; and with a suddenness that startled her they came apart, sliding smoothly and almost noiselessly into the walls of the car.

Unlike the car itself, the turbolift shaft behind the doors hadn't been transplanted from anywhere. It had been carved out of solid rock, with only a light gridwork frame installed to support the repulsorlift and tractor equipment that powered the system.

The clearance between the gridwork and the car was minimal, but adequate. Stepping through the door, turning again to face into the car, she found a toehold on the doorframe lip and got a grip on the doors.

She had them pulled back down to a slight crack when Zothip rounded the corner and stomped into the car.

She froze, abandoning the rest of her effort, her eyes searching the outside of the car now. If Grinner noticed the doors were cracked more than they had been earlier there was going to be trouble. But Grinner hadn't struck her as the observant type, and there was nothing she could do about it now anyway. More important was the fact that if she didn't find a way to hang on, she was going to be left behind.

There were no convenient handholds that she could get to, which meant she was going to have to make some. Timing it to the exact moment when one of the pirates stomped into the car, she jabbed her climbing hooks into the grillwork behind two of the glow panels. She'd barely gotten them set when there was the vibration of the main doors closing, and they were off.

"So what was at the other end of the tunnel?" she heard Grinner's voice ask through the crack between the doors.

She'd expected the response to come from Zothip, but it was Control's voice that answered. "Looked like some sort of apartment," he said. "Rather nicely appointed."

"Anyone in it?" Grinner asked.

"Not at the moment," Control said. "But whoever was living there liked having his own personal Star Destroyer captain's chair."

"His own *what*?" Grinner growled. "What in Vader's face would anyone want with something like that?"

"Very good," Control said archly. "You've got the question. Now if we had the answer, we'd have a complete set."

"I don't like this," Zothip rumbled. "I don't like any of it. He's playing something real close to the chest, and I don't like it."

"Whatever it is, we'll find out soon enough," Control assured him. "We might want to go in a little quieter than you'd planned, though."

"Oh, we'll go in quiet, all right," Zothip promised darkly. "Don't worry about that. He'll never hear a thing."

CHAPTER

They had made it five blocks—which was four blocks farther than Han had thought they would get—when the whole thing started to unravel.

"Han?" Lando murmured as the three of them hurried across a busy street with a crowd of other pedestrians. "That security landspeeder there to the left just slowed down."

"I know," Han said grimly, peering around the edge of his scholar's hood. Near as he could tell through the curved windows, there were two men in the vehicle. Alert young men, by the looks of them, undoubtedly armed to the teeth. "That's, what, the third one that's taken an interest in us?"

"About that," Lando sighed. "Where's Luke and his Jedi tricks when you need them?"

"Luke *or* Leia," Han added, wishing mightily now that he hadn't argued so successfully against her coming on this trip. They might well have been spotted a lot sooner; but at least when they were they would have had a Jedi here on their side. "He's turning back around—they're on us, all right."

"Well, don't give up just yet," Lando said, glancing around. "You still have official standing with the New Republic—we may be able to talk our way out of it. Especially if they know how Leia reacts when one of her family gets in trouble."

"You mean like when one of the kids gets kidnapped or her husband gets beaten to a pulp or something?" Han growled, feeling his face warm.

"I didn't mean it that way," Lando protested.

"Thanks anyway," Han said, looking around for inspiration. His gaze fell on a tapcafe across the street with a large sign reading SABACC TOURNAMENT TODAY prominently displayed in the privacy-glazed window . . . "Over there." He nudged Lando in the tapcafe's direction. "You have your slugthrower, right?"

"Uh . . . yes," Lando said cautiously. "What exactly have you got in mind?"

"What's the one thing security types can't ever resist?" Han asked. "Especially young, cocky ones?"

"I don't know," Lando said humorlessly. "Working prisoners over?"

Han shook his head. "A good commotion," he said, nodding toward the tapcafe. "You take Lobot into the middle of the place and clear it out. I'll handle the rest."

"Right. Good luck."

They made it across the traffic in one piece and went into the tapcafe. Inside, it was just as Han had hoped: large, well lit, and crowded to the gills with sabacc players hunched over tables and kibitzers standing behind them gazing over their shoulders. Breaking to the right just inside the door, he sidled around behind a wall of observers as Lando and Lobot worked their way in toward the curved bar bulging out into the room from the center of the left-hand wall. By the time they reached it Han had managed to work his way out of his scholar's robe. Kicking it back out of the way against the wall, he rubbed the sweat off his palms and waited for Lando to make his move.

He didn't have to wait very long. "All right, that's it!" Lando abruptly bellowed, his voice cutting through the low murmur of background conversation like a lightsaber through a block of ice. All heads turned toward the bar—

And jerked back in shock and fright as the slugthrower blew a gaping hole in the ceiling.

"We'll settle this right here and now, you mangy kowk brain," Lando shouted over the echoing thundercrack and a handful of gasping shrieks. "Everybody else—*out!*"

It was as unclear to Han as it was to everyone else just who the mangy kowk brain was that Lando was referring to. But if the sudden panicked exodus from the room was any indication, no one seemed eager to accept the title. Drinks, cards, and dignity completely forgotten, the whole crowd made a concerted dash for the door.

Han let about half of them get past him. Then, shoving his way into the stream, he squeezed through the door and out into the street.

He'd been right about the two security men. Their quiet surveillance totally abandoned, they were pushing their way upstream against the crowd toward the sound of the slugthrower shots, their blasters drawn and ready. Elbowing his way crosswise against the flow, Han angled toward them.

Concentrating on the tapcafe, the first one shoved past Han without a single glance. Han waited until the second was just passing him; then, grabbing the kid's gun hand, he swiveled on one heel and drove his elbow hard into the other's stomach. The air went out of him in a loud, agonized *whoosh* that clearly announced he was out of the fight.

Unfortunately, the sound also clearly announced trouble to his partner. Even as Han wrenched the blaster from his victim's limp hand the other security man, still enmeshed by the crowd, turned to see what had happened.

The kid was certainly young and agile enough. But he had turned around to his left, which left his blaster out of line for a quick shot behind him. Han, on the other hand, already had his appropriated weapon aimed. With a silent plea for the complete trappings of civilization to be in place here in the Imperial capital, he fired.

His plea was answered. Instead of the killing flash of full-power blaster fire, the weapon in his hand spat the brilliant blue rings of a stun jolt.

The security man dropped like a rock beneath the flow of the crowd, already scattering away from this new threat to their peace and quiet. Brandishing the blaster high, Han leaped over the prone body and dashed back to the tapcafe.

Inside, the place was deserted. Even the bartender had found somewhere to disappear to. "Not like the old days in the Outer Rim," Lando commented almost wistfully, stripping off his own scholar's robe with one hand as he kept his slugthrower ready.

"Lucky for you it isn't," Han reminded him. "On Tatooine or Bengely there'd have been fifteen blasters on you before you got your second shot off. Come on—back door's that way."

Nevertheless, he felt a twinge of regret of his own as the three of them headed for the back of the tapcafe. Those had indeed been fine days . . .

Bracing himself, Disra lifted his eyes from the datapad. "I don't know what to say, Admiral," he said, careful not to overdo the hurt indignation in his voice and expression. "I categorically deny all of this, of course."

"Of course," Pellaeon echoed, his eyes cool and measuring. "I'm sure it's nothing more than a carefully orchestrated smear campaign against you by your political enemies."

Disra bit down on his tongue in annoyance. That had indeed been the line he'd been planning to run with. Vader take the man, anyway. "I wouldn't go quite that far," he said instead. "I have no doubt that at least some of your sources have been sincere. Whatever their motivations or sincerity, though, their information *is* wrong."

Pellaeon exchanged glances with Commander Dreyf, seated beside him. Patient, knowing glances on both sides. "Really," Pellaeon said, looking back at Disra. "And what do you suggest is the motivation and sincerity of the official trading data Commander Dreyf uncovered on Muunilinst?"

"That's section fifteen on the file," Dreyf offered helpfully. "In case you missed it."

Disra ground his teeth, looking back at the datapad. Vader take Pellaeon *and* Dreyf. "All I can suggest is that someone deliberately planted those numbers," he said.

It was an unbelievably weak defense, and everyone in the office undoubtedly knew it. But even as Pellaeon opened his mouth to most likely point that out, there was a diffident tap from across the room and one of the double doors swung ponderously open. Disra looked up, ready to scorch the person who'd had the temerity to intrude on a private conversation—

"Your Excellency?" Tierce said, blinking with nicely underplayed surprise at the sight of the two armed troopers flanking the doorway, guards Pellaeon had had the effrontery to bring in here with him. "Oh, I'm sorry, sir—"

"No, that's all right, Major," Disra said. "What is it?"

"I have an urgent message for you, Your Excellency," Tierce said, hesitantly crossing toward the desk, his eyes on Pellaeon. "From the palace situation room."

"Well, let me see it," Disra growled, waving the other impatiently forward and trying to cover his sudden misgivings. Tierce could just as easily have called down on the comm with news of their spy search; the speaker focus was set so that no one but Disra could hear. To have come down personally implied that something had gone seriously wrong . . .

Tierce reached the desk and handed Disra his datapad. And something had indeed gone seriously wrong.

> *Enemy spies identified as former New Republic generals Han Solo and Lando Calrissian plus an unidentified man with cyborg head implant. Subjects were spotted and identified at the corner of Regisine and Corlioon, but have broken surveillance and escaped. Capital Security is currently attempting to reestablish contact.*

Disra looked up at Tierce, saw the hard edge to the Royal Guardsman's eyes. "I don't like getting reports like this," he said darkly. "What exactly is the lieutenant doing about it?"

"They're all working on it," Tierce said. "They seem to be doing their best."

"Is there a problem?" Pellaeon spoke up. His question was addressed to Disra, but his eyes—and his attention—were clearly on Tierce. "Perhaps you'd like to see to it personally."

Disra ground his teeth again. Yes, he very much wanted to see what was going on up there. But Pellaeon wouldn't have offered to let him squirm off the hook, even temporarily, unless he had some devious plan of his own in mind.

He suppressed a smile as it struck him. Of course—Pellaeon wanted the chance to pull a quick private interrogation on Tierce, and was trying to get the Moff out of the way.

And it was now equally clear that the hope of dangling that precise bait in front of him was precisely Tierce's reason for delivering the message personally. "Thank you, Admiral," Disra said, getting to his feet. "I believe I will. Major Tierce, perhaps you'll keep the Admiral and his party company until I return."

"Me, sir?" Tierce asked, giving the visitors a simpleminded, wide-eyed expression. "Why, certainly, sir. If the Admiral doesn't mind."

"Not at all," Pellaeon said softly. "I'd be delighted."

"I'll be back soon," Disra promised. "Enjoy yourselves. Both of you."

Thirty seconds later he was back in the situation room. "What in the name of Vader's teeth happened?" he demanded.

"Calm yourself, Your Excellency," Thrawn said, his eyes flashing warningly at Disra. "We've only lost them temporarily."

Disra glared at the other, biting back a blistering retort. If this mess was the con man's fault, he was going to nail him to the wall. "May I inquire how something like this could happen?"

"Solo and Calrissian are combat veterans, highly experienced at survival," Thrawn said calmly. "The security men they came up against were neither." He shrugged, a subtle movement of shoulders beneath the white uniform. "Actually, it was rather instructive, pointing up as it did some obvious deficiencies in Capital Security's training procedures. We'll have to remedy that."

"I'm sure they'll be delighted to have your input," Disra said, looking over at the status board. An overview of the city was currently displayed, along with the locations of all the Capital Security forces scattered around it. "Wouldn't it make more sense to concentrate our surveillance on the spaceport? They're probably trying to get back to their ship."

"I'm sure they are," Thrawn agreed. "However, if they arrive to find a ring of stormtroopers blocking their path, they'll simply find an alternative way off Bastion."

"I suppose you're right," Disra said reluctantly. Tierce's argument, undoubtedly. Most likely his exact words, too; Disra could practically hear the Guardsman's characteristic inflections in the con man's voice. "May I ask what you suggest we do, then?"

Thrawn turned his glowing red eyes toward the status board. "The first step in catching a sentient prey is to think as he does," he said. Again, words that sounded straight out of Tierce's mouth. "What was their mission here, and how did they intend to accomplish it?"

"How about sabotage?" Disra gritted. "That sound like a likely mission?"

"No," Thrawn said firmly. "They wouldn't send men like Solo and Calrissian in as saboteurs. Spies, perhaps, but not saboteurs."

"Admiral Thrawn?" one of the troopers spoke up from his station. "I've got a partial backcheck on the targets now. We've got a droid download that shows they've spent the past three days in the Imperial Library."

"Very good," Thrawn said, looking back at Disra. His head tilted fractionally toward an unoccupied corner of the room—

"I'd like to speak with you a moment, Admiral," Disra said, picking up on the cue. "Privately, if I may."

"Certainly, Your Excellency," Thrawn said, gesturing toward the corner. "Let's step over here."

They crossed to the corner. "Don't tell me—let me guess," Disra muttered, keeping his voice low. "They're here after the Caamas Document."

"What an amazing revelation, Your Excellency," Flim said, not quite sarcastically, his tone changing subtly out of his Thrawn character. "The interesting part is that I've never heard of either Solo or Calrissian having anywhere near the slicing training for a job like that."

Disra frowned. Getting past the con man's impertinence, he had a good point. A *very* good point. Disra himself had worked his way into the Emperor's Special Files, but he'd had years to do it and any number of experts to call on for advice along the way. "Then the slicer must be the head-implant who's with them," he suggested.

Flim's mouth puckered slightly. "No, I don't think so," he said. "They didn't get a good enough look at him for a positive ID, but my guess is that that's Lobot, Calrissian's old administrator from his pre-Endor days on Bespin. As far as I know Lobot hasn't got any slicing expertise, either . . ."

He trailed off, his eyes suddenly narrowing. "What is it?" Disra demanded.

"There's a trick I heard about once," Flim said slowly. "A slicing trick someone in the fringe came up with a few years ago. Now, how did that work? No, be quiet a minute—let me think."

For a dozen heartbeats the only sound in the room was the murmur of background conversation as the men working their boards reported to each other new information as it came in. All of it negative. Disra took deep breaths, concentrating on keeping a firm leash on his impatience. There were enemy spies loose in his city . . .

And abruptly, Flim's eyes focused on him again. "Verpines," he said with a note of triumph in his tone. "That was it. Verpines."

He took a half step past Disra. "Lieutenant, start a wide-spectrum comm frequency scan," he ordered, his voice suddenly that of Thrawn again. "Concentrate on Verpine biocomm frequencies."

The lieutenant's eyebrows didn't even lift. "Yes, sir," he said briskly, setting to work.

"Wait a second," Disra said, almost grabbing at Flim's sleeve and remembering just in time that that would be out of character. "Verpine *biocomm* frequencies?"

"It's really an impressively cute trick," Flim said, dropping his voice again to a level where only Disra could hear. "You have a Verpine slicer sitting off in a hole somewhere while a runner with an implant tuned to his personal biocomm frequency goes to the system you want to slice. With the data flow the implant can handle, the whole thing acts almost like a telepathic link. The Verpine sees through the implant's eyes and works the slicing on his own computer board, and the runner's fingers mimic his on the real system."

"He turns him into a puppet, in other words," Disra bit out, his stomach twisting with distaste. For an alien to play a human being that way, even an implant who was no longer really human, was a vileness that bordered on the obscene.

"Basically," Flim agreed casually. "Like I said, a real cute trick."

"I'll take your word for it," Disra growled. Naturally, to a con man mired in the fringe himself, such obscenities were probably just a commonplace way of life. "So what if they've shut the link down?"

Flim shrugged, the same Thrawn-like gesture he'd used earlier. Out of earshot of the other troopers, he was still cagey enough to stay visually within his role. "Then we crump out, and we'll have to try something else."

Disra looked over at the status board. "What if we try broadcasting on those biocomm frequencies?" he asked. "Maybe tell the Verpine to start up their repulsorlifts or something? That would at least smoke out their ship for us."

"We'd have to know how to encode a message into Verpine," Flim said doubtfully. "I doubt we could find someone who can do it fast enough."

"Couldn't a protocol droid handle the translation?"

"Not without a special module," Flim told him. "Off-the-floor models don't usually come equipped to translate Verpine. Not enough call for it."

He stroked his lower lip thoughtfully. "On the other hand, if Lobot's still got the link open from his end, we might be able to pick up a resonance echo if we hit the right frequency. That was something we used to have to worry about with our comlinks when we were running against some of the more sophisticated planetary patrol groups. If we can get a receiver close enough, and if we're lucky, we might be able to locate them."

Disra felt his lip twist. "An awful lot of *ifs* in there."

"I know," Flim conceded. "But we've got to try something, and that's the best I can do right now." He nodded toward the door. "Maybe you'd better get Tierce back up here. This is tactics, and he *is* our tactics expert."

And Pellaeon had had enough time alone with the man, anyway. "I'll send him up," he said, heading toward the door. "Keep me informed, Admiral."

With one final lurch, the turbolift car came to a halt. "This it?" Zothip's voice growled.

"I expect so," Control said as the doors slid open. "Yes—this should be it."

"So which way?" one of the other pirates demanded.

Easing her head to the side, Karoly lined up one eye with the crack still showing between the back doors. The pirates were half in and half out of the car now, Zothip standing in a narrow passageway outside with his fists set on his hips, all of them looking back and forth both directions down a narrow corridor.

"I don't know," Control said, looking around once himself and then pointing to the left. "Let's try that way first."

"Okay," Zothip said. "Grinner, lock down the car—we don't want anyone coming up behind us."

"Right," Grinner said, doing something Karoly couldn't see with the control board. "Done."

The pirates disappeared out of sight to the left. Karoly gave them a five-count; then, finding a toehold on the doorframe lip, she set her climbing claws into the crack between the doors and pried them open.

She stepped into the car; and she was just starting to close the doors again when she heard the sound of footsteps in the corridor outside.

The pirates were coming back.

There was no time for anything but instinctive reaction. Putting her full strength into the effort, she pulled the doors to within a couple of centimeters of being closed. They hung up there, but there was no time for her to try to free them. Crossing the car in two quick strides, she squeezed herself as invisibly as she could into the front left-hand corner.

Just in time. Even as she pressed her climbing claws firmly against the car walls to avoid the telltale clink of metal on metal should they accidentally brush together, the footsteps reached her.

"I don't see what the big deal is that he's got company," Zothip was muttering as the first puff of air from their passage wafted in through the car opening. "Anyway, I only heard two voices in there."

"That doesn't mean there aren't more," Control said patiently as the group passed the open door and continued down the passageway. "Besides, if we're seen by the wrong people this arrangement of ours goes straight down."

"So what?" Zothip growled, his voice fading as they all continued down the corridor. "Canceling the arrangement—*and* Disra—is the whole idea, isn't it?"

"We ought to at least talk first," Control said. "We might be able to recast the deal."

"Hey, Grinner, you sure know your way around a control panel," another voice put in from the rear of the pack as the group continued on its way. "Did you know that when you locked the car down you popped the back doors?"

Karoly held her breath; but Grinner's response was a brief obscenity and an uninterrupted tread down the corridor. She gave them another five-count; then, pulling off the climbing claws and putting them away, she drew her blaster and headed out after them.

She wasn't more than a few steps into the corridor when a subtle wave of air in her face warned her that somewhere ahead a door had opened. She picked up her pace a bit, and came around a slight curve in the passageway just in time to see a rectangle of muted light close down to a sliver as the pirates closed a door down to a crack. Hurrying silently forward, she stopped at the door and eased her ear against the crack.

"Fancy place," she heard one of the pirates say, his tone a mixture of contempt and envy. "Look at this—Ramordian silk sheets and everything."

"Maybe he'll give you a set for your bunk," Zothip growled. "Where's the—oh, there it is."

There was the soft sound of a chair being pulled back across a thick carpet. Karoly moved her eye around the crack, trying to see what was going on. But from her angle all she could see was a small section of an elaborate wall hanging. "What are you going to do?" Control asked.

"Put in a call to his office," Zothip grunted. "Whoever he's got in there, I figure he can tell them to wait."

"I'm sorry, Admiral," Major Tierce said, his fingertips rubbing nervously at the sides of his pant legs. "But with all due respect, I really don't know what you're talking about. I don't think I've *ever* been to Yaga Minor. If I have, it would have been as part of a training cruise when I was a cadet. Certainly not—what did you say; six weeks ago?"

"About that," Pellaeon said, watching Tierce's face closely and wishing mightily that he had enough evidence on him to order a full verity analysis. The man was lying through his teeth—that much Pellaeon was sure of. But until he could positively identify Tierce as the man who'd sliced into the Yaga Minor computer system, there was nothing else he could do.

Or until that New Republic slicer Ghent found evidence of Tierce's tampering. *That* was a wild card neither Tierce nor Disra knew about.

Behind Pellaeon, the double doors swung open. "I apologize for the delay, Admiral," Disra said, striding past Commander Dreyf and around the side of the ivrooy desk. "That will be all, Major," he added curtly to Tierce.

"Yes, Your Excellency," Tierce said. For the briefest instant their eyes met, and Pellaeon thought he saw Disra give his aide a microscopic nod. Then, moving with the air of a man trying to run from a group of besiioths while still keeping some shreds of dignity, the major crossed the office and escaped.

"I trust Major Tierce was congenial company for you," Disra commented.

"Quite congenial," Pellaeon assured him, studying that twisted face closely. Not so much a face as a mask, he thought, built to conceal the mind behind it.

And he knew what was in that mind. The trouble was, he couldn't prove it. Not yet. But let him have one slip on Disra's part—just one—

"Now, where were we?" Disra asked briskly, leaning back in his chair. The short break had definitely done his confidence a mountain of good. "Oh, yes—those unfounded and slanderous things other people have been saying about me. It's occurred to me, Admiral—"

He broke off as the call signal sounded from his desktop comm. Scowling, he leaned forward again and jabbed the switch. "Yes?" he barked. "What is it—?"

He stiffened, his eyes widening momentarily, his jaw dropping a fraction of a centimeter. His eyes darted to Pellaeon, back to the comm display. "Yes, I'm busy," he growled. "And I don't appreciate being interrupted this way for—"

Abruptly he stopped. Pellaeon strained his ears, but the speaker was focused toward Disra and he could hear nothing from his position on the opposite side of the desk.

And then Disra's eyes widened again . . . and Pellaeon saw something he had never seen before. Something he had never expected to see.

Moff Disra, liar, conniver, and probable traitor, went white.

Dreyf saw it, too. "Your Excellency?" he asked, standing up and starting around the side of the desk.

The moment of shock passed, and Disra's expression of stunned disbelief suddenly changed to that of a crazed rancor. "Back!" he snarled at Dreyf, his hand slashing at him as if trying to ward away a dangerous animal. "I'm all right. Just stay back."

Dreyf stopped, throwing a confused look at Pellaeon. "Is anything the matter, Your Excellency?" Pellaeon asked.

"Everything's fine, Admiral," Disra said, the words coming out like they'd been sent through a grain-grinder. His eyes, Pellaeon noted, were still fixed on the comm display. "If you'll excuse me again, there's another matter I need to attend to right away."

He stood up, keying off the comm with a vicious stab of his finger. "I'll be right back," he growled, heading at a not-quite run toward the double doors.

"Of course," Pellaeon called after him. "Take whatever time you need."

The last word was cut off by the boom as the doors closed behind him. "Well, that was interesting," Dreyf commented, looking at the doors and then back at Pellaeon. "Another trick to buy himself some breathing space?"

"I don't think either of these interruptions has been an act," Pellaeon said, frowning thoughtfully at the Moff's desk. Historically, the majority of people who were able to afford culture-grown ivrooy furniture were wealthy politicians, industrialists, and fringe crimelords. All of whom always had things to hide . . . "No, something's going on out there. Something important."

"Mm," Dreyf murmured. "Shall I wander down the hall and see if I can find out what it is?"

"Maybe later," Pellaeon said. "In the meantime, it seems we've been left alone. In Disra's office."

Dreyf lifted his eyebrows in understanding. "Yes, we have, haven't we," he agreed, looking around the office. His gaze fell on the desk . . . "Of course, it's a little dubious legally," he reminded his superior, throwing a sideways glance at the two troopers guarding the door. "We haven't got a search order, and Disra hasn't been officially charged with anything."

"I'll take the responsibility," Pellaeon said. "Go ahead and see what you can find."

"Yes, sir," Dreyf said, giving him a tight smile as he circled around to the other side of the desk. "It'll be a pleasure."

Tierce was standing near the door as Disra burst into the situation room. "We've got an echo," the former Guardsman murmured, a note of malicious satisfaction in his voice. "Once we triangulate in—"

"Zothip's here," Disra cut him off. "He's in my quarters."

Tierce's smile vanished. "How?"

"How in blazes should I know?" Disra shot back. "But he's there. I recognized the furnishings when he called me in my office."

Tierce threw a look at the consoles, at Flim holding position again behind the lieutenant. "This just gets better and better," he said darkly. "Did Pellaeon hear any of it?"

"I don't think so," Disra said. "That slinker of his—Dreyf—started to come around the desk, but I don't think he could hear or see anything, either."

Tierce hissed between his teeth. "We've got to get rid of him."

"Brilliant tactical thinking," Disra growled. "You have any suggestions as to how? He didn't come alone, you know."

Tierce looked over at the consoles again. "I can't just walk out of here," he said. "Solo and Calrissian are slippery. Until Security actually has them in their sights—"

"We can't just leave Zothip resting his feet in there, either," Disra cut him off. "Don't you understand? He's *in my quarters.* That means he has clear passage to my office. Where Admiral Pellaeon is."

Tierce looked sharply at him. "You left Pellaeon alone?"

"Of course he's alone," Disra snapped. "What was I supposed to do, tell the outer door guards to go in and watch him?"

"That wouldn't have been such a bad idea," Tierce retorted. He held up a hand. "All right, all right, let's take this in order. Pellaeon . . . I suppose he'll keep. Solo and Calrissian—"

"We've got a second biocomm frequency echo, Admiral," one of the troopers reported, looking up at Flim. "Security reports ready to move in as soon as we have a solid fix on the location."

"Thank you," Thrawn said, turning those glowing eyes toward the conversation by the door. "Continue the operation. Is there a problem, Your Excellency?"

"A small problem only, Admiral Thrawn," Tierce spoke up before Disra could answer. "But it may require a few minutes of your attention."

"Certainly," Flim said easily.

"What are you doing?" Disra hissed as the con man crossed the room toward them. "You aren't suggesting—?"

"There are only two ways to deal with someone like Zothip," Tierce said, his voice cold. "Kill him, or scare him." He nodded toward Flim. "Can you think of anything that could possibly scare him more than a Grand Admiral?"

Flim had reached them in time to hear the last part. "Who are we trying to scare?" he asked.

"Captain Zothip," Disra said. "He's in my quarters."

Flim's eyes widened, just noticeably. He looked at Tierce—"You'll be fine," the Guardsman soothed him. "Zothip's in this for the profit, and you're our guarantee there will *be* profit. He's not going to risk hurting you."

"Unless he's here for revenge," Flim pointed out uneasily. "For the job Pellaeon did on him out at Pesitiin, remember?"

"He'll forget all about that the minute he sees you," Tierce said impatiently. "At any rate, I'll be there with you. Whoever he's got in there, I can handle them. You'll be fine."

"What about Solo?" Flim persisted, glancing back to the consoles. "What if they lose him again?"

"How?" Tierce countered. "We've picked up two echoes—we know what part of the city they're in. They'll have them in restraints by the time we get back. Now let's *go.*"

Flim grimaced, but nodded. "Continue the operation, Lieutenant," he ordered, half turning, his calm Thrawn voice betraying none of his obvious nervousness. "I'll be back in a few minutes."

Tierce gestured toward the door, and together the three of them headed out. "I don't know," Flim muttered, just loud enough for Disra to hear. "I don't think I'm going to like this at all."

Their first warning was a sudden, subtle jerking motion from Lobot. "What is it?" Lando asked, peering at the other.

"What is what?" Han asked from Lobot's other side.

"He seemed to hesitate right there," Lando said, pulling back the floppy-brimmed hat that had taken over the job of camouflaging Lobot's head implant and studying the tiny indicator lights there. The pattern wasn't the same one that had been showing the last time he looked.

"Maybe he just stumbled," Han said impatiently, looking around the crowds. "Come on, we've got to keep moving."

"Hold on a minute," Lando insisted, widening his examination to the suddenly introspective expression on Lobot's face. He knew the other far better than Han did, and it was clear to him that both the jerking movement and the other's strange look were indications that something odd was going on. Ignoring it would be just begging for trouble.

"Lando—"

"Just a *minute,*" Lando cut him off. Abruptly, Lobot jerked a second time, the indicator lights again changing their pattern. They held the new array a moment, then changed back—

And with a sudden hollow feeling in the pit of his stomach, Lando realized what had just happened. "They're doing a comm echo search," he told Han. "Keyed to Verpine biocomm frequencies."

"Terrific," Han said, catching Lobot's arm to steady him and frowning under the brim at the implant. "They have the right frequency yet?"

"Doesn't look like it," Lando said, looking around for inspiration.

They were still a half hour away from the spaceport if they stayed on foot. A landspeeder could get them there faster, but that would mean either hiring or stealing one. Each option carried its own set of risks.

His eyes fell on a large, glistening sign over one of the shops just down the street. A sign bragging in large print about hundreds of droids in stock, the best prices in the Empire, and everything on sale for one day only . . .

"Come on," he said, taking Lobot's other arm and pulling him toward the droid shop. "In here. I've got an idea."

They made it inside before the Imperials' frequency search hit the right one again. "What now?" Han muttered, looking around the wall-to-wall crowd of bargain-hunters.

"Over there," Lando told him, shouldering his way toward an over-head sign marking the astromech droid section. "We need about a dozen R2 or R8 models."

"No problem," Han assured him, craning his neck to look over the mass of shoppers. "I see at least twenty of them. I hope you remember what our cash supply is like."

"We're not going to buy them," Lando said. "All we're going to do is talk to them."

They pushed their way through the crowd and into the astromech droid section, which was—not surprisingly—less densely populated than the servant and chef droid areas seemed to be. "Good afternoon, worthy citizens," a silver-colored protocol droid said, stepping up to them. "I am C-5MO, human-cyborg relations. May I assist you in your selection?"

"Yes, thank you," Lando said. "We're looking for a droid that can serve as a long-range comm interface on certain very select frequencies."

"I see, sir," the droid said, half turning to gesture toward the lines of shiny rounded cylinders behind him. "May I suggest something from either the R2 or R8 line. Both lines come with full-frequency comm systems as standard equipment."

"Sounds good," Lando said, stepping toward the line of R8s. "Do you mind if I give them a little test?"

"Of course not, sir," the protocol droid said. "Feel free to administer any test you choose."

"Thank you." Lando gestured to the first R8. "You—first in line—I'd like you to transmit a multitonal signal on the following frequency." He rattled off the number. "Next one: I'd like you to do different tones on a different frequency." He supplied the number.

"Just a moment, sir," the protocol droid interrupted, sounding distressed. "I'm afraid you can't simply transmit unauthorized comm signals in the middle of the city—"

One of the R8s twittered a short message. "Oh," the protocol droid said, somewhat taken aback. "You're certain neither frequency is used here? By anyone?"

The R8 gave an affirmative warble. "I see," the droid said. "My apologies, sir. Please continue."

Lando continued down the line, giving each droid one of the major Verpine biocomm frequencies to transmit on. "All right," he said when he had finished, turning back to the C-5MO. "Excellent. Now, if you'll keep them transmitting, I'll go out to my landspeeder and make sure they're holding the frequencies properly."

"You wish to leave them transmitting?" the droid asked, starting to sound distressed again. "But, sir—"

"You can't expect us to buy such a large order just on your word that they're transmitting correctly, can you?" Han put in. "Don't worry—one of our people will still be here." He pointed across the way at a man in a dark green coat examining the line of servant droids.

"He'll stay here until we get this checked out and get back to you," Lando added. "You *do* extend corporate credit for orders of twenty or more, don't you?"

"Certainly, sir," the droid said, brightening considerably. "You'll simply need to show your corporate authorization when you place your order."

"Good," Lando said, lifting his eyebrows at Han. The other took the hint, easing Lobot toward the nearest exit sign. "We'll be back in a few minutes."

Two minutes later, they were out on the street again. "Nice touch, that bit about leaving someone behind," Lando commented to Han. "Should buy us a few more minutes before they start asking themselves awkward questions."

"As long as they don't start a conversation with the guy, anyway," Han grunted. "So what's the plan? Straight back to the ship?"

"It was," Lando said. "Unless you think it would be worth the time to be a little more devious than that."

"I wonder," Han said, rubbing his cheek. "Those droid transmissions ought to blanket any more echo searches, at least for now. But they *did* already have an idea where we were in the city. If we can hop a cargo carrier, that would let us get around the spaceport and hit it from the other side."

"If we don't get caught," Lando warned. "They take a dim view around here of people riding cargo carriers."

"It's worth the risk," Han said, making it clear that he'd already made up his mind. "Come on—nearest access is this way."

CHAPTER

22

The conversation—or at least the part Karoly had been able to hear through the half-open door—had been short, sharp, and unpleasant.

And very enlightening. The Cavrilhu Pirates, allied with the Empire?

On one level, she supposed, it wasn't that much of a revelation, particularly not after that overheard conversation between Solo and Calrissian. Imperials had been doing under-the-board business with the dregs of the fringe for years, after all, from that accursed murderer Palpatine's cozy relationship with Prince Xizor on down. Now that the vast, star-spanning Empire had been reduced to a pitiful handful of sectors, all the more reason they would have to hire out some of their dirty work.

But on another level, this was indeed something new. Zothip hadn't been talking to Moff Disra as a hireling would to his master, but as a full equal. A very unhappy equal, moreover, if the pirate chief's tone and streams of invective were any indication.

Even more interesting, given Zothip's veiled threats to go public, it would also appear that this arrangement was neither sanctioned by nor even known to the rest of the Imperial leadership.

Karoly had originally followed Zothip with the idea of exacting revenge against the pirates for their part in the Lorardian slaughter three years ago. Now, she had stumbled on something far more interesting.

"You think he'll come?" one of the pirates' voices intruded on Karoly's musings.

" 'Course he will," Zothip grunted. "You think he wants us announcing our deal on the all-Bastion comm broadcast frequency?"

"He won't be coming alone," Control's voice warned. "He'll have guards with him."

"Not many of 'em," Zothip said. "There aren't a lot of people that slug trusts."

"A hidden backup might still be a good idea," Control said, and Karoly could hear the verbal nudging in his tone. "Just in case."

"Oh, all right," Zothip conceded with ill grace. "Crans, Portin—go get back in the passageway. If I whistle, come out and kill everything that's not us."

There was a pair of acknowledgments and the sound of approaching footsteps. Moving with considerably less noise, Karoly retreated around the slight bend in the passageway. The dim light increased as the pirates pulled open the door, decreased again as they partially closed it down.

And she now had a decision to make. Back here, four meters behind the two hidden pirates and their mutterings, she wouldn't be able to hear the upcoming conversation between Zothip and Disra the way she'd like to. Moreover, the thought of even an Imperial Moff getting ambushed by the likes of the Cavrilhu Pirates did not sit well with her.

She smiled tightly in the darkness at the irony of the situation. It was precisely the same thing Shada had objected to back on that windswept rooftop on Borcorash five weeks ago, and the reason Karoly was even here.

But the deep philosophical considerations could wait till another day. In the meantime, the Cavrilhu Pirates owed a death debt to the Mistryl . . . and the first installment would be collected right here and now. Putting her blaster away, Karoly drew a pair of slender knives and moved silently forward.

Crans and Portin, crouched side by side behind the partially open door, whispering and chuckling to each other in grim anticipation of the carnage to come, never even heard her coming.

It was another minute's work to quietly drag the bodies a few meters back in the passageway where they'd be out from underfoot. Then, returning to the partially open door, she crouched down and eased the tip of one of her knives along the thick carpet into the room.

The image reflected in the metal was small and somewhat distorted, but Karoly had done this a thousand times before and knew how to read it. As she'd expected, Zothip and his three remaining men were all facing the ornate door set into the right-hand wall. Zothip was seated rather arrogantly at the Moff's computer desk, the others slouched against walls or pieces of furniture at various other places around the room. All were fingering blaster butts or rubbing gun hands in preparation; all were well clear of her line of fire and the ambush they still thought was set up.

She was just working through her likely attack plan, should it come to that, when there was the soft click of a lock from across the room. Instantly, the pirates' muttered conversation ceased. The door swung open, and two men stepped inside.

The one on the right was Moff Disra; that much was obvious from his age and his robe of office and the arrogant hauteur with which he strode into the room. The second man, on Disra's right, dressed in an Imperial uniform—

Karoly felt her breath catch in her throat, an unpleasant tingling on the back of her neck. The second man was a warrior.

Not a soldier: a warrior. She could see it in his stance, in his walk, in the way he held his hands, in the way his eyes took in the situation in front of him.

Control had warned that Disra would bring guards with him. Dimly, Karoly wondered if any of the pirates was capable of recognizing the warrior beneath the uniform.

Zothip himself, apparently, could not. "Took your own sweet time getting here," he growled as the warrior swung the door closed. "Who's the nerf?"

"Get out of my chair," Disra growled back, ignoring the question and gesturing irritably at the lounging pirate chief.

"I'm doing the talking here, Disra," Zothip said, making no move to vacate the chair. "Wait a minute—I know you," he added, leveling a finger at the warrior. "Yeah—you're the snotter who pulled all my advisers out on me. You rotten, rark-eating sovler."

Karoly winced, half expecting sudden death to be the warrior's response to the insult. But he wasn't so easily provoked. "That's right," he said, his voice glacially calm. "I'm Major Tierce. And as I explained at the time, the Empire had a more pressing need for their services."

"So you just upped and pulled them, huh?" Zothip countered, his voice darkening. "Well, maybe that's how you Imperial dreg-sifters do things. But that's not how it's done in the fringe. You make a deal, you stick with it." He leveled his finger again. "Or you get to spend your last couple of minutes of life regretting it."

"I thought that in the fringe you also didn't lose your nerve," Disra put in disdainfully. "Did Pellaeon scare you that badly?"

"Never mind Pellaeon," Zothip bit out. "I'll deal with him later. Right now *you're* the one in the hot circle. Starting with full compensation for my battlecruiser and the eight hundred men who died with it."

"Apparently, he *has* lost his nerve, Your Excellency," Tierce said. "The sabacc pot's grown too big for his taste, and he wants out."

Zothip snorted. "Words. That's all it is with you, Disra. Words and promises, and we end up doing all the work and all the dying. But not anymore. I figure twenty million ought to cover it—"

"Suppose we can show you we have more than words," Tierce interrupted, an edge of challenge to his voice. "Suppose we can give you proof that the Empire is once again on the rise, and that this time there will be no stopping us. Would you still want to quit?"

Zothip laughed, a thoroughly humorless sound. "Proof, huh? If you think anything you've got can—"

He broke off as behind Disra and Tierce the door again swung open. One of the pirates half drew his blaster—

"Good afternoon, Captain Zothip," the white-uniformed figure said calmly as he stepped into the room. "Permit me to introduce myself. I'm Grand Admiral Thrawn."

It took Commander Dreyf less than a minute to locate the secret drawer hidden away beneath the ivrooy desk's writing surface. It took only two minutes longer, with the help of some rather illegal tools, for him to force it open.

Inside were eight datacards. Three of them carried the labels of official governmental briefings: one from the Ubiqtorate, the other two from Fleet Intelligence.

But the other five . . .

"Make copies of them," Pellaeon ordered as Dreyf slid one of the unlabeled datacards into his datapad. "All of them, even the official ones. We'll see what the *Chimaera*'s decrypt section can do with them."

"Let me try something first, if I may, sir," Dreyf said, pulling a data-card from his pocket and inserting it into his datapad's auxiliary slot. "One of the little extras that fell out of my backcheck of Lord Graemon's finances was the encrypt he was using to communicate back to Bastion. Let's see if Disra was careless or overconfident enough to use the same one here . . . Well, well. Our clever little Moff seems to have missed a bet."

He smiled tightly at Pellaeon. "It's here, Admiral. It's all here."

Pellaeon stepped to his side and looked over his shoulder. It was there, all right: names, dates, amounts, details of the various transactions. Everything. "You'll be able to link this with Graemon's end of the operation?" he asked.

"Easily," Dreyf assured him, still scrolling through the files. "Disra was even kind enough to supply dates on everything. All I really need to do—"

"Wait," Pellaeon cut him off, slapping fingertips at the other's arm. Something had caught his eye as it went past. "Back up a few files. No, try one more. One more."

And there it was: the name Pellaeon had spotted going past. The name, current location, imprisonment order—

"Colonel Meizh Vermel," Dreyf read, frowning. "Isn't he one of your aides, Admiral?"

"He is indeed," Pellaeon said, his satisfaction with the catch they'd just made vanishing suddenly into the haze of dark fury. "He vanished while on a special mission for me."

"Did he, now," Dreyf said, his own voice darkening. "So Disra's branched out into kidnapping now, has he?"

"Only on special occasions," Pellaeon said, looking at the hidden drawer. Dreyf had done an efficient job of forcing the lock, but there was no way the damage could be covered up. The minute Disra opened the drawer again he would know someone had been in there.

And Pellaeon came to a decision. "Never mind copying them," he said, gathering up the datacards. "We'll take the originals."

Dreyf blinked. "Sir? But—"

"And we're leaving," Pellaeon added, looking over at one of the troopers guarding the door. "Signal the *Chimaera*," he ordered. "Captain Ardiff is to prepare for departure as soon as I'm aboard. Then call Lieutenant Marshian at the shuttle and tell him we're on our way."

"Yes, sir." The trooper pulled out his comlink.

"What about Disra?" Dreyf asked. "We haven't settled with him yet."

"Disra will keep," Pellaeon said grimly. "Right now, my main concern is to get Vermel free before Disra decides he's a liability."

"You'll be going yourself?"

"Yes," Pellaeon said, sliding the hidden drawer closed. "Depending on how Disra's set up the imprisonment order, it may take my personal authority as Supreme Commander to get him out. Besides, at this point I don't trust anyone off the *Chimaera* not to be in Disra's pocket."

"Or in Thrawn's?" Dreyf murmured.

Pellaeon grimaced. "If Thrawn is indeed alive," he said. "Regardless, I'm going."

"It could be tricky," Dreyf warned, dropping into step beside Pellaeon as they headed for the double doors. "Rimcee Station is a couple days' flight away. Disra's certainly going to miss these datacards before then."

"Don't worry, I have a few tricks of my own available," Pellaeon said. "Trooper?"

"Lieutenant Marshian reports the shuttle will be ready to fly when we arrive, sir," the trooper reported. "Captain Ardiff reports likewise for the *Chimaera*."

"Good," Pellaeon said, motioning the troopers to open the doors. "Then let's not keep them waiting."

For a few seconds the room was utterly quiet. The silence of a cave, or a forest, or a tomb. Disra let the stillness linger, thoroughly enjoying the look of stunned disbelief on Zothip's face. It was high time the cocky, slime-eating pirate ran face-first into something his noise and bluster couldn't handle.

He would have liked to see the consternation last a little longer. But for reasons known only to himself, the con man chose to break the spell. "You seem surprised by my presence here," he said, his smooth Thrawn voice as absolutely perfect as the silence had been. "I can only conclude you haven't been paying attention to the news coming out of Coruscant."

For a moment Zothip's mouth worked silently, the movement amplified grotesquely by the bushy beard, before he finally found his voice. "No, I heard you were back," he said at last, the words coming out with some difficulty. The sound of his voice seemed to embolden him. "I just didn't believe it, that's all," he added, straightening his shoulders.

"Why not?"

Zothip's eyes darted to one of his men, as if reassuring him that he was the one in control here. "Because I figured anyone who'd gotten away from this slime-hole of an Empire wouldn't be stupid enough to come back," he said, his voice suddenly aggressive again.

On Thrawn's other side, Tierce stirred. But Thrawn merely smiled. "Not bad," he said. "A bit slow, but otherwise not bad at all."

Zothip's eyebrows pressed together. "What are you talking about?"

"The Empire is poised to rise again," Thrawn said, crossing in front of Disra as he gave each of the other three pirates a brief, measuring look. "And while we certainly do not need allies, we are also not averse to having them."

One of the pirates, standing behind Zothip and a little ways toward the right-hand wall, snorted in a refined sort of way. "Is that how you think of us?" he demanded, folding his arms across his chest. "As allies?"

"Control's right," Zothip seconded, jerking a thumb back at the other. "You give the orders and pull the profits while we do the dirty work. What kind of ally is that?"

"The kind of ally who stands to gain position beyond his wildest dreams," Thrawn said, his voice cooling noticeably. "Position, power, and the wealth to buy and sell whole systems."

"And when is all this supposed to happen?" Control put in. He was, Disra noted with a touch of uneasiness, drifting slowly away from Zothip toward the wall. As if distancing himself from his boss in preparation for some kind of action . . .

Tierce saw it, too. Out of the corner of his eye Disra saw the Guardsman take a quiet step that same direction, maintaining his same distance from Control as he simultaneously moved closer to the other pirate leaning against the wall to Zothip's left.

Which left only the pirate standing at Zothip's right out of the Guardsman's quick reach. Disra glanced furtively that direction, hoping Tierce hadn't forgotten about him.

"Quite soon," Thrawn assured him. "Most of the pieces are already prepared and in position. Those which aren't will be soon."

"Those pieces being your other allies?" Control suggested. "Is that how you see us? As pieces in a game?"

"I don't like being called anyone's game piece," Zothip growled before Thrawn could reply. "We're the Cavrilhu Pirates. We don't play any games but our own."

He broke off at a twitter from the computer desk. "You expecting a call?" he asked sarcastically.

Disra ignored the comment, stepping forward and keying the comm as he swiveled the display around to face him. "Yes?"

It was the lieutenant in the situation room . . . and from the look on his face Disra could tell it wasn't good news. "Your Excellency, we have a problem," the other said tautly. "The spies appear to have slipped out of the net."

Disra bit back a curse. "How?"

"They used droids from a shop to blanket the Verpine biocomm frequencies," the lieutenant said, sounding disgusted. "By the time we located the shop and shut off the transmissions, they'd made it out of range of our echo detectors. Is Grand Admiral Thrawn there with you?"

"Yes," Thrawn said, stepping to Disra's side. "I'll be there shortly. In the meantime, disperse your echo detectors into a grid pattern to both sides of their last location and see if you can pick them up again."

"Yes, sir," the lieutenant said.

Disra blanked the display, throwing a quick glare at Tierce. He should never, ever have let himself be talked into this confrontation with Zothip while Solo and Calrissian were still on the loose. "We'd better get back," he said, looking at Thrawn.

"So what, you're just going to leave us here?" Control asked. He had backed away another step from Zothip, his arms still folded across his chest.

"Don't be absurd," Disra snapped, suddenly very tired of Zothip and his pirates. "You don't want to be on the winning side? Fine—there are plenty who do. Major Tierce, call for an escort to show our visitors out."

"You hold it right there," Zothip rumbled, heaving his bulk out of the chair and dropping his hand to his blaster. "We'll leave when I've got my twenty million. Now fork it over or else."

"Or else what?" Disra demanded. "You ungrateful, slimy—"

"That's it," Zothip snarled. Lifting a finger to his mouth, he blew a piercing whistle. The two pirates on either side of him grabbed for their blasters—

And Tierce moved.

The pirate nearest to the Guardsman never even got his blaster clear of its holster before Tierce was on him. A short jab—a blurred movement of hands—a muffled snap of bone—and the pirate crumpled to the carpet like an empty sack. There was a startled curse from his compatriot across at Zothip's right; but even as Disra turned his head to look, there was a whisper of movement from Tierce's direction and the hilt of a knife sprouted suddenly in the man's chest.

A knife that joined the one already sticking out of his neck.

Disra caught his breath, his eyes darting away from the pirate to the tall, slender woman who had suddenly appeared in the room by the hidden doorway. Her hand twitched, there was a flicker of reflected light—

And Zothip gasped with pain, lurching forward directly into the devastating kick Tierce had thrown at his stomach. Another agonized gasp as the kick connected, and the pirate chief sprawled with a thud over the computer desk, his blaster flying out of a suddenly limp hand to land on the floor.

And Disra found himself staring at the knife hilt that had appeared in the center of Zothip's back. A gift, obviously, from the woman.

He looked up at her as she walked quietly to the desk, ignoring the three Imperials. Gripping Zothip's beard, she turned his dulled eyes up to face her. "That was for Lorardian," she said, her voice quiet but bitter.

Zothip's mouth moved once, but no sound came out. The dull eyes became duller, and closed, and as the woman let go of his beard he sagged once more and lay still.

Again a silence descended on the room. And once again, Thrawn was the one who broke it. "Nicely done," he said. "Thank you for your assistance."

"Not that I needed it," Tierce put in tautly. Disra glanced at him, noting with some surprise that the Guardsman had produced a small blaster from somewhere and had it trained on the woman. "Who are you?"

She looked up from Zothip's body, her eyes dark and slightly contemptuous as she looked Tierce up and down. "Apparently, not all your people are as appreciative as you are, Admiral Thrawn," she said, ignoring the Guardsman's question.

"You'll have to forgive Major Tierce," Thrawn said soothingly. "My safety is one of his primary concerns, a responsibility he takes very seriously. But he doesn't understand you the way I do." He waved toward Tierce's blaster. "You may put the weapon away, Major. The Mistryl shadow guards do not kill casually or without cause."

Disra suddenly felt cold. A Mistryl shadow guard? Here in his palace?

The woman blinked, obviously taken aback by Thrawn's revelation of her identity. "How did you know who I was?" she demanded, her eyes narrowing.

"Come now," Thrawn said, mildly reproving as he waved a languid hand around at the carnage. "After that demonstration of your combat skills, who else could you be but a Mistryl? And of course, there was your reference to Lorardian," he added, his voice softening. "My condolences on that."

"Thank you," she said, almost reluctantly tilting her head in acknowl-edgment. "I didn't think anyone else knew or cared what happened there."

"Information is part of my job," Thrawn said.

"I suppose so." The woman nodded to her left. "What are you plan-ning to do with the leftovers?"

"I don't know yet," Thrawn said. "Tell me, Control: what shall we do with you?"

Disra shifted his gaze away from the woman, suddenly and belatedly realizing that the last pirate had indeed not been accounted for.

And with good reason. Control was standing perfectly still in the spot where he'd been when the fight began, his hands held open and empty in front of him, his blaster still in its holster. Yet on his face was not fear or anger, but cool contemplation of the scene. "My congratulations to you, Admiral," he said, nodding at Thrawn and then at Tierce. "And to you, Major. I was expecting stormtroopers in hidden wall niches. Your way was much more subtle and equally effective."

He turned his head to look at the woman. "Your appearance, on the other hand, was completely unexpected. I gather you sneaked in behind us. I'd give a great deal to know how you did that."

"The only thing the Mistryl have to offer the Cavrilhu Pirates is death," she countered coldly. "Give me a reason why I shouldn't start with you."

Control shrugged; but Disra could tell he wasn't quite as calm as he was trying to let on. "Because you've already avenged the Mistryl deaths at Lorardian," he said. "Zothip was the one who forced the issue there. There was nothing any of the rest of us could do about it."

He turned his eyes back to Disra. "Just as he was also the one de-manding revenge on you and Admiral Pellaeon for the fiasco at Pesitiin, Your Excellency," he added. "I'd like to suggest that all such unpleasant-ries can and should be put behind us."

Tierce snorted something under his breath. "Certainly the courageous one, isn't he?"

"You miss the point, Major," Disra said, smiling at Control. Sud-denly, it was all making sense. "Control here isn't scrabbling around des-perately trying to save his skin. He had this whole confrontation mapped out right from the start."

The Mistryl frowned at him. "What do you mean?"

"I mean that he decided he was tired of being second in line," Disra told her, watching Control closely. The slight, knowing smile on the other's lips was all the proof he needed that he had hit it precisely. "All of it was pure politics."

"It was more than just politics, Your Excellency," Control said. "Zothip had mouth and bluster; but he didn't have the brains to run an organization as large as ours. For years now I've been the one who's been holding it all together. It's high time I took over the perks as well as the work."

"How convenient that we've cleared the path for you," Thrawn said. "Is there anything more you want from us?"

"For starters, I'd like to leave here alive," Control said, giving each of the Imperials a smile that managed to be smug and ingratiating at the same time. "Other than that—" He hesitated. "Zothip was right about our arrangement with Moff Disra," he said, turning his attention to Thrawn. "We made out pretty good, but we were also taking too many of the risks. Besides that, the New Republic seems to be on to us now. I think it's time we bowed out."

"Then you forfeit your chance to share in the division of the galaxy at the Empire's victory," Disra warned, wondering why he was even bothering to try to talk Control into this. Certainly he didn't really care if the Cavrilhu Pirates walked or not.

He needn't have worried. "We'll take our chances," Control said. "You may be a genius, Admiral, but frankly I don't think even you can pull it off."

"As you wish," Thrawn said. "You will, of course, still keep the Preybird production line operating."

"We'll keep it running," Control promised. "In fact, I'll give you our interest in the whole operation as a welcome-back present."

He smirked, but in Disra's eyes the expression rang just a little bit hollow. "And as a token of our past association with the Empire, and of our friendly parting of the ways."

"Of course," Thrawn said, giving him a knowing smile in return. "And just in case you're wrong about the extent of my genius?"

The smirk twitched and vanished. "A lot of fringe groups got caught in the middle the last time you went up against the New Republic, Admiral," he said. "I'd rather the Cavrilhu Pirates not wind up in that position."

"I think that can be avoided," Thrawn agreed. "Certainly as long as the Preybirds continue to be delivered."

"You've got a deal," Control said, his eyes flicking to the Mistryl as he cautiously lowered his arms. "If that's all, then, I have an organization to restructure. Good luck to you, Admiral."

"And to you, Captain Control," Thrawn replied, inclining his head slightly. "I don't expect to see you or any of your pirates in Imperial space again."

Control swallowed visibly. "No, sir," he said as he backed toward the door to the secret passageway. "You won't."

He slipped into the doorway and vanished. "I hope letting him go was the right thing to do," Disra muttered. Pellaeon was at the other end of that passageway, and they only had Control's word that he wasn't interested in revenge.

"Don't worry," Thrawn assured him. "As you already pointed out, he put a great deal of time and thought into maneuvering Zothip here this way. No, he'll head directly back to his ship with his tale of woe, and that will be that."

"What about her?" Tierce asked, nodding at the woman. He had lowered his blaster as ordered, but was still holding it ready at his side. "She *did* come in with them."

"I came in behind them," the woman corrected. "I overheard a comment about clones and pirate arrangements with the Empire and—"

"Clones?" Disra cut her off. "Who was talking about clones?"

She regarded him coolly. "A couple of New Republic agents named Han Solo and Lando Calrissian," she said. "You may have heard of them."

"I believe we have, yes," Thrawn said with an easy smile. "Actually, we're trying to make contact with them at the moment."

Her lip twitched. "I'll bet you are."

"But more interesting to me," Thrawn continued, "would be to hear your response to the offer I made to you a few minutes ago."

She frowned. "What offer?"

"Don't you remember?" Thrawn asked. "I pointed out that your recovery to my appearance had been a bit slow, but otherwise not bad. I then spoke of the Empire's wish to acquire allies."

Her forehead furrowed. "What are you talking about?" she demanded. "You made that offer to Zothip, not me. You didn't even know I was there."

"On the contrary," Thrawn said quietly. "I knew full well you were there. And if you'll think back to my offer, you may notice that I never mentioned either Zothip or his pirates."

She stared at him, her face struggling as she obviously tried to sort out whether he was being truthful or feeding her a load of lies. Flim weaving yet another of his spells . . . and even with the audience prejudiced against him, it appeared to be working.

But right now Disra didn't have time to enjoy the show. "I'm sure you and the lady have a great deal to discuss, Admiral," he murmured, taking a step back toward the door. "If you'll excuse me, though, I need to get back to Admiral Pellaeon."

"Certainly, Your Excellency," Thrawn said, dismissing him with a wave of his hand. "Perhaps we'll move to another room to continue our discussion." He lifted an eyebrow at the woman. "Assuming, that is, you're interested in what my new Empire has to offer the Mistryl."

"We've never worked for the Empire before," the woman said cautiously as Disra stepped to the door and pulled it open.

"That was Palpatine's Empire," Thrawn reminded her. "The Empire I propose to rebuild—"

The rest of the sales pitch was lost as Disra closed the door behind him and hurried down the corridors. The secret passageway would have been faster; but Pellaeon didn't know about that, and Disra would just as soon it be kept secret. Switching corridors, rounding the last corner, he headed down the main hallway toward the door guards. "Has Admiral Pellaeon asked about me?" he asked as the guards saluted and stepped aside.

"No, Your Excellency," one of them said as the double doors began to swing open. "Actually, he's already left."

Disra came to an abrupt stop. "What do you mean, he's left?" he echoed, peering in through the opening doors. The office was indeed empty. "Where did he go?"

"He didn't say, Your Excellency," the guard said.

Disra stepped into the office, frowning around the room as the doors closed behind him. This made no sense. Why would Pellaeon and that slinker Dreyf just leave? Surely they hadn't simply decided to let him off the hook.

His eyes fell on his desk . . .

He was around the side of the desk in five quick strides, swearing the whole way, feeling a clammy sweat breaking out on his face. No. They couldn't have.

But they had. The hidden desk drawer had been forced open.

And the datacards were gone.

CHAPTER

23

Disra's groping hand found the comm switch. "Tierce, get in here," he managed, his voice sounding odd through the pounding of his heart in his ears. *"Now."*

He switched the comm to the guards outside. "When did Pellaeon leave?" he demanded.

"Five or six minutes ago, Your Excellency," the voice came back.

Which meant he would be out of the palace by now and headed for the spaceport, with the Capital Security forces who could have intercepted him dispersed uselessly around the city in their hunt for Solo and Calrissian. Disra ground his teeth together, a vision of the grand scheme he'd worked so hard to create collapsing in front of his eyes. Everything was on those datacards—*everything.* Encrypted, of course; but if Pellaeon was able to decrypt them . . .

And then another, even more awful thought jabbed up under his heart. Colonel Vermel, hidden away in a quiet little detention cell on Rimcee Station . . .

It took nearly a minute to get the long-range comm keyed through the various relays to the Rimcee system. And when he did . . .

Across the room, the secret door opened and Tierce stepped into the office. "We have them," he announced with grim satisfaction. "Their ship's in Docking Bay 155—"

"Pellaeon's got the datacards," Disra cut him off viciously.

"What?" Tierce demanded, picking up his pace.

"The datacards, fool," Disra snarled. "The Vengeance scheme, our arrangement with Zothip's pirates, names and details of the industrial/financial web I've been using—everything."

Tierce hissed between his teeth, throwing a look at the empty drawer. "Incredible," he said, almost as if talking to himself. "He actually broke into your private records. I would never have thought him capable of doing that. It must have been Dreyf's idea."

"We can get the details at the trial," Disra snapped. "Forget whose idea it was. What are we going to do?"

"What do we have to do?" Tierce said with a shrug. "They're encrypted, aren't they? By the time Pellaeon decrypts them—"

"He already has," Disra cut him off. "At least well enough. He knows Vermel's at Rimcee Station."

Tierce's face hardened. "How do you know?"

"Because I just tried to get through to them," Disra gritted. "Pellaeon's had all transmissions to the entire system blocked off."

Tierce threw a dark look at the blank comm display. "Fast work," he murmured. "Very good, Admiral."

"Never mind that," Disra snapped, almost shaking with fear and rage and frustration. Didn't Tierce understand the whole plan was about to collapse on top of them? "We've got to stop him. We've got to pull Vermel out before Pellaeon gets there—"

"No," Tierce said, his voice suddenly decisive. "What we have to do is catch Solo and Calrissian before they get to their ship and have our Grand Admiral put on a show for them."

"Are you insane?" Disra snarled. "To Kessel with Solo—this is my neck we're talking about!"

"Calm down, Disra," Tierce said, his voice like a slap of cold water in the Moff's face. "Whatever Pellaeon's got doesn't matter. You understand? It *doesn't matter*. We have the ultimate clear-card: Grand Admiral Thrawn. All he has to do is take command and declare everything we've done to have been at his direction. Now snap *out of it*."

Disra took a shuddering breath, glaring at Tierce in silent, impotent fury. Silent fury that the Guardsman was dismissing so casually all the years Disra had put into this project. Impotent fury because he was right. "Fine," he choked out. "So we forget Pellaeon. What do we do instead?"

"You weren't listening," Tierce said, his eyes still narrowed as he watched Disra's face. "We've got their landing bay number—that Mistryl woman D'ulin rode in with them as a stowaway. The admiral and I have to get there before they get back. You understand?"

"Yes, I understand," Disra growled, his brain only now starting to unfreeze from the shock and panic. "I'm not a child, you know."

"Glad to hear it," Tierce said coldly. "Because while we're out there, you're going to go talk to D'ulin. Find out what she wants and what it'll take to bring the Mistryl onto our side."

Disra felt his mouth drop open a centimeter. The reports he'd heard about the Mistryl— "You want to try to make *allies* of them? Have you lost your mind? They hate the Empire!"

"We need a new fringe group to replace the Cavrilhu Pirates," Tierce said, his voice one of exaggerated patience. "And we do not have time to argue about it. Thrawn and D'ulin are in the library across from your quarters. Go take over so that he and I can get to the spaceport. Understand? Now *move.*"

The snapped command made Disra jump. "Don't ever talk to me that way again, Major," he warned, his voice quietly deadly. "Ever."

"Then don't ever fall apart on me again, Your Excellency," Tierce countered. If he was either impressed or intimidated by Disra's warning, he didn't show it. "Now get moving."

The legion of Imperial troops Han had feared would be ringing the spaceport wasn't there. Neither were the hard-eyed guards he'd expected at the entrypoint, the monitor droids along the access street, or the stormtroopers at the door to their docking bay. In fact, from all appearances it looked like they'd gotten completely away with it.

And that all by itself was enough to worry him. A lot.

Lando felt it, too. "I don't like this, Han," he muttered, glancing around the street behind them as Han unlocked the bay door. "This is way too easy."

"Yeah, I know," Han agreed, taking one last look around as he took Lobot's arm and guided him through the doorway. Lando's on-the-fly changes to his implant's programming over the past hour may have thrown the Imperials off the scent, but they'd also left Lobot rather dazed. If it came to a fight at the *Lady Luck*'s ramp, he was going to be no help at all.

The dark passageway through the docking bay's service and supply area was also deserted. "Soon as we're aboard you get the engines fired up," Han told Lando as they stepped out onto the permacrete beneath the open sky. The *Lady Luck* was still there, looking just the way they'd left her. "I'll handle the weapons. Maybe Moegid can get into the spaceport computer and get us a quick exit slot—"

"That won't be necessary," a quiet voice came from behind them.

Han spun around, yanking out his appropriated blaster. Behind them on the permacrete had appeared the flickering full-sized holo of a man. A man with blue skin, wearing a white Imperial uniform . . .

Lando made a strange sound in the back of his throat. "It's him," he murmured.

Han nodded, feeling numb. It was indeed.

Grand Admiral Thrawn.

"Please lay your weapons on the ground," Thrawn directed. "I'd prefer to speak with you face-to-face, but understandably have no desire to be shot."

"Understandably," Han agreed, keeping a firm grip on his blaster, his eyes darting around the landing bay. There must be some actual troops in here somewhere . . .

The holo smiled. "Come now, Captain Solo," he said soothingly. "Surely you don't think you'll be able to simply blast your way out of Bastion as you have from so many other systems during your checkered career. Don't you wish to see your wife and children again?"

Han adjusted his grip on his blaster, feeling sweat gathering on his forehead. "Yeah, that's kind of the point, isn't it?" he said.

The holo shook his head. "You misunderstand, Captain," Thrawn said. "You have nothing to fear from me. All I want is a few words with you, and then you and your companions will be free to go your way." He nodded toward Lando. "Ask Captain Calrissian. I allowed *him* to leave my Star Destroyer."

"This isn't exactly the same," Lando said tightly. "This is your hidden capital. You aren't going to want anyone knowing where it is."

"Come now, Captain," Thrawn said, rather scornfully. "Do you really think I would expect knowledge of Bastion's current location to die with you? The seat of Imperial authority has been moved before, many times. It can certainly be moved again. Still, you apparently need more persuasion."

A movement at the corner of his eye caught Han's attention. He looked up—

To see a row of stormtroopers lined up along the rim of the landing bay's storage area roof, blaster rifles trained on them.

He sighed. They should have made a dash for the *Lady Luck* when the holo first appeared instead of letting Thrawn stall them this way. Too late now. "How'd you find us?" he asked, setting the blaster's safety and laying the weapon on the ground in front of him.

"It wasn't difficult," the holo said as Lando reluctantly followed suit with his slugthrower. "I knew none of you had the slicing expertise needed to invade the Special Files. I suspected you were using a Verpine for that, and so instructed my men to run a scan on those comm frequencies."

"Looking for an echo," Han said, nodding. "I would have sworn we cut that off before you could get a fix."

"You misunderstand, Captain. I wasn't looking for an echo." Abruptly, the holo vanished—

And from around a stack of storage crates to their right Thrawn himself appeared, his white uniform dazzlingly bright in the afternoon sunlight.

But no more dazzling than the gleaming armor of the six stormtroopers flanking him in guard position. On second thought, Han decided, a mad dash for the *Lady Luck* wouldn't have been such a clever plan after all.

"I was merely seeking confirmation that your slicer was a Verpine," Thrawn continued as he walked up to them. "Once you supplied that confirmation by blanketing those biocomm frequencies, all I had to do was search the spaceport records for a ship that had supposedly landed here eight, twelve, or seventeen days before the drone probe you followed in from the Parshoone Ubiqtorate contact station."

"Wait a minute, you've lost me," Han said, frowning. "Eight, twelve, or seventeen days?"

Thrawn smiled. "Those are important numbers to the Verpines," he said. "Not consciously, perhaps, but nevertheless anchored deeply within them. It was obvious that your Verpine was the master slicer of your group; therefore, he would have been the one to make any alterations in the spaceport records to hide your ship's location. Need I go on?"

"No," Han said, a cold chill running through him. Back at his and Leia's Orowood Tower retreat Lando had claimed to have seen Thrawn; had claimed it, had argued it, had maintained it despite all the evidence and arguments to the contrary. Han had wondered then how his friend could have been so easily spooked.

Now, finally, he understood.

"Good," Thrawn said, peering at him with a depth of understanding Han didn't care for at all. "Then let us get down to business." He raised his voice slightly. "Major?"

From behind another stack of boxes to the left a youngish man wearing major's insignia appeared, his eyes wary on the prisoners. In his right hand he held a blaster; in his left, a datacard.

"As you may recall our last conversation, Captain Calrissian," Thrawn went on as the major walked toward them, "you suggested that if I wanted to save the New Republic from its current crisis I should simply give you a complete copy of the Caamas Document."

"Yes, I remember," Lando said as the major came to a stop a meter in front of him. "You told me that would take too much time."

"Less time than I thought, as it turned out," Thrawn agreed. "There it is."

The major held out the datacard. "What do you mean, there it is?" Lando asked, looking at the datacard like he expected it to explode in his face.

"The Caamas Document," Thrawn said simply. "It's yours. Take it."

Slowly, hesitantly, Lando took the card. "What's the catch?" he asked as the major took a step back.

"There's no catch," Thrawn assured him. "As I told you before, I merely wish to help."

"Sure you do," Han put in, his words sounding harsh in his ears after the Grand Admiral's more urbane tones. "Like you helped wreck the Combined Clans Building on Bothawui?"

The glowing red eyes focused on him. "Explain."

"There was an Imperial team behind that riot," Han said stiffly. Beside him, Lando was making shushing noises, and he had to admit that accusing Thrawn to his face like this was probably not the most politic thing he could have done. But it had been his neck on the line there, his and Leia's, and he was not going to just stand here and let Thrawn get away with making conciliatory noises. Not after all the death and destruction that riot had caused. "We found the redirection crystal they used with their Xerrol Nightstinger sniper blaster."

He had hoped for a flicker of guilt, or at least a twinge of recognition. But instead Thrawn merely gave him a brittle smile. "Yes, a Xerrol Nightstinger," he said, his voice tinged with bitterness. "Apparently still a favored tool of assassins and saboteurs. But in this case, you're looking the wrong direction. The Empire's last five Xerrols were stolen six months ago from a Ubiqtorate cache on Marquarra."

His eyes glittered. "If you want to find them, I suggest you search the private estate of High Councilor Borsk Fey'lya."

Han exchanged startled glances with Lando. "Fey'lya?"

"Yes," Thrawn said. "It was his private army who stole them."

"No," Han said, the word coming automatically. "That's ridiculous."

And yet . . .

Fey'lya had known he and Leia were going to the Combined Clans Building to check out the true state of Bothan finances, a job they'd somehow never gotten around to finishing after the riot. And it *was* just the sort of back-blading stunt the Bothans were famous for.

Thrawn shrugged. "I'm not going to try to convince you. The truth is there for you to find if you care to. In the meantime—" He nodded toward the datacard in Lando's hand. "Good day, gentlemen. Have a good voyage."

Without waiting for an answer he turned and headed for the exit, half of his stormtrooper guard falling into formation around him. The remaining three stormtroopers and the major waited until he was out of sight before turning and following. As they too vanished through the doorway the row of stormtroopers above them turned and headed away across the roof.

And a moment later Han, Lando, and Lobot were alone.

Han turned to Lando, found the other staring at him from under hooded eyelids. "Well, Lando," he said, trying to keep his voice calm. It wasn't one of his better efforts. "I guess I owe you an apology."

"Never mind the apologies," Lando said, stooping to retrieve their weapons as he ran a quick glance around the empty rooftop. "Let's just get out of here, okay?"

"Yeah," Han said, taking Lobot's arm and turning him toward the *Lady Luck*'s ramp. "Let's."

.   .   .

"You should have seen their faces," Flim said, swirling his drink around in his glass, his moody voice in odd contrast with what should have been gloating words. "They were so petrified, and trying so hard not to show it. It was really rather funny."

"I'm sure you could hardly keep from breaking out laughing," Disra said sourly. "The question is, did they buy it?"

"They bought it," Tierce assured him, sliding a datacard out of his datapad and picking up the next one from his stack. Alone among the three of them, he seemed to have no doubts about Flim's performance. "Our Grand Admiral was as smooth as polished transparisteel. He didn't even flinch when Solo threw the Bothawui commando team in his face."

"The Bothawui team?" Disra demanded sharply. "*Our* Bothawui team? Navett's group?"

"Relax—he was talking about them in conjunction with the Combined Clans Building riot," Tierce said. "There was no indication they know Navett's back there now."

"I hope not," Disra growled. On the other hand, that whole scheme was listed on the datacards that Pellaeon had stolen from him. Still, it was unlikely Pellaeon would run straight to Coruscant to warn them, even if he stopped sifting through the financial data long enough to notice it was even there. "How did they find out we staged the riot?"

Tierce shrugged. "Who knows? It doesn't matter, though—the Admiral deflected them nicely." He looked over at Flim. "What was all that about a weapons cache being stolen from Marquarra? I don't remember hearing about that."

Flim sipped at his drink. "You don't remember," he said, "because I made the whole thing up. I figured it would—"

"You made it up?" Disra cut him off. "What kind of fool stunt was that?"

"One that got Solo off my back," Flim said stiffly. "Why? You disapprove?"

"Yes, I disapprove," Disra bit out. "It's out of character. Thrawn didn't go around making things up—if he didn't know something, he said so."

"Calm down, Your Excellency," Tierce said. But he didn't look all that happy, either, as he gazed at Flim. "He had to say *something*—we can't be offering Coruscant the Caamas Document with one hand and helping foment riots with the other. At least he's bought us the time it'll take them to check up on it."

Disra snorted. "However little that is."

"However little it is will be enough," Tierce said firmly. "In seven days the New Republic's civil war is set to begin. At that point, no one's going to care about a few riots and a handful of Xerrol Nightstingers."

He nodded back toward the secret door. "And speaking of buying things, how did your talk go with our guest? Are we going to be able to buy their services?"

"I don't know," Disra said, his mouth tightening briefly. "Mistryl don't work for Imperials—she must have told me that fifteen times. On the other hand, she did agree to call one of their leaders to come talk to us. And there *is* something they very much want, but I wasn't quite able to get her to tell me what that is."

"What they want is revenge," Flim said soberly. "Like everyone else these days."

"Revenge against whom?" Disra asked.

Flim shrugged. "The story around the fringe is that their world was devastated in a war with person or persons unknown some number of decades ago. The money the Mistryl earn hiring out their services still supposedly goes to support the survivors."

"What's the name of the world?" Disra asked.

"I don't know," Flim said. "They keep it very quiet. Probably afraid whoever did it will come back and finish the job."

"She said something about revenge for Lorardian," Tierce mused. "Could that be the system?"

"I have no idea." Flim shrugged. "I don't even know who or what Lorardian is."

"What do you mean, you don't know?" Disra said, frowning. "You sounded like you knew all about it back there."

"I also sounded like I knew she was hiding behind the door the whole time," Flim countered patiently. "The whole trick behind being a good con man is convincing the target you know more than you really do."

Disra grimaced. Con men. "Of course. I forgot."

"Don't go all high and nobly indignant on me, Disra," Flim warned, his face darkening. "Your Cavrilhu Pirate raids on New Republic shipping were as much a con as this is. So is your precious little Vengeance movement, for that matter," he added, shifting his glare to Tierce. "A few Imperial agitators pretending to be a huge group of civilian malcontents. Not to mention this whole Thrawn charade. You don't like cons? Well, too bad. You're up to your necks in them, both of you. Not that you've got any choice. Not with the shape the Empire's in."

He dropped his feet back onto the floor with a muffled thud and stood up. "And I'll tell you something else," he added. "If and when you ever get to the point where you've got all the military strength you want, you're still going to need me."

He slapped at his chest. "*I'm* the only one of this group who knows the fringe. Who the pirates and mercs are, where to find a good bounty hunter on short notice—you want to hire more privateers, you'll have to come to me. *I'm* the one who could finger D'ulin as a Mistryl just by the way she fought."

"We're not arguing," Disra said, a little taken aback by the fire of the con man's tirade. "So what are you trying to say?"

"I'm saying that if and when this Hand of Thrawn of yours shows up, you might not need my Thrawn masquerade anymore," Flim shot back. "But you'll still need *me.*"

For a long moment the room was silent. Flim glared back and forth between the two of them, breathing a little heavily.

Tierce broke the silence first. "You finished?" he asked mildly.

Flim studied his face, and some of the stiffness seemed to leave his back. "Yes," he muttered. "I just . . . this is going to stir the pot, Tierce, from Coruscant to the Outer Rim. Unless the Hand of Thrawn is living under a rock, there's no way he's going to miss this."

"I told you before that we could protect you from him," Tierce said. "And we will. Don't worry about it."

"Yeah." Flim took a long drink from his glass. "Yeah. Sure."

Lando pulled back the hyperdrive lever, and in front of them the stars of Bastion's sky stretched into starlines. "Well," he said. He'd meant the word to come out sounding casual, but all it sounded was hoarse. "I guess he really meant it. About letting us go."

Beside him, Han didn't answer. For that matter, he probably hadn't said ten words since Thrawn had walked out of the docking bay. Lando looked sideways at his friend, wondering if it was time he started worrying about him.

Han must have felt the other's gaze. "It was really him, wasn't it?" he said quietly, his own gaze still on the swirling patterns of hyperspace.

Lando nodded, his throat feeling tight. "Perfectly calm, perfectly in control, three steps ahead of us the whole way," he said. "No one else but Thrawn."

"I wouldn't have believed it." Han looked at Lando, his mouth twitching. "I guess I *didn't* believe it," he amended. "Whatever I said to you back at the Orowood Tower—"

"Forget it," Lando said, waving the apology away. "I was right there that first time, and *I* didn't even believe it. At least, I didn't want to."

Han shook his head. "We're in trouble, Lando," he said. "From now on, we can't trust anything we see. Anything we see, anything we hear, anything we think we ought to do. Not with Thrawn back on the scene."

"I don't know," Lando said doubtfully. "Thrawn or no Thrawn, the Empire *is* still down to eight sectors. Maybe this is really all he's going for, hoping to confuse Coruscant so badly it just freezes up."

"Who knows?" Han growled, some heat starting to seep into his voice. At least he didn't sound dazed and demoralized anymore. About time, Lando thought. "That's what drives you so crazy about him. You try to do something, and odds are it's exactly what he wanted you to do. You stand still and don't do anything, and he runs a smartrope around you."

"So what do you suppose he expects us to do with this?" Lando asked, holding up the datacard.

"I don't know what he expects," Han said, reaching over and taking it. "But I'll tell you what we're *going* to do. First, we're going to read it and see if it gives those names everyone's so hot to get hold of. Second, we're going to call Leia as soon as we're in range of the HoloNet and let her know we've got it. And third—"

He jerked a thumb over his shoulder. "We're going to turn Moegid loose on the thing and have him check it sixteen ways from center. See if he can find whatever surprises Thrawn has tucked away."

Lando eyed the datacard warily. "You think there are surprises?"

"It's Thrawn," Han said simply.

Lando nodded. "Right."

Getting out of his seat, Han gave the instruments one final check. "Come on—I don't trust this thing anywhere near the ship's computer," he said, heading for the cockpit door. "Let's get a datapad and find out what it says."

CHAPTER
24

The first navigational stop the *Wild Karrde* had made after leaving Dayark had showed nothing ahead. Nothing but the twisting glow of the Kathol Rift and the fiery frozen wisps of ionized gas streamers and miniature nebulae that looked as if they'd been torn from it by violence. So had the second stop, and the third, until Shada had begun to wonder if the legendary lost world of Exocron was truly nothing but a myth.

On the fifth stop, they found it.

"It looks quite pleasant," Threepio commented somewhat doubtfully from Shada's side as they gazed out the *Wild Karrde*'s bridge viewport at the small planet rapidly approaching. "I do hope they will be friendly."

"I wouldn't count on it," Shada warned him, feeling an unfamiliar and unpleasant dryness in her mouth. Down there somewhere, if Jade and Calrissian were right, Jorj Car'das would be waiting for them.

At the helm, Odonnl half turned in his seat. "Shouldn't we have the turbolasers ready?" he asked Karrde. "Just in case they're not happy at having their privacy infringed on?"

Shada looked at Karrde. He was hiding his nervousness well, but she herself had no trouble seeing it. "We're here to talk, not fight," he reminded Odonnl, his voice steady. "I don't want anyone down there getting the wrong impression."

"Yes, but after Dayark—"

"We're here to talk," Karrde repeated, his tone leaving no room for argument. "H'sishi, are we picking up any sensor probes? Or transmissions, Chin?"

[No probes yet, Chieftain,] the Togorian said. Her fur, Shada noted, had fluffed out just noticeably. Apparently, she'd picked up on Karrde's mood, too.

"Nothing of transmissions either, Cap't," Chin added. "Perhaps they not see us come in."

"Oh, they see us, all right," Karrde said, a hint of grimness creeping into his tone. "The only question—"

He broke off at a beep from the comm. "Incoming starship, this is Admiral Trey David, second-in-command to Supreme Admiral Horzao Darr of the Exocron Combined Air-Space Fleet," a courteous but firm voice said. "Please identify yourselves."

Chin reached for his board— "No, I'll do it," Karrde told him, visibly bracing himself as he touched his comm switch. "This is Talon Karrde aboard the freighter *Wild Karrde*, Admiral David. Our intentions are totally peaceful. We'd like permission to land."

There was a long pause. A *very* long pause, in fact. Shada rubbed her knuckles gently, visualizing a heated argument going on in the Exocron Combined Fleet office . . .

"*Wild Karrde*, this is Admiral David," the voice came back. "I'm told you're here to see Jorj Car'das. Can you confirm that?"

Shada watched Karrde closely. But aside from a brief twitch at the corner of his mouth there was no reaction. "Yes, I can," he said, his voice a little hollow but under control. "There's a vital matter I urgently need to discuss with him."

"I see." There was another pause, shorter this time. "Is he expecting you?"

Another twitch of the lip. "I don't know if *expecting* is the proper word. I do believe he knows I'm coming."

"Do you," David said, his voice suddenly sounding a little odd. "Very well, *Wild Karrde*, you're cleared for Circle 15 at the Rintatta City military landing field. Coordinates are being sent to you now."

"Thank you," Karrde said.

"Got it," Odonnl muttered, studying his nav display. "Looks pretty straightforward."

"We have an escort on the way," David continued. "I trust I don't have to tell you to cooperate with them."

"I understand completely," Karrde said. "Will I be seeing you there?"

"I doubt it," David said; and this time there was definitely a darkness in his voice. "But perhaps we'll all be lucky. You never know. David out."

For a moment the bridge was quiet. Shada looked around at the others, at their tight faces and tense shoulders and grim expressions. If they hadn't known before what they were getting into, she decided, they knew now.

And yet, she saw no indication that any of them were even thinking of trying to back out. A truly loyal, close-knit crew, completely dedicated to their chief.

Much as Shada herself had once been dedicated to the ideals of the

Mistryl. Even when the Mistryl themselves had all but forgotten those ideals.

Even in the face of the looming danger ahead, the memory of that loss still hurt.

"Instructions, Captain?" Odonnl asked quietly.

Karrde didn't hesitate. "Take us down," he said.

Rintatta City was a middling-sized cluster of military-style buildings interspersed with about fifty landing pads of varying sizes, many with ships already settled down onto them. The military areas were in turn surrounded by a wide ring of civilian-style homes and businesses and community buildings. The whole thing was nestled up against the base of a short but rough-sided ridge of mountains, the city giving way to a grassy plain on its other sides.

There was no shakedown like there had been at Pembric 2. Nor was there any sort of customs or entrance inquiry at all as the *Wild Karrde* headed in to the surface. The two aging system patrol ships that Admiral David had sent escorted the freighter to its assigned landing circle, watched as it set down, then headed off again into the sky without comment. Around the other ships, hundreds of men and women and dozens of small vehicles were hurrying about various tasks of their own, completely ignoring the offworld ship that had set down in their midst. From all appearances, Karrde thought as he and the others started down the ramp, all of Exocron might be trying to pretend the visitors didn't exist.

With one notable exception.

"Good day, Captain Karrde," Entoo Nee beamed from the foot of the *Wild Karrde*'s landing ramp. "Welcome to Exocron. I see that even without my help you were able to find us. Hello, Shada; hello, Threepio."

"Hello, Master Entoo Nee," Threepio replied, sounding distinctly relieved to see a familiar face. "I confess I had not expected to find you here."

"There was some question about you, as well," Entoo Nee said cheerfully. "When I last saw you on Dayark, you seemed to be having pirate trouble." He took a step closer to the ramp and peered up into the ship. "Will your charming Togorian be joining us?"

"No, H'sishi will be staying with the ship," Karrde told him, eyeing the little man with some bemusement. H'sishi was an increasingly valued member of his crew, but *charming* was not a descriptive term that would have automatically sprung to mind.

"Too bad," Entoo Nee said, looking at Shada and Threepio again. "Is this it, then? You don't want to bring any others along?"

Karrde felt his muscles tense up again, despite all his efforts to relax them. Certainly he wanted to bring more people along. The *Wild Karrde*'s entire crew, for starters, plus the crews of the *Starry Ice* and the *Etherway*, General Bel Iblis's complete New Republic task force, Rogue Squadron, and about four clans' worth of Noghri warriors.

But even if he had had such resources, it would be a futile gesture. Car'das was waiting for him, and bringing more people would only mean putting more people at risk. That wasn't why he was here. "Yes," he told Entoo Nee. "This is it. Do I assume you're here to take us to Jorj Car'das?"

"If you wish to see him," the little man said, his eyes thoughtful on Karrde's face. Once again, as on Dayark, glimpses of the true Entoo Nee were peeking through the carefully crafted facade of harmlessness. "Well. Shall we go?"

He led the way to an open-topped landspeeder at the edge of the landing circle—a landspeeder, Karrde noted, that despite Entoo Nee's apparent surprise at the small size of the party was only a four-seater. Weaving his way expertly in and out of the rest of the traffic, the little man headed off toward the mountains. "What's going on here?" Shada asked, gesturing around them as Entoo Nee dodged around a particularly slow-moving fuel truck.

"They're preparing for some sort of maneuvers, I expect," the other said. "Military people are always maneuvering one direction or another."

"How far is it to where we're meeting Car'das?" Karrde asked, not particularly interested in what the Exocron Combined Air-Space Fleet had on its agenda for the day.

"Not far," Entoo Nee assured him. "Do you see that light blue building straight ahead, the one just a bit up the slope of the mountain? That's where he is."

Karrde shaded his eyes from the sunlight. From this distance, at least, it was not a very impressive place. Not a fortress; not even a mansion.

In fact, as Entoo Nee cleared the military area and started across the more sparsely trafficked civilian section of the city, the light blue building ahead began to look more and more like a simple, unassuming house.

Shada was apparently thinking along the same lines. "Is that where Car'das lives, or just where we're meeting him?" she asked.

Entoo Nee threw her a quick smile. "It's always questions with you, isn't it? Such a good, thoughtful mind."

"Asking questions is part of my job," Shada countered. "And you haven't answered me."

"Answering questions isn't part of my job," Entoo Nee said. "Come now, there's no need for impatience—it's only a little farther. Just relax and enjoy the trip."

The blue house continued to look smaller and less impressive the closer they got. Smaller, less impressive, older, and considerably shabbier. "As you can see, it was built right up against the cliff face," Entoo Nee commented as they drove past the last cluster of other houses and started across a grassy field with a rapid creek running through the middle of it. "I believe the original owner thought that would provide extra stability during the winter winds."

"What happened to the left side?" Shada asked, pointing. "Did a wing get torn down?"

"No, it was never built," Entoo Nee told her. "Car'das once began to add on to the house, but—well, you'll see."

An unpleasant tingle ran down Karrde's back. "What do you mean, we'll see? What stopped him?"

Entoo Nee didn't answer. Karrde glanced over at Shada, found her looking at him with an odd expression on her face.

A minute later they were there. Entoo Nee brought the landspeeder to a smooth halt in front of a once-white door whose paint had chipped and faded with age and neglect. "You lead the way," Shada said to Entoo Nee, sliding herself deftly between Karrde and the house. "I'll be behind you; Karrde will be behind me."

"Oh, no, that won't do at all," Entoo Nee said. He shook his head, a quick, nervous-looking movement. "Only Captain Karrde and I will be able to go in."

Shada's eyes narrowed. "Let me put it another way—"

"No, that's all right, Shada," Karrde said, moving around her and taking a step toward the door. Away from the center of the group, with nothing between him and the blank and empty windows, he felt painfully exposed. "If Car'das only wants to see me, then that's the way it has to be."

"Forget it," Shada said flatly, catching hold of Karrde's arm and hauling him bodily to a stop. "Entoo Nee, either I go in with him or he doesn't go in at all."

"Shada, this isn't helping," Karrde growled, glaring at her. Did she want all of them to be summarily shot down before he even had a chance to plead the New Republic's case? "If he wanted me dead, he could have done it at any of a hundred points along the way. He could certainly do it right here."

"I know that," Shada shot back. "And it doesn't matter. I came along as your bodyguard. And that's what I'm going to do."

Karrde stared at her, a sudden strange sensation running through him. Back at that Orowood Tower meeting with Solo, Organa Solo, and Calrissian, Shada had merely agreed to come along on this trip to help out. When during the two and a half weeks since then had that grudging agreement transmuted into the far deeper commitment of bodyguard? "Shada, I appreciate your concern," he said, quietly but firmly, reaching up to where she still gripped his arm and putting his hand gently on top of hers.

"But you need to remember the big picture. My life, and what happens to it, isn't the most important thing at stake here."

"I'm your bodyguard," Shada said, just as quietly and just as firmly. "It's the most important thing to me."

"Please," Entoo Nee spoke up. "Please. I think you misunderstand. Captain Karrde and I must go in first, but you may certainly come in right behind us. It's simply that—well, you'll see."

Shada still didn't look happy, but she gave a reluctant nod. "All right, fine," she said. "Just remember that if anything happens, you personally will be directly in my line of fire. You two first, then me, then Threepio."

"Really, Mistress Shada, I'm sure it's not necessary for me to come in with you," the droid hastened to assure her, taking a shuffling step back toward the landspeeder. "Perhaps I should remain here and guard the landspeeder—"

"Actually, he may be useful," Entoo Nee said, smiling reassuringly. "Come, Threepio, it'll be all right."

"Yes, Master Entoo Nee," Threepio said in a resigned tone. Moaning almost inaudibly to himself, he shuffled to a spot half a meter behind Shada. "But I must say, I have a bad feeli—"

"Good," Entoo Nee said cheerfully. The solemn moment past, he was radiating his usual harmlessness again. "Shall we go?"

The door was unlocked. Karrde followed the little man in, feeling more vulnerable than ever as they stepped out of the sunlight into a dank, gloomy room.

A room that, to his surprise, had apparently not been used for some time. The few pieces of furniture scattered about were old and dusty, with the same signs of long neglect that they'd seen in the exterior of the house itself. The three windows, which from the outside had seemed so dark and threatening, could now be seen from this side to be merely incredibly dirty, with the slight frosting effect that came from years of wind-driven dust or sand slashing across them. In the shafts of dim sunlight that managed to penetrate the grime, long strands of cobweb could be seen stretching from some of the chairs to the ceiling.

"This way," Entoo Nee said quietly, his voice an intrusion in the eerie atmosphere as he led them across the room to a closed door. "He is here, Captain Karrde. Please prepare yourself."

Karrde took a deep breath. Behind him, he heard the faint scraping sound as Shada's blaster came free of its holster. "I'm ready," he said. "Let's get it over with."

"Indeed." Reaching past him, Entoo Nee touched the door control. With a faint squeak, it slid open.

It was the smell that hit Karrde first. An odor of age, and distant memories, and lost hopes. An odor of sickness and tiredness.

An odor of death.

The room itself was small, much smaller than Karrde would have expected. To both sides built-in shelves covered each of the side walls, on which were stacked a strange assortment of small art objects, useless-looking knickknacks, and medical vials and equipment. A large bed took up most of the rest of the space, the foot coming to within a meter of the doorway and leaving barely enough room left over for two people to stand.

And lying in the bed beneath a stack of blankets, humming softly to himself as he stared at the ceiling, was an old man.

"Jorj?" Entoo Nee called softly as he stepped through the doorway. The humming stopped, but the man's gaze remained on the ceiling. "Jorj? There's someone here to see you."

Karrde stepped in beside him, squeezing into the remaining space, his mind spinning. No. Surely this couldn't be Jorj Car'das. Not the vigorous, hot-tempered, ambitious man who'd almost single-handedly created one of the greatest smuggling organizations ever known. "Jorj?" he called carefully.

The wrinkled face frowned, and the head lifted up. "Mertan?" a quavering voice asked. "Mertan? Is that you?"

Karrde let his breath out in a tired sigh. The voice, and the eyes. Yes, it was indeed him. "No, Jorj," he said gently. "Not Mertan. It's Karrde. Talon Karrde. You remember?"

The old man's eyes blinked a couple of times. "Karrde?" he said in the same uncertain voice. "Is that you?"

"Yes, Jorj, it's me," Karrde assured him. "Do you remember me?"

A tentative smile started on the old man's face, fading as if the muscles were too old or too tired to hold on to it. "Yes," he said. "No. Who are you again?"

"Talon Karrde," Karrde repeated, the bitter taste of defeat and disappointment and utter fatigue in his mouth. All this way. They'd come all this way to see Car'das and plead for his help. All of Karrde's fears about this meeting—his fears, his regrets, his guilt—all of it for nothing. The Jorj Car'das he had lived in quiet terror of for so many years was long gone.

In his place was an empty shell.

Dimly, through the darkness swirling through his mind, he felt a hand on his shoulder. "Come on, Karrde," Shada said quietly. "There's nothing here anymore."

"It was Karrde, right?" the old man asked. A thin arm came up from beneath the blankets, flailing a bit before the hand was able to tuck the pillows tighter behind his neck. "Tarron Karrde?"

"It's *Talon* Karrde, Jorj," Entoo Nee corrected, his voice that of a patient parent to a very young child. "Is there anything I can get for you?"

Car'das frowned, his head settling back onto the pillow, his eyes again drifting to whatever it was he saw on the ceiling. *"Shem-mebal ostorran se'mmitas Mertan anial?"* he muttered, his voice almost inaudible. *"Karmida David shumidas krree?"*

"Old Tarmidian," Entoo Nee murmured. "The language of his childhood. He's been slipping into that more and more lately."

"Threepio?" Shada prompted.

"He's asking if Mertan has been by here today," the droid translated. For once, there was no mention of how many types of communication he was fluent in. "Or that nice Admiral David person."

"No, neither of them," Entoo Nee said to the figure in the bed, motioning Karrde to back out of the room. "I'll be back later, Jorj. Try to get some sleep, all right?"

He followed Karrde out of the room and reached for the door control. "Sleep?" The old man snorted weakly, giving a cackling laugh. "Can't sleep now, Mertan. Too much to do. Far too much to—"

The door slid shut, mercifully cutting off the rest. "You see, now, how it is," Entoo Nee said quietly.

Karrde nodded, the taste of ashes in his mouth. All those years . . . "How long has he been this way?"

"And why did you even bother bringing us here in the first place?" Shada demanded.

"What can I say?" Entoo Nee said. "He's old—very old—with the many and varied afflictions that so often come of long age." His bright eyes shifted to Shada. "And as for bringing you here, *you* were the ones who wanted to come."

"We wanted to see Jorj Car'das," Shada bit out. "What's in there is not what we had in mind."

"It's all right, Shada," Karrde said. All those years . . . "It's my fault, not Entoo Nee's. I should have come here years ago."

He blinked sudden tears from his eyes. "I suppose there's only one more question to be asked. Entoo Nee, Car'das once had a huge datacard library. Do you have any idea where it might be?"

Entoo Nee shrugged. "Whatever he did with it, he did it long before I came to be in his service."

Karrde nodded. So much for even their last hope of finding a copy of the Caamas Document here. Wasted fears, and now a wasted trip. Suddenly, he was feeling very old. "Thank you," he said, pulling out his comlink and keying it on. "Dankin?"

"Right here, Chief," Dankin's voice came promptly, an edge of tautness to it. "How are things?"

"Running quite smoothly, thank you," Karrde said, giving the all-clear code response. "The mission is over. Get the ship ready; we'll be leaving as soon as we get back."

"Yeah, well, that might be a bit tricky," Dankin said, his voice turning grim. "There's something about to happen here, Chief, something big. Every ship on the field's getting tooled up for combat."

Karrde frowned. "Are you sure?"

"I'm positive," Dankin said. "There are racks of missiles being taken aboard, gunner-type flak-vac suits—the works. And they seem to be arming a lot of civilian ships, too."

"It's Rei'Kas and his pirates," Entoo Nee murmured quietly at Karrde's side. "It would appear one of them followed you in."

Karrde grimaced, yet another piece of his carefully built up mental picture crumbling to dust. He'd been so sure that Rei'Kas had been hired and brought here by Car'das. "No one should have been able to follow us," he told Entoo Nee. "We always watch our backtrail very closely."

Entoo Nee shrugged again. "I don't know how they did it. I only know that they did. According to Admiral David, their entire fleet has now left its hidden base and is on its way to Exocron."

"You knew about this before we even landed?" Shada demanded. "Why didn't you say something?"

"What should I have said?" Entoo Nee countered. "The damage had already been done. They had found Exocron." He gestured upward. "In fact, that was why I wanted to bring you here myself from Dayark, Captain Karrde. They wouldn't have been able to track my ship."

Karrde grimaced. As if his guilt burden hadn't been heavy enough, now this. "How long before they reach the planet?"

"Excuse me," Threepio spoke up before Entoo Nee could answer. "But if pirates are on their way, shouldn't we be planning our departure?"

"He's right," Entoo Nee agreed. "Still, there's no particular hurry for you. They won't be here for at least another eight hours. Possibly more."

"What about you?" Shada asked.

Entoo Nee's mouth puckered. "I'm sure we'll be all right. I'm told the Combined Air-Space Fleet is quite good."

"Maybe against the occasional smuggler or rock-dodger," Shada said darkly. "But this is Rei'Kas we're talking about."

"It's our trouble, not yours," Entoo Nee said firmly. "You'd best make preparations to go."

The comlink, Karrde suddenly realized, was still on. "Dankin?" he called. "You get all that?"

"We got it, Chief," Dankin confirmed. "You still want me to get the ship ready?"

Karrde looked past Entoo Nee at the room's darkened windows. Beyond those windows were people his actions, however unintended, had put in deadly danger.

Which meant there really wasn't any decision here to be made. "Yes, get it ready," he told Dankin. "But get it ready for full combat."

He looked back at Entoo Nee. "We're going to stay and fight."

CHAPTER

25

It was, Booster Terrik thought, about as chaotic aboard the *Errant Venture* as he'd ever seen it. And considering this was the *Errant Venture* he was talking about, that was really saying something.

They were all over the place: New Republic techs and workers and officer types, thousands of them, crawling around every corner of his Star Destroyer. Fixing things, adding things, taking things out, upgrading things, and occasionally changing things around just for the fun of it. His own people had been overridden, nudged aside, superseded, or flat out run over as this oversized rancor of a restoration crew lumbered through his ship.

And moving around the center of it, like the single calm spot in the middle of a circlestorm, was General Bel Iblis.

"Five more warships arrived in the system last night," a harried-looking aide was saying, hurrying to keep up with Bel Iblis as the general strode briskly along the Starboard-16 weapons emplacement corridor. Booster, with his longer legs, had less of a problem in that department. Still, in his opinion, Bel Iblis had a lot more energy than anyone had any business having this early in the morning. "The *Freedom's Fury, Spirit of Mindor, Starline Warrior, Stellar Sentinel,* and *Welling's Revenge.*"

"Good," Bel Iblis said, stopping beside a turbolaser monitor panel. "What about the *Garfin* and *Beledeen II*?"

"No word on them yet," the aide said, checking his datapad. "I've also heard rumors that the *Webley*'s here, but so far they haven't checked in."

"They're here," Booster spoke up. "Captain Winger is, anyway—those mechanical fingers of hers leave pretty distinctive marks on metal ale tubes."

The aide's eyes darkened. "All incoming ships are supposed to check in immediately—"

"It's all right," Bel Iblis calmed him. "Don't worry, they'll surface in plenty of time. Alex probably just wanted her crew to get some rest before the orders started flying."

"They're not the only ones who could use some rest," Booster muttered under his breath.

Bel Iblis frowned slightly, as if only now noticing the big man's presence. "Was there something you wanted, Terrik?" he asked.

"Just wondering when the work on my ship will be finished," Booster said.

"We're almost there," Bel Iblis said. "Lieutenant?"

"Looks like the major refitting will be completed inside of twelve hours," the younger man confirmed, studying his datapad. "There may be a few odds and ends left, but they can be finished on the way to Yaga Minor."

Bel Iblis looked at Booster. "Was there anything else?" he asked.

"Yeah, there was," Booster said. He stopped, looking significantly at the aide.

Bel Iblis took the hint. "Lieutenant, go check on the Number 7 tractor beam emplacement," he said. "Make sure the balance adjustments are being made properly."

"Yes, sir," the aide said. Throwing a speculative look at Booster, he headed at a quick walk down the corridor.

"Why don't we step in here out of the way," Bel Iblis suggested, crossing to a door with the bright red markings of an emergency med station.

They went inside. "Up to now, you've been pretty quiet about what your plan is for this little raid," Booster said when the door was sealed again behind them. "I think it's about time I heard some details."

"There's not much to tell," Bel Iblis said. "We'll be taking the *Errant Venture* in past their sentry line and, hopefully, through their main defense perimeter. Once we're inside, the rest of the task force will come in behind us from hyperspace and attack the perimeter. If we're lucky, the Imperials will be so busy with them they won't give us a second look."

"That assumes their first look doesn't pin us to the wall, of course," Booster pointed out darkly. "Assuming that, what then?"

"Yaga Minor has a peculiarity that as far as I know is unique among Imperial installations," Bel Iblis said. "There are a pair of outrider computer stations set up at the end of a corridor/walkway tube that extends about a hundred meters out from the main orbiting Ubiqtorate station."

Booster frowned. "Odd design."

"The idea was to give high-ranking civilian researchers access to the computer records system without having to let them into the Ubiqtorate base proper," Bel Iblis told him. "Grand Moff Tarkin ran a lot of his more private stuff through Yaga Minor, and he didn't want his political enemies getting even a glimpse of what he was up to."

"Okay, so there's a convenient remote connection to the computer," Booster said. "I don't suppose it happens to have an equally convenient access hatchway where we can get to it."

"There are hatchways, but unfortunately they're not at all convenient," Bel Iblis said, his voice turning grim. "We'll probably have to blast a hole in the side of the walkway tube and send in our slicers in vac suits."

Booster snorted. "Right—blow a hole in the side of the station. *That'll* sure go unnoticed."

"It could," Bel Iblis said. "The main force will be firing barrages of proton torpedoes at the time. The Imperials may assume that was one that got through."

"And if they don't?"

Bel Iblis shrugged. "Then you and I and the rest of the *Errant Venture*'s crew start earning our pay the hard way. We'll have to hold them off long enough for the slicers to pull up a copy of the Caamas Document and transmit it out to the attacking ships."

Booster snorted again. "No offense, General, but that has to be the worst plan I've ever heard in my life. What happens to us once we've got the document?"

Bel Iblis looked him straight in the eye. "What happens to us doesn't matter," he said bluntly. "If they accept our surrender, fine. If not . . . they turn the *Errant Venture* into scrap around us."

"Hold it a second," Booster said, frowning. Buried in among all that breathtakingly lousy strategy he'd suddenly noticed a highly important word. "What do you mean *us*? I thought you were going to be out there with the main fleet."

Bel Iblis shook his head. "This ship is the key to the operation," he said quietly. "This is the ship that has to survive long enough to first get the Caamas Document and then punch it out through whatever jamming the Imperials have going. This is where I'm needed the most. So this is where I'll be."

"Now, wait just one mradhe mucking minute," Booster growled, pulling himself up to his full one-meter-nine height. "This is *my* ship. You told me I would still be her captain."

"You're still the captain," Bel Iblis agreed. "I'm simply the admiral."

Booster let out a long, hissing breath. He should have known Bel Iblis hadn't really given in on anything. He should have *known* it. "And if I refuse to give you command?"

Bel Iblis lifted his eyebrows slightly. Booster nodded, a sour taste in his mouth. With the *Errant Venture* crawling with Bel Iblis's people, the question wasn't even worth answering. "Right," he muttered. "I knew I'd regret this."

"You can stay here if you want," Bel Iblis offered. "I'm sure Coruscant would compensate you for—"

"Forget it," Booster bit out. "This is my ship, and you're not taking it into combat without me. Period."

Bel Iblis smiled faintly. "I understand," he said. "Believe me, I understand. Was there anything else?"

"No, that ought to about do it for now," Booster said glumly. "You might want to see if you can come up with a better plan in the next three days."

"I'll try," Bel Iblis promised. Turning, he headed for the door—

"Wait a second," Booster said as a new thought struck him. "You say we're going to blow a hole in that outrider computer station. What happens if someone's in there at the time?"

"I'm not expecting anyone to be there," Bel Iblis told him. "I doubt it's used much anymore. Besides, I can't see any other way to do this."

"But what if there is someone?" Booster persisted. "You said yourself the place was only used by civilians. You blow a hole in the wall and you're going to kill them."

A shadow seemed to cross Bel Iblis's face. "Yes," he said quietly. "I know."

"Well," Klif said, consulting his chrono. "It's been four hours. What do you think—another two before the panic call comes?"

Navett shrugged, running through a quick mental calculation of his own. He and Klif had been conspicuously elsewhere at the time, just in case backchecks were made, but according to Pensin the subtle transfer of their little organic time bombs to the Bothan techs' clothing had gone as smooth as spun gemweb. Four hours now since those techs had vanished into the Drev'starn shield generator building; give them another hour to make their presence known, two more after that for the Bothans to become fully aware of the magnitude of the problem and to exhaust all other possibilities for dealing with it . . . "I'm guessing at least three," he told Klif. "They aren't going to be in a hurry to call in offworlders."

"Well, the stuff's ready whenever they do," Klif said with a shrug.

Across the shop, the annoyingly cheery chime rang out as the door swung open. Settling his face into what Klif had dubbed their earnest-but-stupid expression, he looked up.

And felt the expression freeze across his face. There, walking into the shop, were their two New Rep military types.

Beside him, Klif made a faint choking sound in the back of his throat. "Quiet," Navett murmured, adding a slightly dopey smile to his expression and bounding eagerly around the end of the counter toward their visitors. "A day of fun and profit to you, or however that goes," he said, keying his voice to the pleasant yet vaguely pushy tone of a merchant determined to make a sale. "Can I help you?"

"Just looking, thanks," one of the men said as they wandered down the row of cages. They were two of a kind, Navett noted: both somewhat short, both with slightly graying brown hair, the speaker with brown eyes while his companion had green.

And seen up close, Brown Eyes especially looked familiar.

"Sure, sure," Navett said, hovering nearby in traditional shopkeeper style. "Anything special you're lookin' for?"

"Not really," Green Eyes put in, gazing down into the polpian cage. "What are these? Polpians?"

"Sure are," Navett said. Both of them had faint Corellian accents, too. "You know your petstock."

"I know a little," Green Eyes said, gazing at him with a glint in his eye that Navett didn't care for at all. "I thought Bothans are allergic to polpians."

"Yeah, some of 'em are, I suppose," Navett said with a shrug.

"And yet you brought them to Bothawui?"

Navett put on a bewildered expression. "Well, sure," he said, trying to sound slightly wounded. "Just 'cause some people are allergic to something doesn't mean someone else won't wanna buy it. Not all Bothans are allergic to 'em, either, and anyway there are lots more people here than just Bothans—"

He broke off as Brown Eyes sneezed. "There—see?" he said, jabbing a finger toward the other as if the sneeze was a sort of vindication. "Probably something in here *he's* allergic to, too. But you still came in, right? And I'll bet I can find something that'd make a really great pet for you."

The door chime sounded again, and Navett turned to see a thin old woman come in. The fringe companion Klif had mentioned? "Hi, there," he said, nodding to her. "A day of fun and profit to you. Can I help you?"

"I hope so," she said. "You have any ratter thists?"

Navett felt his throat tighten. What in blazes was a ratter thist? "Don't think I've ever heard of 'em," he said carefully, knowing better than to pretend knowledge he didn't have. "I can check the lists, though, see if we can get 'em from somewhere. What kind of critter are they?"

"They're not all that popular, really," the woman said. Her voice was casual, but she was watching him as closely as Green Eyes was. "They're small and agile, with tan-striped fur and retractable claws. They're sometimes used as livestock border guards in mountainous terrain."

"Oh, sure," Klif called from the far side of the counter. Leaning casually on it, there was no sign of the datapad he undoubtedly had going out of sight under the flat surface. "You're talking about Kordulian krisses."

"Oh—Kordulian *krisses*," Navett said with a knowing nod. He'd never heard of those, either, but Klif's cue was obvious. "Sure. I just never heard of 'em by that other name before. Klif, can we get 'em in?"

"Let me check," Klif said, making a show of pulling the datapad up onto the counter and pretending to turn it on.

"What are these?" Brown Eyes called. He was standing over the mawkren tank, looking in with a somewhat leery expression.

"Baby mawkrens," Navett told him, stepping to his side and looking fondly down through the clear plastic at the tiny lizards scrabbling restlessly around on top of each other. "Just whelped this morning. Cute, huh?"

"Adorable," Brown Eyes said, not sounding like he meant it.

"Here it is," Klif called. "Kordulian krisses. Let's see . . ."

There was a beep from Navett's comlink. " 'Scuse me," he said, pulling out the instrument, a sudden feeling of dread coming over him. If this was the call they were expecting . . . "Hello?"

"Is this Proprietor Navett of the Exoticalia Pet Emporium?" a stiff but harried-sounding Bothan voice asked.

"Sure is," Navett said, striving for earnest-but-stupid cheerfulness. It was the call, all right; and with all the rotten luck it had come with a pair of New Rep agents standing right there listening. "What can I do for you?"

"We have a small but troublesome insect infestation problem," the Bothan said. "Our attempts to eliminate them have so far proved futile. As a dealer in exotic animals, it was thought you might have some suggestions."

"Probably," Navett said. "Klif and I did some bug-squash work before we got into the pet business. What kind are they?"

"They're unfamiliar to our experts," the other said, sounding disgusted. "All we know is that they're very small, do not respond to any of our extermination methods, and at random intervals all begin making a loud humming noise."

"Could be skronkies," Navett suggested doubtfully. "They make a pretty annoying noise. Or aphrens, or—wait a minute. I'll bet they're metalmites. You got any electronics or heavy machinery in the area?"

There was a sort of strangled sound from the comlink. "A considerable amount of it, yes," the Bothan said. "What do metalmites do?"

"Chew through metal," Navett said. " 'Course, they don't actually *chew* through the stuff—they've got enzymes that—"

"I don't need the physiological details," the Bothan cut him off. "How do we eliminate them?"

"Well, let's see," Navett said, rubbing his chin thoughtfully for the benefit of the New Rep agents. Green Eyes had that glint in his eyes again . . . "First thing you gotta do is some spraying. You got any—let's see—any CorTrehan around? That's cordioline trehansicol, if you need the whole name."

"I don't know," the Bothan said. "But I'm sure we can get some made up."

"Before you do, make sure you got someone who knows what they're doing," Navett warned. "Won't do you a bit of good to just slather the stuff around."

There was a brief pause. "What do you mean?"

"I mean you can't just slather the stuff around, that's what," Navett said, letting a little impatience creep into his voice. "You gotta get all the spots where they're going to feed, but also leave 'em enough bare spots—" He sighed. "Look, this isn't something for amateurs to mess around with. We've got the equipment to spray with—we use 'em to disinfect our cages and stock. You get us the CorTrehan, and Klif and me can do the job for you."

"Impossible," the Bothan said sharply. "Offworlders cannot be permitted in that area."

"Oh. Okay." Navett shrugged. He'd expected the automatic rejection of his first offer. "Just trying to help. You'll have plenty of time to get rid of a single brood before it does much damage."

He frowned, as if something had suddenly occurred to him. "It *is* just a single brood, isn't it? When they hum, do they all make one note, or are there a couple of different pitches?"

There was a short pause. "There are several different notes," the Bothan said. "Five, perhaps six."

Navett let out a low whistle. "*Five* of 'em? Ho, boy. Hey, Klif—they got five different broods in there. Well, good luck to you. I sure hope you can get someone on 'em before the brood war starts."

He keyed off the comlink. "Five broods," he murmured, shaking his head. "Wow."

"Shocking," Green Eyes agreed, the glint still in his eyes. "Pretty exotic pests, metalmites."

"They come in on ships sometimes," Navett said, wishing he could read that face. Green Eyes was suspicious, all right. But was he suspicious of Navett personally, or just the general metalmite situation? "I've heard of 'em riding mynocks, too. Sort of scavenging along behind as they—"

There was another beep from his comlink. " 'Scuse me again," he said, pulling it out. "Hello?"

"This is Field Controller Tri'byia again," the same Bothan voice came, sounding disgusted. "I spoke with you a few moments ago."

"Yeah, sure," Navett said. "What can I do for you?"

"I've been instructed to ask how much you would charge for getting rid of the metalmites," Tri'byia said.

"Oh, not much," Navett said, carefully suppressing a smile. From the tone of Tri'byia's voice, it was clear the sudden official change of heart wasn't his idea. "Matter of fact, as long as you spring for the CorTrehan—

well, look. The guy at Customs said we're gonna need a special merchant's license to sell our pets outside Drev'starn. You get us that license, and we'll do it for free."

"For free?" Tri'byia repeated, the pitch of his voice dropping a few steps. "Why so generous?"

"Listen, I've seen what metalmites can do," Navett said stiffly. "If you think I want to run a business in a town where they've gotten a foothold, you can think again. And the faster we get started, the easier it'll be to get rid of them. You get us a merchant's license and the juice, and we'll call it even."

"I believe that can be arranged," Tri'byia said reluctantly. "You and your equipment will have to submit to a full scan before you can be allowed into the facility."

"No problem," Navett said. "Actually, this'll be kind of fun—just like old times. When do you want us?"

"A landspeeder will pick you up in thirty minutes," the Bothan said. He still didn't sound happy, but there was a cautious note of relief in his voice. "Be ready to go."

"We will," Navett promised.

The Bothan clicked off without bothering to say good-bye. "Man, you just never know, do you?" Navett said philosophically, sliding the comlink away. "Sorry, folks. Did you want us to order some of those krisses for you, ma'am? Klif, you find anything on the lists?"

"Looks like we can get 'em from a supplier on Eislo—have 'em here in two or three days," Klif reported. "Or we can get 'em shipped in straight from Kordu itself. That'll probably be a little cheaper, but it'll take longer."

"You want to order today?" Navett asked hopefully. "You only have to put a tenth down up front."

The old woman shook her head. "I think I'll see if anyone else in town has them in stock first."

"Well, if you don't find anyone, come on back," Klif called as the three of them headed for the door. "We can get express service for a pretty reasonable fee."

"We'll keep that in mind," Brown Eyes promised. "Thanks. We may be back."

They filed out, passing across the front window and out of Navett's view as the door closed behind them. "I'll just bet you will," he said softly to himself.

He shook his head, dismissing them from his mind. Fringe lifters and even New Rep agents were completely unimportant right now. What was important was that their little metalmite time bombs, introduced into the shield generator techs' clothing, had done their job.

And now it was time for Klif and him to do theirs.

"Let's get ready," he said, heading briskly toward the back room. "Mustn't keep the Bothans waiting."

"And here," General Hestiv said, keying a combination into the keypad, "is where you'll be working."

"Okay," Ghent said, glancing nervously down the long corridor behind them. It was a long way back to the main base, and Hestiv had assured him that hardly anyone ever came out here anymore. But there was a whole Imperial Ubiqtorate station back there, and he couldn't shake the feeling he was being watched by unfriendly eyes.

With a puff of slightly stale air the door swung open. "There we go," Hestiv said, gesturing him forward. "Go on in."

Ghent stepped into the doorway, throwing Hestiv a sideways glance as he passed. Admiral Pellaeon had vouched for him, he knew. But the man was still an Imperial officer, and Ghent was from the New Republic. If this Moff Disra person wanted to do away with him, this would be a perfect place to do it.

And then he got his first glimpse of the room itself . . .

"This is your new temporary home," Hestiv said from behind him. "What do you think?"

Ghent hardly heard him. Could hardly believe his eyes, for that matter, as he looked around the tiny room. Crammed into it were an Everest 448 DataSifter, a pair of Fedukowski D/Square decrypt/decipherers, five Wickstrom K220 heavy-duty peripheral processors, a Merilang-1221 full-spectrum numerical analyzer—

"The equipment's probably nothing like what you're used to," Hestiv said apologetically. "But hopefully it'll do."

—and there as a centerpiece, nothing less than a brand-new Rikhous Masterline-70 OcTerminal. A *Masterline-70*! "No, not really," Ghent managed, still staring goggle-eyed at the shining array. And they were going to let him have this whole room? All to himself? "But it'll do just fine."

"Good," Hestiv said, crossing the room in front of him and keying open another door Ghent hadn't yet noticed. "Your living quarters are in here, so you won't have to leave this section at all. In fact, you might want to change the coding on the door lock after I leave so that no one can even accidentally walk in on you."

"Sure," Ghent said, his nervousness about this place already forgotten. "I can seal it up real tight. Okay if I get started?"

"Whenever you're ready," Hestiv said. Dimly, Ghent was aware the other was staring at him oddly. "You know how to get hold of me if you need anything. Good luck."

"Sure," Ghent said as Hestiv stepped back through the doorway. There was another puff of air, and Ghent was alone.

Dropping his carrypack to the floor, he shoved it with his foot in the general direction of the living area. Imperial Moffs, lurking danger, and even imminent civil wars all but forgotten, he pulled out the chair in front of the Masterline-70 and sat down.

This was going to be fun.

It took an entire hour of scans and examinations under the watchful eyes and ungentle hands of what seemed to Navett to be half of Drev'starn's contingent of Bothawui Security. But at last, with the obvious reluctance of a being who heartily dislikes a situation but has no better alternatives available, Field Controller Tri'byia finally led him and Klif down into the lower levels of the shield generator building.

Into the very center of the Drev'starn defense system.

"Impressive stuff," Navett commented to his glowering guards as he glanced casually around the room. "I can see why you wanna get rid of 'em fast."

He hoisted the tank of CorTrehan a little higher on his shoulder. "Okay," he said, waggling his slender sprayer loosely in his hand. "First thing is for you to show me anything really delicate or critical you don't want 'em getting into."

"We don't want them getting into *any* of it," Tri'byia snapped, his fur rippling.

"Yeah, sure, sure," Navett soothed. "I just meant where do you want us to start spraying? We should do the most delicate stuff first."

Tri'byia's fur rippled again. "I suppose that seems reasonable," he said unhappily. Clearly, the last thing he wanted to do was point out the most important parts of their precious shield generator to a couple of humans. "This way."

Not that it mattered, of course. Navett knew perfectly well what everything in this complex was, and neither he nor Klif needed the Bothans to point out the kill-points to them. But it was something an earnest but stupid pet shop owner might be expected to ask. Besides, he was curious to see how honest the Bothans might get in the middle of a crisis like this.

"You may start there," Tri'byia said, stopping and pointing to a completely nonvital backup comm console.

"Okay," Navett said. Apparently, not very.

They'd been spraying for fifteen minutes, laying out the elaborate curlicue chemical trails that were the only way to effectively kill metalmites, when things finally began to get interesting. "This one next,"

Tri'byia said, laying a hand protectively on the edge of one of the consoles responsible for maintaining the power-frequency coupling between the various poles of the planetary shield.

"Right," Navett said, his heart starting to beat faster as he stepped over to the console. This was it: the first blade thrust into the heart of the species whose actions had cost the Empire so much over the years. The Bothan techs had already removed the access panels; shifting his grip subtly on the sprayer as he crouched down, Navett eased the tip into the maze of electronics and gave it a delicate squirt.

Only this time he left more than just the metalmite-killing CorTrehan to bead up on the circuit cards and drip slowly down onto the power supplies and ventilation fan casings below. This time, his new grip had allowed the slender tank built into the sprayer handle to dribble some of its own special contents into the mix.

The hour-long examination the Bothans had put their equipment through had scanned for everything those paranoid minds could have thought of: weapons, spy equipment, explosives, poisons, soporifics, acids, wire-spinners, and probably fifty other potential threats.

But nowhere in all those multiple layers of precautions had anyone thought to program a check for food.

Not that anyone in the generator building would have found this particular brew even remotely appetizing, not even the metalmites. In fact, now that the rotten little vermin had played their part, it was time for them to die.

He and Klif spent the next two hours moving systematically through the complex, laying down their poison trails and, at perhaps twenty carefully selected points, adding in a squirt of their liquid nutrient. By the time they finished, the thick, sweet-sour smell of the CorTrehan was almost like a physical barrier that had to be pushed aside as they walked through it.

"Okay," Navett said cheerfully as they were finally escorted back into the security entrance area. "First step's done. Now all you gotta do is put a loudspeaker on that's blasting out the broods' different carrier pitches. That keeps 'em from talking back and forth inside their groups, and *that* keeps 'em from breeding faster so they can fight with the other broods. Gives the CorTrehan time to work. You see?"

"Yes," Tri'byia said, looking marginally less unhappy now that the offworlders were no longer in direct contact with his precious machinery. "How long will this be necessary?"

"Oh, a week ought to do it," Navett said. "Eight or nine days just to be on the safe side. Some broods are harder to kill than others. Don't worry, though—they won't be eating anything during any of that. Mostly, they'll just be dying."

"Very well," Tri'byia agreed reluctantly. "I have only one more question, then. I am told these pests are quite rare. How is it they were able to find their way in here?"

Navett shrugged as casually as he could. The groundwork had been laid, but that didn't mean they were out of the snake pit yet. If the Bothans decided to be suspicious enough to go back in and clean out everything he and Klif had just laid down, this whole setup would have been for nothing. "You got me," he said. "You bring any new equipment in here in the past week or two?"

The Bothan's fur rippled uncertainly. "There were two pieces of equipment that arrived seven days ago. But both were scanned thoroughly before they were brought in."

"Yeah, but I'll bet your scanners aren't programmed for heavily metal-based life like these things," Navett pointed out. It was a safe bet; certainly the Bothans' scanners hadn't spotted the little beasts riding in on their incoming techs' clothing. "Tell you the truth, I don't know if anyone really knows where they come from or how they get around. They just pop up now and then and make trouble. They probably came in with that equipment, though. You might want to catch a couple of 'em and use 'em to reprogram your scanners so they can't make any more trouble."

"Thank you," Tri'byia said, a bit huffily. Apparently, Bothans of his stature were not used to having the obvious pointed out to them.

"No problem," Navett said cheerfully. Earnest but stupid, he was the type to take everything at full face value, without noticing any undertones. "Glad we could help. And you'll get that merchant's license for us, right?"

"I will do what I can to help with it," Tri'byia said.

Which was, Navett noticed, not precisely what he'd originally promised. But that was all right. In six days, if all went according to plan, Tri'byia would cease to exist, along with the city of Drev'starn and as much of the rest of Bothawui as the Imperial Star Destroyers hidden out there could manage.

And on that day, Navett planned to look down on the shattered world from one of those Star Destroyers and laugh. But for now, all he needed to do was smile. "Great," he said cheerfully. "Thanks a lot. And if you guys ever need anything else, just give us a call."

He and Klif didn't say anything to each other on the ride back to the pet shop. Nor did they speak once they were there, at least not about anything of substance, until they'd gone over each other thoroughly with the spy-mike detector hidden in the bottom of the dopplefly cage.

But if Tri'byia didn't especially like them, he apparently wasn't overly suspicious of them, either. The spy scan came up clean.

"Sloppy," Klif grunted as they returned the detector back to its hiding place. "You'd think they'd at least want to hear us slapping each other on the back about getting our license so cheap."

"I'm sure they backchecked our records before they called us in,"

Navett said, sniffing in disgust as he slapped at his shirt. That blasted CorTrehan stuck to everything. "Did you get a chance to see where our power conduit came into the building? I never got to that side of the building."

"I saw it." Klif nodded. "They've actually got a splice going off one of the power cables, probably ready to go to the new equipment Tri'byia mentioned."

"But they hadn't opened the wall any?"

Klif shook his head. "They're not *that* stupid. No, the whole wall's still there."

"Fine," Navett said, shrugging. It would have been handy to have some of that meter-thick, reinforced, heavily braced, multiple-layered, impenetrable wall out of their way. But it certainly wasn't necessary.

"*I'm* just worried about it taking another six days before we can spring this," Klif continued. "Won't the stuff we left start to deteriorate?"

"Not a problem," Navett assured him. "The tricky part now is going to be digging down to the power conduit from that Ho'Din place and then cutting through it without setting off sensors from here to Odve'starn."

"You think they've wired the conduit itself?"

"I would if I were in charge," Navett said. "Horvic and Pensin can get us into the place after hours, but we won't have much time each night to work. Slow and steady is the way to go, and six days should be just about right."

"I suppose," Klif said, sobering. "Of course, that assumes we even *have* six more days. Or have you finally decided to do something about those New Rep agents?" Abruptly, he snapped his fingers. "Oh, *blast*—I just made that face. Wedge Antilles."

"You're right," Navett said, grimacing as the name belatedly clicked with Brown Eyes's face. General Wedge Antilles, leader of that multicursed Rogue Squadron. A single insignificant group of X-wings that had probably caused the Empire more trouble than all the Bothans in the galaxy put together. "And that's going to make things that much more awkward. Even without New Republic celebrities involved, a triple murder would create a major fuss."

He let his eyes drift around the shop, taking in the rows of cages, the subtle mix of smells and sounds. Surely Antilles wouldn't see any threat in a harmless pet shop.

But no. They'd been standing right here when the call came through, and knew he and Klif had been invited into the shield generator building. No, they'd have the pet shop marked now for sure. "But I don't suppose we can afford to let them poke around anymore, either," he conceded. "I guess it's time we took them out."

"Now you're talking," Klif said with dark approval. "You want me to take care of it?"

Navett cocked an eyebrow. "What, all by yourself?"

"Hey, they're just X-wing jocks," Klif said. "At least Antilles is. Outside their cockpits they're babes in arms."

"Maybe," Navett said. "But they found *us* okay. And that old woman looks like she knows her way around, too."

"Meaning?"

Navett gave him a tight smile. "Meaning you don't take them out by yourself," he said. "We'll do it together."

Moranda sipped at her blue-green liqueur. "I don't know," she said, shaking her head. "I can't say that any of them really leaped up and waved at me."

"That's one way to put it," Wedge said sourly, massaging his aching temples with thumb and middle finger. Fifty different shops, businesses, service spots, and eating establishments. All of them set up in Drev'starn since the warships began gathering overhead; all of them visited personally by him, Corran, and Moranda in the past four days. The business turnover rate on Bothawui must be astronomical. "Another way is to just admit we've hit another dead end."

"I'm not sure I'd go quite that far," Corran said slowly, meditatively swirling his drink around in its glass. "There were a couple of places that were definitely more on edge than others. That Meshakian jewelry owner, for one."

"Stolen goods dealer," Moranda dismissed him with a flip of her hand. "And he spotted us right off as anything but casual customers, by the way. You've really got to learn how to rein in that straight-backed CorSec stance of yours, Corran."

"And that Ho'Din tapcafe," Corran continued, ignoring her as he ran a finger down their list. "It's sitting right on top of one of the power-cable conduits to the generator building."

"And has been there for ten years," Moranda reminded him.

"Except that the day manager mentioned they'd just hired a couple of humans for the late cleanup shift, remember?" Corran countered. "There's something about that that bothers me."

Wedge eyed him over his cup. Corran, he knew, had never had much luck with the mind-reading aspects of the Force, not like Luke or Leia. But if he couldn't retrieve other people's thoughts, he could still pull out impressions and hints and textures. Combined with his old CorSec detective training, it meant that anything that bothered him was worth taking a hard look at.

"And then, of course," Corran added, "there are our friends at the Exoticalia Pet Emporium."

Wedge looked at Moranda, waiting for her rebuttal. But it didn't come. "There's them, all right," she said instead, frowning down at the tabletop. "I don't like that one at all."

"I thought you said none of them had jumped out at you," Wedge reminded her.

"No, they didn't," Moranda agreed. "That's just the point. The pet guys acted just perfect. But how many pet shop owners do you know who also happen to be experts at getting rid of vermin? And exotic ones like metalmites, yet?"

"We should be able to backcheck them and see if that kind of experience shows up in their records," Corran said. But he didn't look any happier than Moranda did. "I just wish we knew where exactly this metalmite invasion had taken place."

"Has to be someplace with really high security," Wedge said. "They weren't even going to let them in at first."

"And at the same time, that decision got overruled real quick," Moranda said, nodding. "Someplace with ultra high security, but yet extremely sensitive and vital."

For a moment the three of them looked at each other. Corran broke the silence first. "It's the shield generator building," he said. "There's nothing else in Drev'starn that fits."

"Agreed," Moranda said, sipping at her drink. "Question now is, was the metalmite incursion the attack or the bait? If it's the attack—"

She broke off at a muffled beep from Wedge's comlink, buried deep in a pocket of his jacket. "Who knows you're here?" she asked.

"Our shuttle," Wedge told her, digging out the instrument. "We set up a relay for any incoming transmissions." Thumbing it on, he keyed for low volume. "Go Red Two," he gave the codeword.

The message was very short. "This is father," Bel Iblis's familiar voice said. "All is forgiven; come on home."

Wedge squeezed the comlink hard. "Acknowledged," he said. "On our way."

He keyed the comlink off and looked up to find Corran's gaze hard on him. "Dad?"

Wedge nodded. "Dad," he confirmed. "Time to go home."

"Meaning?" Moranda asked.

"Meaning we have to leave," Wedge told her. "Right now."

"Oh, that's convenient," Moranda growled, glaring at him. "What about the shield generator?"

"From now on the Bothans are on their own," Wedge said, draining his drink and sorting out coins onto the table. "I'm sorry, but we were only on temporary loan anyway."

Moranda grimaced, but nodded. "I understand," she said. "Well, it was fun while it lasted."

"You should probably give Bothan Security a call," Wedge said, standing up. "Point them to our friends at the pet shop."

"Whatever," Moranda said, waving a hand. "Happy flights."

"Thanks," Wedge said. "Come on, Corran."

"Just a second," Corran said. He hadn't moved from his chair, and there was a glint in his eyes as he looked at Moranda. "I want to know what Moranda's going to do now."

"Oh, go on," she chided him, making little shooing motions with her hands. "I'll be fine."

"In other words, you're going to stay on this," he said bluntly.

She lifted her eyebrows. "That's *very* good. CorSec teach you how to do that?"

"You haven't answered the question," Wedge said, sitting back down again. "You *are* going to call Security, aren't you?"

"And tell them what?" she countered. "We don't have a scrap of proof. It's worse than that, really—they presumably already did a backcheck on Navett and his buddy, and they *still* let them into the generator building."

"So what are you going to do?" Wedge persisted. "Stay on this by yourself?"

Moranda's mouth set itself into hard lines. "I was given an assignment, Wedge," she said quietly. "I'm supposed to stay here and watch for Vengeance attempts against Bothawui."

Corran shook his head. "That's not a good idea," he said. "If Vengeance is being driven or guided by Imperials—"

"So where are you two off to?" Moranda demanded scornfully. "A vacation on the beaches of Berchest? I'll lay you fifty-to-one it'll be a lot more dangerous wherever you're going than anything I'm likely to run into here."

"Moranda—" Wedge began.

"Besides which, you don't have time to argue about it," she cut him off. "If 'Dad' is who I think he is, he's not going to be happy if you two get home late. Now scoot, both of you. Thanks for all the drinks."

Reluctantly, Wedge stood up again. She was right, of course; and she was certainly more than old enough to make this kind of decision for herself. But that didn't mean he had to like it. "Come on, Corran. Moranda . . . you watch yourself, okay?"

"You, too," she said, smiling up at him. "Don't worry about me. I'll be just fine."

CHAPTER

26

There was a strange, almost unworldly aroma tugging at her senses as Mara drifted toward consciousness. Something strange, yet vaguely pleasant . . .

"Good morning," Luke's voice came through the haze. With a jolt, Mara came fully awake.

And in that first disorienting moment wished she hadn't. Even as she opened her eyes to the dimly lit gloom around her, she suddenly became aware of a hundred sparks of pain jabbing through her muscles from her heels through her legs and back and right to the nape of her neck. "Ow," she grunted under her breath.

Luke's face appeared overhead, looking down at her with concern. "Is your shoulder still hurting?" he asked.

Mara frowned, blinking away a little more of the haze clouding her mind. Right—her badly burned shoulder. Craning her neck down, focusing eyes that still weren't entirely awake, she peered down at her charred jumpsuit.

At her charred jumpsuit, and the smooth, unmarked skin showing through the hole there.

"No," she said, not quite believing it. "The shoulder feels just fine. It's—oh, right. Your healing trance."

"Some disorientation is normal when you first come out of it," Luke assured her. "Don't worry."

"I wasn't." She eased her shoulders around, trying to ignore the extra wave of tingles the movement sent running through her back. Luke's hand was there, gripping her arm and helping her sit up. "You said it was morning?"

"Well, afternoon, actually," Luke amended. "But Han once told me that anytime you woke up was technically morning."

"That sounds like his casual slant on things," Mara said. "How long— in real time—have I been lying there?"

"About five days," Luke told her. "Easy, now."

"Oh, you bet," she agreed, wincing as muscles that had been laid on for five straight days continued to complain loudly about their mistreatment. "I'm impressed. I don't think even a bacta tank would have done the job that fast."

"You have a strong Force gift," Luke said, his hand hovering ready by her arm. "That usually helps the healing process."

"It's definitely one I'm going to have to learn," she decided, looking around. That aroma she thought she'd dreamed was still there . . .

"It's some kind of roast avian," Luke explained, nodding toward the back of the landing. "A wake-up gift to you from the Qom Jha."

"Really," Mara said, hoisting herself carefully to her feet and hobbling over there on unsteady legs. It was a roast avian, all right, simmering on a cooking pad. "Awfully nice of them. Where did you get the cooker?"

"I sent Keeper Of Promises back to your Defender for the rest of the survival gear," Luke explained. "I'd rather have sent them back to my X-wing—the spare kit Karrde put together was a lot more complete. But after our brush with the Threateners they're not all that eager to go roaming around outside."

"This from the species that eats fire creepers raw?" Mara pointed out as she eased back into a sitting position by the cooking pad. "Pretty selective skittishness."

"It's a little more complicated than that," Luke said, seating himself cross-legged on the floor across the cooking pad from her and gesturing toward the food. "Hence the gift, actually. They've come to the conclusion that you saved their lives in there."

"I don't know how they figure that," Mara grunted, tearing off a piece of the roast. "We were the ones being shot at, not them."

Luke's lips puckered. "Actually, there's some question about that. Splitter Of Stones thinks it was the Qom Jha who the Threateners were firing at, not us, at least until you started shooting back. And as I've gone back through my memories of the battle, I think he's right."

Mara took a careful bite. The meat was a little overcooked for her taste, but not bad for all that. Anyway, as her loudly growling stomach reminded her, a person who hadn't eaten in five days couldn't afford to be too choosy. "Interesting thought," she said, "but I'm not sure where it gets us. Whoever they were shooting at, the fact is, they're still touchy about strangers."

"Maybe," Luke said, his tone odd. "But maybe not. Haven't you wondered why the Threateners never came into the cave looking for you after you knocked yourself out?"

"Are you sure they *didn't* come in?" Mara countered around a mouthful of food.

"The Qom Jha say they didn't," Luke told her. "There were a couple of flybys with their ships, and that was it. In fact, as far as Child Of Winds knows, they never even conducted an outside ground search of the area."

Mara chewed thoughtfully, resisting the urge to point out that Child Of Winds was not exactly the most reliable source of information around. "Okay," she said. "Let's assume the Threateners lost interest in me. Where does that get us?"

"If they simply lost interest, I don't know," Luke said. "But what if they *didn't* lose interest, but just decided to wait until you found your own way into the High Fortress?"

Mara took another bite. That was a disturbing thought. In fact, it was an extremely disturbing thought. All the more so since that exact course of action was one she had actually considered early in her captivity. "I don't know if Karrde mentioned it to you," she said slowly, "but the way we found this system was by tracking the escape vectors from two of their ships to an intersect point. My assumption has always been that they simply didn't know we could track their vector for a few microseconds after they jumped to lightspeed. But now I'm not so sure."

"You think they wanted you to come here?"

"It would fit with them not searching all that hard for me after I landed," Mara pointed out. "Of course, if we argue that direction we then have to come up with an explanation as to why they tried to shoot *you* down."

"Maybe they're not interested in having more than one guest at a time," Luke suggested, gazing out into space. "Or maybe they don't want to talk to anyone from the New Republic until they've talked to you first."

Mara eyed him closely. There had been a flicker in his emotions just then . . . "Is that just off the top of your head?" she asked. "Or are you getting something from the Force about it?"

He shook his head, still gazing at nothing. "I'm not sure," he admitted. "But I have the feeling . . . no, never mind."

"No never mind what?" Mara demanded suspiciously, pressing at the corners of his mind. "Come on, we don't have time for games."

A muscle in his cheek twitched. "I get the feeling it's you they want to see," he said. "You, specifically."

Mara lifted her eyebrows. "I'm flattered. My fame just continues to spread."

"Eater Of Fire Creepers did say they'd heard the Threateners talking about you," Luke reminded her. "I wish we knew the context of the conversation."

There was a flapping from the stairway, and one of the Qom Jha appeared. It spoke—"Thank you, Flyer Through Spikes," Luke said. "Go see if Keeper Of Promises has any news, if you would."

The Qom Jha replied, and with a flurry of wings was gone down the stairway. "I've had some of the Qom Jha patrolling the upper areas of the stairway and listening for activity outside the doors," Luke explained. "Flyer Through Spikes tells me the upper areas of the fortress were active for a while this morning, but they seem to be quiet again."

"Ah," Mara said, tearing off another bite with perhaps a bit more force than necessary. Those blasted Qom Jha and their blasted unintelligible voices—

"Something wrong?" Luke asked.

Mara glared at him. "You know, Skywalker, it's really hard to keep any thoughts to yourself when you're around."

He gave her an innocent look that had far too much amusement in it for her taste. "Odd. I seem to remember a situation not too long ago when you couldn't wait to unload some of those choicer thoughts on me."

Mara grimaced. "Feeling a little more cheerful about our past mistakes this morning, are we?"

He sobered. "Not cheerful, no," he said. "Just learning how to acknowledge them, learn from them, and then pick up and move on. I've had a lot of time for thinking during these past five days, you know."

"You reach any particular conclusions?"

He looked straight at her. "I know why you didn't turn to the dark side," he said. "And why you keep coming up against limits on what you can do through the Force."

With a casualness she didn't especially feel, Mara took another bite and settled her back against the stone wall behind her. "I'm listening."

"The essence of the dark side is selfishness," Luke said. "The elevation of yourself and your own desires above everything else."

Mara nodded. "Fairly obvious so far."

"The point is that all the time you were serving the Emperor, you were never doing so out of selfish motives," Luke said. "You *were* serving, even if it *was* Palpatine and his own selfish ends. And service to others is the essence of being a Jedi."

Mara thought about that. "No," she said, shaking her head. "No, I don't like it. Service to evil is still evil. What you're saying is that doing something wrong isn't really wrong if your motives are good. That's nonsense."

"I agree," Luke said. "But that's not what I'm saying. Some of the things you did were certainly wrong; but because you weren't doing them for your own purposes, the acts themselves didn't open you to the dark side."

Mara glowered at her food. "I see the difference," she said. "But I still don't like it."

"Actually, it's not that much different from the situation with the *Jensaarai* that Corran and I ran into on Susevfi," Luke said. "They didn't know how to be Jedi, but were still serving the best they knew how."

"And in the process had gotten themselves so bent around that you were years untwisting them," Mara reminded him tartly. "Anyway, they at least had the memory of a role model to follow, didn't they? That what's-his-name Jedi?"

"Nikkos Tyris," Luke said, nodding. "Which brings up an even more interesting thought. Maybe *you* had a role model, too."

Mara shook her head. "Not a chance. There wasn't a single person in the inner court with a scrap of what I'd consider virtue or morality."

"Then maybe it was someone in your life before you were taken to Coruscant," Luke suggested. "Your parents, or some close friend."

Mara bit off the last bite of her meal and tossed the carcass back into a corner. "This is a dead-end conversation," she declared firmly, wiping her hands on her jumpsuit legs where the oils and grime would eventually flake off. "Let's get back to the job at hand. Where did you stash my blaster?"

Luke didn't move. "I know you don't remember much about your past," he said quietly. "For whatever it's worth, I understand how you feel."

"Thanks," Mara growled. "That certainly helps."

"Would you like to have that past back again?"

She frowned at him, conflicting emotions surging suddenly against each other. "What do you mean?" she asked cautiously.

"There are techniques Jedi can use to pull out buried memories," he said. "And you could be a Jedi, Mara. You could be a powerful Jedi."

"Right," Mara bit out. "All I have to do is declare I'm ready to serve the galaxy, right?"

Luke's forehead creased, and she caught the flicker of puzzlement from him. "What is it about that that scares you?" he asked. "You've served and worked with people all your life—Palpatine, Karrde, Leia and Han and me. And once you've offered your loyalty, it's for keeps. You can do this—I know you can."

Mara squeezed her hand into a fist, half minded to close the subject again and this time make sure she sat on the lid. But deep inside she knew he deserved an answer on this one. "I can't just offer that kind of blank-line invitation," she said. "Sure I can be loyal; but only to the people *I* choose to be loyal to. I'm not ready to open myself up to anyone who walks in off the street."

She grimaced. "Besides, I keep remembering stories about how the last step to becoming a Jedi is usually making some supreme and rather ugly personal sacrifice. I'm not crazy about *that* one, either."

"It's not always as bad as it seems," Luke said, and Mara could sense his discomfort as unpleasant memories of his own floated back to the surface. "Just before he died, Master Yoda told me that before I would truly be a Jedi I needed to face Vader again. I jumped to the conclusion that that meant I had to either kill him or let him kill me. As it turned out, it didn't happen either way."

"But you had to be willing to make that sacrifice if necessary," Mara pointed out. "Thanks, but I'm not interested."

"Then you automatically limit your capabilities," Luke said. "If you aren't willing to make a commitment—"

"Commitment?" Mara snorted. "*You're* the one telling *me* about commitment? What about Callista, or Gaeriel, or any of the other women you've brushed paths with over the past ten years? Where's been the commitment there?"

Luke's flash of anger was so sudden and so unexpected it physically shocked her back against the stone wall. "You should talk," he snapped. "What about Lando? Huh?"

For a long moment they just glared at each other. Mara held her breath, bracing herself for another outburst, stories of uncontrolled Jedi anger running ominously through her mind.

But instead, she felt his anger drain away, replaced by shame and a deep embarrassment. "I'm sorry," he said, dropping his eyes away from her face. "That was uncalled for."

"No, I'm the one who should apologize," Mara said, trying to hide her own guilt feelings from him and knowing she was being only partly successful. She knew better than to fight like that. "I know how you felt about those women, and what happened to them. I'm sorry."

"That's all right," Luke murmured. "What happened to them was probably partly my fault. Maybe even mostly my fault. I'm the one who dabbled in the dark side, not them."

"You acknowledge your mistakes, and learn from them," Mara reminded him. "Then you pick up and move on. It's time to pick up and move on."

"I suppose." Still not looking at her, he climbed to his feet. "You're right—we should get moving. I had the Qom Jha make some measurements while you were sleeping, and it looks like the upper door out of here should let us out in one of the top three floors of the fortress. Let's try that approach."

"Just a second," Mara said, looking up at him. She had promised herself—rather cavalierly, she realized in retrospect—that she wasn't going to tell him this until he point-blank asked her about it. But her silence was childish. Anyway, the accusation he'd just thrown in her face was probably close enough. "You wanted to know about Lando and me. Right?"

She saw the twitch in his neck. "That's all right," he said. "It's really none of my business."

"I'm making it your business," Mara said, getting to her feet so she could look him straight in the eye. "What was between Lando and me was . . . absolutely nothing."

His eyes flicked suspiciously to hers. "What do you mean?"

"I mean just what I said: absolutely nothing," she repeated. "Karrde had an important mission for me to carry out, and because Lando had supplied the starting point he invited himself along. The—well, personal aspects to the whole thing were nothing but window dressing to keep people from figuring out what we were up to."

She could feel Luke probing at the edges of her mind. "You could have told me," he said, not quite accusingly.

"You could have asked me," she countered. "You never seemed all that interested."

He grimaced, and she could feel a fresh wave of embarrassment wash over him. "I didn't, did I?" he admitted.

"You learn, and move on," Mara reminded him. "Actually, if you want to come right down to it, you were the one who got the whole thing started in the first place. Remember that beckon call you found on Dagobah and took to Lando's place on Nkllon?"

Luke looked at her sharply. "Yes. In fact, I was just thinking about it a few days ago. I wondered why it had suddenly come to mind."

"Proddings of the Force, no doubt," Mara said. It was as good an answer as any. "It turns out that particular beckon call used to belong to someone Karrde once knew who had dropped out of sight some years back. Fellow named Jorj Car'das—ever hear of him?"

Luke shook his head. "No."

"Apparently, not a lot of people have," she said. "Made things so much more challenging. Anyway, with the beckon call we had a starting point, and Karrde asked me to try to track him down. And as I said, Lando—smelling profit, no doubt—insisted on tagging along."

"Must have been a long search," Luke murmured. "The stories of you and Lando . . ."

"It took some years," Mara said. "Off and on work, of course." She lifted her eyebrows. "For whatever it's worth, the romance part of the cover story drove me crazy. But finding Car'das was important to Karrde, so I stuck with it. Like you said, loyalty."

She hissed gently between her teeth with the memories. "Though it did prove exceptionally embarrassing at times. There was one particular week on M'haeli where Lando was trying to sugar-talk the Vicebaron Sukarian out of some information we needed. I had to become a giddy, vacant-brained bit of decorative fluff, because Sukarian automatically put that class of woman beneath his contempt and the role gave me the freedom of movement I needed. The worst part was that Solo caught me in the act with a comm relay when I thought it was Sukarian calling. I've never quite had the nerve to ask him what he thought of that."

"I don't think it would have ruined his opinion of you," Luke said, his voice an odd mixture of support, gallantry, and lingering embarrassment. "Though I imagine Sukarian's opinion is probably beyond repair at this point."

"Oh, I don't think so," Mara assured him. "I usually wore one of Lando's shirts during Sukarian's late-night visits and comm calls, and I made sure to leave one of them hanging on the open door of his private office safe. After I'd gutted it."

Luke smiled. A tentative, still somewhat shamefaced smile, but a genuine smile nevertheless. At this point, that was enough. "His reaction must have been interesting."

Mara nodded. "I like to think so."

"Yes." Luke took a deep breath, and she could sense him forcing old memories and extraneous thoughts to the back of his mind. "But as you said, we've got a job to do," he said briskly, "and it's going to be a long climb. Let's pack up the gear and get going."

It was, as Luke had estimated from the numbers the Qom Jha had gathered for him, indeed a long climb. Nearly as long as it had been from the bottom of the hidden stairway to that first door, in fact. And with Mara's muscles still recovering from five days of idleness, and Luke himself therefore handling Artoo and all the rest of their equipment, it should have been something of a strain.

But to his mild astonishment, it wasn't. And it didn't take any deep Jedi insight to understand why.

The barrier he had set up between him and Mara was gone.

The odd part was that he hadn't even realized there had been a barrier there. The communication they had together—their ability to sense each other's thoughts and emotions—had been so close that he'd simply assumed that was as strong as it got.

He'd been wrong. He'd been *very* wrong.

It was an exhilarating experience; and yet, at the same time, a somewhat intimidating one as well. He'd experienced close-mind contact with other people on occasion, but never to the same level as he was experiencing now. Mara's thoughts and emotions seemed to flow over him, their level and intensity now seemingly limited only by her personal barriers, as his own thoughts and emotions flowed the other direction back to her. There was a new rapport between them, a deepening of their old relationship that he only now realized how sorely he'd missed.

Confession, apology, and forgiveness, Aunt Beru had been fond of reminding him, were the tools friends used to break walls down into bridges. Seldom if ever in his life had he had that truth so graphically demonstrated.

With concern for Mara's physical condition and stamina foremost in his mind, he made sure the party took frequent rest breaks as they climbed, a policy that drove Mara just slightly less crazy than it did the Qom Jha. But he insisted, and as a result it took them nearly an hour to reach their target door. But when they did, at least, Mara was fully ready to go.

"All right, here's the plan," Luke told her, stretching out with the Force. As near as he could tell, the entire area outside the hidden door was clear. "We'll leave Artoo and the Qom Jha in here and do a little reconnoiter on our own."

"Sounds good." Mara pulled out her blaster and checked it, and Luke could sense her working to control her private misgivings about going back in there. Understandable, of course; she was the one who'd gotten shot. Luke had had something of the same trouble the first time he'd gone back to visit Cloud City. "How about leaving one of our comlinks here with them?"

"Good idea," Luke agreed, pulling his comlink from his belt and putting it in Artoo's light-duty grasping arm. "Don't forget and turn it off," he admonished the droid.

Artoo warbled indignantly, the translation scrolling across the datapad. "Yes, I know," Luke assured him. "I was just kidding."

"What?" Mara asked.

"He said turning off comlinks at critical moments was Threepio's trick," Luke told her. "Private joke. You ready?"

He could sense her reaching out to the Force for calm. "Ready," she said. "Let's do it."

The secret door, gratifyingly enough, opened as quietly as the other one had. With Luke in the lead, they stepped out, closing the door behind them.

"Now *this*," Mara said quietly in his ear, "is like the Hijarna fortress."

Luke nodded acknowledgment, looking around. They were in a vast chamber, with short wall segments scattered around apparently at random linking the floor with the relatively low ceiling. The shiny wall coverings, elaborate flooring, and wall sconces they'd seen below were absent, leaving nothing but unadorned and unrelieved black stone. Despite that, though, the place seemed oddly airy. "Doesn't look like our friends downstairs are using this area," he said. "I wonder why."

Mara took a few steps to the side and pointed around the end of one of the wall segments. "There's your answer," she said. "Come on—let's go see."

She disappeared around the wall. Luke followed, noticing for the first time a gentle flow of air coming from that direction.

And the reason for it was quickly clear. Beyond the wall, at the far side of the room, the black stone had been gashed open to the sky.

"Collateral damage from the battle that knocked down that tower, I'll bet," Mara said, already crossing to the gash.

"Be careful," Luke warned her, hurrying to catch up.

"Yeah, yeah," Mara said. She reached the gash and cautiously looked out. "I was right," she said, pointing. "There it is. Or what's left of it."

Luke reached her side and looked out. They were looking across a vast, circular rooftop that slanted downward from their position at a reasonably steep angle. The stub of Mara's ruined tower was ahead of them and slightly to the left, eighty meters or so away. The distance and dim sunlight made it hard to tell for sure, but to Luke's eye the jagged edge looked slightly melted. "And you say this stone absorbs turbolaser fire," he said.

"Like a very dry sponge," Mara agreed grimly. "Whoever the builders of this place were, they must have had some impressive enemies."

"Let's hope they were satisfied with wrecking that one tower and then went away," Luke said, giving the rest of the rooftop a quick but careful examination. Symmetrically placed on the right side of the slanting rooftop was another tower, this one undamaged, stretching a good ninety meters into the sky and topped with a ring of ominous-looking protrusions. Weapons systems, undoubtedly. At the far end of the roof, almost two hundred meters from where he and Mara stood, he could see twin bumps that seemed to extend outward from the roof and then continue down the wall on that side. Twin guardhouses, possibly, flanking the main entrance. Beyond the roof, he could see a smooth surface stretching through the craggy mountaintop away from the fortress that could only be an access road. In the center of the fortress was a thirty-meter-long structure whose flat-topped roof extended horizontally out from the main rooftop, making the whole thing look rather like a round-cornered wedge that had been stuck on as an afterthought.

"There's a landing pad on top," Mara said, pointing to the structure. "You can just make out the markings."

Luke nodded. The markings were dim, but visible enough when you knew to look for them. "They probably have lights they can turn on when something friendly is on its way in."

"With turbolasers ready at the top of that tower in case they're not so friendly." Easing through the gap in the wall, Mara took a few steps out onto the rooftop, peering toward the landing pad. "Looks like the area under the pad is open in front," she reported. "Probably their hangar. Might be a handy place to make for if we ever get caught too far away from our exit." She turned back around—

And her breath caught, a surge of surprise shooting through her. "Whoa," she said, her eyes tracking upward. "Come take a look at this."

Maneuvering through the crack, Luke crossed to her side and turned around. Rising from atop the room they'd just been in was yet another tower.

And it had friends. Spaced around the curve of the fortress rooftop to the left were three more, all of the same design. Even with Luke's skewed perspective, he could tell that these four rear towers were both thicker and a good twenty meters taller than the single one standing below them.

And as with the one below, each of these was also crowned by a ring of weapons emplacements.

"This must have been one impressive place in its heyday," Mara commented. Her voice was steady, but Luke could tell that she was feeling the same vague uneasiness he was. "Like the one on Hijama. I wish to blazes I knew what they were built to protect."

"Or to defend against," Luke added, taking one last look around the rooftop. No lights; no movement; no signs of life at all. "Let's get back inside and find the way down."

The way down was on the far side of one of the other wall segments: a smaller version of the spiral slideway they'd used in the barracks section down below. Unlike that one, though, the slideway here wasn't moving. "Either damaged or shut down for lack of use," Mara said, easing a cautious eye over the edge. "Next level down doesn't look inhabited, either."

"This whole section is probably out of use," Luke said as they started down. "The way the roof slopes toward the broken tower, each of the levels ought to have a little more floor space as we go down. They've probably set up shop on the larger levels."

"Makes sense," Mara agreed. "Let's keep going until we reach a floor with a working slideway somewhere on it. That should be either their highest working level or close to it."

The floors did indeed extend farther outward as they continued down, with the pattern of random wall segments changing with each level. It wasn't until the fourth level that Luke finally caught the faint hum of working machinery. "I think we're here," he murmured, shifting his grip on his lightsaber and stretching out with the Force. There still didn't seem to be anyone nearby.

"Looks like it," Mara agreed, cupping a hand around one ear. "That sounds like one of the slideways. Shall we take a look?"

Luke nodded. "I'll go first. You stay behind me."

He headed out, moving as silently as he could across the empty space, trying to ignore Mara's annoyance from behind him. She could call it overprotectiveness if she wanted—and she undoubtedly was calling it exactly that—but after watching her do five days in a healing trance he much preferred to err on the side of caution. He reached one of the rare—at least on this level—wall segments and eased an eye around it. Beyond it, set right up against the far wall, was the spiral slideway they had heard. "All right," Luke murmured over his shoulder. "Real easy, now—"

He sensed Mara's emotional call; but it wasn't coming from directly behind him. He glanced around, feeling a flash of annoyance of his own as he spotted her standing at the corner of one of the other wall segments twenty meters off to his left. She beckoned to him, a quick, impatient gesture.

And there was a sudden sense of dread in her emotions . . .

He made it to her side in less than ten seconds. "What is it?" he hissed.

She nodded toward the wall, a silent churning in her eyes and mind. "Around there," she said.

Lightsaber ready in his hand, Luke slid around the end of the wall segment.

Beyond it was a large open space that had been set up as a sort of command center, though it was currently as unoccupied as everywhere else they'd been today. Two circles of command consoles had been laid out, the boards and displays winking status lights toward the empty chairs in front of them. To one side, a larger and more elaborate chair ringed by its own status boards had been set up on a meter-high platform where it could overlook the entire operation.

And in the center of it all was a sight that sent a shiver of memory along Luke's spine: a holographic map of the galaxy, with the sectors of the New Republic, the Empire, and the rest of the known regions marked out in a bewildering array of a dozen different colors. The whole variegated mosaic stretched across perhaps a quarter of the huge spiral, fading into neutral white where the edges of the Outer Rim Territories gave way to the vastness of the Unknown Regions beyond.

It was a duplicate of the galactic holo Emperor Palpatine had had in his throne room in Mount Tantiss.

Luke swallowed, tearing his eyes away from the holo to give the surrounding equipment a closer look. Yes, the consoles were indeed Imperial issue: status and computer-access boards from a Star Destroyer or other major capital ship. The chairs, likewise, were straight from a Star Destroyer's bridge crew pits.

And the overseer chair and boards were those of an Imperial fleet admiral. Such as the one Grand Admiral Thrawn would have used.

He felt the whisper of air as Mara came up close beside him. "I think we've found our link to the Imperials," he told her. "It looks like even Palpatine may have had a hand in this place."

Her hair swished against his shoulder as she shook her head. "You're missing the point, Luke," she muttered. "Look at that holo. I mean really *look* at it."

Luke frowned, focusing on the galactic spiral again. What in space was she referring to?

And then, abruptly, he caught his breath. No. No—he was seeing things. Surely he was seeing things.

But he wasn't. At the edge of the known galaxy, where Palpatine's holo had shown only the white stars of the Unknown Regions, an entirely new area had been colored in.

A *huge* new area.

"Funny, isn't it," Mara said, the dread still swirling through her. "He was exiled from the Imperial court, you know. Just summarily thrown out."

"Who was?" Luke asked.

"Grand Admiral Thrawn," she said. "Picked the wrong side in one of the political battles that were always going on there and lost. Everyone else in the cabal wound up demoted or imprisoned or else reassigned to a semiprivate torture chamber like garrison duty in the Outer Rim. But not Thrawn. Oh, no. Even the Outer Rim was too good for this ungrateful alien who'd been accepted into Imperial society and paid them back for their kindness with a slap in the face. No, they had to come up with something very special for him."

"And that something was exile to the Unknown Regions?"

Mara nodded. "If the Outer Rim was a torture cell, the Unknown Regions was a fully populated rancor pit," she said. "So with some prodding—and probably a lot of deal-making—they got Palpatine to put him aboard a Star Destroyer and send him on a one-way trip past the Outer Rim."

She snorted out a derisive laugh. "And just to add insult to injury, they managed to make it a mapping expedition. Imagine—one of the best strategists the Empire had ever known being reduced to mapping duty. Ruining his life and his reputation with a single stroke. I'll bet they were chuckling together about it for years afterward."

Luke shook his head. "I seem to be missing the joke."

"So did they," Mara said, her dark mood darkening even further. "The joke is that it apparently never occurred to any of them that Palpatine was always one step ahead of whatever was happening in his court. And if *he* was a step ahead, a strategist like Thrawn was at least *two* steps ahead."

Luke's mouth felt dry. "Are you saying that Thrawn and Palpatine had the whole thing planned out from the beginning?"

"Of course they did." Mara gestured at the holo. "Just *look* at all the territory he opened up. He couldn't possibly have done that by himself, with just a single Star Destroyer. Palpatine must have been feeding him men and ships all along the way."

"But that can't all be Imperial territory," Luke said. "I mean . . . it can't."

"Why not?" Mara countered. "Oh, I agree there probably aren't more than a few actual colonies out there. But you can bet there are Imperial garrisons scattered all over the place, plus intel centers and listening posts and probably a few full-blown shipyards. And if I know Thrawn, probably a whole network of alliances with the natives, too."

"But if that's Imperial territory, why hasn't the Empire made any use of it?" Luke argued. "I've seen the data, Mara—they're down to practically nothing over there."

"It's obvious, isn't it?" she said quietly. "They're not using it because they don't know it's there."

For a long minute neither of them spoke. Luke gazed at the holo, listening to the distant hum of the spiral slideway, the terrible implications of those gently glowing lights tumbling over each other in his mind. There had to be the equivalent of two hundred fifty sectors there—nearly thirty times the Empire's current size.

With thirty times the Empire's number of warships, garrisons, and shipyards? Very possibly. If all those resources were suddenly put at Bastion's disposal . . . "We need more information," he said, starting toward the console rings. "Let's see if there's a computer jack Artoo can plug into."

"Risky," Mara warned. "This is a command center, and command centers always have security flags set up to catch unauthorized access."

He stopped, grimacing. Unfortunately, she had a point. "All right, then," he said, turning again to face her. "What's *your* plan?"

"We go directly to the source." Mara took a deep breath. "I go downstairs and talk to them."

Luke felt his mouth drop open. "And you call *my* plans risky?"

"You have a better suggestion?"

"That's beside the point," he growled. "Anyway, if someone's going to go down there, it ought to be me."

"Not a chance," Mara said firmly. "Point one: they shot at you on the way in, but they didn't shoot at me. Point two: you said yourself you had the feeling they wanted to see me. Point three: if the situation degenerates to the point where a rescue is called for, you and your Jedi skills are better against a crowd than mine. And point four—"

With a tight smile, she unhooked her lightsaber and stepped over to him. "Point four is that they may not know the extent of my Force skills," she said, handing him the weapon. "If shove comes to shake, that may give me the edge I'd need."

Luke fingered her lightsaber, feeling the familiar coolness in his hand. His own first lightsaber, the one Obi-Wan had given him, which he had given her in turn on the palace rooftop on Coruscant. He'd been younger than she was when he'd first taken that lightsaber into danger. Younger, less experienced, and far brasher. But still . . .

"And the last thing I need right now is for you to start getting all overprotective," Mara added, just the hint of a warning glare in her eyes. "I've survived just fine all these years. I can take care of myself."

Luke locked eyes with her. Odd, he thought, that he'd forgotten just how brilliant a green those eyes were. Though perhaps it was just the lighting. "No way I can talk you out of it?" he asked, trying one last time.

"Not unless you can come up with a better plan," she said, pulling out her comlink and sleeve blaster. "Here—there's no point in my keeping these. They'll just take them away from me anyway. I'll keep my Blas-Tech; they'd be suspicious if I came in completely unarmed."

Luke took the comlink and sleeve blaster from her, his hand lingering on hers before she withdrew it, oddly unwilling to let it go. "I wish we hadn't left the other comlink with Artoo," he said. "You could have kept this one and I'd have been able to listen in on what was going on."

"If something goes sour, you might need to whistle up the Qom Jha in a hurry," she reminded him. "Anyway, can't you follow me with the Force?"

"I can follow your presence," Luke said. "I can get your emotions and probably some images that way. But I can't get much in the way of words."

"Too bad you're not Palpatine," Mara commented, busying herself with removing her sleeve holster. "I could talk to him just fine."

Luke felt a stab of guilt and shame, her earlier indictment of his dark side dabbling flooding back. She caught the emotion, or else the expression on his face, and smiled tightly. "Hey, I was kidding," she assured him, handing him the sleeve holster. "Look, you just follow what you can. I'll give you a full report on the details when I get back."

"All right," Luke said. "Be careful, okay?"

To his surprise, she reached out and took his hand. "I'll be fine," she told him, squeezing his hand briefly before letting go. "See you."

And with that she was gone, slipping out of the command center and around the wall toward the slideway.

With a sigh, Luke stepped over to the nearby wall segment and sank down into a crouch with his back pressed against it. Closing his eyes for better concentration, he stretched out with the Force.

In times past, on Dagobah and Tierfon and other places, he'd been able to use the Force to obtain glimpses of future places and events. Now, as Mara headed down the slideway, he tried to focus that same ability onto real-time observation, hoping to be able to see what was happening to her.

It worked, too, at least after a fashion. The image he got of Mara and her surroundings was faint and foggy, heavily colored by her emotions and shifting mental state, and with the same discomfiting tendency to ripple or metamorphose that seemed to be characteristic of Jedi visions in general. But with Mara's mind there to act as anchor, he was able to quickly drag the images back to something at least vaguely understandable. It was hardly ideal, but it seemed clear that it was all he was going to get.

The slideway from this level seemed to be roughly the same size as the one they had used to get down from the roof. Mara moved to the inner section and headed down, apparently making no attempt at concealment. The lack of any sudden combat twinges in her emotions as she reached the next level implied she didn't see anyone, though he had the impression that she was still hearing distant sounds.

She made no move to get off at this level, but let the slideway carry her on down. The next level was more of the same, with no one coming near the slideway. Luke could sense a definite annoyance beginning to seep through the alertness in Mara's mind, an annoyance aimed both at the aliens' seeming disinterest in her and at their incompetence at basic internal security. She passed that level, and the next, and started down toward the next—

And suddenly there was a dizzying jolt that slammed like a groundquake through her emotions, accompanied by a brief flash of pain.

Luke stiffened, eyes jerking open as he scrambled to his feet. But even as he did so he felt a warning flicker of reassurance from her, together with understanding of what had just happened. Without warning, the slideway section she'd been riding on had suddenly reversed direction, yanking her feet out from under her and slamming her flat on her chest on the ramp.

And as the moment of dizziness from the impact faded away, her combat emotions flared to full alertness.

She was no longer alone.

Luke clenched his hands into helpless fists as he rode her emotions to try to pierce the hazy image. There were several people standing around her, of the same species as those they'd tangled with once already.

And as near as he could tell through the wavering view, one of them was calling Mara by name.

For a moment he continued to talk to her, and though Luke couldn't hear any of the words he had the impression that he was asking her to accompany them farther into the fortress. She agreed. There was a flicker of inevitability as they took her BlasTech, and then the whole group was walking away from the slideway down a corridor that Mara recognized as decorated similarly to the barracks area they'd seen farther below.

Soon—all too soon—the group reached an open door. Another exchange of unheard words, a suppressed flutter of uneasiness from Mara, and she stepped alone through the door into the room beyond.

From her thoughts he could tell that there were others waiting inside for her. One of them—possibly more than one—called out to her as she moved farther inside. Mara answered, surges and flickers of emotion marking bits of information that the vagueness of their contact prevented Luke from getting himself. She continued to walk farther into the room—

And without warning, right in the middle of a step, the touch of her mind cut abruptly off, leaving Luke staring at the quiet lights of the command center. Heart pounding in his chest, he stretched out with the Force, trying to reestablish the contact. *Mara? Mara!*

But it was no use. There was no response, no returning contact, no sense of her presence. Nothing at all.

She was gone.

CHAPTER

Mara took in the room in a glance as she stepped through the doorway. It was long and narrow, stretching perhaps fifty meters back from the door but no more than five meters wide. Near the far wall was a solid-looking chair, facing away from her. Five meters beyond that, right at the room's back wall, were six more of the blue-skinned aliens, all wearing the same tight-fitting burgundy patchwork-design outfits as the ones who had escorted her here from the slideway. And like her escort, each of the aliens was wearing Imperial ranking bars on their chests beneath the high-topped black collars.

But even as her glance took in those details, her main attention was caught by the man in the center of the group, seated in a duplicate of the empty chair facing him a few meters away. His hair was gray, his skin lined with age; but his eyes were alert and shrewd, and his back was straight and proud.

And he was wearing the uniform and insignia of an Imperial admiral.

"So here you are at last, Mara Jade," he said, waving her forward with a gnarled hand. "I must say, you took your time."

"Sorry to have kept you waiting," Mara countered with an edge of sarcasm as she walked toward them. She could feel Luke's concern and nervousness at the back of her mind, and tried to send him a reassurance she didn't entirely feel. These people knew who she was and presumably what she was; and yet here they were, letting her move freely toward them. It all looked far too casual, and she didn't like it one bit. "If your people hadn't been so trigger-poppy, I'd have been here a lot sooner."

The admiral bowed his head briefly. "My apologies. For whatever it's worth, it was an accident. Please, come sit down."

Mara continued forward, trying to watch all of them at once, her senses alert for trouble. If they had a trap set, it would be sprung somewhere before she got too close to them . . .

And without warning, right in the middle of a step, Luke's presence suddenly vanished from her mind.

Her brain froze in shock, sheer momentum keeping her feet moving. *Luke? Luke! Come on, where are you?*

But there was no response. No emotion, no sense of mind or thought, no sense of presence at all. Incredibly, impossibly, he was gone.

Gone.

"Come sit down," the admiral said again. "I imagine you must be quite worn out after all you've been through."

"You're too kind," Mara said, the words sounding distant and mechanical through the pounding of blood in her ears as she forced her feet to keep moving her forward. What in the worlds could possibly have happened to him?

There could only be one answer. Somehow, they'd gotten past his Jedi senses, had penetrated his Jedi powers, and had launched a sudden, undetected, and unblocked attack.

And Luke Skywalker, Jedi Master, was unconscious.

Or dead.

The thought slashed into her mind, cutting through her heart like a jagged blade. No—it couldn't be. It *couldn't.* Not now.

The gray-haired man was still gazing at her, a thoughtful look on his face, and with an agonized effort Mara shoved the fear and pain away to the back of her mind. If Luke was merely unconscious, they could still get out of this. If he was dead, she would most likely soon be joining him. Either way, this was no time to let her emotions muddy her thinking.

She made it the rest of the way to the chair and sank carefully into it. "You don't need to look quite so worried," the admiral said soothingly. "We have no intention of harming you."

"Of course not," Mara said, hearing the bitterness in her voice. "Just like you had no intention of harming me on my last trip in here?"

The admiral's lip twitched. "As I said before, that was a regrettable accident," he said. "They were shooting at the vermin flying around near you—we've had some problems in the past with them getting inside. When you started shooting back, I'm afraid they jumped to the wrong conclusion. My deepest apologies."

"That makes me feel so much better," Mara growled. "Now what?"

The admiral seemed mildly surprised. "We talk," he said. "Why else do you think we gave you our location in the first place? We wanted you to come see us."

"Ah," Mara said. So her guess earlier had been right—those two ships *had* deliberately flown off on vectors that would lead her here.

Unless, of course, he was lying after the fact to cover up his pilots' blunders. "You could have just sent me an invitation," she told him, feeling her forehead crease slightly as she stretched out toward him with the

Force. Odd; for some reason, she couldn't seem to touch him. Not him, not the aliens flanking him. "Or would that have been too straightforward and easy?"

The admiral smiled knowingly. "With an open invitation I doubt you would have come alone. Something more vague seemed a better arrangement. I apologize for not having an escort waiting, by the way—your landing caught us a bit by surprise."

"As did your arrival earlier inside the fortress," the alien standing at the admiral's right added, his voice smooth and cultured, his glowing red eyes steady on Mara. "If we'd known you were coming our people would have been much more careful with their charrics. May I ask how you managed to penetrate the fortress without being spotted?"

"We turned ourselves into vermin and flew in, of course," Mara told him. "It was faster than walking."

"Of course," the admiral said with a smile. "Or perhaps you scaled up the side of the fortress and came in through one of the cracks?"

Mara shook her head. "Sorry. Trade secret."

"Ah," the admiral said, still smiling. "It's not important; I was merely curious. The point is that you *are* here, Mara, just as we wished. May I call you Mara, by the way? Or would you prefer Captain Jade or some other title?"

"Call me anything you want," Mara told him. "And what should I call *you*? Or doesn't anyone in this place have a name?"

"All thinking beings have names, Mara," the man said. "Mine is Admiral Voss Parck. It's a pleasure to meet you at last."

"Likewise," Mara said, staring at him as a ripple of shock went through her. Voss Parck: the Victory Star Destroyer captain who had found Thrawn on a deserted world and brought him to the Imperial court. And who had subsequently joined him in his shame and supposed exile from the Empire.

But the man in front of her . . .

"I imagine I look rather older than you might have expected," Parck said offhandedly. "Assuming you had any expectations at all, of course. I may have overly flattered myself to assume the Emperor's Hand would even remember my name, let alone my face."

"I remember both," Mara said. "You were one of the people every faction in the court used as an example of what not to do in the middle of a political fight." She glanced at the aliens. "But then, those were the same people who also thought Palpatine sent Thrawn out here as a punishment. So what did they know?"

"And you think Mitth'raw'nuruodo's mission was otherwise?" the alien at Parck's right asked.

"I know otherwise," Mara assured him, looking him up and down. "Tell me, Admiral, does the whole race talk like Thrawn? Or is this some special cultural training you give your troops in case they're all invited out for High Day drinks?"

The alien's eyes narrowed—"Calm yourself, Stent," Parck said dryly, holding up a hand. "You must understand that one of Mara Jade's most subtle weapons has always been her talent for irritating people. Irritated people don't think clearly, you see."

"Or maybe I just don't like any of you very much," Mara said, feeling a touch of annoyance at Parck's quick and casual insight. Usually her enemies didn't figure that one out nearly so quickly. The slower ones never figured it out at all. "But enough about me. Let's hear about this grand push of yours out into the Unknown Regions. You gave up a lot, after all: Coruscant, the status and camaraderie of the Imperial Fleet—" Deliberately, she looked at Stent. "Civilization."

Stent's eyes narrowed again, but Parck merely smiled. "You've met Thrawn," he said, his voice softening to near-reverence. "Any true warrior would have given up whatever was necessary for the chance to serve under him."

"Except those of his own people, I gather," Mara countered. "Or did I hear the story wrong of how he wound up on Coruscant?"

"No, I'm sure you heard correctly," Parck said with a shrug. "But like everything else people think they know about Thrawn, that particular story is somewhat incomplete."

"Is it, now," Mara said, leaning back in her chair and crossing her legs, a posture designed by its apparent helplessness to put suspicious people at ease. With the same motion she surreptitiously rocked the chair back a bit, trying to gauge its weight. Very heavy, unfortunately, which eliminated it as a grab-and-throw weapon. "I seem to have some time on my hands. Why don't you start at the beginning?"

Stent laid his hand on Parck's shoulder. "Admiral, I'm not sure—"

"It's all right, Stent," Parck calmed him, his eyes steady on Mara. "We can hardly expect her help unless she has all the facts, now, can we?"

Mara frowned. "My help in what?"

"It started better than half a century ago," Parck said, ignoring her question. "Back when the Outbound Flight project was preparing to fly, just before the Clone Wars broke out. Well before your time, of course—I don't know if you'd even have heard of it."

"I've read about the Outbound Flight," Mara said. "A group of Jedi Masters and others decided to head out to another galaxy and see what was there."

"Ultimately, their destination was indeed another galaxy." Parck nodded. "But before that particular expedition began, it was decided to send them and their ship on a, shall we say, shakedown cruise: a great circle through part of the vast Unknown Regions of our own galaxy."

He waved a hand back toward Stent and the guards. "A route, as it turned out, that was to bring it across the edge of territory controlled by the Chiss."

Chiss. So that was what they called themselves. Mara ran the name through her memory, searching for any reference the Emperor might have made to them. Nothing. "And the Chiss didn't feel like being good hosts that day?"

"Actually, the ruling Chiss families never had the chance to decide one way or the other," Parck said. "Palpatine had already decided that the Jedi represented a grave threat to the Old Republic, and had sent an assault force into the region to quietly take care of Outbound Flight when they showed up."

"And there they were, busily setting up their ambush, when Thrawn found them."

He shook his head. "You have to understand the situation, Mara, to truly appreciate it. On one side were handpicked units of Palpatine's own private army, equipped with fifteen top-line combat ships. On the other side were Commander Mitth'raw'nuruodo of the Chiss Expansionary Defense and perhaps twelve small and insignificant border patrol ships."

"I appreciate it just fine," Mara said, suppressing a shudder. "How badly did Thrawn slaughter them?"

"Utterly," Parck said, the ghost of a smile creasing his face. "I believe only a single one of Palpatine's ships remained capable of flight, and that only because Thrawn wanted some of the invaders left alive to interrogate.

"Fortunately for that remnant, and perhaps one day for the galaxy as a whole, among the survivors was the leader of the task force, one of Palpatine's advisers. A man named Kinman Doriana."

Mara swallowed. *That* name she most certainly *did* remember. He'd been Palpatine's right-hand man, supposedly one of the grand architects of his rise to power. "I've heard it, yes," she said.

"I thought you would have," Parck said, nodding. "Very much a shadow adviser—few people ever even heard his name, let alone knew his true position and power. But among those who did it was sometimes speculated that his untimely death left a gap which Palpatine ultimately tried to fill with three other people: Darth Vader, Grand Admiral Thrawn—" He smiled again. "And you."

"You're too kind," Mara said evenly, not even a whisper of pride rising within her at such a statement. So she had indeed had position and authority in Palpatine's eyes, perhaps more than even she had realized.

But it didn't matter. That part of her life had died, unmourned, a long time ago. "You're very well informed, too."

"This was Thrawn's personal base," Parck said, waving a hand around him. "And information, as you may have noticed, was one of his few obsessions. The databases in the fortress core below us are possibly the most extensive in the galaxy."

"Magnificent, I'm sure," Mara said. "Too bad all his knowledge couldn't keep him from getting killed."

She had hoped to spark some kind of reaction from them. To her surprise, though, none of them so much as blinked. Parck, in fact, actually smiled. "Never assume, Mara," he warned. "But that's getting ahead of the story. Where were we?"

"Doriana and Outbound Flight," Mara said.

"Thank you," Parck said. "At any rate, Doriana explained the entire situation to Thrawn and convinced him that Outbound Flight had to be destroyed. Two weeks later, when the ship arrived in Chiss space, Thrawn was waiting."

"Good-bye, Outbound Flight," Mara murmured.

"Yes," Parck agreed. "But though that was the end of that, it was the beginning of trouble for Thrawn himself. The Chiss military philosophy, you see, did not recognize the morality of preemptive strikes. What Thrawn did was, in their minds, equivalent to murder."

Mara snorted gently. "No offense, Admiral, but it sounds to me like it's *your* perceptions that need an overhaul. How can the slaughter of a bunch of Jedi Masters minding their own business be anything *but* murder?"

Parck looked at her gravely. "You'll understand, Mara," he said, his voice almost trembling. "In time, you'll understand."

Mara frowned. The man was either a terrific actor or there was something buried in all of this that had him well and truly terrified. Again, she stretched out with the Force; again, she couldn't seem to touch him at all.

With an obvious effort, Parck pulled himself together. "But again, I'm getting ahead of myself. As I said, Thrawn's action did not sit well with the ruling Chiss families. He was able to talk his way clear and retain his position, but from that point on they watched him very carefully.

"And eventually, as he dealt with some of the Chiss's enemies, he pushed things just a little too far. He was brought up on charges, stripped of all rank, and sent into exile on an uninhabited world at the edge of Imperial space."

"Where who should show up but a Victory Star Destroyer," Mara said. "Captained by a man willing to take the risk of bringing him back to Coruscant." She raised her eyebrows. "Only it wasn't nearly as much of a risk as everyone thought, was it?"

Parck smiled. "It most certainly wasn't," he said. "In fact, I learned later that Palpatine had made at least two unsuccessful attempts over the years to contact the Chiss and offer Thrawn a position with his soon-to-be Empire. No, he was most pleased with my gift, though because of the political realities of the court he had to keep that pleasure hidden."

"So Thrawn went into private military training and eventually rose to the highest rank Palpatine could offer," Mara said. "And then, what, arranged to have himself sent back here so he could make the Chiss ruling families pay for what they'd done to him?"

Parck looked shocked. "Certainly not. The Chiss are his people, Mara—he has no interest in hurting them. Quite the opposite, in fact. He came back here to protect them."

"From what?"

Stent gave a contemptuous snort. "From what," he bit out harshly. "You soft, complacent female. You think that because you lounge around your quiet worlds behind a ring of warships that the rest of the galaxy is a safe place to live? There are a hundred different threats out there that would freeze your blood if you knew about them. The ruling families can't stop them; neither can any other power in the region. If our people are to be protected, it's up to us."

"And you are? You specifically, I mean?"

Stent drew himself up straighter. "We are Syndic Mitth'raw'nuruodo's Household Phalanx," he said, and there was no mistaking the pride in his tone. "We live only to serve him. And through him to serve the Chiss."

"Whether they want your help or not, I guess," Mara said, noting the alien's use of the present tense. There it was again: the assumption or belief that Thrawn wasn't dead. Could they be that out of touch? "Do they even know you're out here?"

"They know the forces of the Empire are out here," Parck said. "And while the ruling families pretend they don't know Stent and his unit are working with us, the average Chiss does in fact know. We have a steady flow of young Chiss arriving at our various bases and garrisons to enlist in our fight."

Mara suppressed a grimace. So they did indeed have bases out here. "Palpatine wouldn't have been very pleased to see aliens mixing with Imperial forces," she pointed out. "I doubt the current regime on Bastion would, either."

Parck's expression sobered. "Indeed," he said. "Which brings us to the problem and situation we now face. Many years ago Thrawn told us that if he was ever reported dead we should keep at our labors here and in the Unknown Regions, and to look for his return ten years afterward."

Mara blinked in disbelief. They really *were* out of touch. "It's going to be a long wait," she said, trying not to sound too sarcastic. "He was stabbed in the chest, right through the back of his command chair. Most people have a hard time recovering from that kind of treatment."

"Thrawn is not most people," Stent reminded her.

"Was," Mara said. "Not is; *was.* He died at Bilbringi."

"Did he?" Parck asked. "Did you ever see a body? Or hear anything about his supposed death that didn't come from the Imperials' own news sources?"

Mara opened her mouth . . . paused. Parck was leaning slightly toward her, a glint of anticipation in his eye. "Was that a rhetorical question?" she asked. "Or are you expecting me to have an actual answer?"

Parck smiled, leaning back in his chair again. "I told you she was quick," he said, looking up at Stent. "As a matter of fact, yes, we thought you might. You have complete access to Talon Karrde's information network, after all. If anyone would know the truth, it would be you."

A sudden jolt of understanding shot through Mara. "You weren't hunting Imperial connections when you buzzed the Cavrilhu base and Terrik's Star Destroyer, were you? You were hunting *me*."

"Very good, indeed," Parck said approvingly. "In fact, when Dreel spotted you near that Star Destroyer he thought you and Thrawn might already have come to an arrangement. Hence, his transmission asking Thrawn to make contact."

Mara shook her head. "Look, I know you've been out here a long time, and I realize it must have been hard for you. But it's time to face the hard, cold facts. Like it or not, Thrawn *is dead*."

"Really," Parck said. "Then why is the HoloNet buzzing with the news that he has returned and is making alliances?"

"And that he's been seen by many planetary and sector leaders," Stent put in. "Including the Diamalan Senator to Coruscant and former General Lando Calrissian."

Mara stared at him. *Lando?* "No," she said. "You're wrong. Or you're bluffing."

"I assure you—" Parck broke off, his eyes shifting to a point behind Mara as a breath of air on the back of her neck announced the door behind her had opened.

She turned, tensing. But it was only a youngish middle-aged man, walking with a slight limp along the left-hand wall of the long room toward her. Despite his age he wore the uniform of an Imperial TIE fighter pilot; between his graying goatee and similarly graying shock of dark hair he wore an almost unheard-of rarity: a black patch over his right eye. "Yes, General?" Parck called to him.

"Mid-course transmission from Sorn, Admiral," the man said, his one eye trained unblinkingly on Mara as he strode past her. "His pass through the Bastion system was inconclusive. Lots of rumors and speculations, but no hard evidence." He paused. "But the rumors *do* say Thrawn is currently there."

"Wait a minute," Mara put in, frowning. "You know where Bastion is?"

"Oh, yes," Parck assured her. "Thrawn anticipated that the seat of government might periodically change, and he wanted us to know where it was at any given time. So he had a special homing device installed in a dummy file in the central Imperial Records Library, reasoning that where the government went the library would soon follow."

"It's a device of Chiss design," Stent added with clear pride. "Totally dormant except when in hyperspace, a time when virtually no one thinks to do scans for such things. We've followed Bastion's movement from system to system with a great deal of interest."

"Indeed." Parck looked at the pilot again. "Is Sorn on his way back?"

"He'll be here in about three hours." The pilot nodded at Mara. "Has she given you anything useful?"

"Not really," Parck said, looking at Mara as he gestured to the newcomer. "But I'm forgetting my manners. Mara Jade; this is General Baron"—he paused dramatically—"Soontir Fel."

Mara kept her face expressionless. Baron Soontir Fel. Once a legendary TIE fighter pilot, later turning his back on the Empire to become a member of Rogue Squadron, he had vanished years ago into a trap set by Imperial Intelligence Director Isard and never been heard of again. The general assumption had been that Isard had had him summarily executed for treason.

Yet here he was, apparently once again flying with Imperial forces. And a general, yet. "General Fel," she nodded acknowledgment. "Do I take it from the admiral's tone that I'm supposed to be impressed?"

The young Fel, she suspected, would have taken instant offense at that. But this older version merely favored her with a faint smile. "There's no time for pride out here, Jade," he said gravely. "Once you've joined us, you'll understand."

"I'm sure," Mara said, folding her arms across her chest and squeezing her hands tightly into fists with the effort as she stretched out with all her strength. The Force was there—she could feel it flowing through her. Yet for some reason she still couldn't touch any of them, human or Chiss. It was almost like the Force-suppressing effect of those sessile Myrkr creatures called ysalamiri. But that couldn't be it, because she could still feel the Force perfectly well. Besides, there weren't any of the creatures in the room with them—

She swallowed a sudden grimace, feeling like a fool as she focused on Parck and the Chiss standing with their backs to the wall. Of course there weren't any ysalamiri in the room—they were one room over, pressed up against the other side of the wall where they could protect her interrogators from her mind probes. They'd probably put the creatures along the sides, too; probably why Fel had been so careful to hug the wall on his way across the room. Maybe even scattered some above the ceiling—

She took a deep breath, a huge part of the tension in her chest abruptly easing. Of course there were ysalamiri in the ceiling. That was how and why her link to Luke had been so abruptly cut off.

Which meant he was still alive.

She took another breath, suddenly aware that Parck and Fel were both staring at her. "Such a gracious invitation," she said, trying to pick up on the threads of conversation before her silence became too blatant. "Sorry to disappoint you, but I already have a job."

But too late. "I see she's figured it out," Fel said conversationally.

"Yes," Parck said. "I'm rather surprised it took her this long, actually. Particularly since she noticed the ysalamiri effect as soon as she came within the effect of their shroud. I could see the break in her step."

"At least it proves she has Jedi abilities," Fel said. "Just as well we were prepared."

"I congratulate you all on your cleverness," Mara said, putting some scorn into her voice. "You are indeed the true heirs to Thrawn's genius and military might. Let's stop dancing around, shall we? What exactly do you want from me?"

"As General Fel has already said," Parck said. "We want you to join us."

Mara felt her eyes narrow. "You *are* joking."

"Not at all," Parck said. "In fact—"

"Admiral?" Stent interrupted, his head tilted slightly to one side as if listening to something. "Someone's just tried to access the Upper Command Room computer."

"Skywalker," Fel said with a nod. "Nice of him to save us the trouble of tracking him down. Have the Phalanx bring him here, Stent. Remind them that only those carrying ysalamiri are to approach him."

"Yes, sir." Stent stepped past Fel and headed along the wall at a fast walk, speaking rapidly in his own language as he headed for the door. As he passed Mara, she caught a glimpse of a small device in his ear—the Chiss version of a comlink, no doubt.

"He'll be joining us in a few minutes," Fel said, looking back at Mara. "You must rank very highly indeed in Coruscant's eyes for them to send Luke Skywalker himself to rescue you. I hope he won't resist to the point of the Chiss having to hurt him."

"I hope for the Chiss' sake they haven't bitten off more than they can swallow," Mara countered, trying to sound more confident than she felt. Luke had had to function under the handicap of ysalamiri before, but that had been a long time ago. "Speaking of getting hurt, General, what happened to your face? Or is that patch just something you wear to impress the natives?"

"I lost my eye in our final battle against one of the many would-be warlords out here," Fel said, his voice calm but with an edge to it. "Our medical replacement facilities are limited, and I opted to forgo a new eye in favor of others of my pilots who might need the operation." He smiled tightly, a glimpse of the younger, brasher Fel showing through the age and maturity. "Besides, even with one eye I'm still the best pilot around."

"I'm sure," Mara agreed. "But imagine what you'd be like with two of them again. And the way the war with the New Republic has dwindled down to basically nothing, I imagine the Empire's got a pretty good surplus of spare prosthetics. All it would take is you showing up and asking for one."

She looked back at Parck. "But of course, that would mean letting Bastion in on the big secret, which is apparently something you don't want to do. Why not?"

Parck sighed. "Because everything we've done here—everything we have here—really belongs to Thrawn. And at this point, we frankly don't know which side of your conflict he's going to come down on."

Mara blinked. "Excuse me? An Imperial Grand Admiral, and you don't know which side he's going to take?"

"The Empire has been whittled down to eight sectors," Fel reminded her. "Militarily, they're no longer a power even worth considering."

"And as you've already pointed out, they still have a lingering problem with anti-alien biases," Parck added. "On the other hand, Coruscant has serious problems of its own, most notably its inability to keep its members from fighting with each other."

"Which is where you come in," Fel said. "As the Emperor's Hand, you knew a great deal about the Empire and those in power there. On the other hand, as a friend of Skywalker and his associates, you're also well acquainted with the New Republic regime on Coruscant."

He smiled tightly. "And of course, as Talon Karrde's second-in-command, you know a great deal about everything else. You'd be invaluable in helping us end the conflict, unify this region, and begin preparations for the challenges ahead."

"Your expertise and knowledge are very important to us," Parck said. "Our attention has been necessarily turned outward, with the result that we're somewhat out of touch with matters in this part of space. We need someone who can fill that gap."

"And so naturally you thought of me," Mara said sardonically.

"Don't be so flippant," Fel admonished.

"I'm not being flippant; I'm being disbelieving," she countered. "I hardly think Thrawn would have approved of you hiring me as your local affairs adviser."

"On the contrary," Parck said. "Thrawn regarded you quite highly. I know for a fact that he intended to offer you a position with us once the Empire had regained its territory."

One of the Chiss beside Parck stirred, tilting his head as Stent had done earlier. "Admiral?" he said softly, squatting down beside the chair and whispering something into Parck's ear. Parck replied, and for a minute they held an inaudible conversation. Mara ran her eye over Fel and the five Chiss, mentally mapping out how she might be able to take them down if it came to a fight.

But the attempt was little more than a mental exercise, and she knew it. With their eyes steady on her, and their hands resting on their holstered weapons, there was no chance she could take out all of them before they got her. Not without the Force.

The conversation ended, and the Chiss stood back up and strode rapidly away along the wall. "Please excuse the interruption," Parck apologized as the alien left the room.

"No problem," Mara said. Down to four Chiss now, plus Fel and Parck. Still rotten odds. "Having trouble pinning Skywalker down?"

"Not really," Parck assured her.

"Glad to hear it," Mara said, wishing more than ever that she could pick up something of his thoughts. That exit hadn't looked like the departure of someone who wasn't really having trouble. If she only had some idea what Luke was up to . . . "So Thrawn intended to offer me a commission, did he?"

"He did indeed," Parck said. "He knew who all the best people were, both in overall skills and the kind of mental toughness he needed." He gestured toward Fel. "General Fel is a good example. His rebellion against Isard was of no consequence to Thrawn. What mattered was his feelings for the people and worlds of this region. So after Thrawn had Isard capture him—"

"Wait a minute," Mara interrupted. "*Thrawn* was involved with that?"

"It was entirely his plan," Fel said. "You don't think Isard could have come up with anything that clever, do you?" His mouth tightened, his remaining eye gazing away thoughtfully into the distance. "He brought me out here," he said quietly. "Showed me what it was we faced, and what we'd have to do to stop it. Showed me that even with all the resources of the Empire and New Republic combined, and with himself at the head, there were no guarantees of victory."

"On the contrary, he's already made contingency plans for defeat," Parck added soberly. "Ten years ago he had sleeper groups of the best of his cloned warriors scattered around the Empire and New Republic, ready to form the nuclei of local resistance forces should Bastion and Coruscant fall. Men who loved their homes and their land and their worlds, and who would give their lives in their defense."

"Yes," Fel said. "Once I understood—once I *really* understood—I had no choice but to join him."

"As you will, too," Parck said.

Mara shook her head. "Sorry. I have other plans."

"We'll see," Parck said calmly. "Perhaps Thrawn will be able to convince you himself when he returns."

"And what if he doesn't return?" Mara asked. "What if the rumors are just that: rumors?"

"Oh, he'll return," Parck said. "He said he would, and he always kept his promises. The only question is whether or not this particular rumor is actually him."

He looked up at Fel. "And under the circumstances, I suppose the only way we're going to find out for sure will be for me to finally make a trip to Bastion. If Thrawn has indeed set up a headquarters there, that should answer the question of which side he'll be working from."

Mara felt her hands tighten into fists. "You don't know what you're saying," she said. "You can't just turn all of this over to the Empire. All these resources, bases, alliances—"

"They won't misuse them," Parck said, his voice grim. "We'll make sure of that. The task ahead of us is far too serious for anyone to waste time on anything as petty as politics or personal gain."

"If you think *that,* you *are* out of touch," Mara snapped. "Try to remember back to Palpatine's court, and what the taste of power did to those people. Personal gain is all some of them ever think of."

"It's a risk we'll have to take," Parck said firmly. "We'll be careful, certainly—we'll speak with Sorn when he gets back and sift through the data he collected from his pass through the Bastion system. But unless there's something that positively quashes the rumors of Thrawn's return, it's time to make that contact."

Mara took a deep breath. "I can't let you do that," she said.

"*You* can't let us do it?" Fel asked pointedly.

"No," Mara said. "I can't. You give this to Bastion, and the first thing they'll do is turn it straight against Coruscant."

"Don't worry," Parck said. "We won't give anything away until we're sure Thrawn is with them."

"On the other hand, we may do well to worry about *her,* Admiral," Fel pointed out, eyeing her thoughtfully. "Someone as vehemently opposed as she is to our contacting Bastion could be trouble."

"I suppose you're right," Parck said reluctantly. He levered himself out of his chair, one of the Chiss stepping to his side and offering him a supporting arm as he stood up. "I'm afraid, Mara, that you and Skywalker will have to be our guests for a while."

"And if Thrawn *is* back, and I still don't want to join up?" Mara demanded. "What then?"

Parck's lips compressed briefly. "I'm sure it won't come to that," he assured her. But his eyes didn't quite meet hers as he spoke. "We'll have it all sorted out within a few days. Certainly no more than a month at the most."

Mara snorted. "You aren't serious. You really think a couple dozen ysalamiri are going to hold Luke Skywalker and me that long?"

"She's right, Admiral," Fel agreed. "It's going to take more to keep the two of them quiet."

Parck studied Mara's face. "What do you suggest?"

Fel gestured to one of the Chiss. "Brosh, your charric. Set for level two."

"Wait a second," Mara said hastily, jumping to her feet as the Chiss drew his hand weapon. A brief flood of emotion surged through her— *Stall*, the urgent thought leaped into her mind—"Wait just a Hoth-frost *second*. I'm an unarmed prisoner."

The other Chiss were drawing their weapons now, too. "I know," Fel said. He sounded genuinely regretful, for whatever that was worth. "And I'm deeply sorry about having to do this. But I've had some experience with Jedi, and the only way I can think of to keep you a proper prisoner for a few days is to force you to go into a healing trance." He looked over at Brosh—

"Wait a minute," Mara said. *Stall, stall, stall.* "You said you wanted to make a deal with me, right? Well, I can tell you flat out that shooting me will definitely not get any such negotiations off on the right foot. In fact, I'd go so far as to say that it might put me off working for you entirely."

"It won't," Fel assured her darkly. "Not when you know the full extent of the threats facing us."

"Maybe it will, and maybe it won't," Mara countered. "And don't forget Karrde, either. If you really want information, he's the one you're going to have to deal with. And Karrde does *not* take kindly to anyone who takes potshots at his people. I've seen him take whole organizations apart for that sort of crime. In fact, there was one particular Hutt group—"

"Yes, I'm sure," Parck interrupted, frowning. "Really, Mara, you're making far more out of this than you need to. Charric burns are certainly serious, but that's hardly even a consideration for someone with the Jedi skills of pain suppression and healing. And General Fel is right: we *do* need to keep you quiet for a while."

"Yes, I understand that," Mara said. "And it's a brilliant idea—really it is. There's just one small problem: I don't know how to do either the pain suppression *or* healing tricks."

"Come now," Parck said reproachfully, gesturing toward the black-edged hole in her jumpsuit. "Your shoulder indicates otherwise."

"Skywalker put me into the trance," Mara said, consciously relaxing her muscles in anticipation. "And he's not here. I could die of shock, or bleed to death—"

"You'll do neither," Fel assured her. "I know both the power and limitations of Chiss weaponry. Think of it as an added incentive for Skywalker to surrender to us."

He caught Brosh's eye and nodded. The Chiss nodded back and lifted his weapon—

And from it came a brilliant green flash.

CHAPTER

Without warning, right in the middle of a step, Mara vanished. *Mara?* Luke thought desperately toward her, stretching out to the Force. *Mara!*

But there was no response. Somehow, they must have gotten past her danger sense and combat skills and had launched a sudden and overwhelming attack.

And she was unconscious. Or dead.

"No," he whispered aloud, his pulse pounding in his ears. Once again, a person he'd cared for . . .

"No!" he bit out between clenched teeth, the agony in his heart swirling into something dark and deadly as the pain turned into a growing fury. Deal out casual death, would they? If death was what they wanted, he would show them just what death looked like. In his mind's eye he saw himself striding down the spiral slideway, throwing the aliens aside like sand dolls, their bodies slamming against the unyielding black stone and dropping crumpled to the floor. His lightsaber would flash through their ranks, cutting through weapons and bodies and leaving more death in its wake—

His lightsaber.

He looked down at the lightsaber in his hand. Not the weapon he himself had made in the oppressive heat of the Tatooine desert, but the one his father had made so many years before. The weapon he had given to Mara . . .

He took a deep breath, letting go of the rage and hatred, a cold shiver running through him as he realized the magnitude of what he had almost done. Once again, he had come to the very brink of giving in to the dark side. Had nearly surrendered to hatred and the lust for revenge, and the overwhelming desire to use his power for his own selfish ends.

If you honor what they fight for . . . Master Yoda's words echoed hauntingly through his mind. "All right," he murmured aloud. No, he would not avenge whatever had happened to Mara, at least not for vengeance's sake. But he would seek out the truth of her fate.

With an effort, he cleared the last lingering emotion from his thoughts, Mara's picture of songbirds singing inside an ore-crushing facility flickering once through his mind as he did so. Stretching out with the Force, he focused his mental probe toward the spot where Mara's presence had vanished. Unless they had already taken it away, he should at least be able to sense her body . . .

But there was nothing. Not Mara, not the humans or aliens she had supposedly been moving toward when she disappeared.

In fact, within a certain area, he could detect nothing at all. Almost as if something was blocking his access to the Force . . .

Abruptly, his breath went out of him in a rush, relief and chagrin flooding into him in equal quantities. Of course—the aliens had moved ysalamiri into the space between him and Mara. Even given the four-floor distance between them, he should have immediately recognized what was happening. Once again, it seemed, he was having to relearn Yoda's warning against acting while in the grip of strong emotion.

But there was no time for self-recrimination. Within the ysalamiri effect, Mara's fledgling Jedi powers were useless; and it was up to him to get her out.

He pulled out his comlink and thumbed it on. "Artoo?" he called softly. "I need you down here—take the nonmoving spiral slideway behind the wall to the right of the hidden exit doorway and come down four floors. Splitter Of Stones, leave someone behind in the stairway to seal the door, and the rest of you come with Artoo. Got that?"

There was a twitter from the droid and a chirp from the Qom Jha. Luke returned the comlink to his belt and walked slowly across the floor toward one of the level's back corners, stretching out beneath him with the Force as he moved. He could sense beings on the next level down, but none of them seemed to be in this particular area.

That could be misleading, given that he still didn't have a clear reading on this species. But he would have to risk it. Igniting Mara's lightsaber, the feel of the weapon bringing back a flood of old memories, he gripped it with both hands and dug the blue-white blade into the floor.

His big fear had been that like the cortosis ore in the cave below, the strange black stone would resist the lightsaber in some way. But though it felt rather like dragging a tree branch upstream through a rapidly flowing river, the blade sliced through the stone without trouble. Walking in a tight circle, beveling the edge inward so that the plug wouldn't fall through to the floor below, he carved out a round hole a little wider than Artoo.

Finishing his cut, he confirmed one final time that no one seemed to be below him. Then, stretching out to the Force, he lifted the stone plug out.

It was heavy—far heavier than anything of such a small size had any business being. Maneuvering it off to the side, he set it down with its edge just overlapping the hole, then dropped flat to the floor and peered carefully down.

The area did indeed appear to be deserted. Getting a grip on the rim, he eased himself in to hang full-length through the hole. Bracing himself, drawing on the Force to strengthen his muscles, he let go.

The floor was about four meters down, a trivial fall for a Jedi. He let his legs collapse as he hit, absorbing the impact and dropping him into a hopefully unobtrusive heap as he stretched out his senses for any sign he'd been seen or heard. But there was nothing. Getting carefully to his feet, he looked around again—

Master Walker Of Sky?

Luke looked up. Keeper Of Promises was in the room above him, peering down through the hole in the floor. "Keep quiet," he warned the Qom Jha. "Where are the rest of your people?"

They are coming in a flanking curve, Keeper Of Promises said. *Some guard your machine—it is the slowest.*

"Let me know when he gets there," Luke told him, stretching out with the Force. There were, he could tell, more of the aliens on the next level down, but again they didn't seem to be too close to him. Igniting the lightsaber again, he began cutting a new hole directly beneath the first one.

He'd finished the hole and had dropped to the next floor down when a quiet whistle from above signaled Artoo's arrival. "Great," Luke called softly, looking up at the blue-and-silver dome peering cautiously over the lip two floors up as he pulled out his comlink and thumbed it on.

The droid backed out of sight, and there was another acknowledging whistle from the comlink. "All right," Luke said, glancing around. He'd come down into a deserted room this time, but through the open door he could see glimpses of moving shadows. "You see the control boards over there? I want you to go find a computer jack you can access and plug into it. Try to get a floor plan of the fortress if you can; if you can't, just look around and see what else you can find. When I signal you again, unplug and get back over to the hole as fast as you can. Got all that?"

There was a slightly nervous-sounding twitter, and the comlink went dead. Gripping Mara's lightsaber, trying to get a feel for all the minds around and below him, Luke waited.

When it happened, it happened all at once. Suddenly, virtually in unison, all the alien minds changed, their various tones and concerns and textures all shifting to focus in the same direction. Not with fear, concern, or even surprise, but with the calm, deadly purpose of professional soldiers.

Artoo had tripped the flags Mara had warned him about, and the fortress was mobilizing for action.

Luke crouched a little closer to the floor, acutely aware that everything now hinged on what exactly that action would consist of. If all the aliens merely settled in where they were and braced for possible attack, he would have no choice but to fight his way through them to get to Mara. If, however, they instead concentrated on the slideway ramps and the floor where the attempted break-in was occurring . . .

And they did. Even as Luke held his breath, he could sense the aliens below moving purposefully toward the slideway Mara had taken earlier. If he was careful—and quick—the path to her might just be open.

Especially if he was quick. Igniting the lightsaber, he set to work carving yet another hole in the black stone.

He had finished the opening and dropped through to the next level down when his probing senses picked up the cue he'd been waiting for: the subtle change in the alien minds as the assembled assault teams readied themselves. "Now, Artoo," he called softly into the comlink. "Send the Qom Jha to me down the hole, and get over there yourself."

The droid acknowledged, and Luke stepped beneath the hole to wait. The Qom Jha weren't wasting any time; already they were dropping through like leaves blown from a tree, folding their wings tightly as they passed through each successive hole, opening them up between floors to regain control of their flight. Through the flurry of falling Qom Jha he spotted Artoo's dome lean cautiously over the edge, and caught an echo of the surprised and nervous twitter as the droid saw how much farther down Luke was now than the last time he'd looked.

A twitter that turned into an electronic gasp as Luke reached out with the Force to pick him up and drop him wheels-first through the hole.

Luke winced at the noise; but fortunately Artoo quickly realized what was happening and quieted down before the sound of a descending electronic scream could give the whole thing away. Luke got the droid safely to the floor beside him, then stretched out again to the edge of the stone plug he'd left poking over the side of the first hole above. At this distance it felt even heavier; but with alien warriors presumably even now fanning out toward the command center, he had great motivation for speed. Three seconds later, the plug was securely back in place.

Fifteen seconds after that, working his way down, he had all the rest of the holes sealed as well. "Mara's one more level down," he told Artoo and the huddled group of Qom Jha, stretching out with the Force. All the aliens below were gone, and there hadn't been any changes in the overall mental state that would indicate they'd tumbled to his trick.

Though oddly enough, he could no longer sense the assault teams themselves. Equipped with ysalamiri, perhaps?

Probably. But for the moment, those groups were too far away to worry him. "Stay close to me," he said, igniting the lightsaber and starting his final cut. "We'll try to keep this as quiet as we can, for as long as we can."

But if they discover us? Child Of Winds asked anxiously.

Luke frowned at him in mild surprise. He hadn't realized that the young Qom Qae had come in with the Qom Jha. In fact, he'd intended to give instructions that the child stay behind with whoever had sealed up the hidden door. Clearly, it had slipped his mind; just as clearly, it was too late to do anything about it now. "If the alarm goes up, you're to split up and create confusion," Luke told the aliens. "Draw them as far away from me as you can, then find your own ways out of the fortress and head back home."

We will obey, Splitter Of Stones said, fluttering his wings.

"And try not to get hurt," Luke added, finishing the cut and lifting the stone disk out of the hole. "Child Of Winds, you stay with Artoo and me."

He leaned down for a quick visual scan of the empty room below. "All right," he said, slipping his feet into the opening and bracing himself for another drop. "Let's go."

From the hazy look he'd had of this floor before his contact with Mara had been cut off, it had seemed fairly well structured, with rooms and wide corridors instead of the random wall segments they'd encountered upstairs. Not exactly an ideal arrangement for quiet skulking.

But for the first few minutes it seemed to work. Luke led the way cautiously toward the blank spot that marked the cluster of ysalamiri, splitting his attention between the area around him and the various warrior groups assembled near the slideways. Only half a dozen of the aliens wandered near enough to pose potential problems, and he was able to get his party past them unseen using Force-created noises and other distractions. The warriors on the command center level were clearly the methodical types, and as Luke neared the ysalamiri he began to think he might actually be able to burst in on Mara and her captors unannounced.

Han might have been that lucky. Luke, unfortunately, was not. They had nearly reached their goal when the illusion abruptly crumbled.

"They're on to us," he murmured.

Do they know where we are? Flier Through Spikes asked.

"I don't know," Luke said, stretching out to the Force and trying to decipher the sudden turmoil in the emotions of the aliens around him. There was no way to tell whether the assault team had discovered the hole he had cut or had simply found the level deserted and come to the logical conclusion.

What he *could* tell was that whatever it was they had discovered, their consternation had spread rapidly to the rest of the group. Clearly, they had a superb communications system in here.

Which meant that Mara's captors almost certainly also knew he was loose in the fortress.

Which meant he was out of time.

"I'm going in," he told the Qom Jha tightly, easing an eye around the end of the corridor. Just to the right, on the far side of a cross corridor, he could see an unmarked door. At the far end of that room, as near as he could tell, were the ysalamiri. "Artoo, Child Of Winds—come with me. The rest of you, scatter."

We obey, Walker Of Sky, Builder With Stones said; and with a multiple flutter of wings they were off.

"Stay behind me," Luke warned the droid and Qom Qae; and with a quick glance down the corridor he launched himself at the door, igniting Mara's lightsaber as he ran. He grabbed the release lever, twisting it and pushing the door open in a single motion, and leaped inside.

Only to find that he had miscalculated. The room he was in was long and dimly lit, with most of the left half filled with stacks of crates, and no sign of Mara.

But a second glance showed he hadn't miscalculated as badly as he thought. Laid out side by side, a group of ysalamiri on nutrient frames had been leaned against the back wall.

Artoo warbled questioningly. "She's in the next room over," Luke called over his shoulder as he raced toward the row of frames, a plan of action starting to take shape in his mind. Unless her interrogators were themselves Force-sensitive, they would have no way of knowing whether or not their protective barrier was still in place. If he could move enough of the ysalamiri out of the way to give Mara access to the Force again, the two of them together should be able to turn the tables on her captors and get her out of there. Skidding to a halt in front of one of the frames in the middle of the wall, feeling the sudden disconcerting silence in his mind as he stepped inside the meter-wide range of the creatures' effect, he set the lightsaber down on the floor and lifted up the frame.

Fortunately, given that there was no way for him to enhance his muscular strength this close to an ysalamir, the frame wasn't very heavy. He carried it a few steps away from the wall and propped it up against the nearest crate. Stepping back to the next one in line, he picked it up and crossed toward the first—

With his Jedi senses blinded by the ysalamiri effect, Artoo's sudden squawk was his only warning. He looked up, dropping the frame and leaping backward, his hand instinctively stretching back toward the lightsaber on the floor. One of the blue-skinned aliens was crouching in a marksman's stance in the open doorway, another of the nutrient frames strapped to his back, his weapon up and tracking. Luke took another step backward, the Force suddenly flooding in around him again as he moved out of the ysalamir's range. He felt the power tingling through his hand as he again called the lightsaber to him, wondering why it wasn't already in his hand—

And with a burst of understanding it belatedly hit him. He himself was clear of the ysalamiri effect, but the lightsaber wasn't.

The alien's weapon was lined up on him now. "Do not move," he ordered in accented Basic, his tone making it clear he was serious. Artoo started to roll cautiously toward him; the glowing red eyes flicked warningly toward the droid—

And with a screech that was half challenge and half pure terror, Child Of Winds dropped from the ceiling to land in full-taloned grip on the alien's gun arm.

The weapon fired, a brilliant blue flash that went wide, slicing past Luke into one of the nutrient frames along the wall. Luke dived backward in the opposite direction toward the cover of the stacked crates, grabbing for his own lightsaber still hanging from his belt and yanking it clear. His momentum slammed him into one of the other frames, sending it crashing to the floor.

And for one brief second, as he caromed off the wall and back toward the crates, he could feel Mara's presence again.

The touch didn't last long, perhaps half a second before he bounced back into range of the two ysalamiri he had set down beside the crates. But it was long enough. He could sense that she was all right, felt her own flash of relief that he was similarly unharmed, caught a sense of humans and aliens lined up along the wall in front of her. He had time for a single emotional instruction—Stall!—before the contact was cut off again. Digging his feet into the floor, he ignited his lightsaber and charged past the frames, wondering if he would make it through to the other side of the bubble before the alien got his aim back.

It was a close thing, and for a painful heartbeat he thought Child Of Winds's act of bravery was going to cost the Qom Qae his life. Instead of trying to wrench his winged assailant off his right arm, the alien had merely slammed his left hand into Child Of Winds's throat in an attempt to stun him, then transferred his gun to that hand. For an instant his first inclination seemed to be to use the weapon to kill the sharp-taloned nuisance clinging to him; but as he caught sight of Luke charging toward him with drawn lightsaber, he shifted his aim to the more threatening target and fired.

But he was too late. Luke was past the last of the ysalamiri now, and with access to the Force again there was no way a single gunman could penetrate his defenses. He sprinted forward, anticipating and sweeping his lightsaber across each of the alien's shots with practiced ease. Still firing, the alien dodged to the right, crossing behind Artoo. Luke switched direction to match his movement, wondering if the alien was planning to duck down and use the droid as a shield.

If so, he never got the chance. From midway down Artoo's body came the flash of an arc current—

And with an abrupt jolt of twitching leg muscles, the alien stumbled off balance and fell heavily sideways to the floor, taking Child Of Winds down with him. Luke leaped over Artoo, landing with one foot on the gun and feeling the sudden blindness again as he came within range of the ysalamir backpack. The alien's glowing red eyes gazed up with an unreadable expression as Luke raised his lightsaber high and brought it sweeping down. Seeing his own death arcing down toward him—

And then, midway through his slash, Luke closed down the blade, and instead of decapitating the alien merely slammed the heavy metal of the handle across the back of his head. Without a sound, he collapsed limply to the floor, unconscious.

"You all right?" Luke asked Child Of Winds, helping pry the other's clenched feet off the gunman's arm. The points where the Qom Qae's claws had been, he noticed, were oozing with slowly growing spots of red.

I am unhurt, Child Of Winds said shakily. *Why did you protect his life?*

"Because there was no need to kill him," Luke answered, looking up at Artoo. The droid seemed a little shaky, too, but game as always as he retracted his arc welder back into its compartment. "Thanks for the assist—both of you. Come on, Mara needs us."

Running back to the wall, he began grabbing the nutrient frames and hurling them away behind him, all thoughts of subtlety replaced now by a desperate need for speed. That quick kaleidoscopic glimpse he'd had into Mara's mind had included the threat of drawn weapons. He threw three of the nutrient frames aside, risked taking the time to get rid of the one next to where Mara's lightsaber still lay on the floor, then stepped close to the wall.

And realized with a surge of fear that he had cut it a little too close. Filtered through the emotional haze and clipped tactical thinking roiling together in Mara's mind, he could sense an indistinct, wavering image of the four aliens with their weapons pointed at her. Touching his forehead to the wall, he ran through his sensory enhancements . . .

"Skywalker put me into the trance," he heard her voice faintly through the thick stone. "And he's not here. I could die of shock, or bleed to death—"

"You'll do neither," another voice said. "I know both the power and limitations of Chiss weaponry. Think of it as an added incentive for Skywalker to surrender to us."

Luke didn't wait any longer. Straightening up, he drew back his lightsaber, stretching out to the Force as he pointed the tip of the glowing green blade at the wall, agonizingly aware that he would have only one shot at this. But if the Force could guide him with the pinpoint precision necessary to block blaster bolts . . .

And then, with a clarity that was startling in its unexpectedness, an image sprang into his mind: an alien standing with his back toward Luke, almost in front of him, raising a weapon toward Mara. Setting his teeth, Luke thrust his lightsaber through the wall to slash the green blade into the upper part of the alien's weapon.

And on the far side of that wall, he sensed the neatly arranged little scene dissolve into chaos.

Luke pulled the lightsaber downward, slicing an opening for himself as quickly as the stubborn black stone would permit, the emotional turmoil of sudden combat flooding over him as Mara exploded into action. He sensed a dizzying spin as she spun around and dropped into a crouch behind her chair, stretching out with the Force for her enemies' weapons. She yanked one straight out of its owner's hand—twisted another to the side to send his shot harmlessly into the ceiling—ducked back as another shot splattered across the corner of her chair back, sending tiny agonizing drops of liquid metal grazing across her cheek—

And then Luke's section of wall collapsed with a thud into the chaos. He caught Mara's eye as she crouched behind the chair and threw his lightsaber to her, stretched out with the Force to snatch hers from the floor behind him—

And with the old weapon flashing memories of Tatooine and Hoth and Bespin through his mind, he strode into the midst of the fight, the blue-white blade spattering bolts of enemy fire and shattering across the weapons themselves. One of the aliens leaped at him, a knife flashing into his hand; Luke grabbed him bodily with the Force and slammed him back against two others preparing for the same maneuver—

"Stop!" an authoritative voice ordered.

The aliens froze in their tracks, their eyes focused unblinkingly on Luke. Luke eyed them warily in return, his lightsaber held at the ready. Out of the corner of his eye he got a glimpse of the speaker: a gray-haired man wearing an Imperial admiral's uniform. "There's no point in anyone throwing their lives away here," the admiral said sternly. "Let them go."

Luke stretched out toward him with the Force, trying to gauge his sincerity. But both he and the other Imperial in the room were still being shielded by the remaining ysalamiri behind the side wall. "Mara?" Luke asked, risking a quick glance at her.

"What do you think?" she said with a snort as she came to his side, the green blade of his lightsaber held crossways at the ready between her and the aliens. "He's trying to save his own neck."

"Of course, I am," the admiral conceded without embarrassment. "As

I'm also attempting to protect the necks of my troops. If there was one thing Thrawn made certain his officers clearly understood, it was never to waste people for no reason." He smiled. "And it is well known that the Jedi Master Luke Skywalker does not kill needlessly or in cold blood."

"He's also stalling," Mara added. "They're probably setting up some kind of trap right now."

"Then we'd better get moving." Luke nodded at the group. "You think we should take one of them as a hostage?"

Mara hissed between her teeth. "No," she said. "Parck is too old—he'd slow us down—and I don't trust any of these Chiss not to be more trouble than they're worth. That goes double for General Fel."

Luke blinked, focusing his attention for the first time on the younger Imperial's face. Baron *Fel*? "Yes, it's me, Luke," Fel confirmed. "It's been a long time."

"Yes, it has," Luke murmured. Baron Fel, working for the Empire again?

Mara nudged him in the side. "Let's save the Rogue veterans' reunion for another time, okay? We've got to get moving."

"Right," Luke said, stepping back toward the wall and the opening he'd cut.

"Do think about our offer, Mara," the admiral called after them. "I think you'll find our struggle out here to be the most vitally important challenge you could ever face."

"And *you* think about my warning," Mara countered. "Stay away from Bastion."

The admiral shook his head minutely. "We'll do what we have to."

"Then so will I," Mara threatened. "Don't say I didn't warn you."

Fel smiled at her. "Take your best shot."

"Perhaps your fear of what the Empire might do with our information will be an added motivation for you to join us," Parck added. "At any rate, I'm certain we'll see you again."

"Right," Mara said. "I'll look forward to it."

Luke waited until Mara had ducked through the opening before backing out of the room himself. "I believe this one's yours," he told her, shutting down her lightsaber and handing it across.

"Thanks," she said, taking it as she passed his back to him. "Interesting grip yours has got. I think I like it better than mine."

"You can keep that in mind when you get around to making your own someday," Luke said, digging her sleeve blaster out of his jacket and tossing it to her. "Here's your blaster. Watch out—some of their people come equipped with ysalamir backpacks."

"I know," Mara said. She was at the door now, looking carefully out into the corridor. "Looks clear, but that won't last long. What's the plan? Back to the stairway?"

"Unfortunately, I had the Qom Jha lock it down," Luke told her, stepping into the doorway beside her as he threw a last glance back at the opening he'd cut. He'd have thought one of the aliens—the Chiss, Mara had called them—might try for a final shot, but they had apparently decided to stay put.

Which meant Mara was right. They had something else planned.

He looked down the corridor, stretching out with the Force as well. "Child Of Winds, stay on top of Artoo," he told the Qom Qae. "I don't want you getting lost."

"Or getting in the way," Mara added. "So where *are* we going?"

Before Luke could answer, Artoo rolled out into the corridor, heading confidently off to the left with Child Of Winds balanced precariously atop his dome. "I guess we're following Artoo," Luke said, setting off after them. "He must have been able to download the floor plan like I asked him to."

"That, or he's looking for a recharger," Mara muttered as she fell into step beside him. "How good are you at spotting individual ysalamiri?"

"Not as good as I am with groups of them," he conceded, stretching out with the Force. He could sense the grim activity all around them as the Chiss mobilized for combat . . .

The small empty space to their right was so subtle that he nearly missed it. "Watch out!" he snapped to Mara, skidding to a halt and spinning to face that direction. Even as he brought his lightsaber up, a half-meter-square concealed wall panel popped open and a weapon poked out. Behind it in the shadowy alcove he caught a glimpse of glowing red eyes and the glint of a nutrient frame above them—

From behind Luke came the flash of blaster fire; not targeted between the glowing eyes, as he might have expected, but above them. There was a sudden howl in his mind—

And the zone of silence around the gunman abruptly vanished.

There was a flash of blue as the alien weapon spat its fire toward Luke's chest. But too late. With the ysalamir's bubble collapsed, Luke blocked the shot with ease. The gunman got off two more shots, also blocked, before the collapsing blue circles of a stun blast sent him slumping out of sight to the floor of his guard alcove.

"Oh, good," Mara said, hefting her blaster and working the select switch. "The stun setting works on them."

"That could be handy," Luke agreed, glancing around with eyes and mind. There were no other threats he could detect, at least not in the immediate area. "Any reason in particular why you didn't kill him?"

"Hey, *you're* the one who wants me to start acting like a Jedi," Mara retorted, starting down the corridor again. Artoo had gotten a few meters ahead, and was twittering with nervous impatience as he swung his dome back around to look at them. "Problem is, the stun setting on this thing has about the range of a thrown bantha. If they're smart enough to keep their distance, you'll have to block their shots while I pick off the ysalamiri."

"Right," Luke said, frowning as he picked up his pace. There was something ominous growing behind the protection of Mara's mental barrier: a dark thought, or equally dark purpose. For a moment he considered asking her about it; but the fact that she was hiding it from him strongly suggested he should leave it alone. "Any idea what their plan is?" he asked instead as they caught up with Artoo.

"Short-term, to put us in deep storage for a few days," Mara said. "They figure making us go into healing trances is the easiest way to do that; hence, the gunfire."

"Friendly sorts," Luke murmured.

"Yeah," Mara agreed. "Long-term, they're waiting for Thrawn to return." There was a momentary flicker in her emotions, a deepening of that hidden darkness . . . "And since they think he may have popped up at Bastion, Parck's decided to head out there and talk to them."

Luke felt suddenly cold. "And turn this place over to the Empire?"

"The place, and everything in it," Mara said grimly. "That may not be what they *think* they're going to do; but once the Empire knows they're here, they'll get hold of it. One way or another."

Ahead, Artoo warbled and made a right turn into a cross corridor. "Where *are* we going?" Mara demanded as they followed.

"I don't know," Luke said, frowning. Twenty meters ahead, the corridor ended in a T-junction, and for some unknown reason his mind flashed back to the Cavrilhu Pirates' asteroid base and the very different T-junction at the far end of the Jedi trap they'd lured him into. Somewhere directly ahead, he could sense the blank area created by a group of ysalamiri.

And then Artoo twittered uncertainly and rolled to a stop, facing the wall blocking their corridor in obvious confusion . . .

"Artoo, get back!" Luke snapped, bringing up his lightsaber and taking a long step to put himself in front of Mara. "It's a trap!" Directly ahead, the wall exploded into a shower of dazzling sparks and completely disintegrated—

And standing shoulder to shoulder together in the corridor behind what was left of the false wall, a dozen ysalamiri-equipped Chiss opened fire.

Artoo squealed and swiveled around, racing back toward Luke as fast as he could, Child Of Winds scrambling frantically to hang on. Luke barely noticed them, his whole attention focused ahead on the Chiss. He forced himself to relax, letting the Force guide his hands as it had in so many such battles, swinging his lightsaber into blocking position in front of each shot.

But with the area around the Chiss closed to that subconscious prescience, a precious split second was being shaved off his normal preparation time. Behind him, Mara's blaster was flashing steadily over his shoulder, methodically picking off ysalamiri. If he could keep up their defense long enough for her to finish the job . . .

Somewhere at the edge of his mind he could hear Child Of Winds screeching something, but he had no concentration to spare for a translation. Ahead, through the massed line of Chiss he could see what appeared to be movement behind them; and then, without warning, they dropped in unison to one knee—

Revealing another line of troops that had come up behind them.

And suddenly there were twice as many bolts blazing his direction. Bolts he was slowly but steadily losing the race to stay ahead of.

Behind him, Mara barked something, and through his haze of concentration Luke saw one of the standing aliens jerk back and collapse as Mara abandoned her nonkilling policy. Luke clenched his teeth and leaned into his effort, dimly realizing that if Parck sent a team in from behind them right now, he and Mara would be finished. Child Of Winds screeched again—

And then, sweeping in from both directions down the cross corridor ahead, a group of Qom Jha dove straight into the middle of the battle.

The Chiss had no chance to react. Sweeping at full speed just over the heads of the standing warriors, the Qom Jha grabbed the tops of their nutrient frames, the momentum yanking the gunmen off their feet and slamming them hard onto their backs on the floor.

"Let's go," Luke heard himself shout, breaking into a cautious jog toward the remaining row of kneeling Chiss. If he could get close enough to get them in range of Mara's stun setting . . .

Half a corridor away, the Qom Jha braked from their mad rush, swiveled around with impossible grace, and charged back at the kneeling gunmen from behind. Again they grabbed the nutrient frames as they passed, pulling the frames and the attached Chiss sprawling onto their faces.

Luke let his lightsaber come to a stop, arm muscles starting to tremble with adrenaline and suddenly released tension. Mara had already sprinted past him, waving the Qom Jha aside as her blaster swept its rings of blue stun fire across the downed Chiss. Even as Luke reached her side, the last of the gunmen twitched and stopped moving.

"That was fun," Mara gritted between clenched teeth, throwing a quick glance both directions down the corridor as she again worked her blaster's select switch. "I hope they haven't got many more of these little traps set up."

"I don't think we've got far to go," Luke said, looking at Artoo. The little droid was already rolling down the cross corridor to their left, heading toward a large, heavy-looking door blocking off the end of the passage fifteen meters away. A door, he noted, equipped with the same locking wheel and hand-grip release system as those of the hidden stairway far behind them. "Splitter Of Stones, get your people together and follow us."

He ran forward, closing down his lightsaber and clipping it onto his belt, reaching Artoo as the droid slowed to a stop in front of the door. Turning the wheel, Luke squeezed the grips and pulled. The door swung ponderously open, letting in a rush of cool air—

Skies of red blood, Keeper Of Promises muttered in amazement. *What place is this?*

"Our way out," Luke told him, feeling a touch of the same awe as he gazed across the view in front of them. Stretching away across the black stone floor, parked close together like troops on parade, were multiple rows of small starships like the pair that had attacked him on his way to the planetary surface.

Beside him, Mara whistled softly. "The hangar didn't look this big from the outside," she said.

"It must stretch back farther than its roof indicated," Luke agreed, wondering how such a closely packed group of ships could ever be properly serviced. A glance upward gave him his answer: the entire area beneath the high ceiling was crammed with service, monitor, and fueling equipment, all held together by metal frames and a network of catwalks. "There must be a hundred of them here."

"At least," Mara agreed . . . and as she spoke, Luke could sense that secret darkness deepen within her. It was about time he asked her about it—

There was a sudden flicker of sensation from behind him. "Look out!" Mara snapped, spinning around and firing a pair of quick shots past his shoulder through the open door.

Luke turned, too, snatching up his lightsaber and igniting it. A handful of Chiss were in the intersection they'd just left, scrambling reflexively out of the way of Mara's shots. "Keep firing," Luke told her, giving the door a quick look. There was no locking wheel on the hangar side, but there was a small hole where one had apparently been removed. Experimentally, he turned the wheel a few degrees; through the hole, the central axle of the locking mechanism could be seen turning.

Perfect. He turned the wheel back to full-open again and with a quick slash of his lightsaber sliced it off flush with the door. Ducking under Mara's covering shots, he pushed the door closed.

But it is still unlocked, Flier Through Spikes objected. *They can use the grip-rocks to open it again.*

"Not for long," Luke assured him. Crouching down, he gazed through the hole at the central axle and stretched out to the Force. Without the wheel's leverage it was much harder to turn, but the thought of armed Chiss descending on the hangar was more than enough incentive. Ten seconds later, the door was securely locked.

"That won't hold them for long," Mara warned. "If nothing else, they can head over the roof on foot and come in the other end."

"I know," Luke said, craning his neck to peer past the parked ships. She was right: as they'd guessed from their first look at the place, the whole front of the hangar was wide open, with only a slight overhang to protect it from rain or attack. The fortress's designers, he decided, must not have intended for their hangar to be packed this full. "But it should slow them down long enough for us to borrow a ship and get out of here."

"Then all we'll have to worry about is whatever they've got in those towers," Mara said tartly, pushing past him and ducking between two of the ships. "We'll have to take something from the front," she called back over her shoulder. "I'll try to get one started. You make sure that door is secured, then find a way to keep the rest of that front row from taking off after us."

"Got it," Luke said. "Artoo, take Child Of Winds and follow Mara—give her a hand figuring out the flight systems. Splitter Of Stones, you and your people had better head out while you can. Thank you for your help."

Our part is paid, Master Walker Of Sky, the Qom Jha said, his tone just slightly ominous. *It will now be your part to rid us of the Threateners as you promised.*

With that, he and the others flapped away over the parked ships. "We'll do our best," Luke murmured.

He double-checked the door, then took another moment to stretch his thoughts back into the corridor. It was empty. Apparently, the Chiss knew better than to waste their time with the impenetrable stone.

Particularly with such an obvious alternative available. Thirty seconds later, following the sound of Artoo's wheels across the black stone, he reached the front of the hangar.

Artoo and Child Of Winds were there, the latter again scrabbling for balance on top of the droid as the dome swiveled back and forth. Luke looked along the front line of ships, noting a gap in the neat array where one was apparently missing.

Mara, however, was nowhere to be seen. "Artoo, where's Mara?"

The droid warbled a negative, still looking around. Luke peered out into the dim sunlight and stretched out with the Force—

"What are you waiting for?" Mara demanded as she ran up from behind him. "We need these ships disabled."

"We were waiting for you," Luke told her, frowning. The dark secret still loomed in her mind; but there was something new to the texture now. All tinges of uncertainty or doubt had disappeared, replaced by a heavy cloud of deep and bitter sadness. Something vitally important had just happened . . .

"Well, don't," she growled, slapping a release panel on the side of the nearest ship. Above them, a hatchway swung open and a ladder unfolded to the floor.

"One of the ships seems to be missing," Luke pointed out.

"I know—Parck mentioned it was on its way in," Mara said, swinging herself up onto the ladder. "Nothing we can do about that one. Go on, get busy."

She disappeared inside. "Right," Luke murmured, reaching out with the Force to lift Artoo up and into the hatch behind her. Then, stepping to the next ship in line, he ran a quick eye over it. The fighter was three times the size of an X-wing, with a set of four TIE-fighter solar panels melding into a disturbing flow of alien lines.

And presumably with a set of repulsorlifts on the underside . . .

He ducked under the bow. There they were, one pair running longitudinally along each side of the centerline: the subtle but distinctive diamond pattern of repulsorlifts. Four quick slashes with his lightsaber, and they were no longer functional. Ducking around the landing gear, he moved on to the next ship.

He had disabled seven of them, with another seven to go, when he caught the change in Mara's emotional texture. Slowly, with the slightly awkward movements that came of a pilot unfamiliar with her craft, the ship lifted half a meter off the floor and eased forward. His comlink beeped—"We've got company," Mara's voice announced tightly; and as Luke concentrated he could sense both wary Chiss minds and ysalamiri-created blank areas approaching over the rooftop. "Snap it up—I'll try to keep them busy."

And she did. The interior of the hangar was flickering with reflected light from the firefight by the time Luke finished disabling the last of the fighters: soft blue flashes from the Chiss hand weapons, a sharper and brighter blue from Mara's ship. *Ready,* he thought toward her, sprinting across the line of disabled ships toward the end of the hangar opening where most of the brighter flashes seemed to be coming from. He reached it, eased a careful eye around the corner—

Get ready, Mara's acknowledgment flowed into his mind; and with a sandstorm blast of backwash, the ship dropped past the overhang and bounced to a rough landing in front of him.

Luke was ready. Even as the ship bounced up again, he was sprinting around its tail to its far side. The hatchway Mara had used earlier was standing open; throwing Jedi strength into his leg muscles, Luke leaped upward, catching the door and pulling himself inside to land in an undignified sprawl on the deck. "Go!" he shouted, stretching out with the Force to pull the hatch closed.

Mara needed no encouragement. Already the ship was jumping toward the sky, the roar of repulsorlifts not quite drowning the pinging of Chiss shots slapping into the underside and back.

Are we safe? Child Of Winds asked anxiously. He was pressed into the aft-most seat, his claws gripping the safety straps.

"I think so," Luke soothed him, listening to the fading pings of heat-stressed metal as Mara pulled for altitude. "All they seem to have is anti-personnel weapons down there. Unless they can get their heavier stuff on line quickly—"

"Luke, get up here," Mara's taut voice called back from the flight deck.

Luke scrambled to his feet, his mind reaching out to Mara's. The dark thought was still there, lurking in the back of her mind. But it had now been superseded by something else, a tangle and mixture he couldn't decipher. He dodged past Artoo, gurgling pensively in a droid alcove, and dropped into the copilot seat beside Mara. "What is it?" he snapped.

"Look at the fortress," Mara told him, turning the ship into a slow rotation.

"What, the weapons towers?" Luke asked, stretching out with the Force as he looked down at the structure turning lazily into view out the canopy. He couldn't see or sense any indication they were preparing to fire. He glanced at Mara's board, searching for the sensor displays—

"Forget the logistics and strategy for a minute," Mara said curtly. "Look at the fortress. Just *look* at it."

Luke felt his forehead wrinkling as he gazed down through the canopy again. It was a fortress. Walls; a flat, roundish, angled roof with a hangar in the middle; four weapons towers following the curve of the roof in back, one intact tower farther down in front—

"Look at it," Mara said again, very softly.

And with a sudden shock, he saw it. "Stars of Alderaan," he breathed.

"It's almost funny, isn't it?" Mara said, her voice sounding strange. "We automatically dismissed the whole idea that it could be some kind of superweapon. Thrawn never used superweapons, we all said.

"And yet, that's exactly what it is. The only kind of superweapon someone like Thrawn ever used. The only kind he ever needed."

Luke thought about that galaxy holo in the command center, and all the planets and resources Thrawn had gathered under his control. Enough to tip the balance of power in any direction its inheritors chose. "Information," he said, a shiver running through him.

Mara nodded. "Information."

Luke nodded back, gazing down at the fortress now receding into the surrounding hills as Mara pulled the ship away again. The flat-roofed fortress with its four towers in back and one in front stretching upward toward the sky. Looking for all the world like four fingers and a thumb reaching to pluck the stars from the sky.

The Hand of Thrawn.

Just under a kilometer away from the fortress, shielded from view by a craggy ridge, was a deep indentation in the cliff face. Mara maneuvered the ship carefully in beneath the overhang and eased it as far back against the wall as she could. "That's it," she said, shutting down the repulsorlifts and feeling herself slump with fatigue and released tension. For the moment, at least, they were safe.

For the moment.

From the aft seat, Child Of Winds said something. Almost intelligibly this time, but Mara was too tired to even try to decipher it. "What did he say?" she asked.

"He asked what we're going to do now," Luke translated. "A good question, actually."

"Well, for right now, we're just going to sit here," Mara said, running a critical eye over Luke's outfit. There were a half-dozen new scorch marks where the Chiss' charric shots had made it through his defenses, and she could sense his automatic and almost unconscious suppression of the pain. "Looks to me like you could use a few hours in a healing trance."

"That can wait," Luke said, gazing through the canopy at the landscape beyond the overhang, fading into the growing darkness of evening. "My damage to their repulsorlifts won't hold them for long. We have to get back in there before they can mount an aerial search for us."

"Actually, I don't think they'll bother," Mara said, waving at her control board. "For one thing, the sensors on these things seem to be pretty useless for close-order ground searches. My guess is that they'll move troops into the areas where they think we stashed our ships and leave it at that."

"You don't think they'll worry we might get back inside?"

"And do what?"

Luke frowned. "What do you mean?"

Mara took a deep breath. "I mean I'm not sure we should even try to interfere with what they're doing."

Child Of Winds made a noise like a choked-off comment. Luke glanced back at him, then turned again to Mara. "But they're enemies of the New Republic," he said. "Aren't they?"

Mara shook her head. "I don't know. Just because they're in Imperial uniforms . . ."

She sighed. "Look. Baron Fel was in there. The same Baron Fel who turned his back on the Empire years ago when he finally recognized how corrupt and vicious things had become under Isard and some of Palpatine's other successors.

"Yet here he is, wearing an Imperial uniform again. Braintwisting is useless against a man like him—you'd ruin the fine combat edge that makes him useful to you in the first place. Something must have happened to legitimately change his mind."

"Thrawn?"

"In a way," Mara said. "Fel said Thrawn took him to the Unknown Regions and showed him around . . . and that that was when he agreed to rejoin."

She could feel Luke's emotions darken. "There's something out there, isn't there?" he said quietly. "Something terrible."

"According to the Chiss, there are a hundred terrible somethings out there," Mara said. "Of course, that *is* only the Chiss talking. Odds are that a lot of the dangers would be pretty harmless to something with the size and resources of the New Republic. Threats we could swat without any trouble if they ever ventured in past the Outer Rim."

She shrugged uncomfortably. "On the other hand . . ."

"On the other hand, Fel knows our resources as well as we do," Luke finished for her. "And yet he's here."

Mara nodded. "He and Parck are both here. And neither of them seems to have any interest in wasting their resources in actions against the New Republic. That says a lot right there."

For a long minute the ship was silent. Then Luke stirred. "Unfortunately, there's still one more point we have to consider," he said. "Bastion and the Empire. You said Parck was going to open contact with them?"

"Yes," Mara confirmed, the quiet ache within her deepening. "And I don't trust the current Imperial leadership to see things with the same long-term perspective that Fel does. You give them the Hand of Thrawn and they *will* move against Coruscant."

Luke gazed out the canopy again. "We can't let that happen," he said quietly. "Not with the New Republic in the state it's in."

"Especially not if those resources are needed to battle some other threat," Mara agreed, unstrapping her restraints. "Which unfortunately means we have to get back in there and pull copies of that data for ourselves. At least then we'll have a chance of blocking whatever Bastion does to pull them in on the Imperial side."

She could sense Luke forcing the tiredness from his mind. "You're right," he said as he started unfastening his own straps. "If we can get Artoo to a computer jack so he can download everything—"

"Hold it, hold it," Mara said, reaching over and putting a restraining hand on his arm. "I didn't mean right this minute. We're not going anywhere until you get those burns healed."

"They're nothing," Luke protested, glancing down across the scorch marks. "I can handle them."

"Oh, bravely said," Mara said, fatigue and her private pain adding an unintended note of scorn into her voice. "Let me rephrase that: *I'm* not going anywhere with you until you're healed. You were just barely able to keep ahead of that last attack—I don't want any of your attention wasted on old injuries you could have gotten rid of with a few hours' rest. Understand?"

He glared at her. But behind the glare, she could sense his grudging agreement. "All right, you win," he said with a sigh, resettling himself into his seat. "But you wake me right away if anything happens. I'll set up the phrase 'welcome back' to snap me out of it."

Mara nodded. "Got it."

"And even if nothing happens, wake me up in two hours," he added, closing his eyes. "It won't take them more than a few hours to get enough of the damaged ships out of the way to free up the ones in back. We'll need to get back there before then if we're going to stop Parck from handing all this over to Bastion."

Without waiting for a reply, he took another deep breath and leaned back against the headrest. His thoughts and emotions cleared and faded, and he was gone. "Don't worry about Bastion," Mara said softly. "I'll take care of it."

For a moment she sat there in the silence, gazing at his sleeping face, a tangle of emotions twisting through the darkness of her private agony. Ten years now they'd known each other, years that could have been filled with camaraderie and friendship. Years Luke had effectively wasted with his own lonely and arrogantly stupid wanderings through completely unnecessary pain and doubt.

She ran a fingertip gently across his forehead, brushing back a few loose strands of hair. And yet, after all that, here they were together again, and the man she'd once so highly respected and cared for was finally back on his proper path.

Or perhaps it was the two of them together who were on *their* proper path.

Perhaps.

Behind her came a tentative questioning warble. "It's just a healing trance," Mara assured the droid, pushing the last of her straps away and getting out of her seat. "He'll be all right. You watch over things in here, okay?"

The droid twittered again, his tone suddenly suspicious. "I'm going outside," Mara told him, making sure her sleeve blaster and lightsaber were secure. "Don't worry, I'll be back."

She slid past him, ignoring his sudden flurry of comments and questions and popped the hatch. Child Of Winds brushed past her as the ladder unfolded, chirping rapidly for a few seconds and then flapping off into the deepening darkness.

A darkness matched by the ache deep within her.

For a moment she looked back at the top of Luke's head, visible over the chair's headrest, wondering if he had guessed her plan. But no. She'd carefully held it secret within her, behind the mental barriers Palpatine had so long ago taught her how to create.

The old Luke, the one obsessed with solving every problem himself, might have forced his way in through those barriers to demand the truth. The new Luke, she knew, would never do such a thing.

Later, probably, he would regret not having done so. But by then it would be too late. The simple fact was that Parck and the Chiss had to be prevented from giving the Empire the secrets of this place.

And it was up to her to stop them. However she could. Whatever the cost.

The droid had run out of words and was watching her, his stance somehow reminding her of that of a frightened child. "Don't worry," she soothed him quietly. "It'll be all right. Watch over him, okay?"

The droid gave a forlorn moan of agreement. Stretching out with the Force, Mara turned and headed down the ladder.

However she could. Whatever the cost.

CHAPTER

30

Even late at night the Drev'starn spaceport was a bustling hive of activity, the pedestrians and vehicles casting long shadows in the bright light of the glow lamps as they hurried about their business. The same bright light, Navett thought as he strode along, that would make the spaceport an ideal target for the warships orbiting high above them.

He wondered if that same thought had occurred to the rest of the hurrying crowds. Perhaps that was one of the reasons they were hurrying.

He reached the target zone and gave a soft whistle. It was answered immediately from a stack of shipping crates to his right. Stepping around the stack, he found Klif waiting. "Report," he murmured.

"We're set," Klif murmured back. "She went in about an hour ago and shut things down. I shorted out one of the glow lamps to give us an approach."

Navett edged an eye around the crates for a cautious look. The old woman's Sydon Pacifier was squatting silently in its landing circle, with nothing but parking lights showing. A long strip of shadow thrown by another stack of crates led nearly to its sealed hatchway. "Looks good," he said. "What about the New Rep agents?"

"Well, now, that's an interesting question," Klif said. "I did a quick slice into the spaceport computer; and according to its records, they're gone."

Navett frowned. Gone? Now? "Where?"

"No idea," Klif said. "But I ran a global against both their registration and engine ID, and there's no indication they might have circled around and landed again, not here or anywhere else on Bothawui."

"Interesting, indeed," Navett murmured, stroking his chin as he gazed at the Pacifier. "Either we fooled them completely, or else they suddenly had something more urgent to do. Rogue Squadron's attached to Bel Iblis these days, isn't it?"

Klif nodded. "You think Bel Iblis is up to something?"

"That walking sack of annoyance is always up to something," Navett growled. "However, he's not our problem. We'll send word to Bastion and let them figure him out. Right now"—he slid his blaster out of its concealed sheath—"we've got our own sack of annoyance to deal with. Come on."

They slipped out into the concealing shadow and headed for the Pacifier, eyes and ears alert for any sign of trouble. None came before they reached the ship, dropping into combat crouches on opposite sides of the hatchway. "Pop it," Navett muttered, blaster held ready as he tried to watch everywhere at once. Antilles could conceivably have sent in other New Rep agents on his way out . . .

There was the muffled clicking of Klif's lockjim followed by a soft hiss, and the top of the hatchway swung smoothly down to the permacrete, its inside surface forming a ramp. Giving the area one final scan, Navett rose from his crouch and ducked up the ramp into the ship.

Inside was darkness, with only dim walk-lights marking the corridors. He could hear Klif's soft breathing behind him as he eased down toward the living section. Still no signs of life; the old woman must already be asleep. He eased to the first door in line, eased it open . . .

And abruptly, all around them, the lights blazed on.

Navett dropped instantly into a crouch, cursing under his breath as he blinked against the sudden glare. There was a bump against his shoulders as Klif dropped into a mirror-image crouch at his back. "No one here," Klif hissed from behind him.

"Not here, either," Navett said, frowning as his eyes finished adjusting to the light and realizing that what had seemed so bright when they came on were apparently only the normal shipboard lights.

No gunmen, no automatic weapons, not even any eye-burning flash-flare defensive lights. What was going on?

"Good evening, gentlemen," a voice spoke up into the tense silence. The old woman's voice.

"Klif?" Navett hissed, looking around again. There was still no one visible in his direction. "Anyone?"

"No, I'm not here," the voice assured him smugly. "I'm a recording. You wouldn't hurt an innocent little recording, would you?" She snorted. "Of course, considering who you are, maybe you would."

"There," Klif said, pointing. Half hidden behind a cable conduit was a small datapad with a recording rod sticking out of it.

"You must think you're pretty hot stuff," the woman continued. "Strutting around in plain sight, bamboozling the bumbling Bothans—hey, that's kind of cute—and in general running rings around everyone and everything."

Navett stepped over to the datapad. It was jammed into the space between the conduit and the wall as if hurriedly slapped in there.

On the other hand, it *had* been keyed to come on with the lights . . .

"Well, I'm sorry to so rudely pop your bubble," she said. "But you're not as smart as you think. Not *nearly* as smart as you think."

Navett caught Klif's eye and nodded toward the sleeping rooms. Klif nodded back and slipped down the corridor toward the farthest one. Putting his back to a wall, Navett leveled his blaster along the corridor leading to the flight deck. This could still be nothing but a distraction.

"You see, I talked to a couple of friends this afternoon," the recording went on. "They tell me that every time they try to get a handle on this big, loud Vengeance organization that's been making so much noise, it just kind of evaporates into nothing. Kind of like the bubble I just mentioned—nothing but hot air. Hot air blown by—dare I say it?—a handful of Imperial agents."

There was a flicker of movement at the corner of Navett's eye. He glanced over to see Klif emerge from the sleeping room area and shake his head. He nodded in the direction of the cargo hold and lifted his eyebrows questioningly.

"So I guess that means it's down to just you folks and me," the old woman said. "My New Rep friends have left—which you probably already know—and the vast organization you've been pretending to be doesn't exist. So. You and me. Should be fun."

Klif was staring at Navett, a bewildered frown on his face. "What in blazes is she talking about?" he hissed. "Is she *challenging* us?"

Navett shrugged.

"Oh, and help yourself to something in the galley if you want," she added. "Especially whichever of you was stuck out there watching my ship today. Stakeouts can be such thirsty work. Just put everything back in the cooler when you're done, okay? Well, see you later. Which is not to say you'll see me, of course."

There was a soft click, and the recording stopped. "This woman is nuts," Klif declared, looking around. "Does she have any idea at all who she's dealing with?"

"I don't know," Navett said, eyeing the datapad thoughtfully. "She implied she knows we're Imperials; but she never once said anything about our covers here. Or whether she even knows she's talked to us."

Klif grunted. "So she's fishing."

"She's fishing," Navett nodded. "More to the point, she's fishing alone. If she had any proof or official backing she'd have had more than just trick lights and a recording waiting here. Sounds like her plan now is simply to draw us out."

"So what do we do?" Klif demanded. "Keep after her?"

Navett rubbed his chin. "No, I think we'll back off," he said slowly. "If she starts wandering in too close again, we can reconsider. But with Antilles and his partner gone, she's not going to be all that effective."

He peered down the corridor toward the flight deck. "Unless she's still in here somewhere trying to get a look at us," he amended, hefting his blaster. "In which case, she's automatically vaped."

"Now you're talking," Klif growled.

"Just watch it," Navett warned. "She might have set up some booby traps."

They were there another hour, running a fine mesh over the ship before they finally gave up and left. Only three or four times after the recording shut off did they get close enough to the comlink hidden in the datapad for Moranda to pick up anything of what they were saying.

In most of those brief snippets, they were sounding pretty irritable.

Watching through her spy hole from inside the empty crate she'd set up on top of a stack of similar ones fifty meters from her ship, she watched the two of them slip out again into the bustle of activity. So she'd been right, she and Corran and Wedge. The Imperials were here, and they were planning something nasty.

And they were sufficiently rattled that they were willing to risk a murder right in the middle of the spaceport. *That* was very interesting.

And unless her ear had totally failed her, that careless and highly unprofessional conversation beside her rigged datapad had given her their identities: the earnest but stupid proprietors of the Exoticalia Pet Emporium.

Of course, knowing was one thing. Proving was something else entirely. And for possibly the first time in her life, that vast legal gap was going to work against her.

The Imperials had joined the pedestrians on one of the major walkways now, their postures and strides midway between casual and decisive. Imperial Intelligence, most likely, or even some of the folks from the Ubiqtorate underhanded tricks division. Either way, definitely experts who knew what they were doing.

Unfortunately, the New Republic rep in Drev'starn wouldn't be interested in any of this without proof. Neither would the Bothans.

In fact, come to think of it, there were probably still a couple of warrants outstanding against her on Bothawui. That definitely let out the Bothans.

The Imperials were gone now, vanished toward the western entrance and presumably out of the spaceport. Still, as Moranda had long ago learned, "presumably" never fed the sabacc pot or took the pets for a walk. Her new playmates might just have been irritated enough by her sneaking out on them to have left a spotter behind.

Opening her pocket flask, she took a sip of the tangy blue liqueur and consulted her chrono. Another two hours, maybe three, and it should be safe to move.

Taking another sip, she resealed the flask and settled herself comfortably against one of the corners of the crate. It was a long time since she'd dealt with an opponent of this caliber, and as long as she was stuck in here anyway she might as well start working out her next move.

"It's so good to hear your voice again, Han," Leia's voice came over the *Lady Luck*'s speaker, and there was no mistaking the relief in her tone. "I've been so worried about you."

"Hey, hon, it was no big deal," Han assured her, only fudging the truth a little. There would be plenty of time to tell her the whole story of their little trip to Bastion when he could hold her hand while he did it.

And besides, the last thing he wanted to put out on a HoloNet call, even an encrypted one, was the fact that Grand Admiral Thrawn was indeed still alive. "The point is that we got in and out okay and we're heading home," he went on.

"I'm glad you're safe," she said, a cautious hope creeping into her voice. "Did you—I mean—?"

"We got it," Han told her. "At least, I think we got it."

There was a short pause. "What does that mean?"

"It means we got what we went for," Han said. "And it all looked all right to me. But . . . well, there were a couple of complications. Let's leave it at that for now, okay?"

"Okay," she said reluctantly. Clearly not happy about letting it go like that, but as aware as he was of the limitations of HoloNet security. "But don't go to Coruscant. I'm on my way to Bothawui."

"Bothawui?"

"Yes," she said. "I was heading for Coruscant when I found out President Gavrisom was there trying to mediate this whole war fleet thing."

"Ah," Han said, frowning at the speaker. Considering he'd left her on Pakrik Minor ten days ago, she should have already *been* on Coruscant, not just on her way there. Had something happened with that meeting with Bel Iblis? "Your visitor get delayed or something?" he asked obliquely.

"The visitor arrived right on schedule," she said. "Only it wasn't exactly who I was expecting. And I then wound up taking a little side trip."

Han felt his hands curl into fists. "What kind of side trip?" he demanded. If someone had tried to hurt her again—"Are you all right?"

"No, no, I'm fine," she hastened to assure him. "Things just went differently than I was expecting, that's all. It's all tied in with why I have to talk to Gavrisom right away."

HoloNet security. "Yeah, all right, we'll head for Bothawui," Han said. "It'll be another couple of days before we can get there."

"That's fine," she said. "I won't be there until tomorrow myself."

Han grimaced. It would have been better if he could have gotten there ahead of her. From everything he was hearing, the sky over Bothawui was a flash point just begging to happen. "Well, you be careful, Leia, all right?"

"I will," she promised. "I'm just glad *you're* safe. I'll call Gavrisom right away and give him the good news about your mission."

"And tell him I'm not going to give it to him unless he promises you some real vacation time when this is over," Han warned.

"Absolutely," she agreed.

"Okay. I love you, Leia."

He could almost hear her smile. "I know," she said in their private joke. "I'll see you soon."

With a sigh, Han cut off the comm. Another two days to Bothawui, with Leia getting there a day ahead of them. Maybe Lando could get a little more speed out of this crate. He swiveled his chair around—

"So how's Leia?" Lando said from the bridge doorway.

"She's fine," Han assured him, studying his friend's face. There was something very unpleasant lurking there behind his eyes. "Sounds like she had more than just a straight run home from Pakrik Minor, though, and we have to change course for Bothawui to meet her. What's up?"

"Trouble," Lando said darkly, jerking his head over his shoulder. "Come on back a minute."

Lobot and Moegid were waiting in the aft control room when he and Lando arrived, sitting on opposite sides of the computer table. Lobot just looked like Lobot, but Moegid's antennae were twitching in a way Han had never seen a Verpine do before.

And lying on the table between them was the datacard Thrawn had given them.

"Don't tell me," he warned as Lando picked up the datacard and slid it into the computer reader. "You said it was clean."

"We thought it was," Lando said, pulling up the Caamas Document on the large plotting display. "But then Moegid thought of something else to try." He pointed to the display. "Turns out it's been altered."

A whole string of Corellian curses ran through Han's mind. None of them was adequate for the situation. "Altered how?" he asked, just for the record.

"You have to ask?" Lando growled. "The list of the Bothans involved in the attack has been changed. The one thing we absolutely needed."

Han stepped closer, peering at the display. "You're sure," he asked. Again, just for the record.

"Moegid is," Lando said, looking down at the Verpine. "It's a masterful job, but there are some tricks the Verpines have come up with over the years." He pointed at the display. "Remember how surprised we were when we first looked it over and saw how many of the top Bothan families were implicated? Well, now we know why those names are there."

"A little something to stir the pot a little more," Han said with a grimace. "And to make the rest of the New Republic trust the Bothan leadership even less than they already do."

"You got it, old friend." Lando pulled out one of the other chairs and sat down. "Which means we're right back at square one."

Han pulled out a chair for himself. "We're not even that lucky," he said glumly. "I already told Leia we've got the document."

"You don't think she'll keep that information to herself?"

"Normally, yes," Han said heavily. "Unfortunately . . . she already said she was going to give Gavrisom the good news."

"And he won't keep it to himself?"

Han shook his head. "He's on Bothawui, trying to keep a war from starting. And he's not the type to not use every tool he's got."

"So in other words, we're going to show up at Bothawui with everyone expecting us to be the heroes of the day." Lando shook his head. "Where's an Imperial ambush when you need one?"

"I wouldn't joke about that if I were you," Han warned him. "You can bet that Thrawn will be keeping the Empire off our backs on this one; but there are a lot of people on *our* side who won't want to see the Bothans getting the chance to slip off the hook."

Lando winced. "I hadn't thought about that. Though come to think of it . . . no."

"What?"

"I was just thinking about what Thrawn said about Fey'lya's people stealing those Xerrol sniper blasters," he said slowly. "But if he was lying about the Caamas Document . . ."

"Doesn't necessarily mean he was lying about that, too," Han said. "For that matter, we don't have any proof that Thrawn was even the one who changed those names."

Lando snorted. "You don't really believe that, do you?"

"*Someone's* going to bring it up," Han pointed out. "I can guarantee that one."

Lando muttered something under his breath. "This just gets messier and messier. So what do we do?"

Han shrugged. "We go to Bothawui on schedule and pretend nothing is wrong. Maybe the Bothans really do know who was involved. If they do, maybe we can bluff them into coming clean."

"And if they don't, or we can't?"

Han got to his feet. "We've got two days to come up with something else. Come on, let's go turn this crate toward Bothawui."

.   .   .

"That's it," Tierce said with grim satisfaction, waving at the display. "They've come."

"I'm not convinced," Disra growled, peering at the computer-enhanced image on the display. "Fine, so whoever they are seem to be using TIE fighter technology. That doesn't prove a thing."

"They flew past Bastion," Tierce pointed out. "Clearly looking us over. And we've never seen anything like this anywhere else—"

"That doesn't even prove it was from the Unknown Regions," Disra sniffed. "Let alone that it was Parck or the Hand of Thrawn or whoever."

"—and Bastion is where Thrawn was last reported being seen," Tierce finished with a note of finality in his voice. "Doubt all you like, Your Excellency, but I can tell you right now that the scheme has worked. Thrawn's old allies are finally nosing around the bait."

"I hope you're right," Disra said. "With the Bothawui flash postponed, and with Pellaeon probably springing Vermel from Rimcee Station right at this moment—"

"I told you not to worry about that," Tierce said with some asperity. "There's no way he can hurt us."

"Who can't hurt us?" Flim's voice asked from off to the left.

Disra turned to see Flim emerge from the secret door. The con man had been doing a lot of that lately, he'd noticed: skulking around quietly eavesdropping on his two partners. As if he didn't trust them. "Admiral Pellaeon," Tierce told him. "We were just speculating that he and Colonel Vermel will probably be coming by at some point to demand an explanation for how we've been mistreating them."

"And were you also speculating about that alien ship that buzzed past Bastion a couple of days ago?" Flim demanded. "Or were you going to wait until the Hand of Thrawn knocked on the palace gate before you mentioned it?"

"I can assure you that the first thing they do will *not* be to show up here in person," Tierce said. "These are very cagey people, Admiral. Which, considering the card they're holding, they have every right to be. No, their first contact will be a cautious transmission from somewhere in deep space where they can make a fast escape if they decide it's necessary."

"I fail to see how that helps us any," Flim said icily. "One way or the other, they're still going to want to talk to Thrawn."

"Of course they are," Tierce explained patiently. "But calling in from off-planet allows me to take a message for you *and* to shake some useful information out of them along the way. Trust me, Admiral, I've been planning for this moment for a long time."

Flim grimaced. "That's going to be very comforting if Parck sees straight through it and blasts Bastion to rubble."

Tierce shook his head. "These people were extremely loyal to Thrawn, Admiral," he said. "No matter how cautious and skeptical they appear on the surface, they *want* Thrawn to have survived Bilbringi. You're a con man; surely you understand the effect wishful thinking has on a target."

"Oh, it's very useful," Flim grumbled. "It also means they're twice as dangerous when you finally pull the rug out from under them. Speaking of dangerous, did either of you know that General Bel Iblis has disappeared?"

Tierce and Disra exchanged glances. "What are you talking about?" Disra asked.

"We got a message from the strike team on Bothawui a couple of hours ago," Flim said, strolling forward and tossing a datacard onto the desk. "He said a couple of Rogue Squadron pilots who'd been sniffing around had suddenly pulled out and left the system. He suggested that might mean Bel Iblis was up to something."

"Could be." Tierce nodded, stepping to the desk and picking up the datacard. "Let me check on it."

"I already did," Flim said, pulling over a chair and sitting down. "The official story is that Bel Iblis is out at Kothlis putting together a New Republic force to protect Bothawui. But if you start poking through the data, you can't find any evidence that he's anywhere near Bothan space."

"How did you learn about all this?" Disra interrupted.

Flim lifted his eyebrows in polite surprise. "I'm Grand Admiral Thrawn, Your Excellency," he reminded him. "I called Intelligence and asked."

"Did you get a written report?" Tierce asked him. He had the datacard in his datapad now and was skimming through it.

"It's at the end of that record," Flim told him. "They were quite helpful, actually—asked me if I'd like someone to do a flyby around Kothlis and see what they could find out."

"Waste of time," Tierce said, his voice starting to sound a little odd. "If Kothlis is a cover story, Bel Iblis will have made it far too vac-tight for any casual flyby to pick up on."

"That's exactly what I told them," Flim said smugly. "I'm starting to pick up a genuine feel for tactics, if I do say so myself."

"Don't flatter yourself," Tierce said absently, gazing at the datapad. "And in the future, kindly do not interact with anyone without Moff Disra or myself present. Now be quiet and let me think."

Disra watched the Guardsman's face, an unpleasant sensation creeping over him. Tierce seemed to be doing more and more of this sort of thing lately, this staring off into space as if in some kind of trance as he thought. Was the pressure and strain starting to get to him? Or had he always been this way and Disra simply hadn't noticed?

Abruptly, Tierce's head snapped up. "Admiral, you said that the D'ulin woman had called one of the Mistryl leaders to come talk with us?"

"Yes," Flim said. "Last I heard, she was on her way here."

"Have D'ulin get in touch with her and tell her to change course," Tierce instructed him. "Tell her we'll meet with her instead at Yaga Minor."

"Yaga Minor?" Disra repeated, frowning.

"Yes," Tierce said, smiling tightly. "I believe we may be able to give the Mistryl a live demonstration of Thrawn's tactical genius. *And* help convince Captain Parck that Thrawn is indeed back; *and* deliver a humiliating blow to one of Coruscant's best and brightest in the bargain."

"Wait a minute, wait a minute," Disra protested. "You've lost me."

"I think he's trying to tell us Bel Iblis is going to be insane enough to hit Yaga Minor," Flim said, staring in obvious disbelief at Tierce.

The Guardsman inclined his head slightly. "Very good, Admiral. Only it's not insane—it's their very last chance to avert a civil war. Who better to send than Bel Iblis?"

"I think Flim was right the first time," Disra said. "You're talking about the Caamas Document; but they've already got the copy we gave Solo and Calrissian."

"But Bel Iblis doesn't know about that." Tierce tapped the datapad. "According to the report, he vanished to this supposed Kothlis buildup eight days before that traitor Carib Devist brought his falsified data to the Parshoone Ubiqtorate station, which was how Solo found Bastion. Assuming Bel Iblis has been basically out of contact with Coruscant—and that's the likely situation—he won't know anything about Solo's Bastion trip."

"And what if he checks in before he leaves for the attack and they tell him to stand down?" Disra countered.

"Then we simply impress the Mistryl with the size and power of an Imperial Ubiqtorate base," Tierce said. "They don't need to know we're expecting an attack until it actually happens."

He looked at Flim. "It's a classic con technique," he added. "If the target doesn't know what's supposed to happen, he can't be disappointed if it doesn't."

"He's right about that," Flim agreed.

"All right, fine," Disra said. "And what if Coruscant changes its mind and sends Bel Iblis to attack Bastion instead?"

Tierce shrugged. "On what grounds? We've given them the Caamas Document—"

"Altered."

"Which they don't know about and have no way of proving," Tierce reminded him. "The point is that if Bel Iblis so much as pokes his nose into this system they'll be handing us a propaganda weapon they'll regret for years to come. Give me some holos of an unprovoked New Republic attack on Bastion, and I'll have a thousand systems seceding from Coruscant in the first month alone."

"Besides, Your Excellency," Flim said with a casual wave of his hand, "even if Bel Iblis did hit Bastion, the three of us will still be safe at Yaga Minor. Unless you're so attached to your comforts here you couldn't bear to give them up."

"I was merely pointing out," Disra said stiffly, "that it would look bad for Thrawn to be somewhere else when the Imperial capital was under attack."

"Don't worry about it," Tierce said with a tone of finality in his voice. "Bel Iblis won't hit Bastion; and he *will* hit Yaga Minor. And once we've defeated him, we'll see the Empire's prestige rise considerably."

"We might also finally push Coruscant into launching a full-scale attack at us," Disra warned.

Tierce shook his head. "In five days Coruscant will have a civil war on its hands," he said. "And long before they're ready to turn any attention this direction, we'll have Parck and the Hand of Thrawn."

His eyes glittered. "And this time, there will be nothing that can stop us. Nothing at all."

The corridor was long and drab and gray, lined with equally drab doors. Locked doors, of course—this *was* a prison, after all. The walls and ceiling were solid metal, the floor a metal grating that gave off a pair of hollow-sounding clinks with every footstep.

They were certainly making a lot of those clinks at the moment, Pellaeon thought, listening to the sound echo off the walls as he strode down the corridor toward the secondary security post just around the corner at the far end. It sounded like a parade, in fact, or a sudden burst of rain on a thin metal roof.

And those ahead had taken notice of the commotion. Already four of the guards had poked black-helmeted heads around the corner to see what all the commotion was about. Two of those guards were still visible; the others had ducked back out of sight, presumably to report to whoever was manning the security post.

The other two guards had reappeared by the time Pellaeon reached the corner, all four of them now standing stiffly at full military attention. Without a word or glance Pellaeon passed through the group and rounded the corner.

Four more guards were standing at attention behind the security post desk, three meters in front of an extra-secure-looking cell door. Seated at the desk, gazing up at Pellaeon with a mixture of uncertainty and surliness in his face, was a young major. He opened his mouth to speak—

"I'm Admiral Pellaeon," Pellaeon cut him off. "Supreme Commander of the Imperial Fleet. Open the door."

The major's cheek twitched. "I'm sorry, Admiral, but I have orders that the prisoner is to be kept strictly incommunicado."

For a few seconds Pellaeon just stared at him, a glare developed and honed and fine-tuned by long decades of Imperial command. "I'm Admiral Pellaeon," he said at last, biting out each word, his tone the verbal counterpart of that blade-edged glare. He'd been willing to give the guards the benefit of the doubt, but he had neither the time nor the inclination to put up with any nonsense whatsoever. "Supreme Commander of the Imperial Fleet. Open the door."

The major swallowed visibly. His eyes flicked away from Pellaeon to the dozen stormtroopers visible in the corridor behind him, his mind perhaps flicking to the other twelve stormtroopers out of sight around the corner that his guards would have told him about, then came reluctantly back to Pellaeon's face again. "My orders come from Moff Disra himself, sir," he said, the words coming out with difficulty.

Beside Pellaeon, the stormtrooper commander stirred. "Moff Disra is a civilian," Pellaeon reminded the major, giving him one last chance. "And I'm countermanding those orders."

The major took a careful breath. "Yes, sir," he said, capitulating at last. Half turning, he nodded to one of the guards.

The guard, who had also been eyeing the stormtroopers and had obviously already done the math, showed no hesitation whatsoever. Stepping quickly to the cell door behind him, he keyed it open and moved smartly aside.

"Wait here," Pellaeon told the stormtrooper commander, rounding the desk and stepping into the cell, his pulse pounding in his neck. If Disra had somehow managed to get word here through the transmission blockade and ordered all witnesses disposed of . . .

Seated at a small table, a hand of single sabacc laid out in front of him, Colonel Vermel looked up, his eyes widening in astonishment. "Admiral!" he said, clearly not sure he believed it. "I—"

Abruptly, he scrambled to his feet. "Colonel Meizh Vermel, Admiral," he said briskly. "Request permission to return to duty, sir."

"Request granted, Colonel," Pellaeon said, not bothering to hide his relief. "And may I say how pleased I am to find you looking so well."

"Thank you, Admiral," Vermel said, heaving a sigh of relief of his own as he stepped around the table. "I hope you didn't come alone."

"Don't worry," Pellaeon assured him grimly, waving Vermel to the cell door. "I haven't exactly taken over Rimcee Station; but my men are in position to do so if any of Disra's people take exception to our leaving."

"Yes, sir," Vermel said, throwing an odd look back at him. "Regardless, may I suggest we hurry?"

"My sentiments exactly," Pellaeon agreed, frowning. There had been something in that look . . .

They passed the major and the guard station without comment and headed around the corner. The stormtroopers, as per Pellaeon's earlier instructions, fell into full escort array with twelve each front and rear. "You didn't sound very confident when I mentioned Disra's people a minute ago," Pellaeon commented as they headed down the long corridor.

"It may not be Disra's authority you'll have to go up against, Admiral," Vermel said, moving a bit closer to Pellaeon as if worried about being overheard. "When Captain Dorja brought me aboard after intercepting my ship at Morishim, he said he'd been personally ordered to do so by Grand Admiral Thrawn."

Pellaeon felt his throat tighten. "Thrawn."

"Yes, sir," Vermel said. "I've been hoping it was just some trick of Disra's—I remember you mentioning how totally against these peace talks he was. But Dorja seemed so *sure*."

"Yes," Pellaeon murmured. "I've heard some of those rumors myself. He's allegedly been seen by various people in the New Republic, too."

Vermel was silent a moment. "But you haven't actually seen him yourself?"

"No." Pellaeon braced himself. "But I think it's time I did," he said. "If he has indeed returned."

"You might be in trouble with him for pulling me out," Vermel pointed out reluctantly, glancing back over his shoulder. "Perhaps it would be better if I went back."

"No," Pellaeon said firmly. "Thrawn never punished his officers for doing what they sincerely thought was right. Especially when he hadn't given them orders or the necessary information to understand otherwise."

They reached the end of the corridor and turned into the main guard nexus. The guards and officers were still sitting where Pellaeon had left them, glowering under the silently watchful eye of yet another contingent of the *Chimaera*'s stormtroopers. "No, we're going to go back to Bastion and see what Moff Disra has to say about all this," he continued as they passed through the nexus and headed toward the landing bay where their shuttles were berthed. "If the rumors are false, then we should have no further trouble with Moff Disra. Commander Dreyf and I have obtained a set of datacards—in Disra's personal encrypt, no less—that lays out his entire operation: names, places, and deals, including all his links to the Cavrilhu Pirates and various shady financiers on both sides of the border."

He felt his face harden. "And including the details of his efforts to incite civil war within the New Republic. That alone should be worth a great deal to us in any future negotiations with Coruscant. It will certainly put Disra away for a long time."

"Yes, sir," Vermel murmured. "And if the rumors are true?"

Pellaeon swallowed. "If the rumors are true, we'll deal with them then."

Vermel nodded. "Yes, sir."

"In the meantime," Pellaeon went on conversationally, "your last report is far overdue. I'd like to hear exactly what happened at Morishim."

CHAPTER
31

The preparations had taken six hours: six hours of frantic work as every flight-worthy spaceship on Exocron was hurriedly fitted out for battle. It took another hour to get the whole ensemble into space, and one more to arrange them into something resembling a combat perimeter. And with that, their estimated eight-hour grace period was over.

And now, with the entire Rei'Kas pirate gang on its way, the most pitiful defense fleet Shada had ever seen stood by in trembling readiness to defend its world or die trying.

Most likely, to die trying.

"Report from ground, Adm'ral David," Chin reported from the *Wild Karrde's* bridge comm station, looking over at the helm. "Supreme Adm'ral Darr says we all in good position. Also says Airfleet ships ready if pirates get past."

Looming over Dankin, his hands clasped stiffly behind his back, Admiral Trey David nodded. "Very good," he said, his formal tone nevertheless hinting at a great deal of energy below the surface. "Signal the rest of the fleet to be ready. They could be here at any moment."

"Oh, my," Threepio said miserably from beside Shada at the spotting station. "I do so hate space combat."

"I can't argue with you on this one," Shada agreed, looking over her status board. She had wondered at first—wondered with a great deal of suspicion, actually—why Admiral David would ask to direct the battle from the *Wild Karrde* instead of one of Exocron's own combat ships. But her subsequent assessment of those ships and their capabilities had unfortunately provided her with the answer.

Eight hours ago, she had snidely suggested to Entoo Nee that the Exocron space force might find anything more formidable than an occasional smuggler beyond its strength. Never before in her life had one of her offhanded comments nailed the truth so accurately.

There was a brush of air beside her. "It becomes a waiting game now," Karrde said, kneeling down beside her seat. "What do you think?"

"We haven't got a chance," Shada told him bluntly. "Not unless Rei'Kas doesn't bother to send anything bigger than the Corsairs he hit us with at Dayark."

She thought she'd spoken quietly enough for only Karrde to hear. David apparently had good ears. "No, he'll bring everything he has," the admiral assured her. "His full armada, with himself at the head of it. He's wanted to get his hands on Exocron's wealth for a long time."

He smiled tightly. "Besides which, I understand from Entoo Nee that you gave him something of a bruised eye at Dayark. For the revenge part alone he'd be sure to be here."

Shada felt Karrde's silent sigh as a breath of warm air on her cheek. "Which may ultimately give us our only real chance," he said. "If we can pretend to start running, we may be able to draw enough of them away for your forces to deal with the rest."

"Possibly," David agreed. "Not that that would do us personally much good, of course."

"It's my fault he's here," Karrde reminded him. "It's not too late for you to transfer to one of the other ships—"

At the sensor station, H'sishi suddenly snarled. [They come,] she announced. [Three Sienar *Marauder*-class Corvettes, four Duapherm *Discril*-class Attack Cruisers, four combat-modified CSA Etti Lighter freighters, and eighteen *Corsair*-class attack vessels.]

"Confirmed," Shada said, running her eyes over her spotting displays, a sinking feeling in the pit of her stomach. The *Wild Karrde* could take any one of those ships or give any two of them a decent fight. But all of them together . . .

"Stand by turbolasers," Karrde said, rising to his feet beside her.

"Turbolasers standing by," Shada confirmed, keying targeting information over to the three weapons stations. Just because it was hopeless didn't mean they shouldn't do their best. "Looks like the Corsairs are forming up a screen around the bigger ships."

"Cap't?" Chin called from the comm. "We getting call from one of the Marauders. You want make him an answer?"

Shada could feel Karrde tense. "Yes, go ahead," he said.

Chin keyed the comm—"Hey, there, Karrde," a familiar gloating voice boomed from the bridge speaker. "I told you you'd see me again before you died, didn't I?"

"Yes, Xern, you did," Karrde agreed, his voice betraying none of the tension Shada knew he was feeling. "I'm surprised you're still alive after that fiasco at Dayark. Rei'Kas must be going soft in his old age."

From the background came a distant flurry of Rodian invective.

"Rei'Kas says he'll maybe save you for last for that one," Xern said. "You like that, huh?"

Across the bridge, David cleared his throat. "Rei'Kas, this is Admiral Trey David of the Exocron Combined Air-Space Fleet," he said.

"Oh, an admiral, huh?" Xern said sarcastically. "You mean this collection of scrap rates a whole admiral?"

"You're in violation of Exocron space," David said calmly, ignoring the insult. "This is your last chance to withdraw peaceably."

Xern laughed. "Oh, that's rich. That's really rich. We *definitely* got to save you for last. Then we can gut you all and feed you to the scavengers."

There was another burst of Rodian. "Hey, we got to go, Karrde—time to make the big scrap into lots of little scrap. See you later, Admiral."

The comm keyed off. "They're sure well stocked in the confidence department, aren't they?" Shada murmured.

"Yes," Karrde said. His hand brushed past her shoulder, hesitated, then came back almost reluctantly to rest there. "I'm sorry, Shada," he said, his voice just loud enough for her to hear. "I should never have brought you into this."

"It's all right," Shada said. So this was it: the end of the long journey. Back at the Orowood Tower, facing the Noghri and their blasters, she had been ready to die. Had almost hoped they would overreact and kill her, in fact. The easy way out, she had thought then.

Now, facing the incoming pirates, she realized that there were no easy ways out. No way of dying that didn't involve abandoning a responsibility, or leaving necessary work undone—

She glanced up at Karrde, gazing out the viewport, his face set in hard lines. Or, indeed, of leaving friends behind.

Distantly, she wondered when in all of this she had started to think of Karrde as a friend.

She didn't know. But it didn't matter. What mattered was doing their best to clean up the mess they'd created here. Shifting her attention back to her displays, she began tagging primary and secondary targets. The leading ships were almost in range . . .

"Signal to all ships," Admiral David announced. "Pull back. Repeat: pull back."

Shada flashed him a frown. "What?"

"I said pull back," David repeated, flashing an almost curious look at her in return. "Which part didn't you understand?"

Shada started to say something blistering; choked it back as Karrde squeezed her shoulder warningly. "She was thinking about the fact that the *Wild Karrde* isn't as maneuverable close in to a gravitational field as it is in open space," he told David. "Neither are most of the ships in your fleet."

"Understood," David said. "The order remains. Pull back."

"Chief?" Dankin asked.

Shada glanced up again. Karrde was looking at David, measuring the man with his eyes. "Transmit the order, Chin," he said, his tone suddenly thoughtful. "Dankin, go ahead and retreat, but keep us in formation with the other ships. Shada, have the gunners lay down covering fire."

"Right." Shada keyed her intercom, her eyes searching the displays as she tried to figure out what was going on. The usual tactical reason for pulling back toward a planetary surface was to lure an enemy within range of either ground-based weapons or a surface-launched ambush. But every ship Exocron had was already up here, and H'sishi's sensor probes would certainly have picked up any ground weaponry powerful enough to reach this far into space.

The fleet was beginning to move now, backing toward Exocron as ordered. Some of the armed civilian ships were already firing uselessly at the Corsairs arrowing silently in at them, wasting energy on out-of-range targets. Shada looked at David, but either he hadn't noticed or didn't especially care what they did. Were the civilians nothing but sacrificial lures to him? "Keep retreating," he said instead. "All ships."

The Corsairs were nearly in range, the larger warships formed up behind them now in a straightforward assault line. Little wonder; considering the opposition, there was no need for them to try anything fancy. A straight slice through the ships arrayed against them, then probably a low strafing loop over Exocron's major population centers, taking out Supreme Admiral Darr's pitiful Airfleet along the way . . .

"Keep retreating," David said again. "Tactical display, please."

H'sishi hissed acknowledgment and the tactical overlay came up. The defenders were all well within Exocron's gravity field now, far too late for any of them to change their minds and try to escape to hyperspace. Was that what David was going for? Shada wondered. Putting them in a position where they had no choice but to fight to the death?

Even as that disturbing thought occurred to her, the last of the pirates passed within that invisible boundary, as well. They were all totally committed to this battle now. Neither the attackers nor the defenders would be leaving Exocron until one side or the other had been destroyed.

"Here they come," David murmured.

Shada looked at him, a bitter retort bubbling in her throat. Of *course* they were coming—

And abruptly, H'sishi snarled in disbelief.

Shada snapped her attention back to the viewport. The pirates were still there, still coming.

But they weren't the ones David had been referring to. Behind the pirates' line, something else had appeared.

It was a spaceship, of course. But it was a ship like nothing Shada had ever seen. Roughly ovoid, half again as big as the Marauders, it was covered with thick hull plates that gave it the appearance of some sort of armored sea creature. Conical projections, possibly exhaust ports or thruster pods, jutted out from the hull with no symmetry or pattern that Shada could spot. A magnified image popped up on one of the displays, showing an intricate array of symbols and alien glyphs covering the hull. At close range, the hull itself looked disturbingly like something alive . . .

Someone on the bridge swore, very quietly. Shada looked at the viewport again, just in time to see three more of the ships wink into existence. Not *jump* in, with the characteristic flicker of pseudomotion of a normal hyperspace jump, but simply appear.

And then, almost casually, the first alien ship drove up behind one of Rei'Kas's Marauders; and with a glittering, filigreed sheet of blue-green energy discharge sliced it in half.

H'sishi snarled. [What are these?] she demanded.

"They're called the Aing-Tii monks," David said, his tone a strange mixture of satisfaction and awe. "Alien beings who spend most of their lives near the Kathol Rift. There's not a lot we know about them."

"Yet they're coming to your aid," Karrde pointed out. "More significantly, you knew they would."

"They hate slavers," David said. "Rei'Kas is a slaver. It's very simple."

A second Marauder flashed with fire and streaming air as one of the other Aing-Tii ships sent another of the strange flower-blossoms of energy through its side. Ahead of the wrecked ships, the confident battle line collapsed as the remaining attackers swung around to face this new threat that had appeared so unexpectedly behind them. But to no avail. The Aing-Tii ships shrugged off the frantic turbolaser fire with ease as they systematically drove through the attackers' ranks, cutting up the larger ships and crushing the smaller ones against their own hulls.

"I'm afraid it's not quite that simple, Admiral," Karrde said to David. "According to Bombaasa, Rei'Kas has been setting up in this area for the past year. Why did your Aing-Tii wait this long to move against them?"

"As I said, they prefer to stay near the Rift," David said. "It takes something special to make them come out even as far as Exocron."

"In other words," Karrde said quietly, "you needed someone to lure Rei'Kas into their territory. And that someone was us."

David didn't move, but Shada could see a subtle new tension now in his face and posture. Perhaps wondering what would happen to him if a bridge full of hardened smugglers decided to be offended at having been used as bait. "It was your actions we used, Captain Karrde," he said. "Your decision to come to Exocron, and your inability to keep Rei'Kas's people from tracking you. It wasn't you personally we were using."

His eyes flicked around the bridge. "Not any of you."

For a long moment the bridge was silent. Shada looked back at the viewport, to find the destruction of the pirates nearly complete. Only three of the Aing-Tii were visible now, and as she watched another of them winked out, leaving as mysteriously as it had arrived. The last two alien ships stayed just long enough to finish their task before they too vanished into the darkness.

"You say *we*," Karrde said. "Is that just you and the rest of the Exocron military?"

"That's an odd question," David said obliquely. "Who else could be involved?"

"Who, indeed?" Karrde murmured. "Chin, open a transmission frequency to the surface. Threepio, I want a message translated into Old Tarmidian for me."

Shada looked up at him. Karrde's face was carved from stone, his expression unreadable. "Old Tarmidian?" she asked, frowning. "Car'das's language?"

He nodded. "Here's the message, Threepio: 'This is Karrde. I'd like permission to come down and see you again.' "

"Of course, Captain Karrde," Threepio said, moving uncertainly over toward the comm station. Chin nodded, and the droid leaned over his shoulder. *"Merirao Karrde tuliak,"* he said. *"Mu parril'an se'tuffriad moa sug po'porai?"*

He looked back at Karrde. "You understand, of course, that there may not be an answer for some time—"

"Se'po brus tai," a voice boomed from the speaker, making the droid jump.

A strong, vibrant voice, with no hint of weakness or illness. Shada looked up at Karrde again, to find his stonelike expression had hardened even further. "Translation?" he asked.

Threepio seemed to brace himself. "He said, sir . . . come ahead."

Entoo Nee was waiting for them as the *Wild Karrde* put down again in Circle 15 of the Rintatta City landing field. His casual manner, his cheerful chatter, and the landspeeder ride along with Shada and Threepio toward the pale blue house against the mountain were like a ghostly repetition of Karrde's last trip through the area a few hours earlier.

But there was one big difference. Then, the driving emotions behind his mood had been fear and dread and the morbid contemplation of his own looming death. Now . . .

Now, he wasn't sure what his mood was. Puzzlement and uncertainty, perhaps, tinged with a hint of resentment at having been twitched along like a puppet.

And overlaying it all a renewed haze of dread. Car'das, he couldn't help remembering, had always spoken fondly of predators who played with their prey before finally killing them.

The blue house itself was unchanged, just as old and sagging and dusty as it had been before. But as Entoo Nee led the way to the bedroom door, Karrde noted that the odor of age and sickness had vanished.

And this time the door opened by itself as they approached. Steeling himself, only vaguely aware that Shada had deftly inserted a shoulder in front of him, the two of them together stepped through the door.

The built-in shelves, with all their useless knickknacks and exotic medical supplies, were gone. The sickbed and its stacks of blankets were gone.

And standing where the bed had been, still just as old but now as vitally alive as he had been feeble then, was Jorj Car'das.

"Hello, Karrde," Car'das said, the vast network of facial wrinkles shifting as he smiled. "It's good to see you again."

"Not that it's been all that long," Karrde said stiffly. "I congratulate you on your amazing recovery."

The smile didn't even falter. "You're angry with me, of course," Car'das said calmly. "I understand that. But it'll all become clear soon. In the meantime—"

He half turned and waved at the back wall; and abruptly the wall was no longer there. In its place was a long tunnel equipped with four guide-rails that faded off into the distance. Just beyond where the wall had been, an enclosed quadrail car was waiting. "Let me take you across to my *real* home," Car'das continued. "It's much more comfortable than this place."

He waved a hand toward the car, and a side door swung invitingly open in response. "Please; after you."

Karrde looked at the open door, an odd tightness squeezing his heart. Predators playing with their prey . . . "Why don't just you and I go?" he offered instead. "Shada and Threepio can return to the *Wild Karrde*—"

"No," Shada cut him off firmly. "You want to show someone around, Car'das, you take me. Then if—*if*—I decide it's safe, I'll consider letting Karrde join us."

"Really," Car'das said, regarding her with such obvious amusement that Karrde found himself cringing. Being amused at someone like Shada wasn't an especially healthy thing to do. "Such quick and short-tempered loyalty you inspire in your people, Karrde."

"She's not one of my people," Karrde told him quickly. "She was asked to come along by High Councilor Leia Organa Solo of the New Republic. She has absolutely nothing to do with me, or with anything I might have done in the past—"

"Please," Car'das interrupted, holding up a hand. "I admit this is highly entertaining to watch. But in all seriousness, you're both worrying about nothing."

He looked Karrde straight in the eye. "I'm not the man you once knew, Talon," he said quietly. "Please give me the chance to prove that."

Karrde let his eyes drift away from that unblinking gaze. Predators playing with their prey . . .

But if Car'das truly wanted them dead, it didn't really matter whether they played along or not. "All right," he said. "Come on, Shada."

"Excuse me, sir?" Threepio spoke up hesitantly. "I presume you won't be needing me any further?"

"No, no, please," Car'das said, waving the droid forward. "I'd love to sit down later and have a chat with you—it's been such a long time since I've had anyone I could speak Old Tarmidian with." He smiled over at Entoo Nee. "Entoo Nee tries, but it's not the same."

"Not really, no," Entoo Nee conceded regretfully.

"So please join us," Car'das added to Threepio. "By the way, you don't also happen to know the Cincher dialectory, do you?"

Threepio seemed to brighten. "Of course I do, sir," he said, pride temporarily superseding nervousness. "I am fluent in over six million—"

"Excellent," Car'das said. "Let's be going, then."

A minute later they were all in the quadrail car, speeding smoothly down the tunnel. "I mostly keep to myself these days," Car'das commented, "but occasionally I still need to deal with Exocron officialdom. I use that house back there for such meetings. It's convenient and keeps them from being overawed by my real home."

"They know who you are?" Shada asked, her tone just short of a demand. "I mean, who you *really* are?"

Car'das shrugged. "They have bits and pieces of my past," he said. "But as you'll soon see, much of that history is now irrelevant."

"Well, before we get to history, let's try some current events," Shada said. "Starting with these Aing-Tii monks of yours. David can spin his anti-slaver slant all he wants, but we all know there's more to it than that. You called them in, didn't you?"

"The Aing-Tii and I have had some dealings together," Car'das agreed soberly, his wrinkled face thoughtful. Abruptly he smiled. "But that's history again, isn't it? All in its proper time."

"Fine," Shada said. "Let's try again. David says you didn't use us to lure Rei'Kas in. I say you did."

Car'das looked at Karrde. "I like her, Talon," he declared. "She has a fine spirit." He shifted his eyes to Shada. "I don't suppose you'd be interested in a new job, would you?"

"I wasted a dozen years with a smuggling gang, Car'das," Shada growled. "I'm not interested in joining another."

"Ah," he said with a nod. "Forgive me. Here we are."

The tunnel had come to an end in a small, well-lighted room. Car'das popped the door and bounded out as the quadrail slid smoothly to a stop.

"Come, come," he urged the others. "You're going to love this place, Talon, you really are. All ready? Let's go."

Almost bouncing with childlike anticipation, he led the way to an archway-topped door. He waved his hand as he approached; and as the wall at the blue house had done, the door simply vanished.

And stretched out beyond the doorway was a dream world.

Karrde stepped through, his first impression being that they had stepped out into the open air into a meticulously tended garden. Directly in front of them was a wide expanse of flowers and small plants and shrubs, all carefully and artistically arranged, stretching for perhaps a hundred meters ahead of them. A winding path led through the garden, with stone benches set at various points along it. At its side edges the garden gave way to a forest of tall trees of dozens of different species, with leaves whose colors varied from dark blue to brilliant red. From somewhere within the forest came the bubbling sound of water running over a rock-bottomed creek, but from their position he couldn't see where it was.

It wasn't until he followed the tallest trees up to their tops that he spotted the sky-blue dome above them. A dome that flowed down into unobtrusive walls behind the stands of trees . . .

"Yes, it's all inside," Car'das confirmed. "Very much inside, in fact— we're under one of the mountains to the east of Rintatta City. Beautiful, isn't it?"

"You tend it yourself?" Karrde asked.

"I do most of the work," Car'das said, starting forward toward the path. "But there are a few others, as well. This way."

He led them through the garden to a concealed door between two red-trunked trees on the far side. "Must have been some job putting all this together," Shada commented as the door again vanished at a wave of Car'das's hand. "Your Aing-Tii friends help?"

"In an indirect way, yes," Car'das said. "This is my conversation room. As beautiful as the garden, in its own way."

"Yes," Karrde agreed, looking around. The conversation room was laid out in more or less classic High Alderaanian style, done up in dark wood and intertwined plants, with the same feeling of expansiveness as the garden outside. "What did you mean by indirect help?"

"It's rather ironic, really," Car'das said, angling off through the conversation room toward a door to their right. "When I arrived on Exocron I started building my home under these mountains purely for defensive reasons. Now that defense is no longer an issue, I find I enjoy the place for its solitude."

Karrde glanced at Shada. Defense no longer an issue? "Was Rei'Kas that much of a threat?"

Car'das frowned. "Rei'Kas? Oh, no, Talon, you misunderstand. Rei'Kas was a threat, certainly, but only to the rest of Exocron. I helped get rid of him in order to protect my neighbors, but I myself was in no danger at all. Come; you'll particularly want to see this."

He waved the door away, and gestured them forward. Karrde stepped inside—

And stopped in amazement. He was standing at the outer rim of a circular room that appeared to be even bigger across than the garden they'd just left. The floor of the room dipped, amphitheater fashion, toward the center, where he could see the edge of what looked like a work station or computer desk. Arrayed in concentric circles around the desk, with only narrow walkways separating them, were circle after circle of two-meter-high data cases.

And filling each of the shelves on each of the data cases were data-cards. Thousands and thousands of datacards.

"Knowledge, Talon," Car'das said quietly from beside him. "Information. My passion, once; my weapon and my defense and my comfort." He shook his head. "Amazing, isn't it, what we sometimes persuade ourselves are the most important things in life."

"Yes," Karrde murmured. Car'das's library . . . and the Caamas Document.

"So Entoo Nee lied to us," Shada spoke up, the edge in her voice cutting into Karrde's sense of wonder. "He said he didn't know what happened to your library."

"Entoo Nee?" Car'das called. "Did you lie to them?"

"Not at all, Jorj," Entoo Nee's distant voice protested from behind them. Karrde turned, to see the little man still on the far side of the conversation room, busying himself with drinks. "I merely said that whatever you had done with it had been done before I came to be in your service."

"Which is perfectly true," Car'das agreed, gesturing them back out of the library. "But come sit down. I know you have so many questions."

"Let me start with the most important one," Karrde said, not moving. "The reason we came here was to look for a vitally important historical document. It involves—"

"Yes, I know," Car'das said with a sigh. "The Caamas Document."

"You know about that?" Shada asked.

"I'm not the frail bedridden old man you met a few hours ago," Car'das reminded her mildly. "I still have a few sources of information, and I try to keep in touch with what's happening back home." He shook his head. "Unfortunately, I can't help you. As soon as the Caamas matter first broke I checked through all my files to see if I had a copy. But I'm afraid I don't."

Karrde felt his heart sink. "You're absolutely sure?"

Car'das nodded. "Yes. I'm sorry."

Karrde nodded back. After all the work and danger in getting here, there it was. The end of the road; and at its finish, an empty hand.

Shada wasn't ready to let it go quite that easily. "And what if you *had* found a copy?" she demanded. "You can talk all you want about keeping in touch, but the fact is that for the past twenty years you've been taking it easy out here and letting everyone else do all the work."

Car'das lifted his eyebrows. "Suspicious and unforgiving both," he commented. "That's rather sad. Isn't there anyone or anything you trust?"

"I'm a professional bodyguard," Shada bit out. "Trust isn't part of the job. And don't try to change the subject. You sat out the whole Rebellion, not to mention Thrawn's first bid for power. Why?"

Something unreadable flicked across Car'das's face. "Thrawn," he murmured, his eyes sweeping slowly around his library. "A most interesting person, indeed. I have most of his history with the Empire on file here—pulled it all out recently, reading through it. There's more to his story than meets the eye—I'm convinced of it. Far more."

"You still haven't answered my question," Shada said.

Car'das lifted his eyebrows. "I wasn't aware you'd asked one," he said. "All I heard were accusations that I'd been letting others do all the work. But if that was intended as a question . . ." He smiled. "I suppose it's true, in a way. But only in a way. I've merely let others do their work, while I've been doing mine. But come—Entoo Nee's *rusc'te* will be getting cold."

He led the way across the conversation room to the sunken circle. Entoo Nee was waiting patiently there, his now loaded tray set on a pillar table. "What have you told the lady about me, Talon?" Car'das asked as he gestured the two of them to seats on one side of the circle. "Just to avoid repeating things."

"I've told her the basics," Karrde said, gingerly sitting down. Despite all of the geniality and surface friendliness, he couldn't shake the feeling that there was something more going on beneath the surface. "How you started the organization, then abruptly left twenty years ago."

"And did you tell her about my kidnapping by the Bpfasshi Dark Jedi?" Car'das asked, his tone suddenly odd. "That's where it all really began."

Karrde threw a glance at Shada. "I mentioned it, yes."

Car'das sighed, not looking up at Entoo Nee as the latter put a steaming cup into his hands. "It was a terrible experience," he said quietly, gazing into the cup. "Possibly the first time in my life I'd felt truly and genuinely terrified. He was half mad with rage—maybe more than half mad—with all of Darth Vader's power and none of his self-control. One of my crewmen he physically ripped to shreds, literally tearing his body apart. The other three he took over mentally, twisting and searing their minds and turning them into little more than living extensions of himself. Me—"

He took a careful sip of his drink. "Me, he left mostly alone," he continued. "I'm still not sure why, unless he thought he might need my knowledge of ports and spacelanes to make his escape. Or perhaps he simply wanted an intact mind left aboard who could recognize his power and greatness and be properly frightened by it."

He sipped again. "We headed across the spacelanes, dodging or avoiding the forces gathering against him. I thought up scheme after scheme to defeat him as we traveled, none of which ever made it past the planning stage for the simple reason that he knew about each of them almost before I did. I got the feeling that my pitiful efforts greatly amused him.

"Finally, for reasons I still don't entirely understand, we made for a little backwater system not even important enough to make it onto most of the charts. A planet with nothing but swamps and dank forests and frozen slush.

"A planet named Dagobah."

There was a whiff of some exotic spice from Karrde's side, and he looked up to see Entoo Nee hand him his cup. The little man's usual cheerful expression had vanished, replaced by a profound seriousness Karrde had never seen in him before.

"I don't know if the Dark Jedi expected to be all alone down there," Car'das went on. "But if he did, he was quickly disappointed. We'd barely stepped outside the ship when we spotted a funny-looking little creature with big, pointed ears standing at the edge of the clearing where we'd put down.

"He was a Jedi Master named Yoda. I don't know whether that was his home, or whether he had just flown in specially for the occasion. What I *do* know is that he was definitely waiting for us."

An odd shiver ran through Car'das's thin body. "I won't try to describe their battle," he said in a low voice. "Even after forty-five years of thinking about it, I'm not sure I can. For nearly a day and a half the swamp blazed with fire and lightning and things I still don't understand. At the end of it the Dark Jedi was dead, disintegrating in a final, massive blaze of blue fire."

He took a shuddering breath. "None of my crew survived that battle. Not that there was much left of what they'd been anyway. I didn't expect to survive, either. But to my surprise, Yoda took it upon himself to nurse me back to life."

Karrde nodded. "I've seen a little of what Luke Skywalker can do with healing trances," he said. "Better than bacta in some cases."

Car'das snorted. "In my case bacta would have been completely useless," he stated flatly. "As it was, it took Yoda quite a while to return me to health. I still don't know how long. Afterward I was able to jury-rig the ship well enough to get it spaceworthy and limp home.

"It wasn't until I was back with the organization that I began to realize that, somewhere in that whole procedure, some part of me had been changed."

He looked at Karrde. "I'm sure you remember, Talon. I seemed to have gained the ability to outthink my opponents—to guess their strategies and plans, to know when one of them was planning a move against me. Abilities I assumed I'd somehow absorbed from Yoda during the healing process."

He looked up at the ceiling, a new fire in his eyes and voice. "And suddenly, there were no limits to what I could do. None. I began expanding the organization, swallowing up any group that seemed potentially useful and eliminating everyone that didn't. Victory after victory after victory—everywhere I went I conquered. I saw the Hutts' criminal cartels and planned how I would take them down; foresaw the gathering of power around Senator Palpatine and considered where and how I could best insert myself into the coming struggle for my own advantage. There was literally nothing that could stop me, and I and the universe both knew it."

Abruptly, the fire faded away. "And then," he said quietly, "without warning, everything suddenly collapsed."

He took a long drink from his cup. "What happened?" Shada asked into the silence.

Karrde stole a look at her, mildly surprised at the intense concentration in her expression. Despite all her professed distrust of Car'das himself, she clearly found his story riveting.

"My health fell apart," Car'das said. "Over a period of just a few weeks, all the youth and vigor that Yoda's healing had woven into my body seemed to evaporate." He looked at Shada. "Very simply, I was dying."

Karrde nodded, the last mystery of that beckon call lying abandoned in the Dagobah swamp suddenly falling into place. "And so you went back to Yoda and asked for help."

"Asked?" Car'das gave a short, self-deprecating laugh. "Not asked, Talon. Demanded."

He shook his head at the memory. "It must have looked quite absurd, really. There I stood, towering over him with a blaster in one hand and my beckon call in the other, threatening to bring my ship and all its awesome weaponry to bear on this short, wizened creature leaning on a staff in front of me. Of course, I was the single-handed creator of the greatest smuggling organization of all time, while he was nothing but a simple little Jedi Master." He shook his head again.

"I'm surprised he didn't kill you on the spot," Shada said.

"At the time, I almost wished he had," Car'das said ruefully. "It would have been far less humiliating. Instead, he simply took the beckon call and blaster away from me and sent them spinning off into the swamp, then held me suspended a few centimeters above the ground and let me scream and flail to my heart's content.

"And when I finally ran out of strength and breath, he told me I was going to die."

Entoo Nee stepped to his side, silently pouring more of the spice drink into his cup. "I thought the first part had been humiliating," Car'das went on. "The next part was worse. As I sat there panting on a rock, swamp water seeping into my boots, he told me in exquisitely painful detail just how badly I'd squandered the gift of life he'd given back to me a quarter century earlier. How my utterly selfish pursuit of personal power and aggrandizement had left me empty of spirit and vacant of purpose."

He looked at Karrde. "By the time he finished, I knew I could never go back. That I could never, ever face any of you again."

Karrde looked down at his cup, suddenly aware he was gripping it tightly. "Then you didn't . . . I mean, you weren't . . ."

"Angry with you?" Car'das smiled at him. "On the contrary, old friend: you were the single bright spot in the whole painful mess. For the first time since I'd left Dagobah, I found myself thinking about all the people in my organization. People who I'd now abandoned to the viciousness of internecine warfare as my lieutenants, most of them as selfish as I was, fought for their individual slices of the fat bruallki I'd created."

He shook his head, his old eyes almost misty. "I didn't hate you for taking over, Talon. Far from it. You held the organization together, treating my people with the dignity and respect they deserved. The dignity and respect I'd never bothered to give them. You transformed my selfish ambition into something to be proud of . . . and for twenty years I've wanted to thank you for that."

And to Karrde's surprise, he stood up and crossed the circle. "Thank you," he said simply, holding out his hand.

Karrde stood up, a terrible weight lifting from his shoulders. "You're welcome," he murmured, gripping the extended hand. "I just wish I'd known sooner."

"I know," Car'das said, letting go and returning to his seat. "But as I said, for the first few years I was too ashamed to even face you. And then later, when your Mara Jade and Lando Calrissian came sniffing around, I assumed you would soon be showing up yourself."

"I should have," Karrde conceded. "But I wasn't exactly eager to do so."

"I understand," Car'das said. "It's as much my fault as it was yours." He waved a hand. "Still, as it turned out, your arrival was just what we needed to eliminate the threat from Rei'Kas and his pirates." He pointed toward the ceiling. "That's one of the many things I've been learning from the Aing-Tii, in fact. Though not all is predetermined, all is somehow still being guided. I still don't quite understand that, but I'm working on it."

"Sounds like something a Jedi would say," Karrde suggested.

"Similar, but not the same," Car'das agreed. "The Aing-Tii have an understanding of the Force; but it's a different understanding from that of the Jedi. Or perhaps it's merely a different aspect of the Force that they relate to. I'm not really sure which.

"Yoda couldn't heal me, you see. Or rather, didn't have the time the task would require. He told me he needed to prepare for what he said was possibly the most important instruction he had had for the past hundred years."

Karrde nodded, another piece of the puzzle falling into place. "Luke Skywalker."

"Was it him?" Car'das asked. "I've always suspected that, but was never able to confirm he actually trained on Dagobah. At any rate, Yoda said my only chance to postpone my death was to seek out the Aing-Tii monks of the Kathol Rift, who might—*might*—be willing to help me."

Karrde gestured toward him. "Obviously, they did."

"Oh, yes, they did," Car'das said, his mouth twisting wryly. "But at what a price."

Karrde frowned, a shiver running through him. "What kind of price?"

Car'das smiled. "Nothing less than my life, Talon," he said. "My life, to be spent learning their ways of the Force."

He held up a hand. "Don't misunderstand, please. It wasn't their demand, but my choice. All my life, you see, I've relished challenges—the bigger the better. Once I'd gotten a taste of what they had discovered out here . . ." He waved his hand around the room. "It was the biggest challenge I'd ever faced. How could I pass it up?"

"I thought you needed a certain amount of inborn aptitude to be a Jedi," Shada pointed out.

"A Jedi, perhaps." Car'das nodded. "But as I said, the Aing-Tii have a different view of the Force. Not in terms of Jedi and Dark Jedi—of black and white, as it were—but in a way I like to think of as a full-color rainbow. Here, let me show you. Would you move your tray, please, Entoo Nee?"

The little man picked up the tray, leaving the pillar table empty, as Car'das set his cup down on the floor in front of him. "Now watch," he said, rubbing his hands together. "Let's see if I can do this." He settled his shoulders and gazed hard at the pillar table . . .

And abruptly, with a sharp pop of displaced air, a small crystalline decanter appeared.

Karrde jerked violently, his drink sloshing up the side of his cup and over the edge onto his fingers. Never in any of his dealings with Skywalker or Mara had he seen anything like *that.*

"It's all right," Car'das said hastily. "I'm sorry—I didn't mean to startle you."

"You created that?" Shada asked, her voice sounding stunned.

"No, no, of course not," Car'das assured her. "I merely moved it in here from the cooking area. One of the little tricks the Aing-Tii taught me. The idea is to see the room, and then envision it with the decanter already here—"

He broke off, retrieving his cup and getting to his feet. "I'm sorry. I could go on all day about the Aing-Tii and the Force; but you're both tired, and I'm neglecting my duties as host. Let me show you to your rooms and let you relax for a while while I see about a meal."

"That's very kind of you," Karrde said, standing up and shaking the drops of spice drink off his fingers. "But I'm afraid we have to leave. If you can't provide us with the Caamas Document, we need to start back to New Republic space right away."

"I understand your commitments and obligations, Talon," Car'das said. "But you can certainly afford to take one night just to relax."

"I wish we could," Karrde said, trying not to sound too impatient. "I really do. But—"

"Besides, if you leave now, it'll actually take you much longer to get home," Car'das added. "I've spoken to the Aing-Tii, and they've agreed to send a ship tomorrow to carry the *Wild Karrde* anywhere you want to go."

"And how does that gain us anything?" Shada asked.

"It gains you because their star drive is considerably different from ours," Car'das told her. "As you may have noticed from the battle. Instead of using the usual hyperspace travel, their ships are able to make an instantaneous jump to whatever point they wish to go to."

Karrde looked at Shada. "You were on the spotter scopes," he said. "Was that what they were doing?"

She shrugged. "It's as good an explanation as any," she conceded. "I know H'sishi scrubbed the data and *she* couldn't figure out what had happened, either." She looked suspiciously at Car'das. "So why can't they do this for us now?"

"Because I told them you wouldn't need the ship until morning," Car'das said with a smile. "Come now, indulge an old man's desire for company, won't you? I'm sure your crew could use a good night's rest, too, after all they've been through on this trip."

Karrde shook his head in defeat. "Still a master manipulator, aren't you, Jorj?"

The smile widened. "A man can change only so much," he said genially. "And while they're freshening up," he added, shifting his eyes to Threepio, "you can come help me cook while we have our talk."

"Certainly, sir," Threepio said brightly. "Do you know, I have become quite a fair chef during my service to Princess Leia and her family."

"Wonderful," Car'das said. "Perhaps you can teach me some of your culinary expertise. Why don't you call your ship, Talon, and tell them to settle down until morning. And then I'll show you and the lady to your rooms."

The starlines collapsed down into stars; and gazing out the *Falcon*'s viewport, Leia inhaled sharply.

"Councilor?" Elegos asked, frowning at her from the copilot's seat.

Leia pointed out at the planet Bothawui directly ahead. The planet, and the vast armada of warships swarming around it. "It's worse than I thought it would be," she said in a low voice. "Look at them all."

"Yes," Elegos said softly. "Ironic, isn't it? All those mighty ships of war, preparing to fight and kill and die. Widespread carnage arising from their deep respect for the Caamasi Remnant."

Leia looked across the cockpit at him. There was a profound sadness in his face as he stared out at the ships, a sadness tinged with an almost bitter acceptance of the inevitable. "You've tried to talk to them," she reminded him. "You and the other Trustants. I'm afraid they're beyond listening to reason."

"Reason and calm are always the first casualties of such confrontations." Elegos gestured toward the gathered warships. "All that's left is the thirst for vengeance and the righting of perceived wrongs. Whether those wrongs exist at all, or whether the object of the vengeance is responsible for them."

He craned his neck. "Tell me, can we see the comet from here?"

"Comet?" Leia asked, glancing down at her midrange display. There was a comet there, all right, below and to portside, blocked by the *Falcon*'s main hull. Rolling the ship a few degrees, she brought it up around and into view.

"Yes—there it is," Elegos said. "Magnificent, isn't it?"

"Yes," Leia agreed. It wasn't as big as some comets she'd seen, nor was its tail much more than average. But its proximity to the planet more than made up for its modest size. Still on its way inward toward its loop around the sun, it had apparently just passed through Bothawui's orbit.

"We rarely saw comets from Caamas," Elegos said, his voice sounding distant. "There were few in our system, and none that came nearly so close to our world as these planet-skimmers do. There are, what, twenty of them in this group?"

"Something like that," Leia said. "I remember hearing once that whole branches of Bothan folklore had grown up around them."

"Most identifying them as omens of momentous or terrifying occurrences, no doubt," Elegos said.

"Having something like that blaze past overhead barely half a million kilometers away would tend to make you worry," Leia agreed. "Especially with them coming by once or twice a year." She grimaced. "Of course, with Bothan back-stab politics the way they are, momentous and terrifying events probably had a hard time keeping up with the comets."

"I imagine so," Elegos said. "I pity them, Councilor. I really do. For all the strength and mental agility they claim their political techniques provide to their species, I see them as an essentially unhappy people. Their whole outlook on life breeds mistrust; and without trust, there can be no genuine peace. Neither in politics, nor in the quiet individuality of the heart and spirit."

"I don't think I've ever thought of it quite that way before," Leia said, rotating the *Falcon* back to its original attitude and putting the comet again out of sight. "Did your people try to enlighten them to all that?"

"I'm sure some of us did," Elegos said. "But I don't think Bothan resentment toward us was the reason they sabotaged our shields, if that's what you were wondering."

Leia felt her face flush. "You sure you don't have any Force sensitivity?"

He smiled. "None at all," he assured her. "But the Caamasi Remnant has thought long and hard about this puzzle ever since our world's destruction."

He gave a full-body shrug. "My own belief is that while the saboteurs were probably threatened or blackmailed into their action by Palpatine or his agents, there was something more personal involved. Some dark secret those particular Bothans held that they feared the Caamasi knew and might someday reveal."

"But you don't know what that secret might be?"

Elegos shook his head. "I don't. Others of the Remnant might have learned that memory, but if so are probably unaware of its significance."

Leia frowned. "Learned the memory?"

"There are certain unique qualities to Caamasi memories," he told her. "Someday, perhaps, I'll tell you about them."

"Councilor?" Sakhisakh's voice cut in sharply over the intercom. "Trouble ahead: twelve degrees by four."

Leia looked out that direction. An Ishori war cruiser on the near edge of the swarm of ships seemed to be drifting toward a pair of much smaller Sif'krie skiffs. "Looks like he's trying to get into a lower orbit," she said.

"Unfortunately, that particular space is already occupied," Elegos pointed out.

"Yes," Leia agreed, frowning. Odd; despite the hopeless mismatch in size and firepower, the skiffs were nevertheless holding their ground . . .

And suddenly she saw why. Coming up fast on the skiffs' far side were a pair of Diamalan blockade carriers.

Elegos saw them, too. "I believe," he said, "someone has decided to force the issue."

Leia glanced across the rest of the gathered ships. Others were starting to react to the imminent confrontation, starting to drift out of their confining orbital slots or opening fighter bay doors or rotating so as to better target the nearest of the opposition.

The Sif'krie skiffs were starting to waver now, clearly not eager to be at the center of a massive firefight. The Ishori, recognizing their hesitation, increased its speed toward them; in response, the two Diamala also picked up their pace, splitting formation into a flank/crossfire stance.

"They're going to run down those Sif'kries," Elegos murmured. "Or else the Diamala will open fire on the Ishori to prevent it. Either way, both sides will claim the other was the instigator."

"And either way, the shooting starts," Leia said tightly, running her fingers down the sensor data. New Republic ships—there had to be some New Republic ships out there somewhere. If one of them was close enough to intervene, or even get in between the Ishori and Diamala . . .

But there were only three Corellian Corvettes carrying New Republic IDs, all on the far side of the pack of ships. No chance at all that they could get to the confrontation in time.

Which meant it was up to her.

"Everyone hang on," she called toward the intercom. Without waiting for a reply from the two Noghri, she turned the *Falcon*'s nose toward the Ishori cruiser and threw full power to the sublight drive.

The engines roared to life, the acceleration pushing Leia momentarily into her seat before the compensators could catch up. "I trust you have a plan," Elegos said calmly over the noise. "Do bear in mind that your High Council authority will not likely be enough to stop them."

"I wasn't even going to bring that up," Leia said, glancing at the nav display and easing the helm yoke back just a bit. The *Falcon* was now on a collision course with the Ishori cruiser's stern. "Take over," she added, pulling off her restraints and snagging her lightsaber as she got up from her seat. "Keep us on this course."

"Understood," Elegos's voice came distantly back to her as she sprinted down the tunnel and skidded past the exit hatchway toward the aft cargo bay bulkhead door. She stretched out to the control switch with the Force as she approached, sending the door sliding open—

"Councilor?" Barkhimkh's anxious voice called from the upper quad laser.

"Stay there," Leia called to him as she ducked into the cargo bay and crossed to the starboard side of the ship. Through one more door, and she came at last to the access grill protecting the starboard power converters and ion flux stabilizer.

Han was going to kill her, but it was their only chance. Igniting her lightsaber, clenching her teeth, she jabbed the glowing blade into one of the power converters and dragged it across into the stabilizer.

And grabbed for a handhold as the *Falcon* bucked like a stung tauntaun. It bucked again; and suddenly the drone of the engines changed to an ominous whine.

Twenty seconds later she was back in the cockpit. "Report?" she asked as she slid back into her seat.

"We've lost starboard maneuvering," Elegos said. "The engines appear to be trying to go into a feedback instability." He glanced at her. "I certainly hope this is part of your plan."

"Trust me," Leia assured him, trying to feel as confident as she sounded as she keyed the comm. "Ishori cruiser, this is the freighter *Millennium Falcon*. We're in serious trouble and urgently request assistance."

There was no answer. "Ishori cruiser—"

"This is the Ishori War Cruiser *Predominance*," an angry-sounding Ishori voice snarled from the speaker. "Identify yourself."

"This is New Republic High Councilor Leia Organa Solo aboard the freighter *Millennium Falcon*," Leia said. "We've lost maneuvering and power control in our starboard engines. Our current course has us passing too close to your hull. I need you to move immediately out of our path while we try to regain control."

There was another long pause. Leia watched the warship looming ever nearer, uncomfortably aware that if the Ishori commander chose he could easily turn this whole thing to his own advantage. He had only to use her request as an excuse to speed up his drive toward the Sif'krie skiffs . . .

"I ask you to please hurry," Leia said. A thought occurred to her, and she reached over to blur the fine-focus of her comm a bit. Just enough to let some of the other ships beyond the Ishori eavesdrop on the transmission . . . "My passenger, Trustant Elegos A'kla, is attempting to effect repairs, but I'm afraid the equipment aboard is not within standard Caamasi technical expertise."

Without a word, Elegos unstrapped and got to his feet, disappearing out through the cockpit door. "Ishori Cruiser *Predominance*, do you still copy?" Leia added. "Repeating—"

"No need to repeat," the voice snarled again. Leia felt automatic anger stirring in response to the tone, forced herself to remember that all the emotion in the Ishori voice meant there was some serious thinking going on. She shifted her eyes to the cruiser again and held her breath . . .

And abruptly, the Ishori's advance toward the skiffs slowed, its stern rotating instead out of the *Falcon*'s path. "We stand ready to assist you and Trustant A'kla," the Ishori bit out, his voice already sounding calmer. The thinking was over, and it was time for action. "Lower your shields and prepare for acceleration impact," he continued. "We will attempt to lock a tractor beam onto you to slow your rush."

"Thank you," Leia said, keying off the shields. They didn't affect tractor beams all that much, but there was no point in making a tricky high-speed grab any harder than it already was. "Once we're in your beam, we'll try a cold shutdown and see if we can bring this under control."

"We stand ready to provide any assistance you and Trustant A'kla require," the Ishori said. "Stand ready . . ."

The *Falcon* jerked as the tractor beam caught it, wobbled a moment, then settled down as the lock firmed. Reaching across to the engine controls, Leia threw the shutdown switches.

The engine whine ran down the scale and faded into silence. On the control board, indicators turned red; around her, the lights flickered once as battery power took over. "We read successful shutdown," the Ishori reported. "If you wish, we will bring you aboard our ship to assist you in your repairs."

For a moment Leia was tempted. Having a Caamasi aboard one of the most outspoken and confrontational species' ships might help stretch the peace out here. But on the other hand, it could also be misinterpreted as Elegos's tacit endorsement of the Ishori's anti-Bothan stance. "Thank you again," she told the alien. "But we have an urgent appointment with President Gavrisom that we can't delay. If you could escort us over to the group of New Republic ships, we would very much appreciate it."

"Of course," the Ishori said with only the barest hesitation. The Diamala had reached the Sif'krie skiffs now, the four of them standing together in quiet defiance against any further action. The chance had been missed, and the Ishori knew it.

As did the rest of the armada. All around them, Leia saw, the other ships were starting to settle back into their taut, watchful waiting.

The flash point was safely past. Or at least, this flash point was.

She keyed off the comm. "You're really taking a beating this trip, aren't you," she murmured, patting the *Falcon*'s control board sympathetically. "I'm sorry."

The door behind her slid open. "I see it worked," Elegos said, slipping into the copilot seat again. "You have a fine and unique gift of diplomacy, Councilor."

"And sometimes I'm just lucky," Leia said.

Elegos lifted his eyebrows. "I thought Jedi didn't believe in luck."

"It comes of hanging around Han and this ship," Leia said dryly. "Where did you go, anyway? Back to look at the stabilizer?"

The Caamasi nodded. "I didn't expect to be able to do anything, certainly not after you'd finished with it. But you'd indicated I was trying to repair it, and I wanted there to be some truth in what you were saying."

"Truth." Leia sighed. "That's what we need here, Elegos. What we need desperately. Truth."

"Captain Solo will have that truth here within another day," Elegos reminded her quietly. "All you and President Gavrisom need to do is hold things together that long."

Leia stretched out with the Force, trying to get a feel for the future. "No, I don't think so," she said slowly. "Something tells me it's not going to be that easy. Not nearly that easy."

Navett and Klif had cut through the floor of the Ho'Din tapcafe's storage subbasement floor their first night of work, a ten-minute task with the fusion cutter Pensin had scrounged from somewhere. But after that the job had switched over to something longer, harder, and considerably more tedious.

"Four more days of this, huh?" Klif grunted, heaving another shovelful of noxious Bothawui dirt out of the chest-deep hole onto the large drop cloth they'd spread out to catch it.

"Well, if we really put our backs into it, maybe it'll only take three," Navett pointed out, scooping up the dirt from the cloth in turn and dumping it into their Valkrex fusion disintegration canister. He sympathized with Klif's frustration, but there wasn't a lot either of them could do about it. The vibrations of their digging were iffy enough; but if they tried operating heavy equipment within range of the power conduit's sensors, they'd bring Bothan Security down on them in double-quick time.

"Thanks lots," Klif said dryly, dumping another shovelful. "You know, I don't mind dying for the Empire, but to Vader with these preliminaries."

"Watch your words," Navett warned him, glancing at the door at the top of the stairway. Pensin was supposed to be keeping an eye on the door to the subbasement, but there were a handful of other staff and night guards still up in the tapcafe, and a wrong word overheard by one of them could ruin everything. He scooped up the next shovelful—

There was a scrabbling sound at the door. Navett let the shovel down silently onto the cloth, dropping to one knee and drawing his blaster in a single smooth motion. He leveled the weapon on the door, then lifted it at the soft two-one-two knock. The door opened and Horvic stuck his head around the corner. "Pack it up," he hissed. "The night guards think they've spotted an intruder, and they might come down here looking."

Klif was already out of the hole, manhandling the square of duracrete floor they'd cut back into place. "They get a good look?" Navett asked, holstering his blaster and giving Klif a hand.

"I don't know," Horvic said grimly. "But personally, my money's on that old woman of yours. I spotted someone with your description of her sitting off in a corner booth when Pensin and I came on duty."

"Terrific," Navett snarled under his breath, leaving Klif to disguise the edges of their trapdoor as he shut off the disintegrator and carried it back to its hiding place behind a stack of vodokrene cases. "Well, don't just stand there—go help them find her."

"Right," Horvic said. "What about you?"

"We'll head outside," he said. "Maybe we can tag her on her way out."

"Happy hunting," Horvic said, and disappeared.

It took thirty seconds to fold up the drop cloth and hide it, and another minute to ease their way up through the main basement to the gimmicked back door. The streets in this part of Drev'starn were mostly deserted at this hour, the high-mounted glow panels dimmed to a fairly low light. "I'll take back here," Navett murmured to Klif. "You circle around front. Don't let anyone see you."

"Don't worry." Moving like a shadow, Klif headed down the side alley and disappeared around the corner of the building. Checking both directions, Navett crossed to a trash container a few meters away. Sinking into its shadow, he balanced his blaster across one knee and waited.

And waited. Occasionally he spotted figures hurrying by in front of the lighted windows of the tapcafe, and several times the Ho'Din or one of his night guards poked their head out the back door, double-checked the lock, and went back in. But no one came out and stayed out. Not the woman or anyone else.

It was an hour before the commotion seemed to finally die down inside. Navett waited another thirty minutes, irritably counting the number of shovelfuls behind schedule this was costing them, before finally pulling out his comlink. "Klif?"

"Nothing," Klif's voice came back. He sounded irritated, too. "Sounds like they've given up."

"Must have been a false alarm," Navett said. "Come on around and we'll get back to work."

A few minutes later they were back in the subbasement. Klif retrieved the drop cloth as Navett headed around the stacked vodokrene cases for the disintegrator.

And paused there. Lying on top of the disintegrator was a comlink. "Klif?" he called softly. "Come here."

A moment later the other was at his side. "I don't believe it," he said, sounding stunned. "How in blazes did she pull *this* one off?"

"Why don't we ask her," Navett said, carefully picking up the comlink. It was a binary-linked type, he noted, the sort typically carried on small starships and connected only to another specific comlink. He gave it a quick once-over for booby traps, then flicked it on. "You're very inventive," he said. "I'll give you that."

"Why, thank you," the old woman's voice came back promptly. "That's very flattering. Particularly coming from an Imperial dirty tricks team."

Navett glanced at Klif. "You know, that's the second time you've accused us of being Imperials," he reminded her. "You *are* just guessing, of course."

"Oh, hardly," she said scornfully. "Who else would be looking to take down the Bothans' planetary shields?"

"You're still just guessing," Navett said, straining his ears for some sign of telltale sounds in the background and wishing viciously he had the equipment that would let him trace the transmission. "If you were sure, you'd have called Bothan Security instead of still skulking around yourself this way."

"Who says I haven't called them?" she said. "Or maybe I like skulking around. It could be I used to do this sort of thing all the time against Hutts and other slime. Maybe I'm looking for a new challenge."

"Or maybe you're looking for an early and violent death," Navett countered. "How did you find us, anyway?"

"Oh, come on," she chided. "You don't really think your cover is *that* good, do you? My New Rep buddies and I had you pegged first time off the rack. So what was the deal with those metalmites at the shield generator, anyway?"

Navett smiled tightly. "Fishing now, are we? Please."

"You never can tell," she said. "Incidentally, whichever of you gimmicked that back door lock needs to do a better job next time—it was so obvious you might as well have hung a sign on it. It did come in handy, though."

"I imagine it did," Navett said. "You're still in the building, aren't you?"

"Now who's fishing?" she countered. "Actually, no, I left some time ago—there's a crawlspace beneath the ceiling that leads to a handy skylight. That was a free one."

"Thank you," Navett said between clenched teeth. Who did this little fringe slime think she was talking to, anyway? "Here's some free advice in return. Go back to your ship and clear off Bothawui. If you don't, you *are* going to die on this dirtball. I will personally guarantee that."

"With all due respect, Lieutenant—or is it Major? Colonel? Oh, well, with the Empire in shambles these days I guess rank doesn't really matter. With all due respect, Imperial, I've been threatened by far more impressive folks than you. Anytime you want to come out and do a face-to-face, I'm ready."

"Oh, we'll do a face-to-face, all right," Navett promised, forcing down his anger. Anger, and the muddled thinking that accompanied it, were exactly what she was angling for. "Don't worry about that. But when we do, it'll be a time and place of my choosing, not yours."

"Whatever you want," she said. "Nighttime would work best—that way you can use that Xerrol Nightstinger of yours to full advantage. You didn't just throw it away after that riot a few weeks back, did you? The one where you framed Solo for shooting into the crowd?"

Navett glared at the comlink. Aside from being a general all-around pain in the neck, this woman was far too well informed. Who in space did she work for, anyway? "You're fishing again," he said.

"Not really," she said offhandedly. "Just putting two and two together."

"Sometimes that kind of math doesn't work the way you think it does," Navett warned her. "And sometimes if the mathematician hangs around where she's not welcome, she doesn't live to finish her sums."

She clucked. "You're starting to repeat yourself, Imperial. If I were you, I'd try to work up some fresh threats. However, it's well past my bedtime and I know you have work to do, so I'll let you go. Unless you'd like to go fetch your Xerrol and come out and play, that is. I'll wait."

"Thanks," Navett said. "I'll pass for now."

"Entirely up to you," she said. "Go ahead and keep the comlink—I've got plenty of spares. Good night, and happy digging."

The transmission clicked off. "And restless and unpleasant dreams to you, too," Navett murmured, dropping the comlink into the disintegrator.

He looked back at Klif. "This," he said darkly, "is just exactly what we needed."

"Oh, exactly," Klif ground out. "So what are we going to do about her?"

"For now, nothing," Navett said, picking up the disintegrator and lugging it over to the drop cloth. "For all her fishing and accusations, she doesn't really know anything."

"Like blazes she doesn't," Klif retorted. "She knows we're digging over one of the shield building's power conduits. What more does she need?"

"My point exactly," Navett said. "She's spotted our digging, but hasn't called Security down on us." He squatted down and eased his shovel blade under the edge of their trapdoor. "Why not?"

"How should I know?" Klif grumbled, getting his shovel into place under the other side. "Maybe she figures she'll pick up a bounty if she can deliver everything in a neat package."

"Could be," Navett said, lifting carefully. The block came up, and he got his fingers under the edge. "I think it's more likely she's got some trouble of her own with the Bothans that means she can't go to them with any accusations."

"That wouldn't stop her from calling in an anonymous tip," Klif grunted as they eased the trapdoor off the hole. "The mood they're in out there, they're probably jumping at every cracked twig."

"No," Navett said, gazing into the hole. "No, she's not the type for anonymous tips. I think that for whatever reason, she's decided to take this whole thing personally. Professional pride, maybe—I don't know. The point is that she's turned this into a private duel between her and us."

Klif grunted. "Pretty stupid."

"Stupid for her," Navett agreed. "Useful for us."

"Maybe," Klif said. "So what now?"

"We get back to work," Navett said, dropping into the hole. "And when we're done," he added, digging his shovel into the packed dirt at his feet, "I'll go retrieve the Xerrol. Maybe tomorrow night we'll take her up on her invitation to come out and play."

Gavrisom looked up from Leia's datapad, his prehensile wing tips flicking restlessly across the desk beside it. "And you truly believe he is sincere about this?" he said.

"Very sincere," Leia said, feeling a frown creasing her forehead. She had expected a considerably more positive reaction to Pellaeon's peace proposal. "And I examined the credentials he brought from the Imperial Moffs. Everything was in order."

"Or so it appeared," Gavrisom said, shaking his mane. "So it appeared."

He looked back down at the datapad, touched the control to scroll back. Leia watched him, trying to understand this strange and unexpected emotional conflict she could sense in him. An end to the long war might finally be at hand. Surely this was news for at least cautious excitement.

So why wasn't he cautiously excited?

Gavrisom looked up at her again. "There's no mention of Thrawn anywhere in here," he pointed out. "Did you ask Pellaeon about that?"

"We discussed it briefly," Leia said. "At that time he'd received no word from Bastion that Thrawn had assumed supreme command. Nor had he had any indication that the Moffs had rescinded his authorization to begin peace talks."

"Neither of which means anything at all," Gavrisom said, his tone suddenly and uncharacteristically harsh. "With Thrawn on the scene, officially or otherwise, this is utterly meaningless." He slapped a wing tip across the datapad.

"I understand your concerns," Leia said, choosing her words carefully. "But if it's not a trick, this may be our chance to finally end this long war—"

"It is most certainly a trick, Councilor," Gavrisom ground out. "That much we can all be sure of. The only question is what exactly Thrawn hopes to gain from it."

Leia drew back in her seat. The flash of emotion right then . . . "You don't want Pellaeon's offer to be genuine, do you?" she asked. "You *want* it to be a trick."

Gavrisom turned his eyes away from her, snorting a soft, whinnying sigh. "Look all around us, Leia," he said quietly, turning his head to gaze out the stateroom viewport. "Look at them. Nearly two hundred warships, dozens of peoples, all ready to begin a civil war over their own individual concepts of what constitutes justice for Caamas. The New Republic is poised ready to destroy itself . . . and there's nothing I can do to prevent it."

"Han has a copy of the Caamas Document," Leia reminded him. "He'll have it here tomorrow. That should defuse a lot of the tension."

"I'm sure it will," Gavrisom agreed. "But at this point I'm not willing to rely on even that to stop them. You and I both know that for many of the potential combatants Caamas has merely become a convenient excuse for restarting old wars with old enemies."

"I realize that," Leia said. "But once that excuse is taken away from them, they'll have to back down."

"Or create a different excuse," Gavrisom countered bitterly. "The fact is, Leia, that the New Republic is in danger of fragmenting, of being driven apart by our own vast diversity. We need time to counter those forces; time to talk, time to plan, time to try to build all these different peoples into some sort of unity."

He waved a wing toward the viewport. "But we no longer have that time—this crisis has snatched it away from us. We need to get it back."

"The Caamas Document will do that," Leia insisted. "I'm sure it will."

"Perhaps," Gavrisom said. "But as President, I can't afford to put all my hopes on it. I must prepare to muster every common purpose I can find for the New Republic. Every common purpose, every common goal, every common cultural ethos."

He tapped the datapad, gently this time. "And, if necessary, every common enemy."

"But they're not a real enemy anymore," Leia said, striving to keep her voice calm. "They're far too small and weak to be any kind of threat."

"Perhaps," Gavrisom said. "But as long as they're out there, we have someone to unite against." He hesitated. "Or even to fight against, if necessary."

"You aren't serious," Leia said, gazing hard at him. "Stirring up action against the Empire at this point would be nothing short of a slaughter."

"I know that." He shook his head. "I don't like this any better than you do, Leia. In fact, I will admit to being ashamed of using the people of the Empire this way. But whether my name and memory are denounced by history is of no importance. My job is to hold the New Republic together, and I will do whatever is necessary to achieve that."

"Perhaps I have more faith in our people than you do," Leia said quietly.

"Perhaps you do," Gavrisom said with a nod. "I sincerely hope you are right."

For a moment they sat together in silence. "I presume you won't be releasing news of Pellaeon's offer," Leia said at last. "With your permission, though, I'd like to begin putting together a list of delegates for a full peace conference. If and when you decide to proceed with this."

Gavrisom hesitated, then nodded. "I admire your confidence, Councilor," he said. "I only wish I could share it. Yes, please assemble your list."

"Thank you."

She got up from her chair and retrieved her datapad. "I'll have the list ready for you by tomorrow." She turned to the stateroom door—

"There is, of course, one other option open to you," Gavrisom called from behind her. "You are merely on leave of absence from the Presidency. Assuming the Senate confirmed the decision, you could resume that office right now."

"I know," Leia said. "But this isn't the time for that. Yours is the voice that has been speaking for Coruscant since the Caamas Document first came to light. It wouldn't be good for that voice to suddenly change."

"Perhaps," Gavrisom said. "But there are many in the New Republic who believe that Calibops are skilled at words and nothing more. Perhaps the time for words has ended, and the time for action has arrived."

Leia stretched out briefly to the Force. "The time for action may indeed have come," she agreed. "But that doesn't mean the time for words is ended. Both will always be needed."

Gavrisom whinnied softly. "Then I will continue with the words," he said. "And will entrust to you the actions. May the Force be with us both."

"May the Force be with us all," Leia said quietly. "Good night, President Gavrisom."

CHAPTER
33

She waited until an hour after the background sounds of the household had quieted down. Then, getting up from her bed, Shada left her room in the vast underground complex that was Jorj Car'das's home and slipped down the darkened hallway.

The library door was closed, and the Aing-Tii hand-waving trick Car'das had used to get inside obviously wasn't going to work for her. However, before saying good night he had showed her and Karrde the more conventional method of opening their room doors, and she was banking on the library being set up the same way. Searching around the stones lining the doorway with her fingers, she found the slightly cooler one and pressed her palm against it.

For perhaps twenty seconds nothing happened. Shada maintained her pressure on the stone, alert for signs of activity in the area and wondering again at this ridiculous procedure. Based on the life story he'd told them, she couldn't see the Jorj Car'das who had first arrived here on Exocron being an overly patient man, certainly not the type to install doors in his home that took half a minute to open. She could only assume his thinking at that time had been that intruders bent on theft or violence would be similarly impatient.

Now, of course, with his Aing-Tii tricks, none of it mattered. At least not to him.

Beneath her hand, the trigger stone gave a gentle bump. Shada held on; and a few seconds later the door finally slid ponderously open.

She'd expected the library to be as dark as the rest of the house, with only a handful of muted glow panels to show the way around. To her uneasy surprise, the room was lit much more brightly than that. Not as bright as it had been when Car'das showed it to them earlier, but brighter than an uninhabited room ought to be. She slipped inside, ducking to the left out of the doorway; and as she did so, she caught a glimpse of a moving shadow in the central circle near the computer desk.

Car'das? She bit back a curse. Karrde had already scheduled an early-morning departure for the *Wild Karrde*'s rendezvous with the Aing-Tii ship. This was her one and only chance to get to the datacard she needed to find.

And then, drifting up from the computer desk, she heard a muffled but very familiar voice: distinctive, somewhat prissy, and quite mechanical. Silently, she detached herself from the wall and made her way down one of the narrow aisles between the data cases and headed to the center.

To find that her ears had indeed not been playing tricks on her. "Hello, Mistress Shada," Threepio said brightly, straightening up from his stooping lean over the computer desk. "I thought you and the others had retired for the night."

"I thought you had done so, too," Shada said, glancing at the nearest data case as she stepped over to him. Each shelf completely packed with stacks of datacards; each stack of datacards standing eight to ten deep. An incredible collection of knowledge. "Or whatever it is droids do at night."

"Oh, I usually close down for a time," Threepio told her. "But during my talk earlier with Master Car'das he suggested I might wish to have a chat with his main computer. Not that the computer aboard the *Wild Karrde* isn't decent company, of course," he added hastily. "But I must admit I sometimes miss Artoo and others of my own kind."

"I understand," Shada assured him, a lump forming in her throat. "It can be very lonely to be somewhere where you're out of place."

"Really," Threepio said interestedly. "I suppose I've always assumed human beings were adaptable to most every place and circumstance."

"Being adaptable to something doesn't necessarily mean you like it," Shada pointed out. "In many ways I'm as much out of place aboard the *Wild Karrde* as you are."

The droid tilted his head. "I'm so sorry, Mistress Shada," he said, sounding pained. "I had no idea you felt that way. Is there anything I can do to help?"

"Maybe help me return to where I belong." Shada gestured down at the computer desk. "Have you gotten to know the computer well enough to be able to do a search of Car'das's library?"

"Certainly," Threepio said, his voice suddenly wary. "But this *is* Master Car'das's equipment. I'm not sure I should—"

"It'll be all right," Shada soothed him. "I'm not going to steal anything. All I want is one small piece of information."

"I suppose that would be all right," Threepio said, still sounding uncertain. "We are his guests, after all, and guests often have the tacit run of the household—"

He stopped as Shada held up a hand. "Can you do the search?" she asked again.

"Yes, Mistress Shada," he replied in a somewhat subdued voice. "What is it you wish to search for?"

Shada took a deep breath—

"Emberlene," a quiet voice came from behind her. "The planet Emberlene."

"Oh, my!" Threepio gasped. Shada spun around, dropping into a slight crouch, her hand diving beneath her tunic to the grip of her blaster—

"Forgive me," Car'das said, coming into view around the inner circle of data cases. "I didn't mean to startle you that way."

"I certainly hope not," Shada said, her grip still on her blaster, muscles and reflexes preparing for combat. If Car'das took exception to her being here . . . "I didn't hear you come in."

"I didn't mean for you to hear me," he said, smiling. "You're not planning to use that blaster, are you?"

So much for Mistryl subtlety. "No, of course not," she said, withdrawing her hand empty. "I was just—"

She broke off, frowning, as the words he had spoken a moment earlier suddenly penetrated her conscious mind. "What did you say when you came in?"

"I told Threepio you wanted to do a search for the planet Emberlene," Car'das said, eyeing her steadily. "That *is* what you were going to look up, wasn't it, my young Mistryl shadow guard?"

Her first impulse was to deny it. But looking into that even gaze, she knew it would be a waste of effort. "How long have you known?" she asked instead.

"Oh, not long at all," he said, waving a hand in an oddly self-deprecating gesture. "I suspected, of course, but I didn't actually *know* until you defeated those four swoopers outside Bombaasa's place."

Shada grimaced. "So Karrde was right," she said. "He thought giving Bombaasa his name would eventually get it back to you."

Car'das shook his head. "You misunderstand. Bombaasa doesn't work for me, nor I for him. In fact, aside from Entoo Nee and the other few in my household, no one actually works for me at all."

"Right—you're retired," Shada growled. "I forgot."

"Or else you don't truly believe," Car'das countered. "Tell me, what is it you want for Emberlene?"

"What everyone else wants," she shot back. "At least what they want for big, important worlds like Caamas. I want justice for my people."

Car'das shook his head. "Your people don't want justice, Shada," he said, an infinite sadness in his voice. "They never did."

"What are you talking about?" Shada demanded, feeling her face warming. "How dare you judge us? How dare you judge *anyone*? Sitting out here all high and mighty, never deigning to get your own hands dirty, while everyone else fights and bleeds and dies—"

She broke off, her rising fury at his attitude battling against her deeply ingrained fear of losing control. "You don't know what it's like on Emberlene," she bit out. "You've never seen the suffering and squalor. You have no business saying we've given up."

Car'das's eyebrows lifted. "I never said you'd given up," he corrected her gently. "What I said was that you didn't want justice."

"Then what *do* we want?" Shada snarled. "Charity? Pity?"

"No." Car'das shook his head. "Vengeance."

Shada felt her eyes narrow. "What are you talking about?"

"Do you know why Emberlene died, Shada?" Car'das asked. "Not *how* it died—not the firestorming and massive air and space attack that finally crushed it—but *why*?"

She stared at him, a dark uneasiness beginning to swirl into the flame of her anger and frustration. There was something behind his eyes that she didn't like the look of at all. "Someone feared our growing power and prestige and decided to make an example of us," she said carefully. "Some think that person was Palpatine himself, which is why we've never worked for his Empire."

The eyebrows lifted again. "Never?"

Shada had to look away from that gaze. "We had millions of refugees to feed and clothe," she said, her voice sounding hollowly defensive in her ears. "Yes, sometimes we worked even for the Empire."

For a moment the room was filled with an awkward silence. "Principles are so often like that, aren't they?" Car'das said at last. "So very slippery. So hard to hold on to."

Shada looked back at him again, trying to come up with a properly scathing retort. But nothing came to mind. In Emberlene's case—in the Mistryl's case—his quiet cynicism was all too true.

"At any rate, that particular principle was of no real value," Car'das continued. "As it happens, Palpatine had nothing to do with Emberlene's destruction."

He stepped past her and around to the data case behind Threepio. "I have the true history of your world right here," he said, waving at the top row of datacards. "I pulled all the information together once I knew you'd be coming here with Karrde. Would you like to see it?"

Automatically, Shada stepped toward him . . . hesitated. "What do you mean by *true*?" she asked. "What does anyone mean by true? We both know history is written by the winners."

"History is also written by the bystanders," Car'das said, his hand still up beside the datacards. "By the Caamasi, and the Alderaanians, and the Jedi. Peoples who had no part or stake in what happened. Would you accuse *all* of them of lying?"

Shada swallowed, fear and a horrible sense of inevitability twisting itself around her throat. "And what do all these disinterested parties say?" she asked.

Slowly, Car'das lowered his hand. "They say that three years before its destruction," he said gently, "the rulers of Emberlene set off on a rampage of conquest. That for the first two and a half of those years they destroyed and conquered and plundered every one of the dozen other worlds within their reach."

"No," Shada heard herself whisper. "No. That can't be true. We wouldn't . . . we couldn't have done something like that."

"The average citizens weren't told the true story, of course," Car'das said. "Though I imagine most could have read between the lines if they'd truly wanted to know what their leaders were doing. But they had triumph and spoils, pride and glory. Why bother with mere truth?"

Again, Shada had to look away from those eyes. *It wasn't my fault*, she wanted to protest. *I wasn't there. I didn't do it.*

But the words were hollow, and she knew it. No, she hadn't been one of those who had toasted Emberlene's conquests and looked eagerly ahead for more. But in dedicating her life to the Mistryl, she had in her own way helped to perpetuate the lie.

All because she had wanted to make a difference.

"You shouldn't take any of this personally, Shada," Car'das offered softly into her thoughts. "You didn't know; and the desire to make a difference is something held deeply within all of us."

Shada looked sharply at him. "Stay out of my mind!" she snapped. "My thoughts are none of your business."

He bowed his head briefly. "I'm sorry," he said. "I didn't mean to intrude. But when someone is shouting, it's usually difficult not to overhear."

"Well, try harder." Shada took a deep breath. "So what happened? How were we finally stopped?"

"Your victims and potential victims were too weak to fight back on their own," Car'das said. "So they pooled their resources and hired a mercenary army. The army was . . . perhaps overly thorough."

Overly thorough. Again, Shada searched for a blistering retort. Again, there was nothing she could say. "And all in the sector rejoiced," she murmured.

"Yes," Car'das said quietly. "But for the stopping of a dangerous war machine. Not for the suffering of the innocent."

"No, the innocent are never a very high priority, are they?" Shada said, hearing the bitterness in her voice. "Does your true history tell who the army was who destroyed us? Or who their sponsors were?"

His face seemed to settle subtly. "Why do you want to know?"

Shada shrugged, an uncomfortable hunching of suddenly tired shoulders. "My people have never known who did it."

"And if I give you that information, what will you do with it?" Car'das asked. "Turn the vengeance of the Mistryl against them after all these years? Create more suffering among still more innocents?"

The words were a sudden stab in her heart. "I don't know what they'll do with it," Shada said, a sudden misting in her eyes blurring her sight. "All I know is that it's the only thing I can take back that might let—" She broke off, swiping viciously at her eyes.

"You don't want to go back to them, Shada," Car'das said. "They're living a lie, whether they know it or not. That's not for you."

"I have to," Shada said miserably. "Don't you understand? I have to work for something larger than myself. I've always needed that. I have to have something to hold on to and serve that I can believe in."

"What about the New Republic?" Car'das asked. "Or Karrde himself?"

"The New Republic doesn't want me," she bit out. "And Karrde . . ." She shook her head, an acid burning in her throat. "Karrde's a smuggler, Car'das, just like you were. What kind of purpose is that to believe in?"

"Oh, I don't know," Car'das said thoughtfully. "Karrde has altered the organization considerably since my days with it."

"It's still the fringe," Shada said. "It's still illegal and underhanded. I want something honorable, something noble. Is that so much to ask for?"

"No, of course not," Car'das said. "Still, Karrde's much more an information broker now than he is a smuggler. Isn't that at least a little better?"

"No," Shada said. "In fact, it's worse. Information brokering is nothing more than selling people's private property to those who don't deserve to have it."

"Interesting point of view," Car'das murmured, his gaze shifting to Shada's right. "Have *you* ever considered it that way?"

"I haven't up till now," Karrde's voice said.

Shada spun around, shaking the last lingering tears from her eyes. Off to her right, dressed in a robe and ship slippers, Karrde was standing just outside the inner circle, regarding her with an odd expression on his face. "Perhaps I need to reassess my thinking," he added.

"What are you doing here?" Shada demanded.

"Car'das called me," Karrde said. He looked at Car'das, his forehead wrinkling. "At least, I *think* he called me."

"Oh, yes, definitely," Car'das assured him. "I thought you should be in on this part of the conversation." He bowed his head to Shada. "Forgive me again, Shada, if I startled you."

Shada fought back a grimace. "He's just full of surprises, isn't he?" she commented.

"He's always been that way," Karrde agreed, stepping over to her side. "All right, Car'das. Your two puppets are assembled and awaiting your commands. What do you want from us?"

Car'das's eyes widened in a look of innocence. "Me?" he protested. "I want nothing from you, my friends. On the contrary, I wish to present you with a gift."

Shada glanced at Karrde, found him throwing her the same suspicious look. "Really," Karrde said dryly. "And what kind of gift might that be?"

Car'das smiled. "You were never one to appreciate surprises, were you, Karrde?" he said. "Not too bad at dealing them out, mind you, but extremely poor at accepting them. But I think you'll like this one."

He turned to the data case behind him and selected two datacards from the top shelf. "This is the gift I offer," he said, turning back to face them, holding one of the datacards in each hand. "This"—he held up his right hand—"is the history of Emberlene I was just speaking to Shada about. Something she very much wants, or at least has thought in the past that she wanted. This"—he held up his left hand—"is a datacard I made up especially for you. One which I personally think will be far more beneficial for everyone in the long run."

"What's on it?" Karrde asked.

"Useful information." Car'das laid them down side by side on the computer desk. "You may have one of them. Please choose."

Beside her, Shada felt Karrde take a deep breath. "It's your choice, Shada," he said quietly. "Take whichever one you wish."

Shada stared down at the two datacards, waiting for the inevitable emotional turmoil to twist through her. Her only hope of rejoining the Mistryl—perhaps her only hope of even staying alive through the death mark they'd put on her—lay there to her left. To her right was an unknown quantity, put together by an old man who might easily be half insane, for the supposed benefit of another man whose whole purpose in life was the antithesis of what she herself had always yearned for.

But to her weary surprise, the turmoil never came. Had Car'das's earlier revelations merely burned all of it out of her, she wondered vaguely, leaving no strength left to drive such emotions as anger or uncertainty?

But no. There was no turmoil because there was no real decision to be made. Car'das was right: she could no longer work with the Mistryl, who served and killed and died so that Emberlene could someday rise again. Not now that she knew what Emberlene had once been.

And certainly not now that she could see what the Eleven might do with the knowledge on that datacard.

The justice she had once thought she was seeking had already been carried out. All that datacard could create was vengeance.

Reaching across the desk, distantly aware that she was now finally crossing the final bridge from her past, she picked up the datacard on the right.

"I'm pleased with you, Shada D'ukal, child of the Mistryl," Car'das said with a warmth she had never heard in his voice before. "I promise you won't be disappointed."

Shada looked at Karrde, steeling herself for his reaction to Car'das's revelation. But he merely smiled. "It's all right," he said. "I've known who you are for a long time."

She looked back at Car'das. "Who I *was*," she corrected Karrde quietly. "What I am now . . . I don't know."

"You'll find your way," Car'das assured her. Abruptly he straightened and rubbed his hands together. "But now, it's time to go."

Shada blinked. "Already? I thought we had until morning."

"Why, it *is* morning out there," Car'das said, coming around the computer desk and taking Karrde and Shada each by an arm. "Close enough, at least. Come, come—there's a great deal yet for you to do. You, too, Threepio—come along."

"What about this?" Shada asked, waving the datacard as Car'das hustled them up the aisle toward the exit.

"You can read it on the way to the rendezvous point," Car'das told her. "Just the two of you together—no one else. After that, I think you'll know what to do."

They reached the door and Car'das waved it open. "What about you?" Karrde asked as the old man steered them back down the hallway, now properly lit again, toward their rooms.

"My door's always open to you," Car'das said. "Either of you, of course. Come back anytime you want to visit. But for now, you must hurry."

An hour later, the *Wild Karrde* lifted from Exocron and headed out into space. An hour after that, after assuring himself they were properly on their way to their rendezvous with the waiting Aing-Tii ship, Karrde took Shada back to his office.

And sitting together in front of his desk display, they read the datacard.

Shada was the first to break the silence. "He was right, wasn't he?" she murmured. "This is incredible. If it's true, that is."

"Oh, it's true," Karrde said, gazing at the display, his mind spinning furiously. Shada had vastly understated the case: *incredible* didn't even begin to cover it. "If he was nothing else in his entire life, Car'das was always reliable."

"I can believe that." Shada shook her head. "I take it we're going to have the Aing-Tii take us straight back to Coruscant with this?"

Karrde hesitated. Coruscant was of course the obvious choice.

But there was a complete range of possibilities here. Some very interesting possibilities indeed.

"Karrde?" Shada cut into his thoughts, her tone suddenly suspicious. "We *are* taking this back to Coruscant, aren't we?"

He smiled at her. "Actually, no," he said. "I think we can do better than that."

He looked back at the display, feeling his smile turn grim. "Much, much better."

Standing astride the command walkway of the Imperial Star Destroyer *Tyrannic,* Captain Nalgol stared out into the blackness beyond the viewports.

There was still nothing to see out there, of course, unless one of their probe ships happened to dip into the edge of the cloaking shield or he wanted to contemplate the dirty edge of the comet at their side. But it was tradition for a ship's captain to gaze at the universe from his bridge, and Nalgol was feeling rather traditional today.

Four days. Four more days and the long, stultifying idleness would finally be over. Just four days, assuming the strike team was still on schedule.

Four days.

From the far end of the command walkway he could hear Intelligence Chief Oissan's slightly clunky footsteps approaching. Nearly ten minutes late, he noted with disapproval as he glanced at his chrono. "Captain," Oissan said, puffing slightly as he came up beside Nalgol. "I have the latest probe ship report for you."

Nalgol turned to him, noting the slight redness of Oissan's face. "You're late," he said.

"There was more analysis required than usual," Oissan said stiffly, holding out a datapad. "It seems the ships over Bothawui nearly started the war a few days early."

Nalgol felt his eyes narrow as he took the datapad. "What are you talking about?" he demanded, keying for the proper file.

"One of the Ishori warships decided to push at the Diamala," Oissan said. "He came within half a blink of pushing them into open combat."

Nalgol swore under his breath, glancing over the report. If those hotheaded alien fools started their hostilities before the strike team was ready—"What stopped them?" he asked. "Never mind; there it is," he added, skimming the section. "Interesting. Did anyone get an ID on that freighter?"

"None of the probe ships were close enough for a positive ID," Oissan said. "But the follow-up comm traffic through the fleet said it was High Councilor Organa Solo. That's unconfirmed, though."

"But highly likely," Nalgol grunted. "Here to help Gavrisom calm everyone down, no doubt."

"No doubt." Oissan lifted his eyebrows. "The rumors also say she brought a Caamasi Trustant with her."

"Do they, now," Nalgol said, feeling a slow smile starting to tug at the corners of his mouth. "Do they really."

"We should know for sure in a day or two," Oissan pointed out. "If Gavrisom has a real Caamasi there with his peace envoy, he's sure to parade him out in front of everybody as soon as he can."

"Indeed," Nalgol murmured. "And if he can keep him here talking peace for four more days, we'll be able to say there was a Caamasi present at the destruction of Bothawui. Present and, by implication, fully approving." He shook his head wonderingly. "Amazing. I wonder how Thrawn pulled *that* one off?"

"It's amazing, all right," Oissan agreed, not sounding nearly so enthusiastic. "*I* just hope he hasn't miscalculated somewhere along the line. A hundred ninety-one warships would be a little much for three Star Destroyers to take on all by ourselves."

"You worry too much," Nalgol chided, handing back the datapad. "I've seen Thrawn at work; and he never miscalculates anything. The strike team will do their job; and then those warships of yours will commence tearing each other apart. All we'll have to do is eliminate the survivors and demolish whatever's left of the planet."

"Or so goes the theory, anyway," Oissan said sourly. "May I recommend, Captain, that you at least put the *Tyrannic* and the others on standby alert for the remainder of our time out here? That way we'll be able to move quickly if things break sooner than expected."

"It'll also mean four extra days' worth of worn-off combat edges," Nalgol reminded him. "I hardly think that will be useful."

"But if things break too soon—"

"They won't," Nalgol cut him off brusquely. "If Thrawn says four days, it'll be four days. Period."

Oissan took a deep breath. "Yes, sir," he muttered.

Nalgol eyed the other, a mixture of contempt and pity flickering through him. Oissan, after all, had never met Thrawn; had never heard the confidence and authority in the Grand Admiral's voice. How could he possibly understand? "All right, we'll compromise," he said. "I'll order preliminary battle prep to begin this afternoon; and one day before the projected flash point, we'll go to standby alert. Will that make you feel better?"

"Yes, sir." Oissan's mouth twitched. "Thank you, sir."

"And *your* preliminary battle prep will begin right now," Nalgol continued, gesturing at the datapad. "I want you to make up a priority/threat list for every one of those ships out there. Put in everything you have about their capabilities, defenses, and weaknesses, and include details of captain and crew species where possible."

He smiled tightly. "When we finally come from under this cursed cloaking shield, I want to be able to slice straight through whatever's left without losing so much as a single turbolaser or Preybird. Understood?"

"Understood, Captain," Oissan said. "I'll have it ready for you by tomorrow."

"Very good," Nalgol nodded. "Dismissed."

Turning smartly, Oissan headed aft at a quick walk along the command walkway. Nalgol watched him for a moment, then turned back to the empty view through the viewport.

Four days. Four days, and they would finally have their chance to slaughter Rebel scum.

He smiled into the darkness. Yes, he was indeed feeling very traditional today.

CHAPTER

With a start, Luke woke up.

For a moment he stayed where he was, fighting against the usual floundering of trance-induced disorientation as he made a quick assessment of his situation. He was seated in a slightly uncomfortable seat, he recognized, with an unfamiliar control board in front of him and a curved canopy in front of that. From somewhere behind him, a handful of soft night-lights glowed; in front of him, outside the canopy, it was completely dark outside . . .

He blinked, coming suddenly fully awake. *Completely dark outside?* He fumbled with his restraints, throwing a glance at his chrono as he did so.

And paused, giving the chrono a second look. He'd been in the healing trance for nearly five hours.

Five *hours?*

"Mara, I said to wake me in *two* hours," he called back toward the rear of the ship, getting free of the restraints and stumbling to his feet. "What happened, you fall asleep back there yourself?"

But there was no answer, only the sudden frantic twittering from Artoo.

And there was also no Mara.

"Oh, no," Luke breathed, stretching his mind out to flick through every corner of the ship. Mara was nowhere to be found. "Artoo, where is she?" he snapped, dropping to one knee and lifting up the datapad translator still hooked up to the droid. The words scrolled across it—"What do you mean, she left?" he demanded. "When? Why?"

Artoo moaned mournfully. Luke gazed at the words flowing across the datapad, his heart sinking inside him. Mara had left five hours ago, right after he'd settled into his trance. Artoo didn't know where she'd gone, or why.

But both of those Luke could already guess.

"It's all right," he sighed, patting the droid reassuringly as he got back to his feet. "I know there was no way you could have stopped her."

He crossed to the hatch, the taste of terrible fear mixing with the bitter knowledge that whatever she had gone off to do, it was far too late now for him to stop her, either. "Keep an eye on the ship," he told the little droid, popping open the hatch. "I'll be back as soon as I can."

He stepped outside, not bothering with the ladder, but simply dropping to the ground. Directly overhead between the surrounding cliff peaks, patches of stars shone brightly down through the gaps between drifting clouds; everywhere else, all was darkness. *Mara,* he called out, shouting her name hopelessly into the silent night with his mind.

It was as if a cloaked and hooded figure had stirred. Somewhere not far away a dark, hiding presence seemed to shift. A crack opened between cloak and hood—*Up here,* her thought came back.

Luke peered up at the blackness of the cliff directly ahead, caught between the sudden relief that she was still alive and the sobering sense that something terrible was still about to happen. The glimpse faded as Mara seemed to pull her mental cloak back around her—

Where are you? Luke sent the thought outward, fighting back the temptation to break through this cocoon she had suddenly and inexplicably retreated into.

He sensed her hesitation, and her almost resigned sigh. Then, flashing into his mind like glimpses seen in a flickering light, he caught a series of images of the rock face in front of him, marking the route she'd taken up. Sending an acknowledgment and encouragement back toward her, he crossed to the cliff and started up.

The climb wasn't nearly as tricky as he had thought it would be, and with Jedi-strengthened muscles behind it the trip took less than ten minutes. He found Mara sitting on a rough ledge near the peak, braced sideways against the partial shelter of a rugged upthrust of rock. "Hello," she called quietly as he came up onto the final ridge. "How are you feeling?"

"Completely healed," he said, frowning at her as he maneuvered his way along the ridge and sat down beside her. Her voice had been quiet and controlled; but beneath the dark cloak of her mental barrier he could sense the edge of an incredible sadness. "What's going on?"

In the faint sheen of starlight, he saw her right hand lift and point ahead. "The Hand of Thrawn's over there," she said. "You can see the four back towers against the clouds when the light's right."

Luke gazed that direction, running through his sensory enhancement techniques. The towers and back wall of the fortress were indeed visible, along with a hint of something between the leftmost towers that was probably the flat roof of the hangar they'd fought their way out of a few hours ago. "What have they been doing?" he asked.

"Nothing much," Mara said. "That ship that was out—remember the gap we saw in the parking array? It got in about three hours ago."

Luke grimaced. A functional ship, sitting right there in front of the ones he'd sabotaged. Ready to head off to Bastion at a moment's notice. "It hasn't left again?"

He sensed the shake of her head. "Not that I could tell. Anyway, Parck said they'd be debriefing the pilot before he made a final decision."

"I see," Luke murmured. A debriefing that, under the circumstances, Parck and Fel would undoubtedly be hurrying along as quickly as they could. A fast decision, a fast lift back into the sky, and the Empire would have the Hand of Thrawn and all its secrets.

And yet here he and Mara sat. Waiting.

But for what?

"It's funny, you know," Mara murmured from beside him. "Ironic, really. Here we are: the woman who's spent ten years trying to build a new life for herself, and the man who's spent those same ten years rushing madly around trying to save the galaxy from every new threat that reared its ugly face."

"That's us, all right," Luke said, eyeing her uneasily. The twisting darkness in her was growing stronger . . . "Not sure I see the irony, though."

"The irony is that with the New Republic ready to tear itself apart, you rushed off to save me," Mara said. "Ignoring your self-delegated responsibilities in order to save that one woman and her one life."

He felt her take a deep breath. "And that one woman," she added, almost too quietly to hear, "is now the one who has to sacrifice that new life she wanted. To save the New Republic."

Abruptly, a distant flash of pale green light illuminated her face. A face carved from stone; a face gazing with terrible pain and loneliness into the night. "Looks like you got here just in time," she said as a faint thundercrack echoed in the distance.

There was a second green flash. With an effort, Luke tore his eyes from her tortured face and turned to look.

The towers were firing. Even as he focused on them, another pair of green turbolaser flashes lanced out from the top of one of them across the sky, followed by a pair from one of the other towers. Firing across the landscape in the opposite direction from where he and Mara sat. "Ranging shots, probably," Mara said, her voice the deceptive calm of an overly taut spring. "Trying to gauge the distance. It won't be long now."

Luke looked back at her. The pain within her was growing, pressing outward against her mental barrier like flood waters against a dam. "Mara, what's going on?"

"It was all your idea, you know," she continued as if he hadn't

spoken. "You're the one who wanted so much for me to become a Jedi."
She sniffed loudly, the sound of someone fighting back tears. "Remember?"

And then, from the fortress, a flurry of turbolaser shots abruptly burst
out, the green fire accompanied this time by a counterpoint of blue from
Chiss-style weaponry. All four towers were firing now, firing madly and
persistently, all in the same direction. Luke craned his neck, trying to see,
wondering what in the worlds they could be shooting at. Had Karrde sent
in a backup force after all? Had the New Republic found them, or the
Empire? Or one of those hundred terrible dangers Parck had talked
about? He looked back at Mara—

And in that single, awful heartbeat, he knew.

"Mara," he breathed. "No. Oh, no."

"It had to be done," she said, her voice trembling. In the backwash of
light from the enemy fire Luke could see she was no longer even trying to
hold back the tears. "It was the only way to keep them from taking all of
this and handing it to Bastion. The only way."

Luke looked back at the fortress, the knife of Mara's grief digging in
beneath his own heart, a sudden frenzy of thought and urgency swirling
through his mind. If he'd woken up earlier—if he'd forced his way
through her mental barriers back in the fortress and learned her private
plan—if he even now stretched out with the full power of the Force—

"Don't," Mara murmured, her voice infinitely tired. "Please, don't.
It's my sacrifice, don't you see? The final sacrifice every Jedi has to go
through."

Her fumbling hand reached out to touch his. It felt very cold.
"There's nothing you can do. Nothing at all."

Luke inhaled raggedly, the cool night air digging like the ice of Hoth
into his lungs, his hands and mind and heart aching with the overwhelming desire to do something. To do *anything*.

But she was right. He could hate it, he could bitterly oppose it; but
down deep, he knew she was right. The universe wasn't his responsibility.
Decisions made by other people—their actions, their consequences, even
their sacrifices—they weren't his responsibility, either.

Mara had made her choice, and had accepted the consequences for it.
And he had neither the duty nor the right to try to take it away from her.

Which left only one thing he could do. Moving closer to her on the
ledge, he put his arm around her.

For a moment she resisted, old fears and habits and loneliness mixing
together with her roiling pain to stiffen her muscles away from him. But
only for a moment. Then, as if that part too of her life had now been lost,
she melted against his side, her so carefully constructed barriers bursting
aside as she finally poured out the grief and loss she had held so deeply
and privately inside her.

Luke wrapped his arm tighter around her, murmuring meaningless words as he fought with her through the storm of pain and misery, absorbing what he could of it and offering what comfort and warmth he could in return. In the distance, the firing from the towers increased—

And then, above the edge of the cliff, he saw it. Cutting low over a distant hill, its hull burnished by the surrealistic effect of full shields operating in atmosphere, it twisted and writhed like a living thing as it evaded or dodged or simply shrugged off the withering firestorm savaging the air around it, firing back steadily but uselessly in return at the impenetrable black stone rising before it. Drawn like a mynock to a power cable by the beckon call Mara had spliced into one of the alien ships' comm systems, it was driving its single-minded way toward the open hangar entrance, the one single weak point in the entire fortress. Mara's personal ship, the one thing in the universe she truly owned.

The *Jade's Fire*.

The tears had stopped now, Mara's shoulders tensing beneath Luke's arm as she leaned tautly forward to watch. The *Fire* was almost to the Hand of Thrawn now, and Luke could see that beneath the burnishing effect the hull had been torn open in a dozen different places, some with the yellow swirling of raging flames blazing behind them. The towers intensified their attack; but it was too late. The *Fire* dipped one final time, vanishing from their view—

And with a brilliant yellow-orange fireball that blasted outward toward the far mountains, lighting up the landscape like daylight on Coruscant, it reached its goal.

The sound of the explosion a second later seemed curiously muffled, as if the containing wall of Hijarna stone was as unaffected by the sound as it presumably had been by the explosion itself. A few seconds later another even softer blast washed over them, echoed back from the mountains. The towers, almost reluctantly it seemed, ceased their firing.

And once again, the silence of the night settled in around them.

They sat there in the quiet a long time, clinging to each other as they gazed out at the twisting yellow glow that was the *Fire's* funeral pyre. Slowly, as the hangar bay fire burned itself out, Luke felt Mara's pain similarly fade away.

But to his surprise, it was not a hopeless bitterness or even simple weariness that rose within her to fill the space left by the pain. She had mourned her loss and spent her grief; and now, as it would always be with her, it was time to put feelings and emotions aside and focus again on the task that needed to be done.

And indeed, a minute later, she stirred in his arms. "We'd better go," she said, her voice slightly ragged with the aftereffects of her crying but otherwise calm and clear. "They're going to be fighting that fire for a while. This is probably our best chance to sneak back in."

. . .

"From the size of that blast, I figure we ought to have knocked out everything in the hangar," Mara commented as they made their way back down the cliff toward their ship. "At least as far as flyability is concerned. There may be something way in the back they'll be able to salvage, but it's going to be a job to even get it out."

She was babbling, she knew, her words tumbling out every which way in the aftermath of the exhausting emotional hammering she'd just gone through. She'd never much liked babblers herself, and the thought that she'd become one, even on a temporary basis, rather annoyed her.

But oddly enough, it didn't actually embarrass her. That part wasn't a mystery, either. If dumping everything on Luke the way she had up there hadn't totally ruined his opinion of her, a little babbling wasn't likely to do it, either.

And it *hadn't* destroyed that opinion. That was probably the most surprising part of it all. It truly and genuinely hadn't. Picking her way down the cliff, she could still feel the same warmth and acceptance flowing from him that he'd wrapped so tightly around her up there.

There was also, to be sure, a bit more concern and overprotectiveness in the mix than she really felt comfortable with. But that was okay. That was just Luke, and it certainly wasn't anything she couldn't handle.

"I still don't know how we're going to do this," Luke said, stumbling briefly on a patch of loose rock behind her before he caught himself. "It'll take way too long to go in through the cave again."

"I know," Mara agreed. "Parck mentioned there were gaps in the wall. I guess we'll have to go cross-country and then somehow climb up the side to one of them."

"That's going to be tricky," Luke warned. "They're not going to be nearly as kindly disposed toward us as they were before."

Mara snorted. "That's okay," she said grimly. "I'm not exactly all that kindly disposed toward them, either."

Ahead and below now, barely visible in the faint starlight, she could see their borrowed ship, just beyond one last narrow fissure in the rock. Gathering herself, she leaped across the gap to a flat-topped boulder—

And abruptly halted, flailing for balance on the rock as shock froze her muscles. Suddenly, unexpectedly, a strange thought or sound had flashed into her mind.

Jedi Sky Walker? Are you there?

She lost the fight for balance and dropped rather awkwardly off onto the ground, barely able to keep her feet under her as she landed. But she hardly noticed. There at the ship, perched atop the TIE fighter–style panels, were a dozen nervously fluttering shadows. Even as Luke landed on the ground beside her, one of the shadows detached itself from the ship and flew to a landing on the rock they'd just vacated. *It is you, indeed,* the thought echoed through her mind, the words framed by excitement and relief. *I saw the great fire, and feared you and Mara Jade had perished.*

It was Child Of Winds.

And she could hear him.

She looked at Luke, saw her own surprise reflected in his face and mind. "You *do* go in for the dramatic changes, don't you?" she managed, nodding toward the young Qom Qae. "Nice touch. Really."

Luke lifted his hands, palms outward. "Hey, don't look at me," he protested. "I had nothing to do with this."

Listen to me, please, Child Of Winds cut in impatiently. *You must go to the aid of the Qom Jha. The Threateners have invaded their home.*

"You mean the cave?" Luke asked, frowning.

"All the way in?" Mara added. "Or are they just at the front?"

There was a flurry of conversation back and forth between the alien and the others still hanging from the ship. *We do not know,* Child Of Winds said. *My friends from this nesting of the Qom Qae saw them enter the cave with large branches and machines.*

Mara looked at Luke. "Large branches?"

"Heavy weaponry, I'd guess," he said. "How long were these branches?"

Some were twice as long as a Qom Qae, Child Of Winds said, stretching out his wings for comparison.

"A little big for cleaning out a cave," Mara said. "Sounds like they've figured out that was how we got in."

"And are setting up in case we come back," Luke said grimly. "Well, we knew we couldn't get in that way, anyway. I just hope the Qom Jha were able to clear out of their way."

"Nothing we can do about it now," Mara said. "And sitting here dithering will only give them more time to get ready for us."

"You're right," Luke said reluctantly. "Let me go get Artoo and we'll get moving."

Do you not go to help the Qom Jha? Child Of Winds asked anxiously as Luke started past him.

"There's nothing we can do," Mara told him. "We have to get back into the High Tower right away."

He stared up at her. *But you promised.*

"We promised only to do what we could," Mara reminded him. "In this case, it turns out we weren't able to do all that much." She sighed. "Look, for what it's worth, the Threateners don't consider either of you to be anything more than large annoying vermin. If you stay away from their ships and the High Tower from now on, they most likely won't bother you anymore."

I understand, Child Of Winds said, his disappointment still heavy in his tone. *I will pass along that message.*

"I'm sorry we couldn't help you more," Mara said. "But it's an imperfect universe, and no one ever gets everything he wants or thinks he wants. Part of growing up is to face that, accept it, and move on."

The Qom Qae straightened up. *And what is it you want, Mara Jade?*

Mara looked over at the ship, at the open hatch into which Luke had vanished. It was, as it happened, a question she'd been turning over in her mind a lot lately. A question swirling with conflicting emotions and contradictory thoughts, with cautious hopes and wary fears.

And a question she was definitely not interested in discussing with some strange junior alien. "All I want right now is a way back into the High Tower," she said, choosing a more immediate goal. "Let's get through that one first, shall we?"

Child Of Winds seemed to shiver. *Back into the High Tower? But why?*

Luke had reappeared in the hatchway now and was using the Force to lower the droid to the ground. "It'd take too long to explain," she said. "But it's vitally important. Trust me."

I do, he said with an unexpected fervor. *I trust you and Jedi Sky Walker both.* He hesitated. *And I can show you a way.*

Mara frowned. "You can? Where?"

That direction, he said, jabbing his head toward a point just to the right of where the Hand of Thrawn would be. *My friends say there is a hole in the rock beside the Lake of Small Fish that will lead to the cavern near where we first entered the High Fortress.*

Mara looked over at Luke, an odd thought beginning to whisper its way into her mind. Maybe tackling the High Tower itself wouldn't actually be necessary. "Is it big enough for us to get through?"

I do not know. Child Of Winds hesitated. *But I am told it is the same passage the fire creepers use when they move under the ground.*

Mara felt her fingers twinge at the memory. The thought of sliding down a hole behind a horde of fire creepers frankly made her skin crawl. But if it was the only way, then it was the only way. "Let me check with Luke."

She crossed over to where he was standing beside the droid and ran him a quick summary. "Sounds worth checking out, anyway," he agreed. "How far away is this lake?"

It will not take long, Child Of Winds assured him. *By flight it is very near.*

"We can't take the ship," Luke told him. "The Threateners would spot us quickly."

I do not refer to the flying machine. Abruptly the Qom Qae seemed to straighten himself up. *I and my friends will carry you there. And we will not be seen.*

Mara and Luke exchanged glances. "Are you sure?" Luke asked, glancing around the group. "There aren't very many of you, and we're not as light as we look. And we'll need to take Artoo, too."

I and my friends will carry you there, Child Of Winds repeated. *Not for hope of gain,* he added hastily, *but because you have risked much already for the Qom Qae, and we have given nothing in return. It is only right for us to do this.*

Luke looked at Mara. "Going underground again will mean another long climb up the hidden stairway, you know," he warned. "You sure you're up to that?"

Mara felt her lip twitch. "Actually, I don't think we'll need to go into the High Tower at all."

Luke's forehead creased. "Oh?"

"I was just thinking a minute ago about that big power source Artoo spotted when we first got into the underground room," she told him. "The one off in the direction Keeper Of Promises said was always fatal to Qom Jha who wandered off that way."

She looked toward the High Tower. "And then," she added quietly, "I started wondering about what Parck said Thrawn had told them. That if he was ever reported dead they should watch for his return ten years later."

She felt Luke's moment of puzzlement, then the tightening of his emotions as he suddenly understood. "You're right," he said, his voice low and dark. "It would be just like him, wouldn't it? Just exactly like him."

"I think it's worth checking out, anyway," Mara said.

"Definitely," Luke agreed, his voice and mind suddenly filled with new urgency. "All right, Child Of Winds, you're on. Get your friends organized and let's get moving."

The major sitting glowering on the *Chimaera*'s aft bridge comm display was middle-aged, overweight, and almost painfully uncultured. And, if his answers were any indication, unimaginative and not particularly intelligent along with it.

But he was also completely and unwaveringly loyal to his superior. The exact type of man, Pellaeon thought sourly, that Moff Disra would naturally choose to run interference for him.

"I'm sorry, Admiral Pellaeon," the major said again, "but His Excellency left no instructions on how he could be reached. If you'd care to talk with his chief of staff, I can see if he's available—"

"My business is with Moff Disra personally," Pellaeon cut him off, already well tired of this game. "And I strongly suggest you remember who it is you're speaking to. The Supreme Commander of Imperial forces is, by law, to have reasonable access at all times to *all* high-ranking civilian leaders."

The major gathered himself into a sort of halfhearted attention. "Yes, sir, I know that," he said, his tone on the edge of insubordination. "It's my understanding, though, that His Excellency is in fact *with* the Supreme Commander."

Pellaeon felt his face darken. "What are you talking about?" he demanded. *"I'm* the Supreme Commander."

"Maybe you need to ask Moff Disra about that," the major said, clearly unfazed by the threat in Pellaeon's voice and face. "Or Gran—"

He broke off, the stolid features twitching as if he'd belatedly realized he'd started to say something he shouldn't. "But I personally have no official information on that," he finished, a bit lamely. "I expect His Excellency back within a few days. You can call back then."

"Of course," Pellaeon said softly. "Thank you, Major, for your time."

He keyed off the comm and straightened up; and only then did he allow the infinite tiredness within him to flow visibly out onto his face.

To his left, standing in the archway leading to the *Chimaera*'s main bridge, Colonel Vermel stirred. "It's bad, sir, isn't it?" he asked.

"Bad enough," Pellaeon admitted, waving at the empty display. "Blatant insubordination from Disra himself I would have expected. But to get the same thing from a relatively minor lackey implies an exuberant confidence in Disra's palace far beyond anything he should have."

He stepped into the archway beside Vermel. "And I can think of only one possible reason for that degree of confidence."

Vermel made a sound in his throat. "Grand Admiral Thrawn."

Pellaeon nodded. "The major nearly said as much—I'm sure you caught that. And if Thrawn is back, and is siding with Disra . . ."

He trailed off, the long years seeming to weigh even more heavily on his shoulders. After all this time, after all his tireless work and sacrifice for the Empire, to be waved so casually aside. Especially for someone like Disra. "If he's siding with Disra," he continued quietly, "then that is what is best for the Empire. And we will accept it."

For a minute they stood together in silence, the muted background of the *Chimaera*'s bridge activity the only sound. Pellaeon let his gaze sweep slowly across the bridge of his ship, wishing he knew what he should do next. If Thrawn was back, of course, he need do nothing—the Grand Admiral would make his wishes and orders known in his own good time.

But if Thrawn *wasn't* back . . .

He stepped forward and gestured to the Intelligence duty officer at his portside crew pit station. "We've intercepted several rumors of Grand

Admiral Thrawn's return in the past two weeks," he said. "Have any of the reports mentioned him being associated with any Star Destroyer other than the *Relentless*?"

"Let me check, Admiral," the officer reported, keying his board. "No, sir, they haven't. All the rumors specify either the *Relentless* or Captain Dorja or both."

"Good," Pellaeon said. "I want an immediate priority records search through Bastion Military Control. Find out where the *Relentless* has gone."

"Yes, sir."

The officer busied himself at his board. "You don't really think Dorja would file a destination plan against Thrawn's orders, do you?" Vermel murmured.

"No," Pellaeon said. "But I'm not convinced any of this heavy secrecy came from Thrawn in the first place. And if it was Disra's idea, he may not have thought to even mention to Dorja that he was hiding from me."

"Yes, but—"

"Here it is, sir," the Intelligence officer spoke up. "The *Relentless*, Captain Dorja commanding, left Bastion twenty hours ago en route for Yaga Minor. Transit time estimated at twelve hours. Passengers listed as Moff Disra—" He looked up, and Pellaeon could see him swallow. "And Grand Admiral Thrawn."

Pellaeon nodded. "Thank you," he said. "Captain Ardiff?"

"Sir?" Ardiff said, looking up from his conversation with the systems monitor officer.

"Set course for Yaga Minor," Pellaeon ordered. "We'll leave as soon as the ship is ready."

"Yes, sir," Ardiff said, turning around and lifting his hand toward the nav station. "Navigator?"

"I hope you know what you're doing, sir," Vermel said uneasily. "If Thrawn and Disra are working together, forcing a confrontation with Disra in his presence may not exactly be a wise career move."

Pellaeon smiled mirthlessly. "Any considerations of career moves are far in my distant past," he said. "More to the point, there's always the slim chance that Thrawn is somehow unaware of the worst of Disra's offenses against the Empire. If so, it's my sworn duty as an Imperial officer to bring them to his attention—"

"Admiral!" a voice snapped from the sensor station. "Ship incoming—fifty-five degrees by forty. Unknown configuration, sir."

"Stand by defenses," Pellaeon replied calmly, eyes searching along the specified vector as he strode down the command walkway toward the viewport. Unknown ships, in his experience, were nearly always false alarms: an unfamiliar angle or modification, or else some obscure design that that particular sensor officer had never run into before. He caught a glimpse of the craft out the side viewport—

And stopped in midstride, staring out at it in disbelief. What in the name of the Empire—?

"Admiral?" the comm officer called tentatively, his voice unnaturally high-pitched. "Sir, they're hailing us. Rather, they're hailing *you.*"

Pellaeon frowned. "Me personally?"

"Yes, sir. He asked specifically for Admiral Pellaeon—"

"Then you'd better put it on for the Admiral, hadn't you?" Ardiff interrupted brusquely.

"Yes, sir," the boy gulped. "Transmission on, sir."

"Hello, Admiral Pellaeon," a voice boomed from the bridge speakers. A male voice, speaking Basic, with none of the more obvious accents or inflections usually associated with nonhuman vocal equipment.

And a voice that seemed oddly familiar, Pellaeon realized with a sudden shiver. In fact, disturbingly familiar. Like an echo out of the distant past . . .

"You won't remember me, I'm sure," the voice continued, "but I believe we did meet once or twice."

"I'll take your word for it," Pellaeon replied, keeping his voice steady. "To what do I owe the pleasure of your visit?"

"I'm here to make you an offer," the voice said. "To give you something you very much want."

"Really." Pellaeon looked at Ardiff, now standing in taut readiness behind the starboard turbolaser command station. "I was unaware I was weighed down by any such unfulfilled desires."

"Oh, you don't know yet that you want this," the voice assured him. "But you do. Trust me."

"I'll admit to being intrigued," Pellaeon said. "How do you suggest we proceed?"

"I'd like to come aboard and meet with you. Once you see what I have to offer, I think you'll understand the need for a certain degree of secrecy."

"I don't like it," Vermel murmured from beside him. "It could be some kind of trick."

Pellaeon shook his head. "With an unknown alien ship as bait?" he countered, gesturing at the vessel hanging motionlessly against the starry background off their starboard bow. "If it's a trick, Colonel, it's an extremely good one."

He cleared his throat. "Captain Ardiff?" he called. "Make preparations to bring our guest aboard."

CHAPTER

35

There had been no attacks against the *Lady Luck* along the last leg of their trip, as Han had half expected there to be. Nor did any of the nearly two hundred warships eyeing each other warily over Bothawui seem all that interested in the yacht as it picked its way carefully across to where the three New Republic Corvettes orbited, huddled together as if terrified of the awesome firepower stretched out across the sky around them.

Which, Han decided sourly, they probably were. Gavrisom, and Calibops in general, were a lot bigger on words than they were on action.

The duty officer on Gavrisom's ship had initially been disinclined to honor their docking request, but a few minutes of arguing—and probably a back-scene discussion or two—had finally changed his attitude.

And as he and Lando ducked aboard through the *Lady Luck*'s docking hatch, and the waiting Leia melted into his arms, the whole annoying hassle suddenly seemed worth it.

"I'm so glad you're back," Leia murmured, her voice muffled by his chest as she clung to him. "I was so worried about you."

"Hey, hon, you know me," Han said, trying for a casual tone but hanging on to her as tightly as she was to him. Suddenly, now that it was all over, it was as if he was finally able to admit to himself what their reckless jaunt to Bastion might have cost. What he might have lost . . .

"Yes, I know you," Leia said, looking up at him and trying a smile that didn't fool him for a second. Maybe she was seeing what they'd almost lost, too. "And I know you've never been able to stay out of trouble in your life. I'm just so glad you got through this one."

"Me, too," Han said honestly, giving her a closer look. "You look tired."

"I'm just up a little early," she explained. "Gavrisom has us on Drev'starn time, and it's just after dawn down there."

"Oh," Han said. It hadn't even occurred to him to ask the duty officer what ship's time was. "Sorry."

"No problem," she said. "Believe me, this was well worth getting up early for." She hesitated, just noticeably. "Did you bring it with you?"

Han glanced over her head at Lando. "Sort of," he said. "Is there somewhere we can go and talk?"

He felt her muscles tighten beneath his hands. "Of course," she said, her voice not betraying any of her sudden concern. "There's a meeting room just down the corridor."

A few minutes later they were seated in deeply comfortable chairs behind a sealed door. "The room's not monitored," Leia said. "I've already checked. What's wrong?"

Han braced himself. "We got the Caamas Document, like I told you," he said. "What I didn't know at the time was that—well, look, let me give you the whole story."

With occasional side comments from Lando, he ran a summary of their trip to Bastion, ending with Moegid's discovery that the document had been altered. "I guess I should have figured he had some con going," he growled, glaring at the datacard on the low central table. Going through the events again had rekindled his embarrassed anger at himself for falling for the whole stupid trick in the first place. "I should have waited until Lando and Moegid had completely cleared the thing before I even said anything to you."

Leia squeezed his hand reassuringly. "It's all right," she said, the set of her mouth making it clear that it wasn't all right at all. "It's as much my fault as yours. I knew Thrawn was back on the scene, too. I should have realized this had been too easy."

"Yeah, but you didn't know he was the one who'd given us the datacard," Han argued, obscurely determined not to let her take any of the blame for this. "All you knew was—"

Across the table, Lando cleared his throat. "Whenever you two have finished figuring out whose fault it is," he said, just a bit dryly, "maybe we can move on to what we're going to do about it."

Han looked at Leia, saw her mouth relax slightly into a wry smile. "Point taken," she said, matching his tone. "And it may not be as bad as it looks. There's still a chance we'll be able to get hold of a copy of the document from somewhere else."

"You mean Karrde?" Han asked.

"No, there's another possibility." Leia hesitated. "I really shouldn't say anything more about it right now, except that if it works it'll probably take a few more days."

"The point is still that we've got to stall everyone off for a while," Lando said briskly. "Now, Han and I had a couple of days to deal all this around the table, and we think we may have a way to at least buy us a little time."

"Right." Han nodded, glad to change subjects. "First off, I'm going to tell Gavrisom he can't have the Caamas Document yet."

Leia's eyes widened. "How in the worlds are you going to justify that?"

"On the grounds that the situation over Bothawui is too tense for my taste," Han said loftily. "I'm going to demand that everyone break it up and go home before I turn the document over to anyone."

Leia's face was a study in stunned astonishment. "Han, you can't possibly get away with that."

"Why not?" Han countered, shrugging. "This is *me*, remember? Everyone expects me to do crazy things."

"Yes, but—" With clear effort, Leia strangled down her objections. "All right, let's assume Gavrisom lets you get away with that one. What then?"

Han glanced at Lando. "Actually, we hadn't gotten much past that part," he conceded. "Moegid says there's an outside chance he can reconstruct the data—depends on how expert the guy was who changed it. And now that we've actually got the document, we might be able to bluff the Bothans into telling us what they know."

"Assuming they actually do know something," Leia pointed out. "If they don't, we're no better off than we were. Worse, really, because someone's bound to accuse the New Republic of making a deal with them to withhold the names."

"I know," Han said, trying to hide his sudden surge of frustration. "But if we just go out and tell them we haven't got anything, they're going to say the same thing, aren't they?"

Leia squeezed his hand again. "Probably," she said, her eyes taking on that faraway look that meant she was thinking furiously. "All right," she said. "The two biggest instigators out there are the Diamala and Ishori. If we can get them to back down, even temporarily, a lot of the others should follow along. That's why Gavrisom came out here, in fact, to try talking to them."

Han grimaced, remembering his own less than successful try at getting the two species to agree. And *that* had just been shipping details. "Just keep them out of the same room," he warned.

"Exactly," Leia said, looking over at Lando. "Lando, are you and Senator Miatamia still on good terms?"

Lando eyed her suspiciously. "I don't know if we were ever on good terms, exactly," he said cautiously. "Especially not after that ride I gave him ended with an invitation for High Day drinks with Thrawn aboard his personal Star Destroyer. What exactly did you have in mind?"

"Miatamia arrived here yesterday evening to look the situation over," Leia said. "He's staying over on one of the big Diamalan warships, the *Industrious Thoughts*. I'd like you to go over there and talk to him."

Lando's jaw sagged. "Me? Leia—"

"You have to do it," Leia said firmly. "Diamala have a strong sense of personal pride, and Miatamia still owes you for that ride. You can use that."

"Look, I don't know what you think my hospitality is worth on the open market," Lando protested. "But—" He took another look at her face and sighed. "All right. I'll try."

"Thank you," Leia said. "Gavrisom and I are already scheduled to go meet with the Ishori leaders over on the *Predominance* later this morning. Maybe together we can come up with something."

There was a beep from the table comm. "Councilor Organa Solo?" the duty officer's voice called.

Leia reached over and touched the switch. "Yes?"

"There's a diplomatic envoy here to see you, Councilor. Are you available?"

Han felt a flash of irritation. Couldn't they *ever* leave her alone? "This is Solo," he called toward the comm. "The Councilor is otherwise engaged—"

He cut off at Leia's sudden squeeze on his arm. There was something in her face . . . "Yes, I'll see him," she said. "Send him here."

She switched off the comm. "Leia—" Han began.

"No, it's all right," she said, that odd look still on her face. "I have a strange feeling—"

She broke off as the room door slid open. Han stood up, automatically dropping his hand to his blaster.

"Councilor Organa Solo," Carib Devist said gravely, stepping into the room. His eyes shifted to Han—"And Solo, too," he added, stepping toward him and extending his hand. "I'm glad to see you made it through Bastion safely."

"We didn't," Han said shortly, making no move to take the other's hand. "We got caught."

Carib froze, his hand still outstretched. His eyes flicked to the still seated Lando, as if noticing him for the first time; then, slowly, he lowered his hand. "What happened?" he asked, his face taut.

"Like I said, we got caught," Han told him. "They chased us around the city for a while, then were sitting there waiting when we hit the ship." He lifted his eyebrows. "Apparently, we rate pretty high over there. Thrawn himself came out to meet us."

He'd thought Carib's face was as tight as it got. He'd been wrong. "Thrawn was there?" the other repeated, his voice barely above a whisper. "It was really him?"

"It sure wasn't a quarter-size holo," Han bit out. "Of course it was him. We had a nice little chat, and then he gave us the Caamas Document." He jabbed a finger at the datacard on the table. "There it is."

Carib looked down at the datacard. "And?" he asked warily.

"It's been altered," Leia said, her voice almost gentle.

Han threw an irritated look at her. What was she doing being nice to this man? "I don't suppose you'd know how they caught on to us or anything?" he growled, turning his glare back on Carib.

The other took it without flinching. "No, I don't," he said. "But given that you weren't picked up the second you stepped off your ship, I'd guess you simply got spotted. And may I also point out," he added with a new edge to his voice, "that tumbling to you means they've also tumbled to me, which means our families on Pakrik Minor are now in danger of Imperial reprisal. For whatever little that means to you."

Han grimaced. "Yeah," he muttered. "I'm . . . well, I'm sorry."

"Forget it," Carib said, the anger still lingering. "We knew what we were getting into."

Deliberately, he turned back to Leia. "Which is why we're here, in fact. We've decided—"

"Just a minute," Lando put in. "The duty officer said you were a diplomatic envoy. How'd you con your way through that one?"

"No con involved," Carib said. "The Directorate wanted someone to come offer our support to President Gavrisom and the New Republic over the Caamas situation. We volunteered. Simple as that."

"And you got all the way up to Gavrisom on your first try?"

Carib shrugged. "We pulled a few strings. But not too many were needed." He smiled sadly. "I get the impression that there aren't a lot of people around these days flocking to offer Gavrisom their unconditional support. We'll probably make for a welcome change."

He looked back at Leia. "The point is, we've discussed it among ourselves, and we've decided that we can't just sit back and watch this play itself out." He straightened into a probably unconscious attention. "So we've come to offer you our help."

Han glanced across at Lando. A bunch of Imperial clones, volunteering to get involved in the Caamas dispute. Just exactly what they needed. "And how do you propose to do that?" he asked.

"Any way we can," Carib said. "And maybe in ways you wouldn't even think of. For instance, are you aware that your mass of ships out there includes at least three Imperials?"

Han felt his eyes narrow. "What are you talking about?"

"I'm talking about three Imperial ships," Carib repeated. "Small ones, barely starfighter class, probably with no more than three or four men aboard each. But they're Imperials, all right."

"You're sure of that?" Leia asked.

Han frowned down at her. There was a strange look behind her eyes, an unexpected tension in her throat.

"Absolutely," Carib said. "We picked up the edge of a transmission on our way in that was using the latest in encrypts from Bastion."

Leia's lip twitched. "I see."

"I presume you got IDs on them," Lando said.

"On the ones we spotted, yes," Carib said, digging out a datacard and offering it to Han. "Of course, there might be more of them out there keeping quiet."

"Of course," Lando said.

Carib shot him a look, then turned back to Han. For a moment he held Han's gaze, studying his face . . . "Look, Solo," he said quietly. "I know you don't exactly trust me. I suppose in your boots, under the circumstances, I wouldn't particularly trust us, either. But whether you believe it or not, we're on your side."

"It's not a matter of mistrust, Carib," Leia spoke up. "It's the whole question of what's real about this and what isn't. With Thrawn pulling the strings, we're not sure even whether we can trust our own eyes anymore, let alone our judgment."

"Which may well be his most powerful weapon," Carib countered impatiently. "The fact that no one's willing to trust their allies or their circumstances or even themselves. You can't live that way, Councilor. You certainly can't fight that way."

Leia shook her head. "You misunderstand me. I'm not suggesting we capitulate to uncertainty, but only explaining our hesitation. On the contrary, we have a plan and will be attempting to carry it out."

"Good," Carib said, and Han thought he could detect a faint note of relief in his voice. "What do you want us to do?"

"I'd like you to go back to your ship and start wandering leisurely around the area," Leia told him, slipping a datacard into her datapad and doing some keying. "Try to find and identify every Imperial ship that's out there."

"What if they don't transmit anymore?" Lando asked.

"Won't matter," Carib assured him. "There are certain ways Imperial pilots tend to do things that makes them stand out of a crowd. If there are any more out there, we'll find them."

"Good," Leia said, sliding the datacard out of her datapad and handing it to Carib. "Be sure to stay in touch with Han or Lando or me—here are our personal comlink and ship's comm frequencies. Other than that, just stand ready."

"We will," Carib promised, fingering the datacard. "Thank you, Councilor. We won't let you down."

"I know," Leia said gravely. "We'll speak more later."

With a short nod, Carib turned and strode from the room. "I hope you know what you're doing, Leia," Han muttered, gazing darkly at the closed door. "I'm still not sure I trust him."

"Only history will be able to judge his actions today," Leia said tiredly. "Or those of any of the rest of us." She took a deep breath and seemed to shake off her weariness. "But we can only do what we can. I need to go talk with Gavrisom about our meeting with the Ishori; and you, Lando, need to call Senator Miatamia and try to get in to see him."

"Right," Lando said, hauling himself with clear reluctance out of the comfort of his chair. "See you later."

He left. "What about me?" Han asked. "What do I do?"

"You give me another hug," Leia said, standing up and moving close to him. "No, seriously, you'd better stay completely out of it," she added soberly. "You're the one holding the Caamas Document, the one standing on the high moral ground. You can't be seen dealing directly with either side."

"Yeah," Han said, grimacing. "I always like standing on the high ground—you make such a good target up there. Come on, Leia—I can't just sit around and do *nothing.*"

Pressed against him, he felt her body stiffen a little. "Well, actually . . . the *Falcon* does need a little work," she said carefully. "We lost the starboard power converters and ion flux stabilizer on the way into the system."

"That's okay, I've got spares for both," Han said. "Any idea what happened to them?"

He could almost feel her wince. "They ran into a lightsaber."

He twisted his neck to look down at the top of her head. "Oh," he said. "Really."

"It was for a good cause," she hastened to add. "Really it was."

Han smiled, stroking her hair. "I believe you, sweetheart," he assured her. "Okay, I'll get right on it. You're docked over on the other side, right?"

"Yes." Leia drew partway away from him. "One other thing. There's a passenger aboard, who we're also sort of keeping out of local politics for the moment. Elegos A'kla, a Trustant of the Caamasi Remnant."

Han lifted his eyebrows, then shook his head. "I can't leave you for a minute, can I?" he said. "I take off from Pakrik Minor on a simple little trip; and the next thing you know you're consorting with high-level Caamasi."

Leia smiled up at him. But the smile had a disturbing brittleness to it. "You don't know the half of it," she said, reaching up to stroke his cheek.

"So tell me."

Reluctantly, Leia shook her head. "We don't have time right now. Maybe after Gavrisom and I get back from the *Predominance,* I can tell you the whole story."

"Okay," Han said. "Sure. I'll just get to work on the *Falcon,* then, okay?"

"Okay." Leia hugged him again and gave him a quick kiss. "I'll see you later."

"Yeah," Han said, frowning. Something had just occurred to him—"Leia?"

She paused at the door. "Yes?"

"You said a minute ago that history would judge Carib's activities today," he reminded her. "Why *today*?"

"I did say that, didn't I?" Leia murmured, her eyes focused on nothing. "I don't know."

Han felt something cold creeping up his back. "One of those Jedi things?"

Leia took a careful breath. "It could be," she said quietly. "It could very well be."

For a few heartbeats they gazed at each other in silence. "Okay," Han said, forcing a casual nonchalance into his voice. "Whatever. I'll see you later, right?"

"Yes," Leia murmured, still looking troubled. "Later."

She turned and left the room. For a moment Han stayed where he was, running the implications of what had just happened through his mind. There were a whole bunch of them, all of them as muddy as swamp water, none of them anything he really much liked.

But there was one thing clear here, as clear as the fact that his wife was a Jedi. One way or another, this looked like it was going to be one very busy day.

Scooping up the Caamas Document datacard, he stuffed it securely into a pocket. And if this was going to be a busy day, he added sternly to himself, there was no way he was going to be left out of it. No way at all.

Heading out into the corridor, he turned toward the docking bay where the *Falcon* was moored. Whatever the speed record was for replacing an ion flux stabilizer, he was going to break it.

The *Errant Venture*'s briefing room was comfortably crowded by the time Wedge and Corran arrived. Bel Iblis was standing behind the holo table, his eyes flicking to each ship captain or squadron commander as they arrived, measuring him or her with that single glance. To everyone else, Wedge supposed, he probably looked perfectly calm.

With his and Rogue Squadron's longer history with the man, though, Wedge knew better.

Predictably, Booster Terrik was the last to arrive. Ignoring the few remaining seats, he took up a standing position alongside the first row directly in front of Bel Iblis and crossed his arms expectantly.

"This will be the final briefing before we arrive at our destination,"

Bel Iblis began without preamble. "Our target, for any of you who haven't already guessed, is the Imperial Ubiqtorate base at Yaga Minor."

From the ripple of surprise that ran around the room, Wedge decided, a whole lot of them had not, in fact, guessed correctly. "Before you start counting our ships and matching them against Yaga's defenses," Bel Iblis went on, "let me reassure you just a bit. We're not trying to take out the base, or even soften it up particularly. In fact, aside from the *Errant Venture* itself, the rest of you will be mostly staying on the outside as a diversion."

He pressed a key, and an image of the Ubiqtorate base appeared over the holo table. "The *Errant Venture* will drop out of hyperspace, alone, at this point." A flashing blue light appeared just beyond the ring of outer defenses. "We'll be transmitting a distress signal indicating that we're running from a large New Republic attack force—that's you—and need shelter. With luck—and assuming the false ID fools them—we'll be allowed to penetrate the outer defenses at this point."

Booster snorted loudly enough for the whole room to hear. "You must be joking," he rumbled. "An Imperial Star Destroyer, running from a motley collection of scrap like this? They'll never believe that."

"Why not?" Bel Iblis asked mildly.

"Why *not*?" Booster waved an all-encompassing hand around the room. "Just look at us. You've got us running full weapons and defenses, a practically full crew complement, spit and polish that hasn't been seen since Palpatine was a prip. Who's going to believe we're in serious trouble?"

Bel Iblis cleared his throat. "I gather you haven't taken a look at the outer hull recently."

Booster's arm froze in the middle of another wave. "What?" he demanded, his voice low and deadly.

"You're absolutely right about our needing to look the part of a ship in distress." Bel Iblis nodded. "I believe you'll find we do."

For a painfully long moment the two men stared at each other, the expression on Booster's face reminding Wedge of an approaching thunderstorm. "You're going to pay for this, Bel Iblis," Booster said at last in a low voice. "You, personally, are going to pay for this."

"We'll add it to the ledger," Bel Iblis promised. "Don't worry, we'll put everything back together afterward."

"You'd better," Booster threatened. "Everything fixed. And a new coat of paint, too." He considered. "Something besides Star Destroyer White."

Bel Iblis smiled faintly. "I'll see what I can do."

He looked around the room again, then keyed his control. On the holo display, the blue light passed the outer ring; and as it did so, a group of yellow lights appeared farther out. "At that same time, the rest of you will drop in and form up into an attack line," he continued. "You will *not* seriously engage the defense perimeter, but merely prod at it enough to keep their attention turned outward. You'll also be firing a full barrage of proton torpedoes, with an eye toward getting some of them through the ring into the base itself."

The blue light came to a halt beside a slender spar sticking out from the main base. "The *Errant Venture* will meanwhile come to a halt here, where we'll launch an assault boat against the computer access extension and attempt to get a slicer team inside. If the Force is with us, we may be able to locate and download a copy of the Caamas Document."

"And then how do you get out again?" one of the other ship's captains asked. "I presume you're not assuming they won't notice you at *some* point."

Bel Iblis shrugged slightly. "We *are* an Imperial Star Destroyer," he reminded him. "I think we'll be able to rancor-roll our way out without too much trouble."

Wedge looked at Corran, saw the set to the other's mouth. No, Bel Iblis was dead wrong on that one. Casual confidence or not, Star Destroyer or not, once the Imperials tumbled to what was going on the old general was going to be in for the fight of his life.

Or else . . .

Wedge looked back at Bel Iblis, a strange sensation in the pit of his stomach. Or else he knew perfectly well there was no way he would ever get out. Knew that all he could hope for was to find a copy of the Caamas Document in time and transmit it out to the rest of the fleet.

Knew that Yaga Minor was, in fact, where he was going to die.

And if he knew it . . .

Wedge focused on Booster, standing with his arms crossed again. Booster's ship, going to its destruction.

With Booster still aboard? Probably. Almost certainly.

Beside him, he heard Corran's sigh. "He's not going all noble and self-sacrificing on us, Wedge," the other murmured. "He's thinking about Mirax and Valin."

"Sure," Wedge murmured back. Booster's daughter—Corran's wife—and Booster's six-year-old grandson. Yes, of course it made sense. The big, noisy, self-centered old pirate Booster Terrik cared deeply about his family, whether he would admit it or not.

And if it cost him his life to try to prevent his grandson from growing up in the middle of a civil war . . .

"I guess we'll just have to make it Rogue Squadron's business to make sure they get out again," Corran went on.

Wedge nodded. "You got it," he promised.

"What about fighters?" A-wing Commander C'taunmar asked from the other side of the room. "You'll want my squadron for screening, I presume?"

Bel Iblis shook his head. "No. If we had some Imperial fighters— TIEs or Preybirds—I'd definitely bring them along. But this whole operation depends on dragging out the bluff as long as possible; and a screen of A-wings or X-wings would wreck that bluff rather quickly. No, all fighters will be staying with the outer attack group."

His eyes found Wedge. "Including Rogue Squadron."

He held Wedge's eyes just long enough to make it clear there would be no argument, then looked around the room again. "Your individual assignments and positions in the battle array will be given you on the way out of the briefing. Are there any further general questions?"

"Yes, sir," someone said. "You said you had a false ID set up for the *Errant Venture.* Is it a real name, or something fictitious?"

"Oh, it has to be real," Bel Iblis said. "Twenty years ago there were enough Star Destroyers that an individual Imperial could never keep track of all of them, and might assume that his database just happened to be missing something. But not anymore.

"Fortunately, Intelligence has picked up on three ships that haven't been heard from for several weeks. Presumably they're off on some special assignment; regardless, the chances are slim that any of them will turn up at Yaga Minor. We'll therefore be running under the name and ID of the Imperial Star Destroyer *Tyrannic*"—he gestured to Booster—"under the command of Captain Nalgol."

Five minutes later, Wedge and Corran were heading back toward the hangar bay where the rest of Rogue Squadron waited. "It's going to be some trick to protect them from outside the perimeter," Wedge commented grimly.

"I know," Corran said, his voice sounding oddly distant. "We'll just have to be creative."

Wedge frowned at him. "Trouble?"

Corran shook his head slowly. "The *Tyrannic*," he said. "There's something that bothers me about Bel Iblis using that name. But I don't know what."

A Jedi hunch? "Well, you better figure it out fast," Wedge warned. "Launch point is only an hour away."

"I know." Corran took a deep breath. "I'll try."

CHAPTER

36

"Navett, wake up!"

Navett came awake in an instant, his hand closing automatically on the blaster hidden beneath his pillow. His eyes snapped open, taking in the scene with a single glance: Klif standing in the bedroom doorway, a blaster in his hand and a furious expression on his face, barely visible in the dim light of Drev'starn dawn streaming through the window. "What?" he snapped.

"Someone's been in the shop," Klif snarled. "Throw on some clothes and come on."

Someone had been in the shop, all right. Navett walked through the store in a stunned daze, crunching datacards and bits of random equipment underfoot, staring in disbelief at the carnage that had been visited on their neat little pet emporium.

"I don't believe this," Klif muttered, for about the fifth time. "I do not *believe* this. How in space did she get in without tripping the alarms?"

"I don't know," Navett said, glancing over one of the rows of cages. "At least she didn't take the mawkrens."

"Near as I can tell, she didn't actually take anything," Klif growled, looking around. "Just quietly took everything apart and rearranged it."

Navett nodded. Yet for all her energy and enthusiasm, it looked as if she'd missed the real prize. The section of back wall beside the power coupling box, where he and Klif had installed their hidden storage compartment, seemed to be untouched. "Well, aside from making a mess, she hasn't really done anything," he said, circling around the sales counter. The computer was on; she must have gone in and poked through their files. A waste of her time there, too.

"Navett."

He looked up. Klif was standing at the prompous cage, gazing down on the shelf beside it. "What?" Navett asked, rounding the counter again and joining him.

Lying on the shelf, laid out in neat rows, were the tiny cylinders that had been hidden in the false bottom of the mawkren cage.

And sitting next to them was another binary-linked comlink.

"You going to talk to her?" Klif prompted.

"And do what?" Navett retorted. "Listen to her gloat some more?"

"Maybe you can get her to tell you what she's going to do next." Klif gestured at the cylinders. "One of them is missing."

Navett swallowed a curse. Picking up the comlink, he thumbed it on. "You've been a busy little girl, haven't you?" he ground out.

"Why, good morning," the old woman's voice came back. Didn't she ever sleep? "You're up early."

"You're up late," Navett countered. "And you ought to take better care of yourself. Unaccustomed exercise could be fatal in someone your age."

"Oh, pish," she scoffed. "A little exercise keeps the old heart running smoothly."

"Until you run it up against a sharp object," Navett reminded her darkly. "There are laws on Bothawui against vandalism, you know."

"Only if you know who to deliver the warrant against," she said airily. "And you don't, do you?"

Navett ground his teeth together. She was right; all their efforts to backcheck her ship ID had come up completely dry. "Then I guess we'll just have to deal with you ourselves," he said.

There was a clucking sound. "I suggested that last night. I do wish you'd make up your minds. Did you fetch your Xerrol Nightstinger, by the way?"

Navett smiled tightly. He'd fetched it, all right. It was sitting right there across the room in their hidden storage compartment, ready to go. "What exactly did you think you would find in here, anyway?"

"Oh, you never know," she said. "I've always liked animals, you know. What are all those little cylinders for?"

"You're the expert on everything. You figure it out."

"My, but you're crabby first thing in the morning," she chided. "Not even a hint?"

"I'll trade you," Navett offered. "Why don't you tell me what you're planning next."

"Me?" she asked, all wide-eyed innocence. "Why, nothing. From this point on it's up to the Bothans."

Navett shot a look at Klif. "Of course it is," he said. "Come on, now—you can't call Security in on this, and we both know it. It's just you and us."

"You go ahead and believe that," she said encouragingly. "Well, I'm a little tired, and you've got company coming. Talk to you later."

The transmission shut off with a click. "Good-bye to you, too,"

Navett muttered, turning off the comlink and setting it down on the shelf. Pulling his knife, he deliberately drove it through the device.

"What did she mean about company?" Klif asked suspiciously as Navett brushed the pieces of the comlink into the waste collector. "You don't suppose she *has* called Security, do you?"

"Not a chance," Navett said. "Come on, we've got to get this place straightened up before opening time—"

He broke off as, across the shop, there was a knock at the door. Frowning, he crossed the room, returning knife and blaster to their hiding places in his tunic. Unlocking the door, he pulled it open.

To find himself face-to-face with a group of four Bothans wearing the wide green-and-yellow shoulder sashes of local police. "Proprietor Navett of the Exoticalia Pet Emporium?" the one in front asked.

"Yes," Navett confirmed. "Shop hours are—"

"I'm Investigator Proy'skyn of the Drev'starn Department of Criminal Discouragement," the Bothan interrupted briskly, holding up a shimmering ID. "We received word that you had had a break-in."

His eyes flicked over Navett's shoulder. "Obviously, the report was accurate. May we come in?"

"Of course," Navett said, stepping back to let them enter, trying to keep his suddenly murderous thoughts out of his voice. No, the old woman hadn't done anything so obvious as calling Security. Not her. "I was just about to call you, actually," he added as the Bothans fanned out across the shop. "We only just discovered it ourselves."

"You have a list of inventory and stock?" Proy'skyn called back over his shoulder.

"I'll get it for you," Klif volunteered, heading off toward the computer.

One of the Bothans had paused beside the prompous cage. "Proprietor?" he called. "What are these cylinders?" He reached down.

"Please, be careful with those," Navett said quickly, hurrying to his side, mind furiously casting about for something that would sound reasonable. "They're hormonal-drip capsules for our baby mawkrens."

"What sort of hormones are required?" the Bothan asked.

"Newborn mawkrens need a particular combination of solar spectrum, atmospheric conditions, and diet," Klif put in, picking up on Navett's cue and running with it as only Klif could do. "You can almost never get the right mixture off their own world, so you use a hormonal-drip."

"That's them over there," Navett added, pointing to the cage with the tiny lizards. "We fasten the cylinders onto their backs with custom-designed harnesses."

"I see," the Bothan said, peering at them. "When will this need to be done?"

"This morning, actually," Klif said. "Sorry, but you'll have to look around on your own for a while, Investigator Proy'skyn, if you don't mind."

"Of course, of course," Proy'skyn said. "Please, carry on."

Navett stepped over to one of the overturned tables, hiding a grimly satisfied smile as he set it upright again. So much for the old woman's attempt at subtlety—clearly, he and Klif could out-subtle her any day of the week. Not only did they now have reason to postpone long official questions, not only had they soothed any possible suspicion by offering the investigators the run of the place, but they would even be setting up the final phase of their plan right under the collective nose-fur of Bothan officialdom.

Of course, they hadn't planned to institute that particular phase for a couple of days yet. But you couldn't have everything.

Setting up the restraint grid, ignoring the quietly bustling Bothans wandering around looking for clues, they set to work.

They had finished fitting ninety-seven of the mawkrens with harnesses and cylinders, with about twenty more to go, when Navett first became aware of the new odor wafting through the shop.

He looked up at Klif, engrossed in attaching one of the cylinders onto the back of the tiny lizard standing in rigid immobility on the restraint grid, then let his gaze shift around the shop. The four original Bothan investigators had long since left, replaced by a group of three techs busily pulling handprints and chemical samples from the various counters and cages. None of them seemed to have noticed the smell.

Klif looked up, caught the expression on Navett's face. "Trouble?" he murmured.

Navett wrinkled his nose. Klif frowned, sniffing the air . . .

And suddenly his eyes widened. "Smoke."

Navett nodded fractionally, his eyes darting again around the shop. Nothing was visible, no flames and no smoke, but the smell was definitely getting stronger. "She wouldn't," Klif hissed. "Would she?"

"We'd better assume she would," Navett said. "Take the mawkrens we've finished and get them over to the tapcafe."

"Now?" Klif glanced at the bright sunshine outside the window. "Navett, there's a full staff at work there right now."

"Then you'd better come up with a really dandy diversion to get them out of the way," Navett shot back. If they lost the mawkrens, this whole thing would have been for nothing. "Wake up Pensin and Horvic; we're in full emergency mode here."

Klif nodded grimly. "Got it," he said. Setting his tools aside, he started putting the last few mawkrens back into the cage—

And suddenly one of the Bothans let out a squawk. "Fire!" he bleated. "The building is on fire! Morv'vyal—call the Extinguishers. Hurry!"

"Fire?" Navett asked, looking around in feigned bewilderment. "Where? I don't see any fire."

"Foolish human," the Bothan snapped. "Can't you smell the smoke? Hurry—leave everything and go."

Navett shot a glare at Klif. So that was the old woman's plan. She couldn't figure out what in the shop their scheme needed, so she was going to force them to leave without any of it. "But my stock is very valuable," he protested.

"As valuable as your life?" The Bothan, ignoring his own advice, was moving rapidly around the outer edge of the shop, hands brushing along the walls. "Go—get out."

"What are you doing?" Klif asked.

"You are right, there is no flame yet," the Bothan explained. "The fire must therefore be inside the walls."

"The Extinguishers are coming," one of the other Bothans reported anxiously, waving his comlink. "But they will not be here for a few more minutes."

"Understood," the first said, pausing at the power coupling box. Abruptly, his fur flattened, and he pulled a knife from his belt. "Perhaps we can help prepare their way."

"Wait a minute," Navett barked, jumping forward. The Bothan had dug the knife between wall panels directly over their hidden compartment. "What the fracas are you *doing*?"

"The fire smells of wiring," the Bothan explained breathlessly. "Here at the power coupling is the likely place for it to be. If we can expose it and bring fire preventers to bear—"

He broke off, staggering as the prying knife unexpectedly shattered through the relatively thin false front of the storage compartment. He caught his balance, gaping at the Nightstinger sniper blaster now visible inside. "Proprietor Navett!" he exclaimed. "What is this weapon—?"

He fell to the floor, question unfinished, as Navett shot him in the back.

The second Bothan got out just a squeak before Navett's second shot dropped him. The third was fumbling frantically for both comlink and blaster when Klif's shot took him out. "Well, that's torn it," Klif snarled, glaring at Navett. "What in the Empire—?"

"She's expecting us to be properly professional about this," Navett ground out. "And professionals never start shooting unless they have to. So fine: we've just gone unprofessional. *That* ought to take her by surprise."

"Oh, terrific," Klif said. "A brilliantly unorthodox strategy. *Now* what do we do?"

"We take it down, that's what," Navett snarled back, thrusting his blaster back into his tunic and stepping over the body to pull the Nightstinger from its hiding place. "Rouse Pensin and Horvic and get your tails out to the ship and into space. You've got two hours, maybe less, to get aboard the *Predominance* and into position."

Nightstinger in hand, he turned back to find a stunned look on Klif's face. "Navett, we can't do it now," he protested. "The attack force won't be ready for another three days."

"You want to try to dodge our lady friend that long?" Navett snapped, dropping the Nightstinger onto the table and starting to scoop the rest of the mawkrens into their cage. "You can see her plan—she's trying to maneuver the police or Extinguishers or Vader knows who else in a uniform into running interference against us for her. We have to move now, when she's not expecting it."

"But the attack force—"

"Stop worrying about the attack force," Navett cut him off. "They'll be ready, all right. Or will get that way blasted quick. You have your orders."

"All right," Klif said, sliding his own weapon away. "I'll leave you the landspeeder—I can lift another one for the three of us. Anything else you need?"

"Nothing I can't get myself," Navett told him shortly. "Go on—the chrono's counting."

"Right. Good luck."

He left. Navett finished getting the mawkrens into their cage, then gathered up the rest of the cylinders and slid them back into the cage's false bottom. Yes, the old woman had forced his hand, and that sudden drastic change in plans was going to cost them dearly.

But if she thought she'd won, she was mistaken. He only wished he could be around to see her when she realized that.

"I'm sure you understand, Admiral," Paloma D'asima said, obviously picking her words very carefully, "how unprecedented this step would be for our people. We have never before had what might be considered close relations with the Empire."

Seated a quarter of the way around the table, Disra suppressed a cynical smile. Paloma D'asima, one of the proud and exalted Eleven of the Mistryl, might well think herself subtle, even clever, in the ways of politics and political sparring. But to him, she was as patently transparent as only a rank amateur could be. If this was the best the Mistryl could do, he would have them eating out of his hand before the day was over.

Or rather, eating out of Grand Admiral Thrawn's hand. "I understand the conflicts we've had in the past," Thrawn said gravely. "However, as I've pointed out to you—and to Karoly D'ulin before you," he added, nodding politely to the younger woman at D'asima's side, "the Empire under my leadership will bear little resemblance to that of the late Emperor Palpatine."

"I understand that," the older woman said. Her face wasn't giving anything away; her hands, though, more than made up for it. "I only bring it up to remind you that we would need more than just your word as guarantee."

"Are you questioning the word of Grand Admiral Thrawn?" Disra asked, letting just a hint of an edge into his voice.

The gambit worked; D'asima was instantly on the defensive. "Not at all," she assured him, too quickly. "It's merely that—"

She was saved by a signal from the conference room intercom. "Admiral Thrawn, this is Captain Dorja," the familiar voice said.

Seated at Thrawn's side, Tierce touched the switch. "This is Major Tierce, Captain," he said. "The Admiral is listening."

"Forgive the interruption, sir," Dorja said. "But you asked to be informed immediately if any unscheduled ships approached the base. They've just received a transmission from the Imperial Star Destroyer *Tyrannic*, requesting emergency assistance."

Disra threw a startled look at Tierce. The *Tyrannic* was one of the three ships lurking behind their cloaking shields off Bothawui. Or at least it was supposed to be there. "Did they specify the nature of their emergency?" Thrawn asked.

"Coming through now, sir . . . they say they've come under attack by a sizable New Republic assault force and have been severely damaged. They say the force is right behind them and that they need shelter. General Hestiv is requesting instructions."

Disra felt a tight smile crease his lips. No—of course it wasn't the real *Tyrannic* out there. Tierce's hunch had been right: Coruscant had indeed launched a mad attempt to steal a copy of the Caamas Document.

And not only was the trap ready and waiting, they even had one of the Mistryl's Eleven here to watch that pitiful attempt turned into a humiliating defeat. The real Thrawn couldn't have arranged things better.

"Instruct General Hestiv to let the incoming Star Destroyer pass the outer perimeter," Thrawn told Dorja. "He's then to put all defenses on full battle readiness and prepare for enemy attack."

"Yes, sir."

"And then, Captain," Thrawn added, "you will similarly prepare the

Relentless for combat. Track the incoming Star Destroyer as it approaches and plot its course, then bring us to stand directly between it and the base. At that point, you will order General Hestiv to bring full inner defenses to bear on it."

"Yes, sir," Dorja said, sounding slightly puzzled but nevertheless unquestioning. "Will you be coming to the bridge?"

"Of course, Captain." Thrawn stood up, favoring D'asima with a slight smile as he gestured her toward the conference room door. "In fact, I believe we all will."

The sudden noise snapped Ghent out of his doze and sent him jerking upright in his chair. He looked around the work area wildly, saw he was still alone. Only then did his sleep-fogged mind realize the sound was some kind of alarm.

He looked around the room again, searching for the source of the trouble. There was nothing he could see. Obviously, it must be elsewhere in the station. A moment's search in the climate-control section of the board, and he found the cutoff switch.

The sound faded away into an unpleasant ringing in his ears. For another moment he looked at the board, wondering if it would be worth trying to tap into the main comm system and find out what was going on. Probably not; whatever it was, it probably didn't have anything to do with him.

He frowned suddenly. The board in front of him seemed to be flickering. Flickering?

The frown vanished into relieved understanding. Of course—he was getting reflections of light coming in through the viewport in the living area behind him. Getting to his feet, wincing as his knees informed him he'd been sitting in one place too long again, he hobbled in through the open door and peered out the viewport.

The source of the flickering light was instantly apparent: an awesome display of multiple turbolaser and proton torpedo blasts coming from the distance near the base's outer defense perimeter.

And framed in the center of all that flashing firepower, bearing inexorably straight down on him, was the huge bulk of an Imperial Star Destroyer.

Ghent caught his breath, staring at the incoming ship. Suddenly all of Pellaeon's and Hestiv's talk about danger and threats, tucked snugly away in the back of his mind for the past few days, came rushing to the forefront again. That Star Destroyer was coming for him—he was sure of it.

Run! the thought flashed into his mind. Run out of here, down the long tunnel into the main base. Find General Hestiv, or that TIE pilot who'd brought him here from the *Chimaera,* or just find somewhere to hide.

But no. Hestiv had warned him about spies inside the main base. If he went there, one of them would surely get him.

And besides, he remembered suddenly, he couldn't go anywhere. He'd triple-sealed the single access door, passwording it with a layer of computer locks that would take any enemy hours to slice through. Even he, who'd set the blocks up in the first place, would probably need half an hour to undo them.

And half an hour would be too late. Far too late.

For another minute he watched the incoming ship, wondering distantly what they would do to him. Then, with a sigh, he turned away. He was trapped here, they were coming for him, and there was nothing he could do.

Returning to the work area, this time closing the door behind him, he went back to his seat. The Wickstrom K220s had finally finished the complex analysis he'd set for them to do before all this happened. Keying the results over to the Masterline-70, pushing the events outside once again into the back of his mind, he got back to work.

It took Navett half an hour to locate and purchase the pressurized tank of flammable fluid he needed and another fifteen minutes to fit it with a sprayer hose. Forty-five minutes gone, during which time the alarm over the dead Bothans in the pet shop had probably spread to every corner of the city.

But that was all right. The ugly furry aliens couldn't stop him now; and the more time it took him to get ready here on the planetary surface, the more time Klif and Pensin and Horvic would have to wheedle their way aboard that Ishori ship overhead.

They would die there, of course. They knew that. But then, he would soon be dying down here, too. What was important was that, before they died, they would complete their task.

The streets around the Ho'Din tapcafe, so quiet and deserted in the late night, were buzzing with activity here in the early afternoon. With the fluid tank pressed into the seat beside him, wedged at an awkward angle against the low roof, Navett drove slowly down the deserted alleys along the sides and back of the tapcafe, systematically spraying a thick layer of the liquid along the lower walls and the ground around them. The front wall, facing as it did onto a busy street, was too public for him to do the same there without arousing instant suspicion. But he had other plans for that area anyway. Returning to the back alley, again making sure he was unobserved, he fired a blaster bolt into the fluid as he drove past the tapcafe.

He took his time circling through the alleyways until he came around again onto the main street, with the result that by the time he let the landspeeder coast to a stop across from the tapcafe the fire he'd started was blazing furiously away along the outer walls. Pedestrians were running frantically to and fro, waving and yelling as they either fled from the flames or formed themselves into ghoulish knots at a safe distance to watch; and as Navett retrieved the Nightstinger from the back seat the tapcafe's front doors swung open and a crowd of equally hysterical customers and waitstaff began streaming out through the smoke. Checking the Nightstinger's indicator, confirming that he still had three shots left, Navett settled down to wait.

He didn't have to wait very long. The stream of refugees from the tapcafe had barely begun to dwindle when a white Extinguisher speeder truck came roaring around the corner and braked to a hard stop at one corner of the building. Through the side window Navett could see the driver gesticulating as his partner scrambled out and started climbing the outside ladder toward the pressure turret on top.

He never made it. Resting the muzzle of the Nightstinger on the seat back for stability, Navett shot him down. His second invisible blast took out the driver; his third and last blew off the speeder truck's filler tube cap, sending the fire suppressant gushing onto the street to flow uselessly away from the flames.

He lowered the now empty blaster onto the floor, giving the crowd around him a quick look. But no one was paying the slightest attention to the human sitting alone in his landspeeder. Every eye was locked solidly on the blazing building, with probably only an occasional brief thought turned to the puzzle of the two Bothan Extinguishers who had suddenly and inexplicably collapsed.

The flow of customers from the tapcafe had stopped now. Navett gave it thirty more seconds, just to make sure everyone was out. Then, drawing his blaster and laying it ready on the seat beside him, he started the landspeeder and eased his way through the crowd toward the tapcafe's front doors.

He was through the main part of the crowd before anyone even seemed to notice what he was doing. Someone shouted, and a Bothan wearing the green/yellow police sash jumped out in front of him, waving his arms violently. Snatching up his blaster, Navett shot him, veered around the body, and leaned hard on the accelerator. Someone behind him was screaming now; bracing himself, Navett increased his speed—

He hit the tapcafe doors with bone-jarring force, smashing them into shards as the landspeeder ground to a halt right in the middle of the destruction. He was out before the debris finished bouncing off the vehicle's roof, snatching the cage of mawkrens from the back and sprinting through the smoke and heat toward the door to the basement and the subbasement beyond it.

He was halfway down the first flight of stairs when, behind him, he heard the explosion as the heat set off the remaining fluid in the pressurized tank he'd left in the landspeeder.

And with the front of the tapcafe now as engulfed in flames as the rest of the building, he was truly and irrevocably cut off from the outside world.

No one in the universe could stop him now.

There was just a hint of smoke in the subbasement—nothing serious, just a foreshadowing of what would inevitably come. Their equipment was just where they'd left it, but he took a minute first to run a quick check on the fusion disintegrator.

It was a good thing he had. The old woman had been here again, gimmicking the device to overload and burn out the main control coil when it was first started. Grinning humorlessly to himself, Navett ungimmicked it, then spent a few more precious minutes reconfiguring the focus to extend the disintegration beam a few centimeters out from the canister mouth.

Finally, he was ready. Strapping the mawkren cage awkwardly to his back, he dropped into the hole he and Klif had dug and turned on the disintegrator.

The beam cut through the soil beneath his feet like a blaster bolt through snow, sending a gale of microscopic dust flowing up past his face. Fleetingly, he wished he'd thought to bring a filter mask with him. Too late now. Squinting against the eye-burning wind, he kept going, wondering what the Bothans were doing about the myriad of alarms he was undoubtedly setting off. Running around uselessly, no doubt, particularly once they saw that the source of the intrusion was totally inaccessible to them.

And some of them would probably sit back and relax, smugly secure in the knowledge that losing the power conduit he was digging toward wouldn't affect their precious shield in the slightest. Possibly they were even having a hearty laugh at the foolish Imperial agent who thought he could shut them down so easily, or who perhaps thought he could crawl through a ten-centimeter-diameter conduit.

They wouldn't be laughing that way for long.

It took only a few minutes to dig the rest of the way down to the power conduit. The conduit shell was heavily armored, and it took nearly ten minutes more for the disintegrator beam to eat its way through. The power cables themselves flash-burned almost instantly once that happened, of course—they were, after all, only normal power cables, not designed to withstand anything more strenuous than high-power electrical current. He kept at it until he had carved himself a decently sized hole in the outer shell, then shut off the disintegrator and switched on the coolant pack built into the bottom. A few minutes of systematic spraying, and the area was once again cool enough to touch.

He shut off the coolant and sat down by the opening . . . and in the sudden silence, he heard a quiet new sound.

The beep of a comlink. Coming from the disintegrator.

He frowned, checking the device. There it was, wedged into the refill intake for the coolant pack. Smiling tightly, he pulled it out and turned it on. "Hello, there," he said. "Everything running to your satisfaction?"

"What in the name of Alderaan dust are you *doing*?" the old woman's voice demanded.

He smiled more broadly, wedging the comlink into his collar and opening the mawkren cage's false bottom. "What's the matter?" he asked, pulling out a small tube of food paste. "I didn't actually take you by surprise or anything, did I? That was a cute trick with the smoke at the pet shop, by the way. I take it you planted that before you left this morning?"

"Yes," she said. "I figured you had all your good stuff upstairs with you, or else had it hidden behind walls or ceilings."

"So you planted a delayed-action smoke bomb so the Extinguishers would come in and open up the walls for you," Navett said, opening the cage and extracting one of the tiny lizards. "Very clever."

"Look, you haven't got time for this chitchat," she growled. "In case you haven't noticed, that building is burning like a torch over your head."

"Oh, I know," Navett said. Holding the lizard with one hand, he dabbed a drop of the food paste onto the end of its nose and set it down into the hole he'd cut, pointing it in the direction of the generator building. A touch on one end of the cylindrical bomb activated it, setting it to explode when the lizard reached the blockage where the conduit passed through the reinforced wall and sent its individual power cables splitting off into a dozen different directions. He released his grip, and the mawkren scrambled away through the narrow space between the power cables and the conduit shell, following the scent it was too stupid to realize was attached to its own nose.

"What do you mean, you know?" the woman asked. "Unless you do something real clever real fast, you're going to die in there. You know *that*, too?"

"We all have to die sometime," Navett reminded her, dabbing the nose of another mawkren and sending it to follow the first. It had barely vanished down the conduit when the faint sound of a small explosion echoed down the tube.

There was nothing wrong with the old woman's ears. "What was that?" she asked.

"The death of Bothawui," Navett told her, dabbing another mawkren and releasing it as a second explosion sounded. Now that the fumes of disintegrated dirt were dissipating, he could tell that the odor of smoke was getting stronger. "You know, we never did figure out what your name was," he added, pulling out another mawkren and wondering uneasily just how fast the fire above him was spreading. If either the flame or smoke got to him before the mawkrens and their tiny bombs were able to blow a hole through the group of unarmored power cables just inside the generator building, he could still lose. "So what is it?"

"What, my name?" she asked. "You tell me yours and I'll tell you mine."

"Sorry," he said, releasing the mawkren. "My name might still be of use to someone down the line, even after I myself no longer am." There was another explosion—

And then, to his relief and immense satisfaction, a breath of cool air drifted up into his face. The power cables had been blown apart inside the wall, and the generator building had been laid open to him.

"Look, Imperial—"

"Conversation's over," Navett cut her off. "Enjoy the fire."

He clicked off the comlink and tossed it aside. Then he tipped the cage over, allowing the rest of the mawkrens to swarm free. For a moment they swirled around his lap and feet, getting their balance and sniffing the air. Then, in a sudden concerted rush, they clawed their way past each other to disappear down the conduit. Drawn now not by food paste on their noses, but by the tiny spots of liquid nutrient he and Klif had so carefully positioned three days ago as they'd sprayed for metalmites.

And there remained just one final task for him to perform. Reaching into the bottom of the cage, he pulled out the last item there: the remote arming signaler to activate the rest of the cylinders now being carried toward their rendezvous with destiny. A few more seconds and his self-guided bombs would be spilling out into the generator building around the startled Bothans' feet, skittering across the polished floor straight to the key points of the whole installation.

Along the conduit, he could hear the faint sounds of explosions now as the mawkrens reached their targets and the cylinders' proximity fuses began to ignite. A few more seconds—a minute at the most—and the section of the planetary shield protecting Drev'starn would collapse.

The death of Bothawui had begun. And with it, the death of the New Republic.

His only regret was that he wouldn't be around to see it all happen.

Overhead, the sounds of flames could be heard now, the crackling noise mixing with the fainter staccato of the bombs still going off in the distance. Smiling up at the ceiling, Navett leaned his back against the dirt wall. And waited for the end.

.   .   .

The discussions aboard the *Predominance* had just entered their fourth round when the deck below them gave a sudden rumbling vibration. A sound and sensation that Leia had become all too familiar with over the years.

Somewhere in the depths of the Ishori ship, a turbolaser cluster had just fired.

The captain was on the intercom even before the rumble had died away. "What is the firing?" he snarled.

The answer tumbled out in Ishori, too fast and too faint for Leia to follow. "What is happening?" Gavrisom demanded. "You agreed there would be no hostilities while—"

"It is not us," the captain snarled, diving for the door. "Aliens have taken over one of our weapons clusters and are firing at the ground."

"What?" Gavrisom asked, blinking. "But how—?"

But the captain was already gone, taking the door guards with him. "Councilor Organa Solo—?" Gavrisom began, breaking off as another rumble rolled through the ship. "Councilor, what is happening here?"

Leia shook her head. "I don't—"

And suddenly she jerked in her seat, inhaling sharply, as a surge of fear and pain and death shot through her. On the planet below, voices were crying out in terror . . .

And in that single, horrifying instant, she knew what had happened.

"The planetary shield's down," she snapped, getting out of her chair and rushing to the viewport. She reached it just in time to see a third massive turbolaser blast burn its way from the underside of the ship toward the surface. There was a flash of white as it sizzled through the atmosphere; and then the distortion cleared, leaving an angry, black-tinged red glow behind.

Drev'starn, the Bothan capital, was on fire.

She turned back, heading for the door. "It's down, all right," she shouted to Gavrisom as she ran past him. "At least over Drev'starn."

"Where are you going?" Gavrisom called after her.

"To try to stop the shooting," Leia called back.

Outside, a dozen armor-clad Ishori were charging down the corridor, blaster carbines at the ready. Pressed against the bulkheads, trying to stay out of the way, her two Noghri guards looked up at her. "Councilor—?"

"Come on," Leia told them. Unhooking her lightsaber from her belt, stretching out to the Force for strength and wisdom, she joined in with the flow.

.   .   .

Han hit the *Falcon*'s cockpit at a full run, skidding to a halt just barely in front of the control board. "Where?" he barked, dropping into the pilot's seat.

"There," Elegos said tightly, pointing through the viewport at the dark ship lying in space not two kilometers away. "I don't know whose ship it is, but—"

He broke off as another flash of red fire cut through the black of space on its way toward the planet below. "There—did you see it?"

"Oh, yeah, I saw it," Han snarled, a hard jab of fear punching up under his heart as he slapped at the emergency start-up switches. Elegos might have lost track of which ship was which out there, but he hadn't. That shot had come from the flagship of the Ishori task force, the war cruiser *Predominance*.

The ship Leia was currently aboard.

There was another flash, again heading down toward the Bothawui surface. "You know how to release a docking collar?" Han snapped at Elegos, his hands darting over the control boards.

"Yes, I think so—"

"Do it," Han cut him off. "Now."

"Yes, sir." Lunging out of his seat, the Caamasi headed aft.

The engines were starting to come up to power now. Han keyed the comm, setting for full-frequency scan. There was going to be hell to pay for this one, all right, no matter what the Ishori thought they were doing. The sync numbers for the stabilizer he'd just installed were coming in now; it seemed to be firming up—

"All ships, this is New Republic President Gavrisom," Gavrisom's taut voice boomed from the cockpit speaker. "Stand your positions and hold your fire; repeat, please stand down and hold your fire. The incident currently under way is not—"

He never got to finish his plea. Abruptly there was a squawk of blanketing jamming static on that frequency, drowning him out—

"Attack!" a new voice bit out. "All Corellian forces, attack at will!"

Han gaped at the speaker. What in blazes was the Corellian doing?

And then the scan locked on to another frequency. "Attack!" a guttural Mon Calamari voice rumbled. "All Mon Cal ships, attack."

[Attack,] a Diamalan voice called calmly in their own language on another frequency.

{Attack,} came the snarling Ishori reply on yet another.

Han looked out at the mass of ships, heart thudding in his throat. No. No—this was insane. Surely they wouldn't.

But they were. All around the area, the various warships were coming sluggishly to life, heading for the better maneuverability of open sky or else simply turning their weapons to target their opponents.

And even as he watched, the first flashes of turbolaser fire began.

Behind him, Elegos charged back into the cockpit. "The collar's released," he announced, breathing heavily as he resumed his seat. "We can leave—"

He broke off, staring in disbelief at the scene outside. "What's happened?" he gasped. "Han—what's going on?"

"It's just what it looks like," Han said grimly.

"The New Republic is at war."

CHAPTER
37

It was a trip of only perhaps fifteen minutes, as the Qom Qae flew, to the far side of the Hand of Thrawn and the lake Child Of Winds had mentioned. At first Luke had been skeptical of the whole idea, concerned about the young aliens' ability to handle the weight of their passengers, not to mention whether or not they would be able to keep out of sight and targeting range of what were surely by now a seriously hostile group of enemies in the fortress.

But the Qom Qae had surprised him on both counts; and as they weaved expertly in and out of the cover of trees and rocks and mountain gullies, he almost began to relax about this phase of the operation. Mara, too, he could sense, had already turned her thoughts ahead to what they would find at the end of the short flight.

The same, unfortunately, could not be said of Artoo. Suspended in the center of the framework they'd rigged out of their last lengths of syntherope, he moaned and gurgled the whole way.

The cut in the rock was no more than ten meters from the edge of the lake, descending at a fairly steep angle from under a partial overhang of grass-clumped soil. "At least the rock isn't too rough," Mara commented, running a hand experimentally along the lower surface. "Probably worn down by years of little fire creeper feet running over it."

Artoo seemed to shudder, warbling uncomfortably. "I doubt we'll run into any more of them this time around," Luke soothed him as he untangled the syntherope and tucked it back into the droid's storage compartment. "Swarms that size can't travel too close together—there won't be enough food for them all."

"Let's just hope they're smart enough to know that," Mara added.

You are fortunate you have come when you did, Child Of Winds said. *There has been much rain in the past few seasons, and the Lake of Small Fish has been growing ever larger.*

"And have the small fish been getting bigger, too?" Mara asked.

Child Of Winds fluttered his wings. *I do not know. Is it important?*
Mara shook her head. "It was a joke. Skip it."

Oh. Child Of Winds looked back at Luke. *I simply meant that soon
this entrance may be covered over with water.*

"I understand," Luke said. "But for the moment it's not, and you got
us here safely."

It was to our great honor, Child Of Winds said. *What do you wish us
to do now?*

"You've done more than enough already," Luke assured him. "Thank
you. Thank you all."

Shall we wait for you? the Qom Qae persisted. *We would be honored
to wait and take you again to your flying machine.*

Luke hesitated. A ride back to the ship could be very useful indeed.
Unfortunately—"The problem is that I have no idea where we'll be coming out," he said.

Then we will watch, Child Of Winds said firmly. *And others will
watch also.*

"Yes, all right," Luke agreed, anxious to cut off the discussion and get
on their way. "Thank you."

"So what's our marching order?" Mara asked.

"I'll go first," Luke said, sitting down on the edge of the slope and
putting his legs into the opening. "Artoo next, you last. I'll watch for
bottlenecks and try to widen them as I pass. If I miss one, you'll have to
deal with it."

"Right," Mara said, pulling her lightsaber from her belt. "Happy
landings, and try not to cut off your own feet along the way."

"Thanks." Igniting his lightsaber, holding the blade ready over his
outstretched legs, Luke eased onto the slope and started down.

It wasn't nearly as bad as he'd feared. Years of little fire creeper feet
might indeed have smoothed down the rock; more importantly, they'd
also worn away most of whatever obstructions might once have existed
there. Only twice did he have to slice out pieces of rock as he slid his
bouncy way down, and in one of those cases it probably hadn't really
been necessary. Behind him, he could hear the much louder metallic clattering as Artoo slid down the slope, almost but not quite covering up his
continual unhappy twittering.

The slope emptied into one of the same sort of tunnels they'd spent
far too much time in over the past couple of weeks. Luke caught Artoo as
he fell out, getting him out of the way in time to give Mara a clear landing
spot. "Well, here we are again," she said, playing her glow rod around.
"Doesn't look particularly familiar. Any guesses as to which way?"

"From the position of the fortress, I'd say that way," Luke said,
pointing to the left.

"Okay," Mara said. "Let's go."

The Qom Qae, whether by design or simple luck, had chosen their entrance well. They had gone no more than a hundred meters along the tunnel when Luke rounded a curve to see an all-too-familiar natural stone archway in the near distance. "We're here," he murmured back toward Mara. "Be ready; if they know about the stairway, they'll probably have guards waiting for us inside."

There were no guards. Fifteen minutes later, having struggled through the narrow gap in the cortosis-laden rock, they were once again standing in the underground room.

"I guess they don't know about the stairway, after all," Mara commented, playing her glow rod across the cut they'd made earlier in the yellow inner wall.

"Or else don't have any way of getting into it," Luke reminded her. "Even the locking mechanism on those doors seemed to be made of Hijarna stone."

"Don't misunderstand—I'm just as happy to give them a miss this time through," Mara hastened to say. "I wonder how many of those power conduits are running at the moment?"

"Probably more than the last time we went through," Luke said, turning his glow rod to point the other way. As before, the far end of the room was lost in the shadows beyond the light. "*I* wonder how long this room is?"

"It can't be *too* long," Mara pointed out. "There's a lake somewhere that direction, remember?"

"Right," Luke agreed. "Got any sage advice before we start?"

"Just that we be careful," Mara said, joining him. "Side by side as long as we can with the droid behind us, lightsabers and senses ready."

"Succinct and practical," Luke said, stretching out ahead of them with the Force. There was no danger yet that he could sense. "Come on, Artoo."

Mara's point about the room's size turned out to be correct. They had gone only a few steps when the back wall came within range of their glow rods. In the center was an open archway leading farther back into the rock.

Not the rough natural rock of the caverns, though. The walls and floor of this passageway were smooth and finished.

"Interesting," Mara said, playing her glow rod around as they stood just outside the archway. "Notice anything peculiar about the ceiling?"

"It hasn't been smoothed down like the walls have," Luke said, eyeing the jutting rock hanging down from the arched ceiling.

"I wonder," Mara murmured. "Artoo, your sensors getting anything?"

Artoo warbled a rather distressed-sounding negative, and Luke leaned over to check the datapad translation. "He says the output from the power generator is masking pretty much everything else," he told Mara. "That's probably where that hum is coming from, too. You think there's something else up there?"

"Keeper Of Promises said this area was lethal to Qom Jha," Mara reminded him. "And we all know how much Qom Jha like to hang from ceilings."

"And we had that cave of predators who eat flying things like Qom Jha." Luke nodded, seeing where she was going with this. "And a bunch of Chiss up in the fortress who think of them as vermin."

"Not to mention that layer of cortosis ore back there," Mara said. "Which I still don't believe got there naturally. This place has defense rings six ways from Coruscant."

"As one would expect with Thrawn in charge of it," Luke said. "Question is, do we try to do something about that ceiling, or assume it isn't something that will bother us?"

"It's never a good idea to leave a danger at your back," Mara declared, taking a step just inside the archway. "Here goes." Igniting her lightsaber, she hurled it expertly up to slice into the rocky ceiling.

There was a brilliant flash, the crackle and stench of high-energy current—

And suddenly the whole ceiling seemed to collapse.

Mara was back out of the room in an instant, even as Luke ignited his lightsaber and jabbed it protectively over where her head had been. The ceiling fell onto it, draping itself over the green-white blade for a second before it was cut through and fell the rest of the way onto the floor.

"How cute," Mara said, peering in over his shoulder. "It's like a sculpted Conner net. A Qom Jha settles to a landing, there's a high-energy discharge that fries him, and the whole thing drops to take out any of his friends who happen to be with him."

"That's cute, all right," Luke murmured, poking at the netting with the tip of his lightsaber. "Question is, is it safe now for us to walk over?"

"Probably," Mara said. "Conner nets are usually single-charge gadgets, and it doesn't do much good to leave it active once it's on the floor."

"Makes sense," Luke said, stretching out to the Force as he eased his foot out over the net. No tingling of danger . . . and sure enough, his foot came down onto the net without even a spark of residual charge. "It's clear," he said.

"Hold it!" Mara hissed, taking a long step forward and putting her lightsaber handle across his chest to stop him, her sleeve blaster now gripped in her free hand. "Something's coming."

Luke stopped, listening to the soft clicking of feet on rock. More than one something, too, by the sound of it. He played his glow rod down the tunnel trying to see what was coming . . .

And abruptly, from a group of narrow side openings he hadn't noticed came a swarm of fist-sized insectlike creatures scuttling rapidly across the walls toward them.

"Watch it!" Mara snapped, her blaster tracking.

"No, wait," Luke said, pushing her arm to the side off target. He'd caught a glint of metal . . . "Just keep moving. Artoo, come on, hurry."

He could sense Mara's strong disapproval, but she did as instructed without argument. The skittering creatures passed them by without slowing, apparently without even so much as a second glance. Luke reached the end of the collapsed Conner net and stepped off onto the stone floor; and as Mara and Artoo did likewise, he turned around to look.

The creatures had grouped themselves around the front edge of the collapsed net. Even as Luke watched, they began to ease their careful way up the walls, carrying the edge of the net with them.

Beside him, Mara snorted gently. "Of course," she said, sounding mildly disgusted with herself. "Maintenance droids, there to get the trap reset. Sorry—I guess I overreacted a bit."

"Considering it's Thrawn we're dealing with, overreaction isn't likely to be a problem very often," Luke said.

"Thanks, but you don't have to try to soothe my feelings," Mara told him, sliding the sleeve gun away and shifting her lightsaber to her right hand again. "Lesson learned. Shall we go?"

"What in the Empire are you talking about?" Captain Nalgol demanded, blinking the sleep from his eyes as he grabbed for his uniform and started pulling it on. "How can they be shooting at each other? The flash point is still three days away."

"I don't know, sir," the *Tyrannic*'s duty officer said tautly. "All I know is that the probe ships report the battle has begun, and that the section of planetary shield over the Bothan capital has collapsed. It's hard to tell from this distance, but they say the capital appears to be on fire in several places."

Nalgol swore viciously under his breath. Someone had blundered, and blundered badly. Either the Intelligence strike team—

Or Thrawn himself.

It was a shocking thought. A shattering thought, even. If Thrawn's timing could be that far in error—

He shook away his misgivings. What was done was done; and whatever mistakes or miscalculations had been made, he was determined that he and the *Tyrannic* wouldn't add to them. "Have the *Obliterator* and *Ironhand* been informed?" he asked, grunting out the last word as he leaned over to pull on his boots.

"Yes, sir. Probe ships report they're coming to full battle stations now."

"Make sure we get there ahead of them," Nalgol told him tartly.

"Yes, sir," the officer said again. "Estimate we'll be at battle readiness in five minutes. Probe ships are continuing to feed us reports."

"Good," Nalgol muttered. Now that the shock of the news was fading, he realized it wasn't quite as bad as it had first seemed. All right, so the battle had started early. The three Star Destroyers were ready, or would be before their presence was needed to eliminate the survivors of the battle raging out there.

And blinded by the cloaking shield as they were, they definitely needed up-to-the-minute reports from the probe ships. The danger was that, with the ships dipping in and out of the shield with that kind of regularity, someone might notice something odd happening around the comet head and come over to investigate.

But there was a way to minimize that risk. "Put all tractor beam operators on full alert," he ordered. "If any ship besides our own probe ships—and I mean *any* ship—pokes its nose inside the cloaking shield, I want it grabbed and held inside out of communication. Make sure that message gets to the other ships, too. *No* one is going to stumble in on us and live to talk about it. Understood?"

"Understood, sir," the officer said.

"I'll be on the bridge in two minutes," Nalgol said, grabbing his tunic and belt. "I want the ship at full battle readiness by the time I get there."

"We will be, sir."

Nalgol slapped off the intercom and headed out the door of his quarters. Fine; so the aliens and alien-lovers couldn't contain their self-destructive hatreds as long as Thrawn had expected. Fine. It just meant that the pent-up boredom and frustration of his crew would get released a little earlier.

Smiling grimly, he headed down the corridor toward the turbolift at a carefully measured walk. This was going to be a pleasure.

A turbolaser flashed, its lethal red beam sizzling perilously close to the *Falcon*'s starboard side on its way toward an Escort Frigate with Prosslee markings. Han spun the ship away from a second shot, dodged the other direction barely in time to avoid a pair of Bagmim customs ships driving with laser cannon blazing toward the Prosslee.

The whole universe had gone mad. With him square in the middle of it.

"What happened over there?" he called toward the comm, weaving between a pair of Opquis gunships.

"According to the Ishori, three humans came aboard about half an hour ago," Leia's voice came back, the sound of an alert tone droning in the background. "They had New Republic tech IDs and a letter from the

Ishori High Conflux authorizing them to examine the *Predominance*'s power couplings for oxidation damage."

"All phony, of course," Han growled, maneuvering the *Falcon* into a relatively clear space and looking around. It was like Endor all over again out there.

Except that this time the Empire was nowhere to be seen. It was Rebels fighting other Rebels.

"We know that now," Leia agreed. "Once aboard, they killed their escort and took over one of the turbolaser clusters. When the Drev'starn shield went down . . . Han, they got eight shots off onto the surface before we were able to cut off power to their cluster. The Ishori still haven't been able to storm the room and get to them, even with Barkhimkh and Sakhisakh helping them."

Beside Han, Elegos murmured something in the Caamasi language. "How bad did Drev'starn get hit?" Han asked. "Never mind—that's not important right now. What's happening with you and the ship?"

"We're under attack," Leia said, her voice tense. "Three Diamalan ships have joined up against us, one of them sitting between us and the planet in case we try to fire on Drev'starn again. No serious damage yet, I don't think, to either side. But that can't last."

"Didn't you tell them what happened?" Han asked.

"I told them, the *Predominance*'s captain told them, Gavrisom told them," Leia said. "They're not listening."

"Or else don't care," Han said, clenching his teeth hard enough to hurt. Leia, trapped aboard a ship under massive attack . . . "Look, I'm going to try to get over there," he told her. "Maybe I can at least get you and Gavrisom off."

"No—stay away," Leia said sharply. "Please. You'd never make it."

Han gazed bitterly out at the swirling battle. She was right, of course; from his new vantage point he could see the *Predominance* now and the storm of turbolaser fire raking across it, and he knew full well the *Falcon*'s shields wouldn't stand a chance in there. But he couldn't just sit out here and do nothing. "Look, I've outfought Star Destroyers before," he said.

"You've outmaneuvered them," Leia corrected him. "There's a big difference. Please, Han, don't try to—"

There was a squawk, and suddenly she was cut off. "Leia!" Han shouted, his chest tightening as he looked back at the Ishori war cruiser. It still seemed intact; but all it would take would be a single lucky shot into the bridge area—

"She's all right," Elegos said, pointing at the comm display. "They're just being jammed again."

Han let out a breath he hadn't realized he'd been holding. "We've got to do something," he said, searching the sky for inspiration. "We've got to get her off that ship—"

The comm crackled back to life. "Leia?" Han called, leaning hopefully toward the speaker.

"Solo?" a male voice called. "It's Carib Devist."

Han grimaced. "What do you want? We're kind of busy out here."

"No kidding," Carib snapped. "And whose fault do you think that is?"

"We already know," Han growled. "Some troublemakers got aboard the *Predominance* and started shooting. Probably Imperials."

"Definitely Imperials," Carib retorted. "And it was other Imperials who stirred the rest of the crowd into doing likewise. Or didn't you hear them broadcasting recorded attack orders in a half-dozen different languages?"

Han threw a glower at Elegos, feeling a stab of chagrin at having totally missed reality on that one. So that was what those small Imperial ships Carib had identified had been hanging around Bothawui for. Obvious.

Or at least it *would* have been obvious if anyone out there had bothered to take a minute to think it through. But nobody had.

"But that can wait," Carib went on. "I called to warn you that I think there's something happening out by the head of that comet."

"Yeah? What sort of something?" Han asked, his attention already back on the *Predominance* and how in space he was going to get Leia off it.

"I don't know," Carib said. "But there are a dozen mining ships fluttering around the area. All of them flying under Imperial pilots."

Han frowned at the comm speaker. "What are you talking about? What would Imperials want with ore buckets?"

"I tell you they're Imperial pilots," Carib insisted. "Their whole flying style just screams it out."

"Okay, fine," Han said, not really interested in arguing the point. "So what do you want me to do about it?"

There was a hiss of exhaled breath from the speaker. "We're going to go check it out," he said, sounding disgusted. "Under the circumstances, I thought you might be interested in taking a look yourself. Sorry to have bothered you."

The comm clicked off. "I'm sorry, too," Han muttered. He glanced at Elegos—

Paused for another look. "What?" he snarled.

The Caamasi lifted his hands, palms up. "I said nothing."

"What, you think I should just take off and head out there with him?" Han demanded. "Just leave Leia and go running off on a wild-tresher hunt?"

"Can you help her at the moment?" Elegos countered mildly. "Can you free her, or defeat the attacking ships, or halt the battle itself?"

"That's not the point," Han bit out. "Ten to one they're just some miners who used to fly for the Empire. There are thousands of them around the New Republic—it doesn't mean a thing."

"Perhaps," Elegos said. "You must balance that against all the rest."

"All the rest of what?"

"The rest of all things," Elegos said. "Your knowledge of Carib Devist and his observational abilities. Your belief—or lack of it—that he did not, in fact, betray you to the Empire while you were on Bastion. Your own experience with Imperial procedure and style, and whether you believe someone of Carib's skills could recognize them. Your trust in your wife and her reading of this man."

He lifted his eyebrows slightly. "And most of all, your innate sense of what is right and good. If there is indeed danger of some sort out there, whether you should leave him to face it alone."

"He isn't exactly alone," Han grumbled. "He's got a whole bunch of his other clones with him."

Elegos didn't reply. Han sighed and did a quick search of the sky. There was Carib's beat-up Action II freighter, all right, driving out past the boundaries of the battle toward the blazing comet in the distance. All alone. "You know, you Caamasi could be a real pain if you worked on it a little," Han told Elegos, turning the *Falcon* to follow and keying the comm to Lando's comlink frequency. "Lando? Hey, Lando, look alive."

"Yes, Han, what is it?" Lando's tight voice came back.

"You back on the *Lady Luck* yet?"

"I wish I were," the other said fervently. "I'm stuck on the *Industrious Thoughts* with Senator Miatamia."

Han grimaced. "That's one of the ships attacking Leia?"

"If Leia's on the *Predominance*, yes," Lando said, his voice both disgusted and more than a little bit nervous. "Han, we've got to get this thing stopped, and fast."

"No argument from me, buddy," Han said, steering clear of a pair of Froffli patrol ships slugging it out with a D'farian starbarque. "Gavrisom's with Leia. If you can get Miatamia to call off their jamming, maybe he can talk this thing down."

"I've already tried," Lando sighed. "I'm the last person aboard anyone's interested in listening to."

"I know the feeling," Han said. "Look, I need a quick favor. I'm heading over to that comet out there with Carib Devist. Put some macrobinoculars on me, will you, just in case we run into trouble?"

There was a brief pause. "Sure, no problem. Exactly what sort of trouble are you expecting?"

"It's probably nothing," Han said. "Carib seems to think there are Imperials out there flying ore buckets around. Just keep an eye on us, huh?"

"I will," Lando promised. "Good luck."

Han keyed off the comm and swerved around the last handful of ships between him and the comet. "Hang on," he told Elegos as he threw full power to the sublight drive. "Here we go."

"Easy, now," Bel Iblis warned from Booster's side. "Take it nice and calm and easy. We're all friends here, with the protection of the outer defense perimeter between us and the nasty Rebel attack force. We're safe now, and there's no need to look like we're hurrying."

"No, we wouldn't want to look like that," Booster growled, staring uneasily at the huge mass of the Ubiqtorate base looming directly ahead of them. Suddenly, his beloved *Errant Venture* didn't seem nearly so big and powerful and safe anymore as it used to.

"Steady, Terrik," Bel Iblis said. His voice, to Booster's thorough annoyance, was controlled and glacially calm. "The big show's going on behind us, remember? The last thing we want to do is draw their eyes our direction."

Booster nodded, glancing over at the aft display. There was a show going on back there, all right, with the New Republic ships taking a real beating from the Yaga Minor defense perimeter.

Or at least, that was how it was supposed to look. If they were following orders, they were actually hanging just far enough back to keep from taking any really serious damage from the massed turbolaser fire. Hopefully, in all the confusion, the Imperials wouldn't notice that. "I don't know," he said. "I don't like this, Bel Iblis. We got in much too easy."

"General, we've got movement," the officer at the sensor station called. "Imperial Star Destroyer, moving up from starboard."

Booster took a few steps forward along the command walkway, peering out the viewport, a bad feeling twisting into his gut. The Star Destroyer had appeared from around the starboard side of the base and had moved across the *Errant Venture*'s vector.

And even as he watched, it stopped there, between them and the base. Floating in space in front of them, as if daring them to pass . . .

"The ship ID's as the *Relentless*," someone else called. "Captain Dorja listed as commander."

Booster's bad feeling turned suddenly even worse. The *Relentless*—

wasn't that the ship that always showed up in the rumors about Grand Admiral Thrawn?

Bel Iblis had come up on Booster's side again. "General . . . ?" Booster murmured.

"I know," Bel Iblis said, the calmness bending just a bit. "But running now would only make us look guilty. All we can do is play it through."

"Transmission from the *Relentless,* General," the comm officer called. "They're asking to speak to Captain Nalgol."

Booster looked at Bel Iblis. "All we can do is play it through," Bel Iblis repeated. "Go on, give it a try."

"Sure." Taking a deep breath, Booster caught the comm officer's eye and nodded. The man threw a switch and nodded back—"This is Commander Raymeuz, temporarily in command of the Imperial Star Destroyer *Tyrannic,*" he called in his best imitation of a typical Imperial's overly stiff speech pattern. "Captain Nalgol was seriously injured in the last attack and is undergoing emergency treatment."

There was a low chuckle from the bridge speakers. "Really," a calm voice said. A steady voice; a cultured voice; a voice that scared Booster clear down to his boots. "This is Grand Admiral Thrawn. You disappoint me, General Bel Iblis."

Booster looked at Bel Iblis. The general was still staring out the viewport, his face not betraying any emotion at all.

"There's really no point in trying to maintain this charade," Thrawn said. "But perhaps you need a more convincing demonstration."

It was as if someone behind Booster had suddenly yanked a carpet out from under his feet. Suddenly he was toppling forward, arms flailing madly as he fought to regain his balance. Around him came the sounds of consternation from the rest of the bridge crew; from somewhere beyond that came the ominous sound of creaking metal.

"A small demonstration, as I said," Thrawn continued, his tone almost bantering. "Your Star Destroyer is now totally helpless, pinned in place by approximately fifty of our heavy-lift tractor beams."

Booster swallowed a curse that wanted desperately to come out. What *was* it with this ship and tractor beams, anyway?

He started as Bel Iblis tapped him on the arm. The general was glaring at him, gesturing him impatiently toward the comm station. Booster glared back, took a deep breath. "Admiral Thrawn, sir, what are you doing?" he called, trying to mix respect and bewildered fear into his tone. The latter part took no acting whatsoever. "Sir, we have injured officers and crewers aboard—"

"That's enough," Thrawn cut him off coldly. The attempt at casualness had apparently been too much for the red-eyed mongrel—it was back to being overbearing again. "I respect your courage in making this attempt, but the game is over. Must I order the turbolaser batteries to commence taking the ship apart?"

Bel Iblis exhaled softly. "No need for that, Admiral," he called. "This is General Bel Iblis."

"Ah—General," Thrawn said. Once again he'd changed tone, Booster noted, this time switching from cold threat to the almost cordial unspoken camaraderie between fellow professionals. The man was nothing if not versatile. "I congratulate you, sir, on your attempt, futile though it may have been."

"Thank you, Admiral," Bel Iblis said. "However, I suggest the success or failure of the operation has yet to be determined."

"Do you, now," Thrawn said. "Well, then, let us make it official. I hearby call on you to suspend your diversion and surrender your ship."

Bel Iblis glanced at Booster. "And if I refuse?"

"As I suggested earlier, General, you're lying helpless before me," Thrawn said, his voice heavy with menace. "At my order, your ship will be systematically destroyed."

For a long moment the bridge was silent. Booster watched Bel Iblis; Bel Iblis, in turn, was gazing out at the Star Destroyer standing in their path. "I need to discuss this with my officers," he said at last.

"Of course," Thrawn said easily. "Take your time. Only I suggest you don't take *too* much time. Your diversionary force is fighting valiantly, if ineffectually, but my patience toward them will not last forever. Interdictor Cruisers are already moving into position to trap them there, and the various fighter commanders are pleading to be allowed to launch their TIEs and Preybirds."

"Understood," Bel Iblis said. "I'll deliver my answer as quickly as possible."

He gestured to the comm officer to cut the transmission. "What are you going to do now?" Booster demanded. The thought of the *Errant Venture* ending up again in Imperial hands . . .

"As I promised, I'm going to deliver my answer," Bel Iblis said coolly. "Tanneris, Bodwae, where are those tractor beams originating? From the base or the defense perimeter?"

"I'm getting thirty-eight from emplacements in the perimeter," Bel Iblis's sensor officer reported.

"Fjifteen more comjing from the base jitself," Bodwae added. "JI have thejir locatjions marked."

"Thank you," Bel Iblis said. "Simons, do we have any freedom of movement at all?"

"Not really, sir," the helmsman said. "We're pinned pretty solidly in place."

"What about rotational? Can we swivel around a vertical axis?"

"Ah . . . yes, sir, actually I think we can," the other said, frowning at his displays. "Probably no more than a quarter turn, though."

"Not nearly enough to turn us around and get the blazes out of here," Booster muttered.

"Getting out isn't the goal," Bel Iblis reminded him. "Simons, bring us around ninety degrees to portside, or as near to that as you can manage. Portside turbolasers and proton torpedo tubes, prepare to fire at the defense perimeter at my command, targeting the tractor beam emplacements holding us here. Starboard weapons, same thing, only targeting the emplacements on the base."

There was a chorus of acknowledgments. Booster gazed out at the base and the Star Destroyer standing ready in front of it; and as he watched, they started moving to the right. Slowly and ponderously, but moving.

He took a step closer to Bel Iblis. "You realize, of course, that you're not going to fool anybody with this," he warned. "Least of all someone like Thrawn. He's going to see us targeting the tractor beams and start slicing the ship up beneath us."

Bel Iblis shook his head. "I don't think so. Not yet, anyway. All the evidence indicates that he's trying to rebuild the Empire, and a mass of wreckage won't help him do that. What he really wants from us is a few high-ranking New Republic prisoners he can parade in front of potential converts to his cause."

"Not to mention picking up an extra Star Destroyer to use against anyone who isn't so easily converted?"

"That, too," Bel Iblis conceded. "Bottom line: he's not going to start shooting until we're nearly free. Maybe not even then."

Booster grimaced. No, Thrawn would be in no hurry. Not with the *Errant Venture* on the wrong side of all that firepower waiting at the perimeter. "So how *are* you planning to get us out?"

Bel Iblis shook his head. "I'm not trying to get us out. I already told you that. We have a job to do; and that job is waiting for us in there." He nodded out the viewport at the Ubiqtorate base.

"With Thrawn and a Star Destroyer sitting between us and it?" Booster snorted. "Don't take this personally, General, and I'm sure you're a fine military mind and all that. But you try to slug it out with Thrawn and we're all roast dewback."

"I know," Bel Iblis said, his voice suddenly very deadly. "That's why we're not going to engage him. At least, not the way he expects us to."

Booster eyed him cautiously. There was something about the other's face and voice that was starting to send shivers through him. "What are you talking about?"

"We have to get past the *Relentless*, Terrik," Bel Iblis said quietly, gazing out the viewport. "And we have to disable it enough in the process that it won't be able to blast our slicers out of the sky before they can get to the computer extension and cut their way in."

"What about the base's own weapons?"

"*And* we have to do it fast enough that the base's own weaponry won't have time to turn on us," Bel Iblis agreed. "Add it all up, and there's only one way we can possibly pull it off."

Still gazing out the viewport, he seemed to brace himself. "As soon as we can break clear of the tractor beams, we're going to turn and drive as hard as we can straight for the *Relentless.*

"And we're going to ram it."

Booster felt the air go out of him in a silent rush. "You're not serious," he breathed.

Bel Iblis turned, looking him straight in the eye. "I'm sorry, Booster. Sorry about your ship; sorry about letting you and your crew come aboard in the first place."

"General?" the helmsman called. "We've got a seventy-nine-degree displacement now. That's the best we're going to get."

For another second, Bel Iblis held Booster's gaze. Then, turning his eyes away, he stepped past him. "It will do," he said. "All weapons: commence firing at tractor beam emplacements."

Abruptly, out the viewport, a firestorm of turbolaser fire erupted, lancing outward from the angled hull in both directions. "And helm and sublight engines," the general added calmly, "stand by for full emergency power."

"There he is," Elegos said, pointing. "Over there, just to starboard."

"I see him," Han said. For a minute there he'd lost Carib's freighter in the swirling glare of the comet's tail. "You see any of the miners he was talking about?"

"Not yet," Elegos said. "Perhaps he was mistaken."

"Not likely," Han growled, the hairs on the back of his neck starting to tingle. He might not agree that Carib could pick out Imperials just by their flying style; but he sure didn't doubt the guy could tell the difference between ore buckets and empty space. "I wonder where they could have gotten to?"

"Perhaps they're being masked by the tail," Elegos suggested. "They may be working on the back quarter of the comet's surface."

"Miners never work back there," Han said, shaking his head. "The dust and ice foul up alluvial dampers something fierce."

"Then where are they?"

"I don't know," Han said grimly. "But I'm starting to get a very bad feeling about it. Key me a transmission to Carib's freighter, will you?"

Elegos keyed the comm. "Ready."

"Carib?" Han called. "You see anything?"

"Nothing," the other's voice came back. "But they were here, Solo."

"I believe you," Han said, throwing a quick look at the *Falcon*'s weapons board. The quads were ready, keyed remotely down here to him. "I think maybe it's time for a real close look at the surface. See what might be tucked away in there out of sight."

"Agreed," Carib said. "You want us to lead the way down?"

"That freighter of yours armed?"

There was just the briefest of hesitations. "No, not really."

"Then I'd better take point," Han said, throwing more power to the sublight engines. "Hang back and let me pass you."

"Whatever you say."

"Do you wish me to go to one of the weapons bays?" Elegos asked quietly.

Han threw him a quick glance. "I thought Caamasi hated killing."

"We do," Elegos said soberly. "But we also accept that there are times when killing a few is necessary for a greater good. This may well be one of those times."

"Maybe," Han grunted, easing way back on his speed as the *Falcon* shot past the Action II. They were starting to get close in to the comet now, and he didn't want to run into some loose piece of rock that might suddenly decide to break off into their path. "Don't worry—whatever they're hiding down there, I should be able to handle it okay by myself. It's not like you can cram a lot of firepower into one of those ore buckets—"

And right in the middle of his sentence, right before his eyes, the comet and the stars beyond it abruptly vanished.

And in their place, its lights glowing evilly in the total blackness around it, was the dark shape of an Imperial Star Destroyer.

"Han!" Elegos gasped. "What—"

"Cloaked Star Destroyer!" Han snapped back, twisting the helm yoke viciously, the whole plan suddenly coming clear. That battle back there over Bothawui—all those ships beating each other into rubble— with a Star Destroyer waiting hidden here, ready to finish them all off and maybe burn Bothawui in the bargain. No survivors, no witnesses, only a battle everyone in the New Republic would blame everyone else for.

And the civil war that single battle would spark might never end.

"Get ready on the comm," he told Elegos as the *Falcon* veered hard around back toward the invisible edge of the cloaking shield. "The second we're clear—"

The order choked off as he was abruptly thrown hard against his restraints. Beneath him, the *Falcon* jerked to the side like a wounded animal, the roar of the sublight engines mixing with the creaking of stressed joints and supports. "What is it?" Elegos gasped.

Han swallowed hard, his hands tightening uselessly on the yoke. "It's a tractor beam," he told the Caamasi, throwing a desperate glance at the sensor display. If it was an edgewise grab, something marginal or tenuous, he might be able to wiggle his way out.

But no. They had him. They had him solid.

He looked up again as a motion caught his eye: Carib's freighter, now inside the cloaking shield with him, twisting helplessly in the same invisible grip. "They've got us, Elegos," he sighed, the bitter taste of defeat in his mouth.

"They've got us both."

CHAPTER
38

They ran into two more of the disguised Conner nets along the way, both of which Mara insisted on tripping and disposing of. Luke wasn't convinced himself that that was necessary; but on the other hand he couldn't see how it could hurt, either. If the first net hadn't triggered any alarms—and there was no indication it had—then taking down the other two probably wouldn't do anything, either. And at least it gave the insectoid service droids something to do that was back out of their way.

The background hum had also increased as they traveled down the tunnel, reaching a volume where Luke could definitely tell it was coming from above them. The fortress's huge power generator, undoubtedly, sealed safely away inside solid rock beyond their reach.

And eventually, after perhaps a hundred meters, the tunnel ended in a large, well-lit room.

"I was right," Mara murmured from Luke's side as they stood together at the archway entrance. "I knew he'd have a place like this stashed away. Even in his own fortress, hidden away from his own people. I just *knew* it."

Luke nodded silently, gazing into the chamber. It was roughly circular, dome-shaped at the top, sixty meters across at the base, and a good ten high at the center, all carved out of solid rock. A three-meter-wide ring of tiled floor ran around the outer edge at the level of the tunnel, dropping then a meter down to the main floor, which was also tiled. Five meters up the sides, behind a protective railing, a balcony deeply indented into the rock ran two-thirds of the way around the room, its inner walls lined with electronic equipment.

On the main floor to their far right was a more modest version of the command center they'd found in the upper floor of the Hand of Thrawn. This one was only a single ring of consoles, centered not on a galactic holo but on the wide, squat cylinder of a superstorage library/computer information base. Again, as in the fortress above, a handful of glowing lights indicated the equipment was waiting patiently on standby. The rest of the main floor was empty except for a row of furniture lined up against one edge of the raised walkway beneath a plastic sheet.

But all of that was just background, things to be peripherally noted and filed away into his mind for later evaluation. From the first moment he and Mara had entered the room, Luke's full attention had been focused on the deep alcove coming off the main room over to their left. Sealed there behind a solid transparisteel wall was a complete cloning apparatus: a Spaarti cylinder wrapped in nutrient tubes and flash-learning cables, surrounded by support equipment, all of it tied into a humming fusion generator.

And floating gently in the center of the cylinder, asleep or perhaps not even yet truly alive, was a blue-skinned adult humanoid. A humanoid with an exceptionally familiar face.

Grand Admiral Thrawn.

"Ten years," Luke said quietly. "Just like you said. Just like you figured. He told them he'd return in ten years."

"The old fraud," Mara muttered, the words in sharp contrast to the reluctant awe Luke could sense in her. He could sympathize; the alcove and its occupant were intimidating in their subtle grandeur, and in their equally quiet threat. "Probably had the cycle set on a ten-year timer and just reset it back to zero every time he dropped by for a visit."

"Probably," Luke agreed, tearing his eyes away from the almost hypnotic sight of the floating clone and looking over at the ring of consoles at the other end of the room. "Artoo, get over there and find a computer jack you can link into. Start downloading everything you can find about the Unknown Regions area Thrawn opened up."

The little droid warbled acknowledgment and rolled past him to one of the half-dozen ramps leading from the outer ring down to the main floor. He made it down the ramp without tipping over and headed for the console ring, his wheels clattering rhythmically across the small gaps between the tiles as he went. He stopped beside one of the consoles, whistled a confirmation, then extended his computer jack and plugged in.

"He's in," Luke said, turning back to the cloning tank. "Come on, I want a closer look at this."

Together, he and Mara circled the room to the transparisteel wall. "Don't touch it," Mara warned as he leaned in close. "It's probably wired with alarms."

"I wasn't going to," Luke assured her, peering inside. From this angle he could see something that hadn't been visible from the archway. "You see what else he's got in there with him?"

"A couple of ysalamiri." Mara nodded. "Just in case a wandering Jedi happened by."

"Thrawn was the type to think of everything."

"He sure was," Mara agreed. "Except maybe that lake out there."

Luke frowned. "What do you mean?"

"Over there," Mara said, half turning and pointing across the room.

Luke turned to look. There was the rock wall, and the furniture beneath the plastic sheet, and the upper equipment balcony running around the dome above it. "What exactly am I looking at?" he asked.

"The water damage," she said, pointing again. "On the wall across from the tunnel mouth. See?"

"I do now," Luke said, nodding. The wall over there was subtly but definitely discolored, the stain marked with multiple vertical lines where water had seeped through the rock and dripped down. In fact, now that he was paying attention, he could see water oozing slowly through the rock in a dozen places. "Child Of Winds said the lake had been expanding," he said. "Looks like it found a way in through the caverns."

He turned back. "I'd say our clone reached his ten-year mark just in time."

"What do you think he'll be like?" Mara asked, her voice sounding odd. "I mean, how close to the original Thrawn will he be?"

Luke shook his head. "That's an argument that's been going on for decades," he said. "With the same genetic structure plus a flash-learning pattern taken directly from the templet, a clone should theoretically be completely identical to the original person. But despite that, they're never *exactly* the same. Maybe some of the mental subtleties get blurred over in transition, or maybe there's something else unique inside us that a flash-learning reader isn't able to pick up."

He nodded toward the clone. "He'll presumably have all of Thrawn's memories. But will he have his genius, or his leadership, or his single-minded drive? I don't know."

He looked at Mara. "Which I suppose leads us to the question of what we do with him."

"Funny you should ask that," Mara said pensively. "Ten years ago, I'd have said flat out we blast our way in and get rid of him. Maybe even five years ago. But now . . . it's not so simple anymore."

Luke studied her profile, trying to sort through the mixture of emotions swirling through her. "You really *were* spooked by all that talk about distant threats, weren't you?"

To his mild surprise, she didn't take offense. "Fel and Parck are worried about it," she reminded him. "You willing to bet they're both wrong?"

"Not really," Luke conceded, looking back at the clone. "I'm just trying to imagine what having Thrawn suddenly show up would do to the New Republic. Widespread panic would be my guess, with Coruscant scrambling to find enough ships for a preemptive strike at what's left of the Empire."

"You don't think they'd listen to what he had to say?"

"The way Thrawn carved his way through the New Republic the last time?" Luke shook his head. "They wouldn't trust him for a minute."

"You're probably right," Mara said. "Parck said there were rumors he'd returned, though how a rumor like that could get started I don't know. But he didn't mention what the reaction had been."

"And rumors are a lot different than if he actually walked in the door," Luke pointed out.

For a minute they stood there in silence. Then Luke took a deep breath. "I suppose it's an academic argument, really, when you come down to it," he said. "Whatever the original Thrawn might have done, this particular being hasn't done anything wrong. Certainly nothing that deserves a summary execution."

"True," Mara agreed. "Though I imagine you'd have trouble convincing some people of that. Next question, then: do we leave him here to wake up normally and join our friends upstairs? Bearing in mind that they're not too happy with either us or the New Republic at the moment? Or do we see if we can speed up the growth process and take him back to Coruscant?"

Luke whistled softly under his breath. "You sure know how to find the hard questions, don't you?"

"I've never had to find a hard question in my life," she countered tartly. "They've always found me first."

Luke smiled. "I know the feeling."

"I'd rather you knew the answer," she said. "Bottom line: could Coruscant handle it?"

From across the room came a sudden flurry of warbling. Luke turned, to see Artoo bouncing back and forth excitedly on his stubby legs. "What is it?" he called. "You find the Unknown Regions data?"

The droid twittered impatiently. "Okay, okay, I'll be right there," Luke soothed him, heading for the nearest ramp down to the main floor. He started to pass the sheet-covered furniture—

And paused, looking at the collection. There were half a dozen chairs of various types under there, plus a bed, a table, and a couple of things that looked like storage end tables. "What do you suppose this is all about?" he called back to Mara.

"Looks like the stuff he'll need to make this place into a cozy little apartment once he's out," Mara suggested, dropping down to the main floor and coming up beside him. "He'll want some time to recover, maybe get caught up with what's been happening out there over the past ten years. In fact, I'd run you ten to one that console ring's got a direct feed from whatever news/data links they've got upstairs."

"Yes, but why is it all piled here instead of laid out waiting for him?"

Luke asked. "It's not like Thrawn wouldn't have known what kind of arrangement his clone would like."

"Interesting point," Mara agreed, her voice suddenly uneasy.

Luke threw her a look. "What is it?"

"I don't know," she said slowly, looking around. "Something just suddenly felt wrong."

Luke looked around the room, too. Nothing seemed threatening . . . but suddenly he was feeling it, too. "Maybe we ought to get Artoo and clear out of here," he suggested quietly. "Take whatever he's got and just go."

"Let's first see how much he's got," Mara said. She turned back toward the droid and took a step—

"Who dares disturb the sleep of the Syndic Mitth'raw'nuruodo?" a deep voice thundered from above them.

Luke dropped into a half crouch, lightsaber reflexively raised above him. He looked up—

To an extraordinary sight. Above the railing and second-level equipment balcony, a large ovate section of the stone ceiling was undulating like some sort of rocky fluid. Even as he watched, it slowly formed itself into a giant face looking down at them. "Who dares disturb the sleep of the Syndic Mitth'raw'nuruodo?" the voice repeated.

"Now *that's* a nice trick," Mara murmured. "Well, go ahead—answer it."

Luke took a careful breath. "We're friends," Luke called. "We mean the Syndic Mitth'raw'nuruodo no harm."

The fluid eyes seemed to focus on him. "Who dares disturb the sleep of the Syndic Mitth'raw'nuruodo?"

Luke looked at Mara. "A recording?"

"Sounds like it," she agreed tightly. "But what good does a recording—watch it!"

But Luke was already spinning around, lightsaber flashing out into defensive position in front of him, as his own senses flared a warning.

There were two of them, standing there on the upper section of floor: a pair of large, thickset sentinel droids on treaded bases, each with a heavy blaster gripped in its right hand.

"Get behind me!" Luke snapped to Mara, taking a short step in front of her.

Just in time. Even as he stretched out to the Force, both sentinels opened fire.

"Stupid, stupid, stupid," he heard Mara snarl from behind him. "A big fat diversion—the oldest trick on the list. And I fell for it like some dumb farm kid."

"Watch your language," Luke warned. The sentinels were good, laying out a systematic targeting pattern that would have quickly taken out most opponents. So far, though, he was easily staying ahead of them. "Can you do anything about them?"

Her reply was a spitting of blaster fire over his shoulder raking across the sentinels' joints and glowing eyes. But there was no effect. "No good—the armor's too thick for my blaster," she said. "Let me try—"

"Watch it—he's moving," Luke cut her off. The sentinel on the left had suddenly started rolling on its treads along the raised floor ring toward the far end of the room, blaster still firing. Luke clenched his teeth, stretching out harder to the Force, feeling sweat breaking out on his forehead. With the source of the blaster bolts now coming from two different directions—and with the separation between them growing ever wider—it was becoming harder and harder for him to physically get the lightsaber blade back and forth fast enough to block the shots. Behind him, he heard the *snap-hiss* as Mara ignited her own lightsaber—

Followed by a sudden yelp and a muffled thud.

"What happened?" Luke snapped, not daring to take his attention off the sentinels.

"Don't try to walk," Mara warned, her voice inexplicably coming from the floor beneath him. "Thrawn left another surprise for unwanted guests."

Luke frowned. "What do you mean?"

Out of the corner of his eye, he saw the blue-white blade of her lightsaber cut across one of the shots from the more distant sentinel, now at the far end of the room. "Okay, I've got this one," she said. "If you can spare a second, take a look at the floor."

Letting the Force guide his hands, Luke risked a quick look down at his feet.

One glance was all he needed. The floor had sprouted loops of green-black cord that had formed themselves into a tangled mass around their feet. "Looks like they extruded themselves out of the cracks between the tiles," Mara went on. "First step I took my foot tried to catch in one of the loops."

"Clever," Luke agreed tightly. "I guess that rules out any chance of running for it."

"At least we know now why all the furniture's stacked off to the side," Mara added. "You don't want to clutter your killing field with a lot of stuff the victims might be able to hide behind. Luke, this other sentinel's still coming."

Luke risked a glance. The second sentinel had rounded the far end of the room and was now rolling steadily around the other side.

And in maybe ten seconds it would reach a point directly across from Mara.

"Quick—before it gets any closer," he told her, easing a little to his left so he could again defend against both sentinels. "Use your lightsaber on it."

"Right," Mara said, and through his haze of concentration he felt her emotional twinge at the memory of her less than perfect handling of the weapon back in the chamber where they'd taken out all of the stalactites and stalagmites together.

But the moment passed; and as he leaned hard into the effort of blocking the barrage of shots he saw the flash as her lightsaber windmilled across the room toward the sentinel. It sliced cleanly into the intersection of head and body—

And then, abruptly, the blue-white blade vanished.

"What happened?" Luke demanded.

"*Blast* it!" Mara snarled. Out of the corner of Luke's eye he saw the blade reappear, swing into the sentinel, and again vanish. "He put a layer of cortosis ore under the armor."

"Then go for the blaster," Luke said.

"Right."

The blue-white blade sizzled out again—there was a crackle of broken metal and plastic—and suddenly that point of danger faded from Luke's mind. "Good job," he called to Mara, shifting his full attention to the sentinel in front of him. "Now get around here and do the same thing to this one—"

He swiveled back again, getting his lightsaber blade around just in time. Suddenly the sentinel on Mara's side had started shooting again—

"Watch it," Mara snapped a belated warning. "It had another blaster holstered for its left hand—oh, *shavit.*"

"What—? Never mind," Luke growled. In response to Mara's attack, the sentinel facing him had now drawn a second blaster from concealment with its left hand.

"He's got a second blaster for the right, too—"

"I got it, I got it," Luke cut her off, leaning still harder into his defense. With twice as many shots coming in now from each of the sentinels, they were in worse shape than they had been before. A missed blaster bolt sizzled painfully across the top of his left shoulder—

"Sorry," Mara said, her back pressing against his now, the hum of her lightsaber like an angry insect behind him. "What do we do now?"

Luke grimaced. The row of ysalamiri-equipped Chiss he'd faced up in the fortress had been bad enough; but at least there they'd had the option of shooting their opponents if defense became too difficult. Here, trapped in the middle of an open room, caught in a crossfire from two tireless droids who couldn't be killed, with tangling cords around their feet precluding any chance of fast escape . . .

"Luke?" Mara called again over the sound and fury. "You hear me?"

"I heard you, I heard you," he snapped back.

"So what do we do?"

Luke swallowed hard. "I have no idea."

Beneath Leia, the *Predominance*'s great bulk shuddered as another proton torpedo got through the Ishori defenses, its violent explosion ripping another piece out of the hull. Ahead out the main bridge canopy, the sky was a tangle of turbolaser blasts splashing across their shields or occasionally burning through to vaporize layers of metal or transparisteel.

But in that sudden, heart-stopping moment, none of that mattered; not the battle, not her own life, not even the terrible threat of civil war. With that flicker of distant emotion, that sudden tremor in the Force, one thing alone had surged to overriding importance for her.

Somewhere out there, Han was in deadly danger.

"Captain Av'muru!" she shouted over the din of the bridge, crossing quickly toward the command console. Two guards raised their blasters warningly; without thinking, Leia stretched out with the Force to turn the weapons aside as she passed. "Captain, I must speak with you right away."

"I am busy, Councilor," the Ishori captain snarled, not even bothering to look at her.

"You'll be busier than you care to be if you don't listen to me," Leia bit out, straining with all her strength toward the wispy, unclear sensation that was Han. His emotions were still seething with danger and threat and helpless fury; but try as she might, she couldn't penetrate through the emotion and the distance to his underlying thoughts.

But there was one thing that *was* very clear. "There's some new threat waiting out there," she told Av'muru. "One you're completely unaware of."

"Other threats are meaningless!" Av'muru all but screamed. "There can be no other concern but the Diamalan attackers around us."

"Captain—"

She broke off at a feathery touch on her arm. "It's no use, Councilor," Gavrisom said, his long face tight and almost bitter. "He can't and won't think that far ahead. Not with his ship under immediate attack. Can you tell me what this threat is?"

Leia looked out the canopy, trying to pierce the dazzlingly lethal light show outside. "Han's in danger," she said.

"Where? How?"

"I don't know," she said, her stomach twisting with her own sense of helplessness. "I can't pick up his thoughts clearly enough."

"Who else might know?" Gavrisom asked.

Leia took a deep breath, forcing calmness into her mind. Gavrisom was right: what Han needed was for her to put aside her emotions and think clearly. "Elegos was with him on the *Falcon*," she said, stretching out again with the Force. But there was nothing. "I can't even sense him."

"Who else might know?" Gavrisom persisted. "Someone closer at hand?"

Leia looked out at the battle again, a sudden tentative flicker of hope stirring in her. "Lando. Han might have said something to Lando."

"Then we must talk to him," Gavrisom said firmly. "I will go speak to the captain about piercing the Diamalan jamming. In the meantime, is there anything your Jedi skills can do about it?"

Leia took a deep breath. "I don't know," she said. "Let me try."

"I tell you, this can't wait," Lando insisted, throwing every bit of urgency and intimidation he could muster into his voice. "I have to speak to High Councilor Organa Solo right away. The whole fate of the New Republic might well hang on the edge. Not to mention your own lives."

"Really," Senator Miatamia said, his voice icy calm. Diamala, Lando knew, were notoriously hard to read, but it was abundantly clear the Senator wasn't impressed. "And what is the nature of this threat?"

"My friend Han went out to take a look at that comet out there," Lando said. "I was watching him on macrobinoculars . . . and he just vanished."

Miatamia's cheeks creased. "You mean he crashed?"

"I mean he *vanished*," Lando insisted. "Right out in the open."

"Yet how truly open is the region around a comet?" the Diamal pointed out, an ear twitching. "He may have veered into the gases of the tail, or you may have lost sight of him briefly in the glare of sunlight from the surface."

Lando grimaced. Not only was Miatamia not convinced, he wasn't even going to give it a fair hearing.

But Lando knew what he had seen. "All right, then," he said between clenched teeth. "In that case, I'm calling in the favor you owe me."

Both ears twitched this time. "What favor is this?"

"I gave you a ride to Coruscant from Cilpar, remember?" Lando reminded him. "You've never paid me back for that."

"You stated at the time that you would not require any payment other than our conversation."

"I lied," Lando said evenly. "And I want my favor now."

Miatamia eyed him darkly. "We are in a combat situation."

"This won't jeopardize that." Lando gestured at the bridge, lying beyond the transparisteel wall of the observation deck he and Miatamia were standing on. "All I want is for the jamming of the *Predominance* lifted, just on Councilor Organa Solo's personal comlink frequency. Just that one frequency—that's all."

The Diamal shook his head. "I cannot gamble that such an action would not create additional danger for Diamalan lives and goods."

He turned away, facing the battle again. Lando swallowed a curse, looking past him and the besieged Ishori ship at the comet glowing with such deceptive serenity out beyond the fighting. Han had asked for his help. Had trusted him.

And he *did* know what he'd seen.

"All right," he said, stepping squarely in front of Miatamia again. It was time to put his money where it counted. "A gamble, you say? Fine— let's gamble."

He pointed out the viewport at the Ishori ship. "Here's the bet. You let me talk to Leia right now; and if the threat turns out not to be as serious as I claim it is, you and the Diamala will get my mining and casino operation on Varn."

The Senator's ears twitched. "Are you serious?"

"Deadly serious," Lando said. "My friend's in danger, and I'm the only one who can help him."

For a long moment the Diamal stared at him. "Very well," he said at last. "High Councilor Organa Solo's private comlink frequency only. And for no more than two minutes."

"Done." Lando nodded. "How fast can you arrange it?"

Miatamia turned toward the observation deck's intercom and spoke rapidly in the Diamalan language. He was answered in kind. There was one more quick exchange—"It is done," he said, turning back to Lando. "Your two minutes are running."

Lando already had his comlink out and keyed. "Leia?"

"Lando!" her relieved voice came back instantly. "I was hoping to get through to you. Han's in trouble."

"I know," Lando said. "He went with Carib to check out the comet and asked me to watch with macrobinoculars. They cut in close to the surface, and then just disappeared."

"What do you mean, disappeared?" Leia asked anxiously. "As if they'd crashed?"

"No," Lando said grimly. "As if they'd dipped inside a cloaking shield."

He heard her sharp intake of air. "Lando, we've got to get over there right away. If there's an Imperial ship hiding out there—"

"Hey, no argument here," Lando said. "But I've already used up all my favors getting this call through."

"All right," Leia said, her voice suddenly dark. "It's up to me, then."

"What are you going to do?" Lando asked.

"I'm going to help Han," she said, her voice as cold as he'd ever heard it. "Stay clear—you don't want to get involved in this."

The transmission clicked off. "Too late for that, Leia," he muttered at the dead comlink. "Years and years too late."

Another barrage of turbolaser fire lanced out from the nearest of the two Golan weapons platforms, the spread targeting the group of starfighters harrying its flank.

Wedge twisted his X-wing safely between the shots and did a quick check of the rest of his squadron. As with the last such salvo, and the four or five before it, none of them had taken any damage.

Neither, as far as he could tell, had anyone else in the attack fleet. Bel Iblis's strategy of staying just at the edge of the Golans' kill zone had so far paid off.

But that strategy was about to change.

"All fighter wings, this is Perris," the voice of the *Peregrine*'s fighter commander came tautly through his headset. "Captain Tre-na has confirmed that General Bel Iblis is definitely in trouble in there."

Wedge grimaced, wondering what about the situation had needed any confirmation in the first place. Nose to nose with another Imperial Star Destroyer, pinned in place by probably every heavy tractor beam the Ubiqtorate base could bring to bear—

"Look—they're firing," Rogue Five snapped. "Everything they've got, looks like."

"I see it," Wedge said, gazing through the separating distance at the blaze of turbolaser fire flashing out from the *Errant Venture,* his last faint hope that Bel Iblis might still be able to talk his way out of this evaporating like morning mist at sunrise. If he'd opened fire on the base, it meant the bluff had failed.

It also meant he was running low on time. That second Star Destroyer, not to mention the Ubiqtorate base commander, wasn't just going to sit there while Bel Iblis vaped their tractor emplacements and got away.

Tre-na and the rest of the fleet command staff aboard the *Peregrine* had clearly come to the same conclusion. "Okay, fighters," Perris said. "The fleet's going in, and we're going in hard. Your job is to draw fire away from the main ships, help wherever you can to punch a hole in the defense perimeter, and be ready to run screen when the Imperials finally launch their own fighters. All wings, acknowledge and prepare."

"Rogue Leader, copy," Wedge said, then keyed for the squadron's private frequency. "Well, Rogues, you've all had a look at the perimeter. Any thoughts on where the weak spots are?"

"Maybe," Rogue Twelve said. "Seems to me the turbolasers on the starboard side of that second Golan have a slight flutter."

"You sure?" Rogue Three asked. "I didn't notice anything."

"It's small, but it's there," Rogue Twelve said. "It may be just enough to leave a small gap between—"

"General Antilles?" a new voice cut in.

Wedge frowned. It was a familiar voice, but not one of his squadron. "This is Antilles," he confirmed cautiously.

"This is Talon Karrde. How are things?"

It took Wedge a second to find his voice. "Karrde, what in blazes are you doing here?" he demanded.

"To be perfectly honest, trying to get past your forces," Karrde said. "Is Commander Horn there with you?"

"I'm here," Rogue Nine said. "What do you want?"

"I want to collect on a favor you owe me," Karrde said. "The one we discussed the last time we were together on the *Errant Venture*, remember?"

There was an exasperated-sounding noise in Wedge's headset. "Karrde, are you crazy? We're in the middle of a battle here."

"Which is precisely why I need the favor now," Karrde said. "I need you to escort me through the New Republic lines."

"To where?" Rogue Nine countered. "In case you hadn't noticed, on the other side of our lines is an Imperial Ubiqtorate base."

"Which, conveniently, happens to be my destination," Karrde told him.

Wedge snorted gently. "The *Wild Karrde* must be a lot better armored than I thought."

"The Imperials won't be a problem," Karrde said. "I have a high-level code for getting through their lines. My problem is *your* lines."

"Look, Karrde, I don't know what you're up to," Rogue Nine said. "And frankly, right now I don't really care. But we have a job to do here."

"Perhaps I can make that job unnecessary," Karrde said, a sudden edge in his voice. "You get me inside, and I may be able to stop this battle completely."

"Really," Rogue Two said, his voice suddenly suspicious. "May I ask how exactly you plan to do that?"

There was a slight pause, and Wedge could picture Karrde smiling that mysterious smile he was so fond of. "Let's just say I'm holding the ultimate bargaining chip," he said softly.

"And that would be . . . ?"

"All wings, this is Perris," the fighter commander's voice came on. "Run to formation; we're heading in."

Wedge took a deep breath. They were under official orders now, with no room for maneuvering or stalling or anything else.

But General Bel Iblis's life was on the line here . . .

"Karrde, this is Antilles," he said. "Where are you?"

"Coming up behind and above the *Peregrine*," Karrde told him. "Are you starting an attack?"

"Something like that," Wedge said, checking his rear scanner. The *Wild Karrde* was there, all right, hanging a respectful distance back from the New Republic sentry line. "Stay put—we'll be right there. Rogues; let's go."

He turned the X-wing hard over and headed toward their rear. There was a click in his headset as someone keyed to his personal frequency— "Wedge, what are we doing?" Rogue Nine demanded. "We're under orders. Look, if this is about this so-called favor I owe him—"

"I'm not worried about favors right now, Corran," Wedge assured him. "But you heard what Karrde said. He's got an Imperial code for getting through the perimeter."

"Yes, I remember. But his having an access code won't do *us* any good."

"Ordinarily, no," Wedge agreed, smiling tightly. "But also remember what Rogue Twelve said about that turbolaser flutter. If we guide Karrde in under that particular bank—and if we then stay clustered real close behind him—?"

Rogue Nine hissed thoughtfully. "That might just do it."

"It's worth a try, anyway," Wedge said. Because if they could get in behind the perimeter, they'd have a far better shot at knocking out the tractor emplacements that held the *Errant Venture* trapped.

And the faster they knocked out those emplacements, the sooner Bel Iblis would be able to turn his ship around and make a run for safety.

"Wedge?" Rogue Nine said, his voice sounding odd. "You don't suppose Karrde really *can* stop the battle, do you?"

Wedge started to shake his head; paused. This was Corran Horn, Jedi, asking the question. "Not really," he said cautiously. "The Imperials want Bel Iblis—that much is for sure. The only reason I can think of why they'd let him go is if they got something they wanted even more."

"That's what I was thinking, too," Rogue Nine said, his voice still odd. "So why am I also thinking Karrde really *does* have a shot at this?"

Wedge felt a shiver tingle the back of his neck. "I don't know," he said grimly. "All I know is that he's our best chance of getting Bel Iblis and Booster out of there alive. Right now that's all I care about."

They had reached the *Wild Karrde* now, and Wedge pulled his fighter around in a sharp turn into forward escort position. "Okay, Karrde, here we go," he said, double-checking that the rest of the squadron was in position. "Stay close, and follow me."

CHAPTER

39

The sentinel droid continued its attack, systematically sending its fiery bolts of death in Mara's direction. Her lightsaber leaped to meet each one, hands twisting and turning and jabbing the weapon at the guidance of the Force.

She knew her hands were moving, just as she knew that her teeth were clenched tightly together and that there were drops of sweat rolling down her face. But she couldn't feel them. Couldn't feel any of it. So focused was her mind, so locked into the terrible struggle for survival, that there was nothing else in the universe that seemed able to penetrate into her consciousness. Not the rest of the chamber, not the shape of the sentinel dimly visible behind the dazzling glare of the blaster bolts, not even her own body. Nothing but the blasters and her lightsaber.

And Luke.

It was a strange sensation, the small part of her mind that was still free to wonder about such things realized. Standing back to back, stretched out so deeply together to the Force, it was as if their minds had literally melded together to become a single entity. She could feel his mental and physical strain as he maintained his own defense; could sense his reliance on the Force, and his desperate search for a plan to get them out of this, and his deep concern for the woman standing there with him.

In one way it was almost like a logical extension of the brief emotional contacts they'd had throughout this trip. But in another way it was something completely new, like nothing she'd ever before experienced.

Because within the depth of that mental rapport, she suddenly and totally knew Luke Skywalker. Knew everything about him: his hopes and fears; his successes and failures; his strengths and weaknesses; his highest joys and his deepest and most private sorrows. She saw into his innermost spirit, to the depths of his heart, to the very core of his being.

And she knew that even as he lay open before her eyes, so also her heart and spirit were open before his.

Yet it wasn't frightening or humiliating as she might have expected. As she would have expected. It was instead something completely exhilarating. Never before had she experienced such a depth and closeness to another person, a person who understood her as intimately as she understood him. Never had she known such a relationship could even exist.

And never before had she realized how badly she wanted such a relationship.

And that was in its way the most surprising part of all: to suddenly realize after so many years how much her determination to lock herself away from others had ended up hurting her. Had stunted her own growth and life just as her stubborn refusal to accept the responsibility of her Jedi abilities had limited their growth.

It was an amazing insight, particularly coming as it did in the midst of the fire and heat of a battle. She could only regret that the understanding hadn't come to her sooner, instead of now.

Now that she was about to die.

Because her death was indeed close at hand, one way or another. Already she could feel her muscles tiring before the sentinel's onslaught, and knew that she couldn't maintain her defense more than a few minutes more at the most. She had to act now, while she still had the strength to do so, or Luke would die, too.

Because while the plan she'd come up with might—*might*—eliminate the threat from the sentinel in front of her, there was no way she could take out both of its blasters fast enough to keep a killing shot from reaching her. Fleetingly, she thought of Corran Horn and his ability to absorb and dissipate energy; but that had never been one of her talents, and there was certainly no time for her to learn the technique now. No, she would throw her lightsaber at her chosen target, and the sentinel would shoot her, and she would die. All she could hope for was to cling to life long enough to finish what had to be done.

No, Mara. No! Was that her thought? she wondered. Or was it Luke's?

I have to, Luke. That one was hers. Through her own fears and regrets she could feel his sudden surge of desperate emotion as he tried to come up with a way she would not have to die.

But there wasn't one. Mara had already considered every possibility, and there simply wasn't any way Luke could hold off four blasters by himself when two of them were firing at his back this way. But if she could just live long enough to carry this through, using her body to shield him until the sentinel facing her could be eliminated . . .

While I still have the strength, she reminded herself. And the time was now. She took a deep breath—

No! the emotion broke through her black determination. *Wait. Look.*

She had no attention to spare to look anywhere but at the sentinel and its blasters. But she didn't have to. Luke had already seen the critical new factor, and now the image flowed through the Force into her mind.

Off to her right, his little electric arc welder extended ahead of him like a weapon, Artoo was rolling determinedly along the upper floor ring toward her attacker.

Her first thought was to wonder what in blazes had taken the little droid so long to get his metal rear over to help, only then realizing how little time had actually elapsed since the battle began. Her second, somewhat irreverent thought was to note that Artoo had chosen her sentinel to attack instead of Luke's, and to wonder if the Skywalker tendency toward overprotectiveness had rubbed off on him.

Her third thought was that Luke was right. This might be the break she needed, the opening for her plan to succeed without her having to die in the process.

Maybe.

Artoo was almost to the sentinel now, a bluish spark arcing across the welder contacts. The sentinel was perfectly aware of him, of course; the only question was what it would do about it . . .

And then an image flashed into Mara's mind. A picture of her and Luke lying on the floor amid the tangle of trip cords down there.

She felt herself gasp. Was that a vision of the future, of them lying dead together? Was her plan doomed to failure?

You see? Luke's emotion broke through the sudden fear. *You understand?*

And then the image cleared, and she indeed saw what he meant. Not a vision of death, but a hope of life: Luke's own last-second contribution to her plan. *Got it,* she sent back her understanding.

Get ready . . .

She felt her teeth clenching even harder, lightsaber still flashing against the sentinel's attacks, and prepared herself. Artoo was almost to the sentinel, his arc welder still sparking—

And with a casual and contemptuous ease, the sentinel swung its left arm over, placed the side of the blaster in that hand against Artoo's dome, and shoved the little droid over to land flat on his back.

And for that half second, only one of his blasters was firing.

Now!

Mara reacted instantly, letting her right leg collapse beneath her to send her toppling over onto her right side. Luke fell right along with her, his back pressed against hers the whole way down. They hit the floor—there was probably a jolt of pain in her shoulder from the impact, but Mara wasn't aware of it—and Luke flipped over onto his back to face upward toward the ceiling.

And with that single move suddenly there were no longer two attacks coming from totally opposite directions. Now, it was merely two attacks coming from a pair of widely spaced opponents, both of whom were effectively in front of him.

And *that* was something he *could* handle.

Go! his command came as the green-white of his lightsaber flashed past over her head, deflecting a shot away from her face. Mara didn't need the prompting; already her lightsaber was spinning its way toward the sentinel. A quick slash, and the blaster in its right hand had shattered to uselessness. Its other hand was already swinging back toward her; the lightsaber changed direction and slashed again, and the sentinel's second blaster was similarly gone.

There was a short, rumbling roar from the big droid—apparently it had enough sentience to be annoyed at having been outmaneuvered this way. But it was also smart enough to know the disadvantage was only temporary, that her lightsaber couldn't harm it directly, at least not fast enough to do any good.

And its designers had also clearly prepared for such an eventuality. Two more compartments along its lower sides had popped open, and the sentinel's hands were already digging into them for another set of replacement weapons.

But with luck, it would never have a chance to use them. Mara had already brought her lightsaber around in front of the sentinel, turning it to point blade-first toward the big droid. Now, grunting with the effort, she drove it forward.

Not uselessly into the sentinel and its cortosis-ore shell, but straight past it, burying the blue-white blade in the water-stained wall behind it.

The jet of water that burst out around the handle was instant and violent, some of the spray reaching all the way to where she and Luke lay on the floor thirty meters away. Mara felt a sudden twinge of uneasiness at the force of the flow; but it was too late to stop now. Holding the weapon in against the pressure, she spun it around in a ten-centimeter-diameter circle, the hilt more than once nearly vanishing from her view behind the widening spray of water coming out through the crack she was cutting. The sentinel turned its head to see what was happening; lifted its blasters toward the lightsaber—

And with a last burst of effort, Mara finished the cut.

The stone plug came blasting out of the wall with the speed of a proton torpedo, slamming directly into the sentinel's thick torso with armor-crushing force and knocking the big droid helplessly off the upper ring down onto the main floor. Mara caught a glimpse of crumpled metal; saw that the stream of water that had driven the plug was now shooting across the room over her head—

And suddenly a foam-crested wave slammed into and over her from the opposite direction.

With her mind still in the tunnel vision of Jedi defense mode, the wave caught her completely off-guard. She felt herself being lifted and thrown by the wild surf as her feet were somehow pushed clear of the tangling trip cords, and scrabbled madly for something to hang on to. Her left hand caught another bunch of the cords, and she hung on grimly, trying to orient herself. Another wave washed over her, tearing her grip away, and once again she found herself being spun around in the turbulence. She clawed her way to the surface, caught a breath that seemed to be half air and half foam, shook the water out of her eyes to see another wave surging toward her—

And then a pair of hands caught her under the arms, and with a tug that felt like it was going to tear her in half she was suddenly arcing upward through the air. There was a jolt as her back slammed into something hard—one of the two hands holding her fell away as the other tightened its grip—

"Here—hold on," Luke shouted in her ear.

She half turned in his single-handed grip, saw the railing to the upper equipment balcony there beside her, and grabbed on to it. "Got it."

"Hang on—I'm going back for Artoo." Letting go of the railing, he dropped back into the water.

With an effort, Mara pulled herself up the railing and over onto the balcony floor. Below her, she could see, the room had become a surging mass of frothing water.

And it was filling up fast. Much faster than it should have, she realized uneasily.

And suddenly she saw why. The small, neat hole she'd cut in the wall was no longer either small or neat. Four or five square meters of the water-stained section had given way around it, and the Lake of Small Fish was pouring in through the opening. Already it was halfway up the wall to the ledge where she sat . . .

A movement across the room caught her eye: Luke, hanging on to some protrusion in the wall, waving toward her. "I'm here," she shouted over the roar of the water. "What do you need?"

In answer, the top of Artoo's dome rose a few centimeters over the waves. Bracing herself, Mara stretched out with the Force and lifted the droid toward her.

It was harder than she'd expected it to be. Far harder than it ought to have been. The droid rose over the water with agonizing slowness, and twice during the procedure she nearly lost her grip entirely. Clearly, the battle with the sentinel droids had taken more out of her than she'd realized.

But finally she made it, and the droid settled down with a pensive gurgle beside her. He'd been battered around by the water and had lost the datapad they'd rigged to him for translation, but otherwise he seemed all right. She looked back down, searching for Luke—

A hand slapped up to a grip on the bottom rail. "You get Artoo up?" Luke gasped, pulling himself laboriously up the railing.

"He's right here," Mara confirmed, reaching over the railing to give him a hand. "You okay?"

"Just fine," he panted as he made it over the railing and collapsed onto the balcony beside her. "Lesson number one," he added between breaths. "A Jedi needs air to function properly."

"I'll make a note," Mara said, peering down through the railing again. "What about that second sentinel?"

"I took care of him," Luke said. Already he was breathing easier. "Here's your lightsaber," he added, pulling both weapons from inside his tunic and handing hers over. "Good job with the wall, by the way."

"Oh, sure—great job," Mara retorted. "There's nothing so brilliant as a plan that ends up almost drowning you. Speaking of which, shouldn't we be getting out of here before it gets any deeper?"

There was a brief pause. "Well, actually . . ."

She looked at him, a sudden flicker of fear touching her heart. "What's the matter?"

He reached over and took her hand. "I'm sorry, Mara," he said. "The water's already above the level of the tunnel. It's already filling that underground room back there."

Mara stared at him—she'd had no idea the water was coming in *that* fast. "All right," she said, forcing her voice to stay calm. Forcing her mind to stay calm. "All right. So the room's filling up. If we can make it across to the stairway, we can at least climb up into the fortress, right?"

A muscle in his cheek twitched. "You don't understand," he said. "It's already above the level of the tunnel. That means traveling that whole hundred meters without air, plus probably having to get the whole way across the underground room, too."

"What about a hibernation trance?" Mara suggested. "Like the one you used to cold-shirt it across to the *Starry Ice* from the pirate base?"

Luke shook his head. "With the underground room filling up, or maybe already mostly full, the water won't be flowing fast enough through the tunnel to push us through in time."

And it was for sure they couldn't swim while in a trance. Mara pushed a lock of wet hair off her face, trying to think.

Beside Luke, Artoo gave a sudden nervous squawk. "I see it," Luke told him.

"See what?" Mara asked.

"The water level's starting to rise again," he said reluctantly. "That means the underground room must be full. The only drainage we're getting is through the two holes we cut, the one into the stairway area and the one back down into the caverns."

Mara swallowed. "Small holes."

"Far too small to handle the amount coming in," Luke agreed soberly. "I'm afraid . . ."

He trailed off. Mara gazed down at the surging water, now high enough to hide the inflow through the hole she'd cut. But it was still coming in; the steady rippling in the surface was enough to show that. "Back when you first came here," she said, "I told you you could go back to Coruscant if you wanted to and let the Qom Jha and me tackle the fortress by ourselves. You said no, that you had to be here, and you said not to ask you why."

He took a deep breath. "I had a vision of you on Tierfon," he said quietly. "Back before I knew you'd disappeared. I saw you lying in a pool of water, surrounded by craggy rock." He hesitated. "And you looked . . ."

"Dead?"

He sighed. "Yes."

For a long moment they sat there together, the rushing of water the only sound. "Well, I guess that's that, then," Mara said at last. "At least I have the minor satisfaction of knowing I did it to myself."

"Don't give up yet," Luke said. But there was no particular hope in his voice that she could detect. "There has to be a way out of this."

"Too bad, too," Mara said. She looked at him, tracing the contours of his face with her eyes. "You didn't know, but after that pirate base thing, Faughn told me you and I made a good team. She was right. We really did."

"We really do," Luke corrected, looking almost nervously into her eyes. "You know, when we were fighting those sentinels down there, something happened to me. To us. We were so close in the Force that it was like we'd become a single person. It was . . . it was something very special."

She lifted an eyebrow, a flicker of amusement worming its way through even the deadly seriousness of the situation. There was such an oddly awkward earnestness to his expression. "Really?" she said. "How special?"

He grimaced. "You're not going to make this easy for me, are you?" he growled.

"Oh, come now," she said, mock accusingly. "When have I *ever* made anything easy for you?"

"Not very often," he conceded. Visibly bracing himself, he reached over and took her hands again. "Mara . . . will you marry me?"

"You mean if we get out of here alive?"

Luke shook his head. "I mean regardless."

Under other circumstances, she knew, she would probably have considered herself honor-bound to make him sweat, just a little. But with the water still rising below them, such games seemed rather pointless. Besides, there was no reason for old defensive patterns to come into play. Not now. Not with him. "Yes," she said. "I will."

CHAPTER

A blast of turbolaser fire shot past, burning a scorch line in the *Predominance*'s bridge canopy. It was like an omen, Leia thought darkly as she stepped past the outer monitor ring and into the central control cluster: an omen of her own impending downfall. What she was about to do, she knew, would most likely be the end of her political career. It could possibly send her to a penal colony. It could even cost her her life.

But Han's own life was hanging in the balance. Against that, nothing else mattered.

She stopped behind the Ishori at the helm station and looked over his shoulder at his control board. The indicators and controls were labeled in Ishori, of course, but the board itself was a straight Kuat Drive Yards design and she knew the layout. Taking a deep breath, she stretched out to the Force and keyed the sublight drive lever.

The helmsman himself was the first to notice something was wrong. Rumbling something under his breath, he pulled the lever back to its original position. Leia pushed it forward again, this time also laying in a new ship's vector toward the comet blazing in the distance. The helmsman rumbled again, louder this time, and again grabbed the lever.

Except that this time it didn't move. Leia held it firm against his struggles; and as he paused, confused, she took the opportunity to push it still farther forward. The helmsman swiveled in his seat to look at Captain Av'muru—

And out of the corner of his eye he spotted Leia standing behind him.

"What do you do here?" he shouted, swiveling farther around to glare up at her. "Guards!"

Leia turned. Two guards were striding toward her, blasters in hand. Stretching out again to the Force, she plucked the blasters away from them and slammed the weapons straight down to the deck with shattering force.

"Councilor!" Av'muru shouted, jumping up from his seat. "What are you doing?"

Leia didn't answer, but reached again for the speed control. "No!" the helmsman screamed, leaping out of his chair with his hands reaching for her throat.

The clutching fingers never got there. Leia caught him in midair in a Force grip, redirecting the direction of his leap to send him soaring instead over the monitor ring to land in a confused heap at the back of the bridge.

"Guards!" Av'muru shouted. "All guards!"

Leia turned back to the helm, again increasing the ship's speed. Her senses flared with warning, and she snatched up her lightsaber just as two other guards on the far side of the room brought their blasters up. They fired, their stun bolts scattering uselessly from her glowing blade. Again she snatched the weapons away, this time bringing them flying across the bridge toward her and slicing them neatly in half with her lightsaber.

"You will stop this at once," Av'muru snarled, stalking with an even, deliberate pace toward her. "Otherwise, I will declare a state of war to exist between the Ishori Confederene and the New Republic."

"This entire system is in deadly danger," Leia said in a loud voice. "You've refused to take steps to oppose this danger. I have therefore done so in your place."

"You risk war between Isht and Coruscant," Av'muru shouted, still coming toward her. "You have until I reach you to cease this action and return this vessel to my command."

Out of the corner of her eye, Leia saw Gavrisom trotting over toward Av'muru's side . . . and there was now exactly one card left for her to play. "There is no need or reason to involve the New Republic," she told the Ishori. "I hearby resign from the High Council, and the Senate, and the Presidency. I am no longer anything but a private citizen."

"Then you also renounce all diplomatic privileges," Av'muru snapped. Gavrisom had reached his side now, pulling slightly ahead of the Ishori as the two of them continued toward Leia. From Gavrisom's gait, Leia could tell he was trying to reach her first. Probably hoping to stop her himself, with an eye toward minimizing the political damage to the New Republic that she had just caused.

But it was too late for that, and Gavrisom surely knew it. "You are aboard an Ishori war vessel," Av'muru continued. "The penalty for mutiny aboard such a vessel is death."

Leia felt her throat tighten. And that, she realized bleakly, was that. The captain had spoken the word "mutiny," automatically invoking the highest level of Ishori war-law. If she didn't back down before Av'muru reached her, he would have no choice but to bring the entire might of his warship to bear against her.

Could they stop her? Probably not. Certainly not before they reached the comet.

But at what cost? Though she could hold them back, she could almost certainly not do so without the eventual shedding of blood. And if her actions led to death, even deaths from ricochet shots from their own weapons, her fate would be sealed. The strict code of Ishori war-justice would demand her death in return.

And for the sake of unity within the New Republic, she would have to submit. Av'muru and Gavrisom were nearly to her now . . .

And then, to Leia's amazement, Gavrisom turned sideways and abruptly stopped, his long flank stretching across the aisle between two consoles, blocking Av'muru's way. "I think not, Captain," he said calmly. "I am declaring this war vessel to be under direct New Republic command."

"So it is treason from the New Republic Presidency as well?" Av'muru screamed, trying to push Gavrisom bodily out of his way. "Move aside or die alongside her."

"There is no treason involved," Gavrisom said. His voice was still calm, but he hadn't budged a millimeter. "Unless you bring such a charge upon yourself by refusing an official New Republic emergency requisition of your vessel as per Section 45-2 of the Treaties of Allegiance."

Abruptly Av'muru stopped pushing. "You speak nonsense," he said, screaming now at the top of his lungs. "There has been no official requisition."

"The Treaties are vague about how such a requisition is to be made," Gavrisom said coolly. "Deliberately so, for an emergency situation by its very nature requires flexibility."

He waved a wing toward Leia. "In this case, the requisition began when High Councilor Organa Solo—"

"She is no longer a High Councilor, by her own statement!"

"When High Councilor Organa Solo," Gavrisom repeated, emphasizing each word, "began moving this vessel toward a perceived source of danger."

Av'muru glared at Gavrisom, transferred the look to Leia, turned it back on Gavrisom again. "You cannot seriously believe the Confederene will accept such a ludicrous claim," he bellowed.

"What they will or will not accept is a matter for future discussion," Gavrisom pointed out. "Regretfully, the Diamalan jamming has eliminated any chance for you to communicate with your governments for counsel."

He tossed his mane. "It is your decision, Captain. You must base it on the requirements of the law, my position as New Republic President, and the word of a Jedi Knight that your ship is in deadly danger."

Av'muru was trembling with emotion, his eyes flicking back and forth between Gavrisom, Leia, and the view out the canopy. Leia stole a glance out there herself, confirmed that the *Predominance* was indeed moving toward the comet.

"Helmsman?" Av'muru shouted.

"Here, my captain," the other replied, stepping hesitantly forward.

"Resume your post," Av'muru ordered, his voice starting to calm down. "Continue on the course which the Jedi Knight Organa Solo has put us on." He paused. "And increase to flank speed."

"Yes, my captain," the helmsman said, brushing gingerly past Gavrisom as the Calibop moved aside. Leia stepped aside as well, and he sat warily down in his seat again. " 'Course and speed as ordered, my captain."

"Come, Councilor," Gavrisom said, gesturing to Leia with one of his wing tips. "Let us move back out of their way."

Together, they retreated again behind the monitor ring. "Thank you," Leia said quietly.

"I was only doing my job," Gavrisom said. "I have often heard it said that Calibops are long on words and short on deeds."

He ruffled his mane. "Sometimes, though, it is the words that must come first."

"Yes," Leia murmured, gazing out the canopy at the comet. She could only hope that the deeds that followed would be in time.

"We have them both, Captain," the starboard tractor beam officer called up to the command walkway. "Two freighters: a YT-1300 and a Corellian Action II."

"Very good," Nalgol said, still seething over the unexpected and unannounced change in their carefully precise schedule. The strike team on the surface, he promised himself ominously, would have some serious explaining to do when this was all over.

But in the meantime, the *Tyrannic* was ready to do whatever needed to be done. And the first job on that list would be to take care of those spies out there. "Bring them in closer, Lieutenant," he called. "Make sure they don't break away."

"They won't, sir," the tractor officer promised.

Nalgol felt a movement beside him. "You sent for me, Captain?" Oissan said.

"That priority/threat list I asked for," Nalgol said shortly. "Where is it?"

"The preliminary list has been filed," Oissan said, sounding a bit flustered. "We were expecting to have more time to complete it."

"Well, you didn't, did you?" Nalgol bit out, thoroughly disgusted. First the strike team, now Oissan. "Get back to work. We still have an hour or two before the battle out there winds down to where we'll be entering it."

"Yes, sir," Oissan said stiffly. "Will you be wanting my staff to interrogate the prisoners?"

"What prisoners?"

"Why—" Oissan floundered. "The crews of those freighters out there."

Nalgol shook his head. "There will be no prisoners."

"But you said—"

"I said to bring them closer, that's all," Nalgol cut him off tartly. "I don't want any debris floating outside the cloaking shield where someone might notice it."

He looked back out the viewport. The YT-1300 was twisting madly in the grip of the tractor beam, still trying to escape, the larger Action II curiously quiet. "Another minute or two," he added, "and they'll be taken care of. Permanently."

"There!" Lando snapped, pointing out the *Industrious Thoughts*'s viewport. "Didn't I tell you? The Ishori have recognized the danger and are heading out to take a look."

"They are merely running in an attempt to save their skins," Senator Miatamia countered calmly. "Or else feel that the heightened maneuverability available in deep space will serve their defense better."

"Fine," Lando said. "Either way, you can't just let them go."

"The Diamala seek no vengeance against anyone," the Senator said. "We have thwarted their unprovoked attack against Bothawui. That is sufficient for now."

"But what about the threat I warned you about?" Lando demanded. "We bet on it, remember?"

"If such a threat exists, and if the Ishori are indeed searching for it, they will surely discover it on their own," Miatamia said equably. "There is no reason for any Diamalan ships to expose themselves to danger."

Lando glared out the viewport at the departing ship. However she'd done it, Leia had gotten the *Predominance* to move against the comet and whatever surprise the Imperials had hidden out there.

But with Thrawn pulling the strings, the surprise was likely to be a memorable one. Almost certainly too big for a single Ishori war cruiser to handle by itself . . . "I see," he said, striving to keep his voice casual, the tone of a disinterested party who has nothing to gain one way or the other. "I'm sure the Ishori are just as happy to get away from you, too."

"What does it matter how the Ishori see things?" Miatamia said.

"Oh, no reason," Lando said with a shrug. "I was just thinking that if they decided they wanted to make a real fight of it, they'd need to call in reinforcements. And of course, once they're out of range of your jamming, they'll be able to do that."

Miatamia's ears curled over. "Surely they would not do such a thing."

"Why not?" Lando said. "Remember, they think the whole Bothan species should pay for their part in the destruction of Caamas. If I were them, I'd figure that the space over Bothawui would be the perfect spot to hash out their differences with the Diamala."

He nodded back in the direction of the planet beneath them. "Especially with part of the planetary shield collapsed the way it is. Any battle debris that falls through that hole is just a bonus as far as they're concerned."

Miatamia was already at the intercom, speaking urgently into it. Lando stared out the viewport, holding his breath . . .

And then, to starboard and portside, he saw the other two Diamalan ships turn ponderously toward the departing Ishori war cruiser and begin to give chase. A moment later, he felt the slight tug of acceleration as the *Industrious Thoughts* followed suit.

"We will keep them silent until the Drev'starn shield generator is repaired," Miatamia said, rejoining Lando. "But when that is done, they will be free to leave if they wish."

"Good enough," Lando said. "You're just bringing the three ships?"

Miatamia gazed out the viewport. "I have suggested to the captain that all Diamalan ships also be summoned to our side."

"Just in case I'm right after all?"

The Senator's ears twitched. "As I have said to you before, the unanticipated may sometimes happen," he said evenly. "The Diamala believe in being prepared for such an eventuality."

"Hang on," Han gritted, throwing the *Falcon* hard over first to starboard and then to port. No good; the tractor beam still had a solid grip on them. Reaching to the weapons board, he shifted the aim of the upper quad laser, now firing continuously toward the Star Destroyer. Like the swivel maneuver, all the firepower was doing no good, either.

"The portside stabilizer is flickering again," Elegos announced, peering at the monitor displays. "You may do serious damage to it if you continue this way."

Han bit back a curse. Yes, he might blow the stabilizers. He might also burn out a section of the sublight drive, or melt the quads, or even crack the hull.

But he had no choice but to do whatever was necessary to get clear, even if he had to tear the life out of the *Falcon* to do it. A cloaked Star Destroyer meant an ambush . . . and the last thing an ambushing Imperial would want would be to leave witnesses behind.

Elegos, though, hadn't figured that one out yet. "Perhaps we should attempt to surrender," the Caamasi suggested.

"Yeah?" Han grunted. "Why?"

"To prevent our destruction, of course," Elegos said. "Besides, Carib and his group seem to have already done that."

"What do you mean?" Han asked, frowning as he searched the sky. Preoccupied with his own part of the fight, he'd completely lost track of the Action II.

"I mean they aren't struggling against the tractor beam," Elegos explained, pointing out the viewport.

He was right. There was Carib's freighter, a little to starboard and considerably closer to the dark hull than the *Falcon* was. Making no attempt at all to escape.

But that didn't make sense. Surely Carib knew even better than he did that there was going to be no such thing as surrender here. Had he and the others already been killed?

Or had their newly professed allegiance to Leia and the New Republic never been anything more than a trick?

"Solo?" a voice crackled out from the speaker. "This is Carib. Get ready."

"Get ready for what?"

"What do you think?" Carib retorted. "And look; if we don't make it, I want you to see to it that our families are taken care of. Deal?"

Han threw a frown at Elegos. What in space—?

"We have a deal," Elegos called toward the comm, looking as puzzled as Han felt but apparently willing to play along. "Don't worry."

"All right. It's been nice knowing you."

The comm clicked off. Han stared out at the freighter, a sudden premonition sending a chill up his back—

And then, all at once, the Action II exploded.

Beside him, he heard Elegos gasp. "What—?"

"Just watch," Han cut him off, gripping the helm yoke. "And like the man said, get ready." The flare and dust of the explosion cleared, blown away by the expanding air from inside or snatched away by the tractor beam—

And suddenly, from the cloud of debris, a dozen TIE Interceptors burst out.

It took the Imperials no more than five seconds to react to this new and completely unexpected threat. But in this case, five seconds was far too long. The TIEs swarmed close in across the hull, dodging through the frantic turbolaser fire with casual ease, systematically blasting the tractor beam emplacements.

Han watched in fascination, memories of Baron Fel's legendary flying skill flooding back. Only this time, it was a dozen Baron Fels running interference for him.

And with a jolt that cracked his teeth together, the *Falcon* was free.

"Hang on!" he snapped, cutting the ship around in a tight circle and pouring power to the sublight drive. The Star Destroyer's turbolasers were starting to open up behind him now as they saw their quarry escaping, and he threw the *Falcon* into a corkscrewing evasive maneuver as he drove hard toward the invisible edge of the cloaking shield. "You still have the comm ready to transmit to those idiots over Bothawui?" he added, watching the rear deflector indicator warily. If the shields collapsed before they made it out, the Imperials could still win.

"I'm ready," Elegos said. "As soon as—"

He broke off with a gasp. Han twisted his head to the side as the familiar shape of a TIE Interceptor suddenly appeared alongside. Reflexively, he grabbed for the weapons board—

And relaxed just in time. Emblazoned on the TIE's solar panels was the New Republic insignia. Beyond the TIE the rest of Carib's unit was forming up on his flank—

And suddenly the darkness around them vanished, and they were surrounded by stars again. "That's it," he said. "Get busy with the comm."

Elegos cleared his throat. "I don't believe," he said, "that that will be necessary."

Puzzled, Han turned to look.

And caught his breath. Driving resolutely toward them from the direction of Bothawui were a group of over a dozen heavy warships.

The comm crackled. "Han?" Lando's voice came.

"Yeah, Lando," Han called back. "Watch yourselves—there's an Imperial Star Destroyer under that cloaking shield."

"Understood," Lando said. "Are those TIE interceptors with you?"

Han smiled grimly. "You bet they are. Can you whistle up some more help?"

"Captain Solo, this is Senator Miatamia," a new voice spoke up. "We are transmitting your warning to all ships allied to the Diamala and requesting their assistance."

"Great," Han said. "I suggest you invite the Ishori in on this party, too. We're going to need all the help we can get."

"Han?" Leia's voice cut in, sounding breathless and relieved and tense all at the same time. "Han, are you all right?"

"I'm fine, hon," he assured her. "You still with the Ishori?"

"Yes," she said. "The captain's still not sure—"

She broke off abruptly. "Leia?" Han barked.

"Never mind," she said, a sudden grim tone in her voice. "I don't think he has any doubts anymore."

Han frowned, swinging the *Falcon* around in a tight circle and looking back. The Star Destroyer, its ambush now thwarted, had dropped its cloaking shield.

Only it wasn't just a single Star Destroyer pulling away from the comet toward the incoming fleet. It was three of them.

He took a deep breath. "Okay," he said. "*Now* it's a fight."

CHAPTER

41

"Report from Base Command, Admiral," the comm officer called from the portside crew pit. "Enemy Star Destroyer has disabled two more of the tractor beam emplacements."

"Have repairs begun immediately on those emplacements, Lieutenant," Thrawn said coolly. "And order Base Command to lock three more beams onto the target."

Standing a little way off to Disra's left, just aft of the command walkway, Paloma D'asima muttered something under her breath to Karoly D'ulin. "A question?" Disra asked, taking a step toward the two Mistryl.

The older woman nodded toward Thrawn. "I was telling Karoly I don't like any of this," she said, her tone disgusted. "He's playing with them. Why not just blast them and be done with it?"

"Grand Admiral Thrawn is a very subtle man," Disra said, hoping the loftiness of his tone would discourage her from asking questions he couldn't answer. As a matter of fact, he didn't understand what Tierce had in mind with this one, either. But the major was standing straight and tall at Thrawn's side, exactly as a good aide should, so presumably everything was still going according to plan.

Thrawn must have overheard the comment. He murmured something to Tierce, got a nod of agreement, and the major turned and walked back to where Disra and the two Mistryl stood. "Admiral Thrawn heard your question and asked me to come explain his reasoning to you," he said, stepping to D'asima's side where he could talk to her while still keeping an eye on Bel Iblis's attempts to break free of the trap. "He isn't interested in destroying General Bel Iblis, you see. On the contrary, he wants the general to surrender his ship and crew intact."

He gestured toward the multiple turbolaser blasts. "But as you can also see, Bel Iblis is a proud and stubborn man. He has to be convinced first that he has no chance against the resources of this base. Admiral Thrawn is therefore giving him a chance to do his best against us."

"Showing him the futility of resistance," D'asima said. She still didn't sound exactly pleased, but at least the disgust was no longer evident in her tone. "And adding salt to the sore by increasing the number of tractor beams each time Bel Iblis knocks one out."

"Exactly," Tierce said, beaming. "Admiral Thrawn has always been one to treat even his enemies with respect."

"Though naturally he treats his allies far better," Disra put in. It wouldn't hurt to remind D'asima why she was here in the first place.

"Admiral?" the comm officer called again. "We're getting a direct transmission from the perimeter defense coordinator. He urgently requests your assistance in dealing with the X-wings that have broken through his line."

Disra threw a startled look at Tierce behind D'asima's head. "X-wings?" he demanded.

"I don't know," Tierce replied, his voice taut. He made as if to hurry back to Thrawn's side, checked himself just in time at a quick warning glare from Disra. It wouldn't do, the Moff had already warned them both, for Tierce to look too vital to the operation. The con man up there knew how to get him back if he needed him.

But for the moment, at least, their Grand Admiral seemed to have it under control. "What X-wings are those, Lieutenant?" he asked, his voice calm but with an edge to it.

"He says he reported the penetration to General Hestiv over ten minutes ago," the comm officer said, sounding confused. "They apparently sneaked in behind one of our freighters."

"One of *our* freighters?" Thrawn asked.

"An Imperial freighter, sir," the officer corrected himself hastily. "Supply run, probably. The coordinator reports it was running all the proper access codes."

"I'm sure it was," Thrawn said, his glowing eyes flashing. "And General Hestiv just happened to forget to pass this information on to us, did he?"

His gaze shifted around, fell on Tierce. "Major Tierce?"

"Yes, sir," Tierce said, stepping briskly forward at the cue. "Shall I locate that freighter for you?"

"Please," Thrawn said gravely, picking up on the cue in turn.

And then, still looking back in their direction, the glowing eyes suddenly widened. Disra frowned—

"Don't trouble yourself, Major," a familiar voice called from behind Disra. "The freighter in question is currently docked in your number seven hangar bay."

Slowly, disbelievingly, Disra turned around. It couldn't be. It *couldn't*.

But it was. There he stood, in the center of the archway leading to the aft bridge.

Admiral Pellaeon.

The element of surprise was gone, the fratricidal battle over Bothawui cut short sooner than the Imperials had most likely hoped. Even now, Leia saw, the last lingering shots of that conflict were dwindling away as the various combatants woke up to the greater danger on their flank.

But even in its brevity the fight had taken a heavy toll, she realized as she studied the *Predominance*'s tactical display. Out of the nearly two hundred ships that had been fighting, fewer than a hundred ten were arraying themselves for battle against the three Star Destroyers now moving toward them.

"We're outgunned, aren't we?" Gavrisom said quietly from her side.

"I'm afraid we are," Leia conceded. "And even the ships that can still fight have all taken damage. Those Star Destroyers are fresh and rested."

"And not all of our ships may actually stay with us once they compute the odds for themselves," Gavrisom said, twitching his wings. "Even with my general summons under Section 45-2, the fact is, we are still asking them to fight in defense of Bothawui and the Bothan people."

Leia nodded grimly. "Something which at least half of them aren't really interested in doing."

"Leia?"

She lifted her comlink. "I'm here, Han," she said. "Are you all right?"

"Oh, sure," he said, dismissing the danger casually. "They gave up shooting at us a long time ago. Look, Elegos has been counting the ships you've got there, and neither of us is very happy with the numbers he's coming up with."

"Neither are any of the rest of us," Leia said. "Gavrisom has a call in to any New Republic forces nearby, but so far there's been no response."

"Yeah, well, maybe I can come up with something," Han said, his tone studiously casual. "You know if Fey'lya's on Bothawui at the moment?"

Leia frowned. "Actually, I believe he is. Why?"

"You know how to reach him?"

"His private comlink frequency's in the *Falcon*'s computer, listed under his name," Leia said. "Why?"

"I'm going to try a little diplomacy," he told her. "See if you can stall off those Star Destroyers a little."

He clicked off. "Right," Leia murmured to herself. "Stall them off."

Beside her, Gavrisom shook his mane. "There is one other matter of immediate concern, Leia," he said. "This fleet is made up of beings who, by and large, do not trust each other. We need someone in command who all will trust, or at least tolerate."

"That one I may be able to solve," Leia said, rekeying her comlink. "Lando?"

"Yes, Leia?"

"Lando, at the request of President Gavrisom, I'd like you to accept immediate reinstatement into the New Republic military," she said. "We need you to take command of this defense force."

There was a short pause. "You *are* kidding," he said.

"Not at all, General," Gavrisom assured him. "As a hero of Taanab and Endor, you are precisely the one we need."

There was a faintly audible sigh. "I'd argue if I thought it would do any good," Lando said reluctantly. "All right, I'll do it. It would have been nice if you could have given me a bigger fleet to work with, though."

"Hey, no problem, buddy," Han's voice broke in. "It's all taken care of. Take a look behind you."

Leia stared at the bridge's aft-view display, feeling her mouth falling open. Rising rapidly from the surface of Bothawui were over a hundred ships, everything from Z-95 Headhunters to Skipray Blastboats to even a few small capital warships. And more were still rising through the atmosphere. "Han!" she gasped. "What in the worlds did you *do*?"

"Like I said, a little diplomacy," Han said. "I got to remembering that Thrawn suggested to Lando and me that Fey'lya had a little private army stashed away. Made sense to me, so I called the little furball and pointed out that any Bothan who helped save Bothawui could really cash in on that when this was all over."

"And Fey'lya came up with all of *that*?" Leia asked, still not believing it.

"Not exactly," Han said smugly. "Turns out there was a lot of signal leakage in my transmission. Battle damage, probably. I figure half the planet must have heard what I said to him."

And finally, Leia understood. "And of course none of them wanted Fey'lya to grab all the glory for himself," she said, smiling tightly. "Have I told you lately that you're brilliant?"

"No," he said. "But that's okay—you've been busy. Are we ready?"

"We're ready," Leia said, nodding. "General Calrissian: your fleet awaits your orders."

For a long minute the bridge seemed to have become suspended in time and space. Moff Disra stood stiffly where he was, a couple of steps away from the two female civilians, his face contorted with disbelief and hatred and perhaps even a touch of fear. Major Tierce had stopped, too, halfway along the command walkway, looking back at Pellaeon with an unreadable expression on his face. Captain Dorja and the officers at the side consoles were staring back at him, and even the men down in the crew pits had somehow sensed something was wrong and had dropped their voices to whispers.

"Admiral Pellaeon," Thrawn's smoothly modulated voice broke the silence. Pellaeon had rather expected him to be the first to speak. "Welcome aboard the *Relentless*. I'm afraid we somehow missed the news of your arrival."

"As I somehow missed the news of your return," Pellaeon countered. Like Tierce, the expression behind those glowing red eyes was unreadable. "An unintentional oversight, I'm sure."

"Are you questioning the Grand Admiral's decisions?" Disra snarled.

"On the contrary," Pellaeon assured him. "I've always had the highest respect for Grand Admiral Thrawn."

"Then why sneak aboard this way?" Tierce demanded, coming back along the walkway and stopping next to the younger of the two women. "Do you have something to hide? Or some dark errand of treason to carry out?"

Deliberately, Pellaeon shifted his gaze from the major to the women beside him. "I'm afraid we haven't been properly introduced," he said, bowing his head in greeting. "I'm Admiral Pellaeon, Supreme Commander of Imperial forces."

"Not anymore you're not," Disra growled. "Grand Admiral Thrawn is in command now."

"Really," Pellaeon said, eyeing him coolly. "I wasn't informed of any change of command. Another unintentional oversight?"

"Take care, Admiral," Tierce warned softly. "You're treading on very slippery ground here."

Pellaeon shook his head. "You're mistaken, Major," he said. "Whatever slippery ground exists here is beneath *your* feet." He looked at Disra. "And yours, Your Excellency."

He shifted his gaze to the man in the white Grand Admiral's uniform. "And yours . . . Flim."

Disra's head jerked as if he'd touched a live power cable. "What are you talking about?" he demanded. But there was a new tremor in the Moff's voice, and his eyes were those of a man seeing sudden destruction coming inexorably toward him.

"I'm talking about an accomplished con artist," Pellaeon said, raising his voice so that the entire bridge could hear. "I have his rather colorful life history right here," he added, pulling a datacard from his tunic and holding it up. "Including detailed holos and a complete genetic profile."

He looked across at Flim. "Would you care to accompany me to the nearest medical station for an examination?"

"But we checked his genetic profile, sir," Captain Dorja objected, stepping away from the side console where he'd been standing. "Captain Nalgol took a skin sample and compared it to Thrawn's official records."

"Records can be altered, Captain," Pellaeon reminded him. "Even official records, if the access codes have been sliced. When we return to Bastion, you can compare the genetic records with those on this datacard."

"Lies can even more easily be created on datacards," Tierce said. His voice was calm, but there was an edge of something vicious beneath it. "This is nothing but a last, pitiful attempt to undermine Grand Admiral Thrawn's authority, driven by Pellaeon's jealous fear of losing his position and prestige."

He half turned. "You see it, Captain Dorja, don't you?" he called. "Thrawn came to you instead of Pellaeon—that's what he can't stomach. He came to you and Nalgol and the others and not to him."

Dorja's eyes met Pellaeon's, his face tight with confusion. "Admiral, I've always trusted your word and your judgment," he said. "But in this case . . ."

"There's one other record of interest on this datacard," Pellaeon said, looking back at Tierce. "Again, from the same source. It's the record and life history of a certain Imperial Major Grodin Tierce."

Slowly, Tierce turned back to face him. And this time there was no mistaking the murder in his eyes. "And what does that record say?" he asked softly.

"It says that Major Tierce was one of the finest combat stormtroopers ever to serve the Empire," Pellaeon told him. "That his successes raised him to command rank far more quickly than even stormtrooper norm. That at the age of twenty-four he was selected to serve the Emperor as one of the elite Royal Guard. That his fierce loyalty to Palpatine's New Order was second to none."

Pellaeon lifted his eyebrows slightly. "And that, as part of a stormtrooper unit involved in Thrawn's campaign against Generis, he died in combat.

"Ten years ago."

Once again, the bridge went silent. But this time it wasn't the silence of surprise. It was the silence of total shock.

"You're a clone." The words had come from Disra, but the voice was so distorted as to be almost unrecognizable. "You're just a *clone.*"

Slowly, Tierce turned his venomous gaze from Pellaeon to Disra. And then, abruptly, he barked out a short, tortured-sounding laugh. "Just a clone," he repeated mockingly. "Just a clone—is that what you said, Disra? *Just* a clone? You have no idea."

He looked around the room. "None of you do. I wasn't just a clone— I was something very special. Something special and glorious."

"Why don't you tell us what that was," Pellaeon invited quietly.

Tierce spun back to face him. "I was the first of a new breed," he bit out. "The first of what would have been a class of warlords the likes of which the galaxy had never seen. Warlords who combined stormtrooper combat strength and loyalty with Thrawn's own tactical genius. We would have led, and we would have conquered, and no one could have stood against us."

He turned around, his movements becoming almost jerky in his agitation. "Don't you see?" he shouted, his eyes darting to each of the officers and crewers staring in fascination or revulsion at him. "Thrawn took Tierce and cloned him, but he put some of himself into the process. He added part of his own tactical genius to the usual flash-learning, combining it with Tierce's own mind."

He spun again to face Disra. "You've seen it, Disra. Whether you know it or not, you've seen it. I was manipulating you from the very start—don't you see? It was me, right from the minute I maneuvered myself in as your aide. All those pirate attacks—the Preybird deals—that was me. All me. You never saw it—you never even guessed it—but I was the one making the quiet suggestions and feeding you the right data in the right order to get you to do what I wanted.

"And all the rest of you have seen it, too," he shouted, spinning around again. "I've been running the tactics here. Not Flim—not that red-eyed figurehead. *Me*. It's always been me. And I'm *good* at it—it's what Thrawn made me to be. I can do this."

His eyes seized on Disra again. "You talk about the Hand of Thrawn, his last ultimate weapon," he said, his voice almost pleading. "I can *be* that Hand of Thrawn. I can be Thrawn himself. I can defeat the New Republic—I *know* it."

"No, Major," Pellaeon said. "The war is over."

Tierce spun back to face him. "No," he snarled. "It's not over. Not yet. Not until we've crushed Coruscant. Not until we've had our vengeance against the Rebels."

Pellaeon gazed at him, pity and revulsion swirling together within him. "You don't understand at all," he said sadly. "Thrawn was never interested in vengeance. His goal was order, and stability, and the strength that comes of unity and common purpose."

"And how would *you* know what Thrawn was interested in?" Tierce sneered. "Do *you* have part of his mind inside you? Well? Do you?"

Pellaeon sighed. "You say you were the first of these new warlords. Do you know why there weren't any others?"

Tierce's eyes seemed to withdraw within him. "He ran out of time," he said. "He died at Bilbringi. *You* let him die at Bilbringi."

"No." Pellaeon lifted the datacard slightly. "You were created two months before his death—there was plenty of time for him to have made others. The fact is that there weren't any others because the experiment was a failure."

"Impossible," Tierce breathed. "I wasn't a failure. Look at me—*look* at me. I'm exactly what he wanted."

Pellaeon shook his head. "What he wanted was a tactically brilliant leader," he said gently. "What he got was a tactically brilliant storm-trooper. You're not a leader, Major. By your own statement you're nothing but a manipulator. You have no vision, only a thirst for revenge."

Tierce's eyes darted around the bridge, as if looking for support. "That doesn't matter," he ground out. "What matters is that I can do the job. I can defeat the Rebels. Just give me a little more time."

"There is no more time," Pellaeon said with quiet finality. "The war is over." He looked over at Ardiff. "Captain Ardiff, please call a security detachment to the bridge." He started to turn away—

And in that instant, Tierce exploded into action.

The young woman standing beside him was his first victim, doubling over in agony as Tierce swung his fist viciously down and back into her stomach. In the same motion he plucked away the blaster that had suddenly appeared in her hand, twisting around to fire a shot at the older woman as the younger collapsed to the deck. He twisted back, bringing the blaster to bear on Pellaeon. There was a flicker of movement at the corner of Pellaeon's eye—

And Tierce jerked back, screaming in rage and pain as his gun hand was slapped to the side, the shot going wide, the blaster itself flying uselessly from his grip to skitter across the deck and down into the starboard crew pit.

And from concealment around the side of the archway behind Pellaeon, gliding silently across the deck, came Shada D'ukal.

Tierce didn't even bother to pull out the lacquered zenji needle now waving bloodily from the back of his gun hand. Screaming incoherently, he hooked his fingers into predator's claws and charged.

Reflexively, Pellaeon took a step backward. But he needn't have bothered. Shada was already there, meeting Tierce halfway.

And in a blurred flurry of hands and arms, it was all over.

"Captain Dorja, call a medical team to the bridge," Pellaeon ordered as Shada stepped over Tierce's broken body and hurried over to kneel beside the injured woman. "Then order all Imperial forces to cease fire immediately."

"Yes, sir," Dorja said hesitantly. "However . . ."

Flim lifted a blue-skinned hand. "What he's trying to find words to say, Admiral, is that they'll expect any such order to come from Grand Admiral Thrawn," he said. His voice had changed, subtly but noticeably; and as Pellaeon glanced around the bridge, he saw that they finally recognized the truth. "If you'll permit me?"

Pellaeon gestured. "Go ahead."

Flim turned to the comm officer and nodded. "This is Grand Admiral Thrawn," he called, once again in that exquisitely perfect voice. "All units, cease fire; repeat, cease fire. General Bel Iblis, please call on your forces to do likewise, then stand by for a transmission from Admiral Pellaeon."

He took a deep breath and let it out; and as he did so, the aura of leadership and command subtly fell away from him. He was just a man again, a man in blue makeup and a white uniform.

And Grand Admiral Thrawn was once again gone.

"And may I say to you, Admiral," he added as he walked back along the command walkway, "how relieved I am that you're here. This whole thing has been a nightmare for me. An absolute nightmare."

"Of course," Pellaeon said gravely. "We'll have to make time later for you to tell me your tale of woe."

Flim half bowed. "I'll look forward to that, sir."

"Yes," Pellaeon said, looking over at Disra. "So will I."

CHAPTER

The loud gushing sound had subsided now to a quiet sloshing as the water continued to creep its slow but steady way up the sides of the room. A sloshing sound that was being rhythmically punctuated by the splashing of chunks of rock as Luke's lightsaber carved a deepening conical pit into the top of the dome.

"I think you're wasting your time," Mara said as the splash from a particularly large chunk echoed through the room. "There's nothing up there but solid rock."

"I think you're right," Luke conceded, shifting his arm to a new spot around her shoulders and trying to hold her a little closer. Soaked clear through, they were both shivering in the cool, damp air. "I was hoping we might be able to punch through to the main power generator area. But I guess if we haven't hit it by now, it's not there."

"It's probably twenty meters behind us," she said, her teeth chattering slightly. "We'd never be able to cut through to it in time. Are your ears starting to hurt?"

"A little," Luke said, reluctantly closing down his lightsaber and calling it back to his hand. Cutting through the ceiling had been his last, best idea. "The air in here's being compressed. The extra pressure should help slow down the incoming water a little."

"Along with making our eyes go all buggy." Mara nodded toward the far wall. "You suppose there's any chance the top of the room's above the level of the lake? If it is, we might be able to cut our way out horizontally."

"And if it isn't, we'd drown ourselves that much sooner," Luke pointed out. "Anyway, I really don't think we're high enough."

"I didn't think so, either," Mara agreed regretfully, leaning forward to look past Luke at Artoo. "Too bad we lost the datapad—we could have asked Artoo to take some sensor readings. We could still ask, of course, but we couldn't understand the answer."

"Wait a minute," Luke said, another idea suddenly hitting him. "What about that passageway where we first came in? We could send Artoo there with my lightsaber to enlarge it."

"No good." Mara shook her head, the movement sending strands of wet hair slapping gently across Luke's cheek. "That whole section is solid cortosis ore. I checked it the first time we went through."

Luke grimaced. "I thought it sounded too easy."

"Isn't it always," Mara said, the faint sarcasm sounding odd coming as it did through chattering teeth. "Too bad we don't have a Dark Jedi handy we could kill. Remember that big blast when C'baoth died?"

"Yes," Luke said mechanically, staring off into space. The insane Jedi clone Joruus C'baoth, recruited to fight against the New Republic by Grand Admiral Thrawn.

Thrawn. Clone . . .

"Mara, you told me cortosis ore wasn't structurally very strong. Just how weak is it?"

"It was flaking off under our boots as we walked through the passage," she said, throwing him a puzzled look. "Other than that, I haven't the faintest idea. Why?"

Luke nodded at the vast pool below them. "We've got a lot of water here, and water isn't compressible the way air is. If we could create a hard enough jolt here in this room, the pressure wave should travel all the way down the tunnel to the passageway. If it's powerful enough, maybe we can collapse that whole area."

"Sounds great," Mara agreed. "Just one problem: how exactly do we engineer this massive jolt of yours?"

Luke braced himself. "We cut through that transparisteel barrier and flood the cloning alcove."

"Oh, my stars," Mara murmured; and even through his mental exhaustion Luke could feel her ripple of stunned apprehension. "Luke, that's a Braxxon-Fipps 590 fusion generator in there. You dump water on that and you're going to have more jolt than you know what to do with."

"I know it's risky," Luke said. "But I think it's our only chance." Letting go of his grip on her, wincing as his wet clothing shifted against his skin, he stood up. "Wait here; I'll be right back."

She sighed. "No," she said, standing up beside him and taking hold of his arm. "I'll do it."

"Like blazes you will," Luke growled. "It's my crazy idea. *I'll* do it."

"Okay," she said, crossing her arms. "Tell me how you do a Paparak cross-cut."

He blinked. "A what?"

"A Paparak cross-cut," she repeated. "It's a technique for weakening a stressed wall so that it comes down a minute or so after you're safely out of the vicinity. Palpatine taught it to me as part of my sabotage training."

"Okay," Luke said. "So give me a fast course."

"What, like a fast course in becoming a Jedi?" she countered scornfully. "It's not that easy."

"Mara—"

"Besides," she added quietly, "when whichever of us goes down pops up again, the other one's going to have to get them back up here out of the way of the blast. I don't think I can lift you that far that fast." Her lips pressed briefly together. "And frankly, I don't want to sit here and watch myself fail."

Luke glared at her. But she was right, and they both knew it. "This is blackmail, you know."

"This is common sense," she corrected him. "The right person for the job, remember?" She smiled faintly. "Or do you need another lecture on that topic?"

"Spare me," he said with a sigh, running his fingertips across her cheek. "All right, I'll lift you over there. Be careful, okay?"

"Don't worry," she said, taking a deep breath and pulling her lightsaber from her belt. "Ready."

Stretching out to the Force, he lifted her over the railing and across the room to the transparisteel wall. Her mind touched his, her thoughts indicating she was ready, and he lowered her into the water. She took a few more deep breaths, then bent at the waist and ducked her head beneath the surface. A single vertical kick of her legs, and she was gone.

Across the ledge, Artoo moaned nervously. "She'll be all right," Luke assured him, gripping the top rail as he stared anxiously at the choppy water. He could feel Mara's thoughts as she maneuvered her way back and forth across the wall, making short, deliberate cuts with her lightsaber. Stretching out harder, he could sense the change in flow against her skin as the water began to seep through the cracks.

And if the water level rose high enough in there to reach the generator before she was finished . . .

"Come on, Mara, come on," he muttered under his breath. "It's good enough—let's go."

He felt her negative thought; the wall wasn't yet shredded to her satisfaction. Luke pressed back his impatience and fear, the faces of Callista and Gaeriel hovering before him. Only a week ago he'd told himself firmly that he could never permit himself to love Mara, that such a closeness and commitment from him would inevitably put her in danger.

And now he'd reneged on that determination. And sure enough, like all the others, his actions or inactions had put her in deadly danger. He felt a flicker in her emotions, mixing with the fear and dread rising chokingly from within him—

And suddenly her head breached the surface. "Got it," she gasped.

He had her moving before the second word was even out of her mouth, pulling her toward him with all the speed he could manage. He flipped her over the railing and lowered her flat on her stomach on the ledge, stretching himself protectively down on top of her as she landed. "How soon?" he asked, reaching out to the Force to try to create a low-level shield that could provide at least a minimal barrier against the impending explosion.

"Could be anytime," Mara answered, her voice muffled by the rock wall she was facing. "And by the way, just for future reference, don't you *ever* not care for someone just because you're afraid they might get hurt in the process. Especially not me. You got that?"

Luke grimaced in embarrassment. "You weren't supposed to hear that." Behind him, he heard the sudden crack and surging of water as the transparisteel wall collapsed—

And with a brilliant flash he could see even with his eyes squeezed shut, the generator blew up.

The sound of the blast itself was almost muffled; but the roar of the wave that slammed over them more than made up for it. The water surged and roiled all around them, effortlessly picking them up and slamming them back and forth between the wall, the ledge, and the railing. Luke held grimly on to Mara, wishing belatedly he'd thought to tie Artoo down somehow.

And then, as suddenly as it had struck, the swirling water fell away, leaving them bruised and drenched but otherwise unharmed. Shaking the water out of his eyes, Luke pushed himself up on one arm and looked out into the chamber.

And caught his breath. Only one of the room's glow panels had survived the explosion; but by its dim light he could see that the water level was rapidly going down. "Mara—look. It worked."

"I'll be Kesseled," she said, spitting out some water. "Now what? We jump in and follow the flow?"

Luke leaned over the railing, trying to see the exit tunnel. If it wasn't still full to the ceiling . . .

But it was. "It's not quite that simple," he told Mara. "The flow should carry us back into the caverns, all right, but there's still the matter of getting through the tunnel and underground room."

"Why don't we just wait until the level goes down far enough?"

"We can't," Luke said. "I don't know why."

"Jedi hunch," Mara said. "Then we're back to hibernation trances. How fast can you put me in one?"

"Pretty fast," he told her. "Take a few deep breaths, and tell me what phrase you want me to use to snap you out of it."

"A phrase, right," she said, inhaling deeply, a strangely cautious mood touching her mind. "Okay. See if you can handle this one . . ."

She told him, and he smiled. "Got it," he said, and stretched out with the Force.

A minute later she was fast asleep in his arms. "You go first, Artoo," Luke told the droid, lifting him up with the Force and easing him over the railing. "We'll be right behind you."

The droid warbled; and then he was in the water, his dome bobbing above the waves as he was swept toward the tunnel. Wrapping his arms protectively around Mara, Luke jumped in behind him. The current grabbed them, pushing them along behind the bobbing droid as Luke struggled to keep their heads above water. The wall and the top of the tunnel archway loomed ahead; and just before they reached it, Luke took a deep breath and pulled them both under the surface.

The rest of the trip was a blur of dizzying speed, continual buffeting of the water, near-collisions with smooth walls and rough stone, aching eyes and lungs. Through his half trance Luke was vaguely aware of where they left the tunnel and entered the underground room; was more sharply aware of where they slammed through the newly enlarged gap in the wall and the protective cortosis ore barrier as the turbulence threw them back and forth against the rock. The torrent dragged them, twisting and turning, through the caverns and tunnels they'd so laboriously picked their way through days earlier with Child Of Winds and the Qom Jha. Dimly through his slow asphyxiation, Luke decided it was just as well that they'd cut away so many of the stalactites and stalagmites that would have been in their way . . .

Abruptly, he snapped awake, half submerged in water, his head and chest resting precariously on a slimy boulder, Artoo's frantic twittering in his ears. "Okay, right," he managed, shaking his head to clear it.

And suddenly stiffened. Mara was gone.

He shook his head again, digging out his glow rod with numb, half-frozen fingers as he scrabbled around looking for footing. He found it immediately; the water he was in turned out to be only waist high. He fumbled the glow rod out at last and flicked it on.

He was standing in a pool just off the edge of the last of the underground rivers he and Mara had passed during their trip through the caverns. Five meters to his left, the torrent that had brought them here had vanished, leaving only the river rippling its sedate way along.

And two meters to his right, bobbing gently in the pool as she floated beside the craggy rock, was Mara. Her eyes closed, her arms and legs limp. As if in death.

The precise image he'd seen of her in that Jedi vision on Tierfon.

And then he was at her side, raising her head out of the water, gazing at her face in sudden fear. If the trance hadn't kept her alive—if she'd struck something hard enough to kill her after he'd lost his grip on her—

Behind him, Artoo whistled impatiently. "Right," Luke agreed, cutting off his sudden panic. All he had to do to bring her out of it was speak the key phrase she'd chosen, the phrase she'd wondered aloud if he could handle. Almost as if she was afraid he couldn't . . .

He took a deep breath. "I love you, Mara."

Her eyes blinked open, blinked again as she chased the water from them. "Hi," she said, breathing heavily as she grabbed his arm and maneuvered herself upright. "I see we made it."

"Yes," Luke said, taking her in his arms and holding her tightly, his tension and fear evaporating into a mist of utter calm and relief. The vision had been passed, and Mara had survived it.

And they were together again. Forever.

"Yes," Mara murmured. "Forever."

They loosened their grips on each other, just slightly . . . and standing together in the cold water, their lips came together in a kiss.

It seemed like a long time before Mara gently pulled away from the embrace. "Not to put a damper on this," she said, "but we're both shivering, and we're still a long way from home. Where are we, anyway?"

"Back at our underground river," Luke told her, reluctantly bringing his mind back to practical matters.

"Ah." She peered toward the stream. "What happened to our personal flood?"

"It seems to have ended," Luke said. "Either we drained the lake completely—"

"Which is *real* unlikely."

"Right," Luke said. "Or else it's gotten stopped up again somehow."

"Probably more of the chamber wall collapsed," Mara said, reaching up to push back some of the hair that had gotten plastered across her cheek. "Or else it's jammed up with what's left of the cloning equipment."

Luke nodded, helping her push the rest of her hair back out of the way. "Good thing we didn't wait any longer to make our exit."

"Sure is," Mara agreed. "Handy things, those Jedi hunches. You'll have to teach me how to do those."

"We'll work on it," Luke promised, wading toward the edge of the pond. "I think the Qom Jha said this river emptied out into a small waterfall."

"Sounds good," Mara said. "Let's go find it."

Another wave of Skipray Blastboats shot past, pelting the *Tyrannic* with laser fire. Behind them, two of the Ishori war cruisers had gotten inside the kill zone and were scattering a dazzling pattern of more powerful turbolaser blasts across the ridgeline. "Two more starboard turbolasers knocked out," the fire control officer called tensely. "Forward ridgeline has been breached; crews are sealing it off."

"Acknowledged," Nalgol said, hearing his voice trembling with a frustrated and wholly impotent fury. It was unthinkable—*unthinkable*—that a fleet of three Imperial Star Destroyers should find themselves fighting for their survival against such a pitiful ragtag of aliens and alien-lovers.

But that was exactly what they were doing. There were just too many of them to keep track of. Too many of them to fight.

And with all his pride in his ship and his crew and his Empire, Nalgol was realist enough to know when the fight had become hopeless.

"Signal to the *Obliterator* and *Ironhand*," he ordered between clenched teeth. "Pull back and withdraw. Repeat: pull back and withdraw."

"Acknowledged, Captain," the comm officer replied.

"What heading, sir?" the helmsman called.

"A short jump in any direction." Nalgol glared out the viewport. "And after that, set course directly for Bastion. Grand Admiral Thrawn needs to hear about this."

And he would indeed hear about it, Nalgol promised himself silently. Yes, indeed. He would hear *all* about it.

The waterfall exit was considerably less cozy than Luke had expected it to be, the hole possibly having been enlarged by the flood that had just forced its way through. There weren't any footholds right at the mouth, but in the dim starlight Mara spotted a likely ledge about five meters to the left. Using the Force, Luke lifted first Mara, then Artoo, across the gap. Then, a bit more tentatively, Mara brought him across to join them.

"Any idea what side of the fortress we're on?" she asked, looking around the darkened landscape. "Or how much longer we've got until dawn?"

"No, to both questions," Luke said, stretching out with the Force. There was no danger nearby that he could detect. "Probably the far side; and probably not more than a couple more hours."

"We'd better use the time to get under cover," she suggested, peering up at the cliff above them. "We don't want to be out in the open when Parck sends out his search parties."

"I just hope he doesn't find the ship we borrowed," Luke said. "Aside from giving him back his quick access to Bastion, it would lose us our only way of getting out of here together."

"Well, if he does, you and Artoo will just have to take your X-wing and go for help," Mara said.

"You mean *you* and Artoo will go," Luke said firmly. "I mean that, Mara. No argument this time—"

Jedi Sky Walker?

Luke looked up. Fluttering to a landing on a boulder above them were a dozen dark shapes.

And the tone and mind of one of them seemed very familiar. "Yes," he said. "Is that you, Hunter Of Winds?"

It is I, the Qom Qae confirmed. *My son, Child Of Winds, informed all nearby nestings of your deeds this night. We have been watching for your return.*

"Thank you," Luke said. "We very much appreciate your efforts. Can you show us to a place of shelter nearby? We need to hide from those in the High Tower until we can make our way back to our ship."

Hunter Of Winds ruffled his wings. *No need for shelter, Jedi Sky Walker,* he said. *We will carry you to your flying machine, as my son and his companions did earlier this night.*

Luke frowned. After Hunter Of Winds's quick and cavalier dismissal of him and his mission when he and Artoo first landed, such magnanimity seemed suspiciously out of character. "You're very kind," he said carefully. "May I ask why you're willing to take such risks for us?"

Hunter Of Winds ruffled his wings. *I have spoken to the Bargainer for this nesting of the Qom Jha,* he said. *Eater Of Fire Creepers has agreed to release you from your promise to help us against the Threateners, provided you leave our world at once.*

Luke felt his face warming. "In other words, our presence here has become a liability to you?"

Child Of Winds has said the Threateners will not harm us if we do not bother them, Hunter Of Winds said gruffly. *It is to that end that we wish you to leave.*

"Nothing like being appreciated, is there?" Mara muttered.

"It's all right," Luke said, touching her hand and her mind soothingly. Reminding her that, embarrassment and even veiled insult aside, this was in fact the result she herself had said she wanted. Parck and the Chiss would now be left alone, unharassed by the Qom Jha and Qom Qae, and free to focus their full energies on their work in the Unknown Regions.

"Fine," she said, and Luke could feel her grudging acceptance. "But he's not Child Of Winds anymore. After what he's been through, he deserves to have a name of his own."

Really, Hunter Of Winds said, giving her a long, thoughtful look. *And what name do you suggest for him?*

"The one he's earned," she said softly. " 'Friend Of Jedi.' "

Hunter Of Winds ruffled his wings again. *I will consider it. But now, let us depart. The night grows old, and you will wish to be gone before the sunrise.*

.   .   .

"I'll look forward to it," Flim was saying as Karrde rounded the archway onto the *Relentless*'s bridge.

"Yes," Pellaeon said. "So will I."

The Admiral turned as Karrde stepped up beside him. "You're late," Pellaeon said mildly.

"I was watching the turbolift," Karrde explained. "I thought Flim and his associates might try to bring a squad of stormtroopers in on their side of the dispute."

"They might have, at that," Pellaeon said. "Thank you."

"No problem," Karrde assured him, looking around the bridge. The Major Tierce clone was lying unmoving on the deck, Shada was across with the other two Mistryl, the con man Flim was waiting with studied unconcern just back of the command walkway, and Moff Disra was a little off to one side, standing as aloof and cold and dignified as a man facing his own destruction could manage. "Besides, it doesn't look like my presence was really needed."

"Not for this part, no," Pellaeon agreed. "Your friend Shada is quite impressive. I don't suppose she'd be interested in a job."

"Well, she *is* looking for a higher cause to serve," Karrde told him. "However, to be perfectly honest, I don't think the Empire is it."

Pellaeon nodded. "Perhaps we can change that."

"Admiral Pellaeon?" a voice called from the crew pits. "I have General Bel Iblis for you now."

"Thank you." Pellaeon looked to Karrde. "Don't run off—I'll want to speak with you later."

"Certainly."

The Admiral headed down the command walkway, passing Flim without a second glance. Throwing one last look at Disra, Karrde crossed to where Shada and the other young Mistryl were helping the older woman to a sitting position. "How is she?" he asked.

"Not as bad as we thought," Shada said, probing gingerly into the scorched tunic. "She was able to twist almost out of the way of the shot."

"Well-honed reflexes." Karrde nodded. "Once a Mistryl, always a Mistryl, I suppose."

The older woman eyed him balefully. "You're very well informed," she growled.

"About a great many things," Karrde agreed calmly. "Among them the fact that Shada seems to have earned your displeasure somehow."

"And what, you think this makes up for it?" the woman snapped contemptuously.

"Doesn't it?" Karrde countered. "If she hadn't stopped Tierce when she did, you two would have been the next to die after Pellaeon. You were the most immediate threats to him."

She snorted. "I'm a Mistryl, Talon Karrde. My life is gladly given in the service of my people."

"Really." Karrde looked at the younger woman. "Do you also consider your life not worth a little gratitude?"

"Leave Karoly out of this," the older woman bit out. "She has nothing to say on the matter."

"Ah," Karrde said. "Soldiers with no voice or opinion. Remarkably similar to the philosophy of the Imperial stormtroopers."

"Karoly allowed Shada to escape once before," the woman said, glowering at her. "She's fortunate she wasn't punished herself for that."

"Oh, yes," Karrde murmured. "How very lucky for her."

The woman's eyes flashed. "If you've quite finished—"

"I haven't," Karrde said. "Clearly, you don't consider Mistryl lives worth anything. What about Mistryl reputations?"

Her eyes narrowed. "What do you mean?"

Karrde waved toward Flim. "You were about to make an alliance with these people. You were about to be taken in by nothing more than slick talk, whipped air, and a dirt-level fringe con man. And don't bother denying it; a member of the Eleven doesn't travel off Emberlene just for the exercise."

The woman's eyes drifted away from his gaze. "The issue was still under discussion," she muttered.

"Glad to hear it," Karrde said. "Because if even your reputation doesn't matter to you, consider what binding the Mistryl to a vengeful man like Moff Disra would have meant. How long do you think it would have been before you became his private Death Commandos?"

"That would never have happened," Karoly put in emphatically. "We would never sink that low, not even under a treaty."

Shada stirred. "What was it you tried to stop me from doing on the Resinem Complex roof?" she asked quietly.

"That was different," Karoly protested.

Shada shook her head. "No. Condoning and cooperating with murder is no different from committing it yourself."

"She's right," Karrde said. "And once you started down that road, it would have meant the end of the Mistryl. You'd have burned your sky-arches behind you with every other potential client; and when Flim's soap bubble collapsed, as it inevitably would have, there would have been nothing left out there anymore for you.

"And with the end of the Mistryl would have come a final end to Emberlene."

He crossed his arms and waited . . . and after a few seconds the older woman grimaced. "What is it you want?"

"I want the Mistryl hunter teams called off Shada," he said. "Whatever her alleged crime against you, it's to be forgiven and the death mark lifted."

The woman's mouth twisted. "You ask much."

"We've given much," Karrde reminded her. "Is it a deal?"

She hesitated, then nodded reluctantly. "Very well. But she will not be reinstated into the Mistryl; not now, not ever. And Emberlene will forever be closed to her."

She turned burning eyes up at Shada. "From now on she is a woman without a home."

Karrde looked at Shada. Her face was tight, her lips pressed tightly together. But she returned his look steadily and nodded. "Fine," he said. "We'll just have to see about finding her a new home."

"With you?" The woman snorted. "With a smuggler and seller of information? Tell me again how low a Mistryl can sink."

There was no answer to that. But fortunately, Karrde didn't have to come up with one. There was a sudden bustling at his side, and then he was gently but firmly shouldered away by the medical team as they gathered around the injured woman. He stepped back out of their way, shifting his attention to the security team that had arrived at the same time. With professional efficiency they scanned Flim and Disra for hidden weapons, put restraints on them both, and escorted them back to the aft bridge turbolift.

Another group, following behind them, was carrying Tierce's body.

"Karrde?"

He turned to see Pellaeon walking back along the command walkway toward him. "I have to go across to the *Errant Venture* and speak with General Bel Iblis," the Admiral said as he reached him. "But before I go, I wanted to discuss the price for the Flim and Tierce information you brought me."

Karrde shrugged. "For once in my life, Admiral, I'm not sure what to say," he admitted. "The datacard was a gift to me. It seems a bit dishonest to turn around and charge you for it."

"Ah." Pellaeon eyed him speculatively. "A gift from those aliens whose ship scared the stuffing out of my sensor officers at Bastion?"

"From an associate of theirs," Karrde said. "I'm really not at liberty to discuss the details."

"I understand," Pellaeon said. "Still, your ethics apart—which I find laudable, incidentally—I'd like to find a way to thank you with something more concrete than just words."

"I'll see what I can come up with." Karrde gestured toward the Star Destroyer visible out the viewport. "In the meantime, may I ask what you're going over to discuss with General Bel Iblis?"

Pellaeon's eyes narrowed slightly. But then he shrugged. "It's still highly confidential, of course," he said. "But knowing you, you'll probably know about it soon enough, anyway. I'm proposing a peace treaty between the Empire and the New Republic. It's time for this long war to finally end."

Karrde shook his head. "The things that happen when I'm out of touch at the edges of known space," he said philosophically. "For whatever it's worth, Admiral, I agree wholeheartedly with your goal. And I wish you luck."

"Thank you," Pellaeon said. "Feel free to leave whenever you wish, or allow your crew to take advantage of any of the *Relentless*'s facilities if they'd like. And again, thank you."

He headed off toward the turbolift. Karrde watched him go, then looked back at Shada. The medical team had finished their preliminary work and were helping the injured woman onto a stretcher. Shada was watching them from a few paces away, an expression of private pain on her face. Like someone watching the last member of her family leaving home.

And then, unbidden, an idea drifted into Karrde's mind. Something larger than herself, she'd told Car'das. Something she could hold on to and serve and believe in. Something more honorable and noble than the life of a fringe smuggler.

Something that would make a difference . . .

"Admiral Pellaeon?" he called, hurrying back to the aft bridge. "Admiral?"

Pellaeon had paused at the open door of the turbolift. "Yes?"

"Let me ride over with you to the *Errant Venture*, if I may," Karrde said, stepping to his side. "I have a modest proposal I'd like to make to you."

Luke's final fear was that the Hand of Thrawn's weapons towers would spot them as they lifted their borrowed ship out of its hiding place, forcing their departure from the Nirauan surface to be yet another mad race against death. But the Chiss were apparently still dealing with the aftermath of the hangar destruction, with no attention left to turn outward.

And so they lifted out into space without challenge; and with Mara's touch on the hyperdrive lever the stars became starlines and faded into the mottling of hyperspace.

And at long last, they were on their way home.

"Next stop, Coruscant," Luke said with a sigh, leaning back tiredly in the copilot's seat.

"Next stop, the nearest New Republic base or one of Karrde's outposts," Mara corrected. "I don't know about you, but I want a shower, some clean clothes, and something besides ration bars to eat."

"Point taken," Luke said. "You always were the practical one, weren't you?"

"And you always were the idealistic one," she said. "Must be why we work so well together. Speaking of practical, remember back in the cloning chamber when Artoo went all squeaky?"

"You mean just before the sentinel droids showed up?"

"Right. We never did find out what was tying him in knots that way."

"Well, let's find out now," Luke said, levering himself out of his seat and making his way back to the droid alcove where they'd plugged Artoo into the ship's computer. "Okay, Artoo, you heard the lady. What was it about the Unknown Regions data that got you all excited?"

Artoo warbled, his words appearing on the computer display. "He says it didn't have anything to do with the Unknown Regions," Luke reported. "Which he says he didn't get more than a general overview of, by the way."

"I didn't think he'd gotten very much," Mara said regretfully. "He wasn't connected to the computer nearly long enough to download everything."

"Well, we're sure not going to go back and get the rest now," Luke said, skimming down the scrolling words. "But there was something he stumbled across in one of the other records . . ."

Mara must have picked up his sudden shock. "What is it?" she asked sharply.

"I don't believe it," he murmured, still reading. "Mara, he found it. He *found* it."

"Wonderful. Found *what*?"

"What else?" Luke looked up at her. "Thrawn's copy of the Caamas Document."

CHAPTER

43

Fifteen days later, in the secondary command room of the Imperial Star Destroyer *Chimaera*, the peace accords between the Empire and New Republic were signed.

"I still say you should have been the one over there," Han groused as he and Leia watched from the back of the room while Pellaeon and Gavrisom performed the ceremony amid the crowd of assembled dignitaries. "You did way more on this than he did."

"It's all right, Han," Leia said, surreptitiously wiping a tear from the corner of her eye. Peace. After all the years, after all the sacrifice and destruction and death. Finally, they had peace.

"Yeah?" Han countered suspiciously. "Then how come you're crying?"

She smiled at him. "Memories," she said. "Just memories."

He found her hand, took it comfortingly. "Alderaan?" he asked quietly.

"Alderaan, the Death Stars—" She squeezed his hand. "You."

"Nice to know I'm in the top three, anyway," he said, looking around the room. "Speaking of old memories, where's Lando? I thought he was going to be here."

"He changed his mind," Leia said. "I guess Tendra wasn't very happy with him heading out to Bastion with you without at least telling her about it. He's taken her art shopping on Celanon to make it up to her."

Han shook his head. "Strong women," he said, mock sadly. "They'll get you every time."

"Watch that," Leia warned, digging her elbow into his side. "You've always liked strong women. Admit it."

"Well, not *always*," Han said. "Ow—okay, okay. I like strong women."

"What's this about strong women?" Karrde's voice asked from Han's other side.

"Just a friendly family discussion," Han assured him. "Good to see you again, Karrde. How come you're not over there with the rest of the high-class people?"

"Probably the same reason you're not," Karrde said. "I don't exactly fit in with that sort of group."

"That'll change soon," Leia assured him. "Particularly now that you're respectable and all. How in the worlds did you talk Gavrisom and Bel Iblis into this joint Intelligence service idea?"

"The same way I talked Pellaeon into it, actually," Karrde said. "I simply pointed out that the key to a stable and calm peace is both sides knowing the other isn't plotting some kind of move against them. Bastion doesn't trust your Intelligence network, and Coruscant definitely doesn't trust theirs."

He shrugged. "Enter a neutral third party—us—who straddle both regimes and are already equipped to gather and assemble information. We'll simply now be supplying it to your two governments instead of to private buyers."

"It could work, I suppose," Han agreed cautiously. "The Bureau of Ships and Services has been operating independently for years without going political, either under the Empire or the New Republic. You might be able to pull it off."

"I like the fact we'll be getting the same information about our own systems that you'll be giving Bastion," Leia said. "It'll supplement the data the Observers are sending us and help us keep track of what the various system and sector governments are up to. That should help us spot problems before they get too big to deal with."

"Yeah," Han said darkly. "Just because the Caamas Document Luke and Mara brought back slowed down a lot of the brush wars doesn't mean they won't start up again."

"Still, I suspect that seeing how easily their old rivalries were manipulated by Disra and Flim has made them more cautious," Leia pointed out. "I know of at least eight conflicts where the participants have now petitioned Coruscant for mediation."

"It may also depend somewhat on how the trial goes," Karrde said. "I was a bit surprised so many of the culprits are still alive."

"Bothans tend to be long-lived," Leia said. "I'm sure that group is regretting that fact."

Across the room, Leia could see Bel Iblis and Ghent talking with Pellaeon now, Ghent looking extremely uncomfortable at his inclusion into such—to his mind—exalted company. A little ways behind them, Chewbacca was riding patient herd on Jacen, Jaina, and Anakin as the children chattered excitedly away to Barkhimkh and two other Noghri about their adventures on this latest visit to Kashyyyk. "Did Luke tell you where he found that copy of the document, by the way?" Karrde asked. "I couldn't get anything out of Mara."

"No, he and Mara have both been very quiet about it," Leia said. "Luke said they have some thinking to do before they give us any details. It most certainly has to do with that odd spaceship they came back in."

"I imagine there's an interesting story behind it all," Karrde suggested.

Leia nodded. "I'm sure we'll hear it eventually."

Han cleared his throat. "Speaking of Luke," he said, "and speaking of strong women," he added, throwing Leia a grin, "how's your organization going to manage without Mara?"

"We'll have some problems," Karrde conceded. "She was running a good deal of the organization, after all. But we'll adjust."

"Besides, he's got someone new to take her place," Leia couldn't resist adding. "Shada's officially joined him—had you heard that?"

"Yeah, I did," Han said, giving Karrde a highly speculative look. "You know, I asked you once what it would take to get you to join the New Republic. Remember? You asked what it had taken to get *me* to join up—"

"Yes, I remember," Karrde cut him off, an uncharacteristic note of embarrassment coloring his voice. "Kindly bear in mind that I have *not* joined the New Republic. And my relationship with Shada is nothing like that."

"Neither was mine," Han said smugly, putting his arm around Leia. "That's okay. Give it time."

"It's not going to happen," Karrde insisted.

"Yeah," Han said. "I know."

On the ship's layout map, the room was called a forward visual triangulation site, for use in line-of-sight weapons targeting if any enemy managed to knock out the main sensor array.

But for tonight, at least, it had become a private observation gallery.

Mara leaned against the cool transparisteel viewport, gazing out at the stars. Wondering at the right-angle turn her life had just taken.

"You realize, of course," Luke commented as he came up behind her with their drinks, "that they're all probably wondering where we are."

"Let them wonder," Mara said, sniffing the air appreciatively over the mug he handed her. The courtiers of Palpatine's court had always been openly contemptuous of hot chocolate, considering it beneath the dignity of elite such as themselves. Karrde and his people, like the good smugglers they were, had turned up their noses at all nonalcoholic drinks in general.

But the drink fit perfectly with Luke's farm boy past. It gave her a warm feeling, evoking a sense of comfort and stability and security. Simple necessities, which she'd missed so much throughout most of her life.

She took a sip. And besides that, the stuff just plain tasted good.

"Has Leia talked to you about the wedding?" Luke asked, sipping from his own mug as he leaned against the viewport facing her.

"Not yet," Mara said, making a face. "I suppose she's going to want some big blowout High Alderaanian ceremony."

Luke grinned. "Wants, probably. Expects, no."

"Good," Mara said. "I'd rather have something quiet and private and dignified. Mostly dignified, anyway," she amended. "With New Republic dignitaries on one side and Karrde's smugglers on the other, we'll probably need a weapons check at the door."

Luke chuckled. "We'll figure something out."

She eyed him over the rim of her mug. "Speaking of figuring things out, have you decided what you're going to do about the academy?"

He turned his head to gaze out the viewport. "I can't just abandon the students I have there," he said. "That much I know. I was thinking maybe I could slowly turn it into—oh, call it a pre-Jedi school. A place where beginning students can get the basics, maybe learning from older students, and do a little practicing among themselves. Once they've passed that stage, you and I and other instructors can complete their training. Maybe in a more personal one-on-one arrangement, the way Ben and Master Yoda trained me."

He looked back at her. "Assuming you want to be involved with the training at all, that is."

She shrugged. "I'm not completely comfortable with the idea," she admitted. "But I *am* a Jedi now—at least, I assume I am—and until we can swell the ranks of instructors I suppose teaching is going to be part of my job." She considered. "At least, it will be once I've got a little more training of my own under my belt."

"Private training, of course?"

"I should hope so," she said. "Before I can do *that*, though, I'll need time to gracefully disengage from Karrde's organization. I've got responsibilities I have to transfer over to other people, and I can't just let them slide." She smiled. "Responsibility and commitment, you know."

There was a flicker in his emotions. "Yes," he murmured.

"Though even when I'm ready to start teaching I don't think I'll want to stay on Yavin to do it," she continued, studying him closely. "Maybe the two of us could travel around the New Republic with the more advanced students, teaching them as we go. That way we'd be available for emergency conflict mediation and conciliation and all the other things Jedi are supposed to do, while at the same time giving the students a taste of real-life situations."

"That would be very useful," Luke said. "I know I could sure have used some of that myself."

"Good." She regarded him thoughtfully. "Now tell me what's bothering you."

"What do you mean?" he asked warily, his thoughts closing in on themselves.

"Oh, come on, Luke," she said gently. "I've been inside your head and your heart. You can't keep secrets from me anymore. Something hit you when I mentioned responsibility and commitment a minute ago. What was it?"

He sighed, and she could sense him give up. "I guess I still have some lingering doubts about why you'd want to marry me," he said hesitantly. "I mean, I know why I love *you* and want to marry you. It's just that it doesn't seem like you'll be gaining as much from this as I will."

Mara gazed down at the dark liquid in her mug. "I could point out that marriage isn't a game of profit and loss," she said. "But I suppose that would just be deflecting the question."

She took a deep breath. "The fact is, Luke, that until that mental and emotional melding we had during the battle in Thrawn's cloning chamber, I didn't even know myself what it was I wanted. Sure, I had friends and associates; but I'd cut myself off so completely from any real emotional attachments that I didn't even realize how much a part of life was missing."

She shook her head. "I mean, look, I cried when the *Jade's Fire* crashed. A ship—a *thing;* and yet I cried over it. What did that say about my priorities?"

"It wasn't just a thing, though," Luke murmured. "It was your freedom."

"Sure," Mara said. "But that's part of the point. It represented freedom, but it was freedom to escape from other people if I decided I wanted out."

She looked out at the stars. "In many ways, I'm still all closed up emotionally. You, on the other hand, have such an emotional openness it sometimes drives me crazy. That's what I need to learn; and you're the one I want to learn it from."

She moved closer to him and took his hand. "But that's just profit and loss games again. The simple, bottom-line fact is that this is the right path for us. Like that Qom Jha proverb Builder With Vines quoted at us in the caverns, the one about many vines woven together being stronger than the same number used separately. We complement each other perfectly, Luke, all the way down the line. In many ways, we're two halves of a single being."

"I know that," he said. "I guess I just wasn't sure you did."

"I know just about everything you do, now," Mara reminded him.

"Faughn was right—we *do* make a good team. And we can only get better at it. Give us a few more years, and enemies of the New Republic will be running for cover like crazy."

"And those enemies will definitely be there," Luke said, sobering as he turned again to gaze out the viewport at the distant stars. "That's our future, Mara—out there in the Unknown Regions. Our hopes and dreams; promises and opportunities; dangers and enemies. And for the moment, we're the ones who hold that key."

Mara nodded, stepping close to his side and putting her arm around him. "We'll have to decide what to do with that overview Artoo downloaded. Maybe send probe ships out to take a look at some of the worlds Thrawn had listed, just to see what's there."

"Sounds reasonable," Luke said. "Either on our own or under New Republic auspices. *And* we also have to decide what to do about the Hand of Thrawn."

"My vote is that we leave them out of it," Mara said. "If they're not interested in talking to us, the last thing we want to do is try to force the issue."

"What if Parck decides to talk to Bastion instead?" Luke asked.

Mara shook her head. "I don't think he will. If he hasn't contacted them by now, it must mean he's picked up the news reports that the Thrawn sighting was a hoax and decided to go back to lying low."

"He could also be plotting how to come after you for what you did to his hangar and ships," Luke warned.

"I'm not worried about it," Mara said. "The ships themselves he can undoubtedly replace, and he ought to be grateful I stopped him from giving the Hand of Thrawn to Disra and Flim."

She shrugged. "Besides, Fel *did* tell me to take my best shot."

Luke smiled. "I doubt that was exactly what he had in mind."

"I'm not responsible for what Baron Fel has in mind," Mara reminded him. "Seriously, I think if they do anything it'll be to try to recruit me again."

"And, of course, wait for Thrawn to return."

Mara thought about the dead clone floating in the flooded chamber. "That could take a while."

"True," Luke said. "Still, I suppose that even if they get tired of waiting and contact Bastion, we have a treaty with the Empire now. Maybe ultimately we'll all head out to develop those regions together."

Mara nodded. "And to face whatever's out there. That could be interesting."

Luke nodded back, and for a few minutes they stood arm in arm looking out at the stars. An almost-vision floated before Mara's eyes, a vision of the future—*their* future—and of what they would face together. Challenges, children, friends, enemies, allies, dangers, joys, sorrows—all of it swirled into a sort of living mosaic, fading away into the distance. A vision like she'd never seen before.

But then, she'd never been a Jedi before. There were indeed going to be interesting challenges ahead.

"But that's the future," Luke murmured, his breath warm on the side of her face. "This is the present."

Mara pulled a little away from him. "And as head of the Jedi academy and brother of High Councilor Organa Solo you should at least put in an appearance at the ceremony?" she suggested.

He gave her a wry look. "Yes, that's just about what I was going to say," he acknowledged. "I can see this is going to take some getting used to."

"There's still time for you to back out," she pointed out.

He kissed her warmly. "Not a chance," he said. "I'll see you later."

Setting down his mug, he headed for the door. "Hang on a minute," Mara said, stepping away from the viewport and her tantalizingly brief vision of the future. As Luke had said, this was the present. The future would take care of itself. "I'll come with you."